MW01174029

THE WEIGHT OF SHADOWS

ANGELA FRANKLIN

BOOK 1

THE STARLIT QUILL

The Starlit Quill

Publishers Since 2025

Published by The Starlit Quill – Ozark, Missouri 65721, USA

Book cover by Angela Franklin with the collaboration of BookBaby cover designs

Book formatting and interior design by the Starlit Quill

Edited by Angelina Flood

First Edition 2025

To my husband, Nicolas,

You are the hero in the most beautiful love story I've ever lived, my muse, the man who makes my heart race even after all these years. Thank you for helping me soar with your unwavering encouragement, endless patience during my countless book discussions, and for always believing in me.

Love

-Angela

And to my children, Elias, Liam, and Sterling,

I don't know that you can ever fully understand how proud I am of each of you, every single day, until you have children of your own. Until then, know that it's immeasurable.

One day, I hope you'll read this book. You'll tell me how much you loved it – and that you covered your eyes during the steamy parts. OK? Thanks.

Love,

-Mom

Acknowledgements

Thank you to my beta and ARC readers for taking the time to read this and offer feedback. And to my street team that has cheered me on and promoted a debut author and book – you all have been so supportive and amazing.

Thank you to the writer's group that accepted me and answered so many questions and the fellow authors that have become friends because of that group – I'm so grateful to consider you friends.

Thank you to my editor for taking on this massive book and helping me perfect this story – I hope the final version makes you proud.

And finally, thank you to my husband, kids, the rest of my family, and friends for being patient with me and excited for this book to come out – I hope when you read it, you'll love it as much as I do.

PROLOGUE

Twigs from reaching branches whipped him in the arms and face as he raced through the darkened woods. His boots hammered out his location despite the pine needle-softened rug beneath them. If his heart wasn't already racing from the fear of being pursued, the shift in elevation, thinner air, and general lack of endurance would have done the job on their own.

Run.

Don't stop; don't look back.

Keep moving forward.

The thoughts were a mantra, a reminder, urging him to follow his instincts.

The blood coursing through his body banged its rapid alert against his eardrums. The fire in his lungs smoldered and crept into the back of his throat. The sear in his side was an intruder slicing its way from the inside out. Every molecule of life within him felt near to bursting, but still he ran.

He felt as though he'd been trying to escape them for days, but surely it had only been hours. His watch had stopped working, the time reflected no longer matched the darkened hour.

He knew he shouldn't have crossed the border, but the temptation had been too great.

He could hear them, their endless pursuit seeming to come from all around, and nowhere at all.

Would they catch him from behind? He risked a glance over his shoulder as he collapsed against a tree, the bark brushing a rough kiss against his cheek as he scanned the way he had just come.

Nobody in sight. He closed his eyes, gasping to quell the ache in his chest.

Keep moving.

He pushed away from the tree, dusting away the crackled scaly remnants that had imprinted on his palms.

A noise to the left.

He whirled toward the sound. Nobody in sight.

He pumped his legs harder, willing the exhausted rubber beneath him to carry him faster, farther. The obstruction was before him before he could react. A searing jolt of lightning shot from his ankle, clawed its way along his shin, squeezed like a vice around his calf, then settled back in his ankle, radiating fiery agony. He fisted his hand against his mouth, stifling the unavoidable scream that escaped, the mist in his eyes blurring his already limited vision.

Don't stop.

He exhaled loudly, the breaths ragged and rattling as they clawed their way along his ribcage.

He focused on a slight glow through the trees ahead. The thought of a road or a house fueled a new hope. The risk of exposure was outweighed by the possibility of flagging a car. He could be mere moments away from a phone and a call for help.

He burst through the trees, a triumphant runner crossing the finish line.

The glow from the moon above taunted him with only a clearing of scraggly brush laughing at him with their windless dance.

There was no road with a car.

There was no cabin with a phone.

He forced his knees not to follow his heart as it sank to the earth. There would be no help here.

He was alone, and they were still coming.

Run.

Crossing the clearing was the only option. He couldn't go around; he'd lose too much valuable time and it could take him directly into the route of his pursuers.

He had to cross.

Thanking, while also cursing, the celestial flashlight he'd now been offered, he checked behind and around him and pushed into the sea of brambles and brush. Wicked vines raked their talon-liked thorns anywhere they could gain purchase, ripping at flesh, tearing at clothes, only to be followed by a featherlight caress of the tallest grass, an apology for its unwelcome neighbor.

Between the protests of his ankle, angrily making its hatred for each step known, and the barbs of the vines demanding he stay, the crossing took longer than he had to spare. If it were daylight, he'd worry about the droplets of red he'd left for them to follow like breadcrumbs marking a path.

Once out of the moonlight, he crashed against the largest tree, a wide, sturdy shield. He braced against the rough bark, each violent inhale a wheeze, each exhale a scratching need to cough. He bent forward at the waist, bracing his hands against his knees, begging his stomach to stop its objection. He leaned back again, closed his eyes and rested his head. His damp hair stuck to his forehead, his clothes to his skin. He swallowed reflexively but only managed to glue his thickened tongue to the roof of his mouth.

He quickly peered back into the wide moonlit open, searching for any sign. They were already close; this break would only bring them closer.

But he needed the rest.

He knew better than to sit. Fear that he wouldn't get back up, whether from exhaustion or anguish, forced him to stay standing. That way, he'd be ready to go. He took the weight off his bad ankle, thankful he was no longer in the moon's glow. He was sure if he allowed himself to look, what he would see of the damage would stop his escape. He leaned his head back again, closing his eyes against the pain, telling his body to slow down the raspy, ragged breaths that were burning their way through his throat, begging his heart to stop trying to beat out of his chest.

Keep moving.

He ignored his warning.

"Please God, if you can get me out of this, I promise I'll be a better person. I'll go to church every Sunday and even volunteer. Just please help me!" he bargained above and then moaned. "What were you thinking coming out here? You know the stories–"

The snap of a stick sounded nearby.

He snapped his mouth shut while his eyes darted wildly, remaining as still as possible against the tree, trying to listen for the hunter over his racing heart and the breaths keeping pace.

He'd luxuriated in too many precious seconds of rest. He had to move.

He risked a glance behind, then stepped away from the tree, immediately stifling a cry, and falling back against the rough wall. He couldn't bear to look, to see the mess that had once been his ankle.

He could hear them getting closer. In no time, they'd be at the clearing, then across, then on top of him, leaning against the tree like an offering.

Move. Now.

He set his foot down again. The flash of fire swallowed his already nonexistent breath, the empty cavern of his stomach threatened to send up any remnants it could find. Silent, tearless sobs wracked his body. He no longer cared what anyone would think coming across a grown man crying in the woods. He'd welcome the laughs or jests, the pity or the concern, as long as there was another person who could help free him from this place.

He stumbled forward, each step more agonizing than before, forcing himself to pick up speed with each awkward burst forward. Branches reached out to yank at his clothes or whack him in the face. Rocks came out of hiding to roll unevenly under his already unstable feet.

He shouldn't have rested so long. He knew better.

Slowing down is how the race is lost.

A noise called from beyond the trees, whispering soft words to him. It wasn't the wind, as the leaves barely stirred in the lifeless air. He followed in the direction of the fuzzy disturbance, his delirious mind racing at the possibilities of what it could be; a TV left on, resorting to a static station; an air conditioner blasting its frigid gifts; water rushing on its hurried way.

Water! The only possibility that would make sense in the middle of the woods.

He imagined the liquid, icy cold despite the aching heat around him, soothing both his raw throat and his angry ankle. The thought of relief, however minuscule, gave him a burst of energy.

He could lose them in the water.

Sounds of pursuit echoed around him. They weren't even trying to mask their chase.

He willed his legs to carry him farther. Even without damage to his ankle, his muscles were spent. Bearing through the agony and his unsteady steps, he burst through the trees. Instantly, he came skidding to a halt and dropped to the ground to catch himself before he could careen over the edge of a rocky cliff.

Indeed, there was water.

He watched as the roaring river shot over the edge, soared in a moment of freedom, and then crashed against the rocks below before continuing to cut its way through the terrain beyond. He desperately searched for a navigable way to the relief the water teased.

The ledge was too narrow and his legs too unsteady.

He leaned forward to check for passage down, but the descent was too steep for him, even if he'd been in prime shape and had climbing gear.

His hopes for water and escape crashed along with the waterfall into the pool hundreds of feet below. He turned back to the trees.

He had to go back in.

Resigned, he took a step and froze.

He could hear them moving through the woods, seeming to spread as wide as he could see.

How many were there?

How had they gotten so close?

He'd never be able to sneak past them to find another way. Desperation steered him around on the edge of the cliff. Frantically he searched for a hidden path, a deer track, something he had missed initially and could follow.

Again, the moon offered its illumination, generously showcasing the stark, steep, and cruel face of the earth. There was nothing, no way down. Too closely behind him came the crashing sounds of pursuit.

He knew what would happen if they caught him. He wouldn't give them the satisfaction.

He'd never give up.

There was only one way out of the Mountain.

He knew nothing would soothe his racing heart, but still, in this last moment of free will, he thought of his parents, and his friends, then breathed deeply.

Jump.

"I'm sorry," he said to the moon, and leapt into the air.

Miles away, a man calmly picked his way among the rocks and through the trees. The town below, sparkling in the moonlight, was visible from the ledge on which he stood.

At this hour she'd be sleeping peacefully in her bed.

She was all that mattered, his sole purpose for being here. He climbed down from the ledge and continued on his path.

He would find her.

ONE

-LILLIAN-

The bell over the door to Wisteria did a little dance as another person entered the diner.

"Have a seat anywhere you'd like. We'll be right with you," Lillian told the couple as she cleared a table. They chose a booth across the diner in another server's section. "Rain, you're needed out here," she called through the kitchen.

She continued to clear, efficiently removing the dishes to the tub sitting in the chair, sweeping away all the crumbs, spraying and wiping clean the surface with disinfectant. She loaded the dirty tub onto the bottom of her cart. Onto the table, she placed four paper coasters, an upside-down glass on each, and four rolls of silverware. She rolled the cart to the next, newly vacated table to do it all again.

She could clear and reset a table in less than thirty seconds when she had to, and today she had to. As far as accomplishments went, it wasn't her most notable, but on days like today, when the bell just kept singing, or when her help was nowhere to be found, she was glad she could.

"Rain!" She called again through the kitchen door.

"I think she's out back," Lana responded from her stainless-steel haven. "Haven't seen her in a while."

Lillian sighed and went back to retrieve her cart so it wouldn't block the walkway. She stopped at the newcomers' table and delivered water, making sure they weren't ready to order, and set off to find the waitress. Since Rain hadn't responded either time she had called for her, and Lana hadn't seen her, she was most likely outside. There was, however, the possibility of her blatantly ignoring the calls, sitting in the tiny break room at the very back. Either place was not where she was supposed to be, which was out front, tending to her tables.

Luckily for Lillian, the diner wasn't a large place and she'd be able to check all possible hiding areas on her walk to the back door. No sight of Rain in the kitchen of course, or beyond in the teeny break room consisting of a very worn sofa, a few lockers for personal belongings, and a small table barely large enough for three chairs to squeeze around. She almost expected to find her napping on the sofa. At this point, it really wouldn't have surprised her.

She checked the office that the owner, Harvey, sometimes used. The light was off, and while Rain had been known to shirk her duties, sitting in the office with the light off would be pushing it, even for her. The door to the employee bathroom was ajar and the light was off as well. Not there either. That left the employee entrance at the very back of the building. She opened the door and poked her head out, scanning the area for the missing waitress. The immediate lot was clear, but she could smell the stench of cigarettes very close.

"Rain," she called and heard a movement on the other side of the door. Rain was leaning against the building, the skin of her bent knee peeking out of one of her pants' many tears, a boot-clad foot resting against the wall, blowing smoke to the heavens as if she had no concerns in the world. "I need you inside now."

"What's the big deal?" she asked, slowly rolling her big brown eyes to look at Lillian. She took a pull on the cigarette, blowing smoke through glossy lips. Lillian watched as it curled toward the door in a slow wave. "I'm on a break, as you can see."

"It's not time for your break," she told her sternly. "Another table just sat down, you have others to check on, and I'm sure more have come in in the time it took me to find you."

"It's not like I left… just needed a smoke, you know?"

"No. I don't know. You can't just leave without getting someone to cover you."

"I told you I was coming out here." She lazily took another pull, clearly not going anywhere until she finished.

"You didn't say anything to me. Otherwise, I would have known where to find you."

"Well, maybe it was Lana then. I don't remember who, but I'm sure I told someone," she said, waving her hand as if it was settled.

"Whatever, Rain," she could hear the exasperation in her voice. "Either way we're swamped and shorthanded. I don't have the time to stand here arguing with you over who you told you were leaving. I need your help. Can you please get in there and help me?"

"Yeah, yeah, I'll be right in."

Lillian started to take a step back through the door when Rain spoke again.

"You know, if we're so busy, Harvey really shouldn't have given Marley all that time off. Seems like this is the worst time for a vacation."

Lillian turned back to Rain, dumbfounded, "Marley is on maternity leave. She's not on vacation. She just had a baby."

"Yeah, but it's been a few weeks, and we're busy, as you keep reminding me. Shouldn't she be back by now? Maybe Harvey should call her in."

"Will you get in here please?" she sighed, no longer willing to argue.

Rain took one last drag off the cigarette, smashed it against the brick wall she had been leaning against, then flicked it at the no-smoking sign posted on the employee entrance door.

"Look at that, all ready to go. You stress way too much, Lil."

She went around Lillian and breezed through the door, the stench of smoke trailing behind as she passed. She went straight into the bathroom.

"Calm down, calm down," she sang before Lillian could protest. "I'll just be a sec." And shut the door in Lillian's face.

"Hurry up, and don't smell like smoke when you come out front," Lillian called through the door.

Lillian rushed to the front, hoping the smell wasn't clinging to her clothes, too. They were really going to need some help, *reliable* help, and soon. Otherwise, the tourist season would be a disaster.

"You find her?" Lana asked as Lillian passed by.

"Out back," she confirmed, then stopped, turning to Lana. "Did she tell you she was taking a smoke break?"

"Not that I remember, and if she had tried, I would have told her skinny little butt to get back out there and help you. Three more tables left, and one more came in while you were out there. I filled their waters and they're looking at the menus."

"Thanks, Lana. You didn't have to do that, you know. You're busy enough here, but I do appreciate your help. Heaven knows I need it."

"Well, I can't feed them if they turn around and leave, now, can I?"

Lillian laughed, "I guess not. I'll go get their orders and have Rain clear the tables when she gets up here. Will you let her know?"

"Sure thing, go get me something to cook," she said, wiping clean her already gleaming surfaces. How she kept everything tidy when they stayed as busy as they did, and still managed to make delicious foods come out on time, Lillian would never know. Sure, she had a crew in there—which she always kept in line, always had on-task—but Lana alone was like having three kitchen workers in one who never seemed to tire.

Lillian went back out to the noisy diner, a medley of voices flowing around the room. Different speeds, pitches, male and female tones, different cadences and accents all merging and separating, mini conversations coming in and out of range as she passed from table to table. She scanned the room as she went, assessing which of the newcomers had been first.

One couple was still studying the menus, discussing what they may or may not want to try today, their waters still full. Not ready yet. She continued to scan. A couple of teenagers were laughing and looking out the window, waving wildly as another teen jogged across the street toward the restaurant. Meeting up with friends, she mused. She'd give them some time. Glancing around again, she saw a pair of regulars sipping coffee, their menus put away. Bingo. She headed toward the elderly couple, already knowing what they'd order.

"Lilly dear," Gran said as Lillian approached, "we've helped ourselves to the decaf and started you a new pot as we took the last of the other. You know what we'd like—"

"Now what if I want something different?" Gran's husband, Pops, interrupted. He pretended agitation but winked at Lillian. The laugh lines creasing his eyes were indicative of years of ornery behavior. "You can't just go on assuming you know what I want all the time, woman."

"You're right, of course," Gran conceded with a look of her own as she handed him one of the menus to decide. Lillian wasn't sure if Gran's hair turned white from old age, or Pops' antics over their many years together. "Don't take all day. Can't you see Lilly here is busy?"

Lillian tried not to chuckle as he made a show of looking over the menu, his eyebrows rising, oohing and aahing as if he found something new. That would only encourage him further and while Gran was a patient person, Lillian didn't want to push the limits. Thankfully Pops was quick in deciding.

"Ah yes, I've got it," he stated with flare, placing the menu back in its holder before taking a quick sip of his coffee and turning to Lillian. "I'll have the usual."

Gran rolled her eyes and shook her head, trying to conceal the smile that Pops always managed to win out of her.

"He's a toddler, I tell you," Gran told Lillian.

"Two usuals coming up," Lillian laughed, perfectly happy to have the banter of the couple that the locals had taken to calling Gran and Pops, over the blatant disrespect and disregard of Rain minutes earlier.

"Looks like you could use some help in here," Gran said, glancing around at the full restaurant and lack of servers.

"Well, you remember Marley just had her little boy a month ago, so she's still out on maternity leave for a few more weeks, and Rain… is here somewhere," she finished weakly, not wanting to speak poorly of the girl, no matter how much she couldn't stand her attitude or poor work ethic.

"What kind of name is Rain anyway?" Pops started up. "It's a goofy name if you ask me. Goofy parents giving their daughter a goofy name." He shook his head. "People who give their kids names like that don't teach values like they did when I was young. No values… that's why she's not out here pulling her weight, leaving it all to Lilly here—"

"Pops," Gran scolded, the tone stopping him from keeping on with his rant.

"What?" He asked with a little extra innocence to his voice.

Just for that, Pops was getting double meat. She knew she liked him for a reason.

"I'll get your order going as quick as I can," Lillian quickly said, breaking away so she could help the other tables that were finally ready. Their conversation faded into the rest of the background chatter.

Still no sign of Rain.

She stopped at the other tables and quickly took their orders, then swung by the order station, pinning the orders to the quaint spinner that nobody wanted to get rid of and let Lana know about the double meat for Pops. Lana informed her that she still hadn't seen Rain to task her with clearing, so Lillian got started on that as well.

By the time Rain finally appeared, all the tables that needed it had been cleared, the orders had been delivered, and Lillian had started rolling silverware into their napkins and rings.

"Where have you been?"

Rain tied on her half apron, tucking her order book and pen into a pocket. "I told you I had to use the restroom. You saw me go in there." She pulled her black hair into a low ponytail, the navy highlights standing out against her white top.

"That was over twenty minutes ago. I needed you out here," Lillian said, trying to maintain her composure.

Rain looked around the room, "Everything looks fine. Oh, except you let that table's drinks run dry," she clucked her tongue in disapproval. "I'll get them some refills for you. Do you remember what they had? Oh, never mind," she interrupted before Lillian could tell her exactly what they were drinking, "I'll just ask them; wouldn't want them to get the wrong drink and they blame me for your forgetfulness."

She walked off, a superior sway to her step as she headed toward the table.

"You want me to whack her over the head with my flipper?" Lana asked through the window. "It won't do much, but I'd enjoy it."

"You and me both," Lillian agreed. "Thanks, but no thanks."

"Just let me know if you change your mind. I'd have to throw out the flipper because it'd be contaminated of course, but it's a sacrifice I'd be willing to make for the greater good of the team."

Lillian groaned and rubbed her forehead. "Oh she really gets on my nerves sometimes."

"Not sure what Harvey saw when he hired her." Lana leaned against the wall as she chatted, folding her long arms in front of her.

"She wasn't always this bad," Lillian said weakly.

"Sure, in the beginning she was just lazy, now she's lazy and rude. Hey, you want a smoothie? Looks like it's slowing down a little, I can make you one real quick."

"Keeping tabs on my meals?" she laughed.

"Nah, I just know you well enough that you'll keep going 'til you drop."

Lillian and Lana had been working together for three years, but Lana had seniority with seven years at Wisteria. When Lillian joined the server staff, Lana already had a reputation for being the kitchen queen. She'd been head chef in a fancy restaurant on the East Coast where the plates dwarfed the sample-sized portions that were served. She gave up the life, the hustle, and the stress to chase the man of her dreams, but realized he was a dud and landed in Juniper Hollow instead. She'd fallen in love with the quaint mountain-style town and the classic American diner that was Wisteria. When she met Harvey, she convinced him to let her cook for him and she never left.

When Lillian met her for the first time, Lana laid out the rules of her kitchen which Lillian accepted since she was no cook herself. Lana sized her up, studied her in earnest, then announced that they were going to be friends. Lillian had laughed and made a comment about knowing nothing about each other. Lana had responded with something along the lines of having to get along due to the close working quarters at Wisteria, so why not just cut out the wasted time of seeing if they *could* be friends and just *be* friends.

Somehow their friendship worked despite being complete opposites, or maybe because of it. Lana was tall and lithe, a natural cross-country runner still into her early thirties, with olive-toned skin, dark brown eyes, and dark curly hair. Lillian always thought Lana looked like a Mediterranean gypsy whereas Lillian's light skin and wavy brown hair made her more akin to a midwestern librarian… maybe if she was lucky, a forest witch. Sometimes it was hard not to feel like the meeker kid sister next to Lana. She wasn't short, but compared to Lana's 5'9", Lillian felt slight.

Lana had sworn off relationships, which only meant she wasn't exclusive to any one man and enjoyed having a good time. Lillian hadn't seriously dated anyone in years with only the random night out here and there at Lana's insistence, warning her that she'd become an old maid by the time she reached thirty if she didn't. Where Lana spoke her mind whether you wanted to hear it or not, Lillian tended to be more reserved. Lana rarely took anything seriously, often pointing out that Lillian carried the burden enough for both of them.

"What d'ya say?"

"What?" Lillian asked.

"You want a smoothie? I've got the time."

Lillian assessed the dining area. "Sure, mix me up something good. I'll go get Rain tasked with something and be right back."

Rain was sitting on the opposite side of the counter, pretending to watch the restaurant, while actually texting on her phone.

"Hey, did you get those drinks?"

"They said no refills," Rain told her phone.

"Okay, why don't you go clean those tables that left, and then roll some silverware."

"What are you gonna be doing then, if I'm doing all that?" she asked petulantly.

One… two… three… Lillian counted in her head. *Let it go. Even if you listed them off, she won't hear the things you did, alone, with a full house, for over thirty minutes.*

She counted to four for good measure.

"Lana is making me a smoothie. I'm going to head to the back and drink it. I'll be right back out," she stated shortly.

"Don't take too long. I don't make enough to do both our jobs…" she mumbled as she headed to get the cart to clear the tables.

Lillian, noticing the searching glances from Rain's table, delivered refills in to-go cups and made apologies for Rain.

Rain looked up as Lillian finally headed to the back, still clearing the first table, slower than a turtle through mud.

"Hmm. I guess they changed their minds," she said, clearing one piece at a time.

"They're ready for the check." Lillian didn't stop to listen to another excuse.

"My flipper's still at the ready," Lana told her when she finally made it back to drink her melting smoothie.

"Don't tempt me."

TWO
-LILLIAN-

She downed the drink in record time and hurried back out front as soon as she was finished, thanking Lana while her head throbbed from the brain freeze. Gran and Pops were just readying themselves to leave as Lillian stepped up.

"Oh, Lilly dear, I'm glad you're here. We need to pay," Gran said, reaching over to squeeze her hand.

"You know you can leave it on the table like always."

"Sure, if we wanted her to get your tip," Pops nodded at Rain across the room, slowly rolling the utensils.

"Well," Lillian sighed, putting on a smile. "We all have to work together, sometimes clearing each other's tables, but we always make sure the tips get where they're supposed to go."

"Not that one," Pops said, eyeballing her as if she was up to no good even as they spoke. "She's been taking the cash and pocketing it, splitting between her apron and her pocket. I didn't see her go to the register once since you were gone. She's probably not even ringing out the cash-only bills. She's a cool one, that girl. Keep an eye on her."

"Don't worry, I will."

"Oh, stop causing more problems for the girl and pay her already," Gran told him.

"I'm not the one causing problems," Pops countered. "Anyway, here's *your* tip, not hers. Don't you split it with her because she hasn't been doing anything anyway."

He slipped a fifty into her apron pocket, her eyes going large at the denomination on a lunchtime meal, then separately gave exact pay for their bill.

"I can't take that, it's too much," she told them wondering if his eyesight was failing and he meant to give her a smaller bill. She reached for the money, but Gran grabbed her hand and gave a little squeeze, her grip surprisingly firm for as soft as her hands felt.

"Don't you even try to give that back. You deserve it," she said as Pops nodded in agreement, still scowling across the room at Rain. "You work harder than anyone here. Go spend it on something nice for yourself, not bills," she lectured.

"Thank you both," she said as they gathered their things. "See you next time."

She made her way over to Rain, who was not even pretending to work anymore.

"I thought they'd never leave," Rain said when she approached, glowering at the elderly couple as the door closed behind them. "They always stay too long, have a superior attitude like they know what's best for everyone, and then they never tip worth a damn. I'm going to tell them next time that Harvey is setting a new rule that people can't stay longer than thirty minutes, that we're just too busy for people to loiter. I mean clearly that's not the case, but maybe they'll get the hint and go somewhere else."

"You'll do no such thing, to any of our customers. They can stay for as long as they want. Another table will open, and you definitely aren't going to be doing that in Harvey's or the diner's name."

She thought of the fifty in her pocket versus Rain's attitude and knew it wasn't Gran and Pops that was the problem.

"Sheesh, no need to get your panties all in a wad. I'm just saying that if some things changed around here, business could be a lot better and we could hire the help you think we need so bad. I mean, we're so dead, I haven't had anything to do all afternoon. I should probably have a talk with Harvey about some new ideas to freshen this place up, bring it up to this century at least, get a younger crowd in here instead of all these fossils. You and Lana have been here so long that you probably don't even see how outdated everything is, how out of style. None of my friends ever even think of coming in here." She looked around the restaurant, seeing none of the charm the place had to offer, only the negative aspects. "If he made a few upgrades, got some better music in here, was more exclusive in who he let in, this place could have so much more business."

Lillian looked around the diner as Rain continued to spew negativity, seeing what Rain wouldn't: the memories this place held. The checkerboard tiled floor and red upholstered booths, iconic of a simpler time. The functioning jukebox that kids liked to stick their quarters into, making a selection just to watch the record be picked and played, even if they didn't know the song they were choosing. The barstools that swiveled along the counter where people could sip their milkshakes served in tall glasses with whipped cream and a cherry on top. The couples that came for coffee served all day long because it's the best in town and has been for sixty years. She couldn't see that it was more than just a restaurant that looked out of its time.

"The diner is nostalgic," Lillian said, "and despite you being bored, we've been slammed all day."

"Hey Lillian," Lana called before Rain could start up again.

Both women turned toward her.

"Can you come in here for a sec? I have a question about one of your orders."

"Be right there," Lillian called back, thankful this conversation with Rain would finally stop.

Rain stood as if she was going to go check on a table, "Oh, here's your tips. I cleared your tables for you. Don't worry, it's okay; you were busy, so I covered for you." She reached into her apron and separated out some bills, passing them over and keeping some for herself, leaving Lillian wondering about the pocketed money.

Lillian glanced at the bills in her hand, noted which tables Rain had cleared and averaged out what tips should have been, which was substantially more than was handed over.

"There's only twenty here, seems low for the tables," she wondered aloud to see what Rain's response would be.

"The rest paid with card, and I did have to cover for you didn't I, so I took my tips out, too. Fair's fair. I wouldn't expect you to work for free while I was gone. You really should go see about that order."

Rain sauntered off to greet an incoming table. Lillian stared after her, choosing not to get worked up over the things Rain did or said. It wasn't worth the energy. She wandered over to see about Lana and the order.

"Hey, what question did you have?"

"Oh nothing, it just looked like Rain was about to get skewered with a butter knife there for a minute. Which, honestly, would be okay by me, but probably wouldn't go over too well with the early bird crowd," she shrugged, like the early birds could possibly go either way, too. "What was that all about?"

"Oh, just Rain being Rain. I can't even repeat most of it; it was that outlandish. The gist of it was that Harvey's running this place into the ground, and despite hating it here, her business degree will make her the perfect candidate to take over and make something of all of this disaster. She somehow knows how to bring the diner into this century and appeal to a more elite crowd. She thinks I can't hack being a server even though, according to her, I've been working here about ten years longer than I've been alive, and all of our customers are older than dirt, excuse me, fossils or dinosaurs, take your pick. Oh, and you're not invited to stay on as an employee when she takes over, but she *might* be able to find a place for *me* if I'm not too old, can keep up, and get my act together."

Lana considered her options, "If I ever had to work for her, I'd probably burn the whole thing to the ground. Oops, must have been a grease fire… clumsy me," she sang.

"Ha," Lillian snorted, "that would never happen. You love it here too much."

"This place, yes. You and Harvey, yes. Her? Absolutely, unequivocally, and most definitely not. Bye-bye diner, it's been fun, but you had a good run," she joked.

"It won't come to that," Lillian said, looking over the restaurant, knowing the plans Harvey had already set into place years earlier, that assuredly did not include Rain as head honcho. "I'll take your flipper to her first, whip her into shape, then we'll take over."

"Oh, a mutiny! I love it," Lana squealed gleefully, then paused. "Wait, isn't she in school to do nails or something?"

"No, she got kicked out, remember? Her dad got tired of paying her way in the city when she wouldn't take anything seriously, so she had to come back home. She lives with her mom now, I think. I guess she thinks business school is going to be easier and a better fit for her."

"Hmm, I'm not worried about our odds."

Rain came to the window then, to put in an order with Lana, "Here's this for that table over there." She turned to Lillian. "I'm going to have to cut out early. Lil, you can cover for me until Gary gets here in an hour, right? Since I covered for you when you had your smoothie break."

"Sure, whatever Rain," Lillian said, happy not to have to put up with her anymore for a day. The crowd was starting to slow down before the dinner rush anyway.

"Cool, thanks. It's really dead out there right now, but if you don't think you can handle it, then I guess I can cancel my night and stay," she said in a tone that didn't suggest it was an option. "Actually," she smiled as the bell rang and another person entered the diner. "I can take one more customer."

Lillian turned to see who Rain would be willing to stay on for. "Well, great," she sighed, but smiled politely as the dark-haired deputy took a seat.

"Mmm. I'd let him handcuff me any day," Rain said, walking over to his table before Lillian or Lana could respond.

"You know she's got a point," Lana said through the window. They watched as Rain greeted him, talked for a moment, and then sauntered back.

"God he's hot. Like hot-hot," Rain said when she returned to lean against the counter and openly stare at him as he studied his menu.

"Ryder never had a problem in the looks department," Lillian murmured as she busied herself topping off saltshakers.

"I don't care what problems he has; sign me up."

"You know he's like ten years older than you, right?" Lana asked her, watching Lillian pretend to be busy.

"Who cares? Hot's hot."

"How long *did* you and Ryder date?" Lana asked Lillian, getting a sharp look in return.

"Yeah… right," Rain snorted, looking Lillian up and down.

"I thought you were leaving," Lillian interjected before Rain could go on about how good the man that ripped out her heart and left it floundering looked with his tousled hair and bad boy grin.

"I mean, yeah, I've gotta get the stench of grease off me, but it can wait. Imma go see if he's ready to order," she said pushing off of the counter.

"Grease she can't handle, but cigarette smell is fine," Lillian wondered.

She glanced over to see Rain rest her hip against his table, initially blocking her view of Ryder. He leaned back in the booth, and she could see him smiling as he talked, Rain laughing a little too encouragingly. His gaze flicked to Lillian, catching her looking, his smile never faltering as his eyes traveled down and then back up, his smile slowly widening before he turned his attention back to Rain.

Lillian turned back to her saltshakers before he could see her cheeks warming.

"Damn girl. If someone just looked at me like that, I'd already be dragging him out back," Lana said, pretending to fan herself in her kitchen.

"You and every other woman in town," Lillian said, screwing on the lid to another container.

"He wants this to go," Rain said, handing the order slip through to Lana.

"Are you going to check on any of your other tables before you go?" Lillian reminded her as one of her orders came up.

"You already said I could go, that you could cover," she said matter-of-factly. "I'm only staying for him," she said, like that cleared her of any other duties.

Lillian sighed when Rain didn't budge from her lean against the counter, not wanting to fight. "Fine, I'll check on them," she said, taking the order with her as she did.

She had hoped checking the other tables would distract her from Ryder.

She was wrong.

Why was he there? He'd never come in by himself in the three years she'd worked at Wisteria. Why did he look at her the way he did? *Because that's what Ryder does. Let it go. He just wants to see if he can get a rise out of you.* Checking the tables didn't take long enough for her to avoid his table on her way back around. Since his food wasn't ready and she'd checked on everyone else, she couldn't intentionally avoid his table. It would be rude and obvious.

"Hey Lilly." He smiled his million-dollar smile.

"Ryder," she greeted, hoping her cheeks didn't flush like he'd always been able to get out of her, even when she didn't want to smile back. "Rain said you're taking your order to go." She nodded to his glass. "Do you want one of those to go as well?"

"That'd be great," he said, never taking his piercing blue eyes off of her. "Can you send a decaf coffee as well, for the sheriff?"

She smiled and glanced toward the door on impulse. "Is he here, too? Why didn't he come in?"

"Nah, I'm headed back. Thought I'd bring him one. You know how much he likes the coffee here."

"I'll pack it up and send it over with Rain. Tell my dad I said hi."

"Or you could bring it over." He smiled again.

"Oh, but it'll make her day," she said overly sweetly and turned before he could say anything more, smirking to herself.

"What did you say to him?" Rain hissed.

"Nothing. He wants a coffee to go, too," she said as she poured and secured the drinks in a carrier.

"You said *something*," she huffed. "He's looking at you like—"

"Like this meal isn't going to satisfy his appetite," Lana finished, setting the bagged food on the window and hitting the bell in front of Rain's face, receiving a glare in return.

"That's just Ryder being Ryder," Lillian said. She wouldn't give him the satisfaction of glancing back. "He looks at every woman that way."

"Oh… goody," Rain smiled, grabbing the drinks and the bag, and sashayed back to his table.

It wasn't long before Lillian heard the bell over the door and Rain made her way back on a huff. "He said to tell *you* bye."

Lana chuckled in her kitchen.

Rain looked at Lillian again. "What did you say? Did you put him up to that?"

"That doesn't even make sense, Rain. Why would I tell him to tell you to tell me 'bye'?"

"What doesn't make sense is him looking at *you* like you're the only one in the room."

"Maybe he's not into blue hair," Lana called through the window as she cleaned her station.

Rain shot her a dirty look but Lana ignored her, dancing to her own tune as she wiped the already shining surface.

"I wouldn't read too much into a look, Rain. Ryder's just a flirt."

She didn't have to see his face to remember his smile or the way his blue eyes sparkled in such stark contrast to his dark hair. She could summon his voice after not hearing it for days, weeks… years. She could remember what it felt like to be touched by him, how her heart would race when he held her close. And she could remember the torment that night when she caught him wrapped around another woman.

"How is it flirting if you aren't paying attention?"

"It's all a game to him," Lillian told her. "He got under your skin by not paying enough attention to you, so now you'll think about him more. Don't even waste your time."

"Whatever. I've got a date anyway. See you tomorrow, unless things go *really* well, in which case, we'll just see if I can make it in." She took off her apron, rolled it up to put back in her locker, then went through the swinging door to the kitchen. She called back, "Oh and Lil, any of my tips that you clear out for me tonight, you can just give to me when I work next. Bye ladies, wish me luck!" She waved over her shoulder as she disappeared out the back exit.

"And are we wishing her luck that her date takes her far, far away from here, so we don't have to deal with her again?" Lana asked.

"I think that would be wishing *us* luck."

"Damn, you're right," Lana admitted. "She was right you know."

"Rain? Right?... About what?"

"Ryder. He was staring hard, and it didn't have anything to do with making Rain jealous."

Lillian gave her the Look. "I've known him a long time. Trust me, it's always a game to him."

"That's not what I saw."

"There's nothing to see… Trust me."

THREE

-Sheriff Bill-

Bill parked the beat-up, older-than-dirt Blazer in front of the station and reached for his thermos. He was about to head inside to see what had called him in an hour early, when one of his deputies came out the door and headed to the window.

"Hey Sheriff, sorry to drag you out of bed."

"You know I'm up with the birds, Simon. What's the big deal?"

"Some campers found a body."

The sheriff sighed and rubbed his forehead, "Alright, get in. Fill me in on the way."

Simon hurried around the front of the truck and climbed into the passenger side. Bill waited and stared.

"Oh, right, seatbelt," Simon said, clicking his on so Bill would pull out of the parking space.

"You know, for an enforcer of the law, you always seem to forget that particular one."

"Just wasn't ever raised with 'em," he said, as if that made all the difference in the world. "Okay, so here's what we've got," he started. "Some kids've been camping out by the Bend for a couple nights, doing some fishing and kayaking, you know, regular stuff. One of the guys gets up to take a leak, sees something across the river, a mess of junk you know, sticks and river debris wedged up." Bill nodded that he understood. "Anyway, kid didn't think anything of it at first, but then an arm or something moved off whatever it was stuck on, fell into the water, and he realized it was a person. The guy yelled at the others to wake up and they got their kayaks out to cross and help the person trapped in the water. Someone stayed back and called 911. Ryder was first on scene, set up a perimeter, but who knows how much the campers messed up already."

"Ryder's good, he'll keep things in line until we can get there."

"He's gunnin' for your job," Simon blurted.

Bill glanced over at the surprising outburst. "I've been sheriff for a long time Simon, and I'm not ready to pass the torch just yet," he told his deputy.

"I don't know. I get the feeling he's gonna try and push you out."

"Ryder's a good cop and ambitious, but he's never overstepped. When it comes time for someone else to take over the reins," he turned to Simon, "many years from now," he said before turning back to the road, "I'd back Ryder." He glanced at Simon again. "What about you? Is sheriff on your list?"

"Me?" he asked, shocked, as if the thought had never crossed his mind. "No. I mean… I've never thought about not working under your lead."

Bill nodded, not surprised that he wasn't interested in leading; some weren't. "You may not see it yet, but Ryder'll make a good sheriff one day."

"But he's nowhere close to what you are, what you do for this community."

"Ryder's not the worst of the bunch and he has plenty of time to keep learning. Like I said, I'm not on my way out any time soon," he said calmly, navigating the still dark morning roads with ease. "Now, you said we had a body, not a rescue. I take it our early morning mystery swimmer didn't make it?"

"I guess not," Simon stated, getting back to business. "I called you when we got the call that there was someone stuck in the water and Ryder was responding. Thought you should be up at least for something like this if reporters start getting involved, but then right before you made it to the station, Ryder called in and said the guy was DOA."

"Any resuscitation attempts?" Bill wondered.

"Not sure. He kinda made it sound like the guy had been in the water a while."

"Alright. We'll see what we see," Bill told him, turning the old truck off the smooth paved road onto the rough terrain that his truck couldn't wait to dig into.

The Bend was exactly what it sounded like, a bend in the river with enough flat area that people could camp. There was a rocky shore that would be littered with coolers, lawn chairs, and plenty of swimmers in a few weeks when the weather warmed up and all anyone wanted to do was peel off their clothes and cool off in the water. This area of the gargantuan river was a great place to put in and take out rafts because the water was calm for a few hundred feet along the long shore. A little farther up, the river and the rapids could get tricky if a rafter didn't know what they were doing. It wouldn't be the first time this river had claimed a tourist who thought they were capable.

Bill could see the lights up ahead on the path, still more illuminating than the slowly brightening sky. He headed toward the colorful array, the yellow tape already gathering an audience, and parked next to the ambulance. He and Simon crossed under the tape and headed down to the shore where Ryder was talking to a small group of what appeared to be teens. He broke away when he saw the sheriff and jogged over to him.

"Morning Sheriff, glad you could get out here so quick," he said, giving an almost imperceptible sidelong glance in Simon's direction.

"Fill us in," Bill told him.

"I already have statements from the three witnesses," he scrolled through his phone and read off their names and ages. "Two nineteen-year-olds and one twenty, all out here for the weekend celebrating the twenty-year-old's birthday. Pretty sure they had some beers, but none of them seem to be involved with the body. They're all pretty shaken up by finding it out there across the water. None of them are local, heard there was good kayaking and fishing out here. Said they heard tourist season kicks off with a bang, staying busy all summer long, so they wanted to check things out early. They didn't hear anything or anyone else out here all weekend."

"Which one found the body?"

"That would be the twenty-year-old, Evan," Ryder pointed out one of the boys sitting on a rock with a blanket wrapped around his shoulders.

Bill made his way over to the boy and squatted down in front of him. The boy looked tired and ashen-faced.

"Evan?" Bill asked, and the boy nodded weakly.

"Yes, sir," he said, the smell of vomit lightly tingeing the air between them.

"Can you tell me what happened here?"

Evan glanced at Bill, then over to Ryder.

"I know you've already given my deputy your statement, and he's filled me in, but I'd like to hear your version directly."

"Oh, yes sir," he sat up a little straighter, realizing he was talking to the sheriff. "Sorry, it's been a long morning already."

"Take your time, tell me from the start."

"Today's my birthday," he said, letting out a breath. "Juniper Hollow was one of those towns we'd heard about back when we were freshmen. It was on some ghost story, creepy town documentary thing. You know, 'cuz of the Mountain… We thought it'd be cool to check out. We never made it out here though… and now we're all graduated…" his thoughts trailed off as if he'd forgotten where he'd been heading. He glanced toward the water. "We're into rafting the rapids, and this river is known for its crazy ride. Then, add in the Mountain, and that makes this place a double whammy of wicked tries." He paused. "After this though… scary stories…" He trailed off, shaking his head clear of the thoughts. "A dead body's a lot for one birthday," he finished, his unfocused eyes turning back in the direction of the river again.

"So, you and your friends came out to do some camping and kayaking," the sheriff prompted.

"Right, yeah." Evan came back to the now. "We spent the first day heading down river from here, heard that was the easier route. It was a pretty good ride, but nothing we couldn't handle. We did some fishing, some drinking," he admitted, "but didn't go back on the water that day. Yesterday we put in farther upriver, and whoa… have you done that part of the water?" he said, a glimmer of the excitable boy showing through. “It’s intense, definitely holds up to its reputation. It had us all cooked by the time we got back to camp. It took everything to catch and make up dinner, then we all called it a night early, maybe eleven o’clock.

“We were beat… at least, I know I was, but then well, nature called, and I got up to, you know, water the grass and that’s when I saw it… him,” he corrected, “caught up in some branches and stuff. I couldn’t really tell what it was ‘cuz it was so dark, but there was light from the moon, and I could tell it was pretty big, not something that was supposed to be there. Like, it didn’t look like a rock or log or nothin’. I guess I was sorta starin’ at it for a while, kinda half asleep, when the guy’s arm flopped off the branch and splashed into the water. I could see it then, him, I mean, like the picture became clear.”

Evan paused, thinking again. “You know when you’re looking at one of those illusion things and just can’t see what it’s supposed to be, but then bam,” he clapped his hands together, “it just appears and you’re like, ‘hey, that’s a lion,’ only this time… it was a person…” he mumbled. “Anyway, I started yelling for the others to wake up and call the police, tellin’ them someone was in the water. It’s a little too far across the water there, and it doesn’t look like much on the surface, but there’s a current under there. I knew I couldn’t swim over to him *and* help him back if I had to, so Brian and I grabbed our kayaks and paddled over.

"At first, I thought I was wrong, that it wasn’t a person, that my eyes had been messin’ with me from so far away. It just didn’t look like a person anymore…” he trailed off.

“Evan,” Bill asked gently, bringing him back to the present again. “Did you try and help the man?”

“Oh no,” he said immediately, shaking his head. “We could tell he was a goner. He had to have been dead for a while, his skin was so… thin…” He shook the image out of his head. “Brian and I looked at each other and knew we shouldn’t touch him since there was nothin’ we could do to help him, you know, contaminating the scene and all that, but we didn’t want to leave him either. What if he broke loose and floated away? So, I stayed over there until the cops came. This one,” he nodded to Ryder, “borrowed Brian’s kayak and came over, asked me a couple quick questions and then sent me back over here to wait for the ambulance. When the rescue boat showed up with more people to get him out of the water, your guy came back across and asked us all more questions. You showed up just after.”

“Okay,” Bill said, standing. “We’re probably going to have to do some more follow-up. Can you and your friends stay in town a little longer?”

“Oh… yeah… sure thing. Like I said, we were planning to stay a few more days, take a hike to the Mountain, but now I’m not so sure…”

“Make sure you all stay nearby and that my deputy has your info.”

“Yes sir, of course.”

“And you do know that the Mountain is restricted land, right? Nobody’s allowed in there, and the stories are just that, stories.”

"That's the great part, the mystery of it," Evan said, the spark returning to his eyes. "I mean, nobody can say what went on in there; where'd all the people go? And still, what happens up there now?"

"Well, I'd hate to catch you up there and have to bring you into the station for trespassing," Bill warned the kid.

"No, sir," Evan sat up straighter again. "This was enough for this trip," he said. He looked beyond the sheriff, his face losing what little color it had left. "Is it okay if I'm not over here right now?" he asked, clenching his jaw.

Bill turned his gaze to where the boy was watching the rescue boat coming ashore, a sheet draped over the shape of a body within.

"Why don't you head over to those trees?" he told the boy, who took off running to lose whatever was left of his fish dinner in the shrubs.

Bill walked over to the boat as the paramedics lifted the body out, already strapped to a board for carrying since the wheels would be useless over the rocks, and hauled it over to load into the silent ambulance. Bill climbed in after them and pulled the sheet back, the face unrecognizable, bloated and bluish. He didn't even know if this man was a local or a tourist. He covered him back up and went to find Ryder and his other deputies.

"All right, this isn't the first body that's washed ashore," he said. "This is a hard float and has claimed more than its fair share. We'll need to search the area for identification. It'll be a long shot in these waters, but maybe there's a campsite upriver or maybe he had a pack. Check the local missing persons reports, as well as in neighboring towns. It's possible nobody knows to look for him yet. Check to see if anyone has reported finding kayaks or other personal belongings washing up on shore. We don't know yet who this is, where he started, or how long he's been in the water. Somebody is missing a son, husband, brother, or dad, and we need to figure out the answer fast. The reporters are going to have a heyday if we don't get an appropriate statement right away."

His team nodded and divided up the tasks. They were good at what they did; he was confident they'd turn up something soon.

"Simon, come with me. We're going to ride back and talk to the medical examiner and see if we can learn some information about our guy in there."

"Sure thing," he said and headed back to the Blazer.

"Ryder, keep this wrapped as tight as you can. I don't need to remind you how fast this can unravel."

"No, sir, I'm on it," Ryder told his superior.

Bill climbed into the driver's seat and sipped his coffee, which was still piping hot. He waited for Simon to buckle up, and wondered about the poor man who wouldn't see the sun come up on another day. Did he have a family? Was he missed yet? Was he involved in the community or just passing through?

No matter how often he'd had to do it, Bill always hated delivering the news of a death to an unsuspecting family. Would this man's wife stare at him with lifeless eyes, not believing the words to be true? Would he have to answer to a son asking why he'd never get to play catch with his dad again? Would this man's mother wail at outliving her son?

It was one of his least favorite parts of his job, but these were his people and he was responsible for them. For the sake of this man's family, he hoped the M.E. could be convinced to make this a priority.

FOUR

-Lillian-

The discovery of a body in the river, combined with the chatter of a small town, was like kerosene to a fire. Everyone wanted to be the first to share the juiciest piece of gossip—no matter how morbid—which meant that Lillian had heard the news by seven a.m. She had stopped checking her messages and got off social media when it was already all she was seeing, all anyone was messaging about, curious to see if she had insider information.

She pulled her car up to the employee entrance to pick up her Sunday morning standing order: Harvey's famous biscuits and gravy with extra sausage and two steaming cups of coffee to go. Harvey was packing up the last of the homemade biscuits into the paper sack, the coffees ready in a carrier, when she walked in from the back.

"I could have brought this out to the car," he told her. "There was no reason for you to come in here on your day off."

"I knew you weren't going to tell me how busy it was, so I had to come see for myself," she told him leaning in to give him a hug and a kiss on his cheek. He smelled of the same aftershave her grandpa had used when he was still alive, or maybe she'd grown so used to Harvey's that she'd merged both scents into one. Something about the spicy musk and subtle clove mixed with cinnamon gave her a sense of calm every time she smelled it. Or possibly it could be how relaxed Harvey always seemed to be, even at the busiest times. She peered through the open window to the dining area to assess if this was one of those busy times, to see if she was needed.

"Of course, I'm not going to tell you if we're busy or not. It's your day off; you need to take one sometimes. When we made our arrangement, you agreed to the terms. If you keep working like you are, you're going to burn out, and if you burn out, I can't leave this place to you. If I can't leave this to you, then I'll have to live forever… or find another replacement." He added the replacement comment as if it was an absurdity that he'd never considered.

She laughed. "Well, too bad for you, we already shook on it, and you've already left it to me, so you can say all you want, but there's no going back now… but it would be okay if you live forever because nobody's going to be able to make me breakfast like you do."

"Take it from me, kid, you have to take a break. Now get out of here with that food before you ruin my good name with cold breakfast."

"Even cold it's the best there ever was," she told him, glancing out the window again making sure everything was in order.

"Out," he ordered with mock sternness. "I've kept her in business for sixty years. I think I can manage another day. Your baby will be just fine until you get back, *tomorrow*."

"*Your* baby Harvey. I'm just the lucky one that gets to take care of her."

"Go eat, tell your parents I said hi, and don't come back in here today."

She opened her mouth to retort but gathered her food instead and blew him a kiss as she went out the back door.

When they'd made their arrangement for her to take over, she'd asked to be trained for the different roles and managing of the business before they told anyone about the transition in ownership. She wanted it to be seamless when he finally stepped away. He agreed, as long as he could come in and have free meals for life once he was out. She agreed that it was the least she could do as long as he didn't leave a stingy tip.

And here they were three years later, Harvey phasing himself out of the business more and more, only cooking on Sunday mornings and guiding her when she had questions about the books or purchasing. She knew it was almost time to take over completely; she'd been running things from behind the scenes for over a year, hardly needing Harvey's help anymore, and Harvey was ready too, but that last little step, becoming the sole owner of Wisteria, still terrified her.

She didn't want to disappoint him and all that he'd built.

She brought herself back to the present as she parked her car in the gravel lot next to the ugliest, beat-up old SUV, wondering why her dad loved it so much, and gathered their breakfast to share. She knew he was already busy, but their Sunday morning ritual was as important as ever. This would probably be the only meal he made himself eat today, what with the investigation going on.

"Hey Lillian," the receptionist, Jane, called from her desk. A phone rested between her ear and shoulder as she typed at the same time. "He's in his office." Jane nodded down the hall like Lillian hadn't been hanging out in the station her entire life.

Lillian smiled and thanked her as she passed.

"Hi Dad," she said as she set the drink tray on the desk, taking the bag off the top. She gave him a hug and started unbagging the meals, popping open the Styrofoam containers to let the steam escape in a deliciously aromatic burst. "I talked to Mom this morning. She says you've had a busy morning already."

"Just Mom?"

"Well, her and about five others by now… and social media… and the radio. Any idea who it is yet?"

"Not a clue. He was in the water too long. We can't identify him through photos, we haven't come across any ID yet, and while there are plenty of missing persons reports that could be our guy, we don't have a timeline to help narrow it down. Rich is putting this as a priority, but he can only go so fast. Technology is helpful, but those things take time, too, so we're playing the waiting game on prints, hoping at some point he got entered into the system for us to find him."

"You'll figure it out, yôu always do," she told her dad, fully confident in his ability to take care of this man, to find who he belonged to, and see him home.

"You always were my own cheerleader," he said with a smile, then turned toward the door at the rap on the other side. "Come in, Simon," he called through the door.

Lillian raised her eyebrows when Simon poked his head into the room before stepping in. It never ceased to amaze her when her dad could do magic. At least, magic was what it had always felt like when she was little. How he knew it was Simon from just a knock, was one of the many things that made him a great sheriff. He paid attention to the little things. It wouldn't surprise her if he knew what each of the officers sounded like from their walk alone.

"Sorry to interrupt your breakfast, Sheriff. Mornin' Lillian," he said giving her a sweetly shy smile. He was thin and she'd bet a full foot taller than she was, but he tended to hunch slightly. She'd always wondered if he did it because he didn't want to be the tallest in the room, the focal point, or if he just had poor posture. He'd never been one for the spotlight. When she'd heard he'd joined the sheriff's department, she'd been genuinely surprised, but then again, he'd always been one to offer a helping hand.

"How are you, Simon?" she asked politely.

"Oh, you know, busy trying to figure out who this man in the water is," he said, sounding official, then his cheeks pinked slightly as he looked at the sheriff then back at Lillian, "I mean, we can't really say much about anything, since it's an open investigation, but I figured you probably heard by now," he said, trying to cover his fumble.

"It's all over the news, Simon, she's heard," Bill said dryly to his drowning deputy. "Did you need something?"

"Oh right, yeah," Simon said, directing his attention back to the sheriff. "I just wanted to update you that Rich called and said that he's cleaned up the body; it's banged up, lots of 'lacerations and abrasions' he said, but he's going to get started right away on identifying him and do an autopsy."

Lillian tried to ignore their discussion, the statement of facts, the cataloging of each detail. In their line of work, she understood they needed to keep a certain distance, an impersonal neutrality so they wouldn't be overwhelmed by emotion every time they had to do the job. But for her, sitting in the office, hearing the report of the deceased, it felt very penetrating. The intimacy of death should be reserved for the deceased, whatever higher power they believed in, and their family. It shouldn't be a spectacle to be solved, a story to be shared by the first person to get the newest information. She wished for the sake of the man discovered, and his family, that he could be laid to rest quickly. She hoped he could find peace in whatever his afterlife looked like despite the unrest that his discovery and the unknown nature of his identity had stirred.

"Thanks Simon, let me know if anything else comes in."

"Sure thing sir, as soon as I hear something, you'll know," he glanced back at Lillian and then the sheriff before stepping back through the door.

"See you later, Simon." She waved as he turned to smile.

"You too," he said, ducking out of the room, and closing the door behind him.

Bill took a bite and smiled, shaking his head as he chewed the biscuit.

"What's funny?" she asked.

"Simon. He always finds some reason to give me a report whenever you're here."

"I don't mind the interruption," she told him. "I know you guys are busy and have to work."

"I don't keep him so busy that he can't wait until you leave the building. That information could have waited." He finished another bite before continuing. "He's had his eye on you since high school."

"Oh, well, he's a really nice guy," she said, surprised by this revelation.

In high school he was a year ahead of her, but it was a small school. Everyone pretty much knew everyone else. Nobody ever had a bad thing to say about Simon, maybe because he was always in the background. He was the quiet type, always kept to himself, yet somehow managed to be involved with everything. If there was a football game, he was running concessions. If there was a theater production, he was helping with lighting or set-up. She seemed to recall he played an instrument in the band, but couldn't remember what. She'd never considered him romantically before, but back then she was with Ryder. Later, he was just another of her dad's deputies.

"I'm sure he's just being nice. He's not into me."

Her dad looked at her with one raised eyebrow. "Trust me, he is. How do you think I knew he was there before he came in?"

"First, you've always had a superpower of knowing things."

"Superpower, eh?"

"I used to think you were magic."

He chuckled. "I remember that."

"And second, it's not like there are a lot of people in here this morning. It was a lucky guess."

He gave her the look again. "Every Sunday. He'll find a reason every time. Pay attention next time."

"Well, even if he is, I'm not really dating right now. There's too much going on to think about juggling a relationship," she said, not wanting to get into the dating conversation again. Her dad wasn't nearly as bad as her mom was, always asking when she was going to find a good man and give her grandkids, but he still asked in his own way now and then.

"You know you're not getting any younger, and Simon's a good deputy."

"Dad! I'm not dating your deputies so you can just stop playing matchmaker."

"You dated Ryder," he countered.

Ryder's smiling face and Lana's words about him watching her ran through her mind at the mention of his name.

"That doesn't count; that was high school. He wasn't a deputy for you then, and he messed up his chance with me when he was caught making out with Emma Sophia at prom."

"And you dumped him fair and square, then ran off to college and the big city, and didn't talk to him for over six years. People change, you know."

"You know, sometimes it's hard having a cop as a dad," she joked, "You always know all my business."

"No, that's just being a dad. Now the background checks that I run on your boyfriends, that's the cop in me."

"Dad!" she exclaimed. "You can't just go around running background checks on people."

"Why not? I'm the sheriff, it's sorta what I do."

"Yeah, when the situation needs it, not for someone who's taking me on a date."

"I'd say anyone who's going to take out my only daughter is exactly the situation that calls for it. There are a lot of weirdos out there. Who knows, it could save your life one day. 'Cop dad catches notorious serial killer and saves daughter from date of doom by simple background check,'" he reported, miming the headline of a newspaper with a wave of his hand in front of him. "I'd be a hero."

"You're already my hero." She laughed at the part of her dad that she was sure the rest of the world didn't get to know as the sheriff. "But you really need to work on your headline skills. That one was terrible."

"Well, you're alive today to tell me that, so you're welcome."

"Thanks… I think," she laughed. "But stop trying to set me up. You'll just have to report back to Mom that you've failed again."

"Got it, old maid, who doesn't care about the hearts of her parents to give them grandchildren; heartless… and after all we've done for you." He feigned sadness.

"Oh my gosh Dad, I'm twenty-nine, hardly an old maid, and when I *do* find someone, I promise," she paused to gather her things, "you and Mom will be the last to know."

He chuckled as he cleared the trash from their breakfast, and got up to walk her out, nudging her discretely with his elbow as they passed through the desks. Simon looked very serious and busy, but happened to glance up just in time to wave goodbye.

She smiled to herself. Her dad was adorable when he tried to pretend he wanted her to find a boyfriend. If they were having a serious discussion about datable men, she was sure he'd have an entirely different tactic about keeping the men away, but since he knew she wasn't interested, it was safe to joke.

He gave her a hug when they reached her car. "Go see your mother soon. She worries about you all alone."

"I did just see her a week or so ago, but I will again soon," she said, hoping to reassure him. "I've been on my own for a long time. There's no need for her to worry."

"Tell me that when you have grown kids of your own if you ever have any!"

"I'm leaving now," she giggled. "Love you. I'll check in with Mom."

"Love you back," he said and headed into the building.

Her phone jingled in her pocket. She fished it out to check the message before getting in the car. She smiled at the silly meme Lana sent of a lazy, disinterested cat lounging on a chair with the description, *I can't even can't even.* With a separate text asking:

Rain?

Not a chance. That 'can't even cat' is way more approachable than Rain.

Lillian shot back her response.

"You always had a great smile," Ryder said, startling her as he walked up from his parked truck. He stopped at her car, leaning against it, his arms casually crossed in front of him as if he stopped to chat all the time.

It didn't completely bother her that he looked at ease. What did, however, was how quickly she noticed how good he looked. He'd always had the confidence of a man who knew how attractive he was. Now, with the added authority of his badge and the gun on his hip, he wore that confidence better than she'd ever willingly admit to him. But he knew. He'd always known, which was half his problem. The other half was that he liked the attention from the women who liked to look and had no qualms about pursuing them.

"I'm surprised you remember, what with all the smiles flashed your way."

"Still mad at me, Lilly Flower? After all these years?"

"No, not mad," she told him, smothering the agitation she'd noted in her voice, scolding herself for allowing a reaction; a reaction that she knew he'd noticed by the slight smirk he gave her now. She got her keys out to leave. "Not *anything* anymore."

"Why didn't you take any of my calls," he asked, an emotion that could quite possibly be sincerity shone in his eyes. "I tried apologizing."

"Ryder it's been a long time since that night," she sighed. She was surprised he was bringing up their past after all this time. She was frustrated that a tiny bit of her heart still ached at his mention of an apology, but mostly it remembered how hurt she'd been because of his actions. "You showed me who you really were, and I didn't like it. There wasn't anything to say."

"I had things to say then, and things to say now."

"I've been back home for three years. You've seen me plenty in that time. Why now?"

She didn't know why she asked. She knew it didn't matter, but a part of her was curious. She wasn't sure how she felt about that part.

"You've been on my mind lately," he stated as if she needed a reminder of his visit to the diner a couple of days ago. "And then we found that body today."

He reached out and casually brushed a stray hair off her shoulder. Her eyes watched his hand. She was irritated at her heart for the traitorous flutter it offered at the slightest brush of his fingers against her shoulder, at the memory it sparked of how gentle his touch could be.

"It really made me think about life," he continued, as if he didn't notice her eyes watching his movements. "We don't know his name, how old he is, if he had a family… It made me realize that life can end in a snap and there're a lot of things I haven't done in mine."

He made eye contact again and smiled the dazzling smile that had caught her eye when she was a naïve young girl, but that still made the butterflies dance in her stomach as a grown woman. Her brain knew better than her heart and reminded it not to trust things just because they were beautiful… probably.

"And then there you were in front of me, looking like the Lilly Flower I used to know, with that smile that could captivate a room, and I knew it was a sign I needed to talk to you."

"Ryder—" she started to protest whatever charm he was about to try on her, that she was afraid her heart's muscle memory wanted to accept, already smothering out any warnings from her brain.

"Don't worry," he told her, cutting her off before she could figure out what to say next, "I only wanted to tell you now, how sorry I am for the idiot I was back then. That's all, nothing more. I just don't want you to hate me forever."

"I never hated you," she said, but at his disbelieving look, she corrected herself. "Okay, I hated you for a little while… and then maybe a little longer, but that was so long ago… it's done and in the past. There's no reason for me to hate you for it now."

He watched her a moment longer, at ease as he assessed whatever he saw. Even though she felt like he was studying her, she didn't feel uncomfortable under his gaze.

"I've got to go Ryder." When he showed no signs of moving off her car and she wasn't sure how much longer she'd be able to keep cool under his penetrating gaze, she added, "And I'm sure you've got a lot to do in there." She nodded to the station behind him.

He stepped away so she could open her door, holding it for her as she got in.

"You look real good, Lilly Flower. I'm glad you were here today."

He gently shut the door and headed to the station entrance without giving her a chance to respond. She saw him look back and flash that smile again before he disappeared inside.

"Don't even think about it," she said aloud as she pulled the car out of the parking lot. "You've been there and done that and he's still the smooth talker he always was. It doesn't matter how nice his butt looks in those pants, or how he can still make your stupid heart flutter with his stupid touch. Reel it in. Get that puddle-your-insides-smile out of your head and let him break someone else's heart."

FIVE

-RAIN-

Rain was bored. Beyond bored. Sundays were only old people who wanted to sit around and talk about boring stuff and drink coffee. All. Day. Long. It was two o'clock, and they were still drinking coffee and talking. Just talking, and all anyone wanted to talk about was some idiot that went and got himself killed.

Come on people, he's dead, it's not that interesting.

The bell chimed and she heard Gary tell whoever came in to have a seat anywhere. She hoped they sat in his section so she wouldn't have to deal with another person before her shift ended in an hour. This had seriously been the longest, most boring day ever. She was never working the weekend ever again.

Gary's voice interrupted her thoughts. "You've got a table."

"'K," she mumbled, scrolling through the feed on her phone, "be there in a sec."

"Be there now," he told her, grabbing the phone out of her hand before she realized and could stop him.

"Give that back."

"When you come back with an order," he said, holding the phone just out of reach. "They're cute," he sang, dancing away from her attempt to grab it from him.

"Who is?"

"Your table, dummy. Go get their order and thank me when you get back."

She looked over her shoulder at the trio that was looking at their menus. *Hmm, not bad for a place like this.*"Phone," she said, holding out her hand.

He wagged his finger and dropped the phone into his apron pocket. He crossed his arms across his chest and nodded toward the table.

"Ugh, you're so annoying," she said as she turned to check on her new arrivals.

Most days she liked working with Gary. He was only a few years older than her and pretty cute. He could be funny but very dramatic. She'd considered him for a fling when she'd first started working with him, just something casual, no strings, but quickly realized they'd be better off as friends.

His relationships could get a little messy.

But she liked that he accepted her the way she was. Even though he was holding her phone hostage to get her to do what he wanted, she knew he'd hand it over the minute she got back. Her parents, not so much. They disapproved of everything she did and if they decided to hold something over head, there was no telling how long it would take to win them over and get it back.

The sooner she put the order in, the sooner he'd give her back her phone.

She assessed the three guys as she walked up. Not local as far as she could tell, and one of them she would have noticed by now if he lived around here. The other two weren't bad-looking either, but the one sitting by himself was fine. She stood closer to him but angled herself toward the other two. "Hi guys, what're you havin'?"

They turned to look at her, giving her a better look at each of them up close—any one of them would be a perfect distraction to this place… and she got three at once. She smiled, glad she'd worn her tight jeans today.

"What's good here?" one of them asked. It was her least favorite question. How would she know what they thought would be good?

"Oh, loads of stuff, but I guess it all depends on what you like," she said demurely, leaning her hip against the table and bending over a little more than necessary to point out a few items on the menu. "What're you all into?" she asked, looking over her shoulder to the hottie she'd yet to make eye contact with and gave him a smile that meant she was asking about more than just what food he wanted to try. She saw him look, knowing he would, and turned her attention back to the other two. She wrote down their drink order, gave a few opinions on the food when they asked what she thought, and jotted down their choices. "I'll get this goin' for you," she told them, smiling again. "You won't be disappointed by *anything* you try in here."

She walked back to Gary, a little more sway in her step. She slapped the order into his upturned palm, then reached into his apron pocket to get her phone back.

He laughed and hung up the order on the wheel and turned it into the kitchen.

"Girl, you're so mean," he told her. "Leaning over, showing them all your… assets," he looked her up and down in an exaggerated way, "and then just walking off, leaving them to stare after you in unfulfillable desire."

"Who says it can't be fulfilled?" she shrugged at his shocked expression.

"Oh! You're so bad," he said with mock horror, but looked back over to the table with the three hunky men. "Which one were you thinking?"

She turned back to look, studying them with him.

"The loner there caught my eye," she told him, indicating the one sitting alone on his side of the table, "but really any of them could be fun… or all of them," she added for shock factor.

His surprised gasp had her smirking as the bell jingled again and they both glanced at the door.

"Sit anywhere," Gary called to the man who'd walked in and glanced around for an empty table. "Oh, please let him sit in my section," he murmured to Rain.

"Sorry, honey, that one's mine too," Rain told him as he chose a table in the back of her section and started looking at a menu.

"No fair," Gary pretended to pout. "Your side looks like a candy store, while little ol' me's left with nothing."

"Be prettier," she told him cattily.

She batted her eyelashes dramatically at him and he swatted her with his order tablet as she sauntered over to take another order.

She turned her attention to the new guy who was reading the menu and didn't notice her soaking up every delicious detail. He was older than the trio at the other table, a little older than she usually went for, but was built much sturdier. He clearly knew his way around the gym. He didn't look like a jock, a type she never went for, but who could resist a man that could pick you up like you weighed nothing at all?

Maybe this day was looking up after all.

"Hi handsome, see anything you'd like?"

He quickly glanced from his menu to her and back again. "No, I need a little more time," he said dismissively but gave his drink order as she turned to walk off.

"Oh… that's not a pretty face," Gary teased after watching her rebuke. "Too bad… he's *way* hotter than the other three combined."

"He's not *that* hot," she said, bitter that he'd barely given her a glance. "He's sorta old anyway. Probably more your type."

She snorted at her joke. Any type was Gary's type.

"If only," Gary sighed dreamily, "I'll just admire him from afar."

Rain scrolled on her phone while Gary watched both of their sections.

"Time for you to go make a fool of yourself some more. His menu's down now, looks like he's ready."

"Ugh, what a nerd," she said, stopping her scrolling to see the new customer reading a newspaper while he waited. "Who even reads the paper anymore? Dodged a bullet there," she said, not willing to admit that she was set back by his obvious disregard. "You take him. I need a smoke break anyway."

"Nuh uh, you're not pulling that crap on me. You have less than an hour left on your shift, your table full of younglings' food just came up, and you need to give that man a drink and take his order. You're not skipping out. Now scoot."

"You could at least help me out," she said, putting on a pouty face with big doe eyes.

"Not a chance. Go."

"Worth a shot," she said and grabbed the order.

She'd see to the guys that clearly appreciated the way she looked before heading over to the bore in the back; let him wait.

"Now you guys better not leave here without telling me how much you like everything," she smiled as she set each of their plates down in front of them. "How long are you in town for anyway?"

"Who says we're not from around here?" Number Two asked. She'd ranked them in order of hotness, One being the best but so far not very vocal.

"Oh, I'd remember seeing you in town," she flirted, "you're definitely not from around here."

Two and Three smiled, no reaction from One who was looking out the window.

Three gave her a more noticeable look over. As he was the one sitting closest to where she was standing, it was pretty obvious. He leaned toward her and then responded, "Maybe you've been looking in all the wrong spots."

Eh, he was still cute, she thought, hoping that by talking with Three, One would notice and pay her more attention. "And where do you suggest I should look?" she asked, lowering her voice and leaning in as well, lightly brushing against him as she did.

"Out by the Bend when you get off work, unless a little yellow tape bothers you," he said nonchalantly.

"Oh, were you all out there when that body was found?" she asked, pretending interest but starting to get bored by more talk of the dead guy.

She was also still waiting for One to pay attention to her.

"Evan there is the one who found him," Two eagerly piped in to take control of the conversation, giving her a name for One. "We both paddled out to help, but when we got there, it was clear he'd been dead for ages. Jack here stayed on shore like a pansy and called the cops," he said, elbowing Three in the ribcage.

"Who are you calling pansy? You're the one who got scared sleeping in a tent."

"I told you it was a bad dream," Two said through gritted teeth.

Jack ignored him, "Yeah, well someone had to wait on shore while you girls were out there too scared to touch him to even get him out of the water. Had to wait for the cops to get there," he chided and turned back to Rain. "If I had gone out, I would have brought him back to shore instead of just leaving him there to bob around with no dignity at all."

"Whatever, you wouldn't even look at him when they brought him ashore," Two razzed Jack.

"He was covered in a sheet, there was nothing to see," Jack said, returning his focus to Rain. "Poor guy probably couldn't handle the rapids. It's a hard ride, we just did it yesterday. Requires a lot of skill, not for amateurs. He probably thought he was good enough, lost control and lost his ride, then drowned in the wild water would be my guess." He leaned toward her again and gave her a long look, smiling slowly. "Do you ride?"

She smiled right back, knowing full well what he was asking but she decided to play coy. She wasn't entirely sure she wanted to win this one over, but Two seemed a little too eager, and Evan still hadn't said anything.

"Well, you'd probably call me an amateur," she pretended at shyness. "I probably need some lessons for the hard stuff," she said innocently, looking around the table. "Maybe someone could teach me?"

"We probably won't go back out on the water today, but we might go out to the Mountain," Two started, but a look from Jack stopped him.

Not so quick on the uptake, Rain mused.

Understanding dawned across Two's face in the form of a nodding smile.

"You can come out to the Bend later and we can see about lessons," Jack told her.

"You guys have been to the Mountain?" she asked, intrigued by Two's comment.

"Not yet," Two told her, happy he hadn't lost her attention by his goof up. He leaned in conspiratorially and whispered, "But we were goin' to today. Have you been?"

She leaned in closer to the two boys, hoping Evan would want to know what she was telling them and finally show some interest.

"I haven't been in, but I want to," she whispered, looking around to make sure nobody was listening.

"It's said that nobody comes out that's gone in," Two whispered back, "that the place is off limits and haunted or something."

She nodded like she had heard the same. "I haven't wanted to go in alone," she said pretending to look nervous. "But..." She looked at the two of them, then glanced at Evan, who was eating a fry. At least he wasn't looking out the window anymore. "Maybe if I had someone to go with me... maybe then I wouldn't be so scared."

"We could keep you safe," Two told her and Jack nodded.

"Come out to the Bend and we'll figure it all out," Jack said.

"'K," she said, giving Evan one last look. He no longer looked simply disinterested in the conversation—he looked unhappy. But she turned back to the other two, who were hers for the taking. "I've got to get back to work," she told them sweetly, tearing off a slip of paper and leaving a pen. "Write down your info so I can find you when I'm off."

They were quick to scribble down a phone number and hand it back. She folded up the paper and tucked it into her apron pocket, then left them to finish their food.

She heard them whispering and laughing as she headed back to Gary, but she still hadn't heard Evan chime in.

"I'm surprised you didn't just climb onto their laps right there," Gary said as she made it back to him.

She laughed at his over exaggeration, as always.

"You're just jealous you aren't invited," she said smugly, then leaned against the wall. "We're going to the Mountain."

"Oh, you are not!" he exclaimed. "You're all talk and no follow-through, just like everyone else around here."

"We're going after I get off work," she stated matter-of-factly. "I'm going to their campsite… at the Bend," she said indifferently, and his eyes grew large.

"Did they see –?" he started excitedly.

She nodded and cut off his question. "Everything. They found the body themselves." Gary was the deepest well when it came to gossip and would want every last, juicy detail, so of course she wanted to play with him. "Oh, but I forgot, I have another table," she said as if she really cared, finally happy that she had something to entertain her until her shift ended and the real fun could begin.

"Nope, stay right there," Gary told her, grabbing her arm when she pretended to leave to go take an order. "Hunky McHotterson got bored waiting on you, and I wasn't about to do your job for you while you were over there flirting up a storm, so he left. Tell me more."

She laughed. "You just let him walk out?"

"I have principles. I told you I wasn't doing your job, so I didn't. Now tell me all of it."

"You better hope Harvey doesn't find out, or worse, Lillian," she said, rolling her eyes. "She acts like she runs the show around here. If she finds out you let a table walk, you'll probably get canned."

"*I* won't," he said matter-of-factly. "It was *your* table. You're the one that sucks. Now stop stalling and tell me what happened over there and what's happening later. Not one thing left out."

"Okay, so here's what I know…" She told Gary what the boys had told her, maybe adding a few details here and there to get a good squeal out of him, as any good storyteller would do.

She smiled inwardly; she could milk this for the rest of her shift and then Gary would be stuck cleaning up all her empty tables while she grabbed the tips on the way out. Win!

SIX

-Lillian-

Lillian chatted with the checker as he expertly loaded her groceries into the reusable bags that she always kept in her car. She was hopeful he'd be able to get all her impulse purchases squeezed into just two bags so it'd be easier to carry. He would have been a master at Tetris. He pieced everything just right so that the small package of cookies she grabbed at the last minute fit like a puzzle piece on the top of the stack. The bananas she had set back would have spilled over.

Clearly, she'd made the right choice.

She paid for her groceries and grabbed the bags, surprised by their weight. It was nothing she and her sturdy bags couldn't handle, but she wondered if she really needed so much. She wished she could say that she used the bags because of how good they were for the environment, recycling, not using so much plastic and so on. Truthfully, they fit a lot, were strong, and would get her down the road to her car without everything falling out the bottom all over the sidewalk.

She liked to be efficient.

She headed away from the tiny, family-owned market toward the parking lot a few blocks away. She could have gone to the big store a little farther out of town. There, she could park close to the building and get in and out quickly. Sometimes that worked best for her schedule, but that always left her feeling detached. Just another head in the crowd. The market had everything she needed, and she always felt welcomed. Plus, she loved being able to walk the main strip back to her car.

She admired the beautifully maintained, oversized flowerpots as she walked. They'd recently been planted with a bright variety of flowers, floral fragrances filling the air. The bright greenery cascading down the sides perfectly accented the arrangements. This was her favorite time of year, when the days warmed up, and the flowers and trees started to bloom. The clear skies and bright sun encouraged people to venture out and window shop, mingling along the sidewalk on both sides of the street. She watched as two women met up in front of a coffee shop, laughed, and embraced each other before heading inside.

Did they meet regularly, or was this the first time in years they'd seen each other?

Across the street, an older couple sat on one of the cozy benches next to a blooming redbud tree, smiling and pointing things out around them as they chatted.

Was this a tradition for them? People watching together, or were they simply killing time before their next appointment?

She neared Wisteria and Harvey's voice sounded in her head, reminding her not to go back in today. She hadn't actually agreed to his suggestion and he wasn't there this late in the day to know.

Just a quick check, to make sure everything was running smoothly.

But she had her bags… and the weight of them was rubbing her arm uncomfortably.

She stopped at a nearby bench, setting the bags down so she could readjust and switch arms for the heavy bag. The front door opened and for an irrational split second, she worried that Harvey had caught her. He'd scold her for sure, knowing her intentions of checking in.

Thankfully, the man that emerged was most definitely not Harvey. She was very happy she'd decided to take a break when she had, delighted by the improvement to the scenery. Had she not stopped, she would have completely missed the insanely handsome man who had stepped out. He was tall and broad-shouldered, with a well-filled-out frame and commanding presence. If he didn't work out regularly, she'd be shocked. Even this slight distance away she could see how defined his arms were. She watched as he put on sunglasses and pulled a map out of the pack he carried.

A map? Who used a map anymore?

He unfolded the little square and looked down the street, away from her, then back at the map. He was probably getting his bearings. She was still admiring him from not so far away when he turned his head in her direction and found her openly staring.

She'd been caught.

He smiled a dazzling smile, his teeth bright white against his tanned skin. He raised two fingers in a slight wave making her forget she was standing in the middle of the sidewalk. She waved back, slightly embarrassed at being caught, hoping she wasn't red-faced as he began walking over to her.

"Please tell me you live here," he said hopefully.

"Most of my life," she said.

"Good," he said with an almost sheepish grin. "I'm about to do what no man in the history of men has ever done… and ask for directions."

She laughed at his honesty, liking him instantly.

"Where do you want to go?"

He turned the local trail map toward her. She could see that it had been folded more than a few times, with areas marked off or circled. She quickly noted that several were the regular tourist hot spots, but more than a few were off the beaten path, only fit for the true adventurer at heart and skill level.

From the look of him, none of those marks would be a problem.

"I've been trying to hit most of the trails around while I'm here, getting a feel for the difficulty," he told her, indicating the spots he'd already tried that were marked off. "So far, they've all been pretty simple, so I wanted to scout out some of the harder areas." The way he said it wasn't pompous or macho, just a statement of fact. "I thought to try this one tomorrow," he pointed to an area farther from the rest, one she knew would be a challenge for most, "but I'm pretty sure I need to grab some supplies for the trip." He looked up and down the road again, and back at his map. "Honestly, I've been on foot most of the day, just checking out the town for a break day, and I got a little turned around."

"Okay, well this is an easy fix," she said. Feeling adventurous but also oddly at ease with him, she took him by the shoulders to reorient him and his map. She pointed ahead of them, in the direction she'd already been headed. "Over that way is where you want to go tomorrow." She leaned a little closer to the map and indicated the route he'd mentioned trying and where they were currently standing. "This spot right here is where you'll find the best hardware store in town. Go in and ask for Ben. He won't look like it, but he's been all over these hills and trails and will know just what you'll need for any of these spots. He'll make sure you're set and won't sell you something you don't need. Plus, he's fair on pricing.

As for food supplies, just a little way back there," she said, pointing to where she had just come from, "is Tiller's Market. It opens at 5 a.m., so if you're just packing for a day trip and can make a stop first, they'll have what you need. Otherwise, if you plan to just get up and go, you'll want to get what you need before it gets too late because they close at dark."

"Literally at dark?" he chuckled.

"Literally." She laughed with him, his low rumble infectious. "The hours say, 'five to dark.'"

"Good to know. So where could I get something good to eat, if I were to sit down and order something?"

"Well, I have to say I'm pretty fond of Wisteria," she nodded to the door he'd recently come out of, "but since you've already been there…" she trailed off, wondering what to recommend. "What sort of food do you like?"

"Oh, a little of everything really. Is Wisteria where *you'd* choose to eat then?"

"I've eaten there a lot, yes." She laughed again. "And not just because I work there. But… if I were going out for a meal." She looked at the map. "Here is a great lunch spot with outdoor seating, since you appear to enjoy the outdoors." She glanced at him, wondering if he was a health enthusiast or preferred a juicy burger. She caught his gaze, and smiled, going with her gut. "Here is a great place for a burger, and here—" She pointed out of town, near the river. "—is a gorgeous place for a nice steak. It was built a few years ago. The inside is spectacular but it has a huge deck with outdoor seating and lights and overhangs the river. The view is amazing. It can be fancy if you go in the evening, but in the daytime you can get away with fairly casual."

As he studied his choices, she leaned back and reached for her bags, "Think you can find your way now?" She didn't really want to end their encounter but knew there was no reason for her to linger.

"I can." He smiled, folding the map back into a tiny square and tucking it away into a pocket. "I imagine it would be too forward of me to ask you to grab a bite to eat at one of those restaurants you mentioned, but surely you'll let me help you carry one of those bags for you as way of thanks?"

Instinctively, she wanted to politely decline, to tell him that she could manage just fine. But how often did you meet a gorgeous, toned, hunk of a man who offered to carry your groceries down the street on a perfectly strollable day? She assessed his relaxed stance and gentle smile; what harm could come from accepting his help in broad daylight?

"That would actually be great," she said as he reached down to grab the heavier of the two bags. "The parking lot isn't too far up, and I don't think you're going to take off with my groceries."

"Not likely very fast," he joked, curling the bag up and down like a weight. She couldn't help but notice the muscles rippling with each movement, or the ease that he lifted the bag. He made it look like it was filled with feathers. "Did you buy bricks?

"No, just everything else in the store." She smiled, trying to keep her eyes on his instead of allowing them to roam over the rest of him. "Never shop when you're hungry. You buy all sorts of things you don't really need and then wind up wondering how something made the cut after you do finally eat."

"Like those cookies?" he asked, nodding to the package on top of her stack.

"Oh no, those are a necessity. They are the best in the world. They're made right here, in Juniper Hollow, and the only place you can find them is at Tiller's Market. People fight dirty when it comes to these."

"Oh yeah?"

"Totally. I once had to cut in front of a little old lady and her walker to get the last box. Granted she was walking in the opposite direction of the cookie display, but it still haunts me to this day that she may have wanted them if she'd only turned around and seen that it was the last box."

"You probably saved her life that day by removing such a temptation."

"Exactly. So now you know. If you see these cookies, you don't pass them up. End of story."

"Good to know." He laughed his low rumble of a chuckle.

She liked how easy he was to talk to as they walked down the street together. There was a definite attraction physically, but he had an easy way about him that made her instantly comfortable. She felt like they'd known each other all their lives.

"You mentioned you've been checking out the trails. Are you here on vacation or visiting anyone?"

"I guess you could call it a vacation. I got tired of the go, go, go lifestyle of the city, and the constant demand of my time. I hated the feeling that I was never in control of my own life, so I decided to take a break. I'm doing a little traveling for a while. To kinda take my life back, you know? Then I'll decide if I want to go back to the grind or find something a little slower pace. It's only been a few weeks, hopping from place to place, but so far, it's much more agreeable than punching a timecard."

"Yeah, I'd say not working and traveling would be a lot more fun, until the bills come in," she said, crinkling her brow as she realized she sounded like a mother hen. "Sorry, that was rude."

"Not at all," he assured her, seeming to have taken no offense. "Good planning was essential, and now I don't have to think about it while I'm out here, and I can just go. It's really freeing, waking up and knowing that whatever I'm going to do today is yet to be determined; there are no deadlines to meet. You should try it sometime," he said as they stopped by her car.

"That would be really amazing," she agreed, opening the trunk to put the groceries in, "but for now, I'll just have to dream about it. Thank you for your help with the bags."

"Thank you again for the directions and suggestions," he said. He stepped back from her car so she could pass to the driver's side.

She studied him standing aside. His hands were in his pockets and he looked completely relaxed in the world with an easy smile on his face. She didn't know if it was the conversation with her dad about dating, the excitement of a beautiful springtime day, or the ridiculously easy and approachable nature of this man, but she decided to be adventurous and do something she never did.

"You're not secretly a serial killer or something, are you?" she asked, recalling her dad's corny newspaper headline.

He laughed. "If I am, am I supposed to tell you?"

She smiled, studying him again, "You said you've been walking around town all day. Can I give you a lift to your car or one of those stores?"

"That's very generous, but I'm just down the road."

He smiled that gorgeous smile again and she knew this was goodbye.

"Don't forget to check in with Ben," she told him, knowing she needed to get her groceries home before they went bad. "He'll be good to you and can help you out if you have any other questions."

"Thank you again for the valuable information. I hope our paths cross again," he told her.

She smiled as she got into her car. "Me too, that would be nice."

It was only after he walked away and she was driving out of the parking lot in the opposite direction, that she realized she hadn't gotten so much as his name, let alone how long he'd be in town. She'd pushed the concept of dating so far out of her mind that her brain had completely abandoned her in his presence. Even if she was bold enough to ask to see him again, she hadn't even thought to ask. And now she'd have no way to get in contact with him.

She watched him getting smaller in her rear-view mirror and contemplated turning around and asking for his number. But she knew she wasn't that courageous, and she didn't want him to think she was a crazy person. She smiled at their short exchange, thankful for their walk and wondered if she'd get to see him again before he continued his journey. From the number of circles still on his map, she was hopeful it would take him a while to mark them all off.

SEVEN

The moon was high and bright, which was helpful despite the thickness of the trees. He could hear thrashing coming toward him. It had to be her. He had only known a date and an approximate area, but out here, that didn't mean he'd be able to find her.

She had to come out. He couldn't go back in. He couldn't risk it.

Other things were far greater than the life of one person.

He heard a scream. The blood-curdling, stop-your-heart kind of scream.

She's not going to make it. Get out of here while you still can.

Out of nowhere, she appeared. She was running straight for him but focused on whatever was after her.

His movements were swift. He stepped into her path and caught her. Without wasting a moment, he sunk the needle containing the sedative into her arm. Before she realized what had happened, before her next scream could escape, her body went limp.

He lifted her small body easily and carried her out of the trees.

EIGHT

-BILL-

Ryder rapped his knuckles against the sheriff's open door, stepping through as he did. Bill looked up from his paperwork as Ryder took a seat in front of the desk.

"The examiner's office just called over. Rich has finished up with our John Doe."

"Okay, did they send over a report?" Bill asked, noticing his deputy was empty-handed.

"Nope. Rich wants to discuss it with you in person before giving the report. Not sure what's so special about a drowning, but we should probably head over and find out."

"We?" Bill raised an eyebrow. This was a task Ryder would normally try to avoid.

"You're always telling me to know all aspects of the job. One day I aim to be Sheriff, that's no secret. This is part of it."

Bill leaned back in his chair. Ryder was trying to be intimidating, so confident about taking over, but all Bill could see was the kid who dropped off his daughter two minutes early after a date because he didn't want to wind up in trouble with the sheriff.

"You're right," Bill agreed. The shock on Ryder's face was quickly replaced with neutrality. Bill stood and grabbed his keys. "I have no doubt that one day I'm going to retire, and you're just as good a candidate to take over as any. But like you said, if you're going to stand out in order to take over, you're going to have to do the hard work now, learn it all. So, let's go."

"Hey Sheriff!" Jane flagged them down as they were walking through.

A man stood in front of her station. The energy of her area was slightly electric, but the man standing aside seemed cool, collected. Bill assessed him, his build and stance. From the looks of him, he could be another cop or ex-military, but, based on his hiking apparel, not on the job now. He noticed Ryder stand a little taller and cross his arms across his chest, sizing up the man as well.

"What's going on, Jane? We were about to head over to see Rich," he said, wondering if this could be delegated to one of the other deputies. Sometimes Jane was excitable.

"Oh no, no, that'll have to wait. This man here's just come in from hiking and says he's found a body out there."

Bill gave the man another look-over. Newcomer, capable of handling himself, and this was the second body in days. Warning bells were ringing in the back of his cop's mind.

"Okay." He turned to Ryder. "Rich will have to wait. Jane, call the medical examiner's office and tell them what's going on. I'll radio over information once I know more, but tell Rich to be ready for another body."

She nodded and started dialing. Bill motioned for Ryder and the newcomer to come with him, leading them out of the immediate vicinity of Jane's desk so she could make her call.

"What's your name?" he asked the man. He held open the door to one of the interrogation rooms, a simple space with a table and three chairs. Nobody took a seat.

"August," the new guy said. Bill saw Ryder note it in his phone.

"August what?" Bill pressed.

"Steele, sir," August said and held out his hand to shake the sheriff's.

A firm handshake, Bill noticed approvingly, but didn't remove him from the immediate suspect list because of it.

"Tell me about this body you found. Why didn't you call it in?"

"I was on a hike and came across him. Hardly any cell service out there. Figured coming in would be just as good since it's not far."

Bill nodded but didn't interrupt.

"It looked to me like he fell, maybe broke his neck. He wasn't alive when I found him though. I know that much."

"How can you be sure?" Ryder asked. He casually leaned against the table, his hands in his pockets.

"It was pretty obvious," he retorted, but quickly continued. "When you see, you'll understand. The way the body is laying is unnatural, but just in case I was mistaken, and he could have still been alive, I called out and got no response. I climbed over to him and checked for breathing and a pulse."

"You touched the body?"

"Yes," August stated. "I wanted to be absolutely sure someone wasn't lying there, praying for help to come along and offer medical assistance, before I walked away and left him for dead."

"Are you a doctor?" Ryder asked him.

"No."

"What qualifies you to offer medical help to anyone?"

August gave a frustrated sigh. "When you do the sort of climbs that I do, basic medical knowledge is necessary. Accidents happen out there, people get hurt, and if you can't patch things up on the spot, you probably won't make it out to find help."

August turned back to the sheriff, who'd been watching his mannerisms and control.

"Look, I saw a map back in the lobby." He motioned toward the door they'd come through. "I can show you on the map where I found the body, but if you're up for a hike, I can take you there myself."

Bill nodded. "Those woods are a big place and even if you showed us down to the closest pinpoint on a map, we could walk right by and not find him. If you can lead us in, that would be helpful."

Bill led them back to the large area map on the wall of the lobby and watched as August studied it for a moment.

"This is where I started." He pointed and Bill and Ryder leaned in for a better look. "I hiked around most of the morning, going off-trail here and there, and I found the body about here. It's pretty rough going, but—" He gave Ryder an obvious assessment and then a quick look-over of the sheriff. "I think I can get you guys into where he is safely. I marked my way out as direct as possible."

"Alright. Ryder, get the gear and meet us out front," Bill told him and led August out to the Blazer. "Grab what you need from your truck and climb in the back. You can ride with us."

August grabbed his pack and loaded it into the back, then Ryder came out with the station gear and loaded it in next to his. August took the back seat and told Bill which trailhead he had hiked.

When they reached the parking lot, Bill and Ryder changed out their boots and all three men loaded on their packs.

"Is all this really necessary?" Ryder asked as he adjusted the weight. "We're just going in for a body, not an all-day trip."

"Always prepare for an all-day trip and then some," August stated. "You never know what could happen, and it's best to be ready. Besides, this is no stroll through the park. I'm taking you on the easiest, most direct route that I could find in a hurry, but there's a good chance some of your men won't be able to make it." He directed the last part to the sheriff in sincerity.

"I've been all through the trails around here and never needed more than a few power bars and water. I'm sure we'll do fine," Ryder goaded him as they started on the cleared path that entered into the woods.

"I hope you're right, but your ignorance isn't going to screw me over out there," August said as he stopped and turned to the sheriff, who'd been silently listening to the two boys find their place. "Here's the marker where I came out and met up with the trail."

"Came out of where?" Ryder asked, looking beyond August into the wild brambles, brush, and branches that showed no sign of ever being touched by anything other than wildlife. "There's nothing there."

August turned to look behind him into the wild, then back to Ryder with an almost pitying expression.

"Everything is there, you just have to find it," he said simply.

"Lead the way," Bill told him, wondering how far they'd get before he'd have to turn back. He was the sheriff and needed to see to his county. But August was right. Every man had his limits, and he was no climber. He wouldn't jeopardize the three of them to save face, which he could already tell wouldn't be the same for Ryder. He could only hope the path in was doable or someone was bound to get themselves hurt.

Ryder grumbled for a bit as branches swung at him, or he stumbled on a rock. The man was quick and agile on pavement or even dirt, but the wilderness was putting up a fight. Eventually he stopped complaining and focused on the work required, letting August lead the way from marker to marker.

"It's right up ahead," August told them after a hard forty-five minutes, stopping to take a drink of water and wipe the sweat off his forehead.

Bill looked around. The trees had cleared out slightly, allowing the sun to shine through the branches above instead of the constant canopy of cover they'd been under. A sheer, steep rock face jutted about thirty feet above them with ledges scattered along and more trees above.

Something about the look of it made him uncomfortable. He couldn't put into words what it was, but something felt *off* about where they were. He'd been around enough dead bodies in his life that he couldn't imagine that was what was giving him a feeling of unease.

Ryder had moved ahead to some of the large rocks that had clearly fallen from the wall above over many years and was studying what had to be the body they'd come for, already taking pictures and assessing the scene.

Bill moved forward to get a better look at the body. The boy was young, maybe late teens or early twenties, but it was hard to really say. It looked like he must have been climbing above, lost his footing, and fell into the rocks. August had been right. The boy's body was splayed on the rocks, his head dangling awkwardly to one side. His open eyes stared at something none of them could see in this lifetime. This person was not alive.

Ryder stepped back and put his camera back in his pack.

"You really climbed in there and checked his pulse? That poor kid is clearly dead."

"If that was you in there, wouldn't you want someone to check?" August asked.

"So, you think he was hiking up there and fell, or do you think he was trying to climb this wall and slipped off?" Ryder asked, shielding his eyes to get a better look.

The sheriff studied the broken boy on the rocks, then looked back up the wall. "I'm betting he came from above. He doesn't have any climbing gear. I don't think anyone would be dumb enough to try and free-climb this wall. A person would need hooks and ropes, right? To climb something like that?" he asked August.

"Some people are real adrenaline junkies and might try without, but most people realize they aren't invincible and need a backup plan. This guy looks fit enough but isn't equipped at all for this kind of terrain." August looked at the boy and above. "I'm betting you're right, Sheriff. This kid was above and landed down here is my thought."

"Do you have a map or GPS on you so we can see exactly where we are?" Bill asked August.

August pulled out a map of the area as well as his compass. "Here's where we parked, the trail we took in, and our path to where we are now."

Bill noticed the gray boundary line printed just beyond where they were standing, the mark August had made to indicate their location nearly touching the line. He shook off the wary feeling behind his shoulder blades.

"What were you doing all the way up here?" Bill asked August.

"I like to explore."

"Mm hmm," Bill looked at the man, considering. "The problem I have, aside from a dead body over there, is that I have two newcomers up here, one of them freshly deceased, and another one that says he just likes to explore… Do you know this man?"

"Today was the first time I recall making his acquaintance."

"And was he alive when you did so? Maybe you were both up above, something happened, and he slipped and fell. There was nothing you could have done to save him from that height, and you couldn't really carry a body out of the woods and go unnoticed, so you came to get help for a 'stranger.'"

Bill noticed Ryder edge a little closer to August, his training to prepare for whatever the man might try.

"Sir, I appreciate that you have to investigate all possible scenarios, but you've got the wrong idea. I've been all over these hills the past few weeks. I'm on an off-grid vacation so-to-speak. It's just me. The first I saw of this boy was when I found him this morning. I immediately hiked out and came straight to your office. Besides, if I was involved in this poor kid's death, one, why would I hike you all right up to him? And two, why would I even say anything at all? You saw how hard it was to get here. The likelihood that anyone would find him anytime soon is slim. If I was involved, I could have just kept moving."

Bill considered the truth of this.

"You understand I'm going to want you to come back to the station to give your official statement, and I'm going to want you to hang around town for a while in case I have more questions."

"I understand. I wouldn't expect anything less," August agreed.

Bill radioed his deputies, informing them of their location and the difficulty of the hike. He gave directions of what to bring to move the body. He looked back at the rock then back to the map with the gray line.

"Are you aware you're hiking near federal property? Restricted land?" Bill asked, gauging his response.

"I am," he stated. "But last I checked, it's not against the law to hike *near* restricted land so long as you don't go in."

"You're correct," Bill mused, "but it's restricted for a reason. People get hurt in there." He nodded to the evidence lying on the rocks just a few feet from where they currently stood.

"I'd heard some stories," August confirmed, "but I assure you, I was on this side of the line."

"Can't say the same for this poor soul," Bill said, looking back up the rock. He shook his head at the thrill seekers and story chasers. They'd never learn.

NINE
-Rain-

"I knew you'd chicken out," Gary mocked as they stood behind the counter during a lull at the diner.

"I didn't chicken out," Rain said, watching him roll silverware into their napkins as she filled him in on her evening with the guys. "Evan, hottie number one, was being moody, and Brian—" She'd finally learned Number Two's name. "—Brian and Jack didn't want to leave him alone. So instead of going out to the Mountain, they added me on RUSH, and then we just partied at their campsite all night."

"Mm hmm. I knew you wouldn't go. What's RUSH?" he asked before she could defend their reasoning again.

She gave him a critical, assessing look. "Of course *you* wouldn't know," she said haughtily, but opened an app on her phone. "It's the *only* way to showcase an adventure lifestyle."

She turned the phone to him, which he instantly grabbed to look. "Let's see how adventurous your life is," he mused, scrolling through the few images on her profile. "Not very," he chided as she snatched the phone back out of his grasp.

She'd only just discovered the app because of the guys, but she wasn't about to admit that to him.

"My life is plenty adventurous without an app, but Brian and Jack wanted to be able to stay in touch, so I joined for them." She flipped through a few more pictures. "Evan was being a wet blanket though and just stayed in his tent the whole night."

"Wait, go back," he said swiping the screen himself to the previous picture, the yellow strip catching his eye. "Is that the crime scene?"

"Well not really," she said. "That's actually across the river. This is just where they brought the body over."

"And you took a picture of it. Tasteful," Gary said dryly. "And probably illegal."

"It's just a picture. That's not illegal."

"No, but you're inside the tape. Isn't that contaminating a scene?"

"If they didn't want people in there, they should have a guard out there."

Was it illegal? she wondered.

"That's what the tape is for. You're supposed to stay out until they take it down."

She shrugged her shoulders as if she didn't care. *Could they get in trouble for being inside the tape?*

"Isn't Evan the one you said found the body?"

"Yeah. So?"

"Well, I'd say he should at least get a few days to process finding a dead person on his camping trip."

"I guess," she said, pretending as if that was a ridiculous reason to get bent out of shape. "But he sure is letting it ruin the rest of the guys' trip too. All they wanted was to bring him out for his birthday. You'd think he'd be a little more grateful."

"Geez Rain, do you even hear yourself talk sometimes? I can't possibly imagine why he's having a bum day," Gary snorted.

Rain rolled her eyes and shrugged her shoulders.

"Don't be such a priss," she told him.

"Well one of us has to," he stated. "Maybe if you were a little more in touch with your emotions, you would have realized that all he needed was someone to hold him and tell him everything would be okay." He stared dramatically and dreamily off, as if he were imagining doing just that. "At least that's what I would have done."

"You're such a girl."

"Again. One of us has to be, and if you're not willing to do what needs to be done… well…"

She laughed at his absurdity.

"Don't worry… there were no complaints," she implied.

Gary's shocked expression was exactly what she was aiming for. He was always easy to razz.

"What?!" he practically squealed. "Tell me more. Which one?"

When she just smiled coyly and shrugged her shoulders, shaking her head that she wouldn't say, he grabbed her wrist.

"All of them?" he assumed, and she didn't correct him either way. "Oh girl, you are *so* bad."

"I never claimed to be good," she told him matter-of-factly.

"So just that night?" he asked, trying to soak up every last detail.

"I've been spending the past few nights out there with them. The sheriff asked them to stick around in case he had more questions. I don't think he meant for this long. Apparently, they've found something in town that they just can't get enough of."

"Whatever," Gary jabbed. "You're just their plaything while they *have* to be here."

"You're just jealous they didn't look your way."

He fanned himself in pretend overheating desire. "Don't you know it."

"Be gayer," she said.

"Be more of a slut," he countered. "I never took you for the camping type."

"Oh, I'm not, but they're hot and this town is dead right now; a girl's gotta have *some* fun. God! I can't wait for real people to start coming through again. I forgot how boring it gets in the off-season."

"Whine, whine, whine, that's all you ever do," he sang as he left their place behind the counter to take refills to his tables.

She laughed, enjoying their easy relationship.

Staying out with the guys this week had been a relief. They accepted her just the way she was. They didn't try to tell her where she was going wrong in life, they just let her be, sort of like Gary. He just let her be. Sure, he gave her a hard time about everything, but that was kind of their thing.

Her parents on the other hand… they only ever wanted to tell her where she was going wrong. They didn't like her hair or the way she dressed. They never approved of any of her friends. They'd never used her chosen name, telling her it was ridiculous. They'd named her Jennifer. Her. She was no Jennifer. Just once she wished they could accept something she'd chosen for herself, but they'd never see her as an adult, just some silly child.

"Hey, space cadet," Gary called, breaking through her thoughts. "Look busy, Lillian's here."

"My God," she sighed. "She's an hour early. Who gets to work an hour early? I swear she has no life at all."

"Whether she does or not, you better get busy before she sees you standing around chatting like a lazy old gossip."

"What are you talking about? You're right here with me. You'll be in just as much trouble."

"Nonsense. While you've been carrying on and daydreaming, I've managed to make sure all my tables are still topped off and happy *and* restocked the shelves. You… not so much."

"Those shelves were already stocked, you just made them look prettier. That doesn't count."

"It most definitely counts when she walks in here in a few seconds and sees me diligently working and you just standing there watching me," he said as he bent down to line everything up just as Lillian walked in.

Lillian

"Hi guys. How's it going in here today? Gary, that looks really nice," Lillian said, noting the newly straightened shelves. "Looks like a few tables over there need some refills or checks. People are looking a little antsy. Who's on which section today?" she asked, but could easily guess.

"They're probably mine," Rain sighed dramatically and pushed herself away from the counter to go check her side.

"How's it been?" Lillian asked Gary again.

"Just fine and dandy, like always," he said. "And don't you just look fine and dandy as well," he studied her closely. "Something's different today."

"Nothing's different," she said, wondering if he had noticed the mascara she'd put on.

Gary leaned forward and inhaled, closing his eyes as he did. "Mmm, you smell like an exotic night flower."

She laughed. "New body wash. I'm so glad it meets your approval," she joked.

"Very sultry," he teased. "Now, why are you here checking up on us an hour before your shift?"

"I'm not checking up," she fibbed, never knowing what state the place would be in with Rain on first.

"You know I always leave this place in tippy top shape before you get here," he said, pretending at offense. "So, you just turn your pretty little self around and go find something else to do for an hour, or," he pretended to gasp, "be late for once in your life."

"There's no reason for me to go. I'm already here."

"No, you're not. You can't be that hard up for money that an extra hour is going to make all the difference. Now get out of here and do something else until you're needed."

"You're seriously booting me out?" she laughed.

"Seriously. You can't live just to work. Go away. Do something silly, like get your nails done, something fun for once."

"I don't have enough time before –"

"You do. Do you see how many empty tables are in here? All day it's been this way. It's not magically going to pick up in the next hour to the point that we can't handle it. Now go."

She considered what she'd do with the extra hour. It might be nice to do a little window shopping…

"Okay, you win, but only because I saw a dress the other day that I wanted to peek at. I'll just run over real quick and check it out."

"Go slow, buy the dress, I bet you'll be fabulous in it."

She laughed again. "You don't even know what it looks like."

"Doesn't matter, you already have a glow about you. The dress will only accent it."

"Okay fine, I'm going. Tell Rain I'll be back." Gary was right, there wasn't a need for her to be on any earlier today. They had it under control.

Rain

"Where's she going?" Rain asked when she got back.

"I told her she was lame for coming to work early and sent her away."

"Thanks, jerk. I could have gotten off early if she were here. We wouldn't all need to be here."

"Oh, I'm aware, but I wasn't about to let you leave me hanging like you did the other day, sneaking out on all your work for me to clean up. Payback and all that," he said.

"You're so vicious," she pouted.

"Yeah, but you know you'd rather finish out your day with me than Lillian."

"You got that right."

"Now, to make up for your rude escape the last time we worked, you're going to clear and reset my dirties while *I* stand here and look pretty and watch *you* work for a change."

"Aww," she said, overly sweet, "you think I look pretty?"

"Har," he chuckled. "I said *I* looked pretty; *you* just don't work."

"Vicious," she restated but grabbed her towel to wipe the tables.

"When necessary," he agreed and scooted her out.

TEN

-LILLIAN-

Lillian immediately found the dress she went in for then doubted it was her style, but the clerk talked her into trying it on and she ended up loving how it looked. She decided to buy it and two other tops before realizing she was nearing the start of her shift. She thanked the flattering and helpful clerk, promising to be back when she had more time, and hurried out the door to get back to the diner before Gary got his way and she was late.

She hoped she still liked the pieces when she didn't have someone telling her how they hugged her body just right or how flattering the color was for her skin tone.

The diner bell jingled, and she slipped through the front door with ten minutes to spare.

"You're still early," Gary said, lacing as much disappointment through his voice as possible as she breezed past him to put her bags in the back.

"You don't see me," she sang.

Rain made no remark and barely glanced up from her phone.

She stowed her bags in the small office along with her purse, made sure she looked ready to work, and grabbed her half apron to tie on as she walked up front. She knew Rain would be itching to leave—she probably already had one foot out the door. Gary had picked up a few hours to help cover for a sick call and would stay through the dinner rush, but then she'd be left for the last few hours on her own.

If she got some downtime, she'd work on writing an ad for help.

"Okay," she breathed when she walked out of the kitchen and into their little hub behind the bar. "I'm officially here."

"So, I can officially leave," Rain said.

Lillian looked around the dining room. Drinks all looked topped off, nobody was trying to make eye contact for the check … everything looked to be in order.

"Yeah, I guess so," Lillian agreed. "As soon as you let your tables know you're leaving and that I'll be taking over your section, I don't see any reason why you'd need to hang around. Looks pretty good out there."

Rain stopped untying her apron and pulled the cords back tight. Lillian pretended not to see the roll of her eyes as she shuffled past to check her tables.

"How's it been today, really?" Lillian asked Gary.

"Just like I told you, pretty slow. Plus it's a Wednesday, so dinner probably won't be too busy either. You just might get to close up early," he told her, knowing those odds were slim with her on duty. "So, did you buy something pretty?"

"I bought the dress, and some tops. Now I just need to find someplace to wear them."

"Done," Rain interrupted. "Can I go now?"

The bell jingled behind them, and Gary turned to tell the customer to sit anywhere.

"You should probably go before you drive this one off again," he said to Rain.

Confused by his comment, Lillian turned to see who'd walked in. He would be hard-pressed to walk into a room without being noticed. Or maybe she just felt that way because she'd been fantasizing about seeing him since their last encounter on the street. Her heart did a little happy dance, and she tried not to let her excitement show on her face when he chose a table in her section.

She turned to question Gary about his comment and caught sight of the back of Rain's distinctive hair as she went through the kitchen door.

"What's all that about?" she asked.

"You know Rain…" he eluded.

"Yes, in fact I do, but why does it feel like I'm missing something. What happened? Why'd she leave so fast?"

"She's just trying to get out of here to meet up with her new boy-toys," he said with a roll of his eyes.

"Okay," Lillian said slowly, not wanting to play the guessing game when she needed to greet her new table. The fact that it was her mystery grocery man just added to her impatience. "So, what was with the 'drive this one off' comment?"

He looked pained, like he didn't want to say anything and was trying to find a way out of it, but she knew him well enough to know that this was just his ploy to get her—or anyone he wanted to gossip with—eager enough to convince him to tell. All she had to do was wait him out.

She smiled at her table and gave him the universal, one finger, just-a-second sign and he held up his menu that he was still looking anyway.

She turned back to Gary, "Spill it, now."

"Okay, fine," he gushed. "So, we were working over the weekend, and it was just a *drag* of a day –"

"The short version," she told him impatiently, indicating that she had to go.

"Okay, okay. The *short* version is that this group of hotties came in and sat in her section. She flirted it up somethin' fierce, then *this* guy," he nodded to the table, "comes in and sits in her section too. I'm jealous because she's getting all the business, and she's on a high because of the hot-stuff brigade. She goes over, expecting to flirt him up as well but he doesn't bite. Barely even gives her a look." He said it as if that was the worst thing in the world. "Of course, she's all pretending like it means nothing, but you can just *tell* that she's upset by the whole thing. I mean," he paused and stage-whispered, "have you looked at that guy? Like, really look. A much better package than the other three combined, and I told her that too." He paused again as if Lillian had interrupted him. "I know, I know, hurry up Gary," he admonished himself. "So, her table of hotness's food is ready, and she saunters over to give them the food even though this guy," he motions again to the table, "has had his menu down *and* had already given her his drink order. She never gave the drink or took his order and flirted for so long with the boys that he finally got up and left. And I was just too busy to help, so I feel just awful that he sat in her section and not mine where I could have taken care of him like he deserved," he finished.

Lillian nodded, frustrated that she was just finding out and that it was *this* guy. Of all the customers, it was him.

"Thanks for telling me, Gary. I'll have to have a talk with Rain," she said as she went to walk by him and get the customer's order.

Gary grabbed her arm as she passed.

"Oh, Lillian," he begged, "please, please, please don't make a big deal out of this. I just know that she'll get mad at me. I only told you because, well, there he is, and in case he says something, you should already know. Right?"

She'd worked with Gary long enough to recognize the false tone of his voice. He could care less if Rain got mad at him as long as he wasn't the one to get in trouble with the boss.

"If she keeps doing stuff like that, nobody will ever want to come back here. It can't go on. That's all I'm going to say to her. It doesn't have to be a big deal. Now, I really need to go see to that table, so he doesn't leave for a second time, thinking all we do is stand around and talk."

He let her go then, wringing his hands as if he were worried that Rain would realize he was the one who told on her. She knew that was also just part of the show. All of the employees had their quirks, and most of the time she ignored them, let the little games they played blow over, but this was going too far. To ignore someone to the point that they got up and left wasn't going to work.

She approached the customer's table and smiled as he put down his menu.

"Hello there stranger," she said. "Finding your way around town okay?"

"You remembered," he said, his smile causing the butterflies in her stomach to wake up.

"I doubt you're forgotten often," she said, surprising herself. "I wasn't sure I'd be seeing you again."

"Well, I have to confess… When our paths hadn't crossed before now, I thought I'd help them along. I realized the only thing I knew about you, besides that you have a sweet tooth and secretly use your grocery shopping as your workout routine, was that you worked here. I didn't even get your name. I decided I'd come in for dinner, and if you were working, then it was fate, and if you weren't, then…"

he paused. "Well, I don't really like waiting around for fate, so if you weren't here today… then I'd just have to come back tomorrow."

She laughed as her stomach did the rest of the butterfly dance.

"Well luckily for you, here I am. But again, I have to ask," she paused. "Remember that whole serial killer conversation?"

He laughed. "Oh right, that… Yikes, straight to the point."

She held out her hand, then withdrew, with a mock quizzical expression. "As long as you're not planning on chopping me up into little bits and burying the pieces somewhere," she said and extended her hand again. "I'm Lillian."

"As long as *you're* not planning on framing me for said serial killer business." He took her hand and shook, his grasp warm and strong, "I'm August."

"Well August, I was just informed that the last time you were in here… you know, that time when we met outside, and you let me believe you had just finished eating? You had the worst service and were never served. I am so sorry that that was your first impression of Wisteria."

"I wouldn't say it was the worst service I've ever had at a restaurant, but I'll admit, it had the best outcome. Just think. If I hadn't decided to leave when I did, I never would have been outside at just the right time to rescue you from all those heavy bags."

"I seem to remember it differently," she teased. "There was something about someone needing directions... But seriously, I am very sorry. That's not the way anyone should ever be treated and especially not the reputation we want for this diner. You can't go wrong with anything on that menu, so whatever you want, it's on me."

"Hmm, a beautiful woman offering to buy me dinner… I think I'll leave restaurants more often."

She laughed, noting the compliment, but determined not to let him see how flattered she was by his easy flirtation. "Was there something in particular you wanted to try?"

He looked at the menu again and then back to her. "How are the burgers here?"

"The best," she told him. "I'll get one started for you."

She got him a drink and put his order in. She checked on Rain's tables, most of which were paying and leaving, and then started clearing out the dirties. She delivered August's food to him as soon as it came up, all while avoiding Gary's penetrating stare.

"Are you just going to leave me hanging?" Gary asked when she wheeled the dirty cart back into the kitchen after clearing her last table, letting August have some privacy while he ate.

"What do you mean?"

"Clearly you know him. How? Who is he?"

"I only just met him," she said evasively, "and I was trying to make this visit more pleasant than his last."

"Nope, uh uh, that was more chat than just met."

"Fine, I *barely* met him a few days ago," she told him. "Literally just walking down the street for a couple minutes and nothing until just now. I didn't even get his name."

Gary studied her, trying to determine if she was telling him the truth or holding something back.

"Hmph," he finally sighed. "It looked like more."

"Nope, sorry," she stated. "How's your side doing?"

"Deader than a doornail; it's a joke really that we're even open."

"You know how it goes this time of year."

"I know, I know. I'll find something to keep busy, but we really don't both need to be seeing to the tables."

They heard the door open and the bell chime.

"I'll see to it, you've already been on all day," she told him and went through the swinging door, back to the diner to see her dad and Ryder taking seats at the counter. "I'll be right over, guys," she called as she went to check on August. "Hey, what did you think?" she asked, nodding at his empty plate.

"I have to say you were right; it pretty much was the best."

"Like I said, I'm buying, so you can just put your wallet away," she said as he started to reach for it.

"I can't even leave a tip?"

"Nope. That's not how it works. Do you need a refill?"

He shook his head. "In order to see you again… should I stop back in tomorrow?"

"I guess you could, but you wouldn't be seeing me unless you're coming for breakfast," she laughed.

"So that would mean you don't work all day?"

"That's correct."

"And if I were to ask to see you in your off time?"

"I'd say I don't really know you."

"And we've established that I may or may not be a serial killer."

"Exactly. So…"

"So, the only way to get to know me better would be to let me repay you with lunch?"

She considered his offer. It had been a long time since she'd been on a date, longer than she cared to count. Why shouldn't she go on a lunch date with him?

"How about I say that I'll think about it," she said.

"I can handle that. Why don't you think about it, and if you're up for it, we can meet at our bench out front when you get off work and we'll go have lunch."

"Our bench?" she smiled.

"Seems as good a place as any," he said as he stood to leave. "Oh, and wear comfortable shoes… that is if you decide not to leave me hanging."

She was still smiling from their exchange, knowing she had already decided to go with him tomorrow, when she went to check on her dad and Ryder.

"Hey Dad, Ryder, how are things going?" she asked as she brought over their usual drinks. "You guys hungry or just taking a break?"

"Nothing for me," her dad said, but he'd noticed a difference in his daughter's smile when she'd talked to August, the same man he had spent the better part of the morning with, next to an unidentified corpse. "You looked pretty friendly with that man," he said lightly.

"I'm friendly with most people who come in here Dad," she told him, playing dumb. "Ryder, you want anything to eat?"

"Nah, I'm all set," he smiled the way he knew she liked, now that they were on better speaking terms. "Unless you've got any more pie hiding back there."

"You still have a sweet tooth?" she laughed and told him what they still had for the night.

"Some things don't change," he told her smoothly.

She laughed and handed him his favorite, a generous slice of tart apple pie, warmed to just the right temperature, with a scoop of vanilla ice cream. She topped it off with a drizzle of caramel syrup and a pinch of sea salt. "Dad, are you sure you don't want something?"

He was studying her, knowing she was avoiding and changing the conversation.

"You need to be careful. Not everyone is who they seem."

"I'm aware of that, Dad. Don't worry, you've taught me well."

Ryder looked between them as he finished his bite. "I feel like I missed something."

"Nothing to miss," she told them both. "Just my sheriff dad being a dad."

"I just want you to be safe," Bill said.

"Dad, it was just friendly conversation. You have nothing to be worried about. I promise."

"Who?" Ryder asked, finally coming to the conversation. "August?"

"You know August?" she asked, shocked that he knew his name when she had only just discovered it.

"Yeah, we spent the whole day with him. He's kind of a pompous ass, if you ask me," Ryder said.

"August? The man that just left when you guys sat down?" The surprise at Ryder's description was clear in her voice.

"Yep, same guy. Says he found a body out on his hike, takes us out into the wild where just about nobody has ever been, and then acts like it's nothing at all."

"Wait." She turned to her dad. "You guys found another body? Where? What happened?"

Bill gave his deputy the *look*. "I can't go into all that right now, and neither should Ryder." He paused. "August didn't say anything about it?"

"Well, that's not exactly polite conversation," she told them. "Maybe he didn't want to scare me off by talking about something like that. Or maybe he didn't want to have to think about it while he was eating."

"But he seemed fine? Like nothing had bothered him about his day?" Bill asked her.

"Dad, this is a restaurant, not the therapist's office. People aren't going to share all their problems with the waitress."

"He looked awful friendly when we got here," Bill observed.

"Yeah, and took off pretty quick, now that I think of it," Ryder mentioned.

"Guys, listen to yourselves," she said, looking at them both. "He came in here, had some dinner and left. He was finished eating, ready to go, and you happened to walk in just as I was going to check on him. It was coincidence."

Her dad looked hard at her. "Just be careful," he said. "Things are a little weird lately and I just want you to keep your eyes open. Okay?"

"Okay. I will, but you really have nothing to worry about."

He studied her a moment longer, his gaze softening slightly.

"You keep saying that now, but one of these days you'll realize that you never stop worrying, even when they're grown and out on their own." He turned to Ryder. "Let's get back. I need to check in with Rich and see if he's still able to meet us this late."

"Right, I'll be right out," he said as Bill got up to head out the front.

Ryder put some bills on the counter for the pie and grabbed his to-go cup, leaning across the counter toward Lillian.

"Your dad's just doing his job," he said gently. "He's just looking out for you." He searched her eyes. "Be careful around that guy, okay? We don't know anything about him, he turns up with a dead body and no answers, and then he's here at the diner. It's no wonder your dad would worry." He looked down at the counter then back up to her eyes, his own serious. "Or that *I'd* worry." He reached over and laid his hand over hers on the counter. She tried to keep her lips from turning up in amusement at his shift in demeanor, the sudden concern for her wellbeing. "If you see him hanging around here, or get scared for any reason, you know you can call me, right?"

"Thank you, Ryder. That's nice of you to offer. Now you better get out of here before my dad comes back in and sees you," she said, looking down at his hand over hers, trying to ignore the tingling sensation caused by his skin against hers. "It'd be like high school scare tactics all over again."

He didn't move his hand or his eyes, not laughing at her attempt to lighten the mood. "Would that really be so bad? A lot's changed since then, but then again, a lot hasn't. We were always good together," he said, squeezing her hand as he did.

"Yeah, until we weren't," she said softly, sliding her hand out from beneath his. It would be too easy to turn her palm toward his, something it remembered doing all too well.

"That's the past, remember? We're not there anymore." He picked up his to-go cup. "Just think about it," he said, studying her and slowly smiling. "Thanks again for the pie, Lilly Flower."

"Bye Ryder," she said neutrally, trying, and failing, not to smile back.

He shook his head, smiled again, and turned to leave.

Maybe she would think about it, or maybe she wouldn't. Ryder had always known how to make her melt, usually just with a look, but she was older now, and a dazzling smile wasn't going to be enough. Not with their history, even though they were supposed to be leaving that history in the past.

And then what about August?

Why hadn't he mentioned anything about his meeting with the sheriff and Ryder? She'd made excuses for him, but now all she had were questions, questions that made her doubt her decision to meet him for lunch. What did she really know about him?

Was it safe?

ELEVEN

-BILL-

The medical examiner, Rich, couldn't get to them the night before with the addition of another body, so Bill and Ryder headed over to his office first thing in the morning. Rich guided them back to the examination room. Crisp, sterile, and silver, always caught Bill's attention when he had to visit, followed closely by the smell of disinfectant. Everything was scrubbed and shining, and despite all the death the room had seen, the only evidence that remained were the two embalming tables draped in fresh, white fabric.

The cold was the third thing Bill noticed.

"I had my assistant set these two up just before you got here," Rich, told them. "I went ahead and saw to your most recent victim last night so I could report to you on both this morning."

"What have we got?" Bill asked. "Ryder said you wanted to go over the first one in person."

"Okay, up first." Rich carefully pulled back the sheet covering their drowning victim. "Poseidon." Bill heard Ryder snort beside him. "Male, aged late twenties to mid-thirties, good physical shape, no underlying health issues. Still waiting on identification; no outstanding birthmarks or tattoos to help in the identification process.

"The poor guy went through a lot. From the looks of things, he'd been in the water a few days before he was found, at least two, although probably not in the brambles he was found in the entire time. But my guess is that he went in farther up and slowly made his way down the river over the course of a few days, meeting up with a lot of rocks and branches along the way."

Rich pointed out several different cuts and marks along the body, all oddly colored with none of the expected redness from wounded skin or leaking blood. "These marks were made after your guy here was already dead. Like I said, he probably was rolled and smacked along the river, getting pretty banged up along the way in some of those really rough patches, maybe even hung up farther upriver, breaking free to move some more, then finally getting caught up where he was ultimately found. Now these," he indicated several other small slashes across the arms, face, and neck, "were made before he died.

"I'd tell you all the medical mumbo jumbo, as Bill calls it, as to how I can determine that, and with him being in the water so long, that was a more difficult task than normal, but I'll keep it simple and tell you that I just know. These here," he indicated the marks again, "and this here," he held up the badly discolored ankle and rotated it delicately as if the body lying in front of them might have pain from the movement, "were all done before death."

"That's a nasty ankle," Ryder commented. "Could it have gotten caught in the rocks when he tipped his raft? Is that what caused him to drown? He couldn't get it to release and drowned but eventually was wedged free and made his way down?"

"That's a pretty sound assumption… *If* your guy had drowned."

"What do you mean *if* he had drowned?" Bill asked, crossing his arms across his chest to look at Rich inquisitively.

"There is no indication that your man here inhaled fluid."

Bill studied the deceased man before him, bruised, beaten, cut, bloated and broken, then looked back to Rich.

"You're sure?"

"The body reacts a certain way when water is inhaled, physically and pathologically, and none of those indicators are here; no indication of fluid in the mastoid cells, no typical ground-glass opacity in the lungs." He stopped then as he noticed their eyes glazing over as he started to get too technical. "As long as we've known each other, Bill, how many times have I been wrong?"

"There's always room for a first," Bill said, still confused that this man wasn't a drowning victim.

"Okay," Ryder finally asked, "how did he die?"

"Massive heart attack," Rich stated. "Like *extreme* heart attack."

"You're sure?" Bill asked, not wanting to offend him, but it was too absurd.

"The waves of confidence are just spilling from you," Rich said sarcastically. "Yes. Again, I'm sure. One hundred percent."

"This just doesn't seem like the heart attack type," Bill told him. "You said it yourself. He wasn't that old and was in good physical shape. It doesn't make sense."

"Could the ankle in the rocks scenario still work with the heart attack situation?" Ryder spoke up and both men turned to him. "Guy flips out of his boat, gets stuck in the rocks, panics and maybe had a heart condition that he either did or didn't know about ahead of time, and winds up having a heart attack, dies, dislodges, floats, gets stuck, then found."

Bill nodded, following Ryder's line of thought. He was mildly surprised at the quick adaptation of Ryder's thought process. He turned to Rich for the answer.

"That is a possibility, although slim. Remember, no indication of fluid inhaled. Even if he didn't die from drowning, a struggle in the water would inevitably cause him to inhale water, and we'd have those physical and pathological indicators," Rich said and moved closer to the body. "I'll need some help here to lift him." Bill moved forward and helped him tilt the body so they could see the backside. "See these marks here?" Rich pointed to some particularly awful looking gashes, then indicated they could lay the body back down. "These are from impact and from the looks of them, and the amount over his body, he fell from somewhere high, landed in a few different places along the way, and ultimately ended up in the water. Those were made at, or very near, time of death. I'm betting your guy was dead before he finished his descent."

"So, he died from a fall? Not watersports at all?" Bill inquired.

"That's what it looks like," Rich confirmed. "This ankle is bad news, but doesn't look like it happened during the fall, looks like it was before death, probably walked on from the mangled mess that it's in. Maybe your guy was hiking, got hurt with the ankle, then took a spill over a ledge into the river below. These marks here though," he pointed at the lesions along the face and arms, "looks like he got whipped and scraped at high velocity, often seen from a tree branch. He could have lifted his arm to shield his face from swats and got those, or just low branches.

"My guess is he was running from something, or even recreationally if that's your thing, but I'm just not feeling this was a jog through the woods. Could have been a bear was chasing him, then he tripped and fell, which hurt the ankle, kept running, didn't notice the edge, and went over into the water below. What I can tell you for certain though is something scared the life out of this man and his heart exploded in his chest."

"Well, I'd say a plummet to my death would scare the shit outta me," Ryder commented.

"Mm hmm," Bill nodded, but was quiet otherwise, contemplating this new development.

"I can see why you'd want to tell us this in person," Ryder said. "We probably would have thought you sent over the wrong report."

"Exactly," Rich said, covering the body with the sheet and moving to the next table. "Now this one, Zeus," he told them, uncovering the body from yesterday in just as delicate a fashion, "is male, late teens to early twenties, peak physical condition, no underlying health concerns as far as I could tell. No identification yet; has a couple tattoos that could help identify him if someone comes forward, but the odds of finding out who he is through those are slim. Dead approximately three days."

"He looked familiar to me, but he could just have one of those faces," Bill said, and Ryder nodded. "There was no ID on him and there's no telling if he's local or tourist, but we've already started his print and missing persons search."

"So, your man here has some similar scratches along his body as our other body." Rich pointed them out along the arms and face and legs. "Doesn't surprise me though, because you found him up in the woods, little scratches like this would be expected on a hike. Why he was wearing shorts, I couldn't tell you, which strikes me as either not being used to being in the woods, or just didn't care about poison ivy, ticks, or sticks and the like that can scratch a person up. That doesn't bother some people, I guess. Me, I'm bug sprayed, tough pants, boots, gear, the whole nine yards when I go on a serious hike, and where this one was found, was a serious hike."

"Or he didn't plan on being in the woods at all," Bill pondered.

"Normally, I'd chalk this death up to impact. He was found at the bottom of a cliff splayed out on the rocks. Pretty cut and dry, if you ask me, except for the height."

"That was a pretty high cliff," Ryder countered.

"Don't get me wrong, a cliff of that height paired with the landing zone could, without a doubt, have done the job, but the evidence isn't there. More than likely, he would have been broken, but the possibility that he was still alive enough to try to move from where he was, even just a little to try and get help, would have been good. There was no movement for this body. It landed and stayed exactly as it was."

"Okay... could the fall have at least knocked him out and then he died from the injuries before he woke up?" Bill asked.

"Yes, that is a possibility, and with the lack of impact-related, obvious causes of death, that's where I initially went with my examination."

"What do you mean by *obvious* impact-related causes of death?" Ryder asked. "It was pretty obvious that he landed from a fall. He was broken and bent awkwardly."

"Broken arms and legs don't kill you," Rich told him. "Surprisingly his spinal column was intact, and his lungs weren't punctured from the fall. His head wasn't split open from impact. By all accounts, he could have survived. He would have had a hell of a time getting out of there on his own, and would have had a long road to recovery, but again, he didn't even move from his landing position."

"What are you telling us then?" Bill asked. "Was he already dead when he hit?"

"Bingo! You're getting the hang of this."

"So, someone hiked his body up there and threw him over?" Ryder asked, looking immediately to Bill, "Who do we know that has hiked that area recently?"

Bill's face was serious and set as he thought about August and his connection to this body and apparently to his daughter.

Another conversation was going to be had very soon.

"Now don't get too ahead of yourselves, guys," Rich pulled them back in. "I said *normally* I would have thought this one was open and shut, but with the weirdness of Poseidon there, I had to be sure. Aside from the obvious wounds from the fall, there are no signs of a struggle that this person fought with someone beforehand, no defensive wounds, just the results of the fall. So, unless your suspect knows how to give out a heart attack, then you can start looking somewhere else."

"Wait," Bill started.

"What?" Ryder asked at the same time.

Rich looked at them both, wondering who was going to go next.

Bill won. "You're saying this kid, this healthy, obviously athletic kid, died from a heart attack, too? How is that possible?"

"Stranger things have happened, but yes, that's what I'm saying. And not just a heart attack—a massive, explosive heart attack."

Bill looked over to the sheet-covered body that Rich had dubbed Poseidon and back to the uncovered Zeus. He rubbed his forehead. "What are the odds that we get two bodies less than a week apart and both dead from massive heart attacks, both falls, and both dead before impact?" Bill asked, perplexed.

"About zero," Rich confirmed.

Ryder stared at the young kid, thinking about where he was at that age, what he was doing. "What about those energy drinks?" Bill and Rich both looked at him, waiting for more. Ryder turned to Bill. "You remember a few years back, kids were drinking energy drinks, like a lot of them, and were having heart attacks because it was too much for their system or something? It was all over the news, scared a bunch of parents. Hell, even my parents called me up and told me to stay away from them. On the surface, this kid doesn't look like the type to be into drugs, but some sort of pre-workout or energy booster before the hike, maybe did his heart bad?"

Bill nodded, Ryder surprising him yet again, and turned to Rich.

"What do you think?" Bill asked. "Is that a possibility? Kid goes for a hike, has too many of those drinks and has a heart attack, goes over an edge and dies on the rocks?"

"I'm going to hire this one to be my assistant," Rich said nodding at Ryder. "It's a good theory, but no energy drink. Toxicology reports only a small amount of alcohol as abnormal. No drugs of any kind either. My guess," he paused again, studying the body, "kid has a few beers with his buddies, having a good ol' time, and gets it in his head to go for a hike. He works off most of the alcohol, based on the small amount in his system at time of death, but could still be a little tipsy and goes over a ledge." He scratched his chin, looking at them seriously. "But that still doesn't explain the heart attack. If he were buzzed, he'd probably register what was happening too late, so panic wouldn't even have time to set in. It just doesn't make sense."

"What about Poseidon?" Ryder nodded to the other body. "Any foreign substance found with him?"

Rich shook his head. "Toxicology was clear on him, too. Dehydrated actually, which is ironic since you found him in the water, but no drugs, no alcohol."

"So, we have two different bodies, found in two different areas, days apart from each other, both of which have no toxicology abnormalities, but suffered massive heart attacks that killed them," Bill stated the facts aloud.

"Both of whom were physically fit and healthy and fell off something high," Ryder added.

"And both had high levels of adrenaline and cortisol at time of death," Rich mentioned, looking down at Zeus. "They were scared—really scared—when they died."

Rich covered Zeus back up since there was nothing more to see. He walked them back out front, the officers still silent in their contemplations.

"I'll let you know if anything more is discovered," Rich told them. "And you know where to find me if you have any questions."

Bill paused outside the building, Ryder just ahead of him, Rich holding the door open.

"I do have one question," Bill asked Rich.

"Sure thing, shoot," Rich said.

"Poseidon, I get… the water," Bill said. "But why Zeus? Is there not a forest god or something more fitting?"

"Oh," Rich chuckled. "That's because you found him on the Mountain."

The chill was unavoidable as it slithered down Bill's spine.

TWELVE

-LILLIAN-

Lillian was sure today she was the worst employee she'd ever been. All morning she'd been stuck in her head, worrying about her date with August—if that's what they were calling it. After her dad and Ryder tried warning her off of him, she worried if they might be right. What did she really know about him?

She cleared the recently vacated table, and wiped it down.

But despite her joking, she hadn't gotten any serial killer or creepy stalker vibes from the two times she'd been around him.

He's considerate, funny, and seems to be easy-going—not to mention HOT.

She placed the rolled utensils onto the table and smiled, recalling how his name sounded in his smooth voice when he finally introduced himself.

August.

What did anyone really know about anyone else before they dated?

She nodded at this logic, deciding she should be allowed to make up her own mind when it came to August. Ryder, with his flirtatious new attitude, wasn't about to cheer her on about going on a date with another man, and her dad was, well, her dad. He'd always want her to be wary and on high alert for any man, local or out of towner.

Both men were terrible references.

This was the first time in a long time that she was nervous about the end of her shift. She'd never told August what time she'd be finished working, they'd only mentioned lunch, which really could be any time.

Would he be waiting?

If he wasn't, how long was she supposed to sit and wait for him if she got off work earlier than his idea of lunch?

She didn't like the idea of sitting there for an undetermined amount of time, and for the second time she hadn't thought to get his phone number. She had no way to contact him.

As she neared the end of her shift, she glanced out the windows discreetly to see if he had arrived at their bench, but each time she looked, no August. When it was finally time to wrap things up, she looked again.

Still no August.

She sighed inwardly as she untied and stowed her apron. She'd brought clothes to change into. He'd said to wear comfortable shoes, so she assumed he had planned to do some walking. That could be anywhere in this town. She hadn't been too sure how a person would dress for a lunch date in comfy shoes. She'd decided on her favorite jeans, broken in that hugged her just right, a loose top that was cut to flatter, and a pair of cute and comfy tennies that could handle whatever he had in mind.

She pulled her hair back into a low pony and grabbed her purse from the office. She touched up her lip gloss and checked that the rest of her make-up was still in place after a full shift that had started before the sun came up. When she couldn't find anything else to fret over, she decided she was as ready as she was going to be, and headed through the kitchen to the front of the diner.

"Look at you," Lana sang as Lillian walked by. "Where are you off to looking all cute?"

"Really? You think it's ok?"

Lana studied her a little further. "Ok for what?"

"I have a… lunch," Lillian said, knowing if she gave her too much, Lana would want to know all the details and now wasn't the time.

"Mm hmm…" Lana mused. She held up a finger and twirled it around. "Give me a spin."

Lillian giggled but complied. "Acceptable?"

"Let your hair down," Lana ordered. Lillian did as she was told, fluffing it from the pony. "Good. Enjoy your… lunch," Lana teased. "Tell me all about it later."

Lillian pushed through the swinging door and headed to the exit.

She could wait for twenty minutes before it looked too desperate, she decided, thirty minutes tops.

But August was already sitting on the bench, leaning back with an ankle resting on his other knee and his arm along the back of the bench, watching the cars go by as if he could do that all day long.

Her heart did a flip and a flop to see him sitting there.

She admired his relaxed nature as she walked up, his confidence to be comfortably at ease wherever he was. She saw plenty of people who couldn't sit alone as if the world around them didn't matter, who couldn't check for the next posted reassurances on their devices. It surprised her at how sexy she found him because of it. Her earlier nerves about whether he'd show felt ridiculous now. He turned his head as she approached, his cool eyes assessing her. His slow smile of approval made her feel more desirable than she had ever felt before.

Her heart beat faster at the thought of his arms around her.

Reigning in her suddenly out of control hormones, she smiled back, wondering if she should have thrown on some jewelry.

"You look great," he said, never taking his eyes from hers.

"Thanks, but you didn't really give me much to go on except for comfy shoes."

His gaze traveled the length of her again down to her shoes and slowly back up.

His voice was smooth and his smile lingered as if savoring the moment. "Don't worry, you're perfect."

The urge to climb into his lap right there on the bench was high, but she figured that wasn't a good idea. Probably not for this first date thing… maybe?

He stood, and her daydream evaporated because real life was so much better. How could someone make jeans and a t-shirt look that good? She hoped they were going somewhere very public because, she realized, standing in the middle of a very busy sidewalk, that it had been too long of a dry spell. She really hoped the heat she was feeling wasn't showing in her cheeks.

"Shall we walk?" he asked and took her hand in his to lead her down the sidewalk.

Her inner high school girl reared her giddy head, hoping all of her girlfriends would drive by at the same time and see her walking hand in hand with the star of the town.

What was wrong with her? She'd been around attractive men before, even ones that tried hard to flatter her and get her into bed, and she'd never had this sort of immediate and undeniable reaction to *them*.

The walk to his truck was quicker than she expected—she felt like she was in a trance. He gave her a lift that lingered just long enough to be noticeable, but not long enough to make her uneasy, then shut the door so he could walk around the front and get into the driver's seat.

"How was your shift?" He asked as he pulled the truck out of the lot.

"Busy. Breakfast is always a hit at Wisteria."

"I'll have to try it sometime."

"So, are you going to tell me where we're going?" Lillian asked after a few moments of driving and chatter about her work.

"Maybe it's a surprise," he told her, glancing over and smiling mischievously.

He'd driven out of town and turned down a gravel access road. She was sure it was near the river, but it wasn't a part she'd been to before.

"And what if I don't like surprises?" She tried to keep the uncertainty out of her voice. Just because she'd made up her mind to come out with him, didn't mean she was completely certain in her choice. She could hear the whispered voices of Ryder and her dad telling her to be alert.

"Well, we're pretty far into it now," he joked but laughed. "Don't worry, it's just up ahead."

He pulled off the narrow road and into the grass, putting the truck into park. She looked around. There was nothing in sight but trees and a little grassy area where they had stopped.

"I thought we were going to lunch?" she asked, trying not to be nervous. She knew where they were, for the most part, and could get back to town if she needed to, but the little voices of Ryder and her dad were growing louder.

August just smiled devilishly and hopped down from the truck. She opened her little bag and made sure her bear spray was easily accessible and closed it back up as he came around to open her door.

"I'll help you down," he said, reaching for her. "There's a little bit of a dip down here."

She eyed him, contemplating telling him to take her back, but in the end, curiosity won, and she decided to see where this would go. His hands around her waist were strong and sure as he helped her down, his arms solid where she held on. He set her on her feet, but he didn't let go as she looked up into his eyes, her hands still holding on to him as well.

"There's just a small hike," he told her, his voice soft in the wide open.

Of course, he'd want to go hiking. Why didn't you bring boots?

"My shoes…" she started.

"Are still perfect."

He finally broke the trance to close the door behind her, but didn't let her go, taking her hand instead.

"Come on, it's just up ahead."

He led her away from the road to a very overgrown trail that nobody would have ever known was there unless they already knew it existed. They followed the trail into the woods, his sure footing finding the easiest path through. When she was just about to ask how much farther it would be, he stopped and turned to her, still holding the hand he had been leading her with.

"If I leave you alone here, will you be scared?" he asked seriously.

She studied his expression of concern, the warmth of his hand in hers, the absolute calm of the trees as a gentle breeze blew through and birds sang in the distance.

"Should I be?"

His smile was perfect and genuine, almost proud.

"Not at all," he stated. He led her to a tree stump and had her sit. "Wait right here. I promise there's nothing to be afraid of. I'll be back in five minutes."

He looked at her again, an admiration in his eyes, then turned and headed farther into the woods.

Once he was gone, she pulled her phone out of her purse to check if she had a signal. Her earlier nerves had faded along their walk. She wasn't afraid, quite the opposite actually; she was intrigued and excited to be out here with him, but still, it didn't hurt to make sure she had service. Three bars, which was better than she could say for some places in the diner.

While she was at it, she checked her notifications. A missed call from her dad. He was probably just checking on her; she made a mental note to call him and Mom when she got back home.

A few text messages from Lana.

Hey girl, thought you'd want to know Rain JUST showed up for her shift.

Oh… 'Lunch' looked… delicious. And you looked damn fine as well, but show off the girls a little more.

You've got it, flaunt it

Lillian snorted in the middle of the woods with nobody to hear. Lana had a point though and Lillian did a little adjusting to perk things up. She pulled her shirt forward slightly to give a hint of cleavage and thought all was pretty set in that department. She had a message from another number that she didn't recognize so she clicked to open.

Hey it's Ryder, your dad gave me your number. I need to talk to you tonight. Can I swing by the house after my shift?

Seeing Ryder's name immediately brought him into the woods with her and her heart fluttered. *Stop it. You're on a date with another man. A very attractive and potentially interesting man that hasn't broken your heart in the past.* But she thought it was odd that Ryder'd want to come over, and considered telling him no, but something about the urgency seemed like it could be serious. Plus, even though she was sure nothing contrary would happen out here with August, she was a cop's daughter, and it would be good to have someone check in on her. She sent him back a quick text.

May not have much service to text/call for a little bit but will be back in a few hours. You can swing by after 7 tonight if that works for you.

She hit send. That would give her enough time to spend with August during the day, find something to eat for dinner, and be back home for Ryder to stop over, but not stay too long. They could discuss whatever it was he needed to tell her, and she'd be in bed at a decent time for her early shift tomorrow.

She could hear August making his way back to her through the trees. She set her phone to silent so they wouldn't be disturbed and tucked it back in her purse, the bear mace still on top, and zipped it closed. She ran her fingers through her hair to make sure she didn't have any leaves sticking in it from their walk and was ready and waiting when he came into view.

"You didn't run off."

"The thought may have crossed my mind," she laughed.

He held out his hand again and she took it, prepared to follow where he led. It was a short walk this time before she could see sunshine ahead through the branches. He stopped again and turned in front of her, blocking her view of what lay beyond.

"We're here," he said and had her looking around for something out of the ordinary that would trigger the *ah ha, I see why you brought me here* reaction but found nothing. He was smiling at her curious expression. "This is where I'd ask if you trust me, but since you barely know me, the answer to that should be no. So instead, I'm going to ask you to bear with me for a minute longer and it will all be worth it."

"I already let you leave me stranded in the woods," she joked. "What's a minute longer of bearing with you?"

"Great. Give me your other hand," he said and held both in front of her. "Now close your eyes and let me lead you."

She glanced around again, not seeing anything overly perilous she should be worried about and decided to be adventurous.

"You're not going to make me trip, are you?"

"Not a chance… In fact," his face changed to mischief again. "Close your eyes," he said again.

"No peeking," he told her when she finally closed her eyes. He let go of her hands, making her worry about how he was going to lead her without holding on to her, but then she felt his breath at her ear from behind, surprising her with his proximity. "Trust me," he whispered, despite saying earlier that she shouldn't, and lifted her into his arms. Hers instinctively went around his neck, a giggle bursting forth. "Keep your eyes closed," he said when she started to open them on impulse.

He carried her as though she weighed nothing, his body hard where she was pressed against him. It wasn't far of a walk before he set her down again, his arms around her waist, hers still around his neck. "Keep them closed," he said, his hands sliding along, slowly guiding her body, turning her around, but still not letting her go. Her back was pressed firmly against his chest, one arm around her waist, the other across her shoulders. His voice was by her ear again, calm and quiet.

"I want you to hold my arms where I'm holding you," he whispered. She did, wondering what was about to happen, but exhilarated by the unknown. "In a second," he told her softly, "I'm going to have you open your eyes, but you have to do two things first. Okay?"

"What two things?" she whispered as well since the moment seemed to call for it.

"First, you're not going to move a muscle, and second, you're not going to panic."

At the mention of the word panic, her heart started racing and she squeezed his arms tighter, feeling him pull her even closer as he held her firmly in place.

"August," she said nervously, now afraid to open her eyes to see what was before them, as if, like the thoughts of a child, if she didn't see it, it couldn't affect her.

"I promise," he whispered in his calm and steady voice, "you'll be safe."

His voice was reassuring, but her heart was still beating fast with the fear of the unknown before her. What had seemed so exciting moments before was now terrifying.

What were you thinking coming out here like this? What have you gotten yourself into?

"Slow your breaths," he said from behind her. She hadn't even realized she had started to breathe faster. "Feel the breeze on your face," he soothed. "There's nothing to be afraid of."

His breath behind her was slow and steady, and she used his movements to match her rhythm again. When he deemed her calm enough, and she still hadn't opened her eyes, more out of that childish fear at this point, he finally spoke, his voice a whisper on the wind. "I've got you. Open your eyes."

THIRTEEN

-Lillian-

"Oh!" she exclaimed and immediately tried to take a step back, but he was there holding her steady and tight. Her heart raced even faster than before.

"Don't move," he reminded her. "I'm right here with you. I've got you," he repeated. "Just look."

She did, for as far as she could see.

They were on top of the world, with everything unfolding below them.

From where they were, she could see for miles. She felt like a bird, above it all, everything miniature, more beautiful than the best photo. They stood together in silence and watched the river run its course and the birds soar overhead. They watched the sun shimmer on fields and hills below then hide as the clouds drifted idly by. The evergreens dominated the hills, but the newly awakening bloomers offered a beautiful array of vibrant pinks, purples, and whites mixed among them.

The world was perfect.

"August," she breathed, at a loss for words. "Oh my God, it's amazing."

"I told you it would be worth it," he said softly.

She leaned against him and felt him hold her tighter. She had wondered what it would be like to be in his arms, and so far, she wasn't disappointed. Standing on the edge of the world wrapped up in him was not what she had expected to be doing today, but real life was infinitely better than her streetside fantasy.

"There's more," his voice startled her out of her reflection. He slowly stepped backwards, taking her with him still in his arms.

For a moment, she had forgotten how close they had been to the edge.

He turned her around and let her walk toward the picnic that he had already laid out. She smiled at the sweet set-up: a classic checkered cloth placed on the ground complete with linen napkins, plates and silverware. He had bottles of water already out and a bucket of ice with wine cooling. She sat down on the cloth, and he took a seat across from her.

He opened the cooler and took out pre-cut, packaged fruit, sliced cheeses and meats, two sealed bags with sandwiches in them, and a bag of cookies.

"I ran into this girl the other day who told me that if I ever saw these peanut butter cookies, I shouldn't pass them up," he told her as he set them out.

"She sounds brilliant."

"I think you're probably right," he agreed. He handed her one of the sandwiches. "Now these are a secret recipe, passed down generation to generation."

Curious, she opened the package and took a bite, covering her mouth and laughing as she chewed. "It's peanut butter and jelly."

"Secret family recipe peanut butter and jelly," he told her, feigning hurt at her comment.

"Of course," she said with faux seriousness. "I can't believe you did all this."

"You're right," he suddenly said. "Eat fast. I found this just sitting here and whoever it belongs to could be along any minute. We better hurry."

She laughed again and he smiled.

"You have a really great laugh," he said. "It hooked me on the street that day."

"Really? Not the smart woman who could give you directions?" she joked.

He smiled and looked down at his plate. Something about the smile reminded her of trying not to laugh at a joke.

"Oh my gosh," she squealed, realization dawning. She covered her face with her hands, peeking through her fingers, then lowered them to just cover her mouth. Muffled, she spoke through her hands, "You never needed directions, did you?" She covered her face again after seeing his attempt to suppress a laugh. "Oh my gosh," she repeated. "You walked us through here like it was no problem. You are an avid hiker from the look of the map you had. There's no way you were turned around on that street."

"Can you really blame me?" he asked, laughing freely now. "There I am, getting situated, and what do I turn to see, but the most beautiful woman gaping at me. Of course, I had to think of a reason to talk to her, and some terrible one liner wasn't going to be good enough."

"I wasn't gaping," she argued.

"Full on ogling," he countered.

She covered her face again, mortified, but couldn't help laughing.

"Excuse me while I go jump off that cliff," she told him.

"Please don't," he said, peeling her hands off her face. He held one in his own, studying it as he ran his thumb over her knuckles. "The beautiful woman caught my eye, but her laugh hooked me," he looked back at her, "and then the confidence you showed talking to some random person on the street as if you already knew him, welcoming him to your town and sharing some of your favorites with him… there's a whole lot more to this woman that I want to get to know."

"I did what any person would do in that situation," she told him.

"I've been to a lot of places, seen a lot of things, and met a lot of people, and can tell you honestly, that no, no they wouldn't. You're genuine and it's refreshing."

She smiled as he watched her, her heart fluttering in a way she didn't mind.

"Do you want some wine?" he asked, motioning to the bottle in the ice. She contemplated the bottle, their location, all the different what ifs, and realized she was an adult on a date with an amazing man. Why shouldn't she treat herself to a glass? "You can say no you know," he said, noticing her inward deliberation.

"I'd love a glass," she told him, shutting up the voice of reason in her head.

He smiled, rooted around in the pocket of the cooler bag and found the corkscrew, popped and poured. She was sure there was etiquette she was supposed to follow, smelling, tasting, etc., but instead she sipped… and cringed. She saw his face when he tasted it, too, and they both laughed.

"It's terrible, isn't it?" he said, picking up the bottle and inspecting the label as if it would offer insight into its awfulness.

"It's not great," she agreed, taking another sip to see if it was better the second time around. It wasn't.

"The guy at the store said it would pair well…"

"With peanut butter and jelly sandwiches?" she finished for him.

"I asked for something that would go with fruits and nuts and cheeses," he said innocently.

She laughed some more, imagining the clerk's face when he realized what he meant by fruits and nuts.

"There it is again. That laugh. It makes this wasted bottle of wine worth it."

"It's not wasted," she told him trying for a third-time's-the-charm sip. "You could probably use it as an insect repellent."

"It's pretty potent, huh?" he said, trying another sip, and shaking his head. "Nope, it's wasted." He tossed the contents in the grass beside him and opened a bottle of water, drinking deep. "That's better."

"The grass will probably never grow there again."

"Sorry, grass," he said and tossed hers as well. He put the cork back in the bottle, not sure what to do with it, but stuck it back in the ice for now. "Well, that's disappointing. So much for the perfect date."

"Oh, I'd say you're doing pretty well, even without the wine."

He smiled, "I wanted it to be memorable. A first date to top all others."

"So, it's all downhill from here?" she laughed.

"Not likely," he told her. "But the goal was to blow all your other firsts out of the water, so this was the one you wanted to remember."

She grinned as she drank from her water bottle. "Should I go ahead and tell you that you've already succeeded, or wait and see what other surprises you've got up your sleeve?"

"Unfortunately, no more surprises, just me and a terrible bottle of wine," he looked around at the spread. "Oh, and supposedly delicious cookies."

She grabbed the bag from his hand. "There's no supposing about it. These are hands down the best." She opened the package and took one out, handing it to him. "Try for yourself."

"They're actually pretty good," he agreed as he chewed.

"The best," she stated, matter of fact. "You're just too stubborn of a man to admit that I'm right."

"Hey, I asked you for directions, didn't I?"

"Fake directions. It doesn't count."

"You didn't know they were fake at the time. I feel like that should count," he reasoned.

"It doesn't," she laughed, enjoying how easy he was to be around. "Can I ask you something?"

"It sounds serious," he replied, picking up on the slight change in her demeanor. "What do you want to know? And no, before you ask again, I'm not going to tell you whether I'm a serial killer or not."

"Well, as long as we got that one out of the way for now… No, what I wanted to ask is why you're here."

"I told you about taking a break from the work world rat race," he started, but she could tell there was more he was keeping back, so she waited. He studied her face. She wondered if he was contemplating how much to share. She studied him right back, noting something change in his eyes, almost sorrowful before he spoke again. "I wasn't planning on sharing this right out, definitely not here and now," he said solemnly. "It's not exactly first-date conversation material."

"I don't scare too easily," she urged him, wondering what had put the anguish in his eyes.

"Okay," he sighed. "I was engaged before."

"Okay… and I gather it didn't work out?" she said, instinctively looking at his hand, wondering if she had gotten involved with a married man, kicking herself for making a mistake she'd vowed never to make again by not investigating him further.

He held up his hand to confirm no ring.

"We didn't make it to the wedding day," he said sadly, and she got the feeling it wasn't by his choice.

"What happened?" she asked as delicately as she could, not knowing what kind or how fresh a wound this might be.

He glanced away for a moment.

"I'm sorry, I shouldn't have pried," she said, feeling like a jerk.

"It's okay really. We were only engaged for a few months before she passed away."

"Oh, August… I'm sorry… I didn't realize." Now she felt like even more of a jerk. She'd practically forced it out of him when he had no plans of sharing this soon. She felt nosy but a little selfish, hoping it wouldn't ruin their light mood.

"There's no reason to be sorry Lil… Lillian," he corrected himself. "You had no idea. It was a freak accident and by the time I got there, it was too late."

She reached over and squeezed his hand, not sure what to say, not sure how to recover their earlier lightheartedness. He squeezed hers back and smiled gently.

"It's been two years since I lost her. It was a rough first year, everywhere I looked I thought I saw her. I'd hear her voice in the other room. I threw myself into work and didn't look up for a long time. When I did, I realized that I was doing exactly what she would have hated—wasting my life away—so I decided it was time to start living it. I took a sabbatical from work, set things up to pay automatically, got rid of all the extra electronic crap that just wears a person down, and pretty much hit the road. Now obviously, I still need things in order to function in daily life and I keep the basics, like a cell phone and atm card, stowed away wherever I stay, but for the most part, I try not to depend on anything like that."

"Thus, the paper map you had the other day."

"Exactly. It's amazing how different the world is when you open your eyes and look around. So, when I opened mine and saw you watching me, I knew I needed to meet you. And I can already predict what you're probably thinking," he said before she could say anything. "Here's a guy that's still hung up on his ex, looking for a good time with the first woman who caught his eye, who's in town for who knows how long… why would anyone want to mess with that?" He looked at her very seriously. "Lillian, I'll be completely honest with you when I tell you I love and miss her very much, but I know that there is no way she is ever coming back. I've had two years to come to terms with that, and it's time that I moved on. She was one of a kind, and I don't ever want to erase the part of her that I got to have, but instead am thankful that I got what I did. I can also tell you that I have no idea how long I'm going to be here, but as it stands, I have no plans to be anywhere else.

"I think you're pretty amazing and I feel a connection with you that I think you feel as well, but if all this is too much, too fast, or just poor timing, tell me, because I really feel like there's something here."

His words settled deep in her chest, making her heart ache at the loss he had been through and wonder at what it had taken for him to move on from a tragedy so deep. She didn't know much about him, but from the few times she'd seen him and the complete openness she felt from him now, she felt that he was being truthful with her, even knowing that it could push her away completely.

His eyes were searching hers for any sign of what she was feeling.

"I wasn't looking for a relationship," she started and saw a slight falter in his gaze. "I even told my dad to stop playing matchmaker the very morning that we ran into each other on the street." She paused again, watching him watch her. He'd been open and direct. She could too. "But I can't deny that I like you, that I instantly liked you, and not just because you were easy to look at."

"Ogled," he corrected.

"I don't want to rush into anything, August," she said hesitantly, "but if you're willing to stick around for a little while, I'd like to get to know you."

His smile could, and probably just did, melt her heart.

"So, we take things slow," he told her, "and see what happens next."

He pulled the hand that he'd been holding loosely between them to him and lightly brushed his lips against her knuckles.

No more heart, it was completely gone, melted into a puddle somewhere in her body.

Before she let herself think about what she was doing and lost all her nerve, she leaned in close to him, pressing her lips to his. Shocked that she'd actually done it, she pulled back, desperately trying to think of an excuse for her actions.

"Sorry," she whispered. "I don't know what I was thinking."

"Don't be sorry," he whispered back, still just a breath away. This close, she could see little flecks of gold in his brown eyes as his watched hers. He raised his hand, gently brushing her hair aside. When she didn't move away, he moved his hand into her hair and pulled her closer. He kissed her again, softly at first, his other hand framing her face as well. She allowed her hands to roam, wrapping them around his sturdy shoulders. The kiss went deeper, gaining in intensity as each took from the moment what they'd been denying themselves. His arms moved around her waist, pulling her in for more, her initial peck innocent and sweet compared to the desperation they both suddenly shared.

She climbed into his lap, no room for surprise by her actions or fear that he'd slow her advance as she felt him embrace her tighter to him. She felt his thumb graze her back beneath the hem of her shirt, tiny currents raced along her skin, electrified by his touch. She moaned involuntarily and she felt his lips pull up in a smile against her own. His hands moved to her hips and squeezed, the small motion triggering her to impulsively move, rubbing against him. It was her turn to smile as he groaned in response.

She pulled at his shirt, breaking for a breath as she tugged it over his head, admiring how he looked without it, then dove back in for more. His hands were warm and strong against her skin as they slid up under her shirt to flick open the clasp of her bra, granting unencumbered access to her breast, his caress gentle yet firm. Her breath caught at his squeeze, and she released him long enough to take her own shirt up and over her head, his mouth expertly exploring as she did so, teeth nipping and tongue tasting.

He was moving containers and plates out of the way, and she was on the checkered cloth, both of them desperate for each other.

"Wait," he said between kisses, "this isn't how I planned the first time to go."

"But you did plan it," she laughed, bringing him back down to her.

He nipped her gently and smiled at her gasp.

"I have a pulse, of course I did… What about slow?" he murmured as he trailed kisses along her neck. "Two seconds ago you said—"

"Screw slow." She breathed in his scent, feeling empowered by how much he was in her thrall and she in his. She'd never felt so comfortable yet completely exhilarated as she did in this moment. Being in his arms felt right. "We can never know what tomorrow will bring. Now stop talking so much." She laughed and kissed him again, flicking off her shoes and unbuttoning her pants.

His hands found hers and brought them up over her head, pinning them as he kissed her deeply, letting them go as he explored her body, planting kisses as he went. His hands stirred up sensations everywhere they touched, the warmth of his tongue a contrast to the kiss of the breeze. She refused to let her mind think about anything other than now, as the first explosive wave primed her system.

There was no time to recover, to begin to doubt what they were doing or how this would make her look, before he was back at her, kissing and caressing. He held her tight, watching her face as she waited, closing her eyes with a sigh as he slowly began moving with her, pushing her closer and closer back to the edge. Not wanting to give in so soon, she rolled him over and took control, his strong hands holding her hips as she set an indulgently languid pace. They were the only two people in the world and she'd never felt so free. She moved with him, as the breeze caressed her bare skin, as his hands slid and squeezed, as she pushed them both beyond, and finally over the edge.

He pulled her back down to him, kissing her sweetly before she rested against him, both needing to catch their breath. His hand smoothed her hair, trailed down her back, then back again in a hypnotizing rhythm that had her dozing off to the beat of his heart against her ear.

"Hey," she sleepily mumbled against his chest.

"Hmmm?" she heard the vibration from within him.

"You're not going to chop me up into bits now, are you?"

"Probably not," he admitted, the smile she could hear in his voice as she let him lazily pet her back. "I've decided," he said as he swiftly lifted her off him and shifted her underneath his body, "that you taste entirely too good to chop into bits."

She curled into him as he took her mouth again, his fingers shocking a sigh from her as they roamed, then a gasp when she realized he was ready again. He locked his hands with hers, his lips caressing her neck and teeth nipping at her ear as he slowly moved above her. She moved to match him, reveling in how it felt deep within, warming her from the inside out.

"I hope you're not having second thoughts," he murmured somewhere against her body, she could no longer be sure where.

"I'm having no thoughts," she said, pulling his face back to hers for a kiss and to watch him watching her as they both floated on the breeze and drifted away.

She smiled at the weight of his head against her chest, finding comfort in each tickling breath against her skin as she watched the clouds roll by above.

"I can feel you smiling," he told her chest.

"I was just thinking that if anyone were to walk by right now, they'd be in for a surprise. It's the middle of the afternoon and we're completely naked on a picnic."

"I told you to hurry up and eat, that whoever this picnic belonged to could be along any second. They're probably wondering why we didn't like their wine."

She laughed beneath him and felt his lips curl up in a smile against her skin.

It couldn't be this easy, she thought, wondering when the self-conscious thoughts would ruin her moment. *Could it?*

FOURTEEN

-Lillian-

Her date with August ran long, and she wasn't about to complain about the reasons why. After packing up their picnic and him giving her a ride back to her car at the diner, she had just enough time to get home and shower. She threw leftovers into the microwave and had started towel drying her hair when the doorbell rang.

Ryder was twenty minutes early… and she was still in her robe… her silky, black, lace-lined robe that barely reached her knees.

She'd been feeling sexy still and hadn't wanted to let go of that exhilaration. She'd thought she had more time before she had to get dressed.

She was wrong.

She considered making him wait while she ran and threw something on, but the bell rang a second time, so she decided to go with her motto of the day and just screw it. She opened the door in her robe and towel wrung hair.

"Oh," Ryder gawked. "Wow."

"Don't get any ideas," she laughed, "but you're early and I wasn't ready yet."

She stepped out of the way so he could enter her house and shut the door behind him.

"Not gonna' lie, Lilly, but it's pretty hard not to get ideas with legs like those and wearing what you are… or aren't," he told her, staring at her legs and back up again. "I mean, really, wow."

"Thank you, Ryder," she replied. She was still floating on the high of her afternoon, the feeling of being desired and well handled—multiple times—and it was hard not to respond to the look in Ryder's eyes as she stood before him in barely a stitch of silky material, leaving nothing to the imagination. She hoped the warming of her cheeks wouldn't show. The last thing she needed was to offer encouragement to Ryder after his compliment and desiring gaze. "Get your mind back to reality while I go get dressed," she said, not sure if it was for him or herself. "I'll be right back."

"Don't change on my account. I don't mind at all," he told her smoothly.

"Ha. Wait out here." She left him to wander her living room while she escaped to put on clothes, still riding the high of feeling desired. *You've ignored yourself for far too long.* Her inner voice sounded a lot like Lana.

She returned barely fifteen minutes later to find him rummaging around in her fridge.

"Make yourself at home," she said dryly.

His head popped around the door. He gave her an assessing look then smiled, "I liked the other outfit better."

"I bet." She laughed. "Is there something I can help you find in there?" she asked, leaning against the counter opposite him and the fridge.

"Nope… all good," he said over his shoulder, grabbed a few things, and shut the door. "You could get me a cutting board and check that water."

She looked to the pot of water that was nearly simmering, and the box of noodles set out next to it. "Not boiling," she told him.

"Board?" he asked, rinsing the vegetables and getting a knife out of the block on her counter. When she just stared at him, he started opening cabinets until he found one. "You need to eat, and whatever that mush was in the microwave doesn't count as food."

She looked over to the microwave, silent now, and remembered she had started it just before he had rung. She walked over to open the door, only to discover it was empty.

"Trash can," he told her as he chopped zucchini, broccoli, some baby carrots and cherry tomatoes she forgot she had "Start those noodles; the water's ready."

"You can't just come in here and throw away my food," she told him, but there was no bite to her bark. She dumped the box into the water, turning it down slightly so it wouldn't boil over. She hadn't been looking forward to eating her poor attempt at an herb chicken risotto, but she hadn't had time to make anything else before he was due to arrive, and she was ravenous.

"Well, if whatever you had planned to eat had looked even slightly edible, I would have left you to it, but as it was, I think it may have been living… after you cooked it. Obviously, you're hungry or you wouldn't have been willing to eat *that*, I'm hungry because I just finished my shift. I'm going to be here for a minute to talk, so why not eat a meal together?" He glanced over to see her skeptical face. "It's just food, Lilly."

He found a pan and started sauteing the vegetables, then stirred the noodles so they didn't clump together. He found some seasonings and sprinkled them on, adding sauce and turned the heat to low to simmer.

"Have any basil?"

She shook her head that she didn't. "I hadn't exactly planned on a pasta party. There might be some dried on the seasoning rack."

"Fresh is better." He eyed the canister before sprinkling it on.

She handed him a strainer when the noodles were done, deciding that if he wanted to take over her kitchen and make her food, why not let him? She *was* hungry after all.

"I have some of those Texas toast garlic bread slices in the freezer," she suggested, her stomach rumbling at the scents in her kitchen.

He opened the oven and took out the pan of pre-sliced garlic bread that she hadn't realized she'd been smelling.

"Already found them."

"Well aren't you resourceful," she said sarcastically.

He smirked as he tossed the noodles and sauce together in a bowl. She went ahead and set the table so they could sit, and he was back in the fridge again, pulling out an already opened bottle of wine, giving her a questioning glance as he held it up. She pulled out two glasses and he split the drink between the two, setting the empty bottle aside. They sat down to eat his makeshift version of pasta primavera, her stomach rumbling and her mouth watering at the first bite.

"I'll admit… this is probably better than my mush."

"No question about it. I couldn't even tell what that was."

"It was risotto. At least it was supposed to be," she admitted. "It wasn't terrible the first time around, but it was edible and I had extras," she reasoned, taking another bite of his pasta. She was surprised that he was able to pull something this delicious together so quickly. "When did you learn to cook?" she asked him between bites. "You never cooked for me before. This is pretty decent," she said, not wanting to make him feel any more overly confident than he naturally was.

"That's because we were in high school. A home cooked meal probably wouldn't win me as many points then as it would now." He smiled devilishly.

"So, it's points you're after?" she asked, eyeing him cautiously.

"Points are always welcome," he said, leaning back in his chair, "but that's not the reason I wanted to talk to you tonight."

"And what reason might that be?"

"Why don't I help clear these away and we can talk in the living room?"

"Why do I get the feeling that you're stalling… and after more of those points?"

"Again, always welcome," he laughed, taking her plate to the sink and starting the hot water.

She studied the back of him as he added soap and started washing the dinner dishes. While she appreciated a home cooked meal, and someone to clean up as well, this didn't feel like normal Ryder behavior. Not that she knew what normal Ryder behavior was anymore, but she didn't imagine he ever worked this hard to win over a woman. Normally, all he had to do was smile at them, and despite his joking about her attire and complementing her the whole time he was there, she didn't feel like he was trying to come on to her. Something else was going on, and he was trying to avoid talking about it.

She took a towel from a drawer nearby, and rinsed and dried the dishes as he finished with them. She put them away and he wiped down the counters. When there was nothing more for him to do, and he had stopped talking altogether, she knew it must be serious.

"Ryder," she said, taking the washcloth from his hand and hanging it to dry. She gave him a towel to dry his hands. "Tell me what's going on," she said gently.

The moment she said it, she could see the lost expression on his face, the realization that he didn't have anything else to occupy the time. The turmoil that was reflected had her heart aching and she didn't even know the reason. He opened his mouth to speak but no words came out. She'd never seen him at a loss for words… ever.

Something bad must have happened.

She knew it couldn't have been at work, or she would have heard it from her dad. Her dad *had* tried to call her though… What if something had happened *to* her dad? She quickly dismissed that thought. Ryder never would have made her wait so long before saying something.

"Ryder… you're scaring me," she told him honestly. She wasn't scared for herself, but panic had started at what could possibly have made him so visibly torn up.

"I didn't see it," he whispered, his voice barely audible.

She moved closer, to stand before him, turning his face to hers. She hoped it would get him to focus on her instead of what he could see that she couldn't. Instead, he placed his hand on the other side of hers, and leaned into them both, closing his eyes, his brow furrowed.

"What didn't you see?" she gently prodded. "What happened?"

His eyes finally opened, glassy and red-rimmed. She searched his eyes, hoping for some hint at his anguish.

"How could I not see it?" he asked. "Him," he corrected. "How did I not know it was him?"

"Who was who? Ryder, what happened? I don't understand what you're trying to tell me."

"Wade," his voice broke on the name.

She searched her mind for the name. The only Wade she could think of was from high school, for *her* at least, but he and Ryder had been inseparable then, like brothers; maybe they were still friends.

"Wade from school?" she asked. The nod he offered was almost imperceptible. "You guys are still pretty close?" she asked, trying to get him to focus and explain what was happening. He nodded again, pinching the bridge of his nose as he breathed in deep, trying to regain his composure. "And something's happened to him?"

His eyes searched hers, desperate and devastated.

"Something pretty bad," she gently concluded and watched him give up and crumble into her. She held him as he cried. He was the confident boy every girl had wanted in high school, the star athlete who turned into the charismatic man who could get anything he wanted. He'd become the strong officer with grand aspirations—the last man you'd expect to break down—and he was standing in her kitchen, crying, holding onto her as if she was the last steady thing.

"I just saw him," he mumbled into her hair. "How did I not see?"

She still wasn't sure what he meant, but she knew that he wasn't going to make much sense until she could get him to focus and tell her what had happened. She pulled back slightly, not letting him go, but so she could look at his face. Maybe if he could see her standing in front of him, she could get him to calm down, get him to explain.

"Ryder," she quietly said, "can you tell me what happened?"

He searched her eyes, his red at the edges.

"You," he paused and started again. "Lilly Flower… you were the first person I thought of when I heard. I knew I had to see you..."

"I'm here," she reassured him. "What happened to Wade, Ryder?"

"He's gone, Lilly," he finally said, "Wade's gone. I just saw him and now he's gone, and I didn't even know it was him. Couldn't tell it was him. The fingerprints… the fingerprints finally told us. Couldn't see it was him…"

He pulled her back in, his body shaking in her arms as she processed what he was saying; Ryder's friend was dead. She squeezed him tighter, trying to soothe his hurt.

She wasn't sure how long they stood together in her kitchen, her hand making comforting strokes along his back while he regained his composure. She felt him take a deep breath and exhale, leaning back to so he could look at her, the anguish still evident.

She realized a moment too late that the look in his eyes wasn't just anguish, and that they were still holding each other as if his life depended on it. Before she could move away, his mouth was on hers. It wasn't demanding or starving. Instead, it was sweet and cautious, yet full of his need for her. He squeezed her tighter to him, one hand coming up to hold her head, gently caressing along her cheek and into her hair as her traitorous body naturally responded, eagerly remembering what it was like to kiss him as if no time had passed since the last time he held her.

But this wasn't right.

"Ryder," she managed on a breath.

"You're all I wanted," he told her, taking her mouth again.

"Ryder please," she told him and broke the kiss, still wrapped in his arms. Confusion and pain swirled in his eyes. "We can't do this," she told him when he finally focused.

His eyes searched hers, and he stepped back, running his hands through his hair just like he used to, "Lilly I'm sorry," he told her. "I don't know what I was thinking. I shouldn't have done that."

"It's okay," she said reflexively, willing her own heart to slow in its race. Her body tingled where she could still feel his warmth. Her lips pulsed when she rubbed them together, despite knowing that she shouldn't be feeling anything for him when she had just spent the afternoon wrapped up in another man.

"No… no it's not okay. I didn't mean for that to happen," he said, pacing in her kitchen. "I thought I only needed to see you. I didn't realize…"

"Ryder, stop. It'll be okay. Come sit down, okay?" she told him, leading him into the living room. He sat on the couch next to her, leaned forward, his head in his hands. She pushed all the fresh feelings aside and forced her brain back into the moment of consoling a friend. She placed her hand on his back and caressed it lightly. "Can you tell me what happened to Wade?" she asked quietly.

"He's dead," he told the floor, then sat back to look at her, patiently waiting on the couch next to him. "I just saw him about a week ago," he said again, but this time his composure was starting to come back, and she thought the worst of it might be behind them. She waited for him to continue. "He was fine, healthy, we had a barbeque. We try to get together a few times a month, but there's work… and life comes up… it'd been a few months, and we finally said we just had to do it, so he came out to the house, and we grilled and had some beers. It was a good time…" He smiled at the memory, but it didn't touch his eyes or linger. "It wasn't weird not to talk for days or even weeks at a time, we did when we could, you know?" She nodded that she understood, still not interrupting now that he was forming coherent sentences.

"We did what we always do and made plans for next time. Sometimes they'd work, sometimes they wouldn't, but this time, we must have had one too many, because we planned this whole elaborate weekend trip, backpacking with tents and catching our meals, the whole deal…

"I don't even own a tent…

"I knew we weren't really going to go; hell, *he* knew we weren't, 'but man, wouldn't it be cool?'" He smiled. "Wade would always say that, 'man, wouldn't it be cool.' He left and we didn't talk or see each other, didn't think anything of it, 'cuz we both knew we hadn't set a real plan, and we'd catch up and do it all over again in a few weeks." He sighed then, running his hand through his hair again. "I don't know, maybe he went on his own, or maybe something else happened. We just don't know yet, but we found his body," he paused again but didn't cry this time, just took a minute to breath, to steady himself before going on. "I didn't know it was his body when we found him," he said. "He was so badly injured and bloated… the water," he said, seeing what only he could see. "We only just found out this afternoon that it was him because the fingerprints finally bounced back. Nobody even reported him missing." His mouth pulled down at the last sentence.

"I'm so sorry Ryder," she consoled him, reaching over to squeeze his hand. "Do you know how it happened?"

He shook his head. "No. None of it makes any sense. The report says he had a heart attack, but he was healthy. I should have been with him, maybe I could have gotten him help."

"You can't do that, Ryder. You can't start blaming yourself for something that was out of your control. For all we know, you could be dead, too, if you had gone."

"I know… you're right, I know… but it's so hard. We thought it would be so funny. Prove everyone wrong…" he trailed off, "I guess he didn't prove anyone wrong. The place really is cursed."

"What are you talking about?" she asked, confused again by his disjointed thoughts.

"Oh," he said, as if he hadn't realized he'd spoken aloud. "It's nothing really… our weekend camping trip." He waved the thought away, but she waited for him to continue. He sighed. "We were laughing it up about all the superstition, the hype and stories about the Mountain that bring the tourists in … you know all the stories, that it's cursed or haunted… how there's only one way out of the Mountain—dead." He smirked. "Hell, I've even heard conspiracy theories about a government alien cover-up…

"Anyway, we were having a good ol' laugh about the stupid things people believe and spread around. We decided we were going to prove them all wrong and go spend the weekend on the Mountain. We'd live it up, have some beers, catch our food." He made air quotes. "We'd do all the 'manly' stuff that we had always talked about doing. When it was all said and done, we'd come back home, living to tell the tale of how the Mountain is just another hill around here, just another place with a story as overexaggerated as its name. We'd be living proof that there was nothing to be scared of. We were going to break the cycle… prove it wasn't cursed… but it is, and Wade's dead because of it."

"Hey," she said, waiting for him to turn his head, to pay attention to her. When he finally did, his brow was still furrowed. "You know as well as I do that there's nothing to be afraid of up there. The stories about the Mountain are just stories. There's no curse, it's all just stories made up for fun…"

She paused to look him in the eye, to make sure he was paying attention. "The Mountain didn't kill Wade."

He closed his eyes at her words. She waited for him to reopen them before she continued on.

"If he died up there, I'm sure there's a reasonable explanation as to how. And even if there's not," she said, holding up a hand when he started to disagree, "there's still the possibility that *you* could have died, too, being up there. You said it yourself; you don't even own a tent. One of the main reasons why the Mountain is restricted, other than being government private property, is because of its extremely dangerous terrain. People get hurt up there because of the very real dangers it holds, not just the made up stories. People play like it isn't, thinking that because they own a pair of hiking boots, they can manage, and that naive mindset is what gets them hurt… or killed." She squeezed his hand again, bringing her other hand in to hold his in both. "I'm really sorry that Wade died… but I'm glad you didn't go up there."

He smiled back at her weakly, his eyes looking heavy, the fatigue from all the emotions he'd been through today catching up to him.

He rubbed his other hand over his face and sighed. "I know you're right," he said, "but there's still that part that wonders if I could have helped him." He turned to her, searching her face. "Thank you for everything tonight. I'm sorry I brought all this to you, but I thought I should be the one to tell you since we used to all be friends. You shouldn't find out through the grapevine. I didn't mean to lose it like I did, or to kiss you." He smiled, just a ghost of his mischievous smirks. "Although, I'm not sure I'm altogether sorry for that one… but it wasn't fair for me to spring it on you like that."

"I'm going to say you're forgiven for that one since you weren't exactly thinking clearly," she told him, releasing his hand and repositioning minutely away. "But… we're not… I'm not…" she hesitated, at a loss of how to tell him now wasn't good timing.

"Lilly Flower," he said, smiling softly, "I sincerely didn't come here tonight for any other reason than I needed the person who used to be my friend. I know I made a mistake too many years ago and I can't expect you to just forget and move on. You may not believe that I'm different, but I hope you can try to be open-minded enough to see that I'm willing to take the time to prove that I've changed. But you were my friend back then and I really needed her tonight. I really am sorry about the way I reacted in there," he nodded to the kitchen, "but it won't happen again until you're ready."

"And if I'm never ready?" she asked. She held her hands steady to keep them from fiddling and showing her nerves, but couldn't help but wonder if his offer of friendship was contingent on receiving his desired benefits.

He searched her face, his solemn. "I really hope that isn't the case," he admitted, "but if you decide that you can't get beyond the mistakes of a hormone-crazed teenager and see that I'm a changed man, one that's willing to be patient and hopeful with you… then I'll respect your decision and leave you alone. But don't think I'm not going to try and prove myself to you in the meantime."

"Ryder," she started, but wasn't even sure what she was going to tell him before he stopped her.

"It's not for now," he said. "Now is for me to say thank you again for being here when I needed you, and now is time for me to go."

He stood and pulled her up as well, bringing her in for a hug. He wrapped her into his warmth, sighing above her as he kissed the top of her head.

"Thank you, Lilly."

She walked him to the door, watching to make sure he got into his car, him waiting for her to shut and lock her door before he drove away.

She walked back to the couch and sat down, leaned her head back and stared at the ceiling. How had she gone from signing off all men earlier that week, to having crazy, passionate, middle-of-the-day, out in the clear open, sex with someone she barely knew, and then making out with her former boyfriend in her kitchen all in the same day?

What was she thinking?

And what was she going to do about either of them?

FIFTEEN

"Hello!? Please! Why are you keeping me here? Please… please just let me go," she begged, her voice hoarse from days of screaming and pleading. "I won't tell anyone… Please just let me go home."

She cried at the sound of the plate scraping against the floor.

There was food.

Every day there was food and water. She had to use a bucket to go to the bathroom, but there was always food and water.

Every day she begged to be set free, but every day he never said a word. At least, she assumed her captor was a man. It was so dark in the room that even when the food slot opened, no light ever entered.

It was like a vacuum, stealing away all the light, all the joy, all the world, leaving her alone with the sound of her heart beating in her ears and her cries echoing off the walls.

But nobody ever answered.

"I haven't seen your face," she whispered to herself as the food slot closed again and the footsteps retreated. "Please…"

SIXTEEN

-Lillian-

"Girl, I need details. You never texted me back yesterday about your *lunch*," Lana ambushed her as Lillian walked in the back door of Wisteria to start her shift.

Lillian laughed, not even sure where to begin, or what to share.

"It was memorable," she said with a slight smile.

"That's it? *Memorable*? I need more than that!"

"There's not much to say," Lillian told her. There wasn't much she *could* say.

"Oh… memorable… meaning it was bad?" Lana said, disappointed.

"I didn't say that," she said, laughing. "It was good, *very* good." She couldn't help but smile at the memory.

Lana gasped. "No!" She covered her mouth on a squeal.

"What?" Lillian asked, trying to sound innocent.

Lana reached out and pulled her out of the hallway, as if it would make their conversation less audible by moving two feet away. "Did you sleep with him?" she whispered excitedly.

"That's not what I said," Lillian whispered back, but she could feel the truth written all over her face.

"You did!" Lana cheered. "Oh my gosh, tell me everything!"

"I can't…"

"You can. Now. Hurry and tell me all the dirty details of your illicit afternoon… or did he stay over, or you at his house? Oh, hurry up already."

"I'm sure there's something for you to do up there," Lillian stalled, pointing to the kitchen.

"Nope. Everyone's fine. It's a weird thing when people do their jobs the right way, you can take little breaks to get the juicy details from your friend when they don't text you back about their steamy date… now spill."

"Okay, but just for a second. I have to get up there and get started before Rain realizes and tries to use it to her advantage."

She tried skimming over the details, but Lana wasn't having it, so she quickly recapped the day with August.

"Oh my," Lana breathed. "That's like right out of a dream, a sexy dream for sure, but that stuff doesn't happen in real life."

"It did yesterday," Lillian laughed. "And no matter how much I think about it, and I'm definitely playing it back on a loop, I can't feel bad about it."

"Why should you?" Lana asked seriously.

"*Because*," she said, as if that was explanation enough, but continued when Lana wasn't satisfied with the blanket excuse. "It was the first date! I don't know anything about him, *and* we did all *that* without even thinking about what happens next."

"Yeah, that sounds great. If you don't want him anymore, send him my way. I could use a wild afternoon of crazy hot, no-strings, sex."

"No, no," Lillian quickly responded, which had Lana laughing immediately. "It's just not something I'd normally do, so I keep thinking I'm going to talk myself into feeling bad about it, but I don't. I just can't. I may never see him again, but still, it feels really good; it feels right." She shook her head. "That probably doesn't make any sense at all does it? I've probably lost my mind at some point."

"Not at all. I think you've found it. Live a little. You're young and he's hot, hotter than hot… on second thought, live a lot."

She was considering telling her how much she had lived that day, albeit unintentionally, when Gary interrupted their conversation.

"Well don't you two look like you're up to no good. What's with the rosy cheeks, Lillian?" he asked, leaning up against the wall to dish with the girls.

"It's warming up out there," she told him as she tied on her apron.

"Mm hmm," he mused, eyeing them both skeptically.

"Did you need something?" she asked him, wondering how much he had already overheard, but she wasn't about to openly share her sex life with the town gossip.

"Well, since you're not going to fill me in on your little secret back here—" He paused giving them time to change their minds. When they didn't bite, he continued on a huff. "Lana, there's some adorable little boy asking for you up front."

Lana looked confused for about a second before realization dawned. "Oh! My nephew!" she exclaimed and turned to Lillian. "You were saying that we need help out front, and he's looking for a summer job. I figured he could come in and see what he thought, and then if he liked the place, I'd have him talk to Harvey and see about putting him to work."

"Oh, that would be great," Lillian agreed, knowing that Lana wouldn't just bring in anybody, unless she could handle working with them. "And if we could get him trained before the season started…"

"Well, he's just up there waiting on you two lollygaggers," Gary interrupted and turned to head back up front.

"He's mad at us," Lillian mused.

"He's just jealous that he doesn't know something that someone else does," Lana corrected. "He'll get over it as soon as the next little bit of gossip comes through those doors. Come on, meet my nephew. He's a good kid."

Ryder

Ryder had the day off. After they got the fingerprint report back identifying Wade as the victim they'd found in the water, Bill, knowing Ryder and Wade had been friends, told him he could take some time off. He didn't intend to. He thought being at work would be better for him, keep his mind busy, but after breaking down at Lilly's the night before, he decided a day off wouldn't hurt.

She had been there for him, despite their rocky road and not knowing where it was leading. While he really hadn't intended to lose control the way he did, she had stayed calm for him.

And that kiss… to kiss her, was infinitely better than he remembered. His next step was to figure out how to get her to *want* to do it again; it was very high on his list of things to do.

He pushed thoughts of her scent and taste out of his mind as he pulled into the driveway of his friend's house.

It looked like it always did.

The grass was recently mowed, the flag was up on the mailbox, the blinds were open. The house was welcoming. He expected Wade to walk out the front door as soon as he put the truck in park, a beer in each hand, one for each of them.

But the front door didn't open, and Wade didn't come out.

He'd never walk through the door again.

Ryder stared at the house. The birds flew in a dance across the front yard. A mail car drove through the neighborhood behind him. Children were playing in the yard just a few houses down.

How could there be no life left in this house?

It wasn't right. It wasn't fair. He was young and healthy. He was happy.

This couldn't be the house of a dead man.

Ryder sat in his truck longer, thinking about just leaving. Wade wasn't in there. There was no reason for him to be here. He needed to put the truck in reverse and leave.

But he *needed* to go in. Something wasn't right.

He turned off the ignition and got out, but he couldn't bring himself to step toward the door. What was wrong with him? He was a cop and would be sheriff one of these days, and he couldn't even walk up to his friend's front door?

"Nobody's home," a voice called out behind him, startling him. He turned to see who had spoken.

The mail lady's car was parked by the box, the flag still up, watching him as he stared.

"Nobody's home," she called again, nodding to the house of the dead man.

"Oh," Ryder said, looking back to the door. "Okay."

She looked at him curiously, "Are you okay?"

"Oh… yeah… I'm fine," he told her, running his hand though his hair and walked toward the woman. Should he tell her that the owner would never be home again? He didn't think it had become official news yet. Bill was going to notify Wade's family yesterday. It shouldn't have been Bill to do it, he knew, but the thought of sitting in the room while Wade's mother cried… it should have been him.

"You sure?" her voice interrupted his thoughts again. "You're not looking too well."

"Yeah… it's just been a rough day or so." He smiled, trying to look less like a miserable wretch when all she was trying to be was nice. "You said Wade isn't home…" he stated, fading off at the end, not sure what he was going to follow it up with.

"Yeah, but he usually is back before my Monday route," she said and nodded to the mailbox. He looked at the box with its flag up then back to her, blankly. She smiled gently. "If you're trying to reach him, he's gone for the weekend."

"Oh," Ryder said, his stomach turning. This happy and helpful woman had no idea that Wade would never be back.

"You don't need to worry about him. He does this often, and only once did he not make it back before my Monday route to put the flag down. Let me tell you, that boy nearly gave me a heart attack that day."

"I'm sorry…?" Ryder started, not following a word she was saying, worried that maybe he needed to take more than just *one* day off work.

She laughed. "The flag," she said and nodded at the raised flag on the box as if that answered his confusion.

He looked at it and back at her, confusion growing with every second.

"Doesn't that just mean the mail needs to go out?"

"Normally yes, but not always for Wade. It's sort of his back-up plan."

"I guess I don't understand," Ryder admitted.

"Are you a friend of his?" she asked suddenly, as if realizing she shouldn't be telling some random person in his driveway about whatever his back-up plan may be.

"Yeah, since middle school," he confirmed, curious to know what she suddenly rethought about sharing.

She sighed, "I figured so, you looked like you knew the place."

He wasn't sure how a person standing in the driveway could look like they knew the place, but he was already confused enough that he didn't ask and let her continue talking.

"You know how outdoorsy he is," she stated, and he nodded that he did. "Well, a few years back he met me out here and said he was going to be gone for the weekend, that I could still put mail in the box, but he was going to leave a letter to be mailed with the flag up. I told him I'd take it right then since I was there; no sense in sticking it in the box if I was already here. He said that he didn't want it to be mailed, that it was his back-up plan, so of course I asked what he meant. He told me that he was going camping for the weekend and the letter had his location and itinerary, that way if he didn't get back when he planned, whoever he was mailing the letter to would know to look for him and where. I told him he could just call and tell the person, or better yet, not to go camping alone, but he said he liked the solitude, and if he called and told anyone, that they would get nervous and try to talk him out of it.

"He had the letter addressed and ready to go with a note that said not to mail until Monday. I told him I'd leave the mail in the box until my Monday route, but that it had better not be there Monday morning, or I was going to be tracking him down myself and giving him a good wallop for going off by himself.

"We had a good laugh, and the letter was gone come Monday and the flag was back down. We've been doing this for about two years now and only once was the mail still there when I came back on Monday. I tell you, my heart just about stopped when I pulled up to the box, but then there he came running out of the house to stop me from mailing it. My hand never shook so badly handing that letter back to him. He'd gotten in late and forgot to take it out of the box."

She shook her head at the memory and Ryder looked at the flag on the box.

"So why didn't you mail it this time?" he asked her.

"Honey, it's only Friday. The note says to wait until Monday."

"Last Monday," he stated. "Why didn't you mail it last Monday?"

"It only went in yesterday," she laughed. "It's kinda hard to mail something that wasn't there."

Ryder looked back at the box, even more confused.

"Like I said, he's gone for the weekend, so I'd check back on Monday if you want to reach him. You're sure you're okay?" she asked him again.

"I'm fine. Thank you for letting me know about his back-up plan," he told her, trying to smile without looking as pained as he felt.

She smiled and nodded, then waved as she drove the short distance down the street to the next box. He walked back to his truck and climbed in, trying to make sense of what she had told him. Why would the flag only be up as of yesterday? They found Wade's body on Sunday, five days ago, and the M.E. said he'd been dead at least two days already.

How did the flag go up yesterday?

Who else knew about his back-up plan, and why would someone want it to look like he was still alive? Did they not want anyone looking before Monday?

Ryder's head was swimming with questions that deserved answers. Something wasn't right, and he was going to get to the bottom of it.

Lillian

Lillian liked Lana's nephew, Josh, from the start. He was seventeen, eager to work, and had shown up dressed well enough to start today if she wanted. She decided to see what he was capable of, how fast he could pick up on things, and paired him up with Gary to show him the ropes.

After the first thirty minutes, he broke away from Gary to seat and tend to his own table. They hadn't discussed wages or hours yet, but she had already made up her mind that he had the job. He'd wanted to stay when she asked if he had anywhere else to be and had been on his own for the past three hours, not asking for a break yet. She hadn't planned on having the help today, so she was finally able to get some work done in the office for a change, occasionally checking on the diner to make sure all was still running smoothly.

"Hey, it's time for my break," Gary said, poking his head around the door.

She'd lost track of time and hadn't realized it was as late as it was.

"How's Josh doing?" she asked as she shut down the computer.

"He catches on just as quick as he is adorable."

"Gary," she admonished.

"What? He's young and cute. The old ladies are practically eating out of his hand. He's a natural. Let's just hope he doesn't get bored like Rain all the time and decide to quit."

"Well, he hasn't officially been hired yet," she laughed, although all she needed for that was a few signatures, which she could get before he left for the day and have him on the schedule immediately.

"Well. He has my vote. Harvey would be out of his mind not to hire that boy," Gary told her, and she had to bite her tongue; nobody knew he didn't do the hiring anymore. "Anyway, I'm going to lunch, and you'll probably want to come out front. Rain hasn't stopped griping about how you're back here sitting on your," he held his hand next to his mouth and whispered, "*ass*—her word, not mine—" he made sure to clarify, "while she's busting hers. She's not of course," he said with a roll of his eyes, "but Josh will basically be left alone with me gone because she's not likely to lift a finger to help now that her boyfriends are out there."

"What do you mean, her boyfriends?" she asked as she came around the desk.

"Oh, you remember I told you about her three amigos. She's been shacking up with them out at the Bend, practically in the crime scene tape. It's real creepy if you ask me, but they're into some weird stuff what with the things she showed me on her RUSH app."

She just stared at him, not understanding a single thing that came out of his mouth, but she wasn't about to encourage what Gary so clearly wanted to gossip about.

"I'm on my way," she said before he could dive in anyway. "I'll see you when you're done. Enjoy your lunch," she told him as she walked through the kitchen.

Josh was clearing off a table and Rain was laughing at a booth in the back with a group of boys. She'd wait and see how things played out before making an issue of it. She already had a list of things she wanted to talk to Rain about, but if she got her act together and did her work, then she wouldn't have to add this to it.

Rain was still talking when Josh brought the dirty cart back to the kitchen, which meant that Lillian would have to add it to her list after all, but it also meant that she could talk with Josh about the position without Rain interjecting.

"So, what do you think?" she asked him.

"Oh yeah, this will be great," he told her. "I mean, if I've got the job."

"You wouldn't mind working with your aunt?"

"Nah, Aunt Lan's cool."

"Then, it's yours if you want it. It may not look like it right now, but we need the help, and tourist season seems to start earlier every year. People pour in from all over and Wisteria is a landmark. Everyone wants to check out a piece of history, whether it's nostalgia, curiosity, or to snap a picture of going back in time. The tables are almost never empty... so you'll be very busy," she stressed.

"Cool. I like to stay busy and that just means more tips."

"Yes," she laughed, appreciating his honesty. "Tips are a plus, and you're going to be thankful for them at the end of a full day running from table to table with people telling you their order isn't right, or that it needs to be made just so, or a kid spilling their drink in the middle of your shift and you have to stop what you're doing in order to get it cleaned up so nobody slips. When you count your tips on those days, it'll be worth it... think you can handle all that?"

"Definitely."

"Great, then I'll get you some paperwork to fill out and get you all official," she reached out her hand to shake his. "Welcome to Wisteria."

"Just like that? I don't need to talk to anyone else or interview or anything?"

"You've been interviewing all day, and as long as you keep working like that, there won't be any issues."

"Awesome," he said, unable to contain a goofy smile.

"When Gary gets back from lunch, we'll go back and get paperwork started and figure out all the details."

"Details on what?" Rain walked up, slapping the order for her table on the window counter.

"Josh is going to start working here, so we were just discussing the paperwork," Lillian told her.

She looked him over, "Huh," she stated, leaning against the counter and folding her arms over her chest. "Don't you think Harvey should have a say in that?"

Josh looked from Rain to Lillian and back again. "Who's Harvey?"

"Only the guy that owns this place, duh."

"So… I'm not hired?" he asked, looking back at Lillian.

"Probably not," Rain told him. "Lillian's just another waitress. She can't hire you anymore than I can even though she seems to think she runs this place."

"You are," Lillian reassured him then turned to Rain. "Can I talk to you for a minute?"

"I've gotta wait for my order," she said dismissively.

"You just put the ticket in. You have a few minutes."

"Ugh, whatever," she huffed and pushed herself off the counter, heading back to the kitchen.

"Josh, Gary will be right back," she looked at the clock. "He's due back any second. I just need to talk to her for a minute, and Lana is right in the kitchen. If you need anything, she can help, but this won't be long."

She looked around the diner. Nobody new had come in to be waited on, and everyone seemed content enough for her to step away, but she hated leaving Josh on his own.

"No problem," he told her. "If things start going crazy out here, I'll just find you."

"Okay, great. We'll be right back."

She went through the kitchen, updated Lana on the situation, then went to find Rain in the tiny breakroom venting to Gary.

"…sits on her ass back here all day doing nothing at all, and now Her Highness wants to talk to *me* like I'm doing something wrong. Who does she think she is?"

Gary coughed delicately and nodded behind her.

"Oh, you're here finally," Rain stated, taking a pull from the vape Lillian hadn't noticed before now.

"Can you come in the office so we can talk?"

"Fine," Rain grumbled, sighing loudly as she passed, then flopped into one of the chairs.

"Are you about finished back here? Josh is alone up front," she said to Gary, glancing at the clock over his head. He was two minutes past his thirty-minute break already.

"I'm all ready to go and would have been out front if Rain hadn't happened," he sighed, as if she was the only reason he was still sitting in the back and not his own manipulation of the time clock.

"Great. Oh, and Rain just started an order for her table. It's for her friends in the back booth if we're not back by the time it's up."

"Fine. I'll cover for her, but she owes me," he said loud enough to get a wave from the chair.

Lillian stepped into the office to grab the new employee documents and handed them to Gary as he was slinking by. "You can give these to Josh and have him start filling them out."

He scanned the papers, eyebrows raising in question. "Harvey approved?"

She just smiled and started closing the office door. "Thanks, Gary. He knows the papers are coming so you can head on up."

When she was confident he wasn't standing outside the door with his ear pressed against it, she went to sit down at the desk.

"So, what do you want?" Rain pouted.

"First, you can't vape in here."

"It's not smoking. I figured this was better than smelling like the smoke that you're so offended by."

"You can't smoke or vape in the building."

"Where does it say that?"

"Rain," she sighed. "Come on. Nobody wants their server blowing smoke all over them or their food while they're trying to eat."

"It's not smoke."

Lillian held up a hand. "No vaping. Period."

"God, fine," she sighed, shoving the tiny pen into her pocket. "Is that it?" she asked, starting to get up from her chair.

"No. We need to talk about your work ethic," Lillian told her.

"Yeah? What about it?"

"You're just not professional," Lillian told her outright, trying not to be frustrated by Rain's attitude.

"Lil, we work in a restaurant. It's not like this is some fancy schmancy super important business. It's food. Nobody cares if you're professional."

"I do."

"So? Nobody else has a problem with me. Harvey doesn't."

"You hardly ever see Harvey," she countered. "Customers have made complaints."

"Who? Those old people from last week? They're just crotchety old geezers that complain about everyone."

"Rain, this right here… you can't talk about people like this."

"Why not? It's not like they're in here and can hear me."

"Not right now, but can you honestly tell me that you don't say things where customers can hear you?"

"So. Maybe they need to hear it."

Lillian rubbed her forehead. This was not at all how she thought this conversation was going to go.

"Rain," she sighed. "You need to stop with the comebacks all the time. Do your work while you're here, then do whatever you want outside of this place. But when you're here, you need to act professionally, whether you want to or not. People deserve to be treated with respect, and if you're ignoring them to the point that they get up and leave, they aren't going to want to come back."

"That little snitch," Rain said in the direction of the door. "Gary told you, didn't he?"

"It doesn't matter," she sighed again.

"He wasn't doing anything that night either. He could have helped that guy, but he wanted to prove a point and now I'm the one getting in trouble for it?"

"Rain, you're not in trouble. You just need to try, especially since Josh is starting now. He's going to need to be trained, and you'll need to set a good example."

"A good example… right," she barked out a laugh. "Why are we even in here anyway? None of this matters, and when I tell Harvey that you're going behind his back to *hire* someone without him knowing and then reprimand *me* like *you* have some sort of authority … You're going to be the one looking for a job."

"Nobody said you need to look for a new job, Rain. But I'll tell you right now that if you go to Harvey with this, it won't work out in your favor. He's not going to fire me."

"You sneaky bitch," she spewed out of nowhere, shocking Lillian with the venom in her voice.

"Excuse me?"

"It all makes sense now. You acting all hoity-toity all the time, hiring that guy out there like you can, sitting in here talking to me like I'm some child… You're fucking him, aren't you?"

"What? Who?" Lillian asked, wondering how her and August's relationship had anything to do with this. As far as she knew, Rain didn't even know they had gone on a date, let alone anything more. And she hadn't told *anyone* about Ryder's kiss last night, so Rain couldn't have been referring to him.

"Harvey," she accused. "You're fucking him, and you think he'll leave this to you because of it."

The laugh slipped out before she could hold it in, but she immediately realized that Rain wasn't joking and tried to hide her amusement. "Rain, I'm not—"

"Well, you can have him and this place! When I first started working with you, I thought your goody-two-shoes behavior was just a show for the customers. I thought you'd be chill like Lana, that we could be friends even. Boy, was I wrong. You're just like my parents. All you ever want to do is tell me where I'm fucking up. Well, I'm over it. I'm over feeling like I can never live up to the *Great Lillian's* standards.

"You know, I was going to take this place over the adult way, but you couldn't handle that, could you? What'd you do? Run right over to his house after I told you my plans for after school, so you could make sure you had the upper hand? To make sure you'd win? Well, congratulations. It's all yours," she spewed, standing and untying her apron. "You can keep this shithole. I won't work for someone who'll fuck her way to the top just so she can boss everyone else around like she's better than them."

She threw her apron across the desk, Lillian barely catching it in her shock. Rain stormed out of the office, slamming the door so hard that it bounced back open. Lillian walked around the desk to the break area to see Rain clearing out her locker, shoving things into her bag, and grabbing her keys to leave.

"Rain, you've got the wrong idea about everything," Lillian tried saying as Rain headed to the back door.

"You may have all of them fooled," Rain said, pointing to the front of the building as she leaned in close to Lillian, "but I know what you are. You're a snake, slithering sneakily along in the grass, just waiting to strike. Well screw you. I'm not putting up with it anymore."

She spun and yanked open the door, nearly dropping her bag as she tried throwing it closed behind her. Lillian stared at the back door, not entirely sure what had just happened or where it had come from; all she had wanted to accomplish was for Rain not to ignore her tables anymore.

"So... What was that all about?" Lana sang from behind her.

"You wouldn't even believe me if I told you," Lillian said, mentally recounting their short conversation.

"Seemed intense," Lana mused.

Lillian turned, "Apparently Rain takes offense that I'm sleeping with Harvey," she said as seriously as she could.

"I see," Lana said, suppressing a smile. "And with the afternoon sexcapades with August, where do you squeeze in Harvey, or does he join in as well?"

"Okay... It was only one afternoon sexcapade—"

"But you did it twice," Lana interrupted.

"Okay, but only one afternoon..."

"So, you and Harvey just have a leisurely affair then?" Lana asked, giving in and laughing at the absurdity. "Harvey? She really thought you were sleeping with *Harvey*? He's old enough to be your grandpa."

"Apparently, I'll do whatever it takes to get this place from her because, remember, she's in business school to take over, and she's not willing to work for the snake that I am."

"Good riddance. You know she wasn't worth keeping anyway," Lana said, turning to get back to work.

"I know... trust me I know," She moaned and rubbed her hand over her forehead, hoping the dull throb she could feel behind her eyes wasn't a headache forming. She dropped her hand to her side. "I don't even know why I kept trying to defend myself, trying to make her see reason. It's not like I really wanted her to stay on anyway... but... I guess I hoped if someone finally brought it to her attention, she'd step it up a little. At least enough to get us through another season before having to train a replacement."

"You always see the good and honesty in people, honey. Unfortunately, some people just suck. Don't let her get you down."

"Oh, I won't. Once I recover from whatever that was, I'm sure I'll find it funny." She paused, biting her lower lip. "But now all I can think is that we're still short-handed. Got any more amazing nephews?"

"I'm fresh out, but I'll keep my ears open."

"I guess I need to go tell them what happened, and hope Josh can take over her shift tonight. Talk about hired on the spot."

She went out front, saw that everything was still running smoothly despite the bomb named Rain that had just gone off in the back. She filled them in on the new situation and Josh immediately agreed to stay and work.

"I'll check around, see if I know anyone needing work," Josh offered.

"That'd be great."

"Wait," Gary interrupted. "She just quit? Just like that? She didn't even come up and say bye. What did you say to her? Why would she just quit?"

"She never acted like she wanted to be here in the first place," Lillian said.

"Yeah, but that's normal Rain. She'd find a reason to complain even if you gave her exactly what she wanted. What did you say to her?" he asked again.

"I only talked to her about her attitude," Lillian told him. "She was obviously looking for an excuse to leave."

"I just don't get it. Why would she leave? She didn't even say goodbye," he repeated, crossing his arms in front of him, and then stalked away to wrap silverware.

"It's not normally this… crazy," she apologized to Josh.

"No worries. That girl didn't seem like she'd be much fun to work with anyway."

"You're sure you don't mind staying to cover her shift? I'm sure this isn't what you had planned when you came in today."

"Yeah, it's good. Is it okay if I work on those papers between checking on tables?"

"That would be great." She smiled, leaving him to monitor his side, while she checked over Rain's now abandoned side.

She saw Gary whip out his phone occasionally, probably texting Rain to get her story… which meant that this time tomorrow, she was sure to be the horrible boss-screwing devil that Rain would depict her as, and Gary would spread it all around.

She didn't have the energy to care.

She sighed. She may not care, but she needed to fill in Harvey. She made sure everything was running smoothly, then headed back to the office to fill him in herself. Better he hear the news from her than it reaching him through the gossip train and the shock of their supposed affair gave him a heart attack.

SEVENTEEN

-Lillian-

"Do you want me to confirm the rumors?" Harvey asked her after she finished updating him on hiring Josh and Rain's sudden departure.

"No, thank you," she laughed.

Of course Harvey would try and make a joke out of this.

"Are you sure? If word gets out that you're playing the field again…" He jokingly left the suggestion hanging on the line between them.

"No," she laughed again.

"And an older man at that. It could really open up your possibilities of eligible bachelors."

"Oh my gosh, no. Just no, Harvey. I don't need any help in that area."

"Clearly not," he agreed. "I'm quite the catch."

"Yes, you are," she told him sincerely. "Helen was a lucky woman."

"I was the lucky one. She was wonderful," he sighed. "You know, I think it's time for me to step away."

"Wait, what?" She objected at his sudden resolution. "No… I can't lose you and Rain in the same day." This was not how the phone call was supposed to go. They were supposed to have a little laugh, make a plan *together,* and move on. He wasn't supposed to *step away*. Her heart began to race. He couldn't leave her, too.

"You know you aren't losing me," he said softly. "You're already doing it all on your own. It's time to tell everyone, make it official."

She didn't know what to say.

"You know it's time. Think it over."

She thought about their conversation as she headed back out front. Was she ready to be *the* owner? It was nice having Harvey there as back-up in case she messed something up.

He's not going to pack up, move away, change his phone number, and completely ignore you if you have questions, she mentally chided herself.

She sighed inwardly, knowing she was the only one dragging her feet. Harvey had complete faith in her that she could do it.

"Those look like some serious thoughts."

She looked up to see her dad seated at the counter, a coffee steaming in front of him.

"Hi, Dad." She smiled warmly. "Just having one of those days. Are you eating something or just having the coffee?"

"I put an order in with your new guy," he said nodding over to Josh, whom Gary was showing how to roll silverware in their napkins. She hoped he wasn't filling Josh's head with lies that Rain had probably already told him. The last thing she needed was for her new employee to think he'd made the wrong choice and quit on her, too.

"If he can make it through today then he'll probably be set," she sighed.

"Been rough, has it?"

"Kinda," she told him, giving him the quick version, but included Rain's outrageous accusation since Gary was far enough away that he wouldn't hear. If, on the off chance that Rain had come to her senses and realized how far off the mark she had been, and hadn't shared that little bit with him, then she didn't want to be the one to start her own rumor.

Her dad nearly spit out his coffee. He coughed a little and cleared his throat. Gary and Josh both turned their heads to make sure everything was alright.

"Now sweetheart, as your father," he began. The tone of his voice whisked her back to her teenage years, back when she knew a lecture was coming just by the way he'd say a couple words. "I feel like your mother will tell you to follow your heart, and love conquers all… but he is entirely way too old for you."

"Thanks," she said dryly, "I'll keep that in mind." She paused, glancing back to make sure Gary was still occupied. "He says it's time… to step away completely."

Her parents were the only people outside of her and Harvey that knew the arrangement. She'd needed to talk it over, and there was nobody she respected more than them. They'd been supportive, but also pointed out the downsides, too. In the end it had been her decision to make, and they had stood with her.

He nodded. "How do you feel about that?"

She sighed, "I think I'm ready… but I guess, a part of me just didn't think he'd ever really leave, that we'd just sort of partner together until he—"

"Died? The man doesn't want to work until the grave. It's time." He put his hand over hers on the counter in front of him. "For both of you. You know you're ready."

"It's a huge step," she said nervously.

"It's not as big as you think. What is he still doing that you haven't taken over yet?"

She thought about all her roles, clearly the basics of waiting tables, but all the managing of the business, the purchasing, hiring… she'd taken over everything.

She smiled. "He still cooks Sunday morning breakfast."

"Oh, well that can't change. He can step down, but he's going to have to stay on for Sunday mornings. Who's going to make the best biscuits and gravy for us?"

She laughed, feeling lighter about the realization that it *was* time.

"I guess we'll have to make an announcement," she finally said, and her dad smiled.

"Congratulations, kiddo."

"Thanks." She beamed, nervous and excited at the same time. "So, what are you in here for anyway? You don't usually stop by in the middle of your shift, or did I miss something?"

"No, I'm still working, but Ryder took the day off… you know, because of Wade? He said he was going to come by and talk to you last night about it." She nodded that he had, not about to go into *those* details with him. "He called me a little bit ago, kind of worked up about something and I was just around the corner, so I told him to meet me here."

"Hmm. Any idea what's going on with him?"

"No, but he should be here any minute; said he wasn't far away. I figured I'd get something to eat. The way he sounded, I may not get another chance anytime soon."

"He was pretty upset yesterday… understandably. I hope everything's okay."

His food came up and she handed it over to him, letting him know that she had to go check on Rain's tables. Josh seemed to be doing well, but she still needed to follow through, to make sure.

"You boys doing okay still? Need any refills?" she asked the three boys sitting in a back booth.

"Nah, we were just getting ready to leave."

"We thought Rain would come back by before we left, but we haven't seen her in a while," another boy said, looking past her as if Rain would walk up at any moment.

"Oh… you must be the friends they told me about." Two of them nodded. "She took off for the day. I don't think she'll be back in."

"Figures," the first boy to speak said to the second. "She's always up to something."

"She'll probably wind up at the site when she gets around to it," he said dismissively.

The third one seemed subdued and didn't say a word.

They got out cash, told her they didn't need change, and headed to the door just as Ryder came in, their paths crossing where the sheriff was seated. She saw her dad glance over at the group as they neared, and a confused expression flashed across his face. It was gone in an instant. If she didn't know her dad so well, she probably would have missed it. The quieter of the three boys said something to him. She watched as her dad responded, patted him on the shoulder with a little squeeze that looked like reassurance, and then the three boys walked away. Ryder sat on the stool next to her dad, leaned in, and said something hurriedly. Ryder barely glanced her way before her dad turned to find her and waved her over.

She knew it shouldn't matter, but it stung a little that Ryder didn't look for her when he came in. She thought after last night, even without the kiss, he would have at least looked for her.

She shook it out of her head. *Don't get worked up over nothing.*

"Hi Ryder. Everything okay?" she asked when she came up to them.

"Yeah, hi," he quickly answered. "Sorry, I've got to steal your dad."

"Oh… I thought you two were meeting here to talk."

"No, we've gotta get going," he said again.

"Alright, you want a drink for the road or anything?"

He shook his head and stood to leave, tapping his fingers against the counter before realizing what he was doing and shoved them into his pockets.

Bill had only eaten half his burger and fries, so she pulled out a to-go container and handed it to him. "You okay?" she asked her dad.

"Yeah, I'm fine. Why?" he asked.

"You looked confused when those boys came up to you a second ago."

"Oh, that was nothing," he said brushing it off. "I thought one of the kids looked familiar but couldn't figure out why at first."

"We *did* spend a morning and then some with them when they found Wade in the water," Ryder said from beside him.

"Yeah, but one of them looked… familiar… I couldn't put my finger on why… that was probably it though," he said, turning to acknowledge Ryder and waving his confusion off. "That's probably all it was, spending that time with them," he sighed. "Getting old, forgetting how I know someone, trying to place faces… who knows, maybe you'll get to be sheriff sooner than I thought." He laughed to Ryder, but the smile Ryder returned was more like a grimace.

"The one you were talking to," she said to her dad, "he's the one that found him? Wade, I mean?" When he nodded, the boy's silent behavior made more sense. She doubted she'd have much to say either.

"He wanted to know if he could go home yet. His buddies don't seem to mind it here, but he's pretty shaken up about it all. I told him I had all I needed, that he could leave town as long as he answers when I call."

"Getting away from here will be good for him to heal, put it out of his mind," she said solemnly.

"Bill," Ryder said, still standing and waiting for the sheriff to get off his stool. "You ready?"

"That's my cue," Bill joked. "Love you, honey. Call your mom."

"I will. Love you too," she told him as he gathered his food. "Bye, Ryder."

He just waved and held the door for her dad, ushering him along.

She hadn't known what to expect the next time she saw Ryder, but that was not it. Was it too much to ask for some sort of acknowledgment of last night? Not the kiss, of course, that was an accident and nothing she wanted to talk about in front of her dad, but what about everything else? Did his crying while she consoled him mean nothing to him?

Had coming over, distraught about Wade, just been his excuse, an act, to be alone with her in her house, to get what he wanted? When she didn't succumb easily, had he decided to move on? Had he realized that she wasn't worth the effort after all, but knowing he'd still have to see her regularly because of her dad, now didn't know how to act in front of her?

His best friend just died. Of course she wasn't the center of his thoughts, she scolded herself, feeling like a jerk. He had every right to be distracted. What was he going to say in front of her dad anyway? "Thanks for letting me cry on your shoulder. Oh, and sorry about the kiss. We good?"

She chuckled to herself, imagining the look on her dad's face. And why was she getting worked up over Ryder when she still had to figure out August?

Admittedly things had moved much faster with August than she typically allowed. While she refused to regret their afternoon, she wondered if they needed to slow things down, give themselves time figure each other out… especially if Ryder was intruding on her thoughts now, too.

She looked down at the counter she'd been wiping, wondering how long she'd been standing around thinking about men, cleaning the same spot.

EIGHTEEN

-BILL-

It was obvious that Ryder was chewing on something, but he'd yet to spit it out. They both parked in the employee parking lot that ran the length of the strip, and took the nearest alleyway back to the sheriff's Blazer. Ryder immediately went to the passenger's side and climbed in, while Bill got into the driver's seat, patiently waiting for Ryder to tell him what was next.

"I don't think you should let those boys leave town yet," Ryder blurted.

Bill had been expecting something different from Ryder's urgency.

"We've kept them here long enough for something they weren't involved in," Bill said calmly. "Unless you know something about them that I don't?"

Ryder shook his head, still stuck in his own thoughts.

"No," he finally said, "but just in case."

"In case of what?"

"In case we have more questions."

"We've got their contact information if we have questions." Bill studied his deputy. "What's going on Ryder?"

Ryder turned to Bill, looking hard, a pleading look in his eyes. "Please just listen for a second before you say anything. Okay?"

Bill nodded.

"I don't think Wade's death was an accident," he said, the words rushing out. "I think someone's trying to make it look like it was, and if you let those boys go, we may never find out who it is."

If Wade hadn't died from a massive heart attack, Bill would wonder what new information Ryder had found to lead him to be suspicious.

But Wade's heart had exploded, *inside* his chest. Even the M.E. said it was a natural—albeit not anything he'd ever seen before—but natural occurrence. There was no *person* to be searching for.

Bill worried that the death of Ryder's friend was hurting him too deeply, that he was seeing things that weren't there. He knew what it was like to try and make sense of a horrible situation, to grasp at every possible answer to an impossible question.

Bill opened his mouth to speak, but Ryder stopped him before he could get a word out.

"You said you would listen," Ryder reminded him. He ran his hand through his hair. "I went to Wade's house today. I don't really know why," he said, letting his hand fall into his lap at Bill's both surprised and pitying expression. "I don't even know what I was going to do when I got there. He lives alone, no pets, nobody there to miss him…" he trailed off. "I have a key… I'd get the mail for him when he'd be gone sometimes, just check on the place. You know? I don't know… I guess I just needed to be *there*. It still doesn't feel real, him being gone."

Ryder stared out the window and Bill got the feeling he'd lost the train of thought that had been driving him. He wondered if he should say anything yet, or just let Ryder process his pain.

"I didn't ever go in the house," Ryder finally told the tree outside his side of the car, then turned to Bill, serious and focused again. "But then the mail lady came and told me something weird."

He proceeded to tell Bill about Wade's back-up plan, the letters and system they'd had for years and how the most recent letter just went into the box the day before.

"Don't you see?" Ryder searched Bill's face. "His yard had just been mowed; it wasn't a week-old growth like it should have been if Wade did it before he left for his trip. His house literally looked like it had just been left the day before. What if the killer was staying there while he knew Wade wasn't coming home and is gone now because the letter went into the box? The mail lady wouldn't suspect anything until Monday when she mails the letter. Wade's killer could be states away by then!"

Bill waited a few seconds to make sure Ryder was finished before calmly proceeding.

"Ryder, Rich said Wade had a heart attack," he gently reminded him.

"See, even that doesn't make any sense. He was healthy, active all the time, he shouldn't have had a heart attack. He wasn't even thirty yet."

"I agree that it's a weird situation, but Rich said there wasn't anything abnormal in his toxicology report."

"Okay, but put aside the heart attack," Ryder countered. "Let's just say we didn't know the official cause of death… doesn't it seem strange that, by all accounts, it looks like he left his house yesterday?"

"There has to be a reasonable explanation for all of it."

Ryder started to interrupt, but Bill held up a hand. "Just listen for a minute."

Even though Bill could tell it took all Ryder had to bite his tongue, he complied. Bill continued gently, "Wade could have a mowing service that comes even when he's not home. A lot of those places send a bill out afterwards, and nobody but Wade's immediate family and friends know that he's passed away. The mowing people probably haven't been updated about his death." He could tell Ryder didn't like the thought, but he knew it made sense, and had he been in his right state of mind, would have already come to that realization himself. "As for the mail, maybe the mail lady was mistaken about when it went in the box." When Ryder started to shake his head and open his mouth to speak, Bill held up a hand to pause him. "Or… maybe someone else was checking his mail at the house for him for this trip, noticed the outgoing letter was ready to go and thought Wade had forgotten to send it before his trip and just happened to put it in the box."

"Yeah, but doesn't it seem a little strange?" Ryder persisted.

"Ryder," Bill said seriously but gently. "What happened to Wade is a tragedy. It's not fair. Naturally, as his friend, you'd want to make his death mean something, but sometimes bad things just happen unexpectantly and there's nothing we can do to change it. I'm really sorry that you're going through this, but Wade died of natural causes."

"What about the high adrenaline that Rich mentioned? Wade was scared. What if someone was after him?"

"You saw how banged up his body was," Bill told him. "He probably got hurt in there, and who knows how long he was alone, looking for help? That's scary. Then if he lost his footing and fell, yeah, I'd be scared out of my wits, too."

Ryder looked out his window again, his brow furrowed. He grabbed the handle for the door and turned back to Bill. "It's not right, something's wrong here. I can feel it."

"What's wrong is that a young person died too soon. Ryder, go home. Get some rest."

Ryder just shook his head and opened the door.

"I don't like it, Bill," he said. "Something doesn't feel right."

He got out of the Blazer and stalked over to his own truck. He got in, started it up, and drove off. Bill watched the dust settle around him, and hoped Ryder could get this theory out of his head.

Nothing good could come from looking at it like it was something it wasn't.

Ryder was a good deputy and would undoubtedly be sheriff one day, but he could also be impulsive and reckless at times. Bill had seen too many people spiral into deep depression when they lost a loved one. He'd seen them cut ties, become hyper-focused on something menial, or give up on aspirations entirely. He hoped that losing Wade, a friend Ryder considered a brother, and now this theory, wasn't the start of that descent.

NINETEEN

"How long are you gonna leave me in here?" she screamed at the sound of the metal food door sliding open. "Please! Just let me out of here!"

She ran toward the sound, but the darkness was too much, and she hit the wall sooner than she'd expected. Her palms stung from the rough surface and the food slide was already closed anyway. She wasn't sure what her plan had been; grab the plate and frisbee it back at whoever was keeping her? It still wouldn't help her get out.

She slid down the wall, thudding on the ground next to the door.

"Please," she cried hoarsely to the dead air. "I just wanna go home."

TWENTY

-AUGUST-

August took a break from his hike to sit on a downed tree and take a drink of water. Lillian told him yesterday that she was working a double shift today, so he'd decided to mark off another trail from his map, but instead of clearing his mind, all he did was think about her.

Seeing her the first day, standing on the sidewalk… every cell inside of him needed to be near her. He couldn't have walked away from her if he'd tried.

To hear her voice, her laugh… it was like waking up from a terrible nightmare.

Things were going well. He'd set the pace—not too needy, casually interested, just the right amount. She couldn't know how much he needed her; it would only scare her off.

But then she changed everything. *What were you thinking, sleeping with her?*

He couldn't help himself. She'd made the first move; one he never foresaw. She hadn't stood a chance as soon as he felt her lips against his, her apology whispered between them as if she had done something wrong. He was the one that had been wrong. Wrong to think taking her out there was a good idea, having her alone, nobody to interrupt, nobody to stop him from having her completely.

He'd ignored everything and took what he so selfishly wanted, what he'd desperately needed.

He needed to see her again. Was it too soon? Should he give her time? Or would time make her doubt, make her see what he'd greedily stolen from her?

He shook his head, looking above him at the sun shining through the leaves.

"We're both adults," he said to the squirrel resting lazily against the trunk of a tree. The squirrel's tail flicked slightly at his words but didn't make a move to run away. "She could have said no and told me to take her home," he said, but wondered if he'd have been strong enough to stop, strong enough to comply.

When it came to her…

He made up his mind. He'd get down from the hill, shower and change, and then see if he could talk her into a late dinner, after her shift was over. He wouldn't stay to eat in the diner, just stop by to ask her out, let her see he didn't regret their time together, that he still wanted her.

He found the trail that he'd followed hours earlier and took it the rest of the way out of the woods to the gravel lot. There was only his truck, an SUV that was there when he got there, and one other truck in the parking lot. Normally he would have kept on his way, except that he recognized the owner of the other truck.

He stepped out of the woods to see Ryder looking in the windows of the SUV, walking around it, assessing it from different angles.

"Everything okay?" August asked as he approached.

Ryder turned and scowled at him.

"It's August," he reminded him, "from the other day?"

"I remember," Ryder stated, leaving the conversation hanging awkwardly between them.

"Okay... do you need any help with anything?" he tried again.

"Sure," Ryder crossed his arms over his chest, widened his stance. "Why don't you tell me what you're doing out here?"

August looked around him and at the gear that he carried.

"Hiking."

"Mm hmm. And how long have you been out here?"

"All day. Why?"

"Have you been out here before? Say, a week ago?"

"Nope. This was a hike I hadn't had a chance to make yet." August crossed his arms, mirroring Ryder. "What's your problem with me?"

"My problem is that I don't know who you are really, where you're from, what you're doing in Juniper Hollow, and now you've turned up at two separate sites of suspicious deaths. Seems pretty weird if you ask me."

"What are you talking about?" August asked, glancing around for the missed crime scene tape. "The only death I know anything about is the one that I hiked you out to, and again, if I had anything to do with that, why would I report the find, and then take you all the way out to it? That makes zero sense."

"Unless you want us to be looking in another direction. Did you know Wade?"

"Who?"

"Have you been staying at his house?"

"What? No. I have my own place outside of town. I don't think I've met a Wade yet. Look, you're starting to confuse me. I don't know what you're talking about."

Ryder studied him, then nodded to the SUV.

"Do you know who this belongs to?"

"No, but I don't know that many people here. I *can* tell you that it was here this morning when I started my hike, and I started early. I figure either someone is in there camping," he indicated the woods all around them, "or it's been abandoned. But I was all over this side of the hill and didn't see anyone else."

Ryder assessed him further, his stance softening just slightly as he looked back at the SUV.

"This truck belongs to my friend, Wade..."

"Okay... the guy you wondered if I'd been staying with while I'm in town."

Ryder nodded.

"Sorry man. I never heard of him. I'm on my own here."

Ryder continued to stare at the SUV.

"You think he got lost in there?" August asked, breaking Ryder's attention from the vehicle.

"What?" he asked, his eyebrows furrowed in confusion.

August motioned back to the woods. "In there. Do you think he's lost in there? I didn't see anyone, but if he's not checking in or whatever, I can help you search for him." He really wanted to get back to Lillian, but if someone was missing, he couldn't just walk away.

"He died about a week ago," Ryder stated.

"Oh... Man, I'm sorry," August told him, looking back at the truck. "Do you need help getting it back to town?"

"What?" Again, Ryder looked confused at the offer to help. "No," he shook his head, "no, that's not why I'm out here... I found a note with a map that he'd left, saying he was going to be in this zone, so I came out to find any clues about his death, and I found you instead." The aggression was back.

"Look, I'm just out here hiking, and I don't know anything about your friend," August told him as calmly as possible.

"How do I know you weren't in there destroying evidence and were coming back for his car?"

"Good God, Man," August sighed, dropping his hands to his sides. "Look. I get it. You're a cop, you've got to consider all angles, but you're looking in the *wrong* place. I don't know him. I don't know why his truck is here. I don't know how he died. I'm just a guy here to hike. That's it."

"Nothing makes sense," Ryder said, turning to look around the lot. "He left a map..."

August watched him, not sure what move to make. Would he be angry again if he tried to talk to him? If he tried to leave, would that look suspicious to Ryder again?

"He was always the adventurous one," Ryder suddenly said. "It was nothing for him to go off on his own, but he always came back."

"But this time he didn't?" August guessed.

Ryder shook his head, "His body turned up earlier this week."

"Wait, the body in the water?" August asked. He'd heard about it around town. Ryder gave him the look again, but August waved him off. "It's a small town, everyone was talking about it. Literally when I walked down the sidewalk, I heard about it." He set his pack on the ground and fished his hiking map out of his side pocket, unfolding it and laying it out on the hood of the truck. Ryder walked over to see what he was up to. "Here's where we are now," he said, pointing to the trailhead nearest to them, "and here's where I heard the body, sorry," he said as he glanced at Ryder. "Where your friend was found." He pointed to the area called the Bend then showed him all the spanning distance between the two points. "If this is his car, and he went in over here, how'd he wind up all the way over there? Plus, this isn't even close to the nearest put in for a raft." His finger skimmed along the edge of the river to the symbol marking a boat ramp. "Why park so far away?"

"He wasn't a rafter," Ryder stated. Nothing more, just the statement, and studied the map in front of him, full of creases from being folded over and over with circles and marks all over. "You've been all over for someone new to the area," Ryder acknowledged.

"It's what I do," August told him. "I'm here to hike; the only way to accomplish that is to get out and do it."

Ryder studied his map a little longer, then looked at August, clearly not liking him for whatever reason. He sighed. "It looks like Wade wasn't supposed to be in the water. The medical examiner ruled his death accidental and thinks that he fell off a cliff and landed in the water."

August nodded his head in understanding. "I see." He paused, assessing Ryder just the same. "Is that public information?"

He shrugged. "The sheriff doesn't think there's anything suspicious about his death. He says I'm looking for something that isn't there in order to explain a horrible situation." He ran his hand through his hair and looked at the map again.

"So, all the questions just now..."

"Have to consider all angles," he told him, using August's own words. "I don't know. Maybe he's right. It just doesn't add up. His car is here, but it doesn't look like it's been here more than a day. There's no dust, no pollen, there'd be something settled on it if it had been out here all week long. And the map," he said, pointing back to the points August had indicated. "How'd he get all the way from here, through all that, and into the water. What was he doing?"

August studied the map along with him.

Ryder continued, "And sure, there are cliffs, if he did make his way through all this mess, but nothing so high that he couldn't swim when he landed."

"I wouldn't be sure about that," August said, interrupting Ryder's thoughts. "There's bound to be some shallow waters here and there, add in a rocky bottom and a decent cliff, and it's possible the fall could kill a person."

"Where?"

"What?"

"Show me on the map where the cliff could be high enough for a death fall."

"Well, I don't know about depths of the water, but this map has elevations, which is why I use it for my hikes. It's important to know what you're hiking into, and digital isn't always reliable in places like that." August followed the river back from where they found Wade's body, "Let's see… Oh."

"What?" Ryder asked, studying the map as well.

"Well, it's hard to say. My map only shows so much area. He could have fallen from somewhere beyond my map… or the water levels could be low enough right now that a lower elevation fall could do it."

"No," Ryder said, looking hard at August again. "No, you see something. What is it? If you don't tell me, I'm just going to get someone else who can. Now what is it?"

"It's probably nothing."

"But it could be something."

August sighed, not wanting to tell him what he had seen, but knew it would only look bad if he didn't, like he was trying to hide something, and Ryder was already suspicious of him.

"Okay… do you see this mark? This gray line that runs through here and along the edge here?" Ryder nodded as he followed as August pointed. "This is the only point on my map, up to where Wade was found, that is high enough to cause a fall to the death. Now if the water was low and he hit a rock or something like that, well, anywhere could have done the trick, but if we're looking for sheer height… the waterfall and the area near to it, that's it."

"Okay. So that's probably it then. What's the big deal?"

"Maybe it's not as big a deal as everyone lets on. I've only been here a little bit, and I've heard more and more stories, some pretty outrageous, but enough to know that the locals know better than to mess around in there."

Ryder looked back at the map and the gray boundary line.

"You're sure?" he asked, and August nodded. "So he did it," he murmured. "Wade was on the Mountain."

"You don't seem very surprised," August said, watching Ryder examine the map.

His hand was back through his hair, fisting at the back of his head as he paced away from the truck.

"It's something we always said we'd do. A joke really. We never really meant it, and the last time we were together, he was really charged up about it. I guess he knew I'd never go through with it, so he went alone."

Ryder sighed again and kicked the tire of the SUV. "I'm still confused by the little things, the map he left, his truck parked here, why he was so far away. You can see it clearly right there." He waved his hand back at the map on the hood. "The Mountain's boundary runs right by here. Hell, you probably even crossed the border on your little trip today and didn't even realize," he said, moving closer so he could point out how close they were to the line on the map, "but it spit you back out, didn't it? Why did the Mountain claim him? And that has to be miles to that cliff. How did he get so far away?"

August wasn't sure what he should say to Ryder, or if he should say anything at all, but he knew how bad it hurt to lose someone and being alone in that desperation was terrible.

"I know you don't know me, or seem to really like me all that much, but if you wanted to get a beer, you could tell me about your friend. Sometimes that can help."

Ryder stared at him like he'd grown a second head.

"Or… maybe it would be best to talk to someone else that knew him, too," he suggested instead. "I can tell you from experience, it sucks at first, but talking it out really can help."

"Thanks," Ryder finally said. "Sorry… I think I probably need to just get home; get him out of my head for a while."

August nodded, ready to get back himself.

"Sorry again for all the," he waved his arm around the area as August folded up his map, "forceful questioning," he finished.

"In your line of work, I'm sure you always have to have your guard up."

"Yeah," Ryder sighed again, staring at the SUV. "Guess I'll need to arrange to have this towed out of here. Thanks for showing me the map."

"No problem," August said, grabbing his pack and heading to load his truck. "You know where to reach me if you need anything."

He watched Ryder climb into his own truck and pull out ahead of him. He hated bringing the Mountain into this again, but facts were facts and there didn't seem to be anywhere else Wade could have gone in from.

Hopefully Ryder would be able to let it go. If the stories of the Mountain were true, it could only bring more death.

TWENTY-ONE

-Lillian-

After the morning excitement at the diner, Lillian was thankful that the afternoon was quiet. Gran and Pops stopped in for their early bird dinner. Gran greeted her with a slight hug when Lillian showed them to their table.

"Lilly dear, something's different," she said, leaning back to look at her, still holding Lillian's arms as she did.

Lillian shook her head, smiling. "Nothing new to report."

"Hmm," she remarked, her expression curious as she studied Lillian, "there's something."

"Oh, leave her be. If she wanted to share her life story with you, she would," Pops razzed as he slid into the booth.

Gran just clucked her tongue at him, sliding in as well.

"Well, we did hire another server today," Lillian said. She glanced over her shoulder to find Josh tending to one of his tables.

Pops looked him over. "He looks acceptable. Better than that blue-haired one."

"Pops." Gran stopped him.

"Actually," Lillian interjected before he could go on a rant again. "She's decided not to work here anymore." She left out the part where she'd spewed accusations like a volcano erupting.

"Good riddance," Pops said, nodding his head once firmly.

"Usuals again today?" she asked, steering the conversation back to easier territory than Rain's departure.

"Actually," Pops started, pausing at a look from Gran. "What?"

"Let her work," she warned.

"How do you know what I was going to say?"

"Because you say the same thing every time."

"I do no such thing," he said, turning to Lillian. "What I was going to say, before I was so *rudely* interrupted," he dramatically said, turning to smile at Gran and then back to Lillian, "is that I want to see what that one there is made of." He pointed to Josh.

"We're in Lilly's section. You can't pick on him," Gran said. "Lord knows he doesn't need to deal with you on his first day working."

"Who said I was going to pick on the boy?" Pops asked innocently, and then waved him over when Josh turned their way.

"Josh, this is Gran and Pops," Lillian said, introducing the couple in the booth.

"Oh cool. Your grandparents?" he asked her.

"How old are you, son?" Pops asked before Lillian could respond.

"Seventeen, sir."

Lillian caught the eyebrow raised in approval.

"Do we look *old* enough to be her grandparents?" he asked him in complete seriousness.

Josh looked from one to the other. Lillian was about to step in and explain Pops' ornery nature when Josh responded.

"She doesn't come close," he said, looking at Gran who smiled in response. He turned to Pops, "but you look older than time itself, so yeah, it could fit."

Pops stared hard at the boy; Josh stared right back.

Pops' guffaw was robust and the hand he slapped on the table, the exclamation point. He looked at Lillian. "This one's my server today," he told her.

Lillian chuckled and shook her head, patting Josh on the shoulder. "Good luck," she said and wandered off. She heard Pops asking what was good here, knowing full well that Josh had no clue.

She glanced around the diner, noting everything was in order, and decided to steal away to the office to finish more of her tasks.

She'd finally been able to write up an ad for help. She posted it on the diner's social media as well as local niche pages and sent it over to the newspaper for good measure. She went through her inventory reports that had been submitted and started a purchase order. She puzzled together a schedule for the kitchen staff to account for some upcoming vacation holes and was getting ready to rough out a schedule for servers leading into tourist season. Marley would be back, and Josh was already proving capable. She hoped she could add at least two more servers to the schedule. She opened a booking website and ran a search of vacancies at the nearby B&Bs, cabins, and local hotels. Most of the weekends were already booked starting next month and the following month only had a few midweek dates available. It was going to be another busy season. She hoped two more servers would be enough.

She made a decent dent in the list, making notes of the rest of her tasks. She glanced up at a light rap on the open door, expecting to see Josh with a question, and was surprised to see Ryder for the second time today.

Her stomach gave a slight quiver at the sight of him.

"Hi," she said, the surprise in her voice unavoidable.

"Hey, they said I could come back," he told her, nodding back up front. "Do you mind?"

"Not at all. Do you want to sit?" she asked, motioning to the empty chair on the other side of the desk.

"Yeah, thanks." He looked around the small space.

It had been Harvey's office for his duration, but when they had made their arrangement for her to take over, she'd slowly made the space her own. She'd switched out the harsh overhead lights for softer floor lamps, and downsized the hideous old file cabinets that lined the walls to a single standing unit. She added art to the bare walls, a few beautiful pieces with a neutrally muted palette that would contribute to the inviting and cozy environment she craved. She hung natural wood shelves and topped them with air plants and nature-inspired trinkets and knickknacks created by local artists. She loved it.

Nobody had noticed.

"This is nice," Ryder said after his assessment. He gave her a quizzical look. "Yours?"

"I made some changes," she said, and he nodded, looking around again.

Of course the detective would notice. But part of her heart warmed at the thought that he had.

"I didn't know you did this sort of thing," he motioned to the computer and around the room. "I thought you just did the tables and diner stuff."

"I'm full of surprises," she joked, but wondered why he was currently sitting in her office. "Is everything okay?"

He leaned forward in his chair, resting his arms against his legs, appearing calmer and more comfortable than he had when she'd seen him earlier in the day.

"Yeah, everything's fine," he sighed it out, as if it wasn't fine but if he said it enough times it would be eventually. "I wanted to apologize for my behavior lately."

"Ryder, you have nothing to be sorry for," she started, but he held up a hand to stop her.

"Yeah, I do. I never should have unloaded on you like I did about Wade's death."

"I'm sure you didn't intend for it to go the way that it did," she offered, "but please don't apologize for having emotions."

He leaned forward. She watched him study his hands in front of him as his arms rested against his legs. Her mind wandered to the way his hands felt in her hair.

"I couldn't tell his parents," he admitted softly, snapping her attention back to him. "I couldn't bear to tell his mom. She's practically a second mom to me and I couldn't tell her that her son was gone. Hell, after the way I broke down telling you, she probably would have tried to tell *me* it was going to be okay, instead of me trying to be there for her."

"It was probably better that it was someone else," Lillian gently agreed, grateful he wanted to talk about that part of the evening instead of their kitchen kiss. This was safer ground than thinking about the feel of his lips—*Focus.* "Besides, you needed to have your turn to grieve, too. You'll see her when you're able to offer her the support you think she needs."

He looked at her, curiously. "Why did I have to tell *you* but couldn't tell his mom?"

"Well… the three of us… we used to all be friends…" she offered as a suggestion.

"So. Your dad could have told you."

"I guess so," she said, uncertainly, not sure why it was such a big deal. Wasn't kissing her in the kitchen a bigger deal than who told her about Wade's death? Why wasn't that eating him up like how she found out was?

"It had to be *me* that told you. You probably hadn't even thought about Wade since school, but the thought of anyone else telling you, or if you found out from second-hand gossip… It had to be me."

Oh. The quiver in her stomach returned but she squashed it down.

"Why did I *have* to tell you but couldn't tell his mom?"

"You already said you wouldn't have been able to offer his mom what she would need. And as for me, I'm glad I heard it from you," she said. "I'm glad I didn't find out from the internet like when his body was found."

She watched as he winced at the memory. They both knew how fast word spread when disaster struck.

"Since you keep excusing my actions, will you at least let me apologize for something that has no excuse, that never should have happened like it did?"

"Okay?" she wondered.

"I'm sorry for kissing you last night."

"Ryder," she started. She couldn't deny that her heart picked up speed when he finally mentioned their kiss.

"Stop. Quit making excuses for me."

"But you were upset and not thinking," she rationally said.

"Oh, I was thinking," he disagreed, sitting back in his chair, staring hard at her. "I was thinking that there hasn't been a day that's gone by since the last time you let me kiss you that I haven't thought about doing it again, and there you were, right there in my arms. Who knew when I'd ever get the opportunity again? So, I took it."

"The last time we kissed was over ten years ago," she said, unconvinced. While she'd been thinking about the kiss, she wasn't about to believe he'd been pining to do it again. *You know better than that,* she reminded herself.

"I'm aware."

"You haven't been thinking of kissing me for ten years," she said dismissively. "You just want to make it sound like what you did last night was more malicious than it was so you can have *something* to apologize for."

"How do you know what I've been thinking?"

"Even living out of town, being split up for as long as we had been, people still seemed to think I needed to hear all about who you were seeing. *All* of them," she told him dryly. "So, no, I don't believe you when you say you'd been thinking about me for ten years. You had an emotional reaction to an emotional moment. If you need me to tell you that you're forgiven, then fine, you're forgiven, but don't make it out to be something it wasn't. You don't owe me any apologies, Ryder."

"They were all just distractions since you," he told her. Her traitor heart quivered this time, but in the same beat, remembered that night and how it wasn't quivering then. It was breaking.

"You must have needed a lot of distraction from what I heard," she retorted. "Sorry," she said, instantly regretting the slip, regretting letting him see there was anything left to feel, "that was uncalled for."

"Lilly Flower… is that jealousy I detect?" A hint of humor in his voice.

"Not at all. There's nothing to be jealous of. You lived your life. I lived mine."

Just because he'd managed to get into her thoughts this week and confuse her heart and brain, didn't mean that what happened then didn't still pang.

He leaned forward in his seat. "You were keeping tabs." His tone a mixture of recognition and amusement.

"I was not," she stated firmly. "People would just *tell* me things… things I didn't ask to hear about. From the sound of things, you were doing just fine." She busied herself straightening random papers on her desk.

So what if she kept tabs for a little bit. That didn't mean she wanted *him* to know that.

"Maybe you shouldn't always listen to things people say," he said softly.

"Ryder, it doesn't matter," she sighed, moving the papers out of reach and folding her hands in her lap. "We've been through this. It's in the past. Let's just leave it there."

"You're right," he agreed, getting up to shut the door. "It is in the past, and we did talk about it, but you gave me some dismissively polite answer, like you are right now, about how it doesn't matter. But it does."

"No, it doesn't, not anymore." She watched as he came around her desk, closing the space between them. Her heart beat faster.

"It does, because until you let go of the image of that stupid teenager that you still see, I'll never be more in your eyes." He braced his hands on the arms of her chair, leaning down to be on her level. "And I fully intend on being more to you."

Her heart was now fully racing at the intensity in his eyes, even though he'd kept his words light.

"Ryder… I already told you that I didn't know if this could go anywhere," she said, hoping her voice sounded smoother than her nerves trying to interject.

"I know, and if you don't get out how you really feel, then it won't ever get the chance to try."

"I don't feel anything," she said, hoping it sounded convincing.

Ryder smiled slowly, watching her for a reaction. "I bet you still remember her name."

"Whose name?" she asked too quickly.

"You know who. Tell me her name."

"No. This is dumb Ryder. I'm not rehashing an old argument with you. We've already been through this. We agreed to put it aside."

She stood, the arms of the chair and his close proximity too confining. He backed away but leaned against the desk, conveniently blocking her from leaving the area.

"No, you pretended like you were fine, when it's pretty obvious that it's still under the surface. And it's not rehashing if we never had the argument."

"Because there was nothing to talk about," she said, throwing up her hands in frustration. "You broke my heart and then screwed the whole town."

"There it is," he said, crossing his arms across his chest. "I knew it was still in there."

"We were together for nearly three years. Three *years*, Ryder. In case you've forgotten, in high school that's like a lifetime. And then, you went and made out with Emma Sophia like the years we spent together meant nothing, and at prom, of all nights! The night I thought we'd finally–" She stopped and closed her eyes. She took a breath, held it, then slowly let it out. She opened her eyes to see the slight smirk on his face. "It doesn't matter. I didn't want to do this then and I definitely don't want to do it now."

"Emma Sophia?" he asked. "You're sure about that one?"

She crossed her arms across her chest and stared daggers at him. "I wanted her to gain fifty pounds and for all her hair to fall out. Yes, I'm sure."

"Not sure what I was thinking there," he said in disbelief.

"You were thinking she was an easy target, an easy way to get what you didn't think you'd get from me. I was young and nervous and wanted our first time to be special and had this whole idea in my head of what it would finally be like, and then there you were, wrapped up with her, and reality came crashing down. You were my best friend. The one person I could trust completely… and then poof, just like that, I realized that what I thought we had meant more to me than it did to you. I was hurt and embarrassed and…"

"And I was mean about it," Ryder finished. "I let you think that it was you that wasn't good enough to be with me, that I could replace you with anyone –"

"And you did, time and time again," she said, hoping her words were cold enough to feel.

"I did, because the reality was that being with you was the best thing that had ever happened to me, and I was scared."

"That makes zero sense. How could you be scared about something good?"

"We were kids, Lilly," he said, pushing off of the desk to pace. "We had the rest of our lives ahead of us. We're not supposed to meet our soulmate in high school. We're supposed to go to college, make stupid mistakes, then finally find someone who smacks some sense into us and makes us realize the idiot we are so we can finally see what's right in front of our eyes."

"That sounds like an elaborate way of saying you weren't ready to be stuck with just one woman."

"No. I wasn't ready for *you* to be stuck with me."

"That wasn't your decision to make."

"Lilly, prom was *the* night. I knew what was going to happen that night. All the signs were there. And I knew that if it went that far, one of two things would happen. You'd pass the point of no return, and no matter what stupid things I dragged you through in life, you'd stick with me, whether I deserved you or not. Or two, you'd finally realize how much better than me you were. You'd realize that I wasn't worthy of you, that you could reach so much higher than the small-town boy I was likely to be, and you'd move on with your life, leaving me all alone," he sighed, running his hand through his hair before putting it in his pocket. "So, I grabbed ahold of the first girl to smile at me and let her believe she was able to seduce me away from you, and made sure that you'd see."

"Why would you do that?" she whispered, the hurt slicing through her heart, fresh all over again.

"Because you deserved something better than me. You deserved to get out of this town, to make something of yourself, to find a good man, to not be stuck here with me, and I knew you'd never go if you loved me like you thought you did."

"But I did love you," she said softly, swiping at a tear that she hadn't intended to shed. "Did you ever think that maybe you *were* a good man? That we would have been good together?"

He nodded. "We could have been good, but then one day you could have woken up and realized that the good was gone, and then you'd have left me. I thought it would be easier to let you go then, to let you hate me. I'd eventually forget about you and move on with my life, just like you would have done. We'd both be spared heartache in the long run, both eventually find happiness, and we'd have chalked it up to just another high school romance." He looked down at the floor, taking a breath before looking back up at her. "I tried to call, but you wouldn't answer… Losing you never stopped hurting. No matter how many times I tried to push you out of my mind, you'd always drag a chair right into the middle of my thoughts and plant yourself on it, forcing me to look at you, to think about how stupid I'd been to let you go."

"And then you found Wade's body and you seized the opportunity to make amends." She dropped into the chair and sighed. "Why couldn't we have just left the conversation at that?"

"Because you didn't have the truth, and without the truth we can't move forward."

"The truth being that instead of talking to me about how you were feeling, or what I was feeling, you decided to sabotage something that could have been great. How does telling me that now help anything?"

"Because I know exactly what I lost when I gave you up. You're still better than I deserve and if I'm ever going to convince you to lower your standards and give me a chance, then I don't want any secrets from our past getting between us."

She smiled at his attempt to lighten the mood. "Ryder—"

"I know," he told her, squatting down in front of her chair. "I know where you stand, at least, as of last night, when you warned me that this could go nowhere at all. I know that what I told you today could have ruined my chances with you altogether, but I couldn't leave it unsaid and try to prove that I'm different now."

"So, great, we've reopened an old wound," she said, attempting a smirk, but her mouth only wanted to pull down at the edges. "Now I know, and it hurts all over again at what we lost." She grabbed a tissue from the box on her desk and dabbed her nose, gripping the tissue as she dropped her hand to her lap. She hated that she felt anything at all, that she didn't mean the words when she said she'd moved on. But where did that put them now? "Just because you've told me, doesn't mean that anything changes. We're two entirely different people and the image you have of me is of an old high school flame… the one that got away." She snorted at the cliché and rolled her eyes. "You don't even know who I am now, the person I've become over the last decade." She chuckled lightly. "You could have just told me all of this, and you may not even like the new me, just the idea of who I used to be."

"We've both changed, Lillian. I know you aren't the same person that you were back then, neither of us are," he paused, his smile sad, his eyes searching hers. "I hung on every word your dad would say about your life, what you were doing, where you were living—" He paused when she looked down at her lap, waiting to continue until her eyes found his again. "—if you were seeing anyone. He was sparse with details when it came to you, or maybe I just thought he was being stingy. When you moved back home, I watched you work hard to overcome whatever you felt you had to run from." He searched her eyes for the answer to the question he didn't ask but softened his tone. "Your dad would never say, but you dug in hard.

"You're independent and determined. You're also more than caring and thoughtful and you love deeply, you always did. You've brought your dad breakfast every Sunday morning since you moved back home. You've never missed a day," he stated. "It's important to you, and while you could make up every excuse in the book to skip here or there, you don't because of how much family means to you and how much you know it means to him."

He chuckled. "Back when you first moved back, first started bringing him breakfast, I *knew* it was only because you wanted a look at me in uniform. I knew you'd been waiting to see me, just as badly as I had been to see you. I *knew* that it was going to be a walk in the park to win you back… but you wouldn't even look my way. It took a year before you looked at me again, another seven months before you said hi to me when I was with your dad. The chill in your voice could have frozen Hell, but it didn't matter. You'd spoken to me, and I'd take that over no looks any day.

"It was another five months before you accidentally smiled in my direction and didn't look away in disgust. Six months ago, you said, 'good morning' when I was the only person around. And then a week ago, I went out on a limb to see you in your space on my own. Not with your dad as a buffer, not with you in the station. Here, on your turf," he smiled mischievously, "but where you would also have to speak to me since you were working. You wouldn't ignore a customer. I can't tell you how disappointed I was when you weren't my server… but you still came by. You talked to me."

"I thought about avoiding you."

He dropped his chin to his chest, his hair falling forward as he laughed lightly. His eyes were light when he lifted his head again.

"But you did."

She crossed her arms. "It would be rude not to."

His smile faded. His eyes focused on hers and his eyebrows pulled together as he continued. "That day, the possibility of you rejecting me and deciding for us to go back to not talking was scarier than anything I could imagine… until we found the body of an unidentified man in the water. But there you were in front of me, leaving your Sunday morning breakfast. Now, granted, I blew through two stop signs to make it to the station before you left, hoping to catch a smile or, if I was lucky, you'd talk to me again.

"But we weren't in your work. We weren't with your dad. It would have just been us. Then, sitting there watching you smile at something on your phone, I realized that the thing that was even scarier than you ignoring me and driving away, was that if that unclaimed body found in the water had been me and I never got the nerve to say the things that I needed to say to you and I died knowing that you thought I was still *that* guy.

"I'm sorry for the way things went so long ago. I'm sorry for not saying anything to you sooner. I'm sorry for kissing you when I shouldn't have last night," he paused, smiling devilishly again, "but not one hundred percent sorry. And I'm sorry that I was so wrapped up in my own theories and thoughts earlier today that I was rude to you. I wasn't in a good place, and I let that get the best of me, but I need you to know that how I was acting earlier had nothing to do with last night or you."

"I'll admit that it did dig a little, especially after last night, but I realized you were distracted… and that we haven't been friends in a long time. As for everything else…" She paused as she considered everything he'd just said. She had no idea he'd given her a second thought other than the fleeting moments he'd had to endure because of her dad. But a part of her worried that it was too much, that he was trying too hard. What if all of it was just a jumble of words that he thought she'd like to hear to… what? Confuse her?

Play a game because she was a challenge he hadn't won yet? *What if he's telling the truth?* The tiniest of voices made her heart thump loudly in her chest. *What if there was more to him than she'd allowed herself to see.* "Ryder, I don't even know what to say," she finally said feeling lame at her lack of words after everything he'd just said to her.

He gave her a small smile. "Will you at least say you'll think about everything we said today? I don't expect you to change your opinion of me overnight, but will you say you won't shut me out completely?"

"I can say that much," she told him tentatively, then eyed him uncertainly when he stood and held his hand out to her.

"I don't bite." He smiled but winked as she took his hand cautiously. "Don't worry. I'm not going to kiss you," he said as he pulled her to him, guided her hand to his back, and wrapped her in a hug.

She stood enveloped in his arms, her stomach a rave filled with butterflies. Her head reasoned with her to step away, warning her not to enjoy the subtle scent of cologne that he'd put on at the beginning of the day, not to notice the toned arms holding her securely against an equally hard body, not to find comfort in his warmth. Her heart thumped wildly against her chest

"I've missed you, Lilly," he told her softly. "I'm done being scared of whether or not you're going to cast me out."

"I find it hard to believe that you've ever been scared of anything in your life," she whispered against him.

"Only you," he whispered back.

"Mm hmm," Lillian said, pulling away from Ryder's embrace while she still could. "You always seemed just as cocky as ever."

"I had to be." He laughed, leaning against her desk again, allowing her to have her space. "Don't you know what it's like out there in the wild? Show any fear, and I'd get eaten alive. You couldn't know I needed you."

"But now I can? Now it's all out there for me to know?"

"It is. Because life's too short and I don't want to live in the past with you anymore."

TWENTY-TWO

-LILLIAN-

"I can't give you anything more than a friend right now," Lillian said to Ryder, watching his face as she forced herself to sit again in her chair, fighting the urge to be back in his arms, wrapped in his warmth. *It would be so easy to close the space—* "I have my own things to sort out and..."

"I know. But now you know."

He moved away from the desk and went to leave. He'd already said more than she knew what to do with for one day. Having to use the chair as an anchor to keep from sliding back into his embrace should have been reason enough to let him go, but curiosity had been eating at her.

"Ryder?"

"Yeah?"

"Can I ask you something?"

"Of course."

"It's none of my business, and you can tell me no, but I was curious..."

"Curious about what?" he asked when her sentence faded off.

"Earlier today," she started cautiously, and recognition crossed his face. "Admittedly, I did think that you didn't know how to be around me after last night," she began. "I started going down the path that you didn't want to *have* to be around me."

"Definitely not," he told her.

"But then I realized that it probably had something to do with Wade's death." She watched him nod, his gaze far away. "Can you tell me what that was about? It seemed important and had you worked up... as a friend," she said carefully, "if you wanted to talk about him, I could listen."

He chuckled lightly, moving to return to the seat in front of her desk. "You're the second person to offer me an ear. Granted you're far more attractive than the first and not a know-it-all douche."

"I don't think my dad would appreciate that description," she said, surprised.

"No." He laughed. "Not your dad, someone else. No, your dad squashed my theory right away, but I wasn't having any of it. I was going to prove that I was right about Wade's death whether he believed me or not." He let out a deep breath. "It was on that path when I ran into someone else, and after basically accusing him of murder, he offered to buy me a beer and to talk about Wade."

"What? I'm more than a little confused right now."

He laughed again. "Yeah, I was sort of a mess earlier."

"I thought you said last night that Wade had a heart attack. Now you think he was murdered?"

He ran his hand through his hair then settled it against his leg, studying his knee as his hand rested against it. "Honestly, I don't know."

"Murder is kind of a big deal. If there were signs pointing you in that direction, why wouldn't my dad hear you out?"

"Oh, he listened, but he had a logical explanation for each theory. Your dad is a smart man." He smiled. "I guess I wanted Wade's death to mean something, and not be some stupid accident."

"Okay… but I feel like you wouldn't just say a person was murdered, friend or not, if there wasn't something that made it look that way… so what made you think it could have been a murder instead of an accident?"

"As your dad pointed out, but I didn't want to recognize, was that all my *facts* were mere coincidences."

"And since that's official police information, you can't tell me what they are," she guessed.

"My theories aren't officially in his case. His death was ruled accidental and natural, not a murder investigation."

"Would you mind telling me then?"

He looked at her curiously. "Why do you want to know?"

"You were very distracted earlier," she told him. "Enough so that even after telling your boss—the sheriff—what you were thinking, you still decided to ignore him and dig deeper. To me, that feels like there was something that could be relevant that shouldn't be overlooked. How can you just discard a theory in one day after one person points out other angles that may or may not be the truth themselves? Or—" She paused, shrugging her shoulders. "I'm not a cop and have no idea how it really works and that's what you guys do and there really isn't anything there. I can't give you more right now about whatever this is between you and me, but I can at least listen to what you needed to say earlier today."

He smiled warmly at her.

"What?"

"Nothing. You really want to talk murder with me?"

"What are friends for?" she joked.

He chuckled. "I don't think friends want it to be this close to real life. Talking over a murder podcast, theorizing from a removed position, is one thing. This is someone you knew."

"Yes. Someone who meant a lot to you, who deserves what you saw to be heard and considered."

"You're sure?"

She nodded.

"Okay." He let his breath out on a sigh and leaned forward in his chair. "The biggest driver behind my doubt that his death was accidental, was that nothing makes any sense." He quickly told her what he noticed at the house and the conversation with the mail lady, and then how he'd relayed that information and his observations back to the sheriff, along with the sheriff's rebuttals and explanations. "When he shut me down, I wouldn't hear it. I went back to Wade's house. I have a key, so I let myself inside. Nothing looked out of place, there was no mail from the week piled on his counter from where someone else was bringing it in for him. There was still grass on the mower in his garage, like it had been used recently, which wouldn't have been there if he had a mowing service. It looked like he had prepared his house for him to be gone for a few days and then left for the weekend. The food wasn't even nearing expiration in the fridge."

"And he wouldn't have someone else coming to check on the house while he was gone?" she asked. "A neighbor kid that could have mowed for him, using Wade's own mower?"

"I guess there's a first for everything, but as far as I know, he never used someone before. He's a low maintenance guy. He's gone on long weekends a lot and the house is always fine for a few days. There wouldn't be any reason to hire someone… I doubt he even ever considered that an option."

She could tell he was thinking things over, so she let him think, wondering at the odd series of events associated with Wade's death. It was confusing.

"Anyway," he finally said, "I was getting more fueled up. This was a murder investigation; it had to be. Someone clearly had been watching him long enough to learn his routine for going out to camp, found the opportunity to kill him and hide the body and hide out in his house as a cover until the letter could be used. That gave the killer time to make a plan and get away before anyone even started a search for Wade."

"But why even put the letter in the box?"

"What?" he asked, startled out of his thoughts.

"Why put the letter in the box in the first place?" she asked him. "If it gives a deadline, why not just get rid of the letter altogether? That way, nobody would look for him where the letter directed. Maybe his body never would have been found, and nobody would notice anything suspicious."

"Except for the mail lady, who would see the box filling with mail, or his family when they couldn't reach him. They'd start looking eventually."

"Right, but if there was a murderer, why force a timeline on yourself? It could take another week before the mail lady caught on. Who knows how often he talked to family or friends? Any of those variables are unknown, but why force yourself into a limited timeline by sticking that letter in the box if you're the murderer who's trying to hide out?"

"I think… *thought*, that maybe the murderer tried to kill him out there. Maybe it was someone he camped with even, and things didn't work out according to plan and Wade escaped him. When he couldn't find the body right away because Wade went over a cliff into the water, maybe he came back to the house. Stayed there trying to make it look like Wade was still there, still alive doing his daily grind, mowing the grass, getting the mail, until it was close enough to when Wade's camp routine could be used. He sticks the letter in the box and high tails it out of here… or is still here trying to finish covering all his tracks so he can at least be gone by the date on the letter." He rubbed his forehead, sighing. "I don't know."

"But Wade's body was found on Sunday, and your letter didn't go in until yesterday… Why wait so long? Obviously a dead person can't put that in the box; it screams suspicious."

"When the body wasn't immediately identifiable, the killer could have realized he could still play off the letter bit. Identification can be a lengthy process, especially in a place like this, where we never know if someone is here recreationally or is a local. Or maybe the killer didn't realize that it was Wade's body that was found and was still playing out his plan; only family has been notified. The public has no idea who that body is or that Wade is dead. So, by all accounts, the killer could still be here and getting ready to run."

He stood to pace, rethinking his day. She could see that where he'd seemed like he'd calmed down this evening, his earlier preoccupied mind was back in gear. This may not have been as helpful as she had thought.

"Okay, so I'm guessing you read the letter in the mailbox… isn't that illegal?"

"Hmm? Oh, yeah, I mean sorta. But this one was addressed to me, so it was going to be mailed to me as his back-up for this trip on Monday anyway… I just sped that part up."

"What did it say? Did it look like his handwriting?"

"Yeah. I mean, I'm no expert on handwriting analysis, but it looked like his from what I could tell. It was a pretty short letter, you know movie theatrics type stuff, 'If you're reading this, I'm probably dead.' He was always a joker, but basically said if he didn't turn up from his trip then we needed to search for him. He marked his trailhead, where he was going to be and for how long. When I went to the site, his SUV was there, looked like it had just gotten there, but no sign of any foul play. It just looked like someone went camping and would be back anytime. Then that guy August comes strolling out of the woods –"

"Wait… August?" she asked, her heart thudding at the sound of his name.

"Yeah, you met him in here a few nights ago, remember? When your dad and I were here, we said to watch out for him," he told her to try and jog her memory.

She didn't need any help remembering.

"Anyway, he's there, which is real weird because there I am, looking into a possible murder and he's already tied to another death. Now he's at another possible scene? Seems strange."

"But I thought you guys said he helped you with the other one?"

"Right, but he could be trying to hide in plain sight… and I told him all that, straight up, and he's just cool as a cucumber and offers to buy me a beer."

"Wait, what? You lost me."

Ryder laughed. "Yeah well, I was there being a hothead, on my mission, accusing him of being involved, and he's trying to help me out. He pulls out his map, shows me where everything went down, and when I'm realizing that I'm grasping at straws, trying to make all my pieces of coincidence fit into the only puzzle I want them to go into, he's standing there offering me suggestions and *then* tells me he'd buy me a beer and talk things out if I wanted. I must have looked as shocked as I felt because I was downright rude to the guy, so he suggested instead that I talk to someone who knew Wade, and I realized that he was right. Maybe I was focusing on all the wrong things. Wade is dead and even though things are still off about the way he died, the heart attack, all the other weird things… they just don't go well together, but the truth is… he had a heart attack. He died. There are more important things that are still in front of my face that I need to see instead of focusing on making something into what I *want* to see."

"So, what do you think?" she asked him, not so sure herself what to think. He was right that things didn't make sense where Wade's death was concerned.

"I'm sad that I lost my friend… and I'm confused that he can just be gone like turning off a light in a room… and I'm angry that there isn't a better explanation for him being gone. And the strange things that I found this afternoon… it isn't a far stretch to realize that your dad is probably right, and I'm trying to make it something it isn't."

"So, you aren't going to pursue a murder investigation?"

He thought it over for a few moments. She let him process, watching his expressions change from doubt and confusion to conviction.

"For now, I'm going to let it rest… but I don't know that I can really put it away completely. It's one of those things that's just too weird, but unless I come across something that can shed some light, I doubt I'll have the sheriff's office to back me on this."

"So, you're going to just let it go?" she asked, surprised at the her own disappointment that he could be so sure in his thoughts and then abandon them before really digging in.

"There are too many things to risk losing by focusing all my attention on something that probably was as simple as an accident, no matter how much I hate to admit that."

"And if he *was* murdered… and nobody is looking because it isn't convenient… what then? What if the murderer is still here?"

"Hey," he said soothingly. "I'm only letting it rest because of the unlikelihood of all those pieces fitting together the way they'd need to in order to be able to call this a murder. Too many people have poked holes in my theories on day one, you included. I want answers to this weird story, that I may never get, but that answer may not be that a murderer is running around causing people to have heart attacks. There's nothing for you to worry about. I'm sorry, I never should have said as much as I did.

"You know, out of all this, what gets me is that he went to the Mountain without me. He really did it, and I didn't get to be there with him. And I don't only mean that because maybe I could have helped him, but he really did it. I wondered, and I know I said some stuff yesterday when I was in a dark place, but he actually did it."

"How can you know for sure?" she asked.

"The only place he could have gone into the water like the medical examiner says he did is an area that's within the Mountain's boundary line. August showed me on the map." He stopped with the explanations, watching her process all that he'd shared with her. "Are you okay, Lilly?"

"Yeah," she finally sighed, knowing if she got freaked out about every possible scenario that could or couldn't be, knowing more than most as the daughter of the sheriff, she'd never stop worrying and would never get anything accomplished. "It's just a lot," she finally told him. "Everything. It's a lot to process."

"You're telling me." He sighed. "I've said enough today. I'm going to get out of your hair now before you decide not to let me come back."

"Ryder?" she asked, as he was turning to leave.

"You said *people* were dying of heart attacks."

"Yeah, it's real bizarre," he said, solemnly shaking his head.

"The other body you guys found. That's how he died, too?"

He nodded. "Yeah, but that's not released yet. Real sad, young kid. It just doesn't make sense, but the reports came back all clear. Natural cause of death." He paused, pursing his mouth slightly, his eyes focusing elsewhere. He shook off his confusion, but not before she noticed.

"What's wrong?" she asked him.

He shook his head again, his eyebrows scrunched. "Just another one of those weird puzzle pieces… might be nothing."

She waited, but she could tell he wasn't going to tell her on his own. "Ryder, what is it?"

She watched him watching her and wondered which side of his internal debate would win. She noticed the slight shake of his head as he raised an eyebrow and sighed.

"The second body that we found?" She nodded, and he continued. "We found him in the woods… it looks like he was on the Mountain, too. I don't know what that means," he finally admitted. "I need to go. I'm sorry I took up so much of your time today. I'll see you around Lilly," he said, and left before she could ask him any more questions.

She'd always dismissed the stories of the Mountain. They were superstition, folklore to lure the tourists, scary stories to tease each other. She thought back to Wade's bonfire stories. She could still hear his words as he'd try to scare them all. '*Everyone knows there's only one way out of the Mountain … Dead.*'

The Mountain had claimed two more lives… but they were just stories.

She felt an icy tickle at the base of her neck.

TWENTY-THREE

-LILLIAN-

The dinner rush hit hard. It was as if the cosmos knew she'd just been given more than enough to think about and it wouldn't let her. Every time her mind drifted to something Ryder had said, his voice, the feeling of his arms around her, another table walked through the door, or an order came up. She was happy for the distractions. The last thing she needed was to think about Ryder. Or a potential murderer.

At the sound of the bell chiming as another table cleared out, she looked around the diner for Josh. She found him clearing off the table that had just left. She'd already noticed that he was quick to clean as soon as a table cleared out. He'd kept up with the crowd all through the rush, and the regulars all seemed to respond well to him.

"Josh, you can head home if you want," she told him after the crowd had died down and his tables were dwindling.

"Are you sure? I can stay on if you need me to."

"You've already done more than enough on your first day."

"Thanks. I know I have a lot to learn, but it was okay?"

"Better than okay, especially because we would have been shorthanded without Rain tonight. You're sure this is going to work out for you? The dinner rush is how it is all day during the summer."

"Yeah, that's awesome. It flew by and the tips were good. I can cover Rain's schedule and pick up extra if you're shorthanded anywhere else."

"Don't burn out on me in the first week," she laughed.

"I'm saving to buy a car, so I could use the work."

"Well, I could use the help," she told him. "I'll mark you in for Rain and we'll see about picking up shifts as you're comfortable."

"Cool. Thanks, Lillian."

"You're welcome, and thank you for working so hard today. It really helped all of us."

He beamed proudly. "Gary showed me an empty locker in the back. Is it okay if I put my stuff in there?"

"Absolutely, and the schedule is posted back there, too, if you want to check for Rain's days."

"Sure thing."

"Have a good night, Josh."

"Yeah, you too." He smiled and jogged to the back to stow his things.

After the rest of the crowd thinned out and their Friday night slowed down, she offered the rest of the servers the choice to stay on or go home. They chose to go home. She closed down half the diner and kept the other side open for the late-night snack and shake stragglers.

In a few weeks, that wouldn't be an option. They'd be lucky to keep up with their own smaller sections.

She checked the work email on her phone, happy to see that she'd already received a few job applications. She shot back some quick responses to schedule interviews. She'd called Harvey right before the rush started, telling him she was ready. He had sounded happy, but not at all surprised.

"I can't believe this is finally happening," she'd told him. "It feels surreal."

"You know it's already yours," he'd said. "We'll just get some papers signed and make it official. Don't worry about a thing. I'll get everything arranged and text you a time."

"Thank you, Harvey, for everything."

She checked her messages now, while sitting at the counter, and saw a new one from him:

> *I've got everything arranged for tomorrow morning. 9 am at Wisteria. Wear something nice for a picture for the paper.*

She almost dropped her phone. Tomorrow? How could he already have everything ready that fast? She'd expected more like a month to get everything sorted.

Tomorrow?

Her heart raced in anticipation, excitement, and a dash of nerves. She nearly missed the jingle of the bell above the door as it opened. Still in shock from Harvey's message, she could only stare as August walked through the door. He stopped walking and turned back to the entrance then looked back at her.

"You're still open, right?" he asked when she just gawked at him, phone in her hand.

She laughed. "Yes, sorry," she said, shaking off her undoubtedly dumfounded expression.

He approached the counter and sat on one of the bar stools.

"Is everything okay?"

"Hmm? Yeah, why?"

"You just seemed surprised to see me. I know we didn't make plans… it's okay for me to be here, right?"

"Why wouldn't it be?" she asked, confused, then yesterday's events came rushing through her muddled brain. Her cheeks warmed. His slow smile told her he noticed and approved that he provoked a reaction in her. "I'm sorry, my brain isn't working apparently," she told him, waving the phone at him. "Yes, it's definitely okay that you're here. I wasn't sure if I'd see you again, but it's nice that you're here."

"I have a confession," he told her solemnly.

"Oh?"

"I drove around a lot trying to decide if I should come in today or not," he paused. "I wasn't sure if you'd want to see me this soon. If I was supposed to wait a few days to call you... but then I remembered, we never actually exchanged phone numbers, so I would have had to call you here and that could be weird..." He trailed off when he could tell she was trying to hold back a laugh. "What's funny?"

"I forgot there were all those *rules*."

"I'm out of practice," he admitted.

"You didn't seem out of practice to me," she told him. "I had a really great time yesterday... and I think that we can safely say we're past the rules and games portion and skip to the part where we get to know each other."

"I'd say we got to know each other pretty well yesterday," he joked, and she could feel the flush returning.

"We probably should slow that part down a little, too," she told him. "Yesterday was really, *really*, nice, but that's not my normal speed. I don't know what happened. It was like I couldn't control myself and just acted on impulse."

"I enjoyed your impulse," he said, studying her intently, "but if you want to tone it down a little, get to know each other, that's fine by me."

She smiled and exhaled the breath she hoped he hadn't noticed she'd been holding. She didn't realize she'd been so worried that since they'd already slept together, he either wouldn't come around anymore like he said he would, or when she told him she needed to take things a little slower, he'd back away completely. Rain's behavior, Josh getting hired, and Ryder's visits today had been a distraction but had also cluttered her head even more. She needed time to sort everything through, and she was worried that if the only time she spent with August was in bed, then she'd never get to know him or what she wanted.

"You look relieved," he said with a laugh. "Did you think I was going to get up and leave if you aren't going to let me get you naked again?"

She laughed, glancing around the diner impulsively.

"Trust me, I definitely want that... but I'm here," he said, nonchalantly. "Let's see how it goes."

Was it too late for her to take back her words? She smiled at how simple things felt with him.

"The reason I came in tonight," he said interrupting her thoughts again, "aside from deciding it didn't matter if it was too soon or not, was to see if you wanted to get a late dinner after you close up here."

"I would really love that," she started.

"But…?"

"But I have an early morning tomorrow and it'll be pretty late when I get off here tonight."

"Okay. And you're already busy tomorrow… so how do I get to see you again? Maybe you need to pull the boss card and have someone cover your shift for a change. Maybe that one with the blue in her hair?" he suggested.

"Sore subject there… she quit today… although I *had* just hired an additional server, but instead of being plus one, I'm still neutral. I have some ads out and already getting some interest, so hopefully there will be some good prospects." She paused, realizing she was rambling. "Tomorrow, though, I'm only busy for a little while in the morning. Wait…" she studied him curiously. "Why did you say I was the boss?"

"What do you mean?" he asked, confused by her sudden shift.

"You said I should pull the boss card… why would you think I'm the boss? You've only ever seen me wait tables."

His smile never faltered, but she noticed it was too perfect, like he was trying to keep it in place. Something she had learned when she was very young was that a smile didn't always mean truth, and a perfectly held smile in the face of a question usually meant they were trying to hide something. What could he be trying to hide?

"I guess I just assumed you did more than wait tables. From what I've seen of you in here, it seemed like this was yours. You have an air about you that says you're perfectly at home, not just that of an employee that's punching her card. There's pride in how you carry yourself and interact with each person like they're in your home, and not just taking an order and handing it over. You care. It's rare, and usually when I see that in someone, they are the owner, and if not the owner, then at least a partner of some sort…" He paused, an apologetic look on his face. "Sorry if that was offensive. I shouldn't have assumed."

"How could that be offensive?" she asked, immediately regretting having doubted him, thinking he was hiding something. "I'm not sure I've had such an observant compliment before. Thank you."

"You're welcome, but anyone can see it. I'm new here and I saw it immediately… So… not the boss?" he asked her, curiously cautious.

She looked around, making sure nobody was in earshot, and leaned over the counter. He leaned closer as well.

"That's what tomorrow morning is about," she said quietly, exhilarated to share her secret with him. "It's sort of a long story, with a rather embarrassing start, but the gist is that I wound up back home, after college and life—" she waved her hand to encompass all the 'life' moments. "—in my own shame, having a pity party in that booth over there." She pointed over his shoulder. "Having a vanilla milkshake for breakfast—you're not allowed to judge—"

"No judgment here," he joked, holding up his hands.

She smiled, continuing her story. "Harvey, being like a grandfather to me since I worked here until I left for college, came to see what was wrong. After talking for quite a while, he offered me something I couldn't refuse." She looked around with pride. "And even though I tried to tell him no, it wasn't an answer he was willing to take. I thought things over, talked it through with my parents, and finally agreed to be his successor."

"But nobody knows?" he asked in disbelief.

"That was one of my requirements. I wanted to learn and have our transition be seamless. He agreed, and over the past few years, I've been taking on more and more responsibilities..." she let out a breath, "so tomorrow when he signs it over to me completely and makes the official announcement, nothing will really change because I've already been doing it behind the scenes. I mean I'll make changes along the way, but I want to keep the historical and nostalgic aspects of this place. It's been here for so long. It's pretty much a monument."

"And you're perfect to take it over. Harvey obviously saw how much you care and knew this place would be in good hands with you. He made a good choice in his successor."

She smiled again at another compliment.

"So, it sounds like tomorrow is a pretty monumental day."

"No, not really, it's just becoming official. Just a few signatures and a picture for the paper because Harvey is old-school, and then I'm available the rest of the day."

"It's a pretty big deal," he told her, sliding his hand over the counter to hold her own. "Tomorrow your secret is out. Everyone will know who the owner of Wisteria is."

"Well not *everyone*."

"Anyone who has been blind to the fact that you already treat this place as special as you do, will have their eyes opened. It's a day for celebrating." His slow smile spread invitingly. "And celebrations are always fun. Let me take you out tomorrow. Let me show you that you're worth celebrating."

She didn't want to say no, every part of her wanted to start the celebration early, but she was the one that said she needed to take things slow. She at least needed to look like she was thinking it over, give him a little bit of doubt.

"My parents will probably want to come to the signing in the morning. They're silly about that sort of thing."

"I'm sure they're proud of you."

"They will probably want to visit with Harvey and me for a while... I'm not sure what time exactly I'll be finished."

"What time is this signing?"

"Nine in the morning."

"Here?"

"Yes... so I can probably be persuaded to spend an evening in the company of someone who keeps raining compliments on me."

"Oh? A whole evening?"

She laughed. "Not the *whole* evening, but a few hours..."

"A few hours I'll take," he said standing from his barstool.

"Oh, you're leaving?" she asked, surprised since he'd only just arrived.

"It's pretty clear that you're too busy for me tonight," he said, looking around at the two other people in the dining room, who were so deep in their own conversation that they probably never even noticed him enter the building. "And I have a celebration to plan, so you'll just have to finish your night here without me."

"Okay, I'll try to make it through," she laughed.

She was leaning forward on the counter still and he leaned across, surprising her that he'd be so publicly affectionate so soon. She expected him to give her a kiss on the cheek from the way he had advanced, but instead she felt his warm breath at her ear, tickling her skin.

"I want nothing more than to kiss you goodbye... but instead I'll hold onto yesterday's memories until I can see you tomorrow."

He pulled back, smiling wickedly, knowing that now she was thinking the same, and strolled out the front door, his scent lingering to torment her.

TWENTY-FOUR

-LILLIAN-

She groaned inwardly as she parked in the employee lot… next to the local news van. Harvey had said there would be a picture for the paper, not a news crew. She was thankful for three things: one, that Harvey had warned her to dress for a picture, knowing that if he told her there was a camera crew, she would have tried to get out of it; two, she had dressed discretely professional in fitted slacks, one of her new silk tops, and low heels, so she didn't look like she was just a waitress trying too hard to fit her new role as owner; and three, she had arrived twenty minutes earlier than Harvey had suggested, so she had plenty of time to let him know how she really felt about having a camera crew on hand.

She got out of her car and made the short walk to the employee entrance, ready to give Harvey an earful. He was already waiting inside when she entered, and immediately scooped her into a hug. How could she be mad at this man? She could hear the clicking of a camera as she hugged him back.

"You lied to me." She laughed as she pulled away.

"You wouldn't have showed up if I told you the truth."

"You're right on that one," she joked.

Her parents were squeezed into the back break room along with the camera crew, Harvey, and her, and came to give her a hug to the sound of clicking and flashing again.

"Thanks for coming," Lillian said to her parents.

"Wouldn't miss it for the world," her dad said, for once not dressed as the sheriff.

"Harvey said he had it all arranged," her mother said, holding her daughter's hand in her own, "but I had no idea there'd be so much stuff."

Lillian turned to Harvey. "You told *them* about the news crew?"

"Of course. They're your parents. They should know what was happening for you," he said with extra innocence.

She shook her head and smiled as another member of the crew popped around the corner.

"We're all set up and ready to go," he said to Harvey, then turned to her. "Good, you're here early. Come with us and we'll make sure you're camera-ready."

She did not like the sound of that.

They took her into the office, where her makeup was touched up, a tiny microphone was attached discretely to her shirt, and she was given pointers for the camera.

"This will be live, so just try and be as calm as you can. Pretend like the camera isn't even there."

"Live?" she croaked, never one for the screen. "Is all this really necessary?"

"Of course it is," the reporter told her. "Wisteria is iconic in these parts. The transfer of ownership is an important part of our community."

"But is it really?" she asked, still uneasy about the prospect of being on live TV, wondering if she was going to get tongue-tied.

"Don't worry," the reporter laughed. "You'll be just fine. We're going to get some footage of Harvey and you signing with the notary. I'll ask each of you a few questions and get some proud parent feedback. I'll sprinkle in some history about the diner and the town, and roll in some tie-ins to the Mountain, because that's always a grabber for these parts, and then we'll get some footage for later with the staff and locals and their reactions to this new change. That'll run on the evening segment."

"Do we have to tie Wisteria to the Mountain?" she asked, slightly unnerved because of the two recent deaths associated with it.

"Of course. The Mountain and Wisteria are the two keys to Juniper Hollow. Everyone eats up the stories about the Mountain, and the fact that nobody remembers whether the stories or Wisteria came first, it's just natural that they go hand in hand. We can probably run a few historical pieces about the start of Wisteria, how it's changed through the years, and how it and the Mountain are two major pulls for tourism in these parts. We can run a little bit every night this coming week. It'll help draw more people into our town as well. You're taking over a piece of history, you know."

"I'm aware," she said, her mouth suddenly going dry.

"Don't worry," the reporter beamed at her. "You just be you and we'll cover the rest."

"I'm just going to sit for a minute," Lillian said, trying to figure out how she could sneak past everyone and out the back door without anyone noticing. "How did you even have time to prepare for this?"

"Oh, honey. It's what we do. We're always ready for a good story, and it may not seem like much to you, but this is big news."

"It's time," the crew member with his headset told them, causing the butterflies to frenzy in her stomach.

"Here we go!" the reporter exclaimed.

Harvey and her parents were ready and clearly excited. She was ready to be done with this part.

"Okay, Lillian, Harvey, you two have a seat at this table here."

She did as she was told, her nerves causing her hands to tremble slightly.

"Just be yourself," Harvey said from across the table, reaching over to give her hand a quick squeeze. "It'll be over before you know it."

She smiled, hoping it was more convincing than it felt.

"Mom, Dad, you two can come over here," Lillian heard someone instruct, and she looked over to see her parents being seated at the old-fashioned bar stools at the counter. She caught her dad's beaming smile and her mom's reassuring grin. Their confidence put her at ease.

She heard the reporter begin the introduction. She let out a breath and smiled at Harvey. He was witty in his answers to the reporter, displaying nothing but confidence in her taking the reins. When the reporter turned to her, she was able to easily answer the questions she'd been asked. By the time the paperwork was presented and the notary came over, she was comfortable, laughing with Harvey as they enjoyed the moment. She focused on signing her pages and could hear the reporter talking to her parents in the background. They moved on to staff, getting pieces of praise and surprise, but nothing but support, which she was thankful to hear. When it was all over, she realized it hadn't been as bad as she thought it was going to be… but was still thankful it was finished.

"That went well," the reporter told her as the crew started packing up their supplies. "Obviously the live version just went out, but we'll run it again throughout the day and have another segment on the evening news."

"Thank you for making that painless," Lillian told her, then turned to the applause in the diner. She hugged everyone from her parents again, to Harvey, Lana, Gary, Gran and Pops, who'd made the trip over, and several of the other regulars. She hadn't been prepared for any of the overwhelming support she felt, thinking nobody would really bat an eye at the switch.

"Thank you for this." She leaned into Harvey.

"No, thank you," he told her sincerely. "It means everything to me knowing that you're the one to keep her spirit alive."

She stayed and visited for the impromptu after party and finally decided to call it quits at nearly eleven o'clock. She was surprised when she checked the clock to realize how much time had passed so quickly. When they'd finally said all of their goodbyes, Lillian and her parents excused themselves through the employee exit. Her dad held the door for them to pass through, laughing at something called from inside the diner. She heard him tell someone goodbye again, chuckling as he caught up to her and her mom at Lillian's car.

"Looks like you have an admirer," her mom said, nodding at her windshield, where a single white rose had been left, secured under her wiper blade with a card attached. Just one word was written on it: *Congratulations*. "Who do you think it's from?" her mom asked excitedly.

"I have no idea," Lillian wondered.

Rain

"Can you believe that shit?" Rain hurled the question onto the sidewalk as she and the trio left their lunch. Her rapid stomps pounded the pavement with each new outburst before any of the guys could respond. "I knew it! I just knew it. I called it. She's sleeping with him, I just know it, and she's going to run that place into the ground. Did you see how uppity they all were, laughing on the screen like they're something special? That's exactly how my parents act. God, I'm so glad I quit when I did. It'll go to shit now for sure. With me running the show, it woulda been fire… but not now… Whatever," she finished, taking a pull on the vape. "What are we doin' today? I need to get *her* outta my head."

"I can think of something to occupy your mind," Jack said, grabbing her waist from behind, picking her up, and spinning her around.

A peal of laughter escaped her in the spin. "I'm sure you could," she told him. "But you guys promised me excitement," she pouted.

"Oh, it'd be exciting," Jack assured her.

"I thought you guys were all about the adventure, but you still haven't taken me to the Mountain. What gives?"

"It's just stories," Evan stated as they climbed into the truck to head to the campsite. "I'm tired of hearing about that stupid place. And you aren't exactly the most athletic. You'd probably just wind up getting yourself hurt and one of us would have to carry you out. No thanks. You can count me out."

"Way to be a downer, Evan. Are you ever any fun?"

"Hey, ease up," Jack told her. "He's had a rough time."

"So have the rest of you, but you're making the best of things. He's been nothing but lame the whole time you've been here. Why are you still here, Evan? Why haven't you already left if you hate it here so much?"

"Rain," Jack said from the front seat. "That's enough."

She slouched against her seat and looked out the window. She thought being with the guys she wouldn't have to sugar coat things like she did with everyone else. Usually she could go 'round with guys easier than with other girls. They didn't get upset at her if she said something stupid or get their feelings hurt if she was honest like a lot of her old girl friends had. Wasn't that what being friends was about? Being able to tell it straight? She'd lost friends because they couldn't handle her telling them what she really felt, and her parents didn't like to hear what she had to say either. She thought with Jack and Brian, even Evan, that she could be real with them. She didn't mean to be mean. She just didn't understand why she had to say something different than what she was really thinking. All her life she heard people complain about other people not speaking their mind, about waiting to say what they really thought behind people's backs. So why did she lose friends or get in trouble at home when she did exactly what she thought she was supposed to do and speak her mind.

They got back to camp and Evan slammed the truck door, stomping to his tent. She watched as he started packing his things.

And there goes another one.

Jack took off after him. She caught a few words Jack and Evan were saying while she and Brian were unloading from the truck. From the sound of things, Jack was trying to talk Evan into staying one more day and she was about to get booted from their boys-only club. She didn't want to go back home yet. She just needed to stay a little longer before going back to all the disapproval and the *looks*.

She watched as Evan set his bag back inside his tent and heard Jack clap and say, "Cool! I'll go tell Brian and get rid of Rain."

She only had one chance at getting to stay a little longer.

"Brian," she sang sweetly. "You want to go to the Mountain, don't you? You were the most excited out of all of them when we first met. Don't you want to see what it's all about before you guys leave me?" She slid up to him, letting him pull her close while she pouted and searched his eyes. "It could just be you and me," she said softly.

"What about the guys?" Brian asked, glancing over her shoulder at Jack strolling over.

"What *about* them? They want to sit around here and be boring." She emphasized the pout then leaned close to his ear. "I know you want me all to yourself," she whispered. "I've seen you watching me. Take me to the Mountain," she said. She nipped his ear and felt his arm tighten around her. He turned and stole a quick kiss, but she surprised him by pouring herself into it. "Is that a yes?" she said huskily when she pulled back.

He nodded. She knew exactly what he was thinking he'd get from her but if it meant she didn't have to leave, she'd let him think it.

"Great," she said, breaking away when Jack approached. "Let's go now."

"Go where?" Jack asked.

"Brian's taking me to the Mountain. You two can just sit around here and be lame. Come on Brian," she said before he could change his mind.

"Just a sec," Brian called to her over his shoulder as Jack pulled him away, but not out of earshot.

"What are you thinking?" she heard Jack ask Brian. "Evan's right, she's not going to be able to handle the hike."

"Exactly, she'll give up before we even get goin' and then she won't want to come back to camp 'cause then she'd have to admit she couldn't do it, so…" Brian's words trailed off, but she heard them chuckle. "We'll just have to find other things to keep us busy until it's been long enough to come back."

"She's not going to sleep with you," Jack scoffed. "She's been just enough of a tease to be fun, but it's getting old. Evan's agreed to stay one more night. Ditch her and stay here with us."

"I'll be back by dark, don't worry. I'll drop her off on the way back and we can still have a last bash guys' night."

Jack laughed. "Okay, but you know this is only gonna end in disappointment."

"Gotta at least try."

"Good luck. Don't get hurt out there 'cause she doesn't know what she's doing."

"I won't," he said as he grabbed his climbing pack, checking to make sure it had all he needed for hiking, as well as what he hoped to be doing instead, and threw it in the back of his truck. "You ready?" Brian asked, grabbing Rain in for another kiss.

"Mmhmm," she said, licking her lips. "Let's go." She climbed into the truck and waved to Evan and Jack. "Bye boys. If you change your mind, you know where to find us."

She didn't always like *how* she had to do things, but she did like getting her way. She laughed as Brian peeled out, dirt and rocks flying behind them. So what if Brian thought he'd get lucky? It's not like he was a bad kisser anyway. Who knows, maybe he'd keep her around longer if she gave him what he wanted.

She could think of worse things to do.

TWENTY-FIVE

-LILLIAN-

Lillian met August in the shuttle parking lot off the main strip at exactly 6:45pm. She wasn't sure where they were going yet, but this time he had told her it would be at a restaurant, so hiking boots weren't required, although a light jacket could come in handy.

"So, is this to be our 'thing?'" she asked when he gave her a hand up into his truck. "You not telling me where we're going and me blindly trusting you?"

"It adds to the intrigue, doesn't it?" he told her as he pulled out into traffic. "I figure if I can get in a few really good dates, then when you realize that I'm just a regular guy, you'll already be hooked."

"Ah, I see. So that means that tonight will be one of the really good ones then, right?" she joked.

"I think it'll be pretty good."

He drove out of town, taking the scenic, winding roads instead of the main route. She enjoyed the hills and trees and occasional glimpses of the river through them. She had a pretty good idea where he was taking her as they gradually made their way up in elevation and finally pulled off the road onto the two-mile long drive that ended at the Overlook. She'd only ever been to the area when it was simply a scenic overlook where people would park and take pictures. She hadn't made the drive since it'd been developed into a restaurant and event venue.

"You know this was quite the scandal when it opened, right?" Lillian asked as they followed the beautiful lane.

"Oh?" August asked. "I wouldn't think people would care too much about a restaurant being built this far away from town."

"It wasn't the distance from town that was the problem. It was the land itself," she told him, catching his gaze. "See, the place that the Overlook was built used to be an actual overlook of sorts. People would bring lunches, take photographs, go hiking…"

"Sounds nice."

"It was. You could see for miles, and the river was right below… It was very romantic."

"Ah. Got it, lover's lane," August laughed.

"Not just that, but yes," she admitted begrudgingly, smiling over at him, "it had a bit of an evening reputation."

"So, people were mad that their nighttime nookie spot was taken."

She laughed. "Yes, I suppose that aggravated more than a few. Anyway, the land had always had a don't ask, don't tell mantra to it." She turned at his raised eyebrow. "Apparently in more ways than one, now that I think about it," she smiled. "Obviously the land belonged to someone, but nobody ever objected to it being used recreationally, and then out of nowhere, the land is claimed, marked as private, and a restaurant was being built. I remember people being furious because they never thought it would change, and then they couldn't even fight the restaurant being built because it was in the county."

"It seems to have a good reputation now," August noted.

"Well, yeah, it's gorgeous from what I hear. It's the place to go for any event or occasion. People couldn't resist once they saw how the place embraces the location and enhances it."

"I thought you'd been here before?" August asked, turning to her. "You recommended it."

"Everyone recommends it. I've just never had the occasion to go. Oh –" she broke off as they rounded the last curve. The trees cleared away to showcase a stunning tiered fountain before them and the elegant building beyond. Flowers and plants in the valet area spilled over each other in an exotic array of color. She expected a red carpet slicing through the lavish covered entrance—a tunnel to a magical world—but the subtlety of the stone pavers was much more suitable, adding to the ambiance.

She smoothed her dress across her lap, and inadvertently touched her hair to make sure it wasn't out of place. She suddenly felt very underdressed.

August reached over and took her hand when he put the car in park, bringing it to his lips and kissing her knuckles. "You look amazing," he reassured her as the valet opened her door first to help her out. August came around and took her hand to lead her inside.

He spoke with the hostess at the front who confirmed his reservation and led them through the majestic indoor dining area. Lillian caught glimpses of velvet-lined chairs, roses in vases and tea lights at each table, a tasteful bar with sparkling glasses dangling overhead and selections lining the wall, as they followed the hostess. She led them to the intimate outdoor seating area on the veranda. She'd seen pictures of course, but seeing in person the oversized and overflowing flower arrangements, the delicate twinkling lights strung about, the tables with their white tablecloths and candles was breathtaking. The hostess seated them at the very end, next to the railing, allowing for an unencumbered view for miles, and directly below, the river flowing lazily by.

"It's lovely to have you dining with us tonight, Mr. Steele," she said, smiling just slightly too long at August.

He didn't seem to notice and smiled in return, thanking her as she removed the "reserved" placard, and placed their menus in front of them both.

"August, this is too much," Lillian said as the hostess stepped away.

"Nothing's too much when you have a life-changing day like you did today."

She looked around at everything, taking it all in. "How did you even get a reservation so quick? This has to stay booked forever."

"Why don't you just let a man have some secrets?" he teased, entwining his hand with hers across the table.

The server came and offered a bottle of wine to sample, which was much better than the failure of a bottle from their first date, and described the specials for the evening. By the time the salads were placed, it was perfect timing for the sun to begin its panoramic descent.

"So," August started as the main course was served. "Tell me how you wound up being picked to take over Wisteria."

"Oh, well, there's not much to say," she deflected.

"Really?" August asked, topping off her wine. "Last night it sounded intriguing."

"Last night I told you it was embarrassing... not intriguing."

August smiled as she took a bite and sighed. The flavor was richer than the scent, and the scent was heavenly. Her steak was cooked to perfection, with a blend of seasonings that enhanced the meat without overpowering the flavor, and was so tender it practically melted on her tongue.

"Oh my gosh, this is really good," she said, covering her mouth with her napkin when she realized she'd started talking with a mouthful of food. She heard his slight chuckle as he cut into his own meal and tried his first bite.

"Flawless," he agreed, "but, I believe you were telling me a story."

"We don't have to talk about my days of poor judgment, not here, not now."

"What better time to hear how you came to take over a monument than on the day we're celebrating."

"I promise you it isn't awe-inspiring," she warned, seeing he wasn't going to give in.

He cut a bite of his food, glancing up with a raised eyebrow and a smile, waiting.

"Fine," she sighed, "but I warned you." She took another drink of her wine, watching as his eyes seemed to laugh in his victory. "It all started when I was fourteen."

"We're going way back," he mused.

"You asked for it."

"That I did. Continue. Fourteen-year-old Lillian."

"Yes, well, I loved the shakes at Wisteria, but my mom would always say no. My dad would sneak me one on occasion, but Mom would never give me money. After school, a bunch of my friends and I would meet there because the shakes have always been the best and it was a safe place to go hang out. But... I had no money." She paused to take another bite, enjoying the smokey, sweet flavor of a crispy, roasted brussels sprout. "So, in order to not be the only one of my friends meeting up, unable to buy a snack for myself, I went to Harvey and asked for a job." She smiled at the memory. "I can still see him sizing me up, a scrawny thing, late for a growth spurt, but he must have seen something because he put me to work clearing tables. The servers would share tips with me, so I earned my shake money."

"I think Harvey had good instincts; he knew you were motivated to work… even if just by milkshakes. How is that embarrassing?"

"If that were all of it, it wouldn't be."

He smiled and settled back in his chair, a hand on the base of his wine glass. "Ah, there's more."

"Unfortunately," she told him, taking another encouraging sip of her wine. "I ended up serving through high school. Harvey worked with my school schedule and events, never batting an eye if I needed time off. It was a dream job really. If we were slow, I could work on schoolwork. If we were busy, I made a lot of extra cash. And Harvey was a lot more involved back then. It was like working with a grandpa."

"I'm not sure I would have wanted to work with mine. When it came to work, he was an iron fist. Get him away from work? Now that was a different story completely."

"Well Harvey was more like the grandpa that would sneak you snacks when your parents weren't looking," she told him chuckling. "Anyway, when it came time to leave for college, I honestly thought I wouldn't be back here. I was young, of course, went through a rough breakup, and because of that, I didn't feel like there was anything left for me here."

"You had your parents, your friends, Harvey."

"Sure," she agreed, "but at eighteen and heartbroken, none of that mattered. So off I went to the city, to be a big city college girl."

"But that didn't work out…"

"It probably could have," she said, frowning as she studied her drink, not taking a sip just yet. "I threw myself into school, wanted to make something of myself, you know?" He nodded as she continued her story. "I graduated a little early, felt like I was something pretty special because of it, and got a decent job right out of the door. I was doing it; the diligent businesswoman with an ego too big for my own good, that only got bigger when I met a man that wanted me to help him build a very promising start up." She crinkled her nose, sheepishly drawing her brows together. "And it didn't hurt that he was as attractive as he was confident. After a few months of him continually complementing me, the mild flirtations when we worked late, the subtle looks I thought he hadn't noticed I'd seen… finally one night, we wound up in bed together." She took a drink of wine.

"Things were exciting for a time. We were building a successful business, building an exhilarating relationship, we couldn't be stopped," she paused, glancing over at him intently listening and let out a breath. "Until his wife found out."

She watched August's eyebrows raise in surprise, but he didn't interrupt.

"I should have known he was married. He only ever flirted with me when it was just the two of us working. He'd never take me out on dates, always coming only to my place, saying he just wanted to stay in our little world, without the stress of work or anyone else getting in our way. I should have seen the signs, but either I was too dumb to see them, or I didn't want to face them." She sighed, turning her glass slightly, watching the wine slip against the side. "Obviously I was fired, cut out completely, although that wasn't difficult since he'd never put me on any paperwork." She snorted, thinking back to the lies he so easily spread. "In the beginning, he'd said how hard a start-up could be and told me he would assume all the risk in case it failed, but if it became successful, he'd make me co-owner. I thought he had been generous and so thoughtful. Again, should have seen the writing on the wall. I retreated home, in my own shame and embarrassment, and found myself sitting in a booth at Wisteria, drowning my thoughts in a vanilla milkshake. Harvey joined me and told me to spill all the dirty details." She chuckled at the memory. "I told him everything and at the end of it all, he asked me what I had learned. I was understandably still sour, so I flat out told him, 'Always get important deals in writing and don't sleep with your boss.'"

"Useful advice," August agreed, smiling as he smelled his wine.

"Harvey considered my words while I drank my shake and then very seriously said, 'Well, I don't think I'm up for starting any new romances at this stage of my life, but I could offer you something in writing if you're up for it.'"

She waited for August to finish clearing his throat after nearly choking on his wine.

"How old is Harvey?" he asked uncertainly.

"Nearly seventy-nine," she assured him.

"Right. That's good." He smiled. "Continue."

"There's not much more to say. He offered for me to take over Wisteria when he was ready. After careful consideration, I agreed. I told him I wanted to take my time, learn all the ins and outs quietly, so that when he was ready, I would be able to seamlessly step in and keep everything as it had been."

"And nobody had any idea?"

"I discussed it with my parents to get their guidance, and of course the attorney, the accountant, those sorts knew… but no, we kept it quiet."

"And here you are, finally out in the open with your secret to be recognized."

"It's nice," she admitted. "I wanted to be sure I knew what I was doing, that way when I took over, there could be no doubt… but I'll admit, there were more than a few times that it would have been nice to be able to say I was the one making the decisions."

August smiled, holding out his glass to hers. "Congratulations."

"Thank you," she told him, smiling in return as she clinked her glass to his.

Their server appeared to clear away their dishes, offering the remainder of the wine. She started to decline, but August's glass didn't take much to top off, and there was only a small amount left in the bottle. She moved her glass closer so he could fill hers. It was a celebration, after all.

"What do you want for dessert?" August asked her when the dishes were removed and the candle between them flickered in the wind.

"Oh no. The dinner was far too much. I couldn't eat another bite."

"Then we'll share. We have to at least try something," he bargained.

"Okay, but you have to choose."

"Me? It's your celebration."

"Yes, but I'm so full, you're going to get stuck eating most of it."

"Oh, that's how it's going to be?"

She smiled. "You're the one insisting on dessert."

When the server returned, describing each delectable morsel in delicious detail, she wanted to try a bite of them all.

The moon had started its ascent at some point during her story, and the stars were starting to pop out one by one. She turned from her view of the river below, growing darker with the evening, to see August studying her.

"I don't see how your story is embarrassing," he told her.

"Unknowingly sleeping with a married man… not covering myself in important business decisions… none of these things make for a solid resume to take over a place like Wisteria."

"So you were deceived and hadn't felt the cruelty of the world to know any better yet. The only person that should have been embarrassed in that situation is the man that thought it was okay to take advantage of someone as amazing as you."

"That's sweet of you to say," she told him, smiling politely, "but I'm just another girl. Nothing amazing."

"The reflection you see must be different than the woman I see before me."

Before the instinct to deflect the compliment could kick in, the server arrived with a large slice of distraction. The chocolate cake was layered with chocolate frosting, sprinkled with raspberries, drizzled with chocolate ganache, and dusted with chocolate shavings, all topped with a sprig of mint.

She took a bite, closing her eyes with a moan. It was just the right amount of bitter and dark combined with the subtle sweetness of the frosting and ganache, complemented by the tart, fresh taste of the raspberries. She couldn't resist.

"Aren't you glad we got dessert?" August smiled as he sampled the cake.

"This is the best cake I've ever tasted," she said, going in for another bite.

"I thought you were full," August teased.

"I decided it would be rude of me to make you eat all of this on your own."

August cut another bite with his fork, studying the cake as he did. "Do you count the cake layers only, or do the frosting layers count too?"

"I have no idea," she told him, giggling as he counted with his fork. "How many?"

"Nine, counting cake and frosting."

"Does the top layer of frosting not count? Wouldn't it be ten?"

"It's quite a bit thinner than the rest of the layers..." he wondered. "Nine and a quarter layers?"

"Good. Now I know to order the nine and a quarter layer chocolate cake next time."

She laughed at the simplicity of discussing their dessert, enjoying his easy company. They chatted about his favorite hikes and how she was feeling about being a business owner. They watched the stars twinkle brighter as the sky turned an inky black. This far removed from the city, the sky was on full display with no distractions.

The cake plate had long since been removed, and they were nearly the only two people left on the veranda. She yawned and immediately apologized. The excitement of her day, paired with the wine from dinner, was finally catching up to her.

"It's getting late," August told her. "I should get you back."

She glanced at her phone to check the time, surprised by the late hour. "Wow, how have we been here so long already?"

"What can I say? I'm good company," August joked as he signed the check, quickly closing the book so she wouldn't see.

"At least let me leave the tip," she told him.

"Not today," he said, standing and extending a hand to her.

He guided her through the dining room, where only a few other groups still lingered, talking quietly as if the late hour couldn't handle more than a whisper.

"Have a good night, Mr. Steele," the hostess purred as they walked up.

"You too, Amelia. Thank you," he told her as they passed.

"You made her day," Lillian noted when they were outside, waiting for the valet.

"Hmm?" August asked, his hand resting lightly against the small of her back, his thumb caressing in a gentle motion, inciting tiny tingles with each pass.

"The hostess," Lillian told him. "You knew her name."

"It's important to know people's names."

"Yes, but *you* knew *her* name."

"So?"

"She couldn't stop staring at you."

"I guess I didn't notice," he said indifferently. "I couldn't stop staring myself."

She turned to him; an eyebrow raised in question.

"You are so beautiful," he said quietly.

The movement against her back had stopped, replaced with a slight pressure, bringing her closer to him. He tilted her chin with his other hand, a question in his eyes, but didn't wait for an answer. He leaned down and kissed her slowly, softly, as she held on to him next to the glow of the fountain. When the approaching truck sounded, he pulled away, bringing her hand up to kiss her like in an old movie, and then led her to the passenger side, opening the door for her to climb up.

The drive back to her car was too quick. The memory of the feel of his lips, of his arms holding her against him, made her wish the night would never end.

"I had a lovely evening," she told him when they were standing together under the moonlight. "So far you're winning at this whole dating thing."

"Good, because I don't know how many more surprises I have up my sleeve," he joked.

"Maybe you let me pick the next one?" she suggested, not sure what she could do to top the two he'd already mastered.

"Ah, so there *will* be a next one," he said, a lighthearted relief to his tone as if he had doubted there would be another.

She laughed. "I think the odds are in your favor, but you'll have to give me a few days to put something together, and I have work. You know… that thing you've decided to step away from for a while? Yeah, some of us still have that."

He just smiled. "I'll make myself available whenever I can get you."

"Not very hard to get, are you?" She chuckled again.

His smile turned serious as he brushed the windblown hair off her face, his eyes settling on hers. "No games. I like you, Lillian. I want to see you again. I wanted to keep driving to my place and keep you until the sun came back up." He paused, and she hoped he couldn't hear the pounding of her racing heart. "But you said you wanted to slow down, and I don't want to rush you."

"Thank you," she managed on a breath, but couldn't risk any more words that might betray her, because all she wanted to do was climb back in his truck and have him take her anywhere but here.

"I need you to get in your car and go home now," he told her softly, moving in closer, his hand sliding around her waist, the tingles returning, dancing up and down her spine at his touch. "Because if you don't leave, it's going to be really hard for me to let you go."

She let him pull her into him, her hands sliding up his chest, remembering the feel of his skin and closed her eyes at the touch of his mouth. His arms wrapped securely around her as they lost themselves in the middle of a moonlit parking lot at midnight. Earlier, the kiss had been soft and sweet. This time, it was intoxicating, a hint of urgency under the surface as his arms tightened slightly. When she leaned farther into him, he stepped back, ending their embrace, and pulled open her door.

"You have to go," he told her, holding on to the door between them instead of reaching out for her again.

It took every fiber of her will to nod and sit down in the car, wishing she had never asked him to slow down... but he was respecting her request... which only made her want him more. She stared up at him, knowing he wanted her just as badly as she wanted him.

"Not tonight," he finally said, but his voice was gruff, and he still hadn't let go of the door.

"Soon," she promised him. He dropped his head, but when he lifted it, he was smiling.

"Text me when you get home?" he asked. "If you don't mind?"

"I can handle that," she told him.

"I want to kiss you again..." he said when he still hadn't closed her door.

"So why don't you?" she whispered.

"You know why. Now drive away."

He closed her door and briskly walked back to his own truck, climbing in and firing it up.

"You're such an idiot," she scolded herself as she drove away in the opposite direction of him. "You know exactly what you're missing out on, and now you're not going to sleep all night because of it. Way to go. At least if you had gone with him, you'd have an excellent reason for being tired tomorrow."

She could feel his lips on hers and the warmth of his arms wrapped around her the whole drive home. She was still smiling when her house came into view. She noticed something on her porch by the front door but couldn't make out what it was. She pulled into the garage and made her way through the house to retrieve what was left.

She opened the door to find a bouquet of white roses. She lifted the box they were in and carried it inside, smiling at the gesture. She set it on the counter and pulled the vaseful of flowers out, setting it next to the single rose from the morning, which she had placed in a smaller vase earlier that day. Curious, she counted the newcomers. Eleven. She smiled and added the single to the bunch, finishing off the dozen. She glanced back into the box as she lifted it off the counter to find a piece of notepad paper with a scribbled note:

I heard about the good news. Sorry I missed you tonight, but I guess you're out celebrating. Congratulations again. -Ryder.

So, he was her mother's so-called admirer from this morning. She'd automatically assumed it had been from August, since he was the only person aside from her parents that she had told. She smiled at the flowers, but sighed as well. Ryder was trying and was living up to his word that he was going to prove himself to her, but August had her heart still racing to be near him, wanting to call him up and give him directions straight to her bed.

But August wasn't from here and she wasn't sure how long he'd stick around.

Ryder wasn't going anywhere.

She looked at the clock and frowned. She didn't need to solve her boy problems tonight. She had only a few more hours until she'd be up and seeing the other man in her life, who would undoubtedly try playing matchmaker again tomorrow. What she really needed to be working on was her poker face for when she tried telling him she still wasn't interested in finding anyone right now.

Across town, another woman was crying herself to sleep alone in a room with no words, no lights, and no sign of escape, wondering why this was happening to her.

TWENTY-SIX
-Lillian-

"Morning Harvey," Lillian said through the open window as he met her at her car with breakfast for her and her dad.

"Running a little late this morning. Have a late night celebrating?" he joked, knowing she went out about as much as he did.

"Maybe I did," she teased right back.

"Well lucky for you, you always order the same thing for your dad, so it's already ready to go and you don't need to come inside to wait on me since *you're* running so far behind."

"I'm only a little late… and why don't you want me to come inside?" she asked, impulsively looking toward the back entrance. "What's happening in there?"

"Nothing to worry about, boss," he smiled. "It's just a full house. People are in, excited about the new ownership."

"They're excited?" she asked, surprised.

"Why shouldn't they be? You're a home-grown local, daughter of the great Sheriff Bill, and you have only ever shown love for her. People are happy that it's one of them that's keeping her going instead of me closing down or selling out."

"I admit I was a little worried they'd have words to say to you about passing her to me, not keeping the place 'til the end, or not giving someone else a run before making our deal pretty much in secret."

"There will always be those that disagree with the decisions people make. One thing you have to remember is that a person's decisions are theirs alone and as long as they think them through and feel confident in their course, considering and weighing the options and costs, then who is someone else to have a say? We had our decisions to make, and I feel confident in mine. Do you in yours?" When she nodded that she did, he continued. "Then don't worry yourself with those that want to cause strife. They need to work out their own issues instead of trying to create them somewhere else."

"I know," she started, "but sometimes their voices are so loud, it's hard to ignore."

"You're worried about Rain's outburst?" he said, the surprise evident in his voice, but shook his head. "She's on a path that she needs to figure out, and hopefully, one day, she'll come to her senses and grow up, but for now, there's no sense in worrying about her uninformed antics. There's nothing but support for our choices inside those walls."

She looked back at the building. *Her* building.

"Do you think they need me to help out today? I don't really have plans and should probably make myself visible, don't you think?"

"Today is your day off. You may be the official boss, but I'm still your elder, and I say get out of here while you can. There's plenty of help in there, people are happy to see me in there cooking like they expect, and you will have plenty of years to be inside. Go have breakfast and enjoy your day off."

"You really are great, you know that, Harvey?"

"Of course, I do," he laughed. "Now go before you serve up cold breakfast."

He turned to head back inside.

"Oh! Hey, I almost forgot," she called after him and he turned back. "I have some ideas for a little redecorating."

"Okay," he smiled, "but I thought you said you wanted the transition to be like nothing happened… What changed your mind?"

"I realized that I want people to know where Wisteria came from and that I cherish that as much as this place. I wonder if you have any old pictures from the start, through the years, that sort of thing, so I can remind people that even though she may not be in your hands anymore, you'll always be her heart."

He smiled. "That's a real nice idea. I have plenty that we've saved through the years, already in albums and boxes. Come by the house anytime and pick out the ones you want."

"How about this afternoon? I'm open the rest of the day."

"I'll have them ready. Now get going before they come searching for me. My boss is going to fire me if I don't get back to work."

It felt good to have the support of her community, and that confidence boost carried her into the sheriff's station. She stopped at Jane's desk when the receptionist motioned her over.

"Good morning, Jane," she said, setting the containers she was carrying on the desk as Jane got up and came around to give her a hug.

"Oh sweetie!" Jane said, pulling back from the hug and squeezing Lillian's hands in her own. "Congratulations! Your dad was all smiles and we're all so proud of you."

"Thank you." She laughed as Jane hugged her again.

"Now, you go on back, I've kept you long enough. I'll make sure the sheriff gets in there."

Breakfast with her dad was relaxed and easy. He told her again how proud he was and how he'd been telling everyone about his daughter, the business owner.

"They're all probably tired of hearing about it by now," he admitted.

"How many people could you have told, Dad? It's only been public for a day."

"Word travels around here, you know that," he told her, pausing and watching her curiously. "Speaking of which, I heard you were at the Overlook last night."

He let the statement hang between them. She sipped her coffee and smiled.

"I was just having a celebratory dinner with a friend," she stated simply.

"A male friend?"

"As I'm sure you already know… yes."

"Anyone I know?"

She just smiled again and took another sip of coffee, just as their conversation was interrupted by a welcome knock on his closed door. Her dad rolled his eyes and mouthed, "Simon," which had her stifling a giggle at the memory of her dad telling her he always found an excuse to say hi when she was there.

"Come in," her dad called.

"Sorry to interrupt," Simon said and turned to Lillian. "Mornin' Lillian. Saw you on the news last night. You looked real good." His cheeks instantly flushed as he glanced from her to the sheriff and back again. "What I mean is you did real well in your interview. It was very professional… congratulations… on being the new owner," he finally finished.

"Thank you, Simon," she told him, "I'm pretty excited to officially take over. You'll have to come in soon, see some of the updates I'm working on."

"That'd be great," he beamed.

"Was there something you needed?" her dad asked him.

"Oh, yes sir. Um, we've got a couple kids out here reporting some friends missing. Went hiking last night but never came back to camp."

"I'll get out of here so you guys can get to work," Lillian said, starting to stand and clear away the mess so they could focus on finding the hikers.

"Oh… well, actually, I kind of wanted to talk to *you* about it," Simon said uncertainly.

"Me?" Lillian asked, surprised, wondering why he'd want to talk to her about some kids.

"What's up, Simon?" the sheriff asked.

"Well, one of the kids is a tourist—he's actually one from the group down at the Bend. You know, the ones that discovered Wade's body?" he said to the sheriff and Lillian's stomach dropped. She knew where this was going. "But the other one's a local. Female," he said and turned to Lillian, who'd sat back down.

"Rain," she stated, and Simon nodded.

"Yes, that's what they called her. The guys said she works at Wisteria. They're out there now, and you're here, so I thought I'd check with you while you're here, see if you've heard from her?"

She sighed. "No, and I'm the last person she'd probably contact anyway. She actually quit in a fit a few days ago. She was pretty mad at me," she told them, quickly explaining the disagreement and the ridiculous accusation Rain had made. "Obviously that is *not* true, but then with the news yesterday, it would've probably just made her angrier. I'm sorry, but I probably won't be much help in finding her."

"The boys did mention that she was pretty fired up about you after they saw the news. They went back to their camp, and then she talked one of the guys into taking her out to the Mountain."

"Wait, why would they go to the Mountain?" she asked. "Rain never really struck me as the hiking type, and... The Mountain? You're sure?"

"Yeah, that's what they said," he told her, looking at the sheriff, who hadn't asked anything yet, so he kept going. "I guess they—the two that are out there now." He pointed back over his shoulder. "They were tired of her hanging around, and after she threw a fit about seeing you on the TV, they were gonna get rid of her anyway. Have a boy's night with just the three of them since one was going to leave this morning."

"Which one?" the sheriff asked.

"Oh." He paused to check his notes. "Evan. He said after everything that had happened on this trip, you had cleared him to leave, and he just wanted to get home."

The sheriff nodded.

"So, they were going to send her home, and she must have realized they were about to ditch her. Brian—that's the one that's missing—came here wanting to go to the Mountain. The others said he was really gung-ho about it. Said he'd done a bunch of research before they came. You know, all the usual conspiracy theory stuff that brings the tourists, and Rain knew he didn't want to leave here without trying. They thought she just wanted to get her way and convinced him to take her so she wouldn't be sent home. Jack, the third boy, said that he warned Brian that it wasn't a good idea, but Brian figured they wouldn't really go hiking and he'd get lucky out there instead." Simon's cheeks reddened slightly, and he glanced at Lillian. "Sorry," he said, holding up the device with his notes, "that's what they said." He glanced back at the sheriff, who motioned for him to keep going. "Um, so when Brian didn't come back to camp last night, they thought—well—that things went the way he wanted, and they assumed maybe they went back to her place, but then he never showed up this morning... so now they're here."

He finished his report and looked at the sheriff.

"Has anyone checked at her house yet?" he asked Simon.

"No, sir, they don't know where she lives."

Both men looked at Lillian.

"I don't know where she lives either, but I'm sure it's in her personnel file."

"Or if you have her last name, we can look her up," Simon suggested, nodding at the computer.

"Oh, right. It's Storm," she told them.

"Her parents named her Rain Storm?" her dad asked, incredulous.

"No," she chuckled at their combined horrified expressions, "sorry. Her real name is Jennifer. She just calls herself Rain, probably because she thinks it sounds cooler with her last name."

Her dad typed the information into the computer, wrote down a phone number and address, and handed it over to Simon.

"Tell the boys to stick around town a little longer in case we need to talk to them again. It'd be good if they got back to camp in case the kids show up. I know Evan's been through a lot and wants to get going, but with this development, I need him to stay," Bill told Simon, who nodded that he understood. "Get over there and see if anyone is at that address, or see if anyone saw anything. There's a good chance these kids just shacked up for the night, and it's still early. They're probably just sleeping it off and have no idea anyone's even looking for them. Let's not get ahead of ourselves too quick until we check on the house."

"I'll get right on it," Simon said, and turned to relay the information and do his job.

"What is it?" her dad asked after Simon left.

"I'm just wondering... what if they *are* lost out there? What if time's being wasted not getting out there immediately?"

"We need to verify that they aren't somewhere local or just at home, before we arrange for a manhunt in the forest, where we don't even know where they entered. It's a big area, and we could be looking for hours in the wrong spot."

She nodded.

"Lillian, you always get this little wrinkle right between your eyebrows when you're upset and worried about something. What else is there?"

She remembered the conversation with Ryder about Wade's death and the possibility of it being a murder, but she wasn't sure if he really should have shared that information with her and if it would get him in trouble to bring it up with her dad, but with Rain missing...

"Lillian," he gently nudged.

She sighed. "I'm just worried..." But he waited, and she knew that he knew she was holding back and wouldn't let her off without telling him what was bothering her. "Ryder had a theory," she started, but once she'd decided to start, all the words came tumbling out, "and he only told me because I pushed him and he said it wasn't an active investigation so it was okay to share with me, and I'm only bringing it up because they're both missing and I don't want him to get in trouble for saying something he shouldn't have... but do you think there could be a murderer in the woods?"

Bill breathed in deep and slowly let it out. "First off, Ryder isn't going to get in trouble for doing his job and thinking about all the angles. He's an officer. That's what he's supposed to do. However, I don't think Wade or our other unidentified body were murdered. I can't go into all the details, but it sounds like you know some things already, and I can tell you that we have to look into all possible scenarios when we investigate a death. These two so far were deemed natural and accidental. The only sort of connection between the two is that they originated in the area of the Mountain. I have no way of knowing if they were actually behind restricted lines or not, but no, I don't think they were murdered."

"But the weird things with Wade's house?"

"Can all be explained logically. Sweetie, the man's best friend died. Ryder wants it to make sense, and a young person dying young never makes sense. I don't want you to worry about a murderer running around these parts. I just don't see the signs."

"Unless the murderer is cunning and is making it look natural. I've heard more about the Mountain these past few weeks and two deaths linked to it… Doesn't that concern you?"

"Of course it does, but you know as well as I do that there's always talk about the Mountain. There's always a segment in a travel show, or a piece on the conspiracy theory sites. The news pulled Wisteria and the Mountain together for your announcement. Anything they can do to keep throwing out the bait and hooking people in. It's publicity, and unfortunately that means that we get a lot more thrill seekers and a lot more accidents to clean up.

"I hate it, but it's as simple as that. Most of the people that we bring down from there aren't from here. It's dangerous and our people know it, but these outsiders think they're invincible and wind up getting hurt. Do they make poor decisions that sometimes cost them their lives? Yes, and it's tragic, but that doesn't mean that there's a murderer hiding out up there.

"I don't want you to be worried about this," he said. "We're probably going to find the two of them back at her place, or they'll turn up at the campsite, confused about why everyone's making a big deal out of it. It happens all the time. But if they don't show up pretty quickly, we'll start our search with the most likely access points. We'll get a group together, those that know the woods, and start looking."

"I hope they're not hurt out there," she worried. "I know Rain and I didn't see eye to eye on a lot, but I don't want her hurt."

"We'll find them," he promised.

TWENTY-SEVEN

-Lillian-

The possibility of Rain going missing was upsetting, and immediately she wanted to reach out to August for his hiking expertise. At least, that's what she kept trying to convince herself she wanted to talk to him about. He'd been on her mind since the moment she saw him on the street… then their lunch date… and then dinner. She couldn't stop thinking about him. This would give her an excuse to call him.

Stop it, she scolded herself as she ran around town marking off her errand list. *For one, using Rain's misfortune as an excuse to talk to August is terrible and will probably bring bad luck. Second, you don't need an excuse to call him, just call him. Third, actually… maybe don't call him. You don't want to scare him off. Just because you can't stop replaying your time with him on a loop doesn't mean he's doing the same, and you don't want to look too needy. Right?*

"Ugh," she sighed, realizing she was being ridiculous. She forced thoughts of August out of her mind, at least for a little while. She'd marked off every item on her list except for the one she'd saved for last, the meeting with Harvey to pick out pictures.

"Thank you for doing this on such short notice," she told him as he let her into his home.

"It's no problem. Helen loved photos and insisted on keeping all these albums," he told her, smiling nostalgically at the three large albums before them. "These are the earliest," he said, opening the books to pages of black and white images all lined up and neatly organized.

She flipped through a few of the pages. "These are great. I'd like to get a few through the years, the different stages, if you don't mind me making some copies."

"I pulled some out for you already," he said, handing them to her one by one, explaining each as he did. "This is the very first space, back when it was still just 'Harvey's.' I served hamburgers and hotdogs out the window. On a nice day, I'd stick some chairs out front in the gravel, but mostly people walked up, got their food, and walked off. It was simple. I was seventeen when I opened it up and did it to spite my parents."

He laughed at his memories from a lifetime ago.

"After about two years working in what felt like a closet, I had enough saved up to put a deposit down on a place just off the main strip, which isn't where it is now, mind you. That all shifted later, talk about luck there." He showed her the second location that had enough room inside for a few tables and an open grill. "This was where my life changed," he smiled at the next one he handed her, showing a very young Harvey with an equally young woman standing next to him. "She came in looking for work. She was new to the area; her family moved here for the Mountain, but she didn't want to live there, so instead of staying on base, she moved into town and needed to find work. I wasn't looking for help. I had things running just fine without figuring out how to pay someone wages. But I took one look at her, and I knew I couldn't let her leave. I hired her that day, and we got married a year later."

"You two look so young." She smiled, staring at the happy couple.

"We were. This was taken right after she started working with me. I would have been, oh, right at twenty."

"I'm so used to hearing stories about the Mountain being this mysterious place that nobody is allowed to go, that I sometimes forget that it used to be a military base."

"Mmhmm, but even back then, there were stories. Nobody in town really knew what they were doing up there, or why they chose such a difficult location for the base. You couldn't get in unless you were military. Even Helen, after she decided not to live with her parents up there, wasn't allowed to go back and visit them at their home. It was very secretive."

"So, she just never saw them again?" She didn't want to think about not being able to pop in and visit with her mom or bring her dad breakfast at the station.

"Oh no, her parents would come to town often. A lot of the men that were stationed there would come down regularly, too. Most of them made my place so busy on the weekends that we'd push the tables and chairs aside and it'd be standing room only. Those were the days that I was thankful for Helen walking in and demanding to be hired."

"The Mountain was just a regular military base then?" she asked, intrigued. For her, the Mountain was a place of mystery, her only knowledge from stories. For Harvey, it was a part of normal everyday life.

"Well, as regular as a top-secret military base could be. We knew not to ask what went on, and nobody would talk if you did. Honestly, I think most of them just wanted to be regular citizens when they were in town. They didn't want to think about whatever it was they were doing up there."

"You don't happen to have any pictures of the base, do you? I don't love the idea of tying Wisteria and the Mountain together all the time, but I've never seen pictures. I bet a lot of people haven't. It would be neat to be able to include some in the history."

"No. Like I said, not only could you not get onto the base itself, but the roads leading up were blocked at the bottom of the hill. All those trailhead lots that you can park at nowadays?" She nodded that she knew the ones close to that area. "Those were the lesser used access trails, not paved like the main road, but occasionally you'd see some jeep-like vehicles coming through. Those were manned with at least two armed guards, twenty-four hours a day, and the actual road in, the paved one that was the only way to get on or off the base officially, had a big double gate with fencing and patrolling guards always. You didn't get on the base. You definitely didn't get close enough for a picture. Honestly, I never even looked for one. It was just there. My whole life, the Mountain was off limits, unless you were to join up and be stationed there. Of course, that's what my dad wanted for me, but I didn't want to go in there and not have my life anymore. I didn't want to never be able to tell my family what I had done at work that day.

"Besides, the Mountain wasn't something you stumbled into as a new recruit. It was considered very prestigious to be chosen to be stationed there. If I had decided to join up, it was possible that I'd never get selected and would have to move away. Even though I was stubborn back then and started Harvey's to prove a point to my parents, the truth of it all was that I didn't want to move far away from them. If I could make it on my own, I could make the choice to stay close by." He sighed. "So many of my friends wanted to get out of the small town, but this was home. I didn't want to go. It took many, many years for my dad to tell me he was proud of what I built following my own path." He shook his head. "Sorry. I'm rambling. Us old guys tend to do that," he joked.

He handed her another photo, this one of Harvey, Helen, and another man standing in the middle of a field, all of them spread wide from each other, arms outstretched as if reaching for one another but not quite making it.

"And this here, is Wisteria as you know it."

"Not exactly," she laughed at the trio in the empty field, off of what appeared to be a gravel drive where the photographer was standing. "What is this?"

"This is where you work, back before anything was there. This guy here, Gus," he smiled and tapped the third person in the image. "He sure had a mind for real estate. He worked up on the Mountain, but never seemed to fit. There was something different about him than the others that came into town. He started using his wages to buy up properties around town, some of the weirdest places too, far out, kind of obscure if you ask me, but it was cheap because of how far out they were. I remember him saying, 'Just wait, the town's going to shift.' He used to tell me to look at how the town was layed out, to imagine it without the base, and how the structure would change if the base wasn't around. Of course, I thought he was crazy most of the time. The base had been there forever. It wasn't going anywhere. Somehow, though, I let him talk me into taking my savings and buying three empty lots along some dusty gravel road. He bought several himself." He smiled at the memory. "I'm sure we made someone's day buying it all up. He was just *sure* the town center would shift, and we'd be in on the ground floor. 'Trust me,' he'd say."

"Gus sounds savvy," she mused.

Harvey chuckled, and Lillian got the feeling she'd missed a joke.

"What?" she asked when he didn't share.

"He hated that name." Harvey chuckled again. "But he definitely had a knack." He turned to her. "He was savvy for sure." He smiled at the photo of the three of them together. "He showed up in Juniper Hollow for the base, of course, coming to town from time to time like the rest of them. He'd come into Harvey's, and we just hit it off. He was a bit older than me, but we were instant friends. I'd only been open about a year at the new location, but business had been good, so when he said we had to buy the lots, it just felt right. I had the money and we desperately needed the space.

"Helen was nervous the whole time, worried we were making a big mistake moving Harvey's farther from the strip, but we did it anyway. I have to admit I was a little nervous for the expansion. It meant a lot more financial responsibility. We were young, newly married, wanted to start a family… But the location? The location didn't bother me. The town wasn't that big, and even though the new spot was on the outskirts, Harvey's already had so much business, I knew people would drive wherever we decided to put it."

He tapped the man in the picture again. "He was right there with us, 'to invest in our future,' he had said. I knew he wanted out of the military. He never really seemed the type to want that life, almost like he was there for something else, but every time I tried to talk to him about it, he'd always get quiet and would say not to talk about it or even go near it." Harvey stared at the photo for a moment. Whatever memory he'd brought forth pained his eyes and furrowed his brow. "The very last time I saw him, he came to me, acting real strange. He asked me to hold onto his property deeds for him and gave me the name of an attorney. He told me that if he didn't get back, then I was to take the packet to his attorney. I told him he was freaking me out and asked him what had happened. He said that he couldn't say, but that, 'they had meddled in something they shouldn't have,' and told me to stay away from the Mountain. 'It'll only ruin anyone that goes in.'"

"That's really strange, what did he mean by that?"

"Don't know. He wouldn't say anything more."

"That was the last time you saw him? Did you ever try to find him, to ask him?" she asked, curious to know what he'd meant, why he'd be so cryptic with his friend. "What happened to him?" Lillian whispered when Harvey just stared at the only picture he had of his friend from so long ago.

Harvey shook his head, eyes still focused on the past. "He died."

"Oh." She breathed out the word. "I'm sorry, Harvey. What happened?"

He didn't answer right away, and she didn't want to push. He looked back at the photos in front of them and took the next one off his pile, showing her the framework of her Wisteria being built, and the next of Harvey and Helen standing in front of the finished space, with the new name above the door.

"Construction had started for the new place pretty quick after we bought the land, and it was almost ready to open when he died, but he never got to see the finished place," he finally continued. "He was on the base that day. It was just another day, middle of the week, middle of the day. There was nothing special about it, no bad weather, no ominous date like Friday the thirteenth, nothing special at all about the day the Mountain exploded."

Lillian's shocked inhale didn't faze Harvey. She had never known what had happened, why it had closed without warning.

"Everyone was going about their day, because it was just another day, and then, all of the sudden, there was the loudest blast I'd ever heard. It shook the buildings, the very ground we walked on. It was so loud and strange. It rumbled for so long. It was hard to even comprehend. Nobody understood what had happened, everyone panicked. Had the base been bombed? Was the town under attack? Or maybe we'd had an earthquake? We'd never had an earthquake before, but people were considering all sorts of things for explanation. Businesses' windows were blown out on the edge of town closest to the road leading up to the Mountain. We couldn't tell what had happened up there, but it quickly became evident that something *had* happened at the Mountain ... But there was no fire, no smoke billowing into the sky, no people bailing from the trees. There was nothing. It was like the base never even existed." He paused to remember the day. "No bodies were ever retrieved," he said quietly.

"None? How's that possible? Helen's parents?" she asked, her heart aching for Helen, realizing her parents probably would have been at the base.

"Not a single one," Harvey said sadly. "It was nearly impossible to get up there, the road from the base was destroyed, spreading down into the town like someone had pulled a string and let the seam unravel. The gate was mangled and bent in a way that didn't seem possible." His tone shifted to one of awe and fear. "I remember when they brought the pieces through town. Sturdy, reinforced steel gates designed to keep heavy machinery out were curled up like when Helen would use her scissors to slide along that plastic curling ribbon stuff to make bows for presents. When those were brought through town..." He gave a slight shudder and shook his head. "I can still feel the tingle at the back of my neck. I didn't know metal could bend like that, at least not in an afternoon." He shook his head again. "Anyway, anyone who was able to make it up there—and the lord knows plenty of search parties were sent out—none of them ever returned."

"I don't understand. How could nobody come back out? How's that possible?"

"Nobody knows. There should have been *someone*, even just one person, to tell us what was happening, but nobody who went in to search came back out—not alive anyway. People got scared. People stopped volunteering for what only appeared to be death missions. They stopped sending search parties. Everyone worried about being bombed, radioactive leaks or... well... we didn't know *what* to worry about. All anyone knew was there was no explanation for the deaths and disappearances. None of us civilians knew what went on in there, after all, so nobody knew what to worry about. Naturally stories started.

"With the base gone, the traffic that was constantly coming and going was gone. The road wasn't worth repairing because it didn't lead anywhere anymore. Over time, the lesser gated entrances—also destroyed from the event—were torn down and became parking lots, and the lower grounds became managed by the conservation department and were converted for hiking.

"Just like Gus had predicted, the part of the town that had led to the base sort of died away like a bad dream nobody wanted to think about. The town shifted, and what you know as the main center of town today started to grow and flourish. I saw him for the last time the night before the explosion. He'd left his packet for the attorney, as if he knew something was about to happen, and when it did, I knew he wasn't coming back. Still, I waited for weeks for him to turn up, but no bodies were being retrieved, no survivors were coming out of those trees… I knew he was gone. I delivered his packet to the attorney, and I guess they took care of everything from there. I don't know that he had any family to leave it to, aside from his girlfriend, but we never saw her again either, which really devastated Helen because the two of them were like sisters, and to lose her parents in the same day… it was really hard on her."

He paused in his storytelling, and Lillian let him remember, not wanting to break his reverie. He looked up at her then, as if realizing she was still there.

"She was the one that named Wisteria. Did you know that?" he asked, and she shook her head that she didn't. "Wisteria, the flower, is said to symbolize long life as well as immortality. With so many lives cut short in a single day, Helen needed something to be able to honor them in her own way, and what better way than to name our place for them? Her parents, our friends, and all the other lives on the Mountain would live on forever through Wisteria."

"That's beautiful," Lillian finally said, speaking softly. "I had no idea the meaning behind the name… or the tragedy. You all lost so much that day."

"We did, but we also gained so much as well. We had a newfound appreciation for life. We poured our hearts into Wisteria and watched it grow. Our investments in the land that seemed scary at the time wound up being extremely profitable, to say the least, which allowed us to do all the things in life we wanted up until the day Helen died. We lived our lives to the fullest, and I'm so thankful to have all the memories I have. Just like I knew Helen was the one for me when she walked into my life, we knew you'd be the one to carry on our dream when you walked into ours. You'll keep Wisteria and all she stands for alive for years to come, and when the time is right to pass her along, you'll know."

"I hope that's a very long time from now," she told him, looking at the books of memories in front of them.

"Why don't you take these albums with you to look through? You might find some others that you like better than the ones I selected. I didn't mean to tell you all that I did and take up your afternoon with the ramblings of an old man."

"I'm glad you did," she told him honestly. "I never knew. Thank you for sharing your story with me." She could tell that their time together had taken its toll on him, and he looked tired. "Are you sure you don't mind if I borrow these?"

"Not at all," he said, delicately placing them into a box to carry out to her car. "Find the ones you want for the restaurant. If you need any information, I'm sure I have a story for you," he chuckled.

"Thank you again, Harvey, for all of this. I can't wait to share a bit of her history."

She hugged him goodbye and drove straight home, eager to get her project underway.

TWENTY-EIGHT

The metal screeched from across the room, but no other sound followed. No food plate scraped against the floor, and she didn't move to race over. She turned her head in the direction of the sound, still unable to see anything in the dark, wondering if it really was as dark as she thought or if she had somehow lost her vision and just hadn't realized it.

Nothing happened where the sound had come from, so she turned her head back toward the ceiling. She was laying on her back, imagining staring up at clouds brewing in the sky above her. She must have imagined the sound of the metal door as well.

"Not much longer," she heard the faintest hint of a whisper in her imagination.

"Okay," she whispered back, her words barely a breath so she wouldn't disturb the dream.

The scrape of the plate sliding through, and the screech of the metal shutting had her turning her head back toward the door.

"Shhh," she whispered and turned back to watch the clouds turn gray and start to rain, her own tears sliding down and pattering on the ground beside her.

TWENTY-NINE

-Bill-

"Still no word from our missing hikers?" Bill asked Simon later in the afternoon.

"Nothing, sir. I contacted her parents, who admitted to a rough relationship. They said they hadn't heard from her for nearly a week." Simon shook his head in disappointment. "They didn't even know she'd quit her job." He sighed, continuing the report. "The boys confirmed that she'd been staying with them at their campsite for the same amount of time. Sounds like she does whatever she wants and doesn't care to let anyone know. Her car is still out at the site, but neither Brian nor Rain have showed back up. I've got bulletins out to find Brian's truck."

"Good job. Thank you, Simon." Bill exhaled, picking up a pen from his desk and twisting it in his fingers before turning his chair in the direction of the map he kept on his wall. "I guess it's safe to say we're going to need to get some hikers together to form a search party. Call in anyone who's able. Civilians, too. They've already been out there twenty-four hours, so we're going to need all the help we can get. Hopefully the truck will turn up before we're fully assembled so we have a starting point, but we need to get a rush on this."

"Yes, sir, I'll get the word out right away."

"Simon?"

"Yes?" he said, stopping and turning just outside the office.

"Don't alert my daughter yet."

"You said you'd keep her updated…"

"There's nothing to update her about yet that won't cause her worry, and I don't want her out in those woods. It's dangerous, and I'll only worry about her getting hurt. Please, as a favor to me. Keep this to just our search and rescue contacts for now."

"Yes, sir, but I think you need to let her know."

"Let's find that truck. If the kids don't show up by dark, I'll let her know."

Lillian

After getting home and looking through the albums, Lillian was eager to see how the pictures she'd chosen would enlarge. She ran back out to drop off the ones she had chosen so far and then headed to the library to see if she could find any old articles on either Wisteria or the Mountain.

She hadn't wanted to link the two during the recent news segment, but they were more intertwined through history than she had realized. As the reporter, and then Harvey, had pointed out, they were both integral parts of the town. She hoped the library would have information on the base, maybe even a picture.

Bill

Bill looked up at the knock on his open door.

"They found the truck," Simon told him excitedly. "It was reported as left overnight at one of the trailheads."

"Show me," Bill said, leading Simon out of his office to the oversized, more detailed map of the area posted on the wall.

Simon searched the map on his phone and then showed Bill on the large copy that he preferred. Bill nodded.

"Bring Ryder to me," he said, still studying the map.

Simon hurried off to find Ryder, and the two of them quickly returned.

"Simon says the truck's been found," Ryder said when he approached.

Bill pointed to the map. Ryder studied the area.

"I want you to call in that hiker," Bill said to the map.

"August?" Ryder asked. "You think he's linked to this?"

Bill noted the slight surprise in his deputy's voice and that he toned it down to a more casually neutral tone when he asked about August being a suspect.

"I'm not thinking anything yet…" Bill trailed off. "One dead body in this exact area, and now two missing kids a week later. We need someone who's been through there and we already know he has. At the very least we'll use him as our guide."

Bill stopped talking, still studying the map.

"Sir?" Ryder asked.

Bill turned to see Ryder waiting for what wasn't said.

"If worse comes to worst and we find those kids out there under questionable circumstances, then we'll have him close at hand already for any questions."

Ryder nodded that he understood and went to call August.

Bill turned to Simon, who was still waiting. "Do you have a team assembled?"

"Yes, sir. We're ready and some are already en route."

"Good. Let's get going. We don't want to waste anymore daylight."

They searched in pairs until it was too dark. They called it a night and planned to reconvene at first light. Bill called his daughter on his way home, but voicemail picked up. The news that someone was officially missing shouldn't be left in a voicemail. He told her to call him first thing in the morning.

He didn't want her to find out through someone else that he hadn't kept his promise.

THIRTY

-Lillian-

She woke before her alarm, hoping she had a few more hours to sleep, but seeing that it was only a few minutes, she rolled out of bed and started her morning routine. She was halfway through her shower, finally awake enough to realize that she'd seen a voicemail notice on her phone. She got out, toweled off, and threw on a thick, warm robe before listening to her dad's voicemail asking her to call him back when she got the message. He sounded tired and sad. She could put two and two together; they hadn't found the hikers.

She pressed talk. She didn't have to worry he'd still be asleep. Always the early riser, he answered on the second ring.

"I got your message. I can't believe I didn't check in before bed. I got so busy that it completely slipped my mind," she said. "I'm guessing you guys didn't find them?"

"Not yet. We're meeting back out there this morning; I'm heading there now."

"I'll come too. I can move some stuff around, switch shifts to work later."

She set the clothes she'd chosen for work aside to find more appropriate hiking attire.

"No," he stated firmly.

"Dad, I can help."

She rummaged through her socks to find a thick wooly pair that would keep her warm. She'd probably regret the choice later, but the mornings were still cool, and it was supposed to drizzle on and off all day. She'd want warm feet out there.

"I know you can, but I don't want you out there."

"But she's only out there because of me."

She went to her closet and pulled out a light, waterproof jacket and her boots.

"That's nonsense, and you know it. She's out there because of her own decisions."

"Yes, but she was angry with me. I don't know why she was so mad at me in the first place, but she was, and then it got rubbed in her face on the news, which just made her angrier and she acted out. She wouldn't have pushed to go if she was happy."

"But that's not your fault."

"I feel responsible though," she told him, "and I want to help find her."

"I know you do, but how do you think I'd feel if you got hurt out there looking for her? This isn't your job. Let me take care of this."

She was silent, dissatisfied, but she knew he was right. She sat on the edge of her bed, staring at the hiking clothes she'd already assembled.

"If you don't want me in there, at least let me help somehow out here," she suggested instead.

"I'm sure Jane can use help with the phones," he told her. "We've had a lot of people calling already, offering to help search. Word travels, you know. She's having a hard time keeping up. Call over to the office and see what she wants you to do, but I don't want you in the woods. Do you hear me?"

"Yes, I hear you," she said, feeling like a little kid all over again. "But Dad… please be careful."

"Don't worry, I will."

She hung up and glared at her hiking boots. She was *capable* when it came to hiking, but that didn't mean she'd be able to help with a search. She picked up the boots and jacket to return them to her closet and called the private line at the station. Jane answered immediately. Her sigh felt like she'd reached through the phone and hugged Lillian tight at the offer of help. She promised to send over a packet with instructions and would temporarily forward one of the lines to Wisteria. Lillian agreed and headed to work early to inform the rest of the crew.

"Morning Boss," Lana greeted her with a hug when she came into the building. "I'm glad it's you who took over instead of an outsider."

Lillian laughed, confused for a moment. "Sorry, my mind's in another place. Thank you," she told her sincerely, "but I need you to gather everyone back here for a quick meeting if you don't mind."

"Already dolling out the orders," Lana joked, but headed to round up the rest of the crew.

When everyone had gathered in the breakroom, she told them the news about Rain and Brian being missing.

"I'm sure some of you may have heard some things through the grapevine already." Several of the kitchen workers and Gary nodded. "I really don't have much to share, but as of this morning, they've been gone for about thirty-six hours. The police don't know exactly where they went, but they were able to find Brian's truck yesterday. I was told that they've been searching in that area. I've volunteered to answer calls here, most of which will likely be offering tips or volunteering for the search. I'll keep a notepad by the phone, and we'll relay the information back to Jane at the station. An officer will be bringing information to share with the search parties, and there's a good chance that we'll have several people in here today looking for ways to help. Hopefully, we can help get these two found."

She was sending everyone back out to work when Ryder knocked and quickly entered from the back entrance.

"Hey," he smiled. "Jane sent me. I've got supplies for your volunteer station."

"I'm surprised you're not out there already." She led the way into her office.

"Your call came through right as I was checking in. I told her I'd run the stuff over to you on my way out there. Thanks for volunteering. Jane's over the moon to have the help… And congratulations, by the way. I saw you on the news. You were great."

"Thank you, and for the flowers as well."

"No problem. I wanted to tell you in person, but you must have been out celebrating," he said, a hint of curiosity ringing through his words.

"They were really beautiful." She smiled, ignoring his unspoken question. "Did Jane send locations? What am I supposed to tell people who call?"

"Right," he said, remembering why he was there. He set the duffle he'd brought on one of the chairs and pulled out a stack of fliers. "These are for anyone who comes in wanting to help pass them out or just needs to know what they look like to help in the search," he said handing over the pile of papers with pictures of Rain and Brian. "And these," he handed her a second stack, "are trail maps closest to where we found Brian's truck, with instructions and contact numbers to call if they get turned around or if they find something."

She looked over the map that had markings on it already, as well as instructions that nobody was to go into the woods without a partner, a pack containing water, energy bars, first aid basics, a compass or other navigational device, a flashlight, flare, and some sort of communication device.

"This seems like a lot to bring on a search," she said reading through the list.

"We can't have them getting lost or hurt themselves, but if they do, or if they find our hikers, any of this will come in necessary. We have a bunch of premade packs since most people won't have this all on hand, and I have a few to leave behind here. If you run out, just send them on out anyway. They have to check in with an officer before they go into the woods, and we have someone at all these areas," he pointed to several marks on the map indicating check-in zones, "and each of them has additional packs as well."

"You guys are efficient," she said, impressed.

"There are protocols in place that we hope we never have to use, but in the unfortunate situations that we do need to use them, it helps to be prepared."

At the sound of a knock, they both turned toward the open door, where Gary was standing.

"There's someone out front asking for you."

"I'll be right up," she told him, surprised that Jane had already sent someone her way.

"Oh, no, he's asking for Ryder," Gary said apologetically.

"Oh, it's my civilian partner. I told him to meet me here instead of the station since I was going to swing by here first and debrief you, that way he wasn't just waiting in the car for me the whole time. I parked in the back. Is it okay if he comes back and we'll just go out that way?"

"Definitely," she told him and turned to Gary. "Have him come on back. I think we've pretty much covered everything, right?"

"Yeah, without knowing where to search, just direct the hikers to each of the officer check-in points. We can sort them out when they get to us."

"Have you checked her RUSH page?" Gary interrupted, still standing in the doorway. "Or even his maybe? She showed me some stuff before she quit. Maybe they posted a picture or something before they went in that could help?"

"What's RUSH?" Ryder asked.

"Oh… it's apparently all the hype for outdoor extremist social media, which makes no sense to me, because if you're out there being extreme in nature or whatever, why do you care about your phone, but who am I to know?" Gary asked.

"Gary," Lillian interrupted. They didn't have the time for storytelling.

"Oh, right, right, sorry. You know me, get carried away sometimes." He breathed deeply and let it out as if mentally telling himself to reset. "Okay. RUSH is basically like any other social media app, but on steroids. It's limited to posting pictures or videos, but the requirement is that it has to be extreme, serious adrenaline junky type stuff. Those guys were all about it, according to Rain, and she opened an account just before she quit here. Maybe there's something on there that you all can… like, I don't know… GPS track or something?"

"That's good to know," Ryder said, making a note of it in his phone. "We haven't been able to track either of their phones yet, but there might be something there. Thank you for the tip."

Gary beamed. "I just hope it helps," he gushed. "I'll go get your friend."

Ryder turned back to her. "Your volunteer station is already working," he smiled. "Thank you again for doing this today."

"Well, since I'm not allowed to be out there on foot, at least I can be here helping still."

"Don't be hard on him. He just doesn't want you to get hurt," he told her softly, "and neither do I. It'll make both of us worry less knowing you're not in there. It's not safe," he whispered. There was so much concern in his voice that she couldn't even argue about being able to keep up or how chauvinistic they were both starting to sound.

"Don't worry," she sighed, resigned. "I'll do what I can out here, but you'll both be getting an earful later."

"I believe it," he told her, staring intently, "but I'd take a tongue lashing from you any day over knowing you got hurt when I could have prevented it." He leaned in and gently kissed her cheek. Leaning back, he smiled softly. "Thank you again for this; it really does help."

"You're welcome," she told him, trying not to react to his gentle touch. "Now go before they send a search party for you and your civilian hiker."

"I'm going, although I figured he'd be in here already. Where'd your guy go to get him anyway?"

They stepped out of the office and Lillian called Lana to send Gary back. He came through the kitchen door and headed back.

"Where's his partner?" Lillian asked, and Gary looked confused.

"What do you mean?" he asked them both.

"You said you were going to bring August back," Ryder told him.

"August?" Lillian asked, the surprise clearly audible.

"Yeah, my civilian hiking partner. Even though I still think he's an ass, there's no denying that he's the best around. We were paired up yesterday, and I swear that man could go in blindfolded, get turned around like it's his turn at a piñata, be given a broken compass, and still find his way out before the rest of us."

"I sent him back just a minute ago." Gary still looked confused. "I told him you were parked out back. Maybe he thought I meant to just go straight out? Oh, I knew I should have walked back here with him, I just didn't think he'd get lost. It's a straight shot."

"It's fine," Ryder told him, trying to stop Gary before he got too worked up. "I'm sure he's just waiting at the truck."

"I'm sorry," Gary said again.

"I'll be right up," Lillian said, dismissing him so he'd go back to the front. "Be careful out there, all of you," she told Ryder.

"Will do," he said, smiling confidently as he went out the back to find his hiking partner.

Lillian wondered at the pairing of Ryder and August. It was curious that August hadn't stopped in to say hi. Obviously, he knew it was her office, even if he hadn't been in it before, and the door was open, so he could clearly see she was inside if he had any doubts. Maybe he hadn't wanted Ryder to know that they knew each other socially and was just keeping whatever was happening between them private for now? She could appreciate that since Ryder would use all the ammunition he could gather to tell her how wrong it would be to date someone she knew so little about. But wasn't that the whole point of dating, to learn about a person? They didn't need to know that she and August already jumped ahead a few stages.

But still… why hadn't he said anything to Ryder that he was passing by, heading to the truck? He could see him just as well as he'd be able to see her.

The kiss. Realization hit as she was gathering the stacks of papers.

Had August seen Ryder kiss her cheek? It was just a small peck, nothing special… but *she* knew that Ryder wanted it to mean something; *she* knew he was working to prove himself to her. Would it have looked harmless to August? Could he have seen it and gotten upset? Should she call him and explain or send him a text? Or would that make it look like there was something to be upset about? And if she was worrying over something that wasn't even an issue, and he really was just trying to keep their business private, and she called him while he was sitting next to Ryder, what happened then?

She sighed, hating the no games rule that she was now second guessing and getting wrapped up in anyway.

She decided she wasn't going to play the game.

You didn't do anything wrong. If he saw something he didn't understand, then he should be straightforward and just ask.

She nodded to herself that she was satisfied with her decision… determined not to make an issue out of something that didn't need to be one.

THIRTY-ONE

-RYDER-

"I'm beginning to get the feeling that these kids just disappeared off the face of the earth." Ryder stopped to take a drink of water and checked where they were on the map.

"People don't just disappear," August said gruffly into the woods, waiting for his search partner to get moving again.

"Well, obviously," Ryder replied, staring at August's back. "Is everything okay? You've been quiet."

"I'm listening for sounds of people in distress. It's usually easier to hear if you're not talking."

"Yeah, well you seem like something's wrong."

August turned toward Ryder. "How would you know how I am when something's wrong?"

"I just mean you're quieter than you were yesterday, barely said two words on the ride over, and hardly anything at all while we've been out here. Isn't hiking your thing?"

August turned back to his search. "Yes, I like hiking. This isn't that. I don't enjoy searching for potential dead bodies of kids that had their whole lives ahead of them."

"There's still a chance they could be alive."

August turned to look at Ryder, still standing with his pack only on one shoulder, pulled forward so he could put the water bottle back in its holder.

"They've been missing, presumably out in these woods, for almost two days, probably without any sort of food, water, or shelter. The boy might have some general outdoor survival knowledge from what he and his friends were here to do in the first place, with the camping trip and all that, but the girl? From what I've gathered, she's just some townie that got fed up with her daily life and started hanging with these guys. She probably doesn't have the slightest idea how to survive without her cell phone, let alone in the wild for days. Do you really think we're going to find them cozied up in a tent somewhere? Because I don't. And forgive me if that makes me think about life and choices and how it's come to be that I'm out here looking for possibly two bodies when I already came across one not far from here. It's not the greatest feeling and doesn't make for a very happy and chatty hike." He turned back to the woods and started walking again. "Now, if you're done worrying about my feelings, maybe we can keep looking?"

Ryder repositioned his pack and trudged after August.

"Hey man, I know this isn't an ideal situation, but at least what you're doing is helping someone."

August sighed. "Not yet it isn't."

Ryder patted him on the shoulder. "Sure it is. You're helping me. I'd be walking in circles if it weren't for you…" he trailed off.

"What?" August said at Ryder's sudden stop. "Do you see something?" he asked, looking around for signs of people.

Ryder shook his head. "No, not that," he said, clearly thinking about something. "You said we're near where you found that other body."

"Yeah, it's just over that way," August said, pointing deeper into the woods.

Ryder fished around in his pack for his phone, pulling it out and hoping for a signal.

"Back at the restaurant, when I was dropping off the papers and packs with Lillian," he glanced up at August. "She's the owner that was in the office at the back." August nodded that he knew who she was, and Ryder continued. "One of her employees told me about this app that Rain told him about, so I went ahead and downloaded it to check her profile to see if there was anything we could use to find her." Ryder scrolled through her page, found the photo he was looking for, and turned the phone so August could see.

"What am I looking at?" August asked, his eyebrows knitted together.

"I guess they thought it would be funny to recreate the crime scene."

"That's just sick," August said, handing the phone back. "What kind of app is that?"

"Some sort of picture drop for adrenaline junkies or some shit. Pretty dumb, if you ask me, but I guess there's something out there for everyone. But this picture got me thinking. If these kids are into that sort of thing, maybe they came out here for another crime scene photo op."

"You think they hiked all the way out here, one of them definitely an amateur, just to pose in another crime scene picture?"

"Well, and the crime scene is right at the edge of the Mountain's boundaries, and we already know they wanted to go there by what the other two kids said in their statement. It's a two-in-one spot and makes perfect sense."

"Did she post a picture at the second site, or in the Mountain?"

"No," Ryder considered. "Maybe they got turned around in here and something happened… but I think you need to take me back to the site where we found the body the other day. Maybe there are clues."

"I guess it's better than wandering around aimlessly," August agreed and started off in the direction of the crime scene.

They walked in silence for a few minutes, searching for anything out of place, Ryder feeling more upbeat now that they had a destination and a plan.

"I feel real good about this. It makes sense. They've got to be over here," Ryder said, but August didn't reply. "Come on man, this is a possible break in the case. At least be a little less grumpy."

"There's still a chance we'll find them broken, just like the last one," August said sullenly.

"And there's a chance we find them lost and confused and *alive*," Ryder countered. "If we find them," he continued a few steps later, "I'm taking Lilly out to celebrate."

August's steps faltered, but he kept moving.

"Careful," Ryder told him, still in better spirits about the possibility of finding the missing hikers. "These rocks are pretty loose, watch your step."

"Wasn't paying attention, I guess," August told him, still leading the way.

"Don't go falling down this hill," Ryder joked. "I still need you to get me back out of here."

"To your celebratory date," August said with just a hint of bitterness in his voice, but Ryder was so amped on the possibility of finding the hikers that he didn't notice.

"Right! If I find Lilly's employee on a tip from one of her other employees, she'd have to agree to at least dinner. Wouldn't you think?"

"I thought you guys said Rain quit her job?"

"Eh, former employee… close enough. It'd still be an in with Lilly."

"So, you and Lilly are a thing?"

"Not really," Ryder admitted. "We have a history."

August nodded, but didn't ask further questions, changing course slightly to keep them on track.

"What about you?" Ryder asked.

"What *about* me?" August asked right back.

"Do you have a girl?"

"Oh," he said. "Not anymore, no."

"She didn't like hiking?" Ryder joked.

"Not exactly," August said, but didn't elaborate.

"Sorry, man. Sore subject?"

"I just don't want to talk about it."

"She did a number on you, huh?"

August stopped walking and turned to Ryder.

"We were engaged, and then she died. Okay? I thought maybe I'd try the dating thing again, but I just don't know anymore. I don't want to talk about it."

He turned and started his hike again.

"Hey," Ryder said, hurrying to catch up, slightly out of breath with the ascent and obstacles to climb over. "I'm sorry, I didn't know. That was a jerk move on my part."

"It's not something I really want to talk about."

"This coming from the same guy that told me talking about Wade would help," he said, holding his hands up in front of him when August looked his way. "I'm just saying, you're the one who told me it can help."

August stopped climbing again and took a drink of his water, sighing when he screwed the top back on.

"She went in without me... on a hike... whatever. They never found her body," he finally told Ryder. "We'd sort of had a fight... disagreement... It doesn't matter. I told her not to go, but she went anyway and without me knowing. She never came back out. We searched and searched and never found a trace... So you can see why I'm not particularly happy to be part of another search party. Why I can't get overly excited about a little tip that could maybe, possibly, hopefully lead to *these* hikers, because if we find them at all, dead or alive, it just reminds me that we didn't find *her*. And if we don't find them at all... well, it all just sort of opens that wound back up either way."

"So why do you do it?" Ryder asked him suddenly.

"You all didn't really give me a choice to be your guide."

"No, I mean, why do you still hike if it brings back such bad memories?"

"Because of all the good ones I have," he stated. He turned to lead the way again.

"See, that's why I need to make things right with Lilly. That history I told you about? It wasn't good. Things didn't end well, and I admit, I sort of dropped the ball on making things right, then years passed, and I still couldn't get her out of my head. The one that got away, you know? So now I'm trying to patch things up, but I can see the doubt all the time, that she doesn't think I've grown up. That was high school. It was years ago. If I can find Rain, I know it will help her see. All these deaths lately, and missing persons, it just makes life more real, sorta opens your eyes and makes you realize that it can be over any second, and you can't waste what time you have. You know what I mean?"

"Trust me, I do," August mused. "We're here," he said as they walked out of the trees to the pile of boulders at the base of a cliff, yellow tape still marking the area.

Nothing appeared to be out of place. They both called out for Rain and Brian, then waited, listening for responses. Nothing.

"Let's spread out and search the immediate area," Ryder suggested. "Don't go out of sight."

They searched the area but still didn't find anything, and met back at the rocks.

Ryder ran his hand through his hair, still looking around, but had lost the extra bounce to his step.

"How long did they search for your girl before they called it?" he finally asked.

"Two weeks," August stated bitterly. "They said they couldn't search anymore, that they couldn't dedicate anymore manpower to the search. There were other things to attend to, and while it was a tragedy, there was just no sign of her anywhere. There was nothing more to do."

Ryder studied him. "How long before you stopped?"

"Who says I did?"

Ryder nodded, knowing he'd never stop looking either if he'd been in August's place.

August looked around, walking over to one of the markers he'd placed to lead the cops in earlier.

"You know," he said, curiosity in his voice. "Their truck was parked a few miles away at a different trailhead. If they *did* decide to make their way over here to this site," he said, waving back to the yellow tape, "it would've taken them a while, especially if they got turned around. Let's say they did finally make it over here though… maybe they followed the markers out of here."

Ryder had come to join him, seeing the path marked away from them and remembering the hike back and forth.

"See, this is why you're on my team," Ryder said, slapping him on the back.

"I recall you not wanting to be paired with me," August laughed.

"Nah, I just don't like you, that's all," he said, upbeat again.

"Oh, well in that case…" August trailed off, chuckling.

"You're growing on me, Gus," Ryder called as he led the way this time.

"Yeah… no. Don't call me Gus. You can just go back to not liking me. Things are better that way."

THIRTY-TWO
-Lillian-

"How can we help?" Gran asked as soon as she saw Lillian, giving her a hug. "Clearly we aren't going to be able to go traipsing around in the woods to search, so put us to work in here."

Lillian led Gran and Pops to the few tables she'd pulled together with the Wisteria phone and a station cell phone that Jane had included for a second line, along with the few remaining hiking packs and the fliers.

"We could use help handing these out, answering phones, and directing people where to go," she explained. With a nod, they both took seats on the other side of the tables, making themselves at home. "With the amount of people stopping in to help or check for updates, we've been busier than ever. If you could help here, we can focus on serving and updating. Do you want anything to eat?"

"We're here to help, not eat," Gran said.

"But a coffee would be nice," Pops added, smiling wistfully.

"I've got it," Lillian's mom called from behind her, appearing instantly with two cups and the pot.

"Good to see you again, Liza." Gran reached over and squeezed Lillian's mom's hand.

"Did Jane send you?" Lillian asked them as her mom poured.

"It's all over town that you're using the restaurant as the official hub for the search," Gran told her.

"So, Jane's spreading the word," she laughed. "Good. I don't know much about *official*, but we're trying to help any way we can, and if this is it, then I'm glad word's getting out. I'm thankful for your help," she told them both appreciatively, "especially since I know Rain wasn't your favorite person around."

"You don't have to like a person to help them," Gran said, "but if you *can* help, you should. We can, so we will. Now you go get back to work and let us do this for you," she said, shooing Lillian away as the station's phone rang.

Ryder

Ryder and August exited the woods. Still no sign of Rain or Brian.

"I've updated the Sheriff," Ryder said as they made their way out to the parking lot. "He should be meeting us over here in a few minutes, so now's a good time for a break."

August found a place to sit and opened his pack for a drink and an energy bar.

"No luck for them either?" he asked, already knowing the answer.

"Nah," Ryder said, sitting near him and opening his pack as well. "I really thought we'd find them on the trail."

"I'm not done searching," August told him.

"Me neither," Ryder agreed. "However long it takes."

August looked up at him, nodding at his resolve. "I wish that was enough, but even then, we may not find them."

They heard the gravel crunching under approaching tires before they saw the Blazer and another truck approaching. The sheriff and Simon got out, along with their civilian hiking partners.

"We didn't find anything down near their truck," Bill said, "but I like your thought about this site. If they were messing around with the other crime scene, there's a possibility that they came down here."

"We didn't see anything," Ryder reminded him.

"No, but the dogs might," Bill said. "They seemed to have their scent and then it disappeared. Maybe out here they can find it."

"I'm up for anything that will find them," Ryder agreed. "What's up with him?" Ryder nodded back to Simon, who had stayed back at the Blazer.

"He wanted to keep searching where we lost the scent."

"So, why didn't you?" August asked. "Maybe they would have found it nearby."

Bill's eyebrows rose in surprise at the interruption. "We tried for a while. We didn't just leave the second they lost the trail."

"So, why's he back there pouting?" Ryder asked.

Bill sighed. "He wanted to go farther to see if we picked it up past where we lost it instead of backtracking like we did."

"That seems reasonable. Why didn't you?" August asked.

Bill looked hard at August. "There're a lot of things you may not know about this area," Bill started, "but from what we discussed before, I know you know that you're not supposed to go into restricted areas." August nodded, realizing why the dogs lost the scent and why Bill didn't want to go farther. "I know you young people like to throw caution to the wind and just ignore the rules, but that's restricted land, and if I want to go searching on it, I have to get a warrant."

Simon approached. "Yeah, and there's not a judge around that wouldn't approve a warrant to search for kids that could be missing in there."

Ryder's eyebrows rose in surprise. He'd never heard Simon disagree with the sheriff before.

"Simon," Bill sighed again. "I've already told you, they won't. I've been at this a long time, and no matter how hard I've tried, how many people I've tried to convince till I'm blue in the face, I can't get in there."

"Then just go. What if they're just over a hill, or right around a tree? We could be feet from them and not even know it, and you won't go in because there's a rule against it?"

"The scent ended at the boundary for the Mountain," Bill stated. "The dogs didn't even want to go in. You saw how skittish they got and led us away from the border. There's no sign they're even in there."

"I still think you need to say screw the rules and just go," Simon said.

"We're searching over here now," Bill told him sternly and walked off to debrief their civilian partners.

Simon scowled at the ground.

"Hey man," Ryder said, getting up and squeezing Simon's shoulder. "We're gonna find them. And I'm glad to see you're finally standing up for what you believe in instead of just doing as you're told, but you know it's not safe to go in there."

"Who are you to talk?" Simon said, shaking off his hand. "You think I don't stand up to the sheriff because I'm too afraid to? I haven't *needed* to stand up to him because I trust his judgment… but this is different. There are lives at stake, and we're just going to stand by and not look for them in there because a line on the map says we can't? It's wrong, and you know it. I thought you would back me up on this at least. That's why I agreed to come over here and meet instead of trying harder back there to get him to go in. I thought you'd say screw it and go in."

"Things change," Ryder exhaled. "Before, I would have said, 'Fuck it, let's get in there,' but the last two deaths we've worked came otta there. Plus, you know the stories."

"You, of all people, are scared off by stories?"

"It's not the stories themselves… more like warnings. It's dangerous. You saw the cliff August found that kid under. It's not safe. And how would the dogs do in there?" Ryder looked to August for help. "You already told us the other day that we weren't up for some of these hikes, and it only gets harder the farther we climb. The Mountain is worse which means we're definitely not equipped for that."

"From what I could see looking in, we'd need a lot more equipment," August said, trying to stay neutral in the heated discussion.

"Whatever." Simon scowled. "I've got to get them ready to go in."

He stalked away to prepare the dogs.

"I've never seen him this worked up about anything," Ryder commented to August, watching Simon take the clothes out of their baggies for the dogs to reacclimate themselves with the scent.

"These sorts of things can change people. Was he close with the girl?" August asked him.

"Not that I know of. She's too young and, from what I've heard, immature, but maybe that's his thing. Honestly, outside of deputy work, I don't know who he likes… well, aside from Lilly."

August turned to him, "The same one you're chasing?"

Ryder laughed. "Yeah, but she's oblivious. He's obvious about it, though. Every time he sees her, he's all smiles and goes to find her like a lost puppy."

August turned back to Simon, who currently looked serious and determined, not at all like a puppy.

"You might have some competition," August said.

"Nah, he's too… I dunno… *safe* for her."

"Maybe she deserves safe. Someone to look out for her."

"I'd look out for her," Ryder said seriously, "but I'd bring some excitement into her life. Simon would be boring. It would never work out."

"Hmm… maybe *she* should get to figure that out."

Ryder laughed. "I'm not worried about a little competition, especially not from Simon. Come on, looks like they might have something."

The dogs had started pulling against their harnesses and Simon called out for everyone to get moving.

"That's a good sign," Ryder commented, watching the dogs head the way they had already come. "Maybe we were right about them coming back this way."

"Only one way to find out," August agreed and shouldered his pack back on to follow the group.

THIRTY-THREE

-Lillian-

As the owner of the restaurant—so publicly announced the other day—and the head of the search center, Lillian had a very long day. She wasn't complaining, because they were busier than ever, but by the time the dinner rush had started to slow down, she'd been back and forth from sunup to nearly sundown, and she wanted nothing more than to call it a day.

"You know you don't have to stay here all day, right?" Harvey asked her when she took a seat next to him at the volunteer table.

She raised an eyebrow at him in a "that's-a-load-of-crap" expression. "You know as well as I do that I *do* need to be here." She sighed. "Rain was my, well, *our* employee before she quit. We just made this announcement about me taking over. How terrible would it look if I went home to relax while the police and volunteers were out scouting for her? That's not the image I want for myself, or Wisteria after I just officially took over." She shook her head. "No, I'm staying until they come in for the night or until they find her."

"At least sit here a little longer with me. You've got a good crew running right now. You don't have to do it all."

She smiled. "That I can do. My feet are killing me," she said as she lifted them under the table to rest on the chair opposite her. "It really means a lot to me that you're in here doing this," she told him. "It means a lot to the community, too, to see that you're still a part of things."

"Just because I've passed the torch doesn't mean I want the fire to stop burning," he said. "Did you get a chance to look through any of those albums?" he asked, changing the subject.

"A little. I took a few over to have enlarged and enhanced. When they get them ready, I'll see how they turned out and probably have you give me some more information about them so I can have a little tag with each so people can learn about our history."

"That sounds real nice," he smiled nostalgically at the thought.

At the sound of the jingling bell, they both turned toward the door. At the sight of an exhausted Ryder and an equally worn out sheriff, she and Harvey both stood and went around the table to meet them as they entered the building.

"What news?" Lillian asked them anxiously, noticing that several other heads had turned their way at the sight of the officers.

"We found Rain," Bill told her.

She looked from one to the other, and Ryder finally finished the sentence. "Alive."

There was a collective sigh through the diner at the news, followed by quick murmurs of excited conversation. She immediately hugged her dad, and then Ryder, since the moment called for it. His embrace lingered, his arms wrapping around her tightly but letting go just before it was noticeably too long.

"This is such great news!" she gushed. "But why didn't you call us? We've been wondering!"

"We came as fast as we could after seeing her safely off in the ambulance and meeting with her mother. Ryder insisted that news like this needed to be delivered in person, and I agree, he was right," Bill told his daughter, smiling at her beaming face.

"What about the boy?" Liza asked as she joined them. She handed a mug of coffee to her husband.

Ryder's smile faded. "He still hasn't turned up."

"Oh… I thought they'd be together," Lillian said. "So, will you go back out tomorrow?"

Her dad sipped the coffee, smiling in thanks to his wife, then nodded. "Yes. When we found Rain, our immediate goal was to get her out and to safety. Some of the others stayed behind to keep searching, but there's nothing so far. We'll be back out there at first light to keep looking."

"That's good." Lillian said. "We'll keep our search station going as well. It's been busy today, but it slowed down a little bit ago when it started getting dark. You guys need to get home and get some rest if you're starting first thing."

"As do you," Harvey interrupted. "You've not had a break all day. You need to go home and rest as well."

She looked around the restaurant. Her scheduled shift had ended hours ago, but she had still kept working.

"They'll be fine. You're not even supposed to close tonight anyway. Go home. I'll update everyone, wrap this up over here, and you can be back at it first thing in the morning. Go," Harvey told her sternly.

"He's right," her dad said, taking Harvey's side. "I'm sure he can handle things," he said, smiling at Harvey.

"Oh… well, I guess so," she said. She was suddenly at a loss for what to do with herself, but could feel her exhaustion from worrying all day about more than just Rain start to catch up with her.

"Come on, we'll walk you out," Ryder said, gently guiding her with a hand on the small of her back.

"Mom," she said, pausing to get her attention, "you should get going, too."

Liza looked around the diner. "Are you sure? I can help Harvey close up."

"No, Mom, go take care of Dad. You've helped so much today."

Liza folded the towel she'd been using to clear the counters. "If you're sure."

Lillian nodded and said her goodbyes out front. Bill, Liza, Ryder and Lillian headed back to the office so Lillian and Liza could gather their things so they could all leave out the back together. Liza retrieved her purse, but Lillian still had to shut down the computer and collect her things.

"You guys can go on ahead. I promise I'm leaving; I just have to shut some things down in here and get my stuff together," Lillian said.

She followed them to the back door, giving her mom a hug. "Thank you for everything today, Mom."

"Anytime, sweetie."

Her dad leaned over to give Lillian another hug and kissed the top of her head.

"Get some rest tonight, Dad," she told him. He looked tired, but she kept that to herself in front of his deputy.

"I'm just going to update her for tomorrow, then I'm off as well. I'll see you out there in the morning," Ryder said as the sheriff headed out to his Blazer.

"Both of you need to get rest," Bill said over his shoulder as he walked hand-in-hand with Liza to the truck. "It's another busy day tomorrow."

Ryder closed the outside door and followed Lillian into her office, closing her door as well.

"I really am leaving," she said, reaching over the desk to shut down the computer.

Ryder took a seat in one of the chairs, leaning his head back and closed his eyes.

"Take your time," he said, eyes still closed. "I'm just gonna make sure you do."

"Clearly," she said sarcastically, and he smiled toward the ceiling, hands resting on his stomach, legs stretched out in front of him. She knew he was tired. He'd spent all day searching through the woods, up and down the hills. It was physically exhausting, not to mention the mental toll of what they could potentially find out there. She was happy for their sake, and Rain's, that they had at least found one of the party alive. She hoped tomorrow would be just as successful.

As she gathered her things, she noticed that a package had been placed on top of her desk with a sticky note attached. *You were busy. Photo guy dropped this off, said to let him know if you need changes. – Lana*

She added it to her pile, eager to look through the images. She was surprised they were ready so fast, but they could wait until she got home. When she had everything shut down and gathered to go, she turned to let Ryder know she was ready and realized he had fallen asleep. His breathing was deep and his face relaxed. Despite the chair he was resting in, which had to be uncomfortable, he looked perfectly at peace. She'd never seen him like this before, so at ease and approachable. She didn't want to wake him. He was clearly drained if he fell asleep that fast in her chair, but obviously he couldn't stay there.

Still… she couldn't resist how peaceful he looked.

"Ryder," she whispered softly, trying not to startle him awake, but he made no indication that he'd heard her. She stepped closer. "Ryder, you need to wake up." She leaned over and whispered again, unable to resist reaching out and gently brushing a stray bit of hair off his forehead.

He reached up and took her hand, eyes still closed, and gently tugged her toward him. His other arm went around her as he guided her into his lap, a slow smile spreading over his face.

"You smell like a flower," he said sleepily.

"Ryder," she started to protest the seating arrangement, but he just held her a little tighter and snuggled in.

"Just a minute… please?" he asked. "It's sorta been a crappy day and all I wanted was to bring you good news."

He sounded so vulnerable, something she rarely heard in his voice, and he smelled of the outdoors. She felt safe and secure in his lap with his arms holding her close. She had to admit that it felt nice.

"I know my timing's been off with you," he finally spoke, tilting his head to look at her, his eyes back to their usual intensity, "and I know you don't know where to start with me," those penetrating eyes searched her own, "but can you answer one question to start?"

"I can try," she told him warily.

"I just want you to think about this moment right here, right now. Don't think about yesterday, tomorrow, years ago, or years from now. In this space, with me, right now, do you feel good?"

"There's more to it than just that," she began.

"I didn't ask you to think about the more," he said, still watching her closely. "Close your eyes," he told her and waited until she finally gave in on a sigh. "Stop thinking about today. Stop worrying about tomorrow. Stop fretting over everything you think you're supposed to consider in life. Just breathe deep and feel…" He leaned his head into the little dip where her shoulder met her chest, listening to her breaths and her heartbeat beneath his ear. "How do you feel right now?"

She liked the feel of him in her arms and resting against her, the sturdiness of his arm supporting her, and the heat spreading slowly where his other hand rested against her hip. She felt warm and wanted. Her heart picked up speed at the realization that she could still be so comfortable in his arms, even after all these years, after all they had been through. His hand moved slowly, slightly, and her breath hitched.

She felt him smile against her, surely enjoying the torment he knew he was causing, but his voice was serious when he asked her again, "Tell me how you're feeling." She tried squirming out of his lap, avoiding his question, but he held her still. "Why can't you just answer?"

"Ryder, let me go," she told him, her tone serious enough that he released her to stand. He watched her pace away from him, arms folded across her chest.

"Why can't you answer the question?" he asked, coming to stand behind her, but he didn't reach out to touch her. "It's not complicated."

She whirled around. "But it is, don't you get it? It's not just about this moment or the next. There are other things to consider. It can't just be you and me and right now."

"But it can be."

"Things aren't that simple," she said, frustrated.

"One thing I've come to realize lately is that things *should* be that simple. Tell me how you felt before you got angry with me."

"It doesn't matter."

"It does."

"Ryder, there's more to life than just how I feel at a particular moment in time," she told him warily, feeling like nothing was going to make him stop asking.

"Life is too short and unexpected not to recognize and enjoy right now." He leaned against her desk, reaching out to grab her hips and tug her to him. "You're adorable when you're worked up," he said with a smile.

"I'm not worked up," she said pushing at him, but he held firm.

"You are, and all I want is a simple answer about a single moment in time. Answer that one question and I'll leave you alone."

"No."

"Why are you so scared to say it?"

"I'm not scared."

"Then why not just say?"

"Because it doesn't serve any purpose."

"Sure it does."

"What?" she asked. "What purpose could it possibly serve for me to tell you about one single moment, when there's so much more to consider?"

"But there's not," he told her seriously. "That's what you aren't realizing. We're right here, right now, and that's what matters. A year ago, hell, only a few months ago, I never thought I'd actually have you this close to me. To just me. Not to me and your dad, or me and another person on your staff. You and me."

"Ryder –"

"Don't tell me what it can't be, Lilly. I'm telling you what it hasn't been and what it is now. It's *something*, when for so long it was nothing. I'm not asking you to tell me how you think you're going to feel next week. I'm asking you for one moment in time."

She stared at him, not wanting to admit that he was right, that it scared her that she could so easily still feel something for him. She liked the way it made her feel to be desired by him, to feel his touch, to know he needed to know, instead of just assuming that anything he did would make her feel how he intended. But it also scared her to think that if she did let him in, even the little bit that he was asking for, that she'd wind up hurt again.

"Ryder, I don't… I can't," she fumbled.

"It's this or dinner."

"What?" she asked, confused by the sudden shift.

Ryder smiled. "Answer the question or go to dinner with me."

"Tonight? What? Ryder, you're not making any sense."

"When I was out there in the woods, all I could think of was you. I know, looking for missing kids, but my brain kept circling back to you. I told myself that if we found them, I was going to risk your rejection and ask you to dinner. A sort of celebration. So here we are. Dinner… or the question…"

She looked at him warily. She wasn't sure how she felt about everything that had changed between her and Ryder lately, and she wasn't sure where things were going to go with August yet.

"I'm not ready for dinner," she said tentatively.

"We did already have dinner," Ryder countered, smiling mischievously.

"Yes, that you sprung on me and which was a distraction. *Going* to dinner would be… different."

He nodded. "Yes." He studied her. "And you're not ready for that yet." He smiled devilishly. "So… the question it is."

"Fine," she exhaled, arms dropping to her side, "It felt good, but –"

"No buts," he said, cutting her off. "In that moment, you felt good. Right?"

"That's what I said," she stated stubbornly.

"Good. Me, too. I'm going to kiss you now."

"No, you're not," she laughed, thinking he was joking and made a move to pull away, but he pulled her closer.

"I am, because it'll feel good."

"Maybe for you," she told him, and this time he laughed.

"You won't have any complaints."

"You can't just decide to kiss me."

"I can, and I have, and you should stop worrying so much about how you *think* you're going to feel, and just feel."

"Maybe I feel like I'm still mad at you for bringing up the past the other day."

"No, you're not."

"How would you know?"

"I just do. I can see it in your eyes. You're curious."

"No, I'm not," she countered, feeling her cheeks warm at the lie. "I already know what it's like to kiss you. There's no reason to feel curious."

"You only think you know. You remember years ago, and you got a reminder the other day, but it was a terrible representation."

"It wasn't terrible."

His eyebrow rose.

"I mean… I'm not saying it was good… but it wasn't…" She crossed her arms. "I don't even know why we're having this conversation. I'm not kissing you."

"I feel I deserve better representation," he chuckled.

"I guess you should have done better when you had the chance before," she countered.

"I never intended for it to happen like that," he told her, his tone going soft, bringing back the memory of why it had all happened in the first place.

"I'm sorry," she told him, "that's not what I meant. I…" She trailed off, not sure what to say anymore.

He searched her eyes. "I'm not going to hurt you, Lilly Flower," he whispered.

"Ryder… we can't…"

He stood, moving closer. "Says who?"

She had too many answers, but also none at all, and just opened and closed her mouth like a fish out of water. He pulled her back into him.

Ryder

"Stop thinking for just a minute," he said. "One kiss isn't going to end the world." He leaned down. When he was a breath away, he paused. When she didn't pull or push away, he closed the distance, gently pressing his lips to hers to see how she'd react. When she didn't bite his lip, he took it as a good sign and took the kiss a little further. He slid one hand slowly from its place against her hip to the small of her back, bringing his other up to gently cup beneath her ear, his fingers trailing into her hair.

He felt the moment she stopped holding back, the moment she let herself relax against him, her arms instinctively going up and around him. He smiled as he kissed her, triumphant that he'd been able to break down another barrier between them, happy for this small victory, that she had let herself live in the moment without worrying about their past. He moved his hand further into her hair, tightening his hold around her waist slightly more.

He was about to stop their embrace, ready to show her that he had only wanted one little kiss to end the day… but then he heard her sigh. That one little breath changed everything, triggered something inside that he had known was there, but that he thought he had under control.

He was wrong.

He pulled her tighter still, the need no longer a lazy pull, but an overwhelming requirement. He needed her as much as he needed air to breathe. He poured himself into her; all the lost years, all the dreams of holding her again, all the desire he felt for her was unleashed, and he didn't want to reel it back in now that he had her.

She matched his urgency, a groan escaping her throat, sending him further over the edge. He led her to the wall of her office, pressing her against it as he reached over to flick the lock on the door, catching the light switch as well and dousing the room in darkness. He breathed in the sultry scent of her, something slightly floral but musky as well. His hand trailed down her thigh and she rose to wrap around him as he gently squeezed. Her breathing was heavy as he left her mouth to trail kisses and taste along her neck. His other hand grazed down her side, slipping beneath the hem of her shirt to touch bare skin. He felt her tremble as his fingers teased the sensitive skin at the curve of her back. She bowed against him, a moan escaping as he took her mouth again.

It was a desperate assault for them both, each eagerly taking from the other.

When her hands found their way into his hair and her leg was still wrapped around him, it took every ounce of his willpower not to unclasp her bra in a move he'd perfected down to record time. Instead, he skimmed past the clasp, up along her spine, to the back of her neck, her shirt sliding up to expose the skin of her stomach. He cruised along the bare skin with his other hand, hearing her breath hitch as he made it to her side, and slid his hand up to tease beneath her breast with his thumb.

She tugged his shirt free of his belt, her hands soft and warm against him. It was his turn to shudder at her touch as her hands skimmed along his skin. On a groan, he hoisted her up, reaching out with his leg behind him to kick the chair around. He brought them both down into the chair, her straddling him on top, still clinging to him, though he doubted she noticed.

He pressed her tight to him as he moved the collar of her shirt to expose her shoulder, following the exposed area with tongue and teeth to nip at her skin, then slowly made his way back to the hollow of her neck and up, tasting and teasing as he went. Her hands were back in his hair as his squeezed along her hips, resisting the urge to touch her bare skin again. She was still tightly wrapped up with him when her kisses turned salty. He brought his hands up to her face, moving her hair and wiping her cheeks.

"Why are you crying?" he whispered against her lips.

"I can't help it," she said softly, squeezing him to her as he stopped. "Don't let go," she begged into the darkness, "not yet."

"I won't," he told her, holding her as she recovered. "Are you okay?" he asked her a few moments later.

"I don't know," she whispered. "What… was that?"

"What our first kiss should have been."

"Ryder… that was…" her voice trembled, "too much."

He tilted her face to his, kissing her softly, sweetly, this time holding back the demand he felt for her.

"Ryder… I can't," she managed between breaths, still not loosening her own grip on him.

"I know," he told her, wondering how long it would take her to realize that she was in control as he held the arms of the chair to avoid pulling at her clothes for real this time.

She didn't pull back from him, but he knew he couldn't push either of them any further.

"Ryder," she started, and he could tell by her tone that she was working up to tell him they couldn't do what they wanted for whatever reasons she had in her head, so he reached out for her hands instead to stop her.

"Hey," he said, bringing one of her hands to his mouth to kiss her palm. He rested it against his cheek before bringing them together in his, holding them loosely between them despite what touching her again made him want to do. "Don't… don't think about anything right now, that's for later. I've been wanting to kiss you for real since the last one that didn't count, and now you know what's here. I won't ask you what you're feeling because I know you felt something. You can't deny that we're good together, that we'd be good together. I know you have all sorts of excuses and reasons and whatever else, but we deserve to enjoy this one moment without them. I want nothing more than to never let you walk out that door, and if we weren't at your work…" He had to let the thought go. "Let's at least have this, as nice as it is, not wrapped up in doubt."

Lillian and Ryder

She stared at what she could make out of him in the dark, those niggling reasons trying to break through. He was right though, there was something still there between them, and it was a lot stronger than she had wanted to admit, and now it was impossible to deny. She had a lot to think over, but right now wasn't the time.

"I won't tell you all the reasons… today…" she finally told him, shifting to try and move off his lap.

She could make out the smile, slow and sly, that one that had always made her heart beat fast against her ribcage, just like it was doing now.

"Nobody said the moment had to end right this second."

"It does, before we wind up somewhere we might regret when the lights come on and reality sets in."

He gripped her and stood. She reflexively wrapped around him to keep from falling. He held her for a moment before slowly lowering her to place her feet on the ground. "The only regret I have is thinking that letting you go was ever a good idea." He bent down to kiss her forehead, not sadistic enough to tempt himself again with her mouth and think he'd be able to stop. "Come on, I'll walk you out to your car. It's dark."

"I've walked to my car in the dark by myself just about every night of my adult life," she told him, lingering slightly in his arms.

"Yeah, but I want to see you in the moonlight."

"Ah. It's all about you," she said lightly, reaching for the door and noticing it was locked. He was close enough to see her questioning expression as she turned back to him.

"I didn't want to be interrupted," he shrugged.

"Mmhmm. You always were a sneaky one."

She led the way out, glancing toward the front of the restaurant, hoping nobody walked by to notice she hadn't left yet. Ryder waited while she locked her office door from the other side then led the way out the back door, walking the short distance to her car.

"It's a good thing you're headed home to your own place and not your parents' like when we were dating," he said as she loaded her things into the car.

"Why?" she asked as she stood back up to find him standing closer than she remembered.

One hand went around her waist, the other in her hair, as he stole another kiss for the evening. He kept it soft, gentle in the dark beneath the stars.

"Because you look like you've been making out all night long," he told her when he finally pulled back. "Your hair's all a mess and your cheeks are rosy. We'd be in trouble for sure," he whispered.

"Well, luckily for me, you're the one that's going to have to face my dad first and keep a serious face when you see him at work tomorrow when memories of making out with his daughter randomly pop into your head."

"Ouch," Ryder laughed, realizing she was right. While they were all adults now, he did just spend the last thirty minutes or so kissing his boss's daughter and would spend the rest of the night wishing he could have done more. "God, Lilly, you drive me crazy," he told her, shaking his head, watching her, wanting to reach for her again. "Will you be here early tomorrow?" he asked and saw the world come back to her eyes.

"Yes, I guess I will be. As long as you all are still out searching, I'll keep the volunteer station going. I hope you guys find him tomorrow."

"Me, too," he said, his mind drifting back to the woods and the search. "It was strange… the way the dogs picked up on her scent so fast when they brought them to where we were looking. We'd already searched the area, but they found her just beyond. August was closest and first by her side. She wasn't moving, and I thought for sure she was gone, but the commotion from the dogs and all of us crowding in and calling for her woke her up. She was confused to say the least.

"Once she was found, we were all hopeful that Brian would be nearby. Even with the refresher of his scented clothes, the dogs just kept going back to an old crime scene. We sorta figured the two of them had gone out there, from what we'd learned about them, which is why we were looking there in the first place, but it's like they had finished their search. Every time we tried to lead them away, they just kept going back." He shook his head and focused back on her. "I guess we'd all just had a long day. We'll try again tomorrow."

"And she didn't say anything at all that could lead you to him?"

"No... she was really messed up about the whole thing. We couldn't even get a coherent statement out of her. We're hoping that a good night's rest will help. She's staying at the hospital tonight, the doctors will look her over, and an officer is there to keep an eye on her. We'll try again in the morning to see what she can tell us."

"That's good. She's probably scared after being lost out there and all alone. I'm probably the last person she'd want to see, but if you need me to talk to her, I can try. Sometimes it's easier to talk to someone you know instead of a police officer."

"We'll let you know if we do," he said and stepped back from her door. "Go home and get some rest. I know it's probably not my place to ask, but will you just shoot me a text when you get there? I'd feel better knowing you made it safely."

"I can handle a text," she said, smiling at his request as she buckled in. "Good night, Ryder."

He smiled and stepped back from her car as she pulled away.

Lillian

Her drive home was short. She carried in all her things, dropping them on the counter to sort through later, and dug through her purse to send Ryder the text that she'd promised. She realized that she'd been so wrapped up in him, literally, that she hadn't heard any of the notifications that were lighting up her screen now. She sent off the text to him and immediately got a response. She noticed that the first missed message was thankfully from Jane, letting her know that the phones were no longer forwarded for the night and that she'd turn it back on when she got into the station in the morning.

She swiped more of the notifications off the screen, most of them just random junk that she didn't worry about, but faltered when she saw the missed call that had come in roughly between Ryder's tongue down her throat and her legs wrapped around him. There was no voicemail or text, just a single missed call with the name "August" identifying it. She checked the time; it wasn't too late to call him back, but what was she supposed to say? "Hey, sorry, new hot guy that I've already slept with. I didn't mean to miss your call, but I was wrapped up at the time in a mind-numbing make out session with my ex like we were eighteen all over again.'

Probably not the best conversation starter.

What was she supposed to tell him? And how had she so completely forgotten to check in with him all day long? She still didn't know if he'd seen the extremely innocent peck on the cheek earlier and if he was mad about it, or if he really was just keeping their relationship private. She knew for a fact that if he *had* seen the peck and *was* upset by it, then what she just spent her evening doing would warrant definite anger… but she didn't want any secrets between them or to play any games… but having the conversation that she just made out with another man while they were supposed to be figuring out what could be between them made her feel sick to her stomach. And what about Ryder? He didn't want her overthinking anything, just living in the moment, but she imagined he'd change his tune if he ever found out that she'd slept with another man while he was pursuing her, let alone the man that he'd clearly said he didn't care for.

She put the phone down again, exhaling deeply as she thought about the mess she'd somehow found herself in. It would be one thing if she could just cast one of them aside, if she didn't feel something for each of them as she did, but they both made her heart race and lose track of the world around her.

How was it fair that two men could consume her so completely and at the same time when she wasn't even looking for a relationship?

She knew she needed to face her problems, but she was afraid of what she stood to lose. She groaned to nobody but herself and left the phone on her counter. She'd have a hot bath, maybe a glass of wine, and then decide if she wanted to think any more about it tonight.

THIRTY-FOUR
-Rain-

"Rain? The sheriff is here and would like to ask you some questions," the nurse said softly. "Is it okay to let him in?"

Rain opened her eyes. They burned at the brightness of the room despite the curtains being closed. She shut them again and nodded for the sheriff to come in. She could hear the nurse speaking quietly at the door as she let him in.

"She's had a rough night, Sheriff. She was in and out of fits all evening; not very restful. It'd be best if you didn't stay too long."

"Did she say anything in the night?" she heard him ask.

"No, just crying and screaming. We almost had to restrain her once when one of the assistants was checking her vitals and she panicked and tried to get away. We finally had to give her a mild sedative and that seemed to help for a little while."

"Okay, I won't be long, but I need to ask her some questions."

Rain heard the footsteps move closer as the door closed across the room. She opened her eyes slightly. The nurse had left and the sheriff and a deputy stood beside her bed. She opened her mouth to say something, but her mouth was too dry to get a word out. The deputy noticed and handed her the cup of water from the bedside table.

"Thank you," she croaked. Her throat was raw, her voice grating to her own ears.

"Rain, my name's Bill," he started gently. "I'm the sheriff and this is my deputy, Simon. We'd like to ask you some questions about where you've been, if that's alright?"

She nodded again and looked around for the button to raise her bed into a sitting position, adjusting the blanket around her as she did.

"Do you mind if we turn down some of the lights?" she asked, still barely opening her eyes to the harshness above.

Simon made some adjustments and, while her eyes still hurt, she could at least open them and see the two men standing in front of her.

"How are you feeling?" Bill asked.

"Tired," her gravelly voice answered. "And my eyes and head hurt."

He nodded in understanding.

"The nurse said you didn't get much sleep last night."

She shrugged her shoulders, not completely sure where her dreams ended and reality began.

"We've been looking for you for a couple days," the sheriff told her. "You and Brian both."

"I haven't seen Brian," she told them quickly. "We got separated."

"Do you know where?"

She shook her head.

"It all looked the same. He was with me and then he was gone. I was alone –" her voice broke on the word.

"Take your time," Bill said calmly. "I'm sure it was scary being in there for so long."

She nodded again, a tear escaping down her cheek. She brushed it off with her hand and took a deep breath.

"Can you tell us what happened before you two got separated?" Simon asked, equally calm. "It may help us figure out where to start searching for him."

The memories came pouring back and she pulled the blanket up to cover more of her body, her breath speeding up at the thought of running through the woods.

She closed her eyes and forced herself to take deep breaths like the nurse made her do last night. She wasn't there anymore. She was found. She was safe in the hospital. There was nothing after her. There was no more nothing. She opened her eyes to see them still standing on either side of her bed, still and sturdy.

"I was being petty," she admitted quietly, shaking her head slightly. "I knew the guys were getting tired of me, but I didn't want to go home. I knew they were going to send me home." She fidgeted with a loose string on the blanket, feeling like an idiot as she said it out loud. "I knew Brian liked me," she smiled weakly. "It was pretty obvious. I used that to get him away from the others. I knew they were leaving soon, and I just didn't want to go back to the way things were yet."

"Rain," the sheriff asked softly when she trailed off and stayed focused on her blanket. "Is there something going on at your home that you want to talk about? Is there something wrong?"

Her mouth turned down at the corners, unable to fake a smile, but she raised a hand indicating herself.

"I'm the something wrong in my life," she told them, finally managing a half-smile. "Look at me... blue hair, piercings, tattoos. I'm not exactly my parents' idea of the perfect child, and they're both pretty open about letting me know." She sighed as she looked back at them. "With Brian, Evan, and Jack, they didn't care. They let me chill and didn't judge. I mean, Evan and I didn't really vibe, but he still let me hang. It was fun... but then they wanted me to leave, and I just couldn't go back to my perfect mom telling me how imperfect I am… or my perfect coworker—ex-coworker I guess—telling me all the things I wasn't doing right, so I convinced Brian to take me to the woods. One last thrill, you know, before going back to the criticism."

She looked back down to her hands, noticing for the first time her jagged nails, the dirt under them, and her chipped fingernail polish. The deputy shifted his weight beside her bed, and she looked back up. She'd nearly forgotten they were still there.

"So, you guys left the campsite," Bill gently prodded and she nodded.

"We had some gear, but not much. I don't think he even changed his shoes…" She trailed off again. "I didn't think we'd get very far because Brian had other things on his mind…" She blushed slightly. "Only because I let him think what he wanted to get him away."

"Did Brian hurt you?" Bill asked softly.

She shook her head. "No. Once we got going, he got all excited about the Mountain. The first time I met him, he'd told me it was one of the reasons they were here. That was part of what I used to get him away from the others. Sure, I've heard stories, I've lived here all my life. There's always a story, and every kid wants to know what's up in there, but honestly, I didn't really care about going… but he did."

She paused, going back to that day in her mind. "I was getting tired. The Mountain is there, don't go in, blah, blah, blah. The stories always made it sound like you could just stumble in there, but the boundary is so far up there and it's a hard climb. It's not like you're just going to accidentally find it… I told him I wanted to go back. We'd been climbing forever, and I was getting bored of it all. I even considered telling him we could do what he wanted back in the truck if it meant getting out of there," she told them, the blush returning to her cheeks.

"But Brian was stubborn. He was obsessed. The closer we got, the weirder he became. 'You feel it right?' he'd ask, or he'd mumble 'almost… so close… it's there'… I don't know what he meant. He was acting crazy, and it scared me. I wanted to turn back, but I didn't know the way. I had to stay with him… And then we were there.

"There was a rock wall that went on for as far as you could see, we followed it until there was a crumbled place, like something had broken out of it…"

She shivered and pulled the blanket around her tighter, her breath hitching at the memory.

"And I could finally feel what he was talking about. It was like the air was dead. It felt… hollow." She looked up at them both, shaking her head. "I know that doesn't make sense… I can't describe it. It was the scariest feeling I'd ever felt. The hair on my arms stuck straight up and my feet wouldn't move." She pulled her knees up to her chest under the blanket, hugging them close, as if making sure she still could. "I told him I was scared," she whispered, "and I tried pulling him back from going in. There was something in there… watching… but when Brian looked at me, he scared me worse."

"What happened next?" Bill asked her gently when she didn't continue, eyes focused beyond them, reliving that day.

"Um..." she could hear the tremble in her voice despite her steadying breath. "I grabbed his arm when he started to go past the wall. I told him to take me back, but he turned on me and his eyes were... just... crazy. They were like the air, dead, but also not. At first, it was like he didn't recognize me, but then he focused and said we'd come this far so we couldn't turn back... But I did turn back. I told him to go fuck himself and I'd find my own way back... sorry for the language," she mumbled. "He grabbed me then and said we *had* to go in, that it *needed* us to go in... he was so scary, and I tried to get away, but he already had one foot through the wall and he was stronger than me. He pulled me in with him."

She hugged her knees tighter and bit her lip, not wanting to remember what it felt like being in there.

"Rain," Bill told her. "If we're going to find Brian, we need to know what happened."

"I don't want you to find him," she finally whispered, shaking her head rapidly.

Simon sat on the edge of her bed, coaxing her hand from around her knees, holding it solidly in both of his own, "What happened in there?" he asked her, firm yet gentle.

She squeezed his hand in her own, feeling it warm and real and here, safe in the hospital room. Safe. She was safe. She saw him watching just her. Her mouth was trying to pull down at the sides again, but he was waiting calmly.

"When we went through—" Her voice shook again. "Everything was different... but not. Everything still looked the same, but nothing was right. It was like someone turned off the TV in the other room that you didn't realize you'd been listening to, but you missed it when it was gone... except someone turned off *everything*. All the good nature sounds, like birds chirping or squirrels running, the feel of the sunshine on your skin or the cool shade of a tree, even the feeling of my own body felt... off.

"It was hard to breathe, like I was breathing through a straw or something. No matter how deep I tried to breathe, I could only get a little bit. And then it felt like something was wrapped tight around me and it kept getting tighter, like it was going to crush me, but I couldn't see anything on me. Then the noises started. They came from all around. Everywhere I turned..." She closed her eyes, covered her ears, and shook her head. "I don't ever want to hear them again.

"I tried again to tell Brian to leave. We'd made it. We went over the line and were in, we could say we did it. We could leave..." She shook her head, remembering the sight of him. "He was heaving out breaths like he'd just run a mile. He kept swatting at himself, like something was crawling on him, then he'd whip his head around like he could hear something, too, but couldn't see it. I begged him to go.

"When he looked at me finally, he didn't know who I was at all. He looked terrified and angry at the same time... He was breathing so hard it sounded like growling. He was standing in front of the broken part of the wall. I knew I couldn't get past him without him grabbing me, but I could hear something coming for us, coming through the woods. It was getting louder and closer, and he looked crazy, so

I took off. I ran along the wall as far as it went, but I kept tripping over everything and there wasn't enough air, and it was so hard to move because my body felt so squished under an invisible weight all over. I could hear the noises behind me, getting closer.

"The wall ended and I thought I could find a way out, but there were only cliffs straight down. Brian was coming, and I knew I couldn't climb down, so I just kept going." She was quiet for a while, remembering the sounds all around her, the terrible aching in her chest and muscles as she kept pushing forward beyond what her body would allow.

"He was screaming behind me, but I couldn't look back... I knew I was going to die," she whispered. "Either I'd fall off one of the cliffs, or whatever was in the woods with us would get me, Brian would catch me, or my heart would give out. Everything hurt so bad, like someone had reached inside of me and was trying to rip everything out all at once... I've never been that scared... I thought my heart..." She trailed off, rubbing at her chest like there was a sore muscle there. "I thought it stopped... I must have passed out from everything because I couldn't hear Brian anymore. The sounds were gone from the woods. It didn't hurt to breathe. My skin didn't hurt from the air. I didn't feel dead anymore..."

She darted glances around the room, her breaths more rapid at the memory of what came next. "But everything was just black. Everywhere I looked, it was black. I called and called for help, but nobody came, and I couldn't see anything, and I was stuck, and I couldn't get out. It was so cold and so dark. So, so dark. It wouldn't let me go! The Mountain wouldn't let me out!" The lights were brighter now than the dark room she'd been stuck in, but the air was getting harder and harder to breathe. She tried sucking in more and more, but she couldn't catch her breath. "And—" she desperately gulped, trying to fill her lungs. "and... Oh God! I'm still there! HELP! Somebody, please help! I'm stuck in the Mountain! Please, let me out! I want out!"

Bill

Bill watched as Rain tried to bolt from the bed, screaming wildly, afraid of something that neither he nor his deputy could see. They grabbed her and held her on the bed just as the nurse and an assistant came rushing through the door.

"What happened?" the nurse asked hurriedly, a needle already ready in her hand.

"What's that?" Bill asked as she plunged it into Rain's IV drip.

"A sedative," she answered without taking her eyes from her task. She turned to help hold Rain steady until she calmed down enough for them to let go. "What happened in here?" she asked again as the assistant verified that Rain's vitals had stabilized.

"She was just going over what happened a couple nights ago, and all of the sudden she got out of control. She started screaming and tried to get up and run away," Simon said.

"I told you she had a restless night," the nurse stated, as if that explained the sudden change in Rain's behavior.

"That wasn't restless," Bill said. "That was terrified and crazed."

"Well, if you'd been lost in the woods for a week, wouldn't you be a little shaken up?" the nurse countered. "She's obviously traumatized. She's going to need time to recover, probably therapy, too."

She ushered them out of the room as the assistant laid the bed back down, tucking a now mumbling Rain under her blanket.

Bill turned to the head nurse, puzzled. "Why did you say she'd been in the woods for a week? She's only been missing a couple days."

She looked confused. "Oh… she said a week… Her mother was here last night when she was brought in," the nurse said. "We had to ask her to leave because Rain had gotten worked up. They argued, and I only heard the last little bit, where her mom accused her of doing all of this for attention. Rain yelled about how she'd been gone for a week, kidnapped, and asked how her mom could think she'd made it all up. Rain was so upset, screaming and crying. Everyone could hear it down the hall."

Bill looked back toward the closed door that Rain was presumably now sleeping behind.

"Did she have bloodwork done when she came in?" he asked. "She mentioned hearing things, the boy she was with acting strangely, her skin feeling weird…"

"You think they took something before they went in the woods?" Simon asked.

"Possibly. It would explain the hallucinations, confusion of time, why Brian became violent so suddenly."

"It's standard for us to start bloodwork on our patients, especially ones that could be nutritionally deficient from being missing, presumably without food or water. We need to know what and how to treat them, especially if the story is incoherent, as hers appears to be," the nurse replied.

"And… did you find anything?" Bill asked when she didn't offer further details.

"Not in the preliminary results," she admitted, "but if that was a few days ago, it's possible it's already out of her system."

"And the reaction in there?" Bill asked, nodding back toward the closed door.

"Could be from the trauma, like I said before. She would really benefit from talking to someone who's trained in that sort of thing. Her doctor can give a recommendation."

"Whoever it is, see if they can get over here soon. We still have one missing hiker and she's the best bet we have of finding him."

"We'll set it up, but Sheriff, these things can take time, and she's really shaken up. I don't know if she's going to be much help anytime soon. Honestly, I'm surprised she talked as long as she did."

"What do you think?" Simon asked the sheriff when they were back in the Blazer.

Bill sighed. "I think she's shaken up and the nurse is right. Whatever happened in there has scared her so much that even if she did know her way around in the woods, she probably won't be able to give us much useable information now."

"Well, we at least know that they started at the broken wall and must have run along it back to where we found her last night, so he's somewhere along there."

"That's if her account is accurate and not recounting a hallucination. We don't know if they were on something or not. Plus, it's been two days since all that she says happened… where is Brian now?"

Simon was tight-lipped beside the Sheriff.

"We can't go in, Simon," Bill told him, guessing his deputy's thoughts. "We aren't military."

"And it's not an active base."

Bill gave his deputy a stern look.

"So, we keep looking where we already have been and hope he turns up," Simon said sourly.

"For now, that's what we have to do… and pray," Bill told him, hating that he didn't have an easy answer for his deputy. "Seatbelt," he said as he fired up the engine.

Simon strapped the belt and looked out the window. "Then I guess we'd better get back over there."

THIRTY-FIVE

-Lillian-

She was a chicken.

She knew she was a chicken. Instead of facing her man troubles last night like she knew she should have, she'd chosen the path of a big ol' chicken. She'd drawn a bath, threw in some bubbles for fun, lit some candles around the room for good measure, almost dipped a toe in the hot water, then quickly retreated to the kitchen for a glass and a bottle of wine. The phone still lay on the counter, silently judging her for not picking it up and calling August back. She stood watching it, wondering if it would ring if she stared at it long enough, but then quickly changed her mind and retreated to her steamy sanctuary to take away all thoughts of the day.

Now, as she sat at the desk in her office with her black coffee and pounding head, she regretted that third glass of wine. If she had stopped there, maybe she wouldn't be angry at the overhead lights today, but after the third glass, there wasn't enough left in the bottle to save, and she didn't want to pour it down the drain, so she finished it off instead. She put her head in her hands, blocking the light from her eyes and wishing she had poured the wine out.

"Let's see… this isn't peppy-sexcapade-Lillian…" Lana mused from the doorway, leaning against the jamb. "And Rain was found alive last night… so why does it look like you spent the evening with an upturned bottle?"

"There were no upturned bottles," Lillian mumbled into her hands.

Lana waited.

"I poured the bottle into a glass…"

"Mmhmm." Lana came into the room, closing the door behind her. She scooted the chair into place in front of the desk and sat down. "And why did you feel the need to drink as much as you clearly did? And without even inviting me over," she said with mock offense.

Lillian leaned back in her chair, the coffee mug held tightly between her hands just beneath her nose so she could smell the warmth before gently sipping, eyes closing as she willed the headache to fly up to the ceiling with the tiny whisps of escaping steam.

"It's inappropriate for a boss to discuss with an employee," she finally said.

Lana snorted. "That just means it's juicy. Tell me."

Lillian opened one eye and peeked over at her friend, lazily sitting in the chair, waiting for her confession.

"Shouldn't you be working or something?"

"I'm on a break," Lana waved away the attempt to change the subject. "You must be really messed up if you don't even know what time it is." She perched forward in her chair. "Which means it's really juicy. Now spill."

Lillian closed the eye again.

"If you don't, I'll just assume the worst," Lana sighed. "That you're devastated that Rain was found because she knew the truth about you and Harvey and now that she's back, she's going to tell the whole town, and you just can't handle that level of embarrassment."

Lillian groaned. "With everything going on, I actually forgot that was why she quit."

"So, what really had you ignoring reality?" Lana asked seriously. "You're not really the drown your sorrows type, so what gives?"

"Boy troubles," Lillian finally sighed, sitting upright in her chair again. She set the coffee back on the desk, hands still wrapped around the soothing warmth of the mug.

"Your guy not all you thought he was?"

She shook her head. "No, not that."

Lana studied her. "Did you break it off with him?"

"No... but I haven't talked to him either."

"In how long?"

"Just a couple days... I was going to call him yesterday... but then I didn't."

"I don't remember a rule book saying you have to talk every day... what's the real problem?"

She exhaled deeply. "He may have seen my ex kiss me. I should have cleared up before it became an issue, but now I think I've waited too long, and things are really going to be messed up."

Lana sat back in her chair, studying Lillian. "Honey," she finally said, "you don't have an ex."

Lillian looked back at her coffee.

"Wait a minute... *ex*?" She emphasized the word. "As in old high school sweetheart who ripped your heart out and stomped it into the ground while he walked away with another girl, but who happens to be hotter now than he could have possibly been back then, filled out in *all* the right places and makes the uniform look good instead of the other way around, and happens to be a deputy that works for your dad, *ex*?"

Lillian nodded sheepishly.

"So, I *obviously* missed something there that you're going to fill me in on eventually." Lana paused. "But apparently we've made it to the part where it's okay for him to be kissing you again… and you think August saw this and you haven't called him to set things straight?"

She nodded again. "It's not that we're to the point that it's okay… it sort of just happened… but, yes he kissed me, and I don't know if August saw or not, but I'm pretty sure there's no way he couldn't have seen, and instead of explaining it, I ignored it, but now I'm thinking I shouldn't have…"

"Okay," Lana exhaled and sat back in her chair. "What kind of kiss are we talking? How bad?"

"It was just a quick peck on the cheek, more of a reassurance than anything else," she told her.

"Oh, well, that's fine. A peck is nothing. Just call him and tell him. I'm sure he'll understand, and you guys can get back to crazy sex."

Lillian felt the heat in her cheeks as she remembered the other, not so innocent kisses.

"Unless…" Lana leaned forward in her chair again. "You're keeping something else. Something that isn't nothing…" She gasped. "Lillian! Are you sleeping with both of them?"

"Shhh," she hissed, immediately glancing to the closed door as if the whole restaurant was standing on the other side listening to their conversation. "No."

"Then what's the big deal? You're not telling me something, and I can't give you advice if you don't tell me."

"I didn't ask for advice," Lillian pouted. "You just want the gossip."

"Well *yeah*, but that doesn't mean I'm going to tell the rest of *them*… You know I only want to help you."

Lillian raised her eyebrow at her friend.

"Okay, and to live vicariously through your apparently exotic life," Lana conceded. "Tell me what happened with Deputy Hotness."

She rubbed her face in her hands. "Hotness is right," she finally admitted out loud and filled Lana in on her evening.

Lana pretended to fan herself and looked around the office. "You should put like a little sofa in here instead of this chair," she finally said, and Lillian threw a pencil at her.

"That doesn't help," she said, but couldn't help but laugh.

"I'm just saying you need more comfortable seating in here is all," Lana said a little too innocently. "So, let me get this straight. You swear off all guys at some point in your life. No more, they're jerks and just cause problems. Then, within a week of each other, you've got two of the best-looking examples of the opposite sex throwing themselves at you, letting you do with them what you want, and instead of taking both of them to bed, you're drinking yourself into a hangover all alone? How is this a problem?"

"I can't take both of them to bed!" Lillian exclaimed.

"Well, I didn't mean at once… but…" Lana's gaze drifted away momentarily, "it wouldn't be a bad way to wake up in the morning."

Lillian threw a pen this time and Lana just laughed, swatting it away.

"Okay, seriously though, it's not like either one of the guys has asked you to be exclusive or anything."

"First of all, I don't think people actually ask that of other people… do they? God," she said into her hands again. "I feel so old, like I don't even know how to do this anymore… But it's about respect, right? I should just choose one because it's not right to be seeing both at the same time."

"Says who? Society?"

"Lana, you know that's not me. I can't string both of them along."

"Who says you're stringing them along? You're simply having a good time with both men, neither of whom has specified that they don't want you to see anyone else. How do you know they're not doing the same thing? You're not married, Lillian. It's called dating for a reason."

"Well, maybe I don't want to do it like that. I don't like the way it makes me feel. I mean, I do. They both make me feel alive and excited, but I've been the one that wasn't in the know before and it doesn't feel good. I just feel like it's not fair to either of them for me to be sneaking around."

"Are you sneaking?"

"Well, not exactly. Things just sort of happened unexpectedly."

"Okay, so how is that sneaking and wrong?"

"Because… neither one of them knows about the other, and that just doesn't feel right to me. That's not the kind of person I am."

Lana sighed. "I know. You're good and all that," she said, waving her hand in the air dismissively, "but maybe *this* is good for *you*. You've been all work for as long as I've known you, and that's been years. I've never heard of a boyfriend or a date—other than ones I have to drag you out on—in all that time."

"I've had dates," Lillian said weakly.

"Right, and I'm celibate," she said, rolling her eyes. "You need to let loose."

"I just feel like I need to say something."

"And how do you think they'll react when August finds out that the little peck was nothing compared to the rest of your night, or when Ryder finds out that all he got was sexy kissing and not sexy sex like August did?"

"Not good… and now you see why the bottle is lying empty on my bathroom floor this morning."

Lana nodded. "I agree. So, you should enjoy them both while you have the chance… but I know you and it'll only eat at you if you don't say anything."

"It already is, especially since August called last night and I avoided calling him back because I don't know what to say."

"So, you can either keep it up with both of them, enjoy it while it lasts until it inevitably blows up in your face…"

"Gee thanks."

"Or you tell them both now and hope that the right one steps up to fight for you. So, I guess you've got to figure out which one you want to win that fight."

Lillian put her head on her arms on her desk and groaned.

"And you care enough to want them both to be happy, don't you?" Lana stood and patted her head. "Unfortunately, not everyone is going to walk away from this with a smile. Someone's going to come out of this with tears. I just hope it isn't you."

THIRTY-SIX

-Ryder-

"So how did it go last night with the notification?" August asked as they were picking through the leaves on the ground, searching for any sign of Brian.

"Hmm? What?" Ryder asked from a few feet away.

"When you guys told Rain's parents that she'd been found. How'd it go?"

"Oh… fine, I guess. It was just her mom there. Her parents are divorced, and her dad lives out in the city about an hour away. He wasn't there."

"That seems strange," August mused.

"Why?" Ryder kicked a log over, not expecting to find anything, but every little bit needed to be searched.

"I'd think that if my kid was missing, I'd be out here, if not helping with the search itself, then at least around for the mom or for quick notification if she turned up."

"Yeah, I see your point, but I guess he's some bigshot and couldn't take the time off work."

"Still, it's his kid. He should be here. What about Brian's parents? Did they make the trip out?"

"Yeah, they showed up last night. I think they're on the other side, where the truck was found, helping search over there."

August nodded to himself. "Good… It's good they're here. I hope we find him soon, so we have some good news for them."

"Yeah, but it's not looking good. The dogs can't find his scent or something. It's weird. I've never seen them act so weird, not wanting to look. You saw them. They just keep going to those rocks. According to Rain's report to the sheriff this morning, they didn't make it to the other crime scene, but the dogs keep going over there like they smell him there. She must be keeping something out of her story."

"Or they really didn't make it over there."

"There's no reason for the dogs to keep going over there. They're trained to pick up scents for miles and for up to two weeks; of course, that's in the best conditions, but we've had those, and these woods are hiked, sure, but not this far out very extensively. There's no reason they could find Rain's smell so easily and not find Brian's. It's like he *was* there and then was moved, that that was the end of his trail."

"You think someone carried him out? There's no way Rain could do that. She's too small comparatively."

"No, not her… but I'm wondering if something bad happened out here and Rain got away. I'm not sure why she wouldn't tell the truth about what happened…" Ryder trailed off.

August stood, watching him process something. "What's in your head?" he finally asked.

"I probably shouldn't be discussing this since you're not on the squad."

"I'm out here *volunteering* my guide skills and helping search for people I don't even know. If there's something else that's connected to the search, I feel like I should be clued in."

Ryder looked hard at August, clearly considering whether or not he should say anything. He finally ran his hands through his hair and trudged over to where August was standing.

"Okay, this is just a theory that I've had. The sheriff thinks it doesn't have any weight and is just because I'm too close to Wade's case and am looking for a reason to explain his death… but I was wondering if there was an outsider murdering people and leaving their bodies in these woods. There seemed to be ties to the Mountain, and all the bodies were found in a manner that could be explained as natural deaths if you didn't dig in further. Hell, even if you do dig in further it still looks natural—odd coincidences—but still natural, which is why the sheriff disagrees with my idea."

"But you're considering it again?"

"Well, what if those two came out here to have a good time, like Rain says, and they stumbled on someone else. Rain manages to get away but gets lost, but the killer gets Brian before he can escape."

"But that's not the story that Rain gave right?"

"Not at all. She says that Brian started acting strange and she ran off."

"Sounds to me like Brian may not be missing at all," August said.

Ryder stared at him, realization dawning on his face. "You think Brian is the Mountain Killer? That when he and Rain got up there, he figured they were far enough away and she'd not be able to find her way back?" He nodded to himself, staring off into the woods as he worked it out in his head. "He turns on her, but she manages to get away. He searches, but can't find her anywhere, and then we're in here looking and he can't keep up his search anymore, so he bails. We can't find his body because he's long gone."

Ryder turned back in the direction of the trailhead.

"Where are you going?" August asked, following him down the now clearly trampled trail.

"I've got to get back to the station and the sheriff. I need to fill him in. I can't believe we didn't see it. It's so obvious. I need to check my notes and see when Brian said the rest of the guys got into town for their birthday weekend. Maybe the other bodies are linked to him. I need to do some research." Ryder was frenzied, hurrying down the trail as quick as his boots and the rough terrain would allow. He stopped mid-step, and August almost ran into his back.

"What's up?" August asked.

"What if it was all three of those guys? The campers. What if they're all working together? They come in to report their friend missing because they know we're going to utilize all of our force as well as any able citizens." Ryder started moving even faster than before, stumbling over rocks and sliding down the hill, catching himself on a branch that would have caught him in the face otherwise. "There'd be nobody to notice or stop them if they used this distraction to all pack up and leave town. We might never find them if they leave here and are able to scatter. I've got to get back to town."

"Don't you have a radio or cell phone?" August asked from behind him. "Call ahead and let them know."

"Oh, right," Ryder said, surprised that he had forgotten his tools at hand in his excitement to get back to town. He dug through his pack, searching for the cell phone. He pulled it out and held it up, only one bar. "Come on, we need to get closer."

They rushed down the wooded hillside as quickly as they could, neither one saying much as they navigated the difficult terrain.

When they reached the public trail, with its cleared and woodchipped path, Ryder checked his phone again. Four bars. He smiled and dialed the sheriff who quickly picked up on the other end.

"Sheriff, I'm headed in, are you at the station?" he paused and nodded to August mouthing the words, 'he's there'. "Okay. I have a theory that I need to discuss with you, but I need you to get someone to bring in the other two campers."

"The boys from the Bend?" Bill asked.

"Yes, sir, Evan and Jack. Is Simon still with you?"

"He is…"

"Okay, send him to bring them in.

"Ryder we've questioned them repeatedly. I can't keep bringing them in for no reason. You need to give me something."

"Just say we need more information to help find their friend." He ran his hands through his hair. "I promise I'll explain everything as soon as I get in, but we *need* those kids."

"I'll send Simon, but I hope you come up with a better cover than needing more information."

"Thank you, sir."

Ryder finished his conversation and turned back to August. "The sheriff didn't want to just pick up the kids for no reason, wants to know what's going on, but if we're wasting time with explanations, they could sneak away, if they haven't already. He agreed though to send Simon to bring them in. Come on, we need to get back before Simon does, if he's even able to find them."

They loaded into Ryder's truck and headed back to town.

"You know," Ryder suddenly said, breaking the silence in the truck. "I actually wondered if *you* could have been up to no good there in the beginning. You were my prime suspect. Loner, outsider, already brought us one body, maybe you were hiding in plain sight by reporting it…"

"You don't exactly sound like you've ruled me out," August said cautiously.

Ryder looked sideways at him, studying him again as another possible suspect.

"Maybe I'll keep you close, just in case."

They pulled up to the station. Ryder turned off the truck and made his way to the station door, pausing to hold it open, knowing August was too smart to take off and look suspicious. August led the way into the building, then followed Ryder through to the sheriff's office.

THIRTY-SEVEN

-Lillian-

After nearly seventy-two hours, the chances that Brian would be found were growing slim. When Rain was brought in, Lillian assumed it was only a matter of time before Brian was found, too, but quick texts from her dad and the periodic news updates made it sound like he'd disappeared completely. Even the phones had slowed down, and while business was still booming, more people were wandering in for the chatter and not so much for aiding in the search. Jane told her she was taking the forward off the line as it wasn't more than she could handle any more, but if any stragglers came into the diner to help, Lillian could send them to the station for updated directions.

It was sad to see how quickly people dispersed. Lillian wondered if it was because Brian wasn't a local; was the desire to help a stranger only so strong? Or was it because of how long he'd been gone already? Did everyone think he was dead and no one wanted to be the one to find the body? Her dad still had small groups combing the woods, but he had limited people and still had a county to watch over.

She was wrapping up her day in the office, finishing calls to set up job interviews, when she saw the photo shop's package under her pile of papers. She'd been carting it around with her, meaning to look over the pictures, but kept forgetting to open it. She grabbed the packet and pulled out the prints, surprised by how well the old photos had been enlarged. She looked at Harvey's young, smiling face, the early versions of the restaurant, and found herself smiling back at the pictures, imagining what it would have been like so many years ago when their town was so different. She gently laid each photo on her desk as she looked her selections over, thinking how great it would be if the library had had a chance to look for any archived information or photos of the base at the Mountain, when one of the smiling faces caught her eye. She peered at it curiously, wondering what about the third person in the photo was drawing her in. The image was clear enough for an old, enlarged print, but the people were slightly out of focus because they were in the distance. It was easy to tell who Harvey was because she knew him, but if she didn't, identifying the people was a challenge. There was something about the third person that she couldn't put her finger on.

Her phone buzzed next to her arm, startling her out of her intense staring contest with a black and white photo. She set the image on top of the rest and looked over at her phone to see a text message from August.

Can I see you tonight?

Her heart did a little quiver, but then her stomach did a flop, reminding her of all the mess she was still in. She started typing an excuse not to see him tonight, then erased it, then started to ask what he'd want to do, then erased that.

She typed:

Yes.

She pressed send before she could talk herself out of it.

Done. She'd agreed to see him, now she'd be forced to face the music. She'd tell him about the kiss with Ryder, and then he could decide how he wanted to continue from there. She didn't want to be in a lie, and Lana was right. Better to fess up now, lay everything out, rather than try and cover it up and wait for it to explode in her face… but part of her worried that it would still explode in her face. She really liked being with August… and Ryder.

"Stop it," she told herself out loud. "Stop getting in your head. You're going to do the right thing and what happens, happens."

She was beginning to feel like a broken record. She stacked all her things, put them into her bag and shut everything down for the day. She would see August and be done with it, just get it all out in the open.

Her stomach did a slow turn that made her want to change her mind and text him again, tell him something had come up. Her phone buzzed again, another message from August.

Do you want to get something to eat?

She groaned inwardly at both the thought of eating right now and creating a scene in a public place. She didn't really think August was the scene-making type, but how did she know how he'd react to finding out she'd been kissing another man?

I'm not really hungry. Go ahead and eat without me. I have some things to wrap up anyway. When you're finished, you can just meet at my house in about an hour or so.

You sure? I can bring something to make.

No, that's okay, really.

She could imagine the potential disaster of him bringing a nice dinner over, cooking for her, all the while having a conversation about Ryder… she could smell the disregarded, burnt food already. Better to just keep tonight as simple as possible.

Just give me an hour to get my stuff done and get back home.

She sent her address.

K. See you soon.

She knew she didn't have anything to do between now and then, other than using the time to get her stomach out of the knot she'd tied it in, and to hurry home to straighten up her house. She liked to keep things tidy, but she needed to make sure before August showed up. She grabbed her bag, locked her office, said her goodbyes, and headed home, the seconds ticking away faster than she was prepared for.

She made it home in record time, hurrying in and putting her things in her tiny home office; she'd sort through it all later. She quickly passed through the house, making sure all was in order, putting away little things here and there on her way back to her bedroom. She hadn't made the bed; she'd rolled out of it this morning with a headache and the need for coffee and had left it disregarded. The memory of last night's therapy session had her hurrying into the bathroom to deal with the bottle and glass, then heading back to her bed to set it right. She didn't necessarily plan for August to be in her bedroom, but she wanted everything in order on the off chance that he did. At the very least, what if he opened the wrong door looking for the bathroom? Best to have it done.

She'd just fluffed and placed the last pillow when the doorbell rang. She checked the clock beside her bed; he was twenty minutes early. She ran into the bathroom to check her reflection. She was a little frazzled-looking from a full day of work and running around the house, but otherwise not bad. She smoothed her hair, closed the door to her bedroom and made it to the front door before he could ring again. She took a deep breath and opened the door.

"Wow, don't look so disappointed to see me," Ryder said.

"Oh… no, just surprised," she responded, trying to ignore the tingle rippling throughout her body at the sight of him. "What's up?"

"I was driving by, thinking we should talk about last night, when I saw a box on your porch. I was going to move it out of sight if you weren't home… but you are, so I can bring it in for you."

"Oh, I didn't know there was a delivery," she said, looking around for the box he had seen.

"You didn't order anything?"

"Not that I can remember."

He leaned down to get a closer look. "There's no mailing label. Someone hand-delivered this. Have any ideas?" he asked as they both looked at the shut and taped box resting next to her front door.

"Nope. I guess bring it in and I'll check it out."

"We shouldn't bring it in if you don't know who it's from."

"You've got your police voice going. There's no reason to worry, I'm sure."

He studied the box and sighed, bending down to pick it up. She held the door open for him and directed him into the office. He set the box on her desk, still looking at it.

"It's pretty decent weight," he told her, stepping back and watching it like it would explode at any minute. "Do you want me to open it for you?"

"Ryder, I'm sure it's nothing to worry about," she told him again. "I'll open it later when I have time to look at whatever is in there."

He broke his gaze away from the box. "You don't have time now?"

"Actually, no," she told him, leading him back to the front door. "I have company on their way over. I'll let you know if it explodes when I open it."

"That's not funny," he said, looking over her shoulder to the office where the box was resting innocently. "I still think you should let me open it."

"I appreciate your concern, but it's probably just something my mom found at a flea market or something. Stop worrying," she laughed.

"You're having people over?"

"Yes, that happens from time to time," she told him, hoping she wouldn't have to tell him who.

He leaned against the door jamb, watching her. "How are you?"

"Fine," she said too brightly, not wanting to get stuck talking this close to August showing up.

His eyebrows rose. "And here I thought I made at least a little bit of an impression."

She chuckled. "Trust me, you did, you just caught me at a weird time, and I don't have time right now to talk about last night."

"You're not going to avoid it like it didn't happen, are you?" he asked, crossing his arms over his chest as he watched her.

"No, Ryder," she sighed. "I just don't have anything to say about it right now. I need more time to process. I wasn't expecting any of this." She waved her hands to encompass everything between them lately. "Or last night, and I just don't know where I am yet…"

He nodded, studying her. "If you need more… *information* to process, I'd be happy to volunteer my services," he smiled. "For the sake of research, of course."

"I'm sure you would," she replied, rolling her eyes but unable to resist smiling at his corny joke.

"Well, next time I come over unannounced, I'll have to make sure it's a day you're not expecting company so I can coax you into letting me make you dinner again," he smiled, stepping away from the door jamb.

His step brought him close enough that she could easily move into his arms if she listened to what her racing heart was willing her to do. She ignored it and the flurry of butterflies that his gaze was bringing out in her and stood firm, looking up into his focused eyes. She knew if she tilted up to him just slightly, he'd accept her invitation. There was a surprising feeling of energy that came with knowing she could have him. As exciting as that was, she needed to figure out how she felt about that before she allowed herself to do anything more reckless than she already had.

"You're so beautiful, Lilly," he said softly as he watched her watching him, reaching out to brush a stray strand of hair behind her shoulder, his fingers trailing ever so lightly across her skin.

She worried he'd move in for a kiss, not sure she'd want to stop him.

"Do me a favor?" he asked her quietly.

"What?" she breathed.

"Be careful when you open that box."

She laughed and he stepped back to grab the doorknob.

"Don't worry, I will."

"Bye, Lilly."

"Bye, Ryder." She smiled, closing the door behind him, thankful she hadn't ended up in a situation where she had both men standing on her porch together.

THIRTY-EIGHT

-LILLIAN-

She checked the clock. She had five minutes before August was supposed to arrive. He'd been punctual before, so she didn't really expect him early, but she wasn't sure how long she had and she was curious about what was in the box.

She headed to her office and studied the box, looking for a scribbled note that she and Ryder may have missed. Nothing, just a cardboard box with a lid taped on top of it. She got a pair of scissors from a drawer and slid the blade under the lip to break the binding. She put the scissors back, closed the drawer, and watched the box.

Nothing happened.

So far so good.

Had Ryder not been there and filled her head with worry, she never would have questioned the box. She would have hauled it in, opened it, and thanked whoever had sent it, but now… What was she going to find in there? She tried to recall a conversation with her parents about them dropping something off for her, which wasn't unheard of, but usually there was a note attached. Unless there had been, and it blew away. Satisfied that this could be a possible answer, she reached out for the lid, hesitated, then blew out her breath and just ripped the lid off.

And laughed.

Inside the box was a stack of printed papers lying on top of what appeared to be old newspapers. A handwritten note on top simply said:

> *Here's as much as I could get together so far. There's so much more, but I figured you could start here while I gather more if you still need it. Happy research, – Dotty.*

Dorothy, who everyone just called Dotty, was the librarian and honorary historian of the town since she was probably the oldest person in town. She knew everyone and everything that had happened since the dawn of time in Juniper Hollow, and had pretty much single-handedly built the library from the single room off the post office that it had been when she came along, to the amazing wealth of literature and knowledge that it was today. People came from three counties away to visit her library. Lillian had known her request would be in capable hands when she contacted Dotty, but she'd had no idea the old librarian be able to compile so much in such a short amount of time.

She knew August was on his way over, but she couldn't resist diving in. She took out a few pages on top, printouts of old newspaper clippings regarding the town and the base. Some of the articles seemed to just be mentions of the Mountain, like how the reporter had mentioned Wisteria and the Mountain in her own interview. Names were listed, but no real substance was given. She set those aside, realizing there'd be more like that and she could read them closely later if she needed to, but for now, she could weed them out.

She was halfway through the box. She had a pile for newspapers that she'd have to go through when she could read them and find the information Dotty thought was relevant enough to send over; a pile for brief mentions of the Mountain; a pile for mysterious deaths and missing people, which was so large it broke her heart; and a very small pile for articles written specifically about the Mountain. Those all seemed to be dated around Halloween and were heavy on the mystery and stories surrounding the place. She doubted she'd gather much factual information from those, but it could be fun to use some vintage spooky stories in her memorabilia and display, especially in the fall when the ghost hunters came to town for the festivals.

The abrupt knock at the door startled her, and she dropped the last few pages she had been sorting. She'd completely lost track of time. It had to be August this time; she rarely had unannounced visitors. She left the room as it was and went to open the front door, warmth spreading through her at the sight of his ruggedly handsome face.

"I bring gifts," he said, holding up a bottle of wine in one hand and a bag full of things hanging off his other arm. "You said you weren't hungry, and I get that, but hungry and snacky can be two very different things, or so I've learned. Since you won't let me make you dinner, and I'm guessing you do what just about every woman I know does and skips meals when she's too busy, I'm betting you'll at least be snacky while I'm here. I've got you covered for when you realize that, and if not, well, it'll keep until you are."

She laughed at his logic and stepped aside to let him in. He handed her the bottle of wine, which was already chilled, and led him through the living room to the kitchen to set the bag on the island.

"Thank you," she told him as he unbagged his snack feast, her stomach speaking up at the sight of the fruit, cheese, crackers, and meats he was unloading.

He raised his eyebrows in response to her sheepish smile.

"See, I knew it," he told her and opened one of the cases full of pinwheels, holding it out to her to eat. She grabbed one and popped it in her mouth, realizing just how hungry she really was as she chewed the delicious bite.

"Oh my gosh, those are amazing," she told him.

"I didn't make them," he confessed, "but was assured that everything here was sure to please."

"It looks like you went down the deli snack section and told them to give you a little of everything," she laughed, admiring the spread.

"Yeah, pretty much," he agreed. "I figured I'd get something right if I brought a variety."

"I'm pretty sure there isn't a single thing here that I don't like," she told him, taking another pinwheel and watching him as he ate as well. "You didn't have dinner after all did you?"

"Guilty," he admitted. "I had this hunch… and it's more fun to eat with you."

She smiled at him, completely at ease at her kitchen island like he'd been there a thousand times before.

"So, what have you been up to?" she asked.

"Well, I've been helping with the search for Rain, who we found, and then Brian, but he's still in the wind."

"I was hoping that finding Rain meant Brian was soon to follow, but Dad made it sound like his trail is cold, which is so weird to me. They went in together, how could they not be found together? Why would anyone split up in there?"

August didn't have a response and instead seemed to be inwardly debating what to say to her.

"What is it?" she asked. He looked over at her, still considering.

"You haven't talked to your dad lately?" he paused. "Or Ryder?"

At the mention of Ryder's name, the knots in her stomach returned, reminding her why she wasn't hungry earlier, and why she was meeting with August. She set her unfinished bite down, no longer able to think about the food.

"Not pertaining to Rain or Brian," she told him honestly, withholding the fact that Ryder was just at her house, and yes, she spoke with him, but that wasn't relevant to the subject at hand in the slightest.

August glanced away as well. "Ryder has a theory… your dad doesn't seem convinced, but humored him this afternoon."

"Really? The last I heard of Ryder's theory, my dad dismissed him, and I really thought Ryder had ruled it out and moved on."

"So, you do know about it?"

"About there being a murderer running around?"

"I don't know how much I'm allowed to say, but yes, that's what he's saying down at the station." He exhaled slowly. "Where I was questioned about my whereabouts during several dates and times."

"I'm sorry, August," she started apologetically, not surprised that her dad would have him questioned, even if only to mark him off the suspect list. "You're an outsider and did find one of the bodies. I'm sure it was just routine though, right?"

"Right. I'm not worried about it."

"But you're making it sound like there's more to the story."

"Well… some of the times that I was asked about, I was with you," he stated, leaving it hanging in the air between them.

"Oh." She paused, thinking about the reaction of the men in her life who didn't know she was seeing August. "So, who did your interview?"

"Your dad."

"Oh."

"Yeah… oh."

She tried suppressing a smile but failed.

"It's not funny."

"It's a little funny."

"I've spent time with him out in the woods, here and there, over the past few days, and he can be completely chill, and then he can be… intense. Guess how he was when I gave him an alibi for some of his dates."

"I can only imagine," she giggled.

"Calm, absolutely no reaction. There was no recognition, no surprise, no anger about me seeing his daughter. That's worse than any intensity I've seen so far, because I don't know what's happening behind those eyes when I informed the sheriff that I'd seen his daughter multiple times."

"He must be really busy because he didn't call to check up yet."

"He's probably waiting until he can do it in person and see your reaction."

"Well, it's not like it's a secret that we're seeing each other… not really."

August looked back down at the counter. "Is it not?"

Her stomach fluttered again.

"Well, not a secret, just… it's my private life and I haven't gone around talking about it with everyone."

"Ryder doesn't know." It was a simply said statement, and when he raised his eyes back to hers, she tried not to squirm, even though her insides had gone to jelly. "So, when I saw him kiss you the other day in your office, I couldn't really be mad at him. I wanted to. I wanted to punch him in the face. I thought about it all morning while I had to hike around with him, but then he made a comment about Simon being the competition, although not really since Simon didn't stand a chance and was more of an innocent infatuation that you'd never consider. He didn't seem threatened by me, which means he's either really sure of himself or didn't know we were seeing each other."

"No, he doesn't know," she admitted.

He nodded. "But you do," he stated. "I know this is still new, and we don't know that much about each other, but I thought we agreed we wouldn't play games." He paused to look over at her, no anger in his eyes, just a sort of hurt confusion. "This is one of those things that I feel we should share with each other if we're going to try and have any sort of chance at something real. And maybe that's not what you're after, maybe you're just looking for a good time, and that's fine for you, but that's not what I'm sticking around for. I don't share, Lillian."

"It's not like that," she started. "I wasn't sure if you saw that the other day."

"So, you just weren't going to tell me?" he asked, pushing away from the island to pace her tiny kitchen. "It's okay not to know if I don't see it for myself?"

"No, that's not what I meant at all," she said, trying to remain calm when she could feel her nerves starting to unravel. If he was this upset over her not telling him about the little kiss on the cheek, how would he respond to the rest? She had to share the rest. "Ryder and I have a history."

"I'm aware, but that doesn't excuse disrespect for me."

"No, you're right, and that's not at all what I meant. I know I should have told you, and planned on it, but didn't know how."

"It's easy… unless it meant something to you, in which case, I could see why it could be a challenge."

She exhaled and stood up from the island as well. Sitting still was making her antsy.

"I don't know what it meant."

"That's answer enough," he stated emotionlessly.

His face was just like he'd described her dad's in the interview: calm, no reaction, no indication of how he was feeling. He was right, it was worse not knowing what was going on behind those eyes.

"No, it's not," she told him, panicking that he might leave without her getting the chance to explain herself. "We dated in high school and things ended badly. We have been absolutely nothing to each other, a completely nonexistent relationship until just recently. It was nothing I ever planned or expected; sort of like you."

"Are you sleeping with him, too?" he asked flatly.

"No," she growled. "I haven't slept with him."

His arms were crossed over his chest and his face was still blank, but she sensed a slight change, possibly satisfaction.

"I wanted to tell you about the kiss, but I wasn't sure if it was even worth talking about. It was a small peck, a reassurance in all this chaos. There was no romance to it."

"Maybe not to you, but it certainly brightened *his* day." He paused, watching her. "But you also didn't seem surprised by it, and I'd say that even if I had reconciled with an ex, a kiss would be a surprise, romantic or not."

"You're right, it would have been." She hesitated, and he waited. "If it had been the first."

His face hardened, but she was all in now, no holding anything back. She hated that this was how the conversation had wound up going, but it was all or nothing at this point. August deserved the truth, and hopefully he'd still be around after it was all said. She hadn't even gotten to the hard part yet, and her stomach was already threatening to give back everything she had eaten in her brief memory lapse.

"Can I explain?" she asked. "Or have you decided that it no longer matters what I have to say?"

He was clearly angry, and she could finally see the war raging in his eyes. She wasn't sure yet which side would win; they didn't have a history, just a short story, easy to walk out on and move on, but she hoped that it was enough of a story for him to want to find out more.

"Please?" she asked quietly.

He dropped his arms and raised his eyes like he was looking to the heavens for an answer to a question she didn't know, but when he lowered his gaze back to her, she could tell a decision had been made.

"Okay," he said as calmly as possible. "Tell me what it is that you think I should know."

"I'm going to tell you all of it," she said, trying to keep her voice from shaking as much as her insides, "even though it terrifies me that after I do, you're going to walk out that door."

He crossed his arms again, shrugged his shoulders and leaned back against the counter, as if to drive home the fact that this was all her doing and he was just here to watch the shit-show that was to come.

She started with Ryder approaching her and apologizing for their past, explaining that she was grateful for the closure, but that she didn't think much would progress from there.

"I could tell he was being sincere for the moment, but Ryder is good at 'the moment.' It's the long term that he, historically, wasn't good at, but that was also ages ago in high school. So honestly, I guess I didn't know what to expect from him. I was surprised when he came to my house."

At August's raised eyebrows she explained about Wade's death and how they had all been friends back in the day and Ryder had wanted to be the one to break the news. She looked away then back again, determined not to shy away as she told him more.

"That was the night he first kissed me. He was upset and I hugged him, just to console him, and then it just happened. It was a shock and he apologized, and I thought it was just one of those in-the-moment things and it was done, over with… but then Rain disappeared, and it was like ripping another bandage off. So many emotions, even if Rain and I didn't see eye to eye all the time. It was still awful that she was missing, and he was trying to reassure me that everything was going to be okay. He kissed my cheek, that was it." She paused. August's face had gone blank again as she told her story. He didn't look overly upset, but he clearly wasn't thrilled either; she considered stopping her story there, but she knew that her conscience would eat at her if she didn't tell him all of it and their relationship continued with that secret between them. She took a deep breath. "And then—"

"There's more?" he said, stepping away from the counter and laughing sardonically.

"Just once more."

"I don't need to hear the details," he said with a sigh.

"Well, I don't really want to share the details of any of this, but you should know about them."

"I'm seeing the picture pretty clearly without hearing more. The first time, he took advantage of an emotional situation to get what he wanted from you. The second time, he showed you his compassionate and reassuring side, the strong shoulder to lean on. The third time, he opened the door that he'd been working the lock on, and must have made some sort of impression, because it's left you conflicted enough to avoid me."

"I haven't been avoiding you," she started.

He raised his eyebrows in disbelief. "You haven't called or texted me since the other day when he kissed your cheek. That feels like avoiding to me, especially if there was a possibility that you thought I had seen. That's pretty much the definition of avoiding, actually."

She didn't say anything, feeling weak that she didn't have a response because he was absolutely right, but she didn't want him to know that.

"Here's what I'm going to do," he said with an overabundance of calm in his voice. "I'm going to go—"

"No, August, please stay. We can talk about this."

"I can't, Lillian," he said, and the way he said it, the emotion that slipped through in that one statement, hurt her more than if he'd yelled at her. "I'm going to go so you can figure out you. I like you. I think I made that pretty clear, and I thought that would reciprocate some respect, but I get it, things change. You know Ryder. You have a history. Hell, did you know Simon wants to be in the running, too? I'm sure there are others if you open your eyes. You have your pick."

"Now you're just being nasty," she said, trying to keep her voice level.

He paused at the front door. "Probably," he said, voice flat, "but here's the thing, Lillian. It's all or nothing with me. I don't share, and I don't come in second."

He didn't wait for a response, just opened the door, walked through, and pulled it silently closed behind him. There was no yelling. No slamming door. No argument. Just simply stated facts with a few side jabs thrown in.

She wished he had yelled… or slammed the door… or told her Ryder wasn't worth a damn.

She could have handled any of those better than him just leaving.

THIRTY-NINE

-BILL-

"Sheriff," Ryder said by way of greeting. "You all done for the night?" he asked, heading into the building as Bill was coming out.

"Yep. Running by Lillian's, then on home. What're you doing back here?"

"Thought I'd ask those kids some more questions," he motioned behind him as if they could see the two boys through the walls.

"I let them go."

"What? Why?" The agitation resounded through his questions. "Brian could be hiding out somewhere and they could know where."

"We went over it all today with them and their stories never faltered. If they knew something, they would have slipped up."

"Yeah, or they could have practiced. What if they leave town?"

"I've told them to stick around and booked them a room at the hotel."

"So now the city's paying for their lodging?" Ryder asked, not even masking his disagreement with his superior's decision. "That'll look great when the press gets ahold of that information. 'Sheriff uses tax-payor dollars to house potential accomplices to multiple murders.' Are you *trying* to be pushed out of office? Because with that move, it won't take much."

Bill grabbed his deputy by the elbow and walked him away from the entrance of the department, his grip firm when he felt the boy try to squirm away on initial impulse. He stopped walking and let go of his arm when they were far enough away not to be easily overheard.

"First of all," Bill calmly stated. "As you just pointed out, I am the sheriff here and *your* superior officer. In all the time that you've been my deputy, you may have had a different opinion on the choices that I made, but you were never disrespectful of the chain of command, which I'm proud of you for. It's no easy feat to disagree with a decision and still follow orders dutifully. This investigation hits home for you because of Wade, and I know you have theories that—I will admit—are looking more possible. Because of the loss of your friend, and what could be considered a grief-induced brain fog, I'm going to give you a little grace in this situation and remind you that these two bodies have been ruled as natural deaths. No rumors of murder have been spread. No suspects are being held against their will on the suspicion of murder or accomplice to murder due to the incredible *lack* of evidence to support that theory.

"What the press *will* see, if they cared enough to look, is that the Sheriff booked a single hotel room on his own dollar, to see that a couple of kids that fell into unfortunate circumstances not once, by discovering a dead body, but twice, by losing a friend and fellow camper, have a comfortable place to stay while we search for their *missing* friend.

"And," he continued before Ryder dared interrupt, "if, in the meantime, we need to ask them any more questions depending on what further evidence we uncover in our continued investigation, the likelihood that they will be more cooperative with those that have been kind in an unknown situation is far higher than if we chose to hold them for 24 hours while we batter them with questions until we ultimately have to release them in a disgruntled state.

"Would you prefer to fire up the press with talk of murder with no hard evidence to support the theory, potentially alienating the closest leads to the case? Or would you rather we utilize patience and the skills you've honed as an investigating deputy to figure out what's really going on here?"

It was obvious that Ryder didn't initially want to agree, but one good thing about Bill's deputy was his typical ability to consider reason. Bill watched as Ryder processed the words he'd said, weighing out what they really meant.

"You're not cutting them loose?"

"For the time being, I've asked them to remain in town. It wasn't hard for them to agree since they still don't have their friend back."

"Who could be a murderer."

"Or could just be good old-fashioned missing."

"But you're willing to keep the investigation into the two bodies' cause of death open?"

"I've already tasked Rich to look again at both of them and report back as soon as he finishes."

"And if foul play turns up?"

"Then we'll already have a few key people to talk to and know exactly where to find them."

"What if Brian is the killer, and the others are just trying to find their chance to skip town?"

"If that is the case, I'm betting they don't want to blow their cover by leaving town when they were asked to stay. That would cause unnecessary attention at a time when they're supposed to be worrying over their missing friend. Besides, they'd have to get past the officer assigned to their well-being."

"Well-being?"

"I can't exactly position an officer on guard to report back to me with regular updates when there isn't an official murder investigation. However, I can provide support in the form of an officer in the immediate vicinity to convey real-time messages if there is an update on their missing friend."

"They make phones for that."

"I like the human approach."

Ryder analyzed the new information before responding. The sheriff was proceeding reasonably, albeit, not the way he'd have done it himself.

"So basically, you're not pushing yourself out of a job," Ryder finally conceded with a casual smile.

"Not any time soon, son. You're going to have to try a lot harder than that to take over."

"Let me guess, 'there's still much to learn.'"

"Of course," Bill replied lightly, authority no longer necessary. "You should always be learning something new, otherwise how can there be new experiences? And without new experiences, where's the thrill of life?"

Ryder just smiled and shook his head. "Well, I guess you're right there. And I guess there's no point in me going back in there," he waved his hand toward the building. "You said you're swinging by Lillian's house? Do you need me to ride along with you?"

"To my daughter's house?" Bill asked.

"Yeah, are you going to discuss the search or instructions for tomorrow? It'd be good for me to get the details as well."

"Oh. No. Jane took the forward back this afternoon, and I don't see any reason to burden Lillian or the diner anymore as a volunteer station unless things change. No. I'm just going to check on my daughter on my way home. This has been a trying time for everyone. I need to make sure she's okay."

"Okay. Tell her I said hi," Ryder said.

Bill noticed the slight twitch of Ryder's mouth at the statement as if he hadn't meant to say anything but it was too late to retract. *Curious.* He watched for changes in body language as he asked, "Do you know if she's been seeing anyone?"

"Lillian?" Ryder stalled. "Why? What have you heard?"

"Nothing really," Bill said, noticing that he hadn't answered the question. "What with her going out to celebrate taking over the diner at the Overlook the other night, and then everything that's happened since then, I haven't had a chance to talk much about her new role."

"The Overlook. Nice. Must have been some night to celebrate there."

Bill had noticed Ryder's changes around his daughter, and while Bill knew from questioning August earlier in the day that he had been her dinner partner, he could tell by Ryder's change in stance that he was curious about who had taken Lillian out. He also knew how much it would bother Ryder to know that Lillian had been with August and figured that, if he suspected August, he wouldn't be so at ease. He wasn't sure yet how he felt about Ryder getting friendly with Lillian again, and judging by Ryder's evasive answers, he wondered how friendly the deputy had already been. But. Ryder he knew, August he didn't. And Bill didn't like how the newcomer kept showing up at the wrong times.

He decided to let Ryder think about the new information and see what came of it.

"Well, I'm going to try and catch her at home before it gets too late," he said, heading to his Blazer.

"She mentioned earlier that she was having company tonight," Ryder mentioned.

"Oh? You talked to her?" he asked, turning back to Ryder.

"Yeah, just in passing with all this," he motioned to the air as if to encompass the situation of the missing hiker.

"Hmm," Bill mused, watching Ryder's brow furrow as he puzzled out something he didn't feel like sharing. "Well, I'm sure she'll have a few minutes for her old man. Have a good night, Ryder. See you tomorrow. We have an investigation to unravel."

"Yeah, see you."

Bill headed to his daughter's house. He now had questions for her regarding two men.

FORTY
-LILLIAN & BILL-

The knock at Lillian's door startled her from her reading. Her confusion deepened when she noticed the clock read 9:32 pm. Who would be coming by without calling her first? She checked her phone for a missed notification. Nothing. Her heart raced at the thought of August coming back to talk things through. Should she let him? She wanted to set things back to rights, but she was also hurt by the way he had just left.

She didn't know what to say this time around.

She'd spent the first thirty minutes after he'd left wondering how she should have done things differently. Maybe he didn't need to know all—well, most—of the details between her and Ryder. It wasn't like she was in a committed relationship with either of them. Granted, August had made it clear he wanted to see where things could go, but that didn't mean they were married, as Lana had pointed out. And Ryder … things with Ryder had all seemed so circumstantial until August had laid out how Ryder had used the situations to his advantage, which admittedly had her upset with Ryder for a few minutes.

Then she reminded herself that Ryder had no idea about August and her, and he'd already made it known that he was interested in making things better between them. She hadn't been as forthcoming with Ryder as she had with August about what she'd been doing in her spare time. She hadn't figured out yet if that was a defense mechanism because of her history with Ryder, or if it meant that what she was feeling for August meant something more than what she was feeling for Ryder. After feeling guilty for how she'd been acting lately and treating them both, then feeling ridiculous for feeling guilty because she was a grown woman who was allowed to have a social life, she decided to put all thoughts of both men out of her mind and dove into work.

Until the knock on her door.

And now, here she was worrying again about how she was supposed to be feeling. At the second knock she sighed, set her paper down and went to answer the door. The lights were all on inside the house, so it wasn't as if she could just pretend she'd already gone to bed and ignore the knocker. Besides, where would that get her anyway?

"Oh," she said, genuinely surprised to see her dad on the other side of the door. Then she remembered that August had come to her house after being interviewed by her dad all afternoon. She sighed again. "I know why you're here. Come on in."

"Don't sound so thrilled to see your old man," he said, following her inside and closing the door behind him. "So, why do you think I'm here?" She raised an eyebrow at the question, and he smiled apologetically, but held out the small bag he carried. "As your dad, I know how to soften you up, but you know I have to do my job as the sheriff and follow up on information."

"That *information* being to ask if I've been spending my *personal* time with August." She looked into the bag and smiled, pulling out her favorite peanut butter cookies from Tiller's Market and sat on the couch.

"Which already tells me that you *have* been because nobody else could have told you that I'd be interested in confirming other than him." He sat opposite her in one of her comfy armchairs, moving the pile of papers to the floor since there was no space on the table between them.

She opened the package and her mouth began to water at the sweet aroma. She plucked a cookie from the bag, offered one to her dad, then set the package on top of her stacks of neatly organized papers.

"So, what do you need to know?" She nestled herself snuggly into the corner of the couch, ready for the questioning.

Her dad flipped open a notepad, an item he was never without, even in today's digital age where he could instantly make an electronic note that could be shared with all his devices and personnel. Much to the aggravation of the younger generation serving under him, he preferred the simplicity of pen and paper. Thankfully, Jane was a wiz when it came to computers and could easily convert and share pertinent information.

"How long have you known August?"

"Not very long. He's new to town. You know that; you saw him in the diner that day and mentioned that."

"So that day in the diner." He looked at his notes. "Last Wednesday, was the first time you'd met him?"

"As I'm sure August already told you, because you are a very thorough officer of the law and leave no stone unturned." She smiled at her dad. "No, that's not the first time I'd met him."

Her dad waited for her to answer the question.

"I met him in passing on the street last Sunday. He needed directions."

"Directions."

"Mmhmm," she said sweetly.

"August."

"Yes."

"Saying August needs directions is like saying the compass didn't point north."

Her dad had figured that out much quicker than she had, although, in her defense, she had only just met the man.

"I guess you could say he needed recommendations, so I gave him some. You know, where to get gear, where to eat, places to see. Stuff like that."

"All that to a stranger."

She raised her eyebrow and cocked her head. "Dad, everyone is a stranger. I talk to people all day, every day, it's my job."

"And it didn't strike you as odd that someone would ask for directions where they can just look it up on their phone?"

"Asks the man that still writes all his notes on a notepad."

"It didn't seem strange that he'd approach *you* for directions?"

"Because I'm a woman who couldn't know which way was which?"

"Because you are a woman all alone on the street encumbered with heavy grocery bags, who could easily be a target to a predator."

"Dad," she sighed. "He's not a predator."

"How do you know? He was just some man on the street that you decided to engage in conversation and then let walk you to your car."

"I see you know all you need to know about when I met August," she said coolly. "And in case you've forgotten, I'm an adult and can talk to attractive men on the sidewalk if I want to."

"Just last week you told me you weren't interested in dating anyone, and now I find out through interviewing a suspect that my own daughter is his alibi."

"Is this about verifying August's whereabouts, or your daughter's social life?"

He leaned forward, elbows on his knees. "It's about you being careful. You knew he was someone I was already concerned about."

"Not then I didn't."

"Things could have gone terribly wrong on that very first day. I thought we taught you better. He could have knocked you out when you got to your car, taken you away. Just like that you'd be another of my missing persons cases, or worse, a murder I'm trying to solve."

She could hear the worry in his voice and see the pleading in his eyes, but she wasn't sixteen anymore. She had plenty of arguments to throw at him, and after the day she'd had, she could feel a bubbling within and was ready to give him an earful.

But she was still his only child.

She squashed the urge to argue for argument's sake, got up and walked to his chair. She squatted down beside it, taking his hand as she did. "I love that you're ready to fight for me. Thank you for always being my protector, but know that you *have* taught me well, and even though it doesn't seem like it to you because you're my dad, I *am* careful. I survived college and the city. I can handle life here, especially when a nice man offers to help me carry my very heavy bag."

He sighed. "Can you at least see it from my point of view and understand why I'd worry?"

"I can, and I understand that anything I do is going to cause you worry."

"Not *anything*."

She waited.

"Just anything like having a stranger carry your bag to a secluded parking lot, all alone, with no witnesses around."

"In the middle of the afternoon, with traffic buzzing by, with the possibility at any moment someone else could walk to their own parked car nearby, or with the security cameras always on record."

"Or when she decides it's a good idea to go hiking in the woods with a man she just met without a text or call to her parents to tell them where she'll be."

She dropped her head to the arm of the chair, smiling as she stood up to move back to her own seat. "Don't worry, Dad. I told Lana I was out." She didn't mention that she hadn't told her where. "And I had plans for later that afternoon that enabled a check-in on my whereabouts. And that was Thursday, by the way, if you want to confirm August's dates." She grabbed another cookie as her dad scribbled in his notepad. "Besides, if I *had* told my parents, they would have tried to talk me out of going. How will I ever have those grandbabies you and mom are always asking about if I don't find a man?"

"You did say you weren't looking."

"And I still haven't said otherwise."

"Yet you've been spending a lot of time with August."

"Yes, because he's enjoyable to spend time with."

Her dad looked at his notepad again. "What time did your date Saturday end?"

"I don't know." She sighed, hating to document her life like this, but her dad just waited, and she knew from childhood that "I don't know" was never an acceptable answer. "It was late. If you haven't already checked them, you can get the time on the security cameras, but for both our sake's, I'd prefer if you don't watch the stream."

"I'm guessing you'd prefer I didn't have Ryder watch it either?" he asked as he looked from his notepad for her reaction.

"So, you've already seen the footage then?" she asked, avoiding the answer.

"Of course. I had to verify dates and times."

"So then why are you here interrogating me if you already know?"

"I'm not interrogating you."

"It's feeling more and more like that."

"Was August your company this afternoon?"

"You already know he told me about being questioned by you."

"That could have been over the phone."

"So, now we're working forward, establishing alibis in case something else comes up? Yes, I saw him briefly this afternoon, but don't worry, we don't have any plans of seeing each other again."

He knew he'd been pushing it with his questions as a cop, but the way her voice grew pained as she answered, had his fatherly role coming to the surface. "Why not, did you break up?"

She rubbed her forehead. "Dad, no, we weren't *together* to break up. We dated a few times." She nodded to the notepad. "You've got it all written down. We've had a good time, but—" She paused, not wanting to go through it all again, and not with her dad.

"But, Ryder got in the way," he finished for her.

"What? No."

He waited, testing his theory.

"No, Ryder and I…" she trailed off. "We're not together. You know that. I've made that very clear."

"Very. For years."

She sighed, rubbing her forehead again. "Dad, I don't want to talk about any of this."

He studied his daughter, a woman now, sitting across from him in her home. She was the owner of a successful business with the future and all its challenges ahead of her, but was still his little girl, and was struggling with something that she thought she had to handle on her own.

"Then we won't talk about it. But." He paused when she gave him a disbelieving look that said she didn't think he could drop the subject so quickly. "Whatever troubles you've got between you and August and Ryder—and don't tell me there's nothing going on with Ryder. As you continue to point out, I'm both your father and a cop, and I know both of you, your histories, and the ice isn't thawing between you, it went straight to summer overnight, so there's something you both aren't telling me. Besides whatever is going on there," he continued, "and whatever is going on between you and August, no matter how much I don't care for that at this moment, you need to remember to be true to yourself. You've always been very independent, but if you're struggling with something, you don't have to do it all on your own. It's okay to ask for help or guidance." He stopped talking, knowing he couldn't say much more and be "not talking about it." He looked around the room at the mess of papers and motioned to them all. "Take this room for example. If you need help cleaning all this up, you know all you have to do is ask."

Her dad was always easy to talk to, but her August-Ryder situation wasn't something she wanted to dig into with him, especially right now. She smiled at his attempt to lighten the mood and grabbed the extended olive branch. She sighed and leaned toward her coffee table and the piles of papers.

"This," she said picking up the closest newspaper, "is research. You're welcome to help."

He took the extended paper, noticing the yellowed edges. "Ah, paper. Old-school. My area of expertise," he joked, glancing over the front page, frowning as he did. "What's your research for?" he asked, looking over the newspaper at her.

"I thought to bring some history into the diner. I had this idea to be nostalgic. Blow-up old photos, find articles about the town, folklore, the diner, the people. You know, sort of a time capsule since the restaurant has been around so long."

He noticed the hesitation in her voice. "That sounds like a good idea. Why are you conflicted?"

She reached out to take the paper back and read a small section from the front page, "Hiker still unidentified after discovery last week. Police have no leads or suspicion of foul play. Citizens are urged to contact authorities with information that could help identify this young man." She set the paper down. "It goes on to provide a basic description in hopes that someone will claim him. Average build, 6'1", dark brown hair, early twenties, tattoo of an anchor on right shoulder." She looked at the sorted piles. "There's just so much loss here. It's sad, going through it all and seeing the history this town's been a part of."

"This town has had a lot of good, too," her dad said. "Yes, this is a sad story, but it's just one story. I remember this one, when the young man went missing. He was home for a holiday, I think, had joined the navy, thus the anchor tattoo. His family was very proud. He went hiking with friends, but wandered off from the group. That was early in my career, every young officer wanted to be the one to find him, to be the hero." He frowned again at the paper in her hand. "I didn't remember him ever being found, but again, that was early on, and we always had a new case. Obviously, they did find him, and just needed to identify the body. I'm sure when they finally identified him, it brought his family some peace by knowing he'd been found. So even though that was a tragedy, that's just one piece of a puzzle that eventually offered closure to that boy's family.

"Don't get hung up on those types of stories, or you'll drown in all the misery. Set those aside and look for the monumental occasions or the quirky things about this town or the restaurant that people want to remember or learn about when they visit. Talk to locals or put out one of those chats online. I bet you can come up with plenty of rich history to share."

"You're right." She set the paper back on the stack and stood up to stretch. "It's getting late anyway, and I need a break to take a fresh look. Thank you for the perspective on the article. You're right, you know, I'm not planning on plastering the walls with missing faces posters. I just got caught up by how many there were." They walked to the door. "I don't know how you do what you do all the time, Dad."

"What do you mean?"

She motioned back to the stack. "That's your life all the time. You wade through all those stories, more the bad than the good, during the height of the emotional turmoil. How do you still manage to laugh and smile and keep going? It's just so sad."

He smiled at his daughter. "I have you and your mom to light my days. And I look for the victories in the tragedies. Catching the bad guy, finding the missing person, bringing closure. Bad things are going to happen, that's a part of life, but life goes on, so we look for the good things, we learn from the bad things to keep them from happening again, and we continue, too."

He gave his daughter a hug and kissed her on the top of her head.

"It's late. You need to get some rest."

"Maybe you're the one that needs the rest."

"Also true. I love you, Lillian."

"Love you, too, Dad."

"Lock this door behind me." He turned back before pulling it closed. "And call your mom. You know she worries."

"I know, I know," she laughed. "Bye, Dad."

He pulled it shut and she locked the bolt, hearing his steps across her small porch.

She walked back to her table to find her phone and text her mom, not wanting to call her this late and cause her to think there was something to worry over.

Dad dropped by, but just left. On his way home. Want to get together soon? Miss you, love you.

She pushed the send button and dropped her phone onto the pile of papers. It immediately buzzed against the stack, its downward facing light illuminating the print around it. The date on the front of the paper caught her eye as she lifted the phone to check her mom's response.

Sounds good. How does breakfast at 9 tomorrow sound before you go to work? Here at the house. Good night. Miss you more, love you too.

Breakfast sounds great.

She looked at the paper again. It was dated over thirty years ago.

Her dad had been through so many experiences just like this. It made her sad to think of all the cases like this he'd been through, solved or unsolved. She shook her head. This one was a long time ago, and like he said, this wasn't the type of story to make the wall anyway. She turned off the light and headed to bed, looking forward to her mom's homemade breakfast.

FORTY-ONE

-Lillian-

Breakfast with her mom was just what she needed. Lately, the days were increasingly overwhelming. She hadn't realized how much she needed a delicious, home-cooked meal and to just relax, putting aside her stressors for an hour with her mom. When she left, it was with an offer of help on her research, and a plan to meet at the library after her short shift. Together, they'd do a more direct search instead of trying to sift through the everything pile that Dotty had so far provided.

"You're bubbly today," Lana greeted her as Lillian dropped her purse in her office.

"I can't tell if you mean that sarcastically or not," Lillian laughed.

"Well, I meant it truthful, you look happy, like you have stories that you should share with your friend." She studied her, considering, "But… your doubting my sincerity has me wondering what stories you should now definitely fill me in on."

"It's not like that," Lillian said as lightheartedly as she could manage. "It's just with everything that's happened around here lately, I haven't been sleeping well, and thought it showed." She decided to omit the personal strife for now, knowing that Lana would be a good sounding board, but would want details and she wasn't up for a recap session. "But I got to see my mom for breakfast this morning, so that was refreshing."

"If that's where you're going to credit the bounce in your step, and not that you're holding back a good story about either handsome –"

"Nope, no stories." She quickly cut off her friend's sentence and headed to the front at the sound of Gary's approach. "Good morning," she said as she passed him. "How's business today?"

Lana returned to her kitchen and Gary turned to follow Lillian back to the front.

"Staying busy. We've had a few people in to offer volunteer services, but I told them we weren't the hub anymore and sent them to the police station."

"That's good. I haven't heard anything new about the search, but I'm assuming they'll still be looking today. It's sad, isn't it, how quickly people move on? There's been much less turn out for keeping the search going for Brian than when Rain was out there, too."

"I think it's just a hard place to look. It's not like just anyone can volunteer to go. Could you imagine being out there?" He leaned over as if to whisper a secret. "There are bears in those woods." He handed her a piece of paper that was on a shelf near the register. "And ticks. Don't even get me started on the bugs."

She glanced over the resume he'd handed her. The candidate looked very promising. Gary was going on about bugs and poison ivy while she looked around the diner in hopes that the applicant was still there.

"Gary," she interrupted. "When was this left here?"

"Hmm?" He looked at her hand as if he'd already forgotten what was written on the paper. "Oh, just a few minutes ago. Why do you think I was coming to get you?"

"Well, you never said anything."

"I handed you that, didn't I?" he answered, as if it was explanation enough.

"Okay," she said simply. "I'm going to call her and see if she can come back for an interview."

"No need. She ordered and is waiting for her food over there," he said, pointing across the room to a back booth.

Lillian took a deep breath. It wouldn't do her any good to tell him how helpful it would have been to lead with that information. He'd only take it as a personal attack and say something defensive.

Instead, she smiled.

"Thank you, Gary. If you don't need anything from me, I'm going to go see if she can interview while she's here."

Before he could manifest something else that would stall her, she thanked him again for the resume and walked to the woman waiting in the booth. Twenty minutes later she was back at her desk printing off new hire paperwork and checking the schedules to see where she could add her to the rotation. She could really use two more solid hires, but she had a little time before that was going to be absolutely necessary. Plus, Marley would be back from maternity leave soon. Things were looking up. She might even get to take a set day off… if everyone worked out well together.

She stayed busy through her shift, felt confident leaving the diner in the hands of the evening shift, and left at the same time as Lana, meeting her again in the parking lot.

"So, are you going to tell me what's really going on with you?"

"What do you mean?" she asked, taken off-guard by the sudden question.

"You're holding something back. I've known you long enough now to know that when you don't want to talk about something, you dig down and work. It wouldn't surprise me if you told me you finished all your tasks for the month in today's shift, so what gives? And don't say you can't share personal information because you're the boss now. We're friends, and if I have to quit right now so you can tell me what's going on, I will." She crossed her arms and planted her feet as if to show she was determined not to take no for an answer. "But, if you could hire me right back after you tell me, that would save me the hassle of job hunting."

Lillian laughed. She was thankful to have such a good group of people to look out for her. Sometimes she'd get so focused, determined to figure things out on her own, that she'd forget she had an amazing support system of friends and family willing to dive in and help.

"First, please don't quit. Ever. I can't find anyone that can run a crew like you *and* be able to cook, too. I'm not even sure you really exist sometimes."

Lana nodded. "True, you'd close the doors in less than a week without me."

"Right, so, no quitting. But also, there's nothing really to say right now either."

"There's always something to say. You've had a lot going on in not a lot of time, and I feel like if I was in your shoes I'd be bursting trying to keep it all in."

"You're right. I do have a lot on my mind with the changeover, Rain and Brian, some things I'm trying to do to freshen up the place," she said, nodding toward the building.

"The two men in your life," Lana continued for her.

"Yes, there's that too," she sighed.

"Something happened," Lana surmised, then continued after a moment. "A not good something and you're trying to suppress it."

"I'm not trying to suppress it." At Lana's disbelieving raised eyebrow, she continued, "Okay, maybe a little bit. I just don't want to think about either of them right now. You know?"

"Not really, no. I'd want to think about either, both, doesn't matter."

She laughed again at how her friend could be so simply blunt.

"Fine," she sighed again, opening the door to her car to put her things inside. "August and I had a little bit of a disagreement last night and he left."

"What sort of disagreement? Like name calling and slamming doors, but flowers and make-up sex is around the corner?"

"Or like telling him about Ryder and cool and collected August left and hasn't called since."

"Ouch."

"Yeah. So, I'd rather not think about how I tried to do the right thing and be honest from the get-go, and now there's nothing left to get."

"Nope."

"No? Why no?"

"Nope, you don't get to mope."

"Who said I'm moping?"

"Me. You're blinding yourself with work, so you don't have to face him. You didn't do anything wrong, yet you're punishing yourself like you did."

"I made out with Ryder."

"So. You already said it, you barely know August. Things happened. Who cares? It's not 1947." At Lillian's confused look, she kept on, "I don't know, *old times*. You're allowed to date. You can date one guy or fifty guys. If that means you canoodle with all fifty guys, so be it. How are you supposed to figure out which to keep and which to toss? Apparently, August doesn't want you to see fifty guys, so now you know, and you can decide if he's worth keeping over the rest."

"Canoodle? Really?"

"Sure, why not?"

"And there's just two guys, not fifty."

"See, August has nothing to complain about."

"The problem is that I knew I wouldn't want him out *canoodling* with anyone else if he was with me, so it's not right that I was the one doing it to him."

"Yeah, I get that. You're on a straight and narrow path, but here's the thing. You've gotta live. You need to figure out you, not what everyone else wants for you, but what you want for you. And that doesn't mean diving into just work so everything else falls away and you're left with nothing. *You* need to figure out what you want and then go for it. If you want Ryder, you know where he is. If you want August, show him you want him. But you have to figure that out."

"Gee, thanks. You make it sound so simple."

"Eh, I do what I can," she smiled. "Seriously though. Don't let this get away from you. This is one of those things you look back on and wish you did differently."

"Ryder or August?"

She mimed zipping her mouth closed and throwing away the key.

"Thanks, so helpful."

Lana leaned over to squeeze her friend in a hug then headed to her own car. "You'll figure it out."

Lillian sat down in her car and checked her phone. No missed calls or texts… from either man in her messed-up life.

She had some thinking to do.

Lana was right. If she didn't fight for what she wanted, she'd be left with nothing, and it would be her own fault… but how did you fight for something when you didn't know what you wanted?

FORTY-TWO

-LILLIAN-

Liza, always the punctual one, waved Lillian over. She had already started going through another of Dotty's boxes of history by the time Lillian had made it to the library.

"I got the best table," her mom whispered conspiratorially as if securing a spot in the library was the challenge of a lifetime. "When I got here and told them what we were looking for, they already had this box ready to be sent to you. I went ahead and started looking through it, but, well, I'm not really sure what you want to find."

"Me neither," Lillian laughed. She picked up more of the same papers that she had at home, still unsure if the project was even worth doing.

"Okay, well, you're not going to get very far if you don't have a goal. What's the simplest version of your idea?"

"I want to remind people of how the restaurant started, how it's changed through the years, been a staple in the community for so long, and as such, incorporate pieces of the community in there, too."

"Okay… let's go simpler than that," her mom said with a smile.

She thought about her project, wondering how to make it any simpler.

"I guess I want to share the stories."

"Perfect. Now we can start."

"We can?"

"Yes. You can easily pick through these things that you know aren't going to be relevant and go straight to the highlight reel. You aren't documenting *all* of history, just picking a few good things to share." Liza glanced at a few different newspapers, putting them in her discard pile until she held one out. "Here, this looks promising."

Lillian skimmed the front page. The title "10 Cents for a Shake or a Shake – Celebrating 10 Years Running" discussed the ten year anniversary announcement for Wisteria. A customer could pay $0.10 for either a milkshake from Helen or a handshake from Harvey. The photo showed a picture of Harvey and Helen in Wisteria. Harvey had his hands raised in question in front of him, while Helen was laughing, handing a shake to a small boy. Her side showed a long line waiting, while Harvey's side had no one. Helen and the option of a sweet treat the clear choice over a handshake. Lillian agreed that it was a fun article and could possibly make the cut.

"Okay, but what about the rest of those? What if there's something deeper inside that could be useful?"

"Highlight reel," her mom reminded her. "If you want to go deeper later, you can, but for now, the big stories of the day will be front page pieces. If you decide you want to hone in your topic even further for more quirky town stories—you mentioned folklore at breakfast—you would probably be better off doing an internet search. Your old university has a great department that you could give them key words and they can probably search through all of this much faster than we could."

Lillian nodded. "It would sure save more time than looking through each and every paper or artifact from this town."

"You can find almost anything online these days."

"True." She sorted out another few papers that didn't show much promise into the discard pile. "The university is a pretty good idea."

"Oh, you know, I have those sometimes," her mom sang cheerily, but then couldn't hold back. "I want to take credit for it, but it wasn't completely my idea. I asked the attendant who dropped off the box if there was a better way to do this and he said most of this stuff and more has been recorded through partnerships with different departments in the university and that you could potentially even talk to the history department professors and get the students to do most of the research for you as part of their semester projects. Really genius if you ask me. They get to get involved with the community, learn a little something, and you could get perspectives of the younger generation on what they think is relevant enough to dig up. The older generation will remember some of the events, so it'll spark memories, but the younger generation will be learning new things."

Lillian considered this new angle. She already had a few pieces she'd like to use and could wait for more. Maybe she could reach out to the university and see what they thought.

"I feel like you probably just saved me a lot of time."

Liza beamed over the box between them. "Good! We can get copies of these so you can think about them, but this way you won't have so much on your plate."

"It's not like I have too much to do, Mom."

"Oh, I know, honey, but with the diner and really being in charge now, you're going to have more responsibilities. It's time to learn to delegate."

"It's not like I haven't already been doing the things, you know."

"I know that," her mom reassured her, "but now, so does everyone else. Things that people may not have said to you before as the waitress, *will* be said to the owner. I just don't want you to get overworked. You need a social life, too. It can't all be work."

"I have a social life," she said, defensive.

"Oh?" her mom asked a little too innocently, studying the paper she was on intently.

Lillian waited for her mom to give in and look up.

"What has Dad told you?"

"Nothing."

She waited again.

"Nothing much, *really*. You know how your dad can be. He's just worried about you. He said you'd had a few dates, but things didn't seem to work out. And that's okay! It seems rough in the moment, but they aren't all going to be *the one*... I'm just happy you're getting out."

"Thank you," she said.

Her mom smiled. "Just be careful, honey."

"Don't worry, I will."

Her mom read over two more front pages before finally giving in. "Are you going to tell me about him?"

"You've been dying all day long, haven't you?" Lillian laughed.

"Yes!" her mom gushed. "Your dad told me last night that he was worried about how you felt about this guy, but wouldn't give me details, and said I couldn't talk to you about it because when you were ready, you'd talk to me, but, oh, I'm just so happy that you're dating again."

"Geez, Mom, you make it sound like I'm a recluse."

"Well, sort of, you are."

"Thanks, love you, too."

"I just want you to be happy, and after Ryder broke your heart, I thought you'd go off to college and meet someone new and forget all about him, but instead you buried yourself so deep in school that you wound up graduating early. Then you got tangled up with that man that never should have led you on like he did, and while I'm happy that brought you back home, you just repeated the punishment of drowning yourself in work. Now, you're getting back out there. It makes me happy to see you finally have a glow about you."

"Why does everyone think I drown myself in work as punishment?"

"Because you do. That's how you've always been." She waved it away, not allowing her daughter to try and change the subject. "Now, since you're dating again, I have a friend from church whose son is just a little bit older than you. He's single of course, has a good job, but –"

"Mom, no. I'm not getting set up."

"He's very nice, I'm sure. I haven't met him myself, but his mother speaks very highly of him."

"Seriously, Mom, I'm not looking."

"No? Then what about your dates?"

Lillian sat down in one of the chairs, studying one of the papers she'd sifted out. "I'm just in the middle of trying to figure out some stuff right now, and I wasn't even looking in the first place," she sighed in exasperation. "And now I've made a mess of things, and I don't know what to do to fix them."

"But you want to fix them?"

"It's complicated."

"How complicated? Simplest version."

"Why do you always do that?" But her mom just smiled, waiting for her to think it through. "There's more than just one guy involved."

Her mom's eyebrows rose in minute surprise. She recovered quickly, but not before Lillian caught the look. "No wonder you don't need me to set you up. So, they found out about each other and you scared them both off?"

"Sort of, but no."

Her mom sat down across the table. "I get the feeling that this is more than just a fling."

"I don't know what it is," Lillian said. "They both just happened, and I never planned it."

"Sometimes the best things aren't planned." Her mom paused. "But, you know, I don't think you should be seeing more than one at a time if it's feeling serious with either one. Getting to know more than one person at once is one thing, but once you start developing real feelings for one, you should have broken it off with the other."

"And what if you never thought you'd develop feelings for the second, and thought you were only getting to know one, but the other sort of snuck in?"

"Sounds like the second one made more of an impression then, if he's causing this much doubt."

"I guess it's just that I never expected it."

"Just because you don't expect or plan for something doesn't mean it's going to be bad."

"I understand that. Look at Wisteria. I never expected such a great opportunity to fall into my lap, and I definitely never planned to run the place."

"But we're not talking about Wisteria. We're discussing your love triangle."

"You have to be in love to have a love triangle." She paused. "And probably be an age that ends in 'teen.'"

"So, what happened between them to get you so upset that you want to waste the afternoon with your mom looking through stacks of newspapers—" She flipped one over to see the date. "—from nearly thirty years ago that really don't mean anything."

"They do mean something," Lillian protested.

"It's work that can be delegated, as we've already discovered."

"And spending time with my mom is never wasted time."

"Right, but spending time with one of these two men should be more exhilarating. So, what messed it up?"

"I did."

"All by yourself?"

"Yes, by getting involved with them both."

"Pouting and putting all the blame on yourself isn't going to solve anything."

"I'm not pouting."

Her mom laid the paper down on the table between them, delicately folding her hands on top, and looked at her daughter with the expression of total disbelief that all mothers seem to be gifted with as soon as they have kids.

"It can't be either of their faults because neither of them knew about the other one, but I did, and I let them both still pursue me. So, yes, it is all my doing."

"Fine. You're a terrible person."

"Mom!" Lillian said, a little louder than she realized, earning herself a glance from one of the other library patrons nearby.

"What?" her mom said innocently. "That's what you want to hear isn't it? That you've done something so terrible, something nobody else on Earth has ever done and survived. You're the worst."

Lillian looked at her mom with disbelief. "I can't believe you're making fun of me right now. What I did was wrong."

"In the great scheme of things that are wrong, I don't think this one is going to land you in prison. Besides, it sounds like you've already punished yourself, and even after this conversation, you'll continue to tell yourself how bad of a person you were, so why would I add to that distress? I'm your mother, and as your mother, I'm going to tell you that you are an adult who found herself deeper in a situation than she realized, is feeling guilty about it now, and needs to find a solution to make things right with herself. In order to do that, you need to figure out what you want."

"Thanks. Why didn't I think of that? That's so easy," Lillian said dryly.

"I never said it would be. Knowing you, you wouldn't be in this much turmoil over two inconsequential people, so I can only assume that they are both worthy of you, probably in different ways from each other. So, you see qualities in both of them that you appreciate and would want in a single package. But that's not the case, so you're holding on to both men to get all those things. But here's the thing, we don't always see a person's full potential in the very beginning. Through time and getting to know them more deeply, you may find that one or the other will have all the qualities you think you see between the two, and you may also find that they don't. You may also discover that they have qualities that you despise. The challenging part of this is that it will take time to figure all that out. Now, tell me about them. Start with person number two."

"You don't want to know about the first one first?"

"We'll get to him, but I'm sure I can figure that one out easy enough. Boy meets girl, they find each other intriguing, they start seeing where it'll go. Boring. I want to hear about the second one that you were surprised by. The one that has you confused."

Lillian let out a breath, not sure what she could tell her mom that would still get an unbiased answer. If she told her who he was, her mom was likely to tell her to kick him to the curb, simply because of their past.

"Well," she started, trying to figure out how to describe him and not give it away.

"How does he make you feel?" her mom prodded.

"Confused," she admitted, "but also curious."

"Confused doesn't sound like enough to cause you this much distress. Confused how?"

"I've known him… around," she waved her hand to encompass that he was a local resident. "And knew that he had a reputation of liking women… a lot." She paused. "And that he wasn't someone I would be interested in being pursued by."

"Understandable. How can you feel unique and special if he's going to chase the next thing that walks by?" Her mom nodded in agreement. "But something about him did strike you enough to keep him around."

"I had my mind made up about him. Easy, he's not for me. Ever."

Liza watched as Lillian studied her hands.

"But then there was a side to him that I'd never considered. He was vulnerable and wasn't afraid to show it. It caught me off guard. Here was this cockily confident man who I had no intention of giving the time of day allowing himself to be completely open and vulnerable with me in a way I don't think he's ever allowed himself to be with anyone else. I guess it pulled at my heart enough to try and look at him in a new light and try to put aside my conceptions of him. I've been honest with him that I don't know if what is between us could go anywhere at all, and he accepts that, but he's still trying to prove himself. He's been caring and protective. He's charismatic and attractive, and despite his reputation with women, he's a good man."

"If we only ever listen to the rumors about people and our misconceptions, never allowing ourselves to dig in and make our own observations and decisions, wonderful things can be easily overlooked. It sounds like you've made an impression on him, too, if he's willing to keep trying for your approval. I think that's a rare thing, especially if a person has a history of being a man-whore."

"Mom!" Lillian said, shocked again, looking around to make sure she didn't disturb another patron, but laughed at her mom's smug expression.

"What?" she said innocently. "All I'm saying is that it sounds like he's putting in an awful lot of work for a quickie if that was all he was after."

Lillian covered her face with her hands, elbows resting on the table, and laughed into her hands. "Mooooom," she groaned. "No."

"Oh, don't be a drama queen. It's sex. Get over it. This second man sounds intriguing, and I can see why he's got you twisted up. There's more to the puzzle than you originally suspected, and now you want to figure him out, to see if he's worth it. Now. Tell me about the first one."

Lillian could immediately feel her heart begin to beat faster, a slow warmth spreading from within. She smiled at the thought of him, but then she remembered their evening, and her smile faltered.

Her mom reached over and squeezed her hand. "Tell me about him," she said softly.

"He's like nobody I've ever met before." She paused. "And I don't even know how to explain it. I'm sure he's like other men, but there's just *something* about him." She smiled, thinking of the first day she saw him standing on the sidewalk, looking lost, but not at all lost at the same time. That it didn't matter where he was supposed to be going, because where he was in the moment was exactly where he needed to be.

"It's not just that he's insanely hot, but from the first time I saw him, I just felt… *drawn* to him. I want to see him again even after I just saw him. I want to hear his voice or watch him smile. I feel so confident when he looks at me, but also get butterflies in my stomach. I feel like I've known him for years, but he's not even from here. He's just passing through." She frowned again and her mom waited for her to go on. "And last night I told him about—" She paused, almost slipping out Ryder's name. "About the second one, because I didn't want secrets between us, but he got mad and left. I don't even know if he's still in town. He may have moved on by now."

"He's not mad," her mom said softly.

"Oh, he was mad."

Her mom reached out and squeezed her hand again. "Honey, he was hurt. Anger can be an expression of pain."

"He wouldn't stay and talk to me."

"Would you have wanted to if you were in his shoes?" Her mom paused again. "Look at your own path. You haven't spoken to Ryder in ten years," she added gently.

Lillian held back her words. Correcting her mom would open an entirely different conversation.

"I guess I see your point."

"You're going to have to make a decision, and it sounds like it won't be an easy one for you. But one thing I'm good at is simplifying, so here it goes. With man number one, he's a completely new story to read, a mystery to unfold. There's only discovery to be had with him, and that's exhilarating. But you hurt him in a way that you've been hurt before and feel from experience the pain all over again, and you worry that the situation is unsalvageable, because that's how it was for you.

"The second one is a challenge to you. You want to be the one person who can win against all the others, the one person that can settle him down. You have to decide if the victory over perception is going to be enough in the long run. But you don't really know either of them, so you have to take a leap into the unknown, and that's a scary thing to do."

Lillian folded her arms on the table in front of her and put her head on them, sighing as she did. Everybody wanted to oversimplify her situation, but the problem was that when it came to how she felt and what her heart wanted her to do, nothing felt simple.

FORTY-THREE

-Bill-

Bill heard his deputy's raised voice and the phone slam into its base. He imagined that if the chair wasn't on wheels, he would have heard it scratch across the floor as well ten seconds before Simon appeared in his office doorway.

"Sheriff, are you busy?" In his distress, it sounded like more of a statement than a question.

"I have time. What's bothering you, Simon?"

Simon trudged over to the seat in front of the desk. Bill could feel the tension the boy was trying to keep under control; not a typical expression for the usually all-too-eager deputy.

"We can't keep waiting for this red tape bullshit... sir." He projected the first statement, but at Bill's surprised look, he added the formality a little more calmly.

"Simon," Bill sighed.

"I know," Simon said, cutting him off before he could say "no" again. "I know what you're going to say, and at a certain point it has to stop mattering. Brian could be in there and could need help. You saw the dogs go to the opening in the wall. Rain even confirmed that that was where they went through. How can we not follow their steps and try to find him? We're the people to call when things like this happen. If we don't do it, nobody will."

"I take it you haven't made it through to anyone to get clearance?"

"Nobody knows anything about it except to tell me it's restricted. Every person gives me the same story with a different number to try. The hold time is a joke, just to be told it's either the wrong department, that they've never heard of the place, or that there is no confirmed ex-military establishment in this area. Just when I think it's enough of a loophole to just go in, at the last minute, they say, 'Oh, looks like that *is* government land. Sorry, it's restricted and I don't have clearance to authorize entry.' But when I ask them who does, all I get is another dead end." He leaned forward in his chair. "Bill," he pleaded, "I see his parents' faces and hear their voices in my sleep. His friends want answers, too, and the only thing I can tell them is that we're doing our best to find him. I'm lying to them because our best would mean that we go through and search the rest of that area."

"Simon, I know, trust me I do."

"Nobody even knows that it's there! Everyone I talk to only *eventually* finds a footnote that the land is theirs. We could go in, search, and be back out without anyone knowing. There are no armed guards patrolling. There's nobody to report it."

"How do you know? How can you be sure there isn't surveillance equipment in there, ready to alert the real people who do know it exists? Just because you can't get ahold of someone who knows doesn't mean that there isn't a department that does. The other thing you need to consider is the reason it's restricted. Nobody knows what went on inside the base when it was operational, just that when it shut down, it went with a bang, literally. There could be unstable explosives in there still to this day. There could be radioactive waste. We. Don't. Know. All we *do* know is that when people go in, they don't resurface, and if someone does come out, they aren't alive to talk about it. That is not a safe environment, and as the sheriff of this county, I can't authorize my officers or volunteers to walk into a potentially unsafe and unstable location."

"The volunteers, I understand, but the officers are trained. A small group of us can go in and search. We can take the dogs. We could be in and out before anyone knew any better."

"You're trained on how to detect if there's radiation?"

"No, but there has never even been rumor of radioactive waste. Wouldn't the government have to notify us if that was the case?"

Bill shrugged his shoulders. "What about identifying buried landmines?"

Simon sat back in the chair and rubbed his forehead before dropping his hand. "Geez Bill, you act like it's a warzone in there."

"How do you know it wasn't? They were top secret when in operation. Nobody knew what was being done in there when it existed, just that it existed. From what I know about the place, it was opened in the early forties. Times were different then. Who knows what they did to protect themselves, and when the base blew up, or whatever happened to it—nobody really knows—I'm willing to bet that they didn't leave someone behind to make sure any defensive implements had been recovered and deactivated.

"The point is, Simon, that with the limited knowledge anyone has of the area, the already tumultuous terrain that we know of from our side of the wall, plus the express lack of permission to enter top secret government land, I cannot authorize a search and rescue."

Simon stood up, the chair scraping back as he did, and pointed at Bill. "This is wrong, and you know it." He lumbered out of the sheriff's office, leaving the door open as he left.

Bill rubbed his forehead and sighed. He did know it and hated having to give every excuse in the book to try and keep Simon from going in. He hated denying him access, but he couldn't risk another person's life when he didn't know where he was sending them.

"What was that all about?" Ryder asked and Bill looked up to see him leaning against the doorway, folders in his hands. "In the five years I've worked with Simon, I've never seen him angry. What's got him all twisted?"

"He wants to get beyond the boundary for the Mountain to search for Brian, but I can't give him what he wants. It's not safe, and I'm not going to go into it all over again with you, so what do you need?"

Ryder tapped the folders against his hand. "Rich sent the reports via courier for Wade and our John Doe. I figured you'd want to see them right away."

Bill held out a hand for the files. Ryder handed them over and took a seat as Bill flipped through the pages in each: the medical report, photos of the deceased, toxicology report… Nothing new. No change. There was a scribbled note attached to the front: *Sorry Bill, nothing different. Full work up, head to toe evaluation as if brand new body. Results the same.*

"Did you look through these?" Bill asked, looking at one of the pictures of the unidentified body.

"No, just saw the note on the front. What do we do now?"

Bill sat back in his chair, looking at the open folder on his desk and knowing he was about to piss off another of his deputies. And in record time; two in less than ten minutes.

"I can't change these bodies to homicides."

"Sheriff, come on –" Ryder raised his arm then dropped it to his lap as he leaned forward.

Bill held up a hand. "I can't do it Ryder. I know what you're feeling, but the evidence isn't here."

"You don't know that," Ryder pressed.

"Their hearts exploded. That is the cause of death for both of these bodies. Have you ever heard of murder by exploding heart? Because I sure haven't."

"They could have been given something to cause that."

"The toxicology report is clear on both."

Ryder stood to pace the room, running his hand through his hair as he did. Bill closed the folders and stacked them as he watched Ryder work through his thoughts, his frustrations.

"Maybe it's some toxin that Rich doesn't know to look for," Ryder finally said, turning back to face Bill. "But even if it isn't that, it could still be murder. What if while they were in there, they had been captured, then escaped and were being chased down? That would explain why John Doe was mangled on the rocks. He fell trying to escape."

Bill took a deep breath and let it out. "There's no evidence that it was a person chasing them. Both Wade and John Doe were somewhere they weren't supposed to be, they were trespassing on restricted land –"

"So, it's okay that they died." Ryder crossed his arms and shook his head in disbelief.

"That's not what I said. But they *were* trespassing in a place—like I just told Simon— that we are completely unfamiliar with. Maybe there is something toxic in there that Rich doesn't know to search for, and that's why their hearts exploded. We may never know, but the fact remains that they went where they weren't allowed to go, something happened, and now they're dead. But—" Bill stopped Ryder's attempted interruption with a stern look. "We don't know that there is a *person* to blame for it. For all we know, they both could have been chased by a bear or other large animal, and they fell because they were in an area with extremely hazardous terrain and weren't prepared for it. You've seen our side of the wall. It's not safe."

"And what about Brian?"

Bill leaned forward, folding his arms on his desk. "There's no evidence that he's anything other than another casualty of the Mountain. I can only hope that he turns up in our search. For his parents' sake, I hope he's alive, but at this rate, I fear that may not be the case."

Ryder moved to the desk, pressing his index and middle fingers into the surface. "And if I find evidence that he's a killer?"

Bill sighed. "Ryder –"

He tapped the files. "If I can find something, will you reconsider these as homicides?"

Bill knew Ryder wouldn't be able to let it go until he'd satisfied his curiosity. That was one of the reasons he was such a great deputy. Bill couldn't give into Simon because his hands were tied with red tape. Ryder he could give a little rope, a little leeway to do his job and investigate, even if Bill didn't think he'd find anything to support his theory.

"If you're going to look, you do it discreetly. I don't want panic spreading and I do not want the parents of our missing teen to hear that we suspect their son is a killer. Do you understand me?"

"Yes, sir," Ryder said, fighting to keep his expression neutral even though Bill could see the fire of determination flash through his eyes. Ryder turned to leave the office.

"And Ryder, I can't give you long, so you better look fast."

Everything about this case felt off, but despite how much Ryder wanted to point the finger of blame at Brian, Bill's gut just wouldn't agree.

FORTY-FOUR

-Lillian-

Lillian hung up the phone and did a little happy dance in her office chair after filling another server position. She was now fully staffed and would be ready for the tourist season. A light knock interrupted her celebration.

"Come in," she called.

Lana's nephew, Josh, opened the door and peered around.

"Hey Josh, what's up? Everything okay out front?"

"Yes, sorry to bother you, but there's someone that wanted to talk to you. Is it okay if he comes back?"

She immediately thought, *August,* and her heart fluttered. She still hadn't talked to him since their argument. She knew she should reach out and try to make things right, but he hadn't either, and she wasn't sure what to say. Nothing had changed for them to discuss.

"Sure, bring him back please," she said, checking her reflection in the nearby mirror when he left.

She heard Josh in the hall tell the person to "go on in," yet the visitor still knocked lightly as they entered the office. She kept her smile in place, hoping the disappointment she felt wasn't written on her face when the boy entered the room.

"I'm really sorry to interrupt you," he started, his voice clear, but he fidgeted with the baseball hat he was holding. "I don't know if you'll remember me. I was here a few times. Um, I… well, my friends and me… we uh… we were the ones that found…"

"Yes, I remember you," she said quickly before he had to say the words that he was obviously trying to avoid. "You're… Evan, right?" she asked, hoping she was remembering correctly.

"Right." He smiled, and for a moment in his relief she caught a glimpse of the secure young man he should be instead of the wary and morose version standing before her.

"Do you want to sit, Evan?"

"Oh, yeah, sure. Thanks." He took his seat but didn't speak up right away. He traced the frayed edges of his hat, clearly a favorite as the once bright colors were sun faded and the brim well bent.

"Is everything okay?" she asked gently. "Was there something wrong with your order?"

"Huh? Oh, no… no. The food was fine. Um… I needed to ask you something." He glanced down at his hat in his lap and then back up to her. "Rain didn't say very nice things about you." He paused, and when she didn't show surprise, he continued. "But she's annoying and doesn't stop runnin' her mouth, so I pretty much just ignored her. I've seen you in here and you seem nice." He paused again, and she gave him time, unsure where the conversation was heading. "I thought it was pretty cool that you ran the volunteer station to look for Brian and Rain, even though you don't know Brian and Rain is awful."

"I would have been out there searching if my dad hadn't insisted otherwise. The volunteer hub was how I could still help."

He nodded. "That's why I needed to talk to you… about your dad. He's been real good to us through everything. I think he's the best policeman I've ever met. I mean, I haven't had run-ins with them or anything, but you hear stories, you know, that aren't always the best and well, dealing with something like this… he's just been good," he finished, letting out his breath. "It's just that… he said we could go home, but now Brian is missing, and he wants us to stay longer. I don't want to leave Brian here, I want to find him, I do, but…" He looked down, picking at his hat again. "I want to see my parents. I want to go home… I know Rain didn't seem to like you, and maybe you hated her, too, but they won't let us in to see her. I just want to know what happened that night, where Brian could have gone. She might have answers or say something that doesn't make sense to people who don't know Brian, but could mean everything to us."

"Just because my dad is the sheriff, doesn't mean I can change his mind about procedures," she told him softly. "Believe me, when I was a little younger than you, I sure tried."

His lips moved in the direction of a smile but didn't make it. "I'm not asking you to convince him to let us talk to her. I thought that maybe since you're her boss—*were* her boss, I guess, and since you're the sheriff's daughter, that you would be able to talk to her."

"Oh," she began, wondering if her dad would let her in if Rain was off-limits. "I don't know how happy she'd be to talk to me."

"I just don't know what else to do," he finally sighed, his shoulders drooping as if they were just too heavy to hold up anymore.

Her heart broke at the sight. "Here's what I *can* do," she told him, and he raised his head. "I can at least talk to my dad and see about getting in to see Rain. I can't guarantee that he's going to say yes," she warned. "He's never had a problem telling me no. I'll also talk to him about letting you two go back home. Again, no promises. He always has a reason for doing things the way he does, but I will do my best."

He let out a small, relieved sigh, "Thank you. It's something. I feel like I have to do something…"

She grabbed a pen and notepad from the desk.

"Can you write down how to reach you guys if I can't convince him? I don't want you to wonder."

He leaned forward to write their information down, thanking her again as he did.

"Oh, you're bleeding," she said, noticing the drop when he moved his arm, handing him tissues from the box on her desk. "Do you need a bandage?"

"No," he told her, lifting the short sleeve and dabbing at the area just below his shoulder that was slowly seeping. "Sorry," he smiled sheepishly. "We wanted matching tattoos. Thought it would be cool. I must have scratched off a scab before I came in here."

"It's a neat one," she told him, and he smiled in thanks, keeping the tissue pressed against his skin. "*If* I can get in to see Rain, and *if* she decides to talk to me, is there anything in particular you want me to ask her? I'm sure the police have already been very thorough though, so I don't know how much more I'd be able to help."

"I know, but maybe she will have remembered something since they talked to her, or maybe Brian said something weird to her that she didn't tell the cops that she could tell you, and then maybe it'll mean something real to us. Sometimes we have our own words for things, not a code or anything, just nicknames, I guess. Maybe it didn't make sense to her either." He sighed again. "I want to find my friend. I want to go home. I want all of this behind me."

He stood up to leave. She held up the note with his contact information. "I'll keep you updated."

"Thank you."

He put his hat on and left the office. She wanted to make all his pain disappear, but she knew that his wounds ran deeper than her potential conversation with Rain could fix.

FORTY-FIVE

-Lillian-

Lillian woke early to the smell of coffee brewing in her kitchen. She'd set the alarm, despite having the day off, but still managed to wake ten minutes before it sounded. She padded barefoot to the pot, pouring the beautiful liquid into her favorite mug and snuggled into her cushy chair to breathe in the steam. She had a clear day ahead of her with only two tasks: try to talk to Rain and figure out what to do about August.

Neither sounded fun.

Even if she could convince her dad to let her see Rain, she didn't think she'd make much progress, but she'd promised to try.

As for August… She'd picked up her phone a dozen times to text him or check for a message from him, and every time, she'd set the phone back down.

She sipped the coffee.

"He hasn't texted you, either," she reminded herself when she started to feel guilty for not reaching out yet, still not sure what to say to him.

The knock at her door startled her, nearly making the coffee slosh out of her mug.

"Ryder? Everything okay?" she asked, unable to keep the surprise out of her voice. He was the last person she expected to see on her front porch this early.

"Yeah, yeah, everything's fine. Have any more of that?" he asked her, eyeing her cup while letting himself inside.

"Come on in," she said sarcastically, closing the door behind them as he led the way to her kitchen, helping himself to his own mug.

He sipped the scalding liquid, watching her over his cup as he did.

"You look great, Lilly."

"Funny."

"What?" he asked as he sipped again, still watching her.

"It's 6:30 in the morning, Ryder. These are my pajamas, and I haven't even brushed my hair."

"So? You can't look great with bed head and silk jammies?"

"They're not silk –" She stopped herself from explaining further. "Since I'm sure you didn't stop by to discuss my sleeping attire or my coffee brewing skills, maybe you could clue me in on why you're at my house this early?"

"Maybe I wanted to talk about what you wear to bed." He smiled as he took another drink.

She tilted her head at him. "Ryder," she admonished, not wanting to discuss sleeping arrangements while she was wearing shorty-short satin jammies and a single look from him caused her skin to tingle with the memory of his touch.

She took a drink of her hot coffee, hoping to drown her wandering thoughts.

"What are you doing today?"

"What?"

"Today. What are your plans?"

"I plan to beg my dad for a favor. Why?"

"What do you need from your dad? Maybe I can help."

"I want to go talk to Rain."

"Why do you need to beg him for that? Just go see her."

"Isn't access to her restricted?"

"Why?"

"I don't know, because she's a victim and a witness? I thought she wasn't allowed to have visitors."

"Who told you that? Your guy Gary was just in there yesterday. He didn't tell you?"

"It must have slipped his mind," she said dryly. "I guess being the boss gets me out of the gossip circle."

"Hmm." He took another drink from his cup, looking into it, then over at the pot. "Why do you want to see her?"

He held up the pot and she checked her own mug. She wandered over to the island, sitting on a stool, putting the large immovable object between them. She hoped it would keep her from reaching out to touch him as her hands were urging her to do. She slid her cup across the surface as he brought over the pot to top off her drink.

"It's a long shot," she said with a sigh, pulling her steamy cup back, the aroma tickling her nose. "But I thought I'd try talking to her. Maybe talking to someone other than the police and doctors might be more comfortable, and she might think of something new to help find Brian."

He took a drink from the cup and leaned against the counter. "That's a good idea. She knows you, maybe she'll open up."

"Well, I don't know how open she'll be with me. We didn't get along all the time, and she quit working in an angry fit. You guys may want to talk to Gary and see what she said to him, although he has a history of embellishing, so I'm not sure he'd be of much use either."

"If you guys didn't get along, why do you want to talk to her? You don't know Brian, and it isn't your job to find him."

"I know it's not, but it feels like the search is dying down and he's still missing. Maybe new information will keep the fire burning, so to speak… and his friends are hurting."

Ryder raised an eyebrow. "You know his friends?"

"Just through the diner; they've come in a few times. But yesterday, Evan talked to me, and he just seemed so lost. I know it's not my job to find him, but I want to help."

"Why did Evan talk to *you*?"

"Because of my connection with Rain and my dad being the sheriff."

Ryder brooded into his mug. "So, he's using you to get information."

"It's not like that. He asked if I would talk to Rain. He wants to find his friend and go home."

Ryder set the empty cup in the sink. "Come on, I'll drive you to the hospital to see Rain."

"What? Ryder, I can drive myself."

"We'll be going to the same place. We might as well take one car."

"Why are you going to see her? Has something come up?"

"Maybe… but I want to see what she has to tell you."

"That kind of defeats the whole point of me talking to her to get her to relax if you're standing there looming over us. Don't you think?"

"I won't loom. What does that even mean anyway? Come on, get your stuff. It's just a car ride."

"I'm not even dressed yet."

"I already said you look great," he smiled again.

"Haha," she said dryly. "I need to take a shower and get dressed. You don't need to wait around for me."

"I'd wait for you." His words were gentle, but his gaze was serious.

She held his stare, not ready to have the conversation they still needed to have.

He leaned on the opposite side of the island, face to face with her. "I didn't come here to talk about the other day, or how you feel about it. When you're ready, we'll talk," he said as if her thoughts had been written on her face.

She was feeling too many things—for him *and* August—that was the problem.

"Why *did* you come over?" She asked to get on more neutral ground.

"I needed to talk to you about other things."

"At 6:30 in the morning?"

"Couldn't sleep."

She gripped her coffee cup in both hands. Even though it was empty, it gave her something to do with her hands. His were so close… within reach. She could slide—

"And what if I was still asleep?"

"Pillow talk would have been fine."

She dropped her head into her hands to hide her smile when he gave her a devilish one.

"I'm kidding… maybe… but the offer stands."

"I'm sure it does. What did you need to talk about if not the other day and not Rain?"

"It can wait. This takes priority."

"It had to be important for you to be up and out this early."

"It'll wait. Besides, it gives me another opportunity to come see you."

"Ah, of course it does."

She stood from her stool, moving around the island to rinse her cup in the sink. She noticed him turn against the island, watching her move, not bothering to hide it or to slide away to give her room. She wasn't about to shy away in her own house, and she figured he planned on that. She stood her ground as she washed out the cup, taking a little longer to wash his as well. She saw him move closer in her peripheral vision and glanced over to see him reach for the towel hanging on her other side. His fingers lightly grazed against her hip as he did. He took the clean mug from her, dried it and the first one, then set them both next to the pot, handing her the towel to dry her hands.

He was still standing close enough that a baby step would put her in his arms. She could feel the heat of him next to her, the warmth she could be wrapped in… the island was sturdy… She cut off her thoughts when she could feel her cheeks start to warm.

"I'm going to go get ready," she told him quickly, not glancing at his eyes to see if he'd noticed. She turned to hurry out of the room.

"Let me know if you need any help," he called after her.

"I'm sure I can manage," she shot back over her shoulder.

She made it to her room, her heart racing at her momentary lapse. She gathered her clothes for the day and took them to the bathroom with her, turning the shower on to warm as she locked the bathroom door. She stared at the knob, thinking about Ryder in the other room. All she'd have to do was call for him… Her body warmed at the thought, the curiosity…

"What is wrong with you?" she asked the air. "Do you have no self-control?"

She leaned her head against the door, a million different scenarios running through her head at once, all giving her immense satisfaction, but it was the after that she was unsure of. What would happen between them if she gave in to what she was feeling? Lana's advice rattled around in her head. She wasn't married. She wasn't in a committed relationship. Why shouldn't she explore?

She could feel his hands sliding up her thighs… slipping under the airy material of her shorts…

"Good grief woman, get a handle on yourself," she said aloud, pushing away from the door to undress and tossing her clothes on the counter. The mirrors had already steamed over so she wouldn't have to see her judgy reflection.

She was two steps from the shower when she walked back to the door and unlocked it. She knew he wouldn't try, but knowing she wasn't preventing him if he did made her shower more exhilarating. She'd blame her rosy cheeks on the heat of the shower and not the heat of her thoughts.

She finished showering and dressing, expecting Ryder to be pacing the floor waiting on her. Instead she was greeted with the delicious aroma of bacon and sauteed veggies.

"That was fast," he said, barely glancing up from the omelet he was preparing. "I was hungry. Figured you'd be too, and you aren't likely to let me take you out yet."

"So, you decided to sneak another meal by me."

"A guy's gotta do what a guy's gotta do."

He split the large omelet between two plates, added bacon and fresh berries, and poured two small glasses of juice. He set both places on the island and her stomach rumbled at the sight.

"See, I knew you'd be hungry. Eat up and then we'll go see Rain."

"Fine, but if you get called out for something, you have to drop me back here before you go wherever you go."

"I'm off duty today. No calls."

He brought her a napkin and sat on the stool next to her, his leg resting comfortably against her own.

"This is really good," she said. "Thank you."

He smiled at her. "I'm gonna start taking offense at the surprise you always seem to have when I cook."

"I just don't picture you in an apron dancing around the kitchen." She took another bite. "I can't even picture you owning pots and pans," she laughed.

"Maybe instead of assuming you know everything about me already, you let me show you a thing or two."

The words were said lightly, but she could feel the weight settling between them.

"I didn't mean –"

"I know you didn't." He finished his plate before she did and went to wash it in the sink, cleaning the pan and putting it back where he'd found it while he was at it. She finished her own plate, and he came to retrieve it.

"I can clean it."

"Of course you can, but so can I." He stood beside her, waiting for her to hand over the dish. When she finally conceded, instead of walking it back to the sink, he set it out of her reach on the island. "I'm not going to disappoint you, Lilly."

"That's not what I'm worried about."

"I know." His eyes softened slightly as he watched her. "You have no idea how much I know."

She tried to break away from his gaze, but she was stuck in the trance that was Ryder. Her heart was racing, but she didn't want to move away. Every molecule inside of her wanted to reach out to him. When he moved slightly toward her, she felt a flutter of panic. Panic because she wanted him to lean into her. She wanted to feel what they had a few nights ago, the whirlwind, the excitement, the passion. But she knew that if she let it happen, this time it wouldn't stop with just a kiss… She didn't want it to stop at just a kiss.

The singular tiny voice at the back of her mind chirped up, a constant reminder of the dagger sharp pain that could be left behind if she gave herself over to him.

Ryder brushed the hair off her shoulder, his hand trailing down her back with her hair. He bent down to kiss the exposed part of her neck, a soft brush of lips against skin. Her skin tingled with the small breath that tickled it. She closed her eyes… all she had to do was turn.

The moment was over as he turned and headed to the sink. Disappointment and relief were at war in her heart.

"There's something damn sexy about seeing you barefoot in the kitchen," he said over his shoulder as he washed the dish, "but if we're going to leave, you should probably put on some shoes."

She instinctively glanced down at her feet before stepping down and setting off to retrieve her shoes. She needed to get out of the house, out of reach of Ryder, before she went crazy with need for him.

By the time she was ready to go, he was waiting in the living room, keys in hand. She grabbed her bag, locked the house, and followed him to his truck.

"You never told me why you came over in the first place," she said, revisiting the subject that he'd skirted earlier and trying to set her mind to anything other than imagining him pulling her across the seat, into his lap… The truck was roomy…

"I'm working on a thought," he said, interrupting her own. "I needed a fresh look. I was going to use your brain, but this takes priority."

"You don't have to go, you know. I can just fill you in if she tells me anything." She buckled her seat belt as he pulled out of her driveway.

"No, this is better. You'll be less likely to forget details if you fill me in right away."

"I'm glad you're taking this seriously, but I feel like there's something else you're not telling me. Earlier, when you got to the house, you seemed… urgent."

"Urgent?" he asked, glancing over at her in the passenger seat.

"Determined, I guess… like there was something important to talk about."

"There's a missing person. If you can get information, that should be urgent right?"

"Well, yes, but it was after you showed up that we decided to go see Rain. Are you sure what you needed to talk about can wait?"

"Of course. This may help shed light on my stuff, too."

"Okay," she said, letting it go for now while she enjoyed the short drive to the hospital.

"Music?" Ryder asked after a few minutes of comfortable silence.

"Sure, if you want."

He fished his phone out of his pocket, used the face lock to unlock it, clicked his streaming app then handed it over to her. "If you don't see something you like, feel free to add another station."

She scrolled through his list of albums and musicians, a wide range of genres from rock, to country, to pop, and even instrumental. She caught herself wondering at when he enjoyed listening to each. Was rock when he was working out, or did the heavy beats help him decompress too? Was instrumental when he needed something playing but didn't want to focus on the words? When had he started listening to country? She clicked that section, noticing that it leaned more toward traditional or contemporary country artists instead of the newer pop-country, but there were a few she'd consider pop-country as well. She never took him for the country type.

"Nothing you like?" he asked, glancing over.

"Oh there's plenty," she said as she continued to scroll, liking nearly all of his choices. She found the 'Today's Hits' section and pressed play.

"Out of all those stations, you take the easy way out with this one?" He tsked his tongue and shook his head as she handed back the phone, pretending at disappointment.

"You're welcome to change it," she joked. "When did you start listening to country?"

"What?" He turned to give her a grin. "You don't think I can pull off a cowboy hat?"

"Never seemed your style."

He just shook his head, smiling still, and turned back to watch the road. "There's a lot you don't know about me Lilly Flower."

She was beginning to realize he was right.

They approached the hospital and he slowed to turn into the parking lot.

"You know I was joking earlier about you getting a call and taking me home first, right? If you want to leave me here you can. I can figure out a way home."

He looked over at her again in confusion. "Why would I do that?"

"It's your day off. I dragged you into work when you had other plans."

She caught his look before he returned his focus to navigating the lot. He didn't shoot her the dazzler of a smile. There was no joke in his eyes. The eye contact following a sweep of her entire body caused her insides to go to jelly and left her wanting.

"If it means spending time with you, I'd gladly give up my day off."

Part of her wondered if he knew the intensity he was putting out, or if she was falling victim to the same charm that he used on all women. *Stop it,* she chastised herself, not allowing herself to go down that avenue right now. She needed to get her head back into the right place.

They pulled up to the entrance and he parked in the reserved space for law enforcement. He turned to her before he turned the truck off, his face and tone serious—down to business. "When you go in, try and keep things light. She gets worked up easily, and then the nurses come in and sedate her. If you can keep her from flipping out, you might be able to get something we can use."

"What do I ask her? Is there anything specific? Is there anything I'm not allowed to ask, that I shouldn't know as a civilian?"

"Just talk to her. If she tells you something that we don't want shared, I'll let you know when I debrief you."

"Debrief?"

"It's just means –"

"I know what it means. It just feels… cold."

"After it's all over, if you need to be warmed up, all you have to do is ask Lilly Flower."

"No," she laughed.

He grabbed at his heart. "Just straight, 'no.' No consideration? As I recall, things can get very warm."

"Ryder."

"I know, just trying to lighten you up before you go in there." But his smile said otherwise. "Just be yourself. Talk to her about what led up to them going, what happened that night, how or why they got separated, and how she was found but he wasn't. See if she has any ideas where he could be. But Lilly… keep her calm. The last time your dad and Simon talked to her, she didn't want him found."

FORTY-SIX

-Lillian-

Ryder was at the nurses' station, talking with them and the officer assigned to Rain when Lillian left Rain's room. The woman he was closest to was leaning toward him, eyes only for Ryder, despite the other officer that was trying to slide closer to her as they all talked. Whatever Ryder said brought color to her cheeks, or maybe just being in his presence did that. Lillian saw her tear off a piece of paper and write something on it, folding it up to hand to him as he turned and caught sight of her. He clapped the other officer on the back with a word and was at her side without so much as a backward glance at the outstretched hand.

"Looks like you forgot something." Lillian nodded back to the nurse's station and pushed the button for the elevator. "You have time," she told him, watching the numbers change on the display.

"Not interested," he said without turning back to look.

"Why not? She's gorgeous," she told the elevator.

"Not even comparable," he said as the doors opened. He extended an arm to block the door from closing and waited for her to enter.

They walked the short distance to his truck in silence, Lillian scolding herself the whole time for getting jealous, reminding herself that he wasn't hers to be jealous over. And he wasn't hers by her own doing.

"You don't think Brian is missing, do you?" she asked as soon as both their doors were closed.

"What did Rain say?"

"Answer the question."

"Lilly," he started, but she waited, watching, not giving in. "I suspect that he's not in the woods." It was all he'd admit.

She tried not to focus on what Rain had said and made it a point to look out the window. She watched as the town changed from business buildings and apartments that surrounded the hospital, to the chain stores and mom and pop shops, but Rain's words kept circling through her head.

"She's terrified that he's going to find her," she finally said. She turned to Ryder. His face was serious as he navigated traffic. "If she told Gary what she told me, and you don't want the whole town to know already, you're going to need to talk to him before you have a mob out searching for Brian and someone gets hurt."

"We already know what she told Gary, and it wasn't much," he said looking over at her when he stopped at a red light. "You're the only person who's been in to see her without a police escort, where she can really talk. I need to know what she told you."

"I'll need to tell my dad, too."

They'd reached the part of town that she lived in with small starter-style homes. She didn't want to call them cookie-cutter houses, because she felt that all the houses in her neighborhood had a unique charm to them, but essentially they were all very similar inside.

"I can tell the sheriff. It's part of my job, you know," he said as he turned onto her street.

He parked the truck in front of her cottage style home, the sight of it bringing her a sense of comfort that she needed after her talk with Rain. Ryder turned and grabbed his duffel from the back seat then followed her into the house.

"Where do you want to talk?" he asked, looking around her living room and the piles of papers stacked on the table and floor.

"It'll be more comfortable in here," she told him, clearing a place for his laptop.

"Kind of a mess you've got here," he mentioned.

"It's a project. One that I've already delegated to the university, but haven't committed to undoing my organization."

He looked around the space, and his expression told her he only saw the disorganized mess of papers.

"There's a method to my madness," she promised.

"I didn't say anything." He held up his hands in defense, but couldn't help but smile as he returned to his computer. "Okay. I'm ready. Are you?"

"Yeah," she said, settling into her favorite spot on the couch and grabbing a throw blanket to have something to hold onto. "Where do you want me to start?"

"Try to go in order." He paused to look up at her. "Sometimes it can be hard to remember, and things get mixed up. The more chronological you can be, the easier it'll be for later, but also it's not a big deal if we have to go back and enter something in later. Just take your time and be as thorough as possible. No detail is too small."

She let out a breath. "I went into her room." She paused when he smiled as he typed. "You said no detail was too small."

"I didn't say anything," he said, still smiling. "Keep going."

"When she saw me, she was surprised."

"Did she say she was surprised, or do you just think she was?"

"Her face looked surprised, and she made a typical Rain snarky comment." He clacked on the keyboard as she talked, but didn't interrupt, so she continued. "She said, 'What are *you* doing here? I figure you'd be the last person to come check on me.' I told her I had been worried about her and wanted to make sure she was okay, to see if she needed anything. She then rolled her eyes and said, 'Oh, I get it. Daddy gives you permission to come in here and take a peek at the crazy person so you can go back and tell the whole town how wonderful you are that you offered to help. Well, you can just leave. I don't need anything from you and I'm not helping make you look better.'"

"She really doesn't like you, does she?" Ryder asked, still typing to catch up.

She let the question go unanswered, continuing her story. "It took me a little bit to convince her that I was there for her, and then, I don't know what happened. I don't know if she was just too tired to keep up with the tough girl act, or if she just needed to tell her story, but she started to cry. I've never seen her cry before..."

Rain

"Nobody cares about me," Rain said through her sniffles.

"That's not true. Plenty of people dropped everything to look for you while you were missing. You have no idea the relief this entire town felt when you were found."

"That wasn't me," she sniffed. "That was a missing person. It didn't matter who it was."

"No, Rain, it was you. People were coming in to the diner, sharing stories about you, spending their time looking for you or answering calls to try and find *you*."

"And Brian," she stated, wiping her cheeks. "But they need to stop looking for him or he'll find me," she said frantically and looked toward the door as if just talking about him would summon him.

"Don't you want him to be found, too?" Lillian asked, confused by Rain's sudden fear.

Rain scooted up in the bed, leaning toward Lillian to whisper loudly. "No!" She glanced back at the door. "They'll make me go back to sleep if they hear me. They don't believe me. They think I'm crazy."

"Nobody thinks you're crazy, Rain," she tried to say soothingly, but Rain wasn't hearing her.

"They don't want anyone to know, but they need to know."

"Know what?"

"That he's not missing. He's evil!" She looked at the door again at her outburst, then scooted closer again. "He's evil," she said quieter this time. "We went to the Mountain, and it turned him crazy."

"What do you mean?"

"There's something out there, and it changed him right in front of me."

"Changed him how? I don't understand."

"You think I'm crazy, too. I already see it on your face. But I'm not crazy. The Mountain is cursed, just like everyone says."

"Those are just stories, made up to keep people from going in and getting themselves lost or hurt."

"No." She shook her head rapidly. "No. They're not stories. It's true. Everything is true! ... You can feel it. It's like it's alive... When we got closer to the opening, all the hairs stood up on my arms and neck. I could feel it pulling at me. It pulled at Brian, too. His eyes," she said, and stared off at something only she could see. "His eyes were like a dead person's when he looked at me," she said flatly. "He was dragging me in even though I didn't want to go. I wanted to get as far away as I could, but he wouldn't let me leave. Then something was coming. Brian was acting weirder each second, and I could hear something coming for us, but I couldn't get past him to get out, and he wasn't listening anymore anyway, so I ran away. He chased me and we ran and ran. Everything hurts in there. Your body feels squeezed tight. The air is too thick to breathe." She rubbed at her chest. "I just wanted to get away. I ran even though I didn't feel like I could run anymore. My legs were like jelly, my heart was beating out of my chest. I knew I was going to die. But he was behind me still, yelling things, and the noise was getting closer and then the trees were gone and there was a drop, and I didn't hear anything for a minute, but I didn't stop running. I didn't look back. I kept going. I had to get away, but then I could hear it again behind me, closer than before, right on top of me, and then it was all black."

She looked at the door again, expecting someone to come in and stop her like they did when she got too loud.

"What happened then?" Lillian said gently, barely more than a whisper so as not to startle her from her memory.

Rain was still facing the door when she started talking again, this time her tone flat, no longer frantic. "There was nothing but black. It was cold... so cold at first. I don't know why I woke up, there were no noises, but then there was a little piece of light. It was small, but it was so dark in there that even in the little bit of light, I could make out that I was in a small room. It was like a prison cell. I found a folded blanket and a sandwich by the light, but the light was only there for a second and then it was gone. I screamed and screamed, but nobody answered."

She stopped talking and pulled her blanket up closer around her, hugging it tight.

"I begged him to let me go. Every day he came with food, but didn't say anything, and I begged. He wouldn't tell me why he took me. I didn't know where I was. But every day he brought me food. I could keep track that way," she whispered quickly, looking back at Lillian finally. "He only came once a day and on the last day, he finally said something. Just a few words..."

"What did he say?" Lillian finally asked when the silence dragged on.

"He said, 'Not much longer.' I can still hear the words floating on the air." She leaned back against her pillow, exhaustion catching up to her, her eyes looking heavy. She yawned. "It was so long, Lil. So scary."

Lillian could see her starting to fall asleep, but she still had questions. "Rain," she said, reaching over and Rain startled back, her eyes focusing, realizing she was still there. "Rain what happened on the second day? How did you get away?"

"I don't know," she said confused. "I guess he let me go. Maybe because too many people were looking, and it wasn't safe for him to keep me anymore."

"Did he hurt you in there?" she asked softly. "Before he let you go?"

She shook her head. "I never saw him. He never came into the room. Just brought the sandwiches." She stared off toward the ceiling. "Six sandwiches and then sunlight. So much bright light… it hurt to open my eyes, but people were near and I didn't want to go back into the dark." She looked back at Lillian again, her eyes a little more alert. "But don't you see? He let me go. I don't know why, but Brian let me go. He didn't do anything to hurt me; he let me go. If they don't stop looking for him, he might come back for me and put me back in the dark. I can't go back in the dark, Lillian!" She sat up and grabbed her hands. "Please tell them to stop looking for him. He's not missing. He's not in there. He let me go. Don't make him come back. Just let him leave. I can't go back!"

"It's okay… shhh… it's okay, Rain. You're not going to go back. There are policemen here to protect you. You went through something terrible, and they aren't going to let him in here to get you."

"They will if they think he was missing with me. They might want to reunite us if they find him. Please! Lillian… your dad! You have to tell your dad! Tell him not to bring him here. Let him go. I can't go back!"

"Okay… it's okay… I'll tell them," she said soothingly. "I'll talk to them, and they won't let him near you. Okay?" She squeezed Rain's hands, hoping the reassurances were enough to calm her down.

"Thank you," Rain finally whispered, sitting back against the pillows again. "Will you go now and tell them? Please. I can't go back there. Please tell them now."

"I will, Rain." She stood to leave. "Try to get some rest. He's not coming for you."

She nodded and closed her eyes as Lillian left the room.

Lillian

Lillian waited for Ryder to finish typing the last of what she told him and then for him to read back over it all. She waited, remembering how frantic and scared Rain had been even after being rescued and safe for days since her abduction.

"Her story has stayed pretty consistent," Ryder said, shutting his computer and sitting back in his own chair.

"You don't sound like that's a good thing. Shouldn't it be?"

"For me, yes, but for the case, no."

"Care to explain?" she asked when he didn't elaborate further.

"The reason I came to your house today was because I needed your help. I'm on a short timeline and not supposed to raise suspicion, so I'm limited in who I can talk to."

"So, how did I make the short list?"

"Because I had already shared my theories with you… well, and August, too, sort of by accident, but I'd rather see you early in the morning to discuss theories and see where they wind up than him."

At the mention of August, her stomach churned a little, but she wasn't going to let it distract her in the moment. She leaned forward, pushing thoughts of him aside for now, thinking back to the theory that he'd shared with her before.

"You think Brian has something to do with Wade, too?"

"Yes. I've been suspicious that someone was lurking around, and when we found Rain, but not Brian, it was pointing me more toward him as the killer."

"But if he was a killer, why would he let her go? Why not just kill her and dump her body like the other two that you guys found? She can identify him."

He rubbed his hand through his hair and sighed. "I don't know. That part doesn't add up, unless he's trying to throw us off. Using your same argument, no killer in their right mind would let a victim go that could ID him, so he could claim that he was just another victim of whatever else was in the woods that night."

"You said her story was good for you, but bad for the case…"

He leaned forward, resting his elbows on his knees. "Her story sticks to the same lines. They went to the Mountain for the kicks; to get to say they'd done it. When they get there, things change. Brian loses his shit and starts chasing her through the woods. This supports *my* theory that he's the killer and she just happened to be the one that got away. However. As she keeps going, her story gets more bizarre, and she talks about being locked up in a room somewhere.

"We didn't find any evidence of her being restrained, no foreign substances on her body or clothes that would lead to a different location being involved, not to mention how difficult it would be for Brian to move her back out to the woods with an active search going on and nobody noticing either of them moving about. She then swears on her life that she was locked up for longer than she really was. They went into the Mountain Saturday evening, were reported missing the next morning and she was found by Monday night. At most, if she *had* been stowed away somewhere, she could only have been kept for two days.

"But her story stays consistent that she was locked up for nearly a week. Every time any of us has interviewed her, she refers to six sandwiches. She told you the same. She swears it was once a day and will not budge on her story. That makes her look unreliable, so it hurts my case that the only witness believes things happened that didn't. How can we pin abduction and two murders on a guy when the only person who can put him there is spewing an unbelievable story?"

"But if she was locked up, and she was as scared as she obviously was, it's not unrealistic that she wouldn't be able to gauge time. If her only measure of time was how often he was feeding her, and all she was left with was blackness and solitude in between, how would she know how long it had been?" She leaned forward on the couch. "Go sit in a dark closet and tell me how long ten minutes feels like."

He wiggled his eyebrows. "Ten minutes in a dark closet with you would feel like no time at all."

"Haha," she mocked. "Seriously though, if he fed her three times a day, she could perceive it as once a day because of how alone she was, when really it was just two. That would still work with your timeline."

He leaned back in his chair, his brow furrowed as he chewed on a thought. "I can't believe we didn't think about that… The timing could work." He mumbled as he processed his thoughts. "And it wouldn't make her look crazy. How would she know how long it had really been?" He stood and grabbed the computer, placing it in his duffle. "I should get back to the station."

"I thought you were off today."

He smiled. "Did you have other plans in mind to keep me here?" he asked, but the flirtation held no real promise. She could tell he was determined again. "I need to update your dad on this new information. It may be enough to change the case, even though the medical examiner doesn't think foul play was involved."

She stood up as well. "I'm coming too."

"You don't need to. I have the transcript. It'll be enough."

"I told Rain I'd talk to my dad."

"Lilly, I can tell him for you."

"I know you can, but I told her I would do it. I need to do it for her."

"Okay, I get it. Let's get going then."

"You head on. I'll follow."

"Had enough of me already?" He feigned being hurt.

"I'm sure you'll be busy after and I'll need to be able to leave."

"I'd make time for you."

"I'm sure you would, but you have more important things to focus on now. I'll be right behind you."

FORTY-SEVEN

-Lillian-

It took longer to get to the station than Lillian had originally intended. She hoped it had been enough time for Ryder to bring her dad up to speed so she wouldn't have to do all the explaining and could just reiterate Rain's fear. Ryder was talking with Jane when she walked up.

"Hey, did you fill him in?"

"No. He has someone in there. I haven't had a chance yet."

"He's talking to that hiker, August. You know the one," Jane said from her seat.

Lillian glanced toward her dad's closed door. Should she make an excuse to leave? She wanted to talk to August, but this wasn't the place. She hadn't planned to see him next in front of her dad and Ryder. Just knowing he was on the other side of the door made her feel like she needed to throw up. All morning long she'd been fantasizing about Ryder, completely having put August out of her mind for the first time since their argument, but now, knowing he was so close, everything came crashing into her like a guilt-riddled wrecking ball. How could she have let herself get so wrapped up in thoughts of Ryder when she still had feelings for August, feelings she still had to sort through?

"You okay?" Ryder asked, stepping close, placing his hand on the small of her back.

"Yeah, I'm fine… I don't know, maybe Rain's story is still getting to me," she lied.

"Do you need me to get you anything?" he asked her softly, leaning in even closer. "We have vending machines, or I can get you a chair so you can sit."

She wanted to move away, not wanting to make a scene for the rest of the precinct, which was sure to be watching, but also in case August were to come out. As if on cue, the door to her dad's office opened and Ryder was still too close, and his hand was still gently resting on her back.

"Will you let me explain things myself?" August was asking her dad as they emerged.

Her dad noticed her before August did, both immediately looking from her to Ryder standing too close and back. Her dad's face was expressionless as he turned back to August to finish their conversation. August's was easier to read, and it made her stomach drop even further than it already had.

"You have your chance," Bill said. "I don't suggest you waste it."

"Sheriff, I need to talk to you about something," Ryder said as he stepped closer to Bill.

"Can it wait a couple of minutes?" he asked, looking from Ryder to Lillian, "Is everything okay with you?" he asked her.

Ryder looked over at her. "Yeah, she's okay. It's been a busy morning. She's here with me," Ryder said, barreling on before she could get a word in. "This is important."

Lillian noticed August's jaw muscles flex as he clenched his teeth. From the look of him, He'd had enough and turned to the sheriff. "If you don't need anything else, I'm going to go." Bill gave him a nod that he was clear to leave. He walked by without looking back at her.

Ryder was already headed into the office, thankfully not noticing her discomfort.

"Lillian, you'll be okay to wait a few minutes while I talk to Ryder?" her dad asked, and she nodded. He didn't say anything more, but glanced toward the front of the building then back at her as he stepped into his own office and closed the door.

Before she allowed herself to think about what she was going to say, her feet were carrying her out of the building. She turned to look for the truck August normally drove, surprised she hadn't noticed it when she pulled up. She watched as it pulled out of the lot and drove away. She hadn't been quick enough.

Her eyes prickled as she stared at her phone.

Why did this have to be happening now? Why did she have to feel so completely drawn to two different men? Why couldn't she have met August before Ryder started being nice? Maybe *she* was being too nice to allow Ryder in at all. What was she supposed to do when being with either of them made her completely forget the world around her?

What did that say about her?

She sat on the bench outside the department, willing herself to call him, but she couldn't press the button to connect.

"Way to go. You win the biggest loser award," she told herself and put the phone back in her bag, knowing she didn't have time to say what needed to be said right now anyway.

It was beginning to feel like time was never on her side.

She went back into the building and waited for the door to open again and for Ryder to wave her in.

Her dad was sitting in his seat and motioned for her to sit as well. Ryder shut the door and left them alone.

"You look awful," her dad finally said.

"Good morning to you, too." She smoothed her wind-blown hair from her quick trip outside, but knew her clothes or hair weren't what he was referring to.

"Did you talk to August?"

"I tried to follow him, but he was already gone."

She caught the slight nod before he continued talking. "He says you haven't talked for a few days."

"Geez Dad." She sighed and rubbed at her temple, wondering how many times August was going to be the target of investigation because he was conveniently new to town during active investigations. "Are you still checking up on him?"

"This was a different kind of check. More of the father check in versus the cop check in."

"Dad, don't tell me you ran a background check on him," she groaned.

"He was a person of interest in this case, *and* he's been seeing my daughter. Of course I ran a background check."

"He's just a guy that happens to have chosen here to vacation. Can't you leave him alone?"

"If his background came back without questions, then yes, I would."

"What do you mean?" She leaned forward in the chair. "What sort of questions?"

"I told him I'd give him a chance to explain them himself." She watched as he studied her, choosing his words. "But since he didn't stick around to talk…" He tapped his pen on the notepad on his desk and she knew he was considering what to tell her.

"You're not going to tell me, are you?" she finally asked.

He set the pen on the notepad before him. "I'll give him a chance to come clean," he finally decided.

"Come clean about what? If he wanted the chance, he wouldn't have driven off as quickly as he did." She motioned behind her to the door as if they could see the parking lot and August's truck missing from it.

"Did you just come here today to discuss the same as Ryder?" he asked.

"Yes," she sighed. He was changing the subject, having made up his mind and she knew he wouldn't be budged. "Sort of. I told Rain I would tell you specifically that she is afraid of Brian and doesn't want him to find her. Did Ryder tell you everything from this morning?"

"Yes, I read the transcript of your conversation. He never should have used you to talk to her."

"He didn't. I was going to come here and ask to talk to her, but he said she was allowed to have visitors, so he took me over… I'm guessing the reason you won't let Evan or the other friend of Brian's in to see her is because of what she's saying about Brian?"

"That and they barely know her. She's allowed to have visitors if she approves them, and she requested not to see them."

"And she pre-approved me?" Lillian asked in disbelief.

"It's not so much that she pre-approved anyone in particular, but you weren't on the denial list. If she didn't want to see you, she only had to push the nurse button, and they would have asked you to leave. I guess she hasn't felt heard yet and that's why she let you stay."

"So, what are you going to do about Brian?"

"You know I can't discuss that."

"Do I need to be worried that there's a murderer on the loose?"

He let out a breath. News was going to spread soon anyway now that Ryder had been given more rope.

"We're not alerting the community that there's anything to worry about at this time, but I'm expanding the search to encompass the town instead of the woods."

"And what are you going to tell his friends? Better yet, what am *I* supposed to tell his friends? They asked me to try and get through to you so they can go home. I need to tell them something."

"Ryder is calling them as we speak to come into the office for a final debriefing. If their story doesn't change, I'll let them go home. I've already spoken with authorities in their hometown to collaborate if Brian appears."

"Already?" She was shocked since Ryder had only just updated him.

"This has been on Ryder's mind for a few days, and if Brian made his way back home while we were searching here, we needed to know that as well. I have the counties between here and there on alert as well. If he shows up, we'll be notified."

"I'm impressed," she told him.

"It's what we do," he said. "Now go on and find more enjoyable things to do and leave the boring police work to us. I'll handle Evan and Jack."

She chewed on her lip, realizing she didn't have any other excuses for the day to continue avoiding August. She'd allowed this to consume her morning, but now that her role was done, she knew she needed to call him. She just didn't know what she was going to say. He wouldn't want to hear about her conflictions when it came to Ryder, that he was still ever-present in her thoughts, and really, maybe that's where she'd gone wrong before. He didn't need to know everything she thought, or felt, or experienced, just as long as when she was with him, she was with him, not having thoughts of Ryder… but she *was* still having thoughts of Ryder on her own time, so what was she supposed to do about that? Were they enough to throw away trying to see how she really felt about August?

Could she be throwing away something good with August because she was confused about Ryder?

"Here," her dad said, breaking her out of her thoughts and handing her a slip of paper with an address.

"What's this?"

"August's address."

She studied the paper again, not immediately recognizing the road.

"It's going to eat at you until you get whatever's between you out and in the open. He knows where you live, it's only fair you know where he does, too."

"His background check…?"

"Despite my fatherly intuition to immediately dislike anyone who shows an interest in my daughter and years of police experience to find anything and everything to hold against him, there was nothing in his report that would make me advise you to stay away from him. However, you do need to know that he hasn't been completely honest with you."

"But you won't tell me what that means."

"That's between you two."

"And you're not going to offer me advice…?"

"I'm sorry, kiddo. The only solace I can offer is at least they're both stand up men that you're considering."

She chewed her lip again. "Do you think it's wrong that there's more than one to consider?"

"I think it would be wrong to disqualify one because of past judgments… but that's not saying I'm pointing you toward one or the other."

She sighed. "I know." She offered a half-smile. "I'm going to go see if I can climb out of the hole I keep digging myself further into."

She stood to leave, but turned back at the door.

"Dad?"

"Hmm?"

"I know Ryder has his theory, and now it sounds like Rain can back him up… but what if Brian is still a victim, too? She did say there was something else out there. She could hear it. What if you move the search and he's still out there, waiting for help?"

"It's my job to worry about those decisions, not yours," he told her gently.

She nodded sorrowfully, hating he had to carry such a burden, and turned to leave once more.

FORTY-EIGHT

-Lillian-

Lillian's car bumped over the gravel drive that seemed to be never-ending. She'd debated calling Lana or even her mom to see what they'd advise her to do. She didn't feel right just showing up unannounced, but she also didn't want to have this conversation with August over the phone… or risk him not answering.

The route to his house had taken her twenty minutes out of town and down a long private drive. She'd had plenty of time to think about what to say to him, but as she pulled up to the picture-perfect cabin in the woods, his truck parked off to the side, all her words disappeared. Her hands were sweating against the steering wheel, and she had no idea what to say.

She saw a curtain move on a front window. Despite the drive out, she was committed now; he'd seen her car and there was no turning back. She turned the car off and got out as he stepped out on the front porch.

"Your dad quite literally meant not to waste time, didn't he?"

"He wouldn't tell me anything," she said, standing at the bottom of the porch steps, unsure if she'd be welcome to go up.

"Then how are you here?"

"He gave me your address, but said it was for you to tell me… You're not married, are you?"

He sighed. "I already told you I'm not."

"My dad said you hadn't been completely honest with me."

"I haven't lied to you, Lillian."

"But you haven't told me everything either, right?"

"We hardly know each other. I'm sure there are things you haven't told me." He crossed his arms and leaned against the front porch post.

She felt awkward standing in his yard below him and could feel the urge to fidget with her hair so she gripped her purse strap to keep from doing so. "I've tried to tell you everything, which, I don't know, maybe I shouldn't have. Maybe that was the wrong move, but I felt like you needed to know."

"Did *I* need to know, or did *you* need to unburden yourself for seeing Ryder and me at the same time?"

"I wasn't *seeing* Ryder. Things just… happened…"

"Things don't just happen, Lillian. It happened because you let it. The part that bothers me is that you let it happen because of what he means to you still."

"You're right, Ryder was a surprise."

His mouth was set in a line. "You and Ryder seemed to be getting along well this morning. Any more surprises since our last conversation?"

"We were working on the case," she said firmly.

"He keeps opening the door and you just keep walking through." He looked up at the trees and took a breath. "I take it you haven't told him about us yet." When she didn't respond he gave a curt nod and continued. "He didn't seem smug to be by your side or worried about how he and I would react to seeing each other, as I imagine *he'd* react if he knew you and I had hooked up. I'm curious why you're honest with me, but not with him."

"There hasn't been a natural time to discuss you and I seeing each other."

"How about any of the times he opens his mouth to talk to you? Shut him down with the good ol' 'I'm seeing someone.' Hell, Lillian, you don't even have to tell him who it is, but, I don't know, the next time he tries to kiss you—because that seems to happen pretty regularly—you hold up a hand and tell him no. All I can think is that by keeping him happy and oblivious means you have him in reserve if things don't work out between the two of us. It's always good to have a backup plan, after all. But I can make it easy for you, Lillian, if that's the struggle. I'll step aside. You can have Ryder, and I'll never let him know there was competition. You never have to see me again."

"That's not what I want."

"Really? Because you looked pretty comfortable next to him this morning. By the way, we were all at the station early, and he was pretty quick to mention that you were with him. Did he stay at your place last night or did you stay at his while you 'worked on the case?'"

"Stop." She'd had enough. She climbed the two steps to his front porch and he shifted his stance to face her. "I don't know why you're being so intentionally mean, but I didn't come out here for you to attack my character. I thought being honest with you about what happened between Ryder and me was important if you and I were going to have any chance at something.

"Yes, he's flirtatious, which is flattering. I'm sorry, I'm human and I responded. I can't go back and change it. I don't want to change it. Just like I don't want to change how things happened between you and me. Yes, Ryder has made it very clear that he has an interest in me, but nothing more has happened, and I don't deserve to be attacked by you.

"I know what I told you before hurt you, and I'm sorry that it did. I didn't tell you to cause you pain. I didn't want there to be secrets between us. I know I shouldn't feel conflicted when I have feelings for you, and maybe it's because I *do* have feelings for you already that I *am* conflicted." She pinched the bridge of her nose, taking a deep breath, then let her hand drop to her side. "It's like you said, I don't know you, and yet I can't stop thinking about you. When I'm with you, it feels right. It feels like you're supposed to be a part of my life, and I don't understand why. It makes no sense that a person I just met could consume so much of my being that it makes me nervous just to hear your name. My phone rings or the doorbell jingles, and I wish it was you on the other side. I'm trying to run a business, and my thoughts stray to you. There's a search for a missing person, and I hope that you have an excuse to slip into the diner so I can see you again. I'm wrapped up in thoughts of you and it's embarrassing how badly I want you.

"I drove out here without any idea what I was going to say to you, trying to rehearse a script, but nothing made sense. I just knew I needed to see you. I needed to be near you. I need you not to hate me, because you hating me is eating me up and it's not fair that you have that sort of power over me. All I know is that I have to make things right with you, even if that means that I leave this porch knowing that you heard what I had to say and we never talk again...

"And I know part of my excuse to come out here was to confront you about whatever secrets you might be keeping back, trying to shift the blame onto you, but the reality is that I don't even care what it is. It's your business, and you'll tell me, or you won't. I know that I've been honest with you, and I've told you how I feel, and if that means that's it and whatever short thing we had is over, then at least I know I tried... but I'm hoping it isn't."

Her heart was racing and she could feel the heat in her cheeks, surprising herself that she'd said all that she had. Part of her wondered how much of what she said was just meant for him and how much was projection from what she felt for Ryder but she couldn't think about that now, not while she was trying to get back on speaking terms with August. It was out now, and there was nothing more to say.

"Anything else?" he asked, when she finally stopped for a breath.

"I don't think –" she started, but before she could finish, he pulled her to him, his hands in her hair before she could think, his mouth moving against her own. "Wait –"

"I've *been* waiting."

He lifted her easily and kicked the door open behind them. A part of her knew she needed to tell him to stop, that they needed to talk about everything, but the other part, the part that was yelling as loud as possible, was telling her to stop listening to her brain and enjoy the moment for once in her life.

After the past few days of not knowing if she'd see him again, the conflicting feelings she had for him and Ryder, the emotions over Rain and Brian, she just wanted to feel something on her terms.

She let him carry her through the cabin to the bedroom. Her only thought was getting out of her clothes as fast as possible. She was undressed by the time he was lowering her to the bed, his strong arms wrapped around her as he dove into her. She clung to him, feeling his firm body move above her own.

Every movement was an assault from both of them, working out their demons through each other. It wasn't soft and romantic, slow or sweet. They took from each other what they needed, until neither could take any more. She cried out just before he gave in and collapsed against her. When it was over, they lay tangled in each other, panting on the twisted sheets.

"You know," she said, breaking the silence after their breaths finally returned to normal, "you can't use mind-numbing sex every time we have a disagreement."

"Why not?"

"It's not fair," she said into his chest, a chill up her back causing her to shiver against him.

He reached around, feeling for the covers, then lifted his head to look. "Hang on," he said and rolled off the bed to retrieve the blanket.

"You should make your bed when you get out of it," she told him, snuggling in as he covered her up and held her tight.

"I did," he said, a lazy smile in his voice. "You unmade it."

"Oh…" She moved to wrap herself around him more. "I'm not apologizing for that."

"I'd never ask you to. So why is mind-numbing sex not a fair answer to a disagreement?" he asked, drawing shapes with his fingers along her back.

"Because we don't know who won."

"That's the beauty of mind-numbing sex. If you don't feel like you won, I'll happily go again until you do. Besides. That was all you."

"Me? You're the one that started it."

"You're the one that drove out here."

"Yeah, to talk. Not for sex."

"Mind-numbing sex," he reminded her.

She smiled but sighed.

"I'm sorry that what I said hurt you," he said softly, kissing the top of her head. "I guess I didn't realize how much it bothers me to see you with him. I need you, Lillian. I need all of you, and it made me crazy to think you couldn't feel the same way."

"Do you think that's just because this is new, and it'll wear off?" she asked him.

He rolled her over and kissed her, moving his mouth to taste along her neck, his hands sliding over her hips and up her back, his mouth working its way to her ear. "If that's a possibility, then we better make the most of the time we have," he whispered.

This time he took his time touching, tasting, a slow embrace allowing them both to feel every minute sensation as they moved with each other. When the end came, it was euphoric.

When she woke up in the darkened bedroom all alone, she imagined she'd dreamed the whole thing. She looked around at the unfamiliar surroundings, laying back against the pillows, assessing her thoroughly ravaged body, and smiled at how real it had been.

She stretched beneath the covers, and realized what had woken her from her splendid dreams. She quietly slipped out of the bed, not sure where any of her clothes had been tossed, to search for his bathroom. After relieving herself, she couldn't help but treat herself to his expansive shower with multiple sprayers and wonderfully scented soaps. She was thoroughly rinsed and heated by the time he joined her, slipping in and hugging her from behind.

"I didn't wake you when I got up, did I?" he asked.

"I don't think so," she said, letting him lather soap onto her body again, enjoying the feeling of his hands slowly gliding against her skin. "Where did you go?"

"Someone left a wake of debris that needed to be recovered."

"Oh?" she innocently asked as he kneeled down to leisurely soap her legs, working his way up inch by excruciating inch.

"I found a sock on the armchair… and a shoe under my coffee table," he said as he slid his hand along the soft section of skin behind her knee. "There was a belt by the front door," he said as his touch traveled along her tender inner thigh. He brushed a kiss where she trembled at his touch.

"I wasn't wearing a belt." The words were barely a breath as his hands caressed higher.

"No." He leaned forward in the spray of water to taste her freshly rinsed body. "That belonged to me." His tongue felt cool compared to the water now beating against her back as she tried to remain standing upright. He cut off the deep exploration of his tongue when her balance faltered, rising to kiss along her neck. "You left your purse on the front porch and your keys were on the stairs," he whispered right before he nipped at her ear. "You should be more responsible with your belongings," he said as he lifted her into his arms, pressed her against the wall, and slid inside of her in one quick move.

"Oh!" The shocked word escaped. "I'll try to keep that in mind." She breathed out the words, already forgetting what she was supposed to remember.

She clung to him as he torturously drew out every desire, awakening sensations in places she never considered sexy until they were sliding along his slickened skin. She wrapped her legs tighter around him as he drove deeper, crying out when she couldn't hold back anymore. He finished on a moan letting the shower rain over them while he held her.

"Is my being naked going to distract you again?" she asked after they'd dried off and were curled up again under the covers.

"I was never distracted," he told her. "I just wanted to make sure you felt like you won."

"How very chivalrous of you," she said, smiling into the darkness.

"We can stay here a little longer," he told her quietly, petting her hair and down her back, "but then we should talk."

She knew he was right, but she didn't want to ruin their afternoon with reality.

The next time she woke, it was to her stomach growling. She could hear August chuckle lightly behind her, still holding her close.

"How long was I out?" she asked him softly.

"Not too long," he told her, leaning back so she could roll over and face him. He propped himself up on one arm and moved the hair from her face with his free hand. "I want to clear the air, and then if you'll still have me, we can go find something to eat."

"Go?"

"I don't have much on hand here other than snacks. I wasn't really prepared for dinner guests."

"I can snack," she said.

"We can't hide out here forever."

Her eyes focused on her hand resting against his chest. She moved it slightly to feel him respond to her touch. "We're not hiding," she said without looking him in the eyes.

"Lillian." He waited until she looked up at him. "I want you. I think that's been made pretty clear by now. I don't want there to be any doubt that you want me too."

"And getting food with you proves that I want you? Not the last few hours?"

"Not worrying about what others will think if they see us together enjoying each other's company."

"Making you and me known, you mean, to someone it *will* matter to." She bit at her lower lip.

"If this, between us, is what you want to figure out, then you have to let Ryder know."

"I know, but he doesn't need me to flaunt a new relationship in his face." She was already feeling anxious about how to tell Ryder. They weren't together, and while they'd only shared a few moments, those moments were intense. She worried what would happen between them.

Was August right? Had she been holding onto him as a backup plan? How could she sleep with August if she really had feelings for Ryder? *Or are you just too scared to let yourself be hurt again to let Ryder back in completely?*

She chose to ignore the inner voice, for now, while she was lying naked with another man. Now wasn't the time to solve Ryder... but she knew she needed to figure it out soon.

"I'm not asking you to call him to meet us for drinks. I'm asking to be able to take you out for a meal."

"You've taken me out before," she reminded him.

"And I want to keep doing it without worrying about hiding us from him. I told you before, I'm not one to share. If you're going to be with me, be with me. Ryder or anyone else has had their chance. Now is for us."

She was silent. He was right, wasn't he? She shouldn't be considering both of them at the same time.

Then why do people date? her inner voice added to her turmoil.

"We can go to dinner," she conceded, shutting up the voice in her head. "I'll figure out what to tell Ryder."

"Thank you," he said, leaning in to kiss her gently, the warmth of him spreading through her.

She pushed against him slightly. "Uh uh, I thought you were hungry. What did you do with my clothes?" she asked, leaning away to look over the edge of the bed, but he grabbed her and shifted beneath her so she was straddling his lap.

"I think you look fine without them," he said, sitting up to kiss her again.

"I thought you said we couldn't hide out here," she said, breaking off the kiss as she felt him stir beneath her, both surprising and exciting her as she rubbed against him.

"You said we weren't hiding." His voice was thick as she continued to tease against him.

He didn't resist as she pressed him back against the bed, and watched him as she shifted to take him in. His eyes closed on a groan as she slowly slid down the length of him, her sigh a whisper between them. She took the lead, slow and steady, long, drawn out motions, taking her time to drive him crazy. His hands gripping her thighs squeezed tighter. He didn't have much longer. She increased her pace, enjoying the empowerment she felt being in complete control. She held out her own finish, finally letting go when she felt him pulse and heard him moan.

His hands were still holding her hips as she laid on top of him, enjoying the feeling of their bodies together. "Okay," she murmured when her brain was somewhat functioning again. "You can feed me now."

"I think you'll need clothes first," he whispered from above her head. She could hear the smile in his voice.

She tilted to rest her chin on his chest to look at him. "You said I looked fine without them."

"And I was right, but if you ever plan to do anything other than letting me explore every part of you—" he slid his hands along her sides and up her back, "—then I suggest you find something to wear… Even then, I can't make promises that it'll be enough."

Her stomach rumbled loudly, interrupting any potential fantasies his hands were stirring up.

"Come on," he said, rolling out of bed and carrying her with him to the shower.

"I can walk you know." She laughed, but didn't really want him to let her go.

"If you still can after everything we just did… I guess I'm not as good as I thought I was."

"Someone's confident," she joked, but squealed as he turned her into the still cold shower spray. "Okay, okay," she laughed, "you're right, you were amazing and my whole body is like jello, never to be used again."

"Oh, I have many more plans for your body," he told her as the water finally warmed and he turned her into the now steamy spray, letting her down so they could soap each other.

"What are you thinking?" he asked as they were drying off.

She smiled, admiring his tanned skin and toned muscles disappearing beneath the towel folded around his waist. He was built, not body-builder large and bulky, but every muscle was strong and defined; the man was beautiful.

"Why is it that when I'm with you, everything just feels right?" she asked him finally. In these moments with August, everything felt like it was meant to be, and only when she dragged Ryder back into her thoughts did she start messing everything up. "Isn't there supposed to be an awkwardness as we figure all this out?"

"Why does there have to be?"

"I don't know. Shouldn't there be? This doesn't feel like real life. I feel like I'm about to wake up from a dream. A really *good* dream… but I don't want to." She used a spare towel to squeeze out the excess water from her hair.

"Then don't. Stay in the dream with me." He sat on the edge of the bed and held out a hand, inviting her over. She moved into reach, still drying her hair, and he pulled her hips to bring her to him. She set the towel next to him and held his shoulders. She looked into his eyes, searching for anything that would tell her that this wasn't real.

"Am I crazy?" She asked finally.

"Not at all. Being here with you is perfect… but I can pinch you if you want." He gave her hips a little squeeze.

"And risk waking up?" She chuckled. "No way."

"Then let's just enjoy the dream. I'll call the Overlook and have them set us a table."

"I'm not dressed for the Overlook," she said, remembering her inconsequential outfit that was somewhere in his house. "We can go somewhere less fancy."

"You're not currently dressed for anything," he joked and stood to leave to retrieve her clothes, while she returned the towel she'd set on the bed to the bathroom. "Besides," he said as he brought in her things, "they won't care what you're wearing..." She'd taken her towel off to trade for the clothes. He leaned against the door jamb, still holding her clothes. He didn't trade.

"I have to wear something," she said, placing her hands on her hips when he stayed leaning, smiling, watching, still not handing them over. She reached out a hand, a laugh in her voice. "Clothes. Food."

His amused eyes finally met hers. "If you insist on wearing clothes, then I insist on the Overlook."

"Fine," she laughed again. "I'll let you take me to a ridiculously expensive dinner at the nicest place in town, dressed in tennies and ripped jeans, and when they laugh at us at the entrance and tell us to leave, we can go through a drive-thru and you can buy me a burger."

"They won't laugh us out," he said as he left the bathroom to go find his own clothes. "It's pretty hard to turn the owner away."

"Wait, what?" she asked, following him back into the bedroom. "What do you mean?"

"Your dad really didn't say anything, did he?"

"No... just that you had something that you hadn't told me. You *own* the Overlook? I thought you were new to town."

"Sort of."

"How can you sort of be new to town if you own the restaurant?"

She tried to think back to when the Overlook was opening, the controversy stirred up about the location. Had she seen his name in the announcements then? Part of the controversy was that nobody seemed to know who bought the land and built the restaurant. She shook her head. *Someone* had to know, obviously, but the town residents didn't and like most gossip, they only wanted to talk about what disgruntled them and not look any deeper for the truth. She heard the gossip but it never fired her up so she never had reason to look into it any deeper. If she had dug into the development of the Overlook, would she have found him sooner?

"I can see your brain whirring," August joked as he pulled on his shirt. "I've been gone for a while, making investments, building a portfolio, so to speak. I've only just decided to come back to stay."

"So, when you told me you were on a vacation and just hiking your way through..."

"That was a version of the truth." He threaded a belt through the loops in his cargo-style pants.

"A version..." She shifted her weight to one side and put her hand on her hip. "Otherwise known as a lie."

"Not a lie, just an omission. I didn't want to lead with, 'Hey, I have a lot of money want to like me for me?'" He sat on the edge of the bed to pull on his socks and boots.

"But maybe you could have let me know that you weren't going to just up and leave on a whim and go back to where you came from."

He reached out and pulled her over, loosely holding her hand between them. "When I came to this area again, I really hadn't planned how long I'd stay. I have a few places, and I'd been wanting to check on the Overlook's progress. It wasn't a lie that I didn't have a planned timeline."

"Oh my gosh," she moaned, covering her face in her hands in mortification.

"What?" he asked confused by the sudden shift.

"Here I am all excited about taking over my tiny diner and I'm dating the owner of the fanciest place in at least a three-hour radius."

"So?"

"So! It's the *Overlook*!"

How did he not see that they were comparing a luxurious vintage wine to a boxed-wine with a pour spout—a damn delicious boxed-wine but boxed nonetheless!

"Wisteria is a gem. It's unique and special just like you. Why would you let my owning a business that I've had nearly no part in developing other than to fund an inspired idea, outshine what you've worked so hard to preserve and maintain? Don't sell yourself short, Lillian. Wisteria has stood the test of time through Harvey's lead, and now you'll keep her alive so more generations can enjoy a piece of history. What you have is something rare."

She groaned and covered her face again. "What now?" he laughed as she peered through her fingers and started giggling.

"I recommended your own restaurant to you… that first day on the street," she said closing her fingers again.

"That's the best kind of review." He moved her hands to kiss them. "Now, while I love what you've chosen for yourself," he leaned back and gave her an exaggerated look-over, "you did agree to get dressed so we could go eat."

She realized he'd been dressing the entire time they had talked. She had not.

"You could have said something sooner."

"I was having a perfectly good conversation. Why would I interrupt it?" he asked innocently. He dodged her playful swat. "Get dressed. I know you're starved and so am I."

FORTY-NINE

-Lillian-

"Did you see the news today?" Lana asked as Lillian stowed her bag in her office.

"No. Why? Is something going on?"

"They called off the search for the missing boy." When Lillian was clearly confused, because her dad said they were widening the search, not calling it off, Lana went on. "Well, not called off-called off, but they're not looking for him in the woods anymore. They seem to think he could be hiding out somewhere else. Your dad didn't tell you anything?"

"He doesn't typically talk about his cases with me," she said evasively, not wanting to accidentally say something she wasn't supposed to know as a civilian.

"I don't know what it all means, but some people are getting confused."

"Why?"

"Well, for one, why would he be hiding somewhere? If he made it out of the woods, why wouldn't he come forward so everyone would stop worrying about him? It makes me think something else is going on. Maybe those kids he hangs around were up to no good. They were the ones that found the first body, maybe they had something to do with that."

"I think you've been listening to too many murder podcasts."

"I'm not the only one that thinks it. You should see the comments online."

"Or maybe they haven't had any luck finding him in the woods and they just needed a wider search area."

"It doesn't make any sense. Rain was found in the woods. He should be there too… unless he has reason to hide. Maybe he tried to kill her and leave her there, but she got away, and he had to flee. He could be anywhere… I need to find my taser."

"You *can* hear yourself, right?"

"What?"

"Just a few days ago, this community was trying to help find a missing hiker, and now you're ready to electrocute him if he walks by."

"There wasn't much information to go off of in the news release. What am I supposed to do?"

"I don't know, *not* jump to conclusions?"

"Where's the fun in that? There are a lot more outlandish theories on the site. You should read them, or at least tell your dad or that hot deputy of yours to give a little more insight."

"He's not *my* deputy," Lillian impulsively responded.

"Hmm, okay…" Lana said, taking a seat across from Lillian. "Sounds like someone made a choice," she mused. "How *is* August?"

Lillian made a point of logging onto her computer and ignoring her friend.

"No comment," Lana mused to the air. "I'm wondering if I should read that as things went very, very badly between you two and you can't stomach saying anything aloud because you ended up blowing it with both men," she said as she turned one hand over. "Or," she said turning to look at her other hand flipped over with imaginary information, "things went very, very well and there's so much to say that you don't know where to start." She paused again to wait for Lillian's terrible poker face to slip. "I'm going to go with option number two. And since you won't talk, I'll just have to make up my own mind about how things went."

Lillian zipped her lips and mimed throwing away the key as Lana had done to her.

"Must have been *very* good," Lana mumbled to herself. "August is pretty fit, I bet he has a lot of stamina."

"You don't even know that I saw August," Lillian finally interjected.

"Shh shh," Lana said, waving her words away. "I'm fine over here, thank you… But Ryder is rocking that police bod… I'd want him in uniform, or at least some of it."

"You're too much," Lillian snorted.

"What?" Lana asked too innocently. "I'm simply piecing together what happened since my friend won't tell me."

"Because it's none of your business… Shouldn't you be cooking something?"

"So wrapped up in her men that she doesn't even realize my shift hasn't started."

"Then why are you here so early?" Lillian laughed.

"Because my friend doesn't return my texts, and I need to live vicariously through her love life."

"No details," Lillian told her again.

"Fine, fine. My version of a reconciliation with August in one of those smutty nineties romance novel embraces, the wind blowing your hair, only to be interrupted by a fully uniformed Ryder, who slowly removes all his clothes but the belt and the gun and joins the party. Sounds much better than whatever dull life you're living. But don't worry, I've taken your place in this fantasy because it'd go against your morals to have two men at once worshiping you."

"Don't you think the gun belt would get in the way?"

"True. He can take that off, too, I suppose."

"And I don't remember the last time I saw Ryder wear an actual uniform."

"Shh. We're fine over here. We don't need your rules and logic."

"Fine, you keep your fantasy, but keep it to yourself. The last thing I need is to have Gary overhear and spread it around town that the newest owner of a good family diner, a long-term symbol of community and stability, is shacking up with two men, one of whom works for her dad. I'm sure there would be all sorts of comments on your site then."

"Oh, those would be much more exciting to read than the alien abduction theories and the curse of the Mountain."

"Aliens?"

"Oh yeah. Check out the page if you need a laugh. Brian is probably in the Bermuda Triangle by now, according to some." Lana glanced at her watch. "Gotta go. The boss'll be mad if I'm late."

FIFTY

-BILL-

As Bill had suspected, changing the search area had started a frenzy in the community. The station received call after call of sightings, some feasible, others simply outlandish. He tried to be open-minded about each tip that came through, but when Jane brought the latest stack of messages and one suggested that the caller was a psychic and Brian visited her in her dreams to tell her of the "other side," he had a hard time letting them hold weight.

He sighed to himself. Each lead had to be followed up on, no matter how crazy it sounded.

"Ryder," Bill called as he watched his deputy pass by the doorway.

"What's up?" Ryder asked as he stepped into the office.

"Take these, and any others that have come in." He handed him the stack of messages. "Divide them up and check them out."

Ryder snorted at one as he flipped through the pile.

"You know, most, if not all, of these, will be dead ends, right? There're more important things to be doing."

"I'm aware, but we have to check them out. Who knows. The alien lifeform that materialized out of thin air only to drown Mrs. Bally's rose bushes could have been a dehydrated Brian searching for a drink and didn't turn off the hose."

"Or she's a thousand and forgot that she left the hose on herself."

"Make the rounds. Split the pile so it'll go quicker."

"You want Simon on this?"

"No, he's still angry I moved the radius. I've allowed him and a small team to stick near the woods."

"Right. I'll let you know if any of these pans out," Ryder said, fanning the pages.

"Be thorough, but quick," Bill called after him, receiving a backward wave of acknowledgement as Ryder walked through the building.

"Sheriff?" Jane appeared in the doorway. "There's someone here to see you."

A man stood behind her.

"Can I help you?"

"I'm Agent Morreau with the federal government," the man told him, presenting identification. "I understand you have someone in your custody who trespassed on restricted government land."

"Do you now?" Bill asked, leaning back in his chair and wondering why, after all these years, the federal government finally showed an interest in the activities of the Mountain.

The man's face was non-descript and showed no expression.

"Your deputy, Simon Harland." He paused as if by saying his name, Simon would appear. "He's been making inquiries. You have a missing person. Correct?"

Bill folded his hands together. "We do. Are you here to authorize entry to search for him within the boundaries? A simple phone call would have been enough."

"That would be unsafe. I need to speak with your deputy, and the surviving trespasser, Miss Jennifer Storm."

"She goes by Rain," Bill told him, standing and getting his keys. "My deputy is currently leading a search and rescue team, and Rain is still in the hospital. I'll drive you over if you need to talk with her, but she isn't in my custody. No charges were pressed."

"That's up to the federal government to decide since the land belongs to it."

Bill studied the man before him. He was well-built, wore a dark suit, and had a strong stance. He'd probably started as military and worked his way through departments. Way too serious.

"Do you have a vehicle, or do you want to ride along with me?"

"We have our own transportation. Your presence is not necessary."

"She may not be in my custody, but as the sheriff of this county, she's under my care and protection. She's scared, and you'll just make her nervous… I'm not asking," Bill told him when Morreau didn't want to move.

He finally yielded, and Bill led the way out of the building, updating Jane as he passed. When they separated into their vehicles, the feds agreeing to follow, Bill immediately got on a call with Ryder.

"I need you to switch gears."

"What about Mrs. Bally's rose bushes?"

"She'll have to wait. The feds are here, and we're headed to the hospital now to talk to Rain."

"What do the feds want with *her*?"

"Not sure, but she was technically trespassing on government land. Hopefully it's a simple interview and they'll move on. I'd prefer they don't overstay what small welcome they have here."

"This is all Simon's fault," Ryder scolded. "If he hadn't made all those calls, nobody would have been wiser. Now they're out here sniffing around. Who knows what kind of mess they're going to make."

"There's nothing to make a mess of Ryder."

"There's always something, even when there isn't. If the town hears that the feds are here investigating… What do you think that'll do?"

"That's why I need you with me at the hospital. Let's keep this simple and under wraps. There's no need to get worked up yet. Let's just give them what they want, let them see there's nothing here, and help them on their way out of town."

"I'm in route."

Bill

Hours later, Bill sat at his desk, combing through his case files when Rich let himself in and took a seat.

"You're running with a strange crowd these days."

"Not by choice. They kick you out?"

"Nah, but they're real curious about Wade and John Doe. They asked all manner of questions, and had their own examiner request to verify my results. It didn't feel much like a request though, so after he started his look over and started waving some wand over them, I cleared out."

"A wand?"

"I don't know some detector stick. It reminded me of movies when they check for radiation, with all the clicking and whistling, but real high tech."

"A Geiger counter?"

"How am I supposed to know. I've never seen one used in person before."

"Do you think they were checking for radiation exposure? There's never been mention of an environmental contaminate up there."

"Whatever toxin they're checking for, I don't have that kind of budget. I'm curious to see what their reports show, but I have a feeling I won't be privy to that information."

"Yeah, me neither."

Rich raised his eyebrows in surprise. "Aren't all law enforcement supposed to play nice and share information?"

"I'm impressed you made it through that with a straight face," Bill sighed. "They wanted to talk to Rain earlier. The survivor." Rich nodded that he remembered. "She talked to them alone for more than an hour, and after they left, she didn't want any more visitors. I tried getting in to make sure she wasn't upset by their visit, but they posted one of their men outside her door and wouldn't allow entry. I left Ryder to report back to me if he gets a chance to see her. After that, I brought them to you and could tell I'd be better use here trying to figure out what the hell is so interesting about this case that would bring them here."

"What did you figure out?"

"A whole lot of nothing. The only reason they have for being here is that someone crossed into government land." He leaned onto his desk, picking up the pen to tap against his case folders. "Have you ever heard of the feds making a house call when their property is breached? A property, mind you, that's been abandoned for nearly sixty years."

"Not my area of expertise," Rich told him. "But no, seems pretty far-fetched to me."

"Well, it is my area, and I can tell you that I've never heard of it. It doesn't make sense."

Rich nodded at the folders on his desk. "You make copies of those yet?"

Bill looked down at the examiner's reports and his own notes, which he'd been keeping throughout his investigation, and looked back at Rich.

"Again, not my area of expertise, but I'd want backups if the feds start cleaning things up."

"You must watch a lot of movies in your spare time."

"Tons... but that doesn't mean they're not good advice."

"If there was something to cover up here, don't you think they would have just blown in and taken everything from the start? Why give us the chance to make copies?"

"That just looks suspicious and puts people on high alert, trying to sneak out whatever they can at the last second. If they're friendly and ask for permission first, you're likely to help them out, that way when they strike, you're less likely to see it coming. When they walk through that door and demand all your files, you're trying to figure out what's changed and you don't think about sneaking anything out. Even if you do try and sneak something, they've already secretly finished all that they're after and are just cleaning up loose ends so there's nothing left to find."

"You spend too much time alone in that metal tomb of yours," Bill told him, and Rich nodded in confirmation, but Bill was thinking over his words. "Jane, can you come in here," he called through his intercom. Rich shook his head as Bill let go of the call button.

"Don't get her involved unless you know she'll lie for you."

"Too many movies," Bill said as Jane opened his office door.

"Do you need something, Sheriff?" she asked, flashing a smile at Rich.

"I'm going to head out a little early today. If our friends from the federal government show up with more questions, just tell them they can check back in the morning. I'm off duty."

"Oh... okay..." she said, a little uncertainly, looking from Bill to Rich and back to Bill again. "Are you feeling okay?"

"Just fine." He smiled, getting up from his desk, and Rich followed. "But if they want to investigate this case, I'll let them. I could use an afternoon off."

He locked the door to his office and said his goodbyes, Rich leaving the building with him.

"You don't think she'd lie to the feds for you?"

"Oh, Jane would take secrets to the grave. I have no doubt about that, but..." He looked back at the building they'd just left. "If there is something else going on here, the less anyone knows, the less they can say."

"All on your shoulders," Rich observed.

"That's the name of the game. Now, I better find somewhere to get some copies."

"You can thank me later when your originals disappear."

"Or you'll never live this one down for the rest of your life."

"Me? You're the one listening to me."

"Touché ," Bill laughed. "Hey, you mind letting me know how things are when you get back to work?"

"Sure thing."

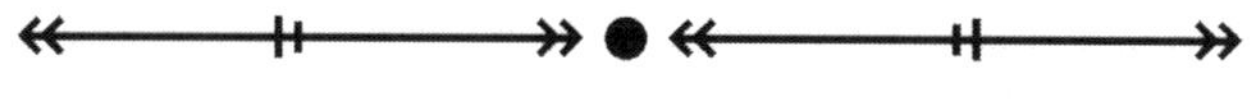

Bill

"Oh, hey, Dad."

"Are you leaving?" Bill asked his daughter, nodding to the keys in her hand.

"Yeah," she said as she automatically glanced to her keys at his look. "You know that history project I've been working on? Well, Mom suggested I use the resources at the university, so I reached out to them. I thought it'd be months before I got anything back, but I guess their tech is pretty efficient, so they already have a bunch of stuff for me to go through."

"You're headed to the university?"

"Yeah, well, things have been pretty smooth here and I wanted to be able to talk to them in person to fine tune things, you know."

"That's a long drive... are you going alone?"

"Dad, I don't need a chaperone."

"I know, I know, but your mother probably wouldn't mind riding with you. It doesn't hurt to have company."

"I do actually have someone coming with me," she admitted.

"Oh?" he asked, wondering why she hadn't said so in the first place.

"Yep, so I'll be just fine," she smiled. "Did you need something, though? I feel bad running off after you just got here."

He held up his accordion holder. "I came to beg to use your copier."

"Of course... everything okay?" she asked as she pointed to the copy machine in the corner of her small office.

"Sure." He smiled as he opened and closed the lid and stared at the buttons, turning back to see her watching him with uncertainty. "Why wouldn't it be?"

"I don't know, maybe because I'm pretty sure you've never copied anything in your life?"

"Sure I have," he told her, holding one of the folders open, "but your machine is a little different than ours at the office. Jane just puts them in, and it spits the copies out."

"If you want efficient, you'd be better off going to the copy store." She walked over and set the first page on the scanner screen. "Here we settle for competent." She closed the lid and showed him the button options. "You can also scan and send it to the computer if you want digital backups."

He looked at her computer with its swirling screensaver. He knew how to use computers, he just hated to depend on them, but she did have a point about a digital backup.

She walked to her desk and wrote her password on a sticky note that she left under the keyboard.

"There. If you change your mind, you can keep it in here until you need it."

He looked warily at the computer, still holding the open folder in his hand.

"I'm the only one that uses this," she told him. "Turn the computer off when you're done and then shred the password when you've finished and nobody else will have access."

"I'll think about it," he finally said, putting the next page on the screen to copy, juggling to put the first page back in the folder.

"Dad," she sighed, walking over to take the folder from him.

"I can do it," he said unconvincingly.

"Scoot." She cleared a place on her desk near the machine, set the folder open on it and set the copied pages face down on one side, the face-up pile ready to go onto the machine. "I have some spare folders in that drawer if you want to keep your copies separated like you have them here."

He walked across the room where she indicated and counted out the necessary folders to keep everything the same.

"I don't have one of those," she nodded to his accordion as another page came off, quickly followed by the next to be copied. "But there's probably a big rubber band in the top drawer that you could use to band them all together."

"I thought you were leaving," he said as she quickly worked through the first folder.

"I'm going to, but I guess my ride-along is running late."

"I can take over," he said as she got to the next folder, removing the copies from the tray so they didn't get mixed in with the first batch.

"It's fine," she said as she opened the file and started copying. "Huh," she said as she worked through copying the pages.

"What is it?" Bill asked.

"Hmm? Oh, nothing," she said, moving another page and copying the next.

"Sounded like something."

"Just one of the pictures looked familiar, but it was nothing."

He walked over to see what folder she was working on. "You shouldn't look at those."

"I'm literally making copies of them. I have to look at them."

"I mean don't look-look at them. They're not pleasant," he said, scooting her out of the way to take over copying the John Doe file.

"It's not like they're gruesome… okay, never mind," she said. The next picture was of his splayed body on the rocks where they'd found him.

"Go sit over there," he said nudging her away.

"It's fine, really," she told him, ignoring his direction. "It's just really sad. I guess I didn't realize this one was so young. I'd heard about the second body you guys found, but it never really clicked that he was just a kid."

"It's unfortunate to go so young, but it was pretty clear he was somewhere he wasn't supposed to be and without proper safety gear. Bad things are bound to happen if you aren't careful… But you said something looked familiar. Do you recognize him? We still haven't been able to identify him."

"It's hard to say," she said truthfully, "and even if I did recognize him, I doubt I'd be of much help. Most of the faces I see in here come and go so quickly. Some are regular enough that I recognize them as local, but don't know them enough to tell you who they are. Or he could have been passing through and was in one time. Either way, I couldn't give you a name."

"But you recognize him enough to know that you saw him in here? Could he be one of the local regulars or a drifter one-timer?"

She studied the medical examiner's image of the young man's face; the lifelessness evident despite the peaceful appearance. She shook her head finally. "No. I can't say. It wasn't this that caught my eye though." She handed him the photo so he could make the copy and turned back to the folder of already copied images, selecting one to hand him. "This was."

He studied the photo of a tattoo of a compass. It was a simple design. "What about it?" he finally asked, looking up to see her studying it as well.

"I saw one recently that looked nearly identical to this one… At least close enough that I thought it was the same. And he was very much alive, so I know it wasn't your guy."

"But you saw this one," he said holding it up.

"If not that one, then it was really close," she said again.

"So, the artist could be local," Bill wondered aloud. "They have those cases full of pictures you can choose from. I wonder if this is a specialty of someone around here."

"Or with everything online now, anyone can have the same picture tattooed."

"The odds that my victim came here from somewhere across the country with the same tattoo as someone you saw locally seem pretty slim… Unless, of course, the victim came with the person you saw."

She shook her head. "No, I don't think so."

"Why not?"

"Because the tattoo I saw was on one of those campers, Evan. Unless there was another person in their group that they never brought around that I never heard about, the only one of the group to go missing was Brian, and that was days after you guys found this boy."

"Yeah, they only mentioned the three of them."

"But," she said suddenly. "You could still be on to something. Evan had scratched at his tattoo and it bled." At his blank expression, she continued. "That means it was pretty fresh and still healing, right? It's like you were saying. This could be a local artist's specialty or on display. If you find out where Evan got his, maybe the tattoo artist will have a better memory of who else has had this design recently. Maybe something was said while this was being done that the artist will remember, and you can identify the body."

"I should hire you as one of my deputies," Bill said, looking again at the photo of the tattoo and making a mental note to have one of his deputies compile a list of tattoo shops within an hours' drive.

"No, thanks. Running this place is exciting enough for me. I'll just bill you for my expert consulting tips."

They both turned at the sound of a light tap at her door.

"Hey," she said with a smile as August walked in.

"So, you're the mystery ride-along," her dad stated.

"I never said it was a mystery… I just didn't say who it was."

"Mmhmm."

"Hi, Sheriff." August reached over to shake his hand. "When she mentioned going to the university, I thought it'd be a good idea to tag along."

"She's a grown woman, August. She doesn't require an escort," Bill said, lacing his statement with disapproval.

He knew by Lillian shaking her head and hiding her smile that she knew he was just being hard on August because he was dating his daughter. August probably knew too. Lillian walked over to the ringing phone on the desk leaving them to figure things out between them.

"No, sir. From what I can tell, she doesn't need for much. She's independent, strong-willed, and just plain incredible." August glanced over to catch her smile as she answered the phone. "Really, I was just looking for an excuse to spend time with her and figured we could learn a lot about each other on the drive."

"Awful risky being stuck in a car with someone you barely know for hours at a time. Careful she doesn't leave you stranded on the side of the road," Bill warned.

"That's a risk I'm willing to take."

Lillian

"That was strange," Lillian said as she hung up the phone. Both men turned from their conversation to her. "That was Rain." She looked at the phone, still confused by their conversation.

"What did she have to say?" Bill asked, his interest piqued.

She looked up at him. "She asked if I'd come visit her," she said. "I was honestly surprised she let me visit the first time. I never expected a repeat."

"Did she say what about?"

"She said she needed to discuss her work schedule… That she was going to need a few more days off before she could return to work."

"I thought she quit," August said, but turned to Bill. "I've heard trauma can block memories… Maybe she forgot?" he said, turning back to Lillian.

"I guess," she said uncertainly. She looked at her dad. "Do you think I should go? I don't really want to hire her back. Things have been much less dramatic with her gone. That's horrible, huh? But if she doesn't remember…" she trailed off, not sure how to handle Rain and not make things worse at the diner.

"I know you two are wanting to get on the road, but I think you should go talk to her."

"What am I supposed to say?"

"Just let her talk to you. If it seems that she's really forgotten, then you can decide if you want to try again with her. She could also not know how to apologize for her behavior before, and this could be her way of asking for her job back."

Lillian chewed on her bottom lip. She hadn't considered adding Rain back to the schedule. How would her newest hires respond to her? The last thing she needed was a crew full of Rains.

"You're right," she told her dad, feeling bad for thinking so negatively about her. "I can at least hear her out." She turned to August. "You don't mind if we post-pone our drive a little do you?"

"Not at all. I'm all yours."

The thought of him all to herself gave her butterflies and she hoped her cheeks weren't turning pink in front of her dad. She looked at her dad and nodded at the folders. "You okay with those if I head over?"

"I'm a pro at this point," he told her, still working on the same page as earlier.

"Call me if you need help, or Josh is working out front. He seems pretty savvy."

"Don't worry about me. I'll be out of here soon. Want me to lock up when I leave?"

She checked for her office key, more from habit than anything else since it was on the same ring as her car key. "That'd be great. Thank you. I'll see you in the morning for breakfast?" she asked, giving him a quick hug before she left.

"You know where I'll be."

"Sheriff," August said by way of goodbye.

"Take care of my girl," Bill replied.

"I intend to."

Bill

When they left the office and Bill was sure they were gone, he took out his phone and dialed Ryder. "Any change at the hospital?"

"None what-so-ever. You want me somewhere else?" The hope and boredom was clear in his voice.

"No. Stay put. Lillian's on her way over."

"Oh?" His voice perked up, but then confusion set in. "Why?"

"Not sure. Rain called her. Said she wanted to talk about work."

"Oh. Not sure that's going to be possible with the guard posted at her door."

"Maybe, maybe not. Lillian isn't an officer," he thought aloud.

"I don't know… I guess it's worth a try. Did you tell her to ask what the feds talked to her about?"

"No. She doesn't know they're involved."

"Huh… I figure that's something you'd give her a heads up on before sending her over."

"The less she knows…"

"Hmm. Well, I guess we'll see what happens. I'm guessing you don't want me to introduce her as the sheriff's daughter when they ask who she is."

"Good point. Maybe it's best to intercept her before she gets to the room. Tell her to keep her relationship to the local authority out of it and just mention that she's Rain's boss and came at Rain's request."

"I think you're going to have some questions to answer by not warning her ahead of time."

"You're probably right. Keep me updated."

"Will do."

FIFTY-ONE

-Lillian-

"Is that Ryder's truck?" August asked as they neared the entrance to the hospital.

"I guess it could be. I wonder if my dad told him to meet us."

"To talk to Rain?"

"He was with me before… but he said she was allowed visitors." She thought back to the conversation she'd had with Rain, realizing that she'd never told August all that was said. "Some of the things she said yesterday were… confusing." She glanced over at him. "Sorry, I'm not sure what I can say or can't."

"You don't have to say anything," he said before she could finish.

"Well, I think it's okay to tell you that because of what she said, they decided to widen the search area for Brian."

He nodded. "I saw that this morning. I wondered if there had been a change somehow or if they were just following protocol to extend the radius after so much time."

She looked back at the truck, fairly sure August was right, and it was Ryder's. She hadn't realized she was chewing her bottom lip when August reached over and gently brushed her cheek.

"I can wait in the car while you go talk to her."

"There's no reason for you to stay here."

"I can think of at least one," he told her, turning to look at the truck that seemed to be growing larger with each second.

"I appreciate that you would stay here to keep from making a scene, but I don't want to hide you away. I wanted to be able to talk to Ryder at an appropriate time, but the reality is that I'd have to specifically set aside a time for him, which would likely give him the wrong impression and then when I told him the truth about us, it would be more likely to blow up. Maybe by you and me just being together, I can have a normal conversation with him, and it won't be a big deal."

She said the words, hoping that it meant it could be possible, but her stomach was already knotting at the thought of seeing Ryder and August together with her stuck in the middle. She was about to rip a bandage off, knowing full well how much it was going to hurt.

August took her hand and brought it to his lips, planting a single kiss on her knuckle. "However you want, I'm with you."

She smiled and leaned across the car to pull him to her, kissing him until her heart was jittery from him instead of what she was about to do. "Okay," she closed her eyes and breathed him in. "Now I'm ready."

They crossed the parking lot quickly and Ryder met them as they were waiting for the elevator.

"Hey Lilly… August…" he added as a slightly confused greeting, turning back to Lillian. "Your dad told me you were coming and wanted me to talk to you before you go up there."

"Oh, he didn't mention anything about that to me."

"Yeah, he called, said you were headed over…" He looked back at August and then at her. "He didn't mention you. Everything okay?" He directed the question to August.

"Everything's fine," August said, a casual air about him as he stood with his hands in his pockets.

Ryder assessed them both, August a little too comfortable, and Lillian a little too uncomfortable. "Huh… so you're the mystery date at the Overlook."

"I didn't realize having dinner in a public place was a secret, but I guess, yes, that would be me."

Ryder gave a snort. "Guess I never stood a chance, huh?"

"Ryde–" Lillian started.

"Nah, it's fine. You tried to tell me from the beginning that there would never be an 'us.' Guess I just didn't want to hear it."

Lillian tried again to say something, but he pressed the button to call the elevator and continued talking like he didn't notice.

"Things have changed with the cases," he stated. "The feds showed up this morning and have been butting in all over town. First at the station, then here with Rain. They went to the medical examiner's, and I heard them mention going over to search the woods."

"Why –" she started to ask, but he kept talking through her as they stepped onto the elevator.

"They're robotic, shut down, and don't answer any questions. We have no idea what they're looking for, but since they questioned Rain, nobody has been in to see her, not even your dad. I was surprised when Bill called to say you'd been asked to come over. I don't know if you'll even be allowed in, but your dad thought it would be best if you tell them you're her boss, not his daughter."

They all stepped off the elevator and Ryder led the way to Rain's room, where Lillian could see the man standing firmly outside her door.

"Hey, Lurch, Rain has a visitor," Ryder said to the guard.

"Visitors aren't allowed at this time," the man said to the wall across from him, not turning to address them.

Ryder held his hand up and dropped it to his side, as if to say, "Told you so."

"I'm her boss," Lillian spoke up when Ryder looked like he was going to start in on the guy. "She's missed a lot of work lately and she called to talk about when she can get put back on the schedule. I wouldn't need much time." When he still wouldn't turn, she moved to be in front of him. "Please, I know she's been through a lot lately and I understand you're just trying to look out for her and make sure people aren't causing her more pain by pestering her with a million questions about what she went through. I only need a few minutes to find out when she thinks she'll be back to work and what kind of hours to work her. We're short staffed, it's almost tourist season, and I need to run a business. Please," she pleaded when she was running low on excuses. "You can come in with me and make sure we only talk about schedules, that I don't cause her extra stress."

She waited for him to acknowledge that he'd heard her, or even that he could see her. After nearly a full minute of silently facing each other, his eyes finally lowered to hers. She hoped her face was adequately pleading and friendly so that he'd allow her entry, without looking desperate.

He let out a breath. "Fine. Just the schedule." He turned to look at the two other men and then back to her. "And just you."

"Thank you," she breathed, turning to look at August and Ryder. "I'll be right back."

"I'll be here," August nodded to her.

"I'll be at the nurses station." Ryder turned, mumbling to himself but loud enough to be heard. "Shouldn't have thrown away that number."

"Ignore him," August said as she watched him walk off. He nodded to the open door. "You better hurry before he changes his mind."

She sighed and entered the dark room, the agent standing at the door watching.

"Rain? Are you awake?" she called softly into the dimly lit room, hoping she wasn't waking Rain up from a nap.

"Lillian?" Rain stirred on the bed, turning to see her and the agent at the door.

"Hey. You called me a little bit ago, remember? You wanted to talk about work?"

"Yeah, I remember." Rain's voice was direct with a hint of snark. "It was only like thirty minutes ago. I'm not senile."

"Right," Lillian responded, starting to walk across the room, glancing back at the agent to make sure it was okay. When he didn't tell her not to, she sat on the couch next to the bed to talk closer to her.

"I know I've missed a few days," Rain said, no apology or remorse to her voice as she motioned the room around her, "but I don't think I'll have to be here much longer, so I'll need to go back to work."

"Yeah, um… well…" Lillian thought she'd be able to come to the right decision when she was face to face with Rain, but just hearing her self-assured tone at the assumption that the job was still hers aggravated Lillian. It wasn't that Lillian expected an apology for the time she was missing, but shouldn't there be some sort of remorse for the way she quit? She couldn't bring herself to openly welcome her back without a second thought.

Lillian also didn't want to be kicked out of the room right away after she tried so hard to get in.

"I'm not sure how many hours exactly I'll need," Rain barreled on, not noticing Lillian's hesitance, "but my dad let me know earlier that I wasn't on his insurance anymore, so none of this hospital stay is covered. Thanks for that, Dad," she said sarcastically to the air. "It's *real* helpful... Anyway. It's gonna cost a fortune, so I need the money. The tips are shitty, but it's better than nothing. It'll do until I can find something better. I figure you need the help anyway since it's gonna get busy soon, so you can't really afford not to have me on full-time anyway, so—"

"You've got five minutes," the agent interrupted.

"Five minutes?" Rain interjected. "You expect her to figure out how to get me the money I'll need in five minutes? Are the feds going to pay for my hospital? Is the sheriff? I don't think so."

"Ten minutes," he said in exasperation. "Not a second longer." He turned to look at Lillian, "Good luck," he said, and she believed for a moment that he actually meant it. Being with Rain for just these few seconds of conversation already had her regretting her decision to walk into the room. He turned and exited.

"Can you believe he was only going to give us five minutes to figure anything out? What could we possibly figure out in five minutes?" Rain asked incredulously as she watched the door close.

"Rain," Lillian sighed, "I'm not sure –"

Rain turned back to Lillian and jumped out of the bed, climbing onto the couch next to her. "Stop, I don't want to work there. You can chill out. Geez, you should see your face."

"What?" Lillian asked, thoroughly confused.

"Shh. I know he said ten minutes, but he could come back sooner. I don't know why I called you, but you were the only one I could think of. Gary would just blather on, and I knew they wouldn't let the guys in here... not that I really want to see them anyway... and then your dad, there's no way. He already tried. I could hear them, and they said *I* said no visitors..." She looked at the door. "But I didn't say no visitors."

"Okay... so what's going on?" Lillian asked, trying to be calm to counteract the electric urgency that was Rain.

"I don't know... but something. They came in here and told me to tell them what happened out there, so I did. I told them the same thing I told you and the police. When it was all over, they said that I must have remembered wrong, that I didn't really go into the Mountain, that I was confused about the boundary line. I told them they were wrong, that we definitely did go in. I told them how it felt different when we did and that Brian was acting weird, and that I could hear something else too. They jumped all over that and said that we probably heard a big animal, maybe a bear, and that it scared us enough to mess with our heads, and that it would explain why Brian was acting strangely, because he was scared of what was coming, so we both ran.

"They told me that was what really happened, and that I needed to stop making up other stories. They said it causes fear, but also makes people curious, and then more people will go up there and more people could get hurt because it's rough and wild and there are dangers in the woods. They said that I wouldn't be able to live with myself if people went up there and got hurt because I was making up stories about the place that weren't true.

"Then they mentioned that if my story *had* been true, and we *did* go into the Mountain, which is highly restricted, government land, blah, blah, blah, I could go to prison for trespassing. They told me they'd hate to see such a young person go away for life because of a made-up story. They made me agree to change my story.

"Lillian, I don't want to go to jail, but I wasn't lying about what happened up there. I don't want anyone else to go up there. There's something wrong up there. But I didn't make it up, and they're saying I did and now they're saying I could go to jail, so I had to say I didn't go." She looked back at the door and back at Lillian. "I don't know what to do, and I had to tell someone."

"Okay… but I don't know what to do either," Lillian immediately said, and Rain's eyes became more frantic than they already were. "But… I'll help figure something out. I think I should tell my dad…"

"I don't know… Do you think he knows and wanted them to say what they did? I don't want him to find out I talked to anyone if he's one of the ones that wants me to change my story."

"One thing I know about my dad is that he believes in telling the truth, even if the truth isn't something anyone wants to hear." She paused to think over telling him. He hadn't told her about the agents being here despite knowing she'd find out as soon as she made it to Rain's door. Was that because he didn't want her to be nervous the whole way over, worrying about whether or not she'd be allowed to see her? Did he suspect that Rain wanted to talk about more than work? He was clearly right, but were his intentions to find out *if* Rain talked, or were they to find out *what* she had to say?

"Lillian," Rain whispered beside her. "I'm scared… I know I can be a lot sometimes… okay, a lot of the time, but it's not enough to go to jail over. I can't go to jail."

"It's okay, you're not going to go to jail. They're just trying to scare you."

"Well, it's working. What am I supposed to say? That nothing happened? That a bear came, and it freaked us out? Those are lies, Lillian. I know I've lied before, but this just feels really wrong. It feels like there's something more, and I'm being told to shut up about it. What if it isn't jail I should be worried about? What if they're going to kill me?"

"Nobody's going to kill you." Lillian was shocked that Rain was considering such an extreme consequence. "They're just trying to sound scary so you won't go back up there again and, like they said, so it doesn't spread more of the kind of rumors that intrigue people instead of deterring them. They don't want people poking around on their land and that's understandable; it's theirs. If someone gets hurt on their land, they have a liability and a responsibility to them. I don't think scare tactics are the way to go about it, but maybe sometimes that's what it takes to get the message through. I'll talk to my dad." She paused at Rain's uncertain look. "I'll talk to him to see what he thinks, but I won't tell him what you've told me unless I completely believe he's on your side. If I feel that he wants the same things these guys do—to scare you off from sharing your story—then I'll make something up about what we talked about."

"You're going to lie to your sheriff dad? For me?" Rain's voice on the last two words was quiet, surprised, as if the offer was the nicest thing anyone had ever done for her.

Maybe it was.

"It's not lying to tell him what a self-righteous pain in my ass you were in insisting I allow you to come back to work and at a higher pay rate than before."

"I never said more money," Rain said smiling weakly. "But if I were to come back it would have to be for more, of course," she said with a little more sass, but without her usual disdain. "Thank you, Lillian… for listening. Yesterday and today." She leaned over and gave an awkward hug, surprising Lillian so she only gave a slight pat back. Rain got up and climbed back onto her bed, repositioning herself as she had been minutes earlier. "I guess this means I need more friends if you're the one I keep calling to talk to."

"I guess so," Lillian agreed. She was just as surprised as Rain that she was the girl's lifeline.

They both heard the handle before the light from the hall could spill through the gap as the door opened.

"So just call when you're released, and we'll start the schedule we discussed," Lillian said, as if their work conversation was ending.

"Make sure you remember to tell the others that I don't have to split my tips. The medical bills are high, you know. They'll understand."

"Time's up," the agent said, looking at Lillian and nodding over his shoulder as if to say, "Let's go."

Lillian rose from the couch and quickly crossed the room. She stole a quick glance back at Rain, small in the big hospital bed and all alone with her fears.

The agent held the door open for Lillian to hurry through. When the door was closed and she was ready to walk away with August, she heard him say, "I'd cut that one loose if I was her boss. Too much attitude."

"It's hard to find help these days," was all Lillian offered back, hoping he didn't want to debrief her like Ryder had done. When he was back to staring at the wall again, she looked to August and mouthed, *Can we go?* He glanced at the guard and back at her, nodding that they should.

She saw Ryder laughing at the nurses' station as they approached and he glanced over, the smile he had for the nurse lingering as he looked at her, waving them in a passing gesture as they neared.

"See you around," he called carelessly over his shoulder, not breaking away from his conversation to see how things had gone.

She wasn't jealous of the nurse. The woman was oblivious to Lillian and Ryder's history, but it stung to see him so casually flirting. August strolled beside her, one hand in his pocket, reaching out to call the elevator with his other. He draped his arm across her shoulders, pulling her in while they watched the numbers progress to their floor. He felt solid and safe. She put her arm around his back and leaned into him. Despite the churning in her stomach and the lump in the back of her throat, she guessed she should feel grateful not to have to figure out how to talk to Ryder about her and August.

August was quiet on the elevator ride down, opening her door for her when they reached her car. She thanked him and pulled out of the lot to head to the university. She kept hearing Ryder's detached voice, seeing his face when the realization hit him. Maybe that hadn't been the best way to let him know after all. Maybe she should have made a point to talk to him alone. Her eyes prickled at the thought of doing exactly what she'd told August she hadn't wanted to do, shove her and August's relationship right into his face.

She felt sick to her stomach. *What were you thinking? He didn't deserve to find out like that.*

Should she call him and try to explain? Would that be better or worse? Would it upset August if she did?

She sighed to herself as she took the ramp to get on the interstate.

"You want me to drive?"

"What?" She noticed his concerned expression, realizing she'd been driving for the past ten minutes, lost in her own thoughts without a word to him since they left the hospital.

"I can drive if you want to think instead of focusing on the route."

"Oh, no… I've made this drive so many times… Thank you though," she said, turning to offer him what she hoped was at least a semblance of a smile even though the last thing she felt like doing was smiling.

"He didn't respond like a man."

"What?" she asked, glancing from the road to August.

"Ryder…"

"Oh," she chewed on her lip. Of course August knew what was clouding her thoughts. "I don't really want to talk about Ryder."

He looked out the window but turned back after only a few moments. "He acted petty, like a child, replacing you with the closest woman around. He wasn't even subtle about it."

She recalled the laughing nurse, Ryder leaning toward her, barely offering a glance Lillian's way, already moving on to the next conquest.

Had that really been all it was for him? Had it been too much work to keep up the charade? Had he really not changed like he'd said he had? If it was that easy to move on to the next girl, should she really be beating herself up over how he got the news?

The pain in her heart was like a slow tearing, a sliver on the surface that kept cutting deeper as it pulled away. She thought she'd been protecting herself, not letting herself fall too far, but after seeing him with the nurse, she knew she'd been lying about how far she'd already let him back in.

She tried to push it all away.

If anything, she should be happy, right? He wouldn't be causing her conflicting thoughts anymore if he was trying to catch someone else. She could focus on August, which was what she'd said she wanted to do.

Right?

"He's not worth your thoughts, either," August said softly beside her when she was silent again.

"I'm sorry." She crinkled her nose and offered him a smile, reaching over for his hand. "I don't mean to be terrible company. I… I guess I need to process what just happened. None of this is fair to you." She stole another glance from the road to see his face. "I never should have let him get under my skin in the first place. It's just that, things ended so abruptly years ago, and then… with him being nice again, I…" She shook her head and sighed. "I don't know, what I expected."

"You're a good person, Lillian," he said, giving her hand a squeeze. "He used that to get back in your good graces and then exploited your feelings. He said it himself, that you told him from the beginning that you guys wouldn't be together. He just wanted to prove you wrong. I'm sorry he had to hurt you again for you to realize that he wasn't worth your time."

She smiled weakly. "Thank you for being understanding when you have every right to be upset."

He brought her hand to his mouth and kissed it. "I'm only upset that he had any sort of reaction from you. Now, can we boot the third wheel and let it be just us? What's the goal for this university trip?"

She smiled again, taking a deep breath and pushed Ryder out of her thoughts.

"I have a plan for renovating with some nostalgic memorabilia…"

"Sounds intriguing."

She laughed. "Probably not, but I have a vision."

FIFTY-TWO

-Bill-

"Ryder said you were able to get in to see Rain," Bill said when Lillian settled into the chair in his office after she'd set up their customary Sunday morning breakfast.

"Yeah, thanks for warning me about the agent standing guard," Lillian said. "What's up with that? Why're they here? Do they get involved often and I just never realized it?"

"No." Bill took a sip of the scalding coffee, setting it back down as he took the top off to allow a puff of steam to burst free of captivity. "I've hardly had to deal with them in person."

"So why now?"

"What did Rain have to say?" he asked instead of answering.

"We talked about her coming back to work."

The eyebrow twitch was the only indication that he was surprised by her response. Otherwise, his face was unreadable. "That was it?"

"It's something we talked about," she answered evasively, scooting her chair close to his desk so she could have a table. "What are the feds doing here?" she asked again, taking a bite of her biscuit and gravy.

"You know I'm not supposed to talk about open cases."

She nodded as she finished chewing. "And you've always told me to keep people's confidences."

He sat back in his own chair, watching his daughter assess him. He glanced over at the office door, expecting the feds to burst through as if talking about them could summon them.

"Something's going on…" she said, interrupting his thoughts. "That's easy enough to figure out. You wouldn't have been making copies at the diner if there wasn't."

The statement hung in the air between them.

He leaned forward, letting out a deep breath after he sipped his coffee again. "I can't tell you anything." He paused, looking sternly at her when she opened her mouth to object. "Because there's nothing to tell. I'm in the dark as much as you." At the slight tilt of her head and raised, disbelieving eyebrow, he amended his statement. "Okay, maybe not as much as you." He sighed, "They showed up yesterday and have been retracing all of our steps. We're trying to figure out what they're after, but nothing about them being here makes sense."

She nodded. "That's pretty much what Ryder told me." At his disapproving look, she added, "Not that I'm in the mood to defend Ryder, but you can't be upset with him. He had to tell me something to explain why there was a guard outside her door, since *someone else* didn't."

He offered a sheepish smile at the second mention of his lack of warning.

"So, why the copies yesterday?"

"Precaution." He waved it away with his fork between bites. "Letting peer pressure get to me," he said, attempting a joke.

"Why did they want to talk to Rain?"

"That's what I was hoping you'd tell me. After she talked to them, nobody else has been allowed in."

"She did talk about work," Lillian started cautiously, "but she said some other things, too."

"Such as?"

"It's like you said, nobody knows why they're here. Maybe it's safer if I keep this to myself until you can figure out what's going on."

"Safer? If she feels unsafe, having all the information will help me do my job better to protect her."

"I understand that, but how long after I walked through those doors as her boss do you think it took them to find out I was your daughter? Ryder specifically told me not to tell them my relationship to you, which means you suspect they wouldn't have let me talk to her if they already knew. Don't you think they'll be coming to you soon to find out what she told me and if I then told you?"

"Now you're protecting me?" he chuckled. "I can handle the feds."

"There's no need to handle anyone if all you know is that I talked to her about work. And let me tell you, she was very convincing. Leave it there for now. Please, Dad. I'll tell you, just not until you know more."

"Knowing what you know could help me figure out more," he reasoned, knowing she was just as stubborn as he was when her mind was made up.

"Or it was the ramblings of a traumatized person that could mean nothing and cause more problems."

"I don't like you feeling torn like this."

Lillian closed the container to her breakfast and leaned back in the chair. "Me neither... So, what are you going to do about these agents?"

"Play nice for the moment. So far, they've just been a rock in my shoe, uncomfortable, but not debilitating. They're covering our tracks but haven't asked for much otherwise."

"Sounds like an audit... Is that a thing in the police world?"

"Sure, there are investigations, but there typically has to be something to investigate."

"Maybe they think there is."

He tapped his fingers on the armrests of his chair, considering what the feds would come all the way out here to investigate. The Mountain had been referenced in the papers and online media a lot lately because of the two recent bodies and the missing persons in proximity. Maybe it was as simple as the government wanted to make sure their area was secure. But why not just say that? Why be evasive and unyielding? *Because they can be*, he thought. He reached over to help Lillian as she started to clear away their mess.

"I've got it," she said, shooing his hand away like her mother sometimes did. He doubted she realized it. "Since you haven't asked, I'll go ahead and tell you. August and I talked the other day… he told me about owning the Overlook and that he's more of a local than I thought." She looked up at him. "Is that what you felt he needed to share with me?"

"For the most part, yes. I didn't think he should let you believe he was a tourist passing through. He needed to be honest with you about who he really was."

"And I agree," she nodded, "but also there's going to be plenty about him that I don't know, and unless there's something that I *should* know, like the really important, could-end-a-relationship type of stuff, I'd like to be able to figure it out the natural way."

"So, you're making things official?"

"You make it sound like we're getting married, Dad. No. We're just… seeing where it goes."

"So, it's okay if people know?"

"Geez, are you just itching to spread the word that your hermit of a daughter finally found a man?"

"I was thinking about your mother…"

"Yes, Mom can know. It's not a secret or anything, but the whole world doesn't need to know every detail of my private life."

"Does Ryder know?"

She stopped cleaning and sat in the chair with a sigh. "Yes, Ryder knows… Don't worry, *he's* fine. He was already flirting with the nurse when I was leaving the hospital."

"How are you?"

"I'm fine," she said without eye contact and a little too much pep to her tone. "Really, I am. August is who I want to be with. There's this… connection… I can't explain it, but it's there, you know?"

"But things were changing with Ryder," he observed carefully.

"We had some… moments, I guess… and things seemed different. I thought he had changed. He did a good job convincing me that he had anyway," she sighed glancing up from the paper coffee cup she'd been turning in her hands. "But I guess it was just the same old Ryder, doing what he does best, and I was the idiot who started to fall for it again." She shook her head and went back to bagging up their trash. "It doesn't matter, really it doesn't, because even with me softening to Ryder, I was feeling more for August. I was just conflicted for a time. I think Mom was probably right. She said I probably saw

Ryder as a challenge and wanted to be the one to finally settle him down. I guess there's some truth to that and being able to reconcile our past."

"Your mom encouraged you to see Ryder?" he asked, unable to contain the shock. "After the breakup you two had, *she* wouldn't talk to Ryder for the first year after he started working for me. Eventually he won her over, but I'm surprised she'd ever approve of him dating you again."

Lillian crinkled her nose. "I didn't give her names."

He barked out a laugh. "You got positive dating advice from your mom about a guy you know she would never suggest for you again. I really do need you on my force. You know you're getting a phone call when she finds out, right?"

"I'm aware," she said dryly. "Feel free to omit that part."

He laughed again. "Oh, I can't wait to see her face."

"Of course… I'm glad I could bring humor to your day," she told him sarcastically, "but I have things to do, and you have cases to solve."

"Back to reality," he said, getting up with her to walk her out of the building. He noticed Ryder walking through the lot, watching as he turned his head, his gaze landing on Lillian's car, then scanned to the front of the building, where he found Lillian. Bill was practiced enough that Ryder didn't notice him watching, as Ryder was practiced enough to shift his gaze from Lillian just before she turned in his direction and saw him approaching. "You're here early," Bill said as they met. "I didn't expect you for another couple of hours."

"I'm going to go," Lillian said, giving her dad a hug. "Bye Dad… Ryder," she added cautiously.

"See you around," Ryder said nonchalantly, keeping his attention turned to Bill. "Evan's on his way to talk about that tattoo, and then if it turns out it's close enough to his, I was going to head over and interview the person that did it. See if we can get an ID."

Bill watched his daughter get in her car, wave, and pull out to drive away. Ryder's positioning gave him a view of Lillian's car leaving the lot, too. He noticed the subtle shift and softening of his eyes as her car turned and drove out of sight. Bill led the way into the building before Ryder could realize he'd seen.

He'd watched the boy his daughter had known grow into the man in front of him, and despite what Ryder was trying to make Lillian think, Bill could tell he was not fine.

FIFTY-THREE

-Ryder-

Ryder led Evan into Bill's office when Jane announced his arrival at the station. Bill thanked him for coming down and motioned for him to have a seat. Ryder directed him into the seat farther from the door in front of Bill's desk. Ryder chose the second seat next to him, blocking his path to the door. Bill handed Ryder the picture of the tattoo from the John Doe case file.

"Do you recognize this?" Ryder asked, passing the photo to Evan. Both men watched as Evan studied the picture.

"Is this some kind of a joke?" Evan asked after a quick study, glancing between Ryder and Bill and back to Ryder.

"What do you mean?" Ryder asked him, looking at the sheriff across the desk for an explanation.

"Do you recognize this picture?" Bill asked Evan again.

"Of course I do. Where is he?"

"Where is who?" Ryder asked instead of answering his question.

"Brian. This is his tattoo, this is him. When did you find him? Why didn't you call us? Is he okay?" He looked around the closed office, an expression of relief on his face as he searched for his friend as if Brian was tucked in the corner waiting to jump out and yell, "Surprise!"

"Was there anyone else in your camping group?" Bill asked him.

"Huh? No. It was just the three of us."

"Someone else didn't leave town before you guys found the body in the water?"

"No," he stated firmly. "It was always just us three." Evan looked from Bill to Ryder—who kept his face as expressionless as the sheriff's. "I don't understand what you're asking. Why can't I see Brian? Oh God." Evan's face went white as he stared at the picture. "Is this… Is he… This is a dead body picture, isn't it? He's dead, isn't he?" He ducked his head into his hand, pinching the bridge of his nose, the photo falling to the floor.

Ryder reached down and put the photo onto the sheriff's desk.

"Evan," Bill said, and waited for the boy to look up at him, his eyes glassy. "Why do you think this is a picture of Brian?"

Evan pointed at the photo, his mouth a slim line. "Because that's his tattoo." He pulled up the sleeve of his shirt, turning his upper body so they could see the area of his deltoid, normally covered by a short sleeve. "Look." He revealed his own similar tattoo. "All three of us got them."

Ryder, being closer to Evan than Bill, picked up the photo and held it next to Evan's arm, analyzing the similarities. "It's pretty close, but not 100 percent," he said, turning back to Bill. "There are a couple minor differences."

"Yeah, all three of ours are a little different, but mostly the same," Evan said, lowering his sleeve to take the photo again. "Jack came up with the design a year ago. We kept saying we'd get them done, but never actually got around to it. The first night we got into town, it was late and even though we were amped about starting our camping trip, we wanted to check out the town, too, but nothing was open. It wasn't a big deal, this trip wasn't about cities and clubs, it was about being men, you know? We're adults, the world is ours, we'll do what we want... all that. We had this dream of rafting the hardest routes. Climbing the steepest cliffs. Going places other people wouldn't dare to go..."

"Sounds very freeing," Bill said when Evan paused in his storytelling to stare at the photo.

"It was supposed to be. Freedom before we had to grow up and get real jobs and be real adults... So, we're heading back out of town to our campsite, and Jack sees the light for this tattoo shop. I don't remember the name, but it's on the way out of town if you're headed out to the Bend, kinda small place. There weren't any cars and Brian joked that they probably just left the light on, nobody was there, to keep driving... I think he was scared to get one," Evan admitted quietly, still talking to the photo.

"Jack insisted we check it out, so we pulled over. Sure enough, the guy was there and said he could do it, so we did—all three of us—but with little changes. They all have the compass in the middle," he said, holding the picture and turning his arm again so they could see them closely together. "The Mountain in the back, the river flowing through, and the trees in the front are all the same. Jack's, though, has a waterfall coming through part of the compass." He smiled to himself. "He's always saying he's going to go over one in a barrel or something like people would do like a hundred years ago... thinks it'd be a rush. We just keep telling him it'll kill him.

"Mine," he said, setting the photo down and pointing to his own, "has these four birds flying. This bigger one is for my dad, this one is my mom, this is for me, and this little one is my kid sister. She's always trying to tag along, that's why hers is real close to mine. And Brian's—" He reached over and picked up the photo again. "Brian's has the river yak. That boy can be pretty goofy and seems like a nerd some of the time, but you put a paddle in his hand and throw him on a raft and he's one with the water. It's somethin' else to watch him know just where the drop will be, which wave to ride... it's like the water talks to him. Meanwhile, Jack and I are getting beat to shit. Sorry," he mumbled, a sheepish expression at the slip of the word, but continued with his story. "No matter how hard we'd try to follow right in his path, do just what he did, one of us would always end up tipping and losing something to the river. He has a gift when it comes to water." He tapped the photo to point out the tiny kayak cruising the river. "That's Brian's. Where is he?"

Ryder looked at Bill, letting him take lead of the interview.

"This tattoo doesn't belong to Brian," Bill told him and Evan sat up a little straighter at the news, but his face remained confused.

"I don't understand. That's Brian's. I'd recognize it anywhere."

"This is a neat design," Ryder said, picking up the photo. "I know the tattoo shop you're talking about… small place, just the owner inside." Evan nodded in confirmation. "He does good work, and this is something I could see him adding to his selection."

"You think he did our tattoo on someone else?"

"Everyone wants to be unique, but this would sell," Ryder told him.

"So, that isn't Brian in the picture? You're sure?"

"This picture belongs to a hiker we found in the woods a week and a half ago," Bill told him and Ryder watched the relief spread over Evan's face.

"Brian's only been gone for a week. He's still alive," he breathed out the words. "I thought for sure…" he trailed off, pointing to the picture. He smiled, then sat back against his seat, taking a deep shaky breath. "God, I thought he was dead."

"We're still searching for him," Bill said, and Evan's face changed from relief back to worry, a reminder that even though the picture wasn't his friend, his friend still hadn't been found.

"Right," he sighed, leaning forward to pick up the photo again. "So, who is this guy?" He looked at the two of them.

"We were hoping you'd have some insight. There were only the three of you?" Bill asked.

He shrugged his shoulders. "Yeah, like I told you."

"Someone didn't come out in the beginning and then have to head back early?" Ryder prompted.

"No. It's always been the three of us, since we were kids." He looked between the two of them again. "Why would I lie? If there were four of us, I'd tell you. There'd be no reason not to, especially if it meant identifying *him*," he nodded to the photo.

"There's all sorts of reasons a person could have for not telling the truth," Ryder started calmly, taking over the interview. "Say four friends go camping, they have a few beers and decide to go hiking, only they've had more to drink than they realize and aren't prepared for the climb. One of them slips. His body is broken, and he doesn't answer when they call. They panic. They're not old enough to be drinking, and now someone's hurt. They could get in a lot of trouble. They leave him, expecting to hide their accident away forever because they're extreme. They go where nobody else can follow. There's no way anyone else will be able to find their mistake. They just have to keep it a secret between friends."

"No. That never happened." Evan looked appalled at the visual Ryder was painting.

"But maybe it's harder to keep the secret than they thought, and it starts eating at them," Ryder continued. "One of them wants to tell the truth, get the cops involved, but he gets talked out of it. Then there's news that the body has been found and that anyone with information to help identify the person should come forward, and the one friend starts to panic again. He wants to tell the truth and says you won't get in trouble if you just tell the truth. It was an accident after all. But he never gets to tell the truth, does he, because he 'went hiking' and never returned. What happened out there Evan?" Ryder picked up the photo and held it closer so Evan would have to look at it. "Who is this, and what did you do with Brian?"

Evan was shaking his head the entire time Ryder was talking, his cheeks reddening as the story progressed. "None of that happened. I don't know who that person is. There were never four of us. Ever. We've told you what happened. Brian *did* go hiking. Ask Rain. She knows better than anyone what happened to Brian. She's annoying and obnoxious, but she'll tell you they went hiking." He turned to Bill. "Please, Sheriff, I don't understand any of this. There are only the three of us, and one of us is still missing. We didn't do any of those things. None of that ever happened. I swear I've only told you guys the truth with any of this."

Bill held up his hand to calm the boy.

"I don't know who that tattoo belongs to if you're sure that body isn't Brian," Evan said again.

"We're sure it isn't Brian," Bill told him reassuringly. "We wouldn't keep that from you."

"But you'll make up stories that we would just leave a friend to die all alone... Who does that?" He looked at Ryder with clear disgust. "You guys have a job to do. You're supposed to be looking for Brian and finding out who that guy is apparently. How about instead of trying to pin whatever that is on me and my friends, you actually do your job and find out what *really* happened? Figure out who that is. Find Brian." He stood up and the chair teetered backward, righting itself before it could fall. He looked at Bill. "Am I free to go, or do you have other theories to make up about us?"

Bill waved a steadying hand at Ryder to keep him from protesting. "You're free to go. Thank you for answering questions about the tattoo."

"I'm sorry I couldn't help figure him out." His voice was strained, but the apology sounded genuine. "I'm guessing you want us to keep staying in town?"

"I told you before that you guys were allowed to leave," Bill reaffirmed.

Evan took a deep breath, still avoiding looking at Ryder. "I don't want to stay here anymore, sir. I know I should stay to find Brian, and it feels wrong to want to go home so bad when he's still lost, but... I want to be in my own house and see my parents and my sister."

"I understand."

"I can stay for a couple more days," he begrudgingly offered. "I hope you guys can find Brian in that time."

"It helps in his case to be able to talk to you, so I thank you for staying," Bill said, the 'good cop' trying to recover some of the boy's trust. "We'll do our best to find your friend."

"I hope that's true," Evan said to Bill, his gaze sliding to Ryder with distrust and dislike and back to Bill. "I hope the next time I have to talk to you is when you're telling me you found Brian."

Evan left without another look at Ryder, closing the door behind him as he went.

"What was all that?" Bill asked.

"Thought I'd see how he'd respond." Ryder shrugged.

"I don't think there were four of them."

"Yeah, me neither," Ryder admitted. "I thought he was going to throw up for a minute. I almost didn't keep going, but figured I was already all in, might as well top it off."

"My gut hasn't pointed me to them for anything other than unfortunate happenstance."

"Then where is Brian? Why can't we find a trace of him? He couldn't have just disappeared."

Bill tapped the photo against his desk. "I don't know… but we're not going to figure anything out sitting in here. Take this to the tattoo shop." He handed the photo across the desk as Ryder stood up. "You said you know the place. See if he can remember who else he gave this tattoo to. If it was Jack's design, the list will be short even if he plastered it on sale and did the tattoo every day since those kids arrived. Verify it was just the three of them," Bill added as an afterthought.

"I thought you said you believed him when he said it was just them three."

"I do believe him, but that doesn't mean I don't want to verify the truth."

Ryder set the photo back on the desk and snapped a picture of it with his phone then handed it back to Bill to return to the case file. "What are you going to do?" he asked.

"Search for a missing person."

"Any new leads?"

"Not a one."

FIFTY-FOUR

-Lillian-

Lillian was kneeling on the sidewalk in front of Wisteria, making measurement notes of the space available to her in front of the diner. Her phone jingled and August's name appeared on the screen. She loved that she couldn't contain her smile as she touched the screen to talk.

"I'm around the corner. I know you said you have a full day of things to do, but I'm sure you need to take a lunch break at some point, and I'm fully prepared to convince you that it should be now, and it should be with me."

"I would love to have lunch with you, but I'm not at my house. I'm already at Wisteria and am currently sitting on the ground while Josh holds the other end of my measuring tape, waiting for me to tell him where to go next."

"Luckily for you, I'm also not at your house, and Wisteria serves amazingly wholesome foods."

The door to Wisteria opened as the call disconnected. She looked up to see August striding out from inside, the sight alone surprising her since she hadn't seen him go in, but he was also holding two potted flowering plants on either hip that were much too large and awkward to be carried together. He carried them with ease. The exotic flowers framed his smiling face as he turned to hand one to Josh. He reached down with his newly freed hand and offered it to her. She took it and he pulled her up in a swift tug, wrapping his arm along her back, and brought her in for a kiss, the flowers tickling her cheek as she let herself feel like a desirable woman, something she had recently realized that she'd put aside for far too long.

"Hi," she giggled. "These are beautiful." She closed her eyes and breathed in the aroma of the vibrant blooms. "But what are you doing here?"

"I told you. Bringing you lunch."

She looked back at the flowers. "These are definitely not lunch."

He released her and set the potted tree on the sidewalk against the building. He turned and took the other plant from Josh, reaching out to shake his hand as the boy's were now freed.

"You're Josh?" August asked, and he nodded, shaking his hand in return. "Thanks for your help there."

"No problem."

August turned back to Lillian. "Mind if I borrow him for a minute?"

"I guess," she said, taking the tape measure from Josh as August opened the door again, holding it for him to pass through.

August leaned over and kissed her again. "Be right back," he told her without further explanation, smiling mischievously. "Wait here."

Left without her assistant to help her measure, she resorted to learning about the gorgeous flowering tree-plant before her. She found the plant descriptor and was reading about the braided hibiscus tree when Gary breezed out of Wisteria to hold open the door, a goofy smile on his face, followed by Josh carrying a café-style metal table and finally, August, carrying the matching chairs.

"What's all this?" she asked as August and Josh assembled them in front of the diner, well enough away from the door not to be a nuisance, and Gary snuck back inside.

"You mentioned yesterday on our drive, that you were envisioning incorporating an outdoor café area, so I thought I'd help you visualize."

August was arranging the trees near the café set up when Gary reemerged from the diner with their lunch, setting the table and then theatrically bowed to her chair, a towel folded over his arm as if he were in a fancy restaurant instead of a quaint family diner. "Madame," he said with a dramatic flair.

She laughed again as she took her seat, thanking Gary as she did. He bustled Josh back into the building, pausing at the door to smooch his fingers into the air like everything was perfect before he whirled in after Josh.

"How did you arrange all of this so quickly?"

"I have my ways," he said mysteriously.

She raised an eyebrow.

"A man should be allowed to keep his sources confidential."

She took a bite of the perfectly prepared chicken salad, her favorite lunchtime meal that wasn't on their menu anymore. She decided it was coming back permanently.

"Gary or Lana?" she asked him.

"Josh," he admitted. At her baffled expression, he continued, "Josh answered the phone at least. At first he was confused, but when I explained that I wanted to surprise you, he caught on. Gary must have been near because then he took over the call and was very excited to be involved." He leaned in to speak more softly even though nobody was around to overhear. "I think he was a little disappointed in my delivery. He had much grander ideas."

"I can only imagine. He's a hopeless romantic."

"I thought about calling in the designers for The Outlook to help your vision come to life out here, but I didn't want to overstep."

"Why would that be overstepping? The Overlook's grounds are phenomenal."

"New boyfriend status… I don't want you to think that I think you can't do all this on your own."

At the word "boyfriend," her heart panicked. She'd made her choice, but hearing the word made it feel real… cemented. Was it too soon to attach a label?

What is your problem? It's just a word. Why should it matter if he wants to call himself your boyfriend? Is this not what you wanted?

She smiled at him, pushing away the unwanted thoughts.

"That's sweet of you. I know I'm capable of handling what this place is going to throw at me… that doesn't mean that I *want* to do it all on my own and reinvent the wheel. Hopefully there doesn't come a day that I turn away help or good advice."

He smiled warmly at her. "Has anyone ever told you that you have an old soul?"

She laughed. "Unfortunately for my not-yet thirty-year-old self, yes, yes they have."

"It's not a bad thing. I happen to like older women," he joked, and she nearly spit out her drink.

"Just because I have an 'old soul' does not mean I'm actually older than you!"

"It wouldn't matter if you were," he told her, watching her enjoy herself on her new patio dining.

"All things aside, I'm sure the Overlook's budget is much higher than Wisteria's, so I'm not sure this project would be worth your designer's time."

"I bet I can get you a good deal," he winked. "At least entertain meeting with her. If you can't come to terms, then I'm sure she could at least give you some ideas to get started. With the ideas you already told me about last night, and her knack for transforming a space, I think you'd get a good head start."

She considered him and the already romantic gesture of trying to help her dream become reality. It was nice not having to be the only one to have an idea, the only one to give the direction, the only one to make sure it was followed through. He wanted to help, and it felt really, really nice.

"I'll meet with her, but no guarantees that I'll use her."

"Good," he said, entwining his fingers with hers across the table, "because I already told her you'd be calling and started her down the path of what you told me."

"You weren't going to take no for an answer, were you?" she said, laughing.

He grinned. "It's not typically a part of my vocabulary."

FIFTY-FIVE

-Lillian-

She hadn't planned on spending her entire day off at Wisteria yesterday, but after the surprise lunch from August, and a call to his designer, Fiona, who agreed to meet with her that afternoon, she'd been able to delegate the task of creating an outdoor dining area, which freed her up to do office work. She would have preferred to go flower shopping and select quaint outdoor seating, look for the perfect lights to create a canopy of stars after sunset, but that was Fiona's area of expertise, and she didn't have anyone to delegate the office work to.

However, one of the perks of being the owner, and finally being fully and competently staffed so she didn't have to wait tables herself, meant that when she finished her work a day early, she unexpectedly had a whole day off today. She would have loved spending the day wrapped up with August, but he was out of town meeting with his attorney and accountant, a quarterly check-in for the management of his portfolio, and she'd barely scratched the surface of the papers that the university had sent her home with.

She eagerly welcomed spending an uninterrupted day researching and was surprised how quickly the hours had passed when she picked up her phone to a series of missed texts and calls. Most were easily and quickly responded to: her mom just checking in; Fiona sending inspiration photos asking for yeses or nos to narrow down options; August telling her about his trip, letting her know the meetings would take all day and that he was staying overnight, but expected to return by tomorrow afternoon, evening at the latest. The rest of the texts and missed calls though came from Ryder. She hadn't expected to hear anything from him, surprised he'd contacted her at all, let alone that he'd asked to see her. She was deciding how to respond when the doorbell sounded and a concerned-looking Ryder was standing on her front porch.

"Ryder?" Even she could hear the confusion echoing through her voice.

"Hey… did you get my texts?"

"Yes… just now… but –"

"I know, I know. You're with August. That's not what this is about."

"Okay…" she said cautiously.

"Something's going on… and then you weren't answering, and… I don't know. I just…" He rubbed the back of his neck, then dropped his hand to his side. "Can I come in?"

"Um, yeah, I guess so," she said, moving aside to let him in. "You're kind of worrying me. Is everything okay?"

"Yeah, I think so. I don't know."

"Why don't you just start with whatever is bothering you."

"It's not so much that anything is bothering me… not really." He sat down on her chair, running his hands through his hair and resting his elbows on his knees. "I mean, yeah, things are bothering me, but I didn't come here to talk about you and August."

"Ryder," she sighed as she took the seat across from him, not really wanting to have this conversation.

"I get it. I mean I don't, but I do. I didn't like him when I first met him, but he has a way of growing on you… plus the guy owns half the town so that's a perk."

"He doesn't own half the town," she countered.

"Right, just the important parts. That's not what I came here for," he continued before she could object. "It really isn't. You tried to be up front with me in the beginning and I thought you were just hesitant about getting involved with me again. I never considered there was someone else. Which is really stupid on my part, because why *wouldn't* there be someone else, a million someone elses?" He paused again. "You could have just told me you were seeing someone, you know."

"Honestly, there wasn't much to say. August and me… things are still early, like really early, but I didn't want –"

"You didn't want to two-time. I get it. I just wish I had made a move sooner instead of wasting so much time. I lost my chance, and someone snuck in while I was thinking I had all the time in the world. I'm sorry for that. I am… I'm also sorry that I was a jerk when you told me. That was an easier reaction than realizing I wasn't going to have a chance. I'm not going to lie. I'm hoping you'll realize August isn't worth a damn and you'll kick him to the curb and give me a real shot, but this is it. This is all I'm going to say on it. You have every right to be happy, and I want that for you. I want you to find the person who makes you smile when you're sad and gives you the world because you deserve no less than everything."

"Oh," she spoke softly, feeling like her heart sighed as well. "Thank you, Ryder, truly."

He sighed, running a hand through his hair before he leaned forward, settling his forearms against his lap as he studied his hands dangling between his knees. He looked up finally. "I guess what I came here for is to see if I've blown things completely and ruined any chance of even just being your friend."

"I don't know," she started tentatively, trying not to fidget in response to his vulnerable gaze. Her hand itched to rest against his unshaved face, an appearance not typical for him. She wanted to feel him lean into her as she soothed his hurt. But she was with August. She held her hands tightly in her lap, pushing aside her thoughts.

He nodded. "I know…"

"I don't know how that would go… if it could work. I know how you feel about me. You know I do have feelings for you." She paused again. "*August* knows about both of our feelings. It wouldn't be fair to him to try to figure out what's between he and I if you and I are friends. You know you wouldn't want August hanging around if you and I had tried to figure things out."

"You got that right, but Lillian, I've already spent so long without you. I've known what it's like to be hated by you, and I don't think I can do that again."

"I don't hate you, Ryder."

"Winning already," he smiled, melting her heart just a little.

"I'm not asking for much. I just want us to get along. I want to know I can talk to you still, see you smile, not have to fake a conversation with another woman to avoid you or pretend not to see you when you walk by. If I promise not to push August off a cliff and blame it on gravity, can you promise that you won't find a reason to hate me again?"

"I can handle that… as long as you promise not to push him off a cliff."

"It's a deal."

She waited a moment longer while she watched him studying his hands. "That's not why you came here though," she prompted, feeling there was something he was holding back.

"I shouldn't be here for why I came here," he finally admitted.

"I don't understand."

He leaned back in the chair and rested his arms on the armrests, but he didn't look at ease; he looked stressed and ready to pace the room.

"It's this case, or really, *all* of these cases lately. I know the movies and shows make the investigation seem so thrilling… mysterious… and when it seems like they're at a complete loss, there's that *one* thing that breaks the whole case open, that solves it all. Nobody could have seen it coming. Congratulations for being the one person to figure it out!" He said theatrically, thinking over the cases he'd been working lately. Wade found in the water. John Doe found on the rocks. Rain and Brian missing. "In real life though, it's not like that. Sure, there are going to be confusing cases and every piece of evidence is important because you never know which is going to be the key, but really, crimes are simple. Something is stolen, we track it down and return it, punish the one who did it. A person goes missing, we look until we find them, dead or alive. A body turns up, we figure out if it was murder or natural causes. If a crime is committed, like a murder, it's with intention. Now granted we don't always understand someone's intentions, but the criminal had something driving them.

"With the technology we have all around us today, the connections are endless. People are eager to help, which sometimes doesn't help at all, but a lot of times, tips will shed light, help us think in a new perspective. But most of the time the trail is pretty easy to follow. What's the motive? Did the suspect have opportunity? Do the pieces fit? But these recent cases... I'm stumped, Lillian. Nothing makes sense... and now the feds are here and that makes things make even less sense."

He went back to studying his hands, the whir of his brain a mystery to her.

"If you came here to talk about the cases," she said tentatively, "I'm not sure how much help I would be. I mean, how much are you allowed to tell me?"

"I know," he sighed, rubbing his hands over his face and up through his hair, resting his head against his hand as he leaned into the chair, as if he didn't have the energy to hold it upright on its own anymore. "I just keep hitting dead ends. Take yesterday for instance. I grilled that guy Evan, really put him through it when he told us the trio of them got matching tattoos. I tried to get him to slip up and say there was a fourth guy in the group, that the tattoo was his, but he wouldn't budge. He stuck to his same old story."

"But that's good right?"

"I guess. But now I'm still at a loss because the tattoo artist said he only did the design for the three of them. I'm at another dead end. Either someone isn't telling me the truth or I'm missing something really obvious. For whatever reason, you were the one I couldn't get out of my mind to talk to about all of this. I know it doesn't make sense. There's a station full of people trained to think about all these things."

"It sort of makes sense," she said, trying not to smile at his quizzical glance. "Even though I didn't follow in my dad's footsteps, you know and respect the man that raised me and know *how* he raised me, so you know the way I think and surmised that I could be a good sounding board to give you a fresh look."

He smiled, but it was a ghost of his usual. "See, my investigative intuition was right."

"Plus, you already brought me in before when you told me your theory about Wade... and then Rain. So, yeah, I guess I've been a little more involved than I realized." She crossed her leg over the other and leaned against them, toward him. "Other than the tattoo, what has you bothered about the cases? I know you didn't think Wade's death was an accident. Have you found anything to help you with that?"

"No, and I've been all through his house." He sat up again, leaning forward as well, letting his arms drape against his knees. "I watched to see if anyone suspicious was around and asked neighbors. Nobody remembers anything out of the ordinary... No strange person or people hanging around. 'Wade was a good neighbor but kept to himself,' is what the people all said. Everybody was shocked when they found out he had died. It was genuine shock, Lillian. More than half of them told me they could have sworn they had just seen him, that it seemed like only a day or two tops, had gone by since they'd seen him driving home, or checking his mail, or just being in the yard. They were genuinely surprised by how long he'd been gone."

"That's not terribly unusual though," Lillian told him. "I'd really have to think about the last time I saw a particular neighbor, and even then, I could be off by a day or two. People get busy, things fade together, time passes quicker than we realize sometimes."

"And then the letter..." he drifted off to his memory again. "The letter still doesn't sit right with me. The mail lady insisted it had just gone in the box. Why would she say that? What purpose does it serve to say that?"

"Well... I know for me, there will be sometimes that I'll go days without having anything in my box. Couldn't it be possible that the mail lady didn't have anything to deliver so she wouldn't have had reason to open the box, and only thought the letter had gone in the day she checked it?"

"She said the flag was up. She wouldn't have ignored a box that had a flag up all week."

"Did you see the flag?"

He looked at her in thought, his brow furrowed as he tried to focus. "I... don't really remember. I was already upset about Wade and then she was there and talking to me... I'm not sure I even paid attention."

"Maybe it had blown over and didn't look like it was up, so she didn't notice it right away. I've had to mess with my flag to get it to stay put sometimes. It could have fallen just enough to not be obvious."

He thought it over, shaking his head that he didn't know. "I hadn't considered that as a possibility," he admitted.

"Which is understandable. You just lost your friend. You wanted a different explanation for his death than some stupid accident."

"That's pretty much what your dad told me, too." He got up finally to pace the room, as if the chair was restricting the flow of his thoughts. "What about the way he died then? He and John Doe, you know, the body we, well actually that August found while he was hiking. Which is also weird. You didn't see the place where he was found. It wasn't easy to get to. What was August doing all the way out there?"

"You'd have to ask him that."

"We have," he told her waving the distracting thoughts away. "He's either very well trained at lying about what he's up to, or he really does just enjoy hiking."

She chose to ignore the comment about him lying, not wanting to drag August into this anymore than he had already been. "What is it about the way they died that bothers you? Being alone in a dangerous place, having an accident, and then dying doesn't seem suspicious."

"On the surface, it looks like that's the case, but the medical examiner's report seemed like something else could have been involved, that the real cause of death wasn't because Wade drowned, even though he was found in the water, and it wasn't because John Doe fell and landed on a pile of rocks. But the toxicology reports on both were clear. It was just coincidence that the autopsies showed anomalies."

"Could it be just that?" she asked, and he paused in his pacing to glance at her. "Could whatever the report showed simply be a coincidence? If there are no other signs that someone or something else was involved, at what point are you looking beyond the obvious, *hoping* for there to be something else that ended their lives?"

"How do you explain a victim found dead in the water with no water in his lungs?"

"Then he clearly didn't die by drowning."

"Exactly. Official cause of death is a heart attack. It doesn't make sense."

"It could be if he didn't know he had a heart condition and he just happened to be on or near the water when he had a heart attack. If it killed him, and he fell into the water, he wouldn't have water in his lungs because he wouldn't have been breathing when he went in."

Ryder stopped pacing and shoved his hands in his pockets.

"That actually works for both victims," he admitted. "If John Doe didn't know he had a heart condition, and an attack happened on his hike or climb or whatever he was doing on the cliff, killing him instantly, causing him to fall to the rocks below, it would explain why he didn't try to move." He started pacing again, waving an arm to the air between them. "But what are the odds that two seemingly healthy people have heart attacks within days of each other and both die that way?"

"I couldn't tell you. It does seem pretty coincidental, but I guess sometimes bad things just happen." She paused, considering a new thought. "If the two deaths had been years apart, would the coincidence of how they died bother you?"

"What do you mean?"

"One death by heart attack, you chalk it up to an unknown condition, or simply bad luck but still a natural occurrence. You close the case and move on. Five years later you have another death, heart attack, another unknown condition. You think, 'How weird. We had one of these years ago.' You think that maybe people should be getting their health checked out before they go do extreme activities so something preventable like this doesn't happen again."

He nodded his head.

"It's perplexing, but you move on because, ultimately, it's a fluke thing, something to warn people about, especially when tourists start flocking to the area. The department makes public service announcements reminding people not to adventure alone, make sure they're up to the strenuous activity they're embarking on, etc."

He chuckled. "Imagine your dad doing a PSA and handing out flyers to always have a hiking buddy."

She smiled as well but continued with her explanation. "Would you be reopening the case from years before just because you happened to have another death that had a heart attack and died?"

"Probably not," he admitted, crossing his arms across his chest, considering where she was directing him to think. "We'd call it natural death, notify and console the family, and close it down."

"Right. The only reason you haven't done that with each of these individual cases is because of how close together in time they happened. Correct?"

"But how do you know that isn't the key?" he countered.

"I don't, but sometimes bad things just happen," she told him again.

He returned to the chair, rubbing his hands over his face, resting his chin against his folded hands. "I don't know," he said, his tone defeated but determined. "I know it doesn't make sense, but it just feels like the timing means something." He looked over at her again, watching him patiently. "Thank you, Lilly."

"For what?" she smiled. "I don't think I offered much in solving these cases."

"But you offered. You could have sent me away, but instead, you listened and gave me a good perspective on the case I hadn't considered. Even if it doesn't align with what I feel for this case, I'm going to think about what you've said."

"I hope you can close these cases soon and move on." She paused, searching his tired eyes. "I hope you can put Wade to rest."

"Me too… but I want to be sure that when I do, it's for the right reason. He deserves his death to be understood so he can fully rest."

"And if it turns out that he really did die from a natural cause, and there is no underlying and more satisfying reason, will that be enough to allow *you* to rest?"

He mulled over her words, the immediate denial that Wade's death was meaningless evident in his pinched brow. "If I exhaust all the resources and keep coming to the same conclusion, then I guess I'll have to accept the way he died."

"For your sake, I hope you can accept his death and start the process of healing."

FIFTY-SIX

-BILL-

"The tattoo was another dead end," Ryder was telling Bill as they went over the case in his office. "But the good news is the guy verified that there were only three of them. He did them all in one sitting, but hasn't drawn up a design to price and sell as a regular option."

"So, either the buddy that came up with the original design –"

"Jack," Ryder interjected.

"Right, Jack. So, Jack either lied about coming up with the design himself, and really found it online and it's tattooed on every outdoor enthusiast, one of which just happened to die in the same town where another person with the same tattoo goes missing days later…"

"Or we're missing something obvious…"

Bill sighed, tapping his pen against the desk. "We could be chasing our tails here, and the tattoo could mean nothing at all."

"It's a pretty weird coincidence. You saw how close it was to Evan's."

"Yeah, I know." Bill shifted forward, leaning into his arms against the desk. "Could be someone saw it on Brian, took a picture, went to a different artist and had it done."

"You don't think Evan would have mentioned that?"

"Not if he didn't know. They were *here* together, that doesn't mean they did *everything* together."

Ryder contemplated this new thought and his hands steepled in front of him. "Rain," he suddenly blurted, his face slightly shocked as if surprised he hadn't thought of her connection earlier. Bill's eyebrows raised at the implication. "I don't mean that she… and all of them…" Ryder said, waving his hand, clearing away the way it sounded. "I mean we know that Brian was at least alone with Rain. So, you're right. He didn't do everything with just the other two. And kids these days are on social media all the time. She could have shared a picture of her and him. Maybe someone saw the tattoo…"

Bill sat back in his chair, swiveling it slightly back and forth as he considered the line of thought. "That's plausible and could explain how another local has the same tattoo, instead of the odds that a random person found the same one online then died within days of Brian going missing."

"Still weird though."

Bill tapped a notepad with his pen. "We should get a list of Rain's friends. See if anyone has been tagging along, shown an interest."

Ryder nodded, making a note on his phone. "She's only been recounting what happened the night of the disappearance. We never thought to ask about anyone from earlier."

"Could be the reason she was found so close to where we found John Doe was because one of her friends had suggested the route."

"That's true," Ryder agreed. "Brian was a tourist. Of the two of them, Rain would have the better resources for the Mountain."

"I'm not so sure about better."

Ryder looked at him curiously.

"He wasn't dressed for it and wound up dead on the rocks," Bill said with reason. "That's not the person I'd be taking advice from."

"But this could work. Rain wants to impress the new guys in town, talks to the only other person *she* knows that *says* he's been out there before, even though they both know he never has. He gets amped and decides to try it out because he's not about to let *her* be the one to do it when he never actually has. He's unprepared and winds up dead. Meanwhile, Rain has no clue any of that's going on because she's having the time of her life with the three amigos and eventually convinces one of them to take her out there. She follows the route he told her about… And we know the rest from there."

"Now we just have to figure out who the mystery friend is."

"Should be easy enough… Shit," Ryder said, dropping his hand to his lap, remembering what Bill had already figured out. "We can't get in to talk to her."

"Heads up," Jane said as she quickly knocked and opened the door to the sheriff's office. "Those cranky looking federal agents are back and headed your way."

Bill stood, moving around to lean against the front of his desk. Ryder stood as well, crossing his arms across his chest just as the two agents entered. Jane narrowly avoiding getting trapped in the office with them all as they pulled the door closed behind them.

"Sheriff Thorne," Agent Morreau said by way of greeting. He nodded at Ryder but didn't acknowledge him verbally or wait for either Bill or Ryder to greet him back. "We've completed our examination of the two bodies held for processing in the medical examiner's morgue." He paused to reference the tablet the other agent handed to him. "Wade Pointe and Paul Slater's identifications have been confirmed and cremation will commence this afternoon."

"Wait," Ryder interrupted, dropping his hands to his side and taking a partial step toward the agents. He looked at the sheriff for clarification. "Cremation?"

Bill shook his head, indicating he hadn't authorized it. "Wade's body is reserved for burial per his next of kin's wishes," Bill said to the agents. "As for the other body, John Doe. You've identified him?"

"As I've stated," Morreau said, without further explanation.

"You've been here a handful of days, and you've already identified him... Just like that?" Ryder asked in disbelief. "We've been searching for over a week."

"We have access to a wide network of resources. Yes, we've identified him." He sighed, turning to read from the tablet in an almost bored tone. "The deceased, Paul Slater, age nineteen of Eminence, Missouri, was reported missing over two months ago when he left home for a cross-country hiking expedition. When he didn't check in with family or friends in over a week, they alerted the authorities. The family has been notified, and the identification has been confirmed." He stopped reading and turned the screen to face them. It showed a grainy copy of a black and white missing poster. He turned it quickly away and tapped the surface to lock it down, handing it back to the silent sentry that had followed him inside. "We will arrange the transportation of Slater's ashes and your department's assistance in locating his body will be mentioned in our press release."

"Missouri? He wasn't a local?" Ryder asked.

"As I've stated."

"I wasn't aware the federal government handled missing persons cases so intimately," the sheriff mused.

Agent Morreau's expressionless eyes slid to Bill's. "We assist when and where it's necessary. We are thankful for the cooperation of your department in expediting the closure of several cases." His eyes never moved from Bill's despite Ryder's derisive snort at the generic, robotic answers. "In addition, we have concluded our interviews with Ms. Jennifer Storm. We believe that due to the trauma of her experience, her memory of the events was inaccurate. It has been determined that neither she nor her partner, Brian Phillips, breached entry to the restricted government lands you all refer to as the Mountain. It should bring you solace to know that the federal government will see no charges be brought against Ms. Storm."

Ryder snorted again, this time unable to keep his mouth closed. "Right, it's kind of hard to press charges if no crime has been committed."

The agent stared flatly at Ryder. "Ms. Storm has been analyzed by professionals. The truth of her story has been recovered. She and her partner did *intend* to enter into restricted government territory, but at the sound of something pursuing them in the woods, they both became scared and ran away. They lost track of each other; Ms. Storm took shelter and was eventually found. Mr. Phillips was not so lucky. Our highly skilled tracker found his remains in a nearby den, belonging to a bear by all appearances. His family has been notified and should be allowed to grieve."

"And at what point were you going to notify me of this discovery?" Bill crossed his arms, and Morreau turned his attention back to him. "I still have men combing the woods searching for him."

"I'm notifying you now, as I have your lead search deputy. We're all on the same side," he added, but it didn't feel that way to Bill. "We are closing these cases and request any documentation you have to add to our own files."

The second agent stepped forward to retrieve the case folders as if Bill kept them on his person at all times. Bill thought of his conversation with Rich and wondered how his friend's workspace had faired after the feds had finished.

"I'll have my assistant make you copies of all that we have," Bill said amiably, ready for the agents to leave, knowing he wasn't going to talk them out of anything they wanted.

"That won't be necessary," Agent Morreau, the only one of the two that seemed to be able to speak told him. "We have state-of-the-art equipment and personnel trained to convert the documents we'll need. I assure you we will return the originals at the earliest opportunity."

Bill nodded slowly. "Of course. How courteous of you to handle such a daunting task."

"We have our own protocols for this sort of thing."

Bill could see Ryder look to the ceiling and back down, shaking his head on a breath. "We'll get you the documents so you can be on your way. Since you closed the opens, there's no further reason for you all to have a presence in my precinct, correct?"

"Correct, Sherriff. Once we have the complete case files we will be on our way."

"Ryder." Bill nodded toward his desk and the accordion holder containing the case folders. "Verify they're all there."

Ryder opened the holder and flipped through, mouthing the names of each tab as he read. "Looks like everything," he said as he rewrapped the string closure.

Bill took the holder and handed it over himself. "If there's nothing else…"

The agent studied the single holder as if it was a foreign substance. "This is all the documentation for Pointe, Slater, Storm, and Phillips? What about digital copies?"

"As you've pointed out, our resources are limited out here. This is everything we've compiled to date. Much to the chagrin of everyone within these walls, I prefer the tangible to the immediately erasable and potentially unrecoverable nature of a digital file. When a case is closed, that is when the information is officially logged, scanned, summarized, and backed up. Up until five minutes ago, our cases were still open."

The agent stared stonily at Bill. He stared right back.

"Thank you for your assistance, Mr. Thorne," Morreau said, addressing the sheriff. You or your precinct will be notified if further assistance is required." The agent turned on his heel to walk away, his hand already on the doorknob.

"Wait," Ryder called, looking back at Bill. "What about Wade… and Brian?"

Both agents turned back, staring at Ryder blankly. "What about them?"

Ryder looked at Bill then back to the agents. "Wade isn't supposed to be cremated. And how do you know Brian was actually whatever you found? Where are *our* reports and documentation? You guys don't have to share with *us*? We just have to give to you?"

"Ryder," Bill warned.

"No, it's not right," he protested. "Wade is supposed to be buried. Why do they get to change how his body is handled?"

"Wade is being cremated because of contaminates found on his person."

"Bullshit. What contaminates? Our examiner ran all the tests and there was nothing abnormal found. And Brian? Dead? Just like that?" He looked between the men with incredulity. "Sheriff, we were all through those woods. Simon's dogs are the best in the state, and they didn't find him. These guys spend a couple days and conveniently find *remains* to wrap this all up and close it down?"

"There's nothing convenient about finding the chewed-on fragments of human remains among the habitat of at least one bear. A bear which could return at any moment, and put my own team in jeopardy," Morreau responded.

"That's not what I mean," Ryder argued, turning back to Bill. "Where is this bear den anyway? Why didn't we come across it in our own search?"

"The woods are large. We have a significant budget and advanced equipment. There is no mandate for us to explain our methodology to you. You may not like the results that we've uncovered, but that doesn't mean that the results are deniable."

Bill watched as Ryder's fists balled at his sides, his nostrils flaring slightly with his outward breath.

"Ryder," he stated calmly, stepping forward to catch his deputy's attention. "If further testing has resulted in more information that could give insight into the two deaths on our hands, identified our John Doe, *and* helped recover a missing person, we should be grateful for the help that has been extended to our department."

"But –"

Bill turned to the agents. "Thank you for your efficiency in helping us close these cases. I look forward to receiving your official reports and the return of our documents." Bill stepped between Ryder and the agents and opened the door to the office, cutting off Ryder's protests.

The agents studied both men a moment longer, and then, without more words, both passed beyond Bill and headed toward the exit.

"Sheriff," Ryder started. "This isn't right."

FIFTY-SEVEN
-Bill-

Bill shook his head, silencing Ryder with a quick movement, watching until the agents exited the building and were out of sight of the windows along the front of the building.

"Jane, get Simon on the phone. I need him right away," Bill directed.

She nodded and quickly dialed, listening for the sound on the other end.

"Send it in here to my phone when he answers," he said, returning to his office, Ryder right behind him.

"Coming through," Jane called after him, and he saw the light blink on his desk phone.

"Ryder, get Rich on the phone right away," Bill told him as he lifted the receiver. "No, Ryder—" he called as Ryder took off to his own desk to make the call. "— use your cell," He watched as Ryder backtracked to Jane's desk and get a slip of paper with a phone number written on it. "I need you with me," he directed to Ryder and then into the phone. "Simon, are you and your team still on site?"

"Yeah. Those feds told us the search was over and to pack up, though. Said they found Brian's body." He paused on the other line. "I'm sorry, sir."

"Sorry for what, deputy?"

"The feds found him on our side of the line, said a bear got him and dragged him off. That could explain why the dogs didn't find more, the bear masked his scent. I shouldn't have been as disrespectful in my insistence that Brian was in the Mountain. He was already gone this whole time."

Bill glanced over when he heard Ryder talking, holding the phone up in a motion that said he had Rich on the line. Bill held up a finger to wait while he finished his conversation.

"There's no need to apologize for fighting for something you believe in. You're an officer who was trying to deliver his best. But," he paused and grabbed his keys from the drawer, tossing them to Ryder and mouthed *start the truck*. Ryder nodded and left the office. "I need you back in the woods."

"What for, sir?" Simon's confusion was clear enough across the line that Bill could imagine his brow furrowing.

"Can your dogs track without a scent?"

"I don't follow."

"Do the dogs have to have something in particular to follow, or can they find a trail and follow the smell on the trail?"

"Well… yes." He paused to think. "Usually, I already have something to guide them to follow, but if the path is fresh enough, they can track the scent—they're trained for that sort of thing—but tracking works best when I have a scent article to reaffirm what they're supposed to be tracking. Why, what are you thinking?"

"I want them to follow where the feds went and find that den."

Simon was silent for a moment. "Do you want to recover remains for the family?" he asked solemnly.

"I want to verify that Brian's actually been found."

Simon was quiet again, confusion still lacing his voice. "What reason would they have for lying?"

"That's another question I'd like answered," Bill stated. "Can you follow their trail?"

"I'll do my best."

"Keep me updated. But Simon—"

"Yeah?"

"Make sure the feds have left before you go back in."

"Of course."

Bill replaced the receiver and told Jane to call him immediately if the agents returned, but not to let them know he'd left the building. She agreed, but he could tell by the way she stood awkwardly beside her desk that she was as lost as she appeared. Hopefully he'd have something worth explaining.

Bill reached the truck and took the driver's seat. Ryder stopped his conversation and turned the phone on speaker, tilting the phone between them as if that made it easier for them both to listen.

"Rich? Are the feds still at your place?" Bill asked as he put the Blazer into reverse.

"They're prepping the two bodies for cremation. I already told Ryder that I've tried to tell them Wade wasn't a cremation—" Rich's voice was as exasperated as Bill currently felt. "—but they're statues, these guys, and their examiner is just a drone going through the motions. Nobody's listening."

"We'll explain it to Wade's family. There's no stopping that now," Bill said regretfully. "Is there any way you can get tissue samples before they're incinerated? I'd really like to know what was so dangerous that it had to be burned away."

"You've met these guys, right? It's my place, but you wouldn't know it by the restrictions they've put on me. There's no way I can get within twenty feet of those bodies."

"You've got to have a trick up your sleeve," Bill said hopefully as he drove through town.

"Sorry. You know I would if I could, but there's just no way. They haven't left the bodies unattended since they got here. There's been an overnight guard."

"Shit," Bill swore and caught Ryder's surprised glance out of the corner of his eye. "Okay. That's okay. When you can get away, I need to talk to you in person."

"I can swing by now. Lord knows they're not going to let me assist in the cremations."

"I don't want you to draw attention by leaving."

"I can manage. See you soon."

"I'm not at the office. I'll have Ryder text you where we're headed."

"Sounds good."

The call disconnected.

"Where should I tell him to go?" Ryder asked, ready to relay the information.

"I don't know yet."

Ryder's phone buzzed. Bill glanced over to see Ryder check the screen but set the phone back down.

"Is that Rich asking where to go?"

"No. Just a personal message," he said, tapping his leg with the phone while he looked out the window. "We could go to my place," he said, turning back to Bill. "If you're just needing somewhere to meet, it'll be fine."

Bill considered the suggestion. He was probably being paranoid by not staying in the office. The odds that the feds would show back up after they'd already taken everything to do with the cases were slim. Rich had sent him down the path of uncertainty when he told him to make copies of the files, and now he'd have to tell him he was right. His gut hadn't followed Ryder down the path of a murderer in their community, but it *was* screaming that some truth was being swept away.

"That's fine." He glanced over at Ryder and nodded to his phone. "Let Rich know, will you?"

Ryder flipped the phone and Bill watched him pause, relay the message, set the phone back down, then pick it back up. But he didn't send another message. Instead, he set the phone down again and went back to staring out the window.

"Everything okay over there?"

"Yeah, why wouldn't it be?" Ryder asked, turning from the window.

"Your phone. You got a message and you're avoiding responding."

"I'm not avoiding responding. I was thinking about the case."

"You're avoiding. You've looked at the message at least twice now and you're itching to look again."

"I'm not itching. I'm fine. I'll respond later."

"Alright," Bill said nonchalantly, rounding the corner and catching Ryder checking his phone again. "Why don't you tell my daughter I'm swinging by her work to grab something?"

"Sir? I thought we were going to my place."

"We will, via Wisteria."

Ryder tapped his phone against his leg, considering, before typing the message. A moment later the phone buzzed. "She's not at the diner."

"Oh." Disappointment laced the singular word. "Okay… Text Rich back, tell him to meet us at the back of Wisteria in twenty minutes."

"Not my place?"

"No. If Lillian isn't at work, we can use her office. It'll save a trip."

"You don't want to check with her first?"

"She won't mind, but we'll need her key. Let her know we're coming by her house, will you?"

Ryder relayed the message and set the phone back down, staring at it instead of out the window.

"How'd you know it was her texting me?"

Bill glanced over. "You just told me."

"No, how'd you know before?"

"I didn't. I need to get my copies from her office. You have a phone and her number."

The silence persisted.

"It was your body language," Bill finally told him, nodding at the phone. "You have tells."

"I do not," Ryder said, immediately defensive.

"You do." Bill chuckled. "For instance, I know if a date was good or not if your phone starts buzzing incessantly and you smirk and send messages back like rapid fire or you roll your eyes and block the number." Ryder opened his mouth to object, but instead smiled and shut it. Bill continued. "My daughter, however, has had you acting out of sorts… slowly since she came back to town, but much more these past few weeks. Now she's told you that she's seeing August, and you've been intentionally dismissive because you think that by pushing her away, you'll be able to get back to the way things were. And maybe things can go back… in a sense… but maybe not for some time.

"And I *suspected* it was her texting because you didn't know how to respond. If it didn't matter, you would have shot a quick response back and been done, but instead, you read it when it came through, again when you texted Rich, and then again, only to set it back down and not respond. It matters."

The silence was their passenger again.

"I don't know *how* you do that." Ryder paused, looking out the window again as they drove. "I thought if I pushed her away, it'd be easier to let her go… I barely made it a day. I've already apologized for being an ass to her," he admitted. "Now she said she needs to talk to me."

Bill glanced over. "About you and her, or her and August?"

"None of that. She's been clear she wants to give them a try." He chuckled. "She made me promise I wouldn't push him off a cliff. No, this felt urgent."

"How does a text feel urgent?"

"She said, 'ASAP.'"

"Huh, that'll do it." Bill nodded to the door as they pulled up to Lillian's house. "Get the key. See what she needed."

Lillian opened the door before Ryder could reach it, waving to Bill before she let him in. Bill used this break to send a message to Rich. The key tapping against his window startled him as he was responding.

"Hey," Ryder said when he rolled the window down, handing the key through. "She says it's fine to use the office; doesn't think anyone will bother you. But she said that if they do, just show them your badge and tell them it's official police business, that you're commandeering the office. Then she asked if commandeering only referred to vehicles or if it could work for an office, too." Ryder chuckled, but his brow was knitted as he leaned against the truck. "You think you can meet Rich without me?"

Bill glanced at his daughter's house, and back to Ryder. "Everything okay with Lillian?"

"Yeah." Ryder paused, leaning back slightly, running one hand through his hair before he continued. "You know how I told you I apologized to her? Well, I also bounced some ideas off her about the cases."

"Ryder…"

"I know, I know. I shouldn't have discussed them with her," he said, then quickly added, "but I had to tell her about identifying Wade, and then when I told her my murder theory, you had already dismissed it at that point, but then it came back around as another possibility, and –"

Bill held up a hand to stop the boy's rambling. "Ryder. I'm fully aware you've discussed these cases with her. So have I. I don't like bringing her into our dark world, but the truth is, she spent so much time at the station when she was younger, she pretty much grew up with this life."

"Right," he said, motioning his hand forward that he agreed. "And she's smart. She shot holes in most of my theories in just one conversation. I didn't altogether like it, but it was a different perspective, and that was what I needed."

"Does what she needs to talk to you about have to do with the cases?" Bill asked, trying to get his deputy back on track.

"Yeah." He motioned back to the house. "It seemed a little urgent, but this is, too, so if you can't cut me loose, I'll just tell her I'll swing by later."

"I could really use you when I meet Rich," Bill started, noticing that even though Ryder's facial expression didn't waver, he hadn't let out the breath he was holding. He glanced back at the closed door of Lillian's house. "But … whatever she's come up with could be useful too." He noticed Ryder was breathing again. "I'll check back after I meet Rich."

"I'll let you know what Lillian's come up with, too. I have my phone if you need me, or I can get Lillian to bring me to you."

"We'll figure it out." Bill put the truck in reverse. "Information, Ryder," he said sternly. "I know that's my daughter in there, but if it doesn't look useful to the case, I need you with me. We need to look into this Paul Slater person, and Rain should be accessible now to verify if she knew him."

"You got it," Ryder tapped the truck as he turned away.

Bill pulled away as Ryder cleared the deck steps in one bound, showing himself in after a quick rap on the door. If it was any other woman, Bill wouldn't leave him here while he needed Ryder's head in the case. He knew he was biased toward his daughter, but she might have seen something they hadn't. And they needed all the help they could get.

FIFTY-EIGHT

-Lillian-

Lillian couldn't help pacing the floor waiting for Ryder to return from talking to her dad. Maybe she shouldn't have said anything. She knew her theory was bizarre…

You'd never let it go if you don't say something.

A porch thud and a quick knock announced Ryder's return.

"Hey, your dad's heading to Wisteria. I'm all yours."

Lillian glanced back at the door, picturing her dad driving away. She chewed her lip. "You're sure he doesn't need you?"

"He'll catch me up. What's going on, Lilly?"

"I'm not sure," she started.

"I know I shouldn't have dragged you into this like I did."

"No," she reached out but quickly retracted her hand. "It's not the case that has me… confused. I mean it is … but it's more."

"Okay … Do you want to sit?" He asked when she started to pace again.

"No." She stopped. He was patiently watching, waiting. "I need you to keep an open mind and not think I'm a crazy person."

"That's pretty easy to do," he chuckled, rocking back on his heels.

"I'm serious."

"So am I."

"And you promise to keep an open mind?"

"Cross my heart," he said, making the motion.

"I should probably get that in writing," she murmured before sighing. "Okay, here goes. Did I tell you I was working on a research project for Wisteria?" She pointed to the piles of papers. "Researching history … the community … all that?"

"You didn't go into detail, but yeah," he nodded at the piles, "you've had these out."

"Okay, well, mostly these are just glimpses into the past, things you'd expect of old papers: stories, current events, just life. You know?" She paused, staring at her piles stacked along the table, thinking of what she'd spent reading into the early morning hours, what nagged her awake only a few hours later.

"Hey," Ryder said softly, gently touching her elbow. "Whatever it is, you can tell me. That's what friends do right?"

She smiled weakly. "There are things…" She struggled to find the right explanation. "There are things that don't make sense."

"Yeah, I get that."

"And if you're living in it, among these things, it's easy to dismiss them, maybe even stay confused, because they just can't make sense."

"I'm following the confusion," Ryder joked.

"But, if you're removed from the … things … and look at it differently, a pattern starts to form."

"Right," Ryder agreed. "That's exactly why I wanted to talk to you about the cases yesterday. I needed a fresh look. But," he paused, considering her struggle, "it sounds like after shooting enough holes in my case yesterday to qualify for the force, you've thought of something new."

"Yes, but remember, you agreed to stay open-minded."

"Got it."

She let out a breath. "First, I have to admit something that I don't want you to tell my Dad."

"Which is?"

She looked at him uncertainly. *You've already come this far.*

She walked across the room and picked up a stack of printed pages. "Second, I owe you an apology."

"I still don't know the first thing, but thanks?"

"These," she held up the pages, but hugged them to herself instead of handing them over, "are what my dad is heading to my office to get."

"You have his files?" He tilted his head slightly, looking at her quizzically. "If you already had them, why did you send him away? It won't take long for him to realize."

"*His* copies are still there. He has no idea I have these … and I don't want you to tell him."

She paused and watched him for a response.

He folded his arms, widening his stance as he settled back on his heels to watch her. "Okay. I'm being open-minded."

"I'm apologizing because I'm asking you not to tell him, which is awful of me since he is your boss, and … well … you're both cops and because I've read your case files, which feels illegal. I'm asking you not to do your job, and I'm sorry for that."

"Since you're telling me all this," he began tentatively, "when you could have destroyed your copies without anyone ever knowing you had them, I'm guessing you found something that we didn't."

She smiled with relief. "Yes, but *this* is where I need you to be open-minded."

"Not when you asked me to withhold information from your dad ... my boss ... the sheriff."

She crinkled her brow in a slight wince. "Right."

"If it helps with the case..."

"These," she reassured him, holding up the stack of papers again, "were really just confirmation. We'd already talked about so much, and then my own conversations, pieced together with my research, led me to reference these." She paused again before diving into her explanation, already knowing he wouldn't believe a word she had to say.

"Lillian," he said softly. "Stop thinking and just tell me what you need to tell me."

"Okay ... I know who your John Doe is."

"Yeah, so do we."

"What?" she asked, taken aback. "You do? How—" She opened her mouth to speak and then closed it again. "You know?" she asked again.

"Sort of. The feds gave us an ID just before we came here. We haven't had a chance to check it, but they say it's been verified."

She chewed her lip, thrumming her fingers against the pages she was still hugging.

"You seem surprised," Ryder said curiously.

She couldn't see the feds coming to the same conclusion that she had, *because* of the conclusion she'd come to ... but if they *had* come to the same conclusion, they wouldn't likely be sharing it with Ryder as she had wanted to. If she were in their position, she'd probably want to cover up what she had discovered, not share it ... There was definitely a reason *not* to share, which was what had already made her question saying anything at all, but if it could answer their questions and close cases, shouldn't she share what she knew? Maybe she *was* going crazy after all.

"Hey," Ryder said, interrupting her thoughts. "Maybe if you let me in on what's going through your mind right now, I can clear some of this up?"

"Who did they ID John Doe as?" she blurted.

"He wasn't a local."

"Right, but what was his name?"

"Nobody you'd find in those pages." He nodded to the stack in her arms.

"You're sure?" she asked him.

"One hundred percent. We'd never heard his name before today, so he's not noted anywhere in that stack."

"Then the agents are lying to you," she said without thinking more about what she should or shouldn't say.

"I haven't even told you the name."

"You told me he isn't in here."

"And you told me that you used your conversations, I'm assuming with Rain, as part of your information to figure out his identity. Up until now, your dad and I thought the feds were lying, too, but we also think Rain had a connection to him. My guess is she told you something that you initially dismissed. All this must have sparked a memory. So, by you confirming that Rain knew him, it confirms what we were already thinking, and the feds just finished it all off by giving us a name."

She shook her head, knowing it would be easier to agree, to let them close the cases and move on, but *she* would still know the truth. "You said his name isn't in here … and it is."

"I promise you it isn't. I'd never heard of Paul Slater until an hour ago."

She closed her eyes and sighed. "John Doe isn't Paul Slater. It's Brian Phillips."

"No," Ryder said, his voice full of consolation. "No, Lilly, it isn't." He moved to her then, leading her to sit in one of her chairs. He squatted down in front of her and took her hands in his. "But the feds did say they found Brian's body. A bear attack," he added gently. "I'll admit, I thought it was too neat and tidy, but now, maybe we just don't want to hear the truth."

Lillian shook her head again. "No, Ryder. They're lying. You need to see what I've found."

"John Doe *can't* be Brian, because Brian was still walking the streets when we found the very dead body."

She looked him square in the eye. "I know."

He dropped his head to his chest. "Lilly," he started.

"You said you'd keep an open mind," she reminded him.

He looked back at her. "Saying that a person was dead *and* alive at the same time is not an open mind. That's … something else altogether," he said.

"That's crazy, you mean."

"I didn't say that."

"That's what *I* said. Over and over, all night, that's what I said. But it adds up and I can prove it."

"Lilly, it isn't *possible*."

"Please. I can *show* you." She watched him study her, hoping her eyes showed she was serious and not as irrational as she felt. "If you don't believe me after I show you, that's fine. I'll understand. You can believe the feds, close your cases, move on, and be happy that you dodged a bullet trying to get involved with crazy ol' me." She tried to smile at her attempt at humor. "But please, I have to show you. I have to get it out. I won't be able to let it go if I don't."

Ryder moved his hands to the sides of her knees, squeezing gently as he moved to sit across from her on the edge of her coffee table.

"I'd be considered crazy, too," he said, "because I'd still want you, crazy or not. I'll keep an open mind. Show me what you found."

"Thank you," she said with a surge of gratitude, reaching across to squeeze his hand and diving in before he could change his mind. "It started with stories in the papers; little things here and there that nobody would notice. Nobody would notice it because it isn't possible. Rain said something that you and I dismissed as delusional, and then, *you* said something about timing being the key, and those words kept nagging at me." She stood then and motioned for him to follow. "It's in here."

She led him to her office where her desk had been moved against the wall, clearing the floor so she could piece together her puzzle.

"I would have used a big board like in the movies when they tape everything and string up connections, but this was all I had to work with," she told him, trying again at humor when her whole body wanted to shake with fear at what she found and how he'd react to it.

"You've been busy," he mused, analyzing the seemingly random bits of paper in front of them.

"More so than I realized," she told him, walking around to pick up an article. "While researching my project for Wisteria, a common thread kept appearing, one that's sad, but a part of life: missing persons notifications. Sometimes I'd find ones like this one, describing the person, giving a name, talking about where he or she was last seen, people they might have been with, or where they might have been going. You know how they read."

He nodded. He was all too familiar with the world of missing persons.

"I'd also come across found persons articles, as I've started to call them. Articles that would ask for help identifying a body. Sometimes there would be a picture, I'm guessing if the deceased wasn't too dead looking."

"Meaning the picture wasn't so graphic that it would send everyone who saw it to the trashcan to lose their lunch."

"Right. Mostly, it was just descriptions of what the dead person looked like, approximate age, gender, what they were wearing, any defining marks to help trigger an identification."

Ryder nodded again but didn't interrupt.

"It was upsetting to see so many of these through the years. And really, I don't know if that's what it's like everywhere, or if it's just here. Maybe there really is a curse around here. They kept coming up and I kept setting them aside because ultimately, they weren't what I was after. I didn't need that information. Read, acknowledge, file aside. That's what I did. Some would sound familiar, but I didn't dig deeper because I didn't need to. There was no reason to. But then we talked.

"You said that the timing felt important, and I don't think you meant it the way I eventually perceived it, but I think you were right. It nagged at me until I dug out my pile and started piecing these together." She handed him the missing person report she'd been holding then turned to find another. "I remembered this one specifically and started with it. That's a report of a missing person. Read the description." She waited while he did. When he finished and looked up, she handed him the next page. "Now read this found report." She waited again.

"This is the same person," Ryder stated when he finished. "That's good."

"Yes, I agree. When I came across each of these on separate days, I remember thinking that this person's family would have received closure. But I remembered this one specifically because I had come across the 'found' report when I was talking with my dad, and he told me this was a big 'missing' case when he was starting out. He was surprised that he couldn't remember the boy being found and chalked it up to it being a long time ago and that a lot of other cases had happened."

"I can see where something could feel big at the moment, but over time, it can get forgotten."

"Right, my dad tried showing me the happy side, that even though he wasn't part of the identification, closure would have been brought to this boy's family." She pointed to each of the pages. "Look at the dates."

Ryder's brow furrowed, looking at the span between them. "This can't be the same person, Lilly," he finally said, looking up at her. "Initially, yes, I thought so based on the description, but this one here," he held up the missing persons article, "is from three years *after* your 'found' person needed to be identified. There's no way someone would not notice someone was missing for that long before reporting it."

"Right ... unless they went missing and were found in a different time."

"Which isn't possible."

"Why?"

He snorted at the absurdity. "Because time moves forward."

"But what if it didn't *only* move forward."

"Lilly, this is just a coincidence," he told her, handing back the pages.

She nodded. "That's what I tried to tell myself, too." She picked up more similar missing and found reports. "Look at these. They all have similar identifiers in the missing and found descriptions, but none of them are close in time." She held them up when his face was skeptical. "How can there be this many coincidences? And this is just one night's research. I bet there are more if I actually tried to find them. What if my dad doesn't remember the anchor man being found because he was found before my dad joined the force?"

"There isn't proof that any of these actually go with who you think they do. They're just a bunch of similarities, and if you look long enough, I'm sure you could find many that go together. There's only so many different ways you can describe a man with brown hair and brown eyes."

"I understand that, but it's the extra descriptions, the scars, the birthmarks."

"None of them are exact," Ryder countered.

"So, because one person writes that, 'a jagged scar crosses through an eyebrow and up into the hairline,' and another description says, 'an uneven scar on right side of the forehead,'" she read from two separate articles, "you're saying it's not close enough to be a match."

"Right. It's close, but that's not evidence enough."

"What about this one and the anchor tattoo?" she asked, holding up the one that reminded her of her conversation with her dad.

"There are a lot of Navy men around here. It's a common tattoo. I'm sorry, Lilly, I just don't see what you do."

She sighed, letting her hands fall to her sides. "It's okay. Really, it is," she told him when he started to speak. "If you can poke holes, then I can let it go. It just means that I need more sleep," she chuckled weakly.

"This just isn't enough to convince me that these are the same people," he told her, pointing to the floor around them.

"Okay … but like I said, this is where it started."

His face was skeptical, but again, he waited to hear what she had to say.

"After putting these together, and staring at them for a long time, I remembered that my dad had made case file copies, and while I didn't know what he did with them, I had shown him how to save them on the computer. I got curious and went to see if he had. I guess he realized it could be beneficial to have a computer backup because they were on my computer."

"Thus, your stack of our open cases."

"Exactly. I remembered Rain saying that she'd been gone for six days."

"We already figured out that math. It was three meals a day for two days, for a total of her six sandwiches."

"Right … unless it wasn't. Unless she was right, and it really was six days."

"She was only missing for two."

"Sure, if time only moves forward." She held up a hand before he could object. "Then I remembered talking to Evan in my office and his tattoo. It was unique. My dad and I discussed it when I saw a similar picture in the case file I was helping him copy. In our conversation, *I* was the one who said it couldn't be Brian because of the timing. But if time wasn't a factor…" She turned again and picked up the picture of the John Doe tattoo, handing it to Ryder.

"Yes, I've seen Evan's and this one side by side. They're similar. *And* I talked to the tattoo artist who said he only did theirs. But Lilly, listen to yourself. It isn't possible."

She turned to pick up two more pieces of paper, this time from the desk to her side, both face down. "I know it *shouldn't* be possible … but what if it is?"

Ryder didn't have a response.

She handed him the image of the face of John Doe. "This is your John Doe, the person the feds are now trying to say is someone named Paul Slater. Correct?"

"Yes," he told her as he glanced at the picture.

"When was the last time you saw Brian?"

"I don't know, probably a day or so before he went missing."

"A week and a half ago then?"

"Yes."

"And you have a good idea of what he looked like?"

"Of course. We have a picture in the missing person's case file."

"You do," she confirmed, handing him the second picture she'd been holding.

He looked at it quickly, as he had the picture of John Doe, but instead of immediately agreeing that the picture was of Brian, he studied it further. Lillian waited, watching the same confusion she had felt when she held the two side by side playing across his face. He looked up at her, both pictures still in his hands.

"Putting everything out of your mind," she started. "If I handed you those two pictures, with absolutely no context, would you say they were of the same person? Don't think about time," she said when she saw him begin to object. "Just look at the people on those papers. Are they the same person?"

"Lilly…"

"Are they the same?"

"Yes," he sighed. "But that isn't possible."

"Because we don't understand it?"

"Because … if this were possible, wouldn't we know about it? How could something like this be kept quiet?"

"You mean stories of weird things happening? Stories about people going places and never coming back out? Dead bodies that show up without explanation? Federal agents having convenient answers to confusing problems?" She took the papers from him, set them aside, and squeezed his hand. "You said that you must have seen Wade longer ago than you realized and that the mail lady's story about when the flag went up didn't make sense with the timing of when he would have died. What if it does? What if you were both right? What if he went to the Mountain when she said he left the note, not long after you saw him, but his body wound up somewhere else in time?"

He ran his hands through his hair and sat against her desk, looking at something beyond her field of vision.

"You think the Mountain is a portal through time."

"I hadn't said it out loud yet … But yes, what if that was the case?"

"And you think the feds know but can't say anything or it would cause panic and riot. People would stream in there like locusts or scream it from the hilltops, fearing the end of the world or some other nonsense, but ultimately, cause more hype about the place, more people..."

"More death."

Ryder looked over. "What do you mean?"

"For one, people can be wild and would probably literally kill to be able to go back in time, change things to make their lives better, or fix something they think should have been different. But two, out of all the stories that come out of the Mountain, the one common thread is death. Nobody goes in and lives to talk about it." She waved her hand at the floor. "If someone did make it back alive, they must have done something right because there's no story about it."

"Except for Rain. She swears she was gone six days," Ryder reminded her. "How did she survive?"

Lillian nodded. "Except for Rain," she agreed. "And she told me the feds told her to change her story. She's just a person who was lost and disoriented. Nobody will believe her story. But maybe there's truth to it that even she doesn't realize."

"What do you mean?"

"She says they went in, that Brian went crazy, so she ran away. She doesn't remember coming out, but she says she was in a dark room for six days where someone fed her sandwiches."

"You think the feds had her?"

"If the feds had her, they would have let her disappear with Brian. I think someone knew how to use the Mountain and saved her. She was released when the time was right for a missing person to be found. She's already known for being unruly and telling outlandish stories, stories that would be ignored if they didn't make sense. As the hype wore off, she'd eventually stop talking and all this would be just another campfire story about the Mountain."

"Okay ... saying all this *is* possible," Ryder said, waving his arm to encompass the room and everything she'd suggested. "How am I supposed to explain this to your dad, who is currently investigating what he suspects the feds are covering up? And two, who is the mystery person that saved Rain from dying the Mountain's death?"

Lillian sighed, feeling exhausted now that everything was out of her mind and in the open and her lack of sleep had caught up. "Those are two questions I don't have answers for."

FIFTY-NINE

-RYDER-

Ryder emerged from Lillian's office twenty minutes later after looking through the timeline she'd compiled to find her cleaning the stacks of paper in her living room.

"What are you doing?" he asked. "You look exhausted. Can't that wait?"

"If I sit down, I'll fall asleep, and none of this is really necessary anymore. I should have cleared it away before now, since I'm using the university, but … I guess, maybe it was waiting for me to realize what it was telling me. I can put it away now and have the university do direct searches if I need more."

"You think that's a good idea? Getting the university to dig deeper? If your theory about the Mountain is true, that's pointing it out, highlighting it for more people to see."

"True," she said, giving up and sitting on the edge of the coffee table. "But, as you aren't quite convinced of my theory, someone who I explained and showed examples to, what do you think a person typing in and printing off search criteria will see? Just some missing and found articles through the years that don't seem to go together. If anyone makes the connection, like you pointed out, it won't be enough to convince them that time travel is real, and they'll chalk it up to coincidence."

Ryder nodded, walking to the pile of papers behind her, nodding to the nearly empty box beside them. "These go in here?"

"Yes, but you don't have to do that. I'll get them," she said, standing again to finish the job.

"You sit. Over there," he said, pointing to the couch. "Let me clean this up while you take a break." She watched him put papers neatly into the box. "Sit," he told her again without looking up from what he was doing. "Let's say I'm leaning toward believing your theory about the Mountain, even though it makes absolutely no sense and can't be possible. Let's just say for current events' sake, that time travel is the answer to all of these cases. Wade being found before he left to camp. Brian being our John Doe and being found before he went hiking. It explains why there was never evidence of a murderer that could be found. It also explains why the dogs stopped searching at the rocks repeatedly." He stopped packing the box and looked over at Lillian. "If the cases progressed as they should have, missing people reported, search, find, the clues would all add up and the cases would be open and shut. Everything is there, it's just out of order."

"My thoughts exactly," she agreed.

He went back to filling the box. "Wade and Brian both still wind-up dead. Nothing really changed, just how it's reported."

He considered his options for trying to explain the possibility of time travel to Bill. It wasn't something he could easily see him accepting, even with the side-by-side photos of John Doe and Brian. It's not something his own brain was wanting to comprehend, let alone the sheriff's fact-based, logic-oriented mind.

"What are you thinking?" Lillian yawned.

Ryder looked up, not realizing he'd finished filling the box. He looked around for the lid and she pointed to the wall behind him where it was propped. "I'm thinking there's no way your dad is going to believe time travel exists."

"Agreed. Which is why I called you and not him."

"And here I thought it was because you couldn't stand to be apart," he said smiling wickedly and loving that she couldn't help but smile back and shake her head at him. "So," he continued, "I'm stuck with what to tell him. He's convinced that the feds are covering all of this up. Which, if your theory is right and they know about time travel and the Mountain, then it explains why they had a neat and tidy story already ready to go. They spend just enough time here going through the motions of investigating, all the while confirming for themselves what they already know, and then deliver the cover-up.

"Unfortunately, I was very convincing this morning that I didn't believe what they were saying, and your dad saw through them as well… He's the best investigator I know and he's not going to be satisfied with their story. So how am I supposed to do my job?" He paused, considering if something like this were to happen again in his career. "If this is a reality, how am I ever going to be able to do the job, knowing that any case that comes across my desk has the possibility of never being solved?"

"Isn't that already a complication of police work? There are so many cold cases that there are whole TV series about them."

"I'm just supposed to be okay with that? I became an officer to help people, to put away the bad guy, to give people closure. If this is real. If time travel is possible, and I figure out that the answer to my case is in the past, how do I close it down? How do I tell a family that wants answers that there isn't anything more to do? How do I watch the station waste resources searching for an answer I already have?"

"If you find your answer in the past," Lillian started, considering a point of view that she hadn't thought of yet, still coming to terms with the possibility herself. "Then *you* at least will have closure. You will continue to do your job and try to find a reasonable answer as if you didn't know about the past, just like you would for any case. And just like you would for any case that can't be solved, you do what

I'm assuming naturally happens. The spark starts to fade along with the trail, it keeps getting pushed to the back of the pile, the more immediate and important cases take precedence, until it's been years and becomes a memory for the community. The family will eventually face the realization that their loved one isn't coming back and will move on."

Ryder picked up the box and placed it against the wall where he'd found the lid, coming back to sit on the chair across from her. He glanced at his phone when a text message buzzed through. "Your dad's heading this way." He looked at Lillian. "I don't want to keep information from him." He paused again, gathering his thoughts, not expecting an answer. "But I don't think trying to explain any of this will help the cases."

"So, what will you tell him about why I asked you over? You know he's going to want to know if it was worth losing you for a couple hours while he's trying to work out a problem."

He thought about everything she'd gone over with him, trying to consider an alternative angle to what she could have wanted to talk about. "The tattoo," he finally said. "You mentioned that you already talked about it to your dad. We discussed it, too, this morning because of the dead-end it provided, but it took us down a different avenue that I was going to look into before the feds gave us their story. We thought that our John Doe was someone that Rain knew, and that was how she ended up where he was found, because he had told her where to go. We suspected that the friend saw Brian's tattoo and got the same one."

"Okay, but you said the feds told you a different name and that he wasn't local. How do I play into this and how do you use what they told you to get my dad to believe them?"

"Rain already befriended one set of out-of-towners, who's to say she didn't meet others? Maybe she meets this Paul Slater, she hits it off with him when he gets into town. Then she meets these other guys, brings Brian around, the connection is made and that could tie the stories together."

"Except that it isn't Paul Slater's body in that morgue, and how will you get Rain to agree that any of that happened?"

He stood up to pace the room, "I don't know. Here in a few hours, there won't be proof that Paul Slater's body was here or not, Brian either for that matter," he said, then realized that she didn't have a clue what he was talking about. "Wade and Paul… Brian, whoever, are being cremated."

"Oh. That seems sudden."

"I think that's the fed's point. They won't let anyone near the bodies to get tissue samples and all we have is their word that he is who they say he is." He stopped pacing and thought about the dilemma of Rain. If he asked her to lie, the truth would eventually come out and then he'd be stuck with the same problem on a different day. "What if Rain had nothing to do with Brian 'meeting' Paul? It was only our theory that Rain would be the source, the connection, since she was local. But the source could have been Brian on his own. The only people who could really confirm if Brian ran into Paul are Brian and Paul, and according to the feds, they're both dead. For all we know, they could have met in a convenience store bathroom and had a five-minute conversation about the Mountain. Paul thought the ink was cool, snapped a picture, and the rest is history. A dead body with a fresh tattoo and a missing Brian. It could work."

"And how do I play into this?"

Ryder looked over at her, considering her alternate role. "You couldn't get the tattoo out of your mind and were convinced that it had to be a key in figuring out who our John Doe was. Your dad already knows that I've talked to you about the cases, but you weren't aware of what the feds had told us up until I got here, so your urgency was warranted in your mind because you wanted to help, but when I filled you in on the feds and what your dad and I discussed this morning, we quickly realized that you were working with old information. It wouldn't be smart of me to just turn around and leave without hearing out your perspective though, since your dad and I suspect the feds are covering this up. Essentially, you didn't really offer more to the case, which is fine because it's not your job to, you were just trying to help, but you were able to help me by giving me a different perspective for an alternate connection for Brian and Paul to have met. That gives me something new to spend my time investigating."

"And ultimately you won't be able to prove the new theory, Rain will deny knowing him, so the only logical thing is that even though the story the feds gave sounds too good to be true, too quick and tidy, you eventually admit that they must have been right and perhaps their perspective from the outside was what you guys needed all along. You don't like it, but you can't poke holes in it, so eventually you are forced to accept their truth."

Ryder sat down again on an exhale. He looked over at Lillian solemnly. "All this for an if. *If* time travel is real." He shook his head. He looked toward her office. "I still can't wrap my head around it."

She sat forward on her couch. "Look at it this way. You can't use a time portal to explain this case, so you have to ignore the possibility and continue investigating as if you never came here. You let my dad direct the investigation and eventually, it will have to be accepted as the feds have presented and closed, or he doesn't accept, and the cases run cold. Or," she paused at the sound of a car door outside, "you could realize that my theory really can't be right because time travel isn't possible, which means that you wouldn't be lying or withholding any information and you get to continue doing work the way you always would."

"You'd let your theory go, just like that?"

"I didn't say *I* would. I said *you* could."

Ryder considered how conveniently the time portal tied everything together, but he wasn't altogether convinced it was *the* answer. Could he really accept that time travel was real? Lillian was right, if he didn't accept it was real, he wouldn't be hiding anything from Bill and could keep on like any other day. He stood up to open the door for Bill when he heard footsteps crossing the small porch.

"Oh. Hey," Ryder said surprised that it wasn't Bill on the other side of the door. He moved out of the way to allow August to pass by.

"Hey yourself," a confused August said as he entered.

"August," Lillian said equally surprised, getting up from the couch. "Hi. I didn't realize you'd be back already."

August looked from her to Ryder, who had closed the door and crossed the room. "So I gather… Someone want to tell me what's going on? What's he doing here?" August asked turning to direct the question to Lillian, but before she could answer, turned back to Ryder, "Where's your car, Ryder?"

"Not here," Ryder said evasively, smirking slightly as he leaned against the wall.

"This isn't what I'm sure you think it looks like," Lillian said wearily. "Ryder and I were just going over the cases."

"Really? Because to me it looks like the guy that has historically used situations to his advantage has used the fact that I was out of town and not expected back until tonight to get you alone, at your house, with no car for him to leave, and this early in the morning. You look exhausted, he looks smug as hell. And last I checked, you weren't an officer of the law, so how *should* I look at this situation?"

"With trust that I've already told you that I'm seeing you."

"And you think that matters to someone like him?"

"He didn't even know you were out of town," she said, her voice strained.

"He's a cop, Lillian. One that can't wait for the next opportunity to get you alone and prey on your vulnerabilities." August looked at Ryder. "How long was it after you realized I was gone that you found yourself here?"

"Just finding out now, buddy, but you keep carrying on the way you are, and I don't think opportunity is going to be much of an obstacle. Not trusting your girl and jealousy aren't good building blocks for a relationship," he said, exaggeratingly whispering the last sentence of advice.

"It's you I don't trust."

"Stop it. Both of you. You aren't going to stand here in my living room and fight about me when there's nothing to fight over. August. I've told you that I'm with you. If you can't trust that I mean it when I say it, then maybe I was wrong about who I thought you were. Ryder knows we're together. He hasn't made a move. He's been respectful of my decision to be with you, even though I know that can't be easy."

"He sure acted respectful the other day," August said, sarcastically, leaving the reminder of Ryder's behavior at the nurse's station in the room between them all.

"And he's apologized for that. But the fact remains, Ryder will always be somewhat a part of my life. He works directly with my dad, in this community. We have to be able to get along."

"No, Lillian, you don't. You just don't want to let him go."

Another knock on the door had them all turning.

"That's probably my ride," Ryder said, looking at them both. "Sounds like I should get out of your hair anyway."

"No, I should be going. I wouldn't want to interrupt important work on a case that you're apparently a part of," August said to Lillian.

"August, just stay, please. This is just a misunderstanding."

August strode to the door and opened it to Bill on the other side.

"Hi, August. Is my deputy in there?"

"Hey, Sheriff. Yeah, he's here." August's voice rang with agitation.

"Don't let me run you off," Bill said as they switched sides of the threshold. "I'm just picking up Ryder and we'll be out of here."

"It's no big deal, I have things to do," August said and cleared the porch, getting into his truck to drive off.

"Hmm," Bill murmured as he looked from August's retreating truck and into the room. "I'm guessing I missed something." When both Lillian and Ryder started explaining at the same time, he held up a hand. "I don't need to know. It's not my business what happens between you three."

"Dad," Lillian started. "It's not –"

"It's not my business," he repeated. "Now," he looked at Ryder. "We have work to do. Are you ready?"

"Yeah," he sighed, running his hand through his hair and clenching his fist at the back of his head. "Can you give me a minute?"

Bill looked from Lillian and then sternly to Ryder. "You have one minute. Not a second more. Lillian. We'll talk later." He turned and shut the door behind him.

Lillian sat on the arm of the couch. "Well, any of that could have gone better. Now I feel like I'm in trouble all over the place."

"Don't," he said softly. "You did nothing wrong. You'll talk it over with August and clear the air. He's just confused by my being here. You'll tell him and he'll see reason."

"I shouldn't have to keep defending myself to him."

"No, you shouldn't. He should see you. That you aren't capable of what he's thinking. You're too good of a person. But he doesn't know you yet. And you don't know him." He brushed the hair from the side of her face, letting it fall behind her shoulder, letting his finger trace along her jaw.

"Ryder," she whispered, "please don't."

"Don't what?"

"This. Don't be nice like this."

"Why?"

"It confuses me."

He raised an eyebrow.

"You want me to go reconcile with August? Why would you suggest that?"

Ryder smiled. "Because I want you to be happy, and for whatever reason, you think he's where your happiness is. Until you figure it out for yourself, I'm not going to get in the way."

The horn honked and they both looked in the direction of Bill and the truck.

"Guess my time's up," Ryder said, smiling mischievously. "Gotta go." But he didn't move away. "What the hell. The good guy only gets so far," he said, and before she had time to think, he leaned in and stole a kiss, her eyes shocked wide by the pulse between them. "Now, I'm leaving," he said and walked out the door before she could tell him all the reasons he shouldn't have done what he did. But if she was determined to choose August over him, he was going to give her a reason to keep him in the running.

SIXTY

-Lillian-

Lillian had had enough excitement for the day, and the day had barely started. She considered going back to sleep, starting over on a second chance, but knew that even though she'd been up all night researching, thoughts of August being upset with her would just keep her awake. Plus, she had to work in a few hours, so she decided on a shower instead. She ran the water as hot as it would go, until the bathroom was nice and steamy, and then she cooled it slightly to get in and let the water fall from above. She closed her eyes and imagined it was the waterfall at the top of the river. The fall was so deafening, even she wouldn't be able to hear her thoughts.

But this wasn't the waterfall at the river, this was the shower in her bathroom, and while the water pressure was good, it wasn't waterfall good. Why did August get to leave and be mad about something that didn't happen? Why did she have to be left with the feeling that she had done something wrong when she hadn't? Why was it now up to her to chase him down and clear her name and prove that he was who she wanted?

Again.

He was the one who misconstrued the situation to his own fears, not her. He should be the one to come back and tell *her* that he was wrong, that he believed her and that she was who he wanted to be with.

But she hadn't walked into his house with another woman that had made her intentions with him very clear, and if she had, she knew she'd probably react the same way.

She sighed, turning off the water to get out of the shower, drying off with the nearby towel before wrapping her hair up and grabbing her robe. Ryder was exciting and unpredictable, but the pull when she was with August was unexplainable. She needed him to understand. Despite feeling like the ball was always falling out of her hands and being frustrated that she had to know all the right moves, all the ins and outs of a game she never asked to be picked for, every cell in her body needed August to understand that she wanted him on her team.

She wiped the mirror with her hand, picked up her brush and stared at the reflection before her.

She imagined Lana would tell her to let August go if he wasn't willing to believe her when she told him her side. She'd push her to go for Ryder. Ryder's advice to make things right with August had surprised her, but then he'd kissed her, so where did he really stand? Her mom would tell her to follow her heart. Right now, even though she was still a little mad that August didn't believe her, her heart wanted to drive out to his house and make things right. She looked at the clock on her wall and calculated. She had enough time to get there and back in time for work, but not enough to really discuss anything.

She grabbed her towel again and squeezed out her freshly brushed hair as she walked through the house searching for her phone. She'd rather see him in person to talk, but a phone call now to hopefully clear the air was better than waiting until after her shift while both of them overthought, potentially making things worse.

She stood in the living room, having already looked in the other few places she'd been that morning. No phone.

"Well, this is great," she sighed, wondering where she should look next. Maybe her phone got mindlessly thrown in the box of papers Ryder had cleared away, or maybe she should go through her laundry basket...

Her thoughts disintegrated at the knock on the door across the room.

"Oh, August, hi," she smiled, surprised but also nervous to see him on her porch. "I was just going to call you."

"Hey," was all he said, his gaze penetrating as she held the door for him.

"Um," she said with slight disappointment, realizing that he was still, understandably, upset from earlier. "Do you want to come in? We can talk."

She stepped back to let him pass into her living room, closing the door behind him softly. The butterflies in her stomach were in a frenzy. This was what she wanted, to talk to him face to face, and *he* came to *her*. This was everything! But the intensity she could feel flowing freely from him was making the room feel much too small, and now that he was inside, he stood across from her and wouldn't look at her. Did he come to tell her that it was over? That it wasn't worth his time to feel like Ryder was a threat? She walked to the arm of the couch to perch, hoping she appeared more at ease than her electrified insides wanted to project.

"Lillian..." he started, glancing at her, the look abrupt before immediately turning away again on a breath and a muffled swear.

The slow ripping of her heart was excruciating as she watched him trying to figure out the words to say it was over. It was more painful to sit calmly and look like she wasn't breaking in front of him.

"I can't –" he started gruffly.

"Please," she interrupted, catching a slight flicker of surprise in his brief glimpse at her. "Before you say what you came here to do, I want to apologize for earlier. I'm not apologizing for what you think happened here, because it didn't, but I do want to apologize for not letting you know Ryder would be here. I wasn't trying to be secretive while you were away. We really were going over case information. I'm connected, and we were just trying to figure out other possible connections now that the feds have been here and are trying to wrap things up. My dad and Ryder both think it's too neat and fast since they've barely been here and have already figured out what the department couldn't and—"

"Lillian," August held up a hand to stop her rambling.

She took a breath. "I just need you to know that nothing happened before you break up with me."

He looked at her ceiling then back to her. "Did you read any of my messages?"

"Huh?"

"I texted you."

"I've lost my phone," she told him, holding up her hands and looking around the room like it would magically appear.

"And now I'm here to end it all…"

"Just because you've already made up your mind and come to terms with it, doesn't mean that I have." She shifted her position slightly on the arm of the couch and he looked away again.

"I texted you," he started again, "because I wanted to talk in person."

"But now you won't even look at me," she said, hurt that she'd told him how she felt, and it hadn't made a difference.

He dropped his head, and she heard a slight chuckle, but when he finally looked at her there was no laughter in his eyes, just the same intensity as before. "I can't look at you," he said, confirming her heart's plummet.

He moved to within arm's reach of her, which had the butterflies in full fury despite her wanting him to just leave so she could be done with this and cry or scream it all out of her system before she had to be at work. He reached toward her and delicately lifted the silky rope tied around her waist.

"I can't look at you," he said again, his voice rough, "because even if I didn't already know how amazing you look under this flimsy swatch of silk, one little tug of this—" He twisted it slowly around his hand, his eyes steadily on her own, and she could feel the material start to slide. "And there would be nothing left between us. I came here to tell you what an idiot I had been, and to beg you to forgive me for being a stupid man … but instead you open the door wearing the whisper of a seductress, apparently without even realizing how tantalizing you look, which is even sexier and tormenting all at the same time. All I can think of is giving this a little tug, wondering which would fall faster, that light as air fabric or me to my knees begging you to take me as the fool that I am and do with me what you will."

She had chosen this robe specifically because she'd wanted to feel exactly as he was describing her now. In her surprise to see him, she'd forgotten she'd been wearing hardly anything at all, and the realization that she had misread his intentions hit her like a bolt of lightning.

She smiled slowly, tilting her head slightly, moving her knee to open the fabric marginally more and watching him watch her as she did. She leaned back just enough that the belt he was still holding slipped, its grip barely a whisper. She tilted her head, tauntingly. "What's keeping y– "

The belt was gone in a whip. It floated to the floor, quickly followed by the rest of the robe as she shimmied out. He leaned into her, kissing and caressing as she wrapped her legs around him to keep from falling off the armrest she was balancing on. Her heart, which had felt like it would shatter moments before, raced to keep up with this new exhilarating rhythm. She squeezed her legs tighter around him as he pulled her against him. He lifted her as if she weighed nothing and carried her through the living room toward the hall.

"Where?"

"That way," she told him between breaths, pointing behind her.

He placed her on the bed and she moved to her knees to help lift his shirt over his head, then held onto him as he kissed her and stepped out of his pants. When he was finally as free from his clothes as she was, he plunged them forward onto the bed, each recklessly devouring the other.

They rolled over the covers, taking turns fulfilling their own desperations and desires, each seeking their own validation. When it was over, they lay in a tangle of rapid hearts and deep breaths.

"So," she finally managed, "you weren't coming to break up."

"No," he breathed. She turned her head toward him. He was also on his back, eyes closed and smiling lazily up at the ceiling. "But, I'm trying to figure out the next fight we can have."

She laughed when he turned to look at her, giving her a devilish smile before grabbing her and rolling her on top of him. "It doesn't always have to be make-up sex you know."

"Why not? You're full of fire when you're upset."

"Sure, rambling incoherently is so fiery."

"It wasn't incoherent…" He paused when she raised her disbelieving eyebrows at him. "Maybe it was, I don't know. It was hard to listen anyway. I was just praying your robe didn't slip while you were passionately giving your speech."

"You were praying it *wouldn't* slip?" she laughed.

"Wouldn't… would… either way," he told her, reaching up to pull her down for a kiss. "Wouldn't meant torture for the way I had acted earlier, for leaving without listening. It was my punishment that I had to imagine what was within reach but not allowed to touch. Every movement you made was a new fantasy. Would the shoulder slip down around your arm, exposing your bare skin that I wouldn't be able to caress?" he said as he brushed his hand ever so lightly along her shoulder and down the side of her arm, brushing the hair back as he did. His finger traced a line just above her breast to the center of her chest, where he planted a kiss. "Would all of this be uncovered, hinting at what was beneath?" He kissed along her collarbone in the area of imagined exposure. "Or," he whispered against her skin, teasing his hand along her thigh as she straddled him, "would you move your leg just right, your robe shifting, opening a door that I couldn't enter." His hand stroked along her hip, up her waist, and gently took her breast. "I could see you before me, but I wasn't allowed to touch." His thumb brushed along her sensitive skin, and she closed her eyes, sighing as she did.

"This still sounds like you wanted it to slip…" Her words caught as she felt the warmth of his breath and the nip of his teeth.

"What can I say…" he admitted. He lifted her and shifted himself inside, both of them moving fluidly, this time taking their time to explore until they each had their fill rather than the onslaught of necessity moments before.

"I have to get ready for work," she mumbled against his chest later, content to stay wrapped in his arms all day.

"Aren't you the boss?" he asked the top of her head.

"Yes, but I'm on tables today." She propped herself onto her elbows to look down at him. "You could come have dinner."

"And eat all by myself? All alone?"

She chuckled at the idea of him having any problem with eating alone. "It's a Tuesday. We probably won't be too busy. I could probably join you."

"Are you asking me on a date?"

"Maybe…" She smiled. "Although not a very exciting one."

"I'll be there. One condition though."

"What's that?" she asked as she headed to the bathroom to shower, looking back and smiling at seeing him propped comfortably on her bed. "You wear something less revealing than that robe."

"You didn't have a problem with me wearing it earlier."

"Obviously I did."

"Hmm," she said, stopping at the door. "I didn't see that as a problem."

SIXTY-ONE

-Lillian-

August had shown up after the dinner rush, when nearly everyone had cleared out of Wisteria. Lillian had been able to sit with him for dinner, checking on her few tables until they all cleared out, and it was just her and August left. She could hear the bustle of the kitchen crew cleaning, and an occasional bark of laughter would ripple to the front. Lana was usually off in the evenings and this crew was a little more raucous than Lana would tolerate, but they were efficient and having fun, which made Lillian's boss's heart happy.

"Hey boss lady," Cole, the cook tonight, poked his head through the kitchen window. "You guys want dessert?"

Her stomach was ready to burst, objecting to her still picking at the sweet potato fries left on the table. "Nothing for me," she called back. She looked to August. "Do you want something?" When he sat back and held up a hand that he couldn't either, she called back to the kitchen. "Nope, nothing tonight."

Cole reappeared. "Nothing? We still have brownies. I make a rockin' brownie sundae." He looked at August. "Nothing for you, my man?"

August shook his head. "I couldn't eat another bite."

"Your loss," his voice called from beyond their sight.

"What time are you done tonight?"

Lillian checked her watch. "We'll start shutting things down a little before closing and be out of here in about two hours or so."

He reached over and entwined his fingers with her own. "You want me to come over?"

She smiled, immediately wanting to say yes, but she shook her head instead. "I open tomorrow. It's straight home and into bed for me."

"I'm fully capable of keeping my hands to myself and letting you sleep, you know… probably."

They both looked over when the door to the diner opened and Simon walked through.

"Hey, Simon," Lillian called, getting up to greet him. She saw him look past her to August in the booth she'd just left, a flicker of recognition and then confusion quickly following then passing.

"Hi, Lillian. Is your dad here yet? He asked me to meet him," he told her, looking over at August again, who had gotten up from the booth to follow her to the counter. "Did he ask you to meet, too?" he asked August.

"No, I was just having dinner," August said. "Any luck with the search?"

Simon looked from August to Lillian and back again. "I guess you haven't heard," he said solemnly. "The feds recovered Brian's body. Well, what was left of him. Bear attack," he added. He turned to Lillian. "I figured the sheriff would have told you."

"He's been preoccupied today," she told him, adding tentatively, "but Ryder had mentioned you were still looking."

"Yeah," he sighed. "There's just nothing out there to find."

He sounded defeated, and why wouldn't he be? He'd been heading the search and rescue for Brian since day one.

"Do you want anything to drink, to eat, while you wait?"

"The burger's a good choice," August suggested, then leaned toward Lillian, placing his hand lightly on her back. "I'm going to get out of here. Text me when you're home?" She nodded and smiled as he told them goodbye.

"A bacon burger and fries would be great," Simon told her, and she wrote it on her slip and clipped it to the order turnstile, dinging the bell as she did. She could have just called it through to Cole, but thinking about how many orders the little gadget had seen always made her smile.

"What would you like to drink with that?"

"A water'll be fine."

She poured him a cup, then topped it off when he immediately drank half the glass.

"Thank you. I ran out of water a while back. I knew it was time to head out, but I just kept thinking maybe we'll find something around this boulder or down the next trail. But even the dogs were done."

"I'm sorry. I know how disappointing that has to be."

"Yeah, and now I have to tell your dad that I'm calling off the search altogether."

"He'll understand."

"I hope." He took another drink of his water, carefully setting the glass back into the ring of water that had already formed on the counter, studying it to make sure it lined up perfectly. "So… you and August?"

"Yes," she said gently.

He nodded then looked up at her and smiled. "That's better than Ryder at least."

She smiled back, wondering if Ryder had said something, or if it was just a general statement. She didn't have long to think about it before the bell dinged behind her.

"Order," the voice called from the kitchen.

She turned to retrieve his burger and set it down in front of him.

"Thanks," he told her. "And sorry," he blurted. "It's none of my business."

"It's okay, Simon. It's not a secret that I'm seeing August. It's just new. Do you need anything for your meal?"

"No, thank you, this is great," he told her, then turned to look at the door when it opened behind him. "Hey, Sheriff."

"Simon. Hey, Lillian," he said, leaning down to give her a hug when she came around the counter.

"Hi, Dad. You want any food, or will you get in trouble with Mom?"

"She said I was on my own this late. I'll do the same," he said, nodding to Simon's plate. "That looks like something your mom would tell me not to have."

She chuckled and wrote it on the slip, turning, then ringing the bell.

"You want a water, too?" she asked him.

"Yeah, water's good. Thanks, kiddo."

"No problem." She filled his glass and topped off Simon's again. "I know you guys have some talking to do. I'm going to clear that table, but let me know if you need me."

"Thanks," Simon told her, waiting for her to walk away before turning to talk with her dad.

She could hear him updating Bill on the search, or lack thereof. He was recommending they call off the search entirely by the time the food was ready and she was setting it on the counter.

"I know you think the feds are trying to wrap this up too fast, but maybe we just have to face the truth. Brian's gone. We weren't the ones to find him, but now we know."

Bill shook his head. "Why won't they tell us where to find the den? What difference does it make if we go and check it out ourselves?"

"I don't have an answer to that, sir, but—" He paused, taking a breath and exhaling slowly. "I'm not taking a team back in."

Bill studied his deputy. "This was your lead."

Simon nodded. "Yes, sir, and I've decided we've done all we can. I believe the feds found his body, or parts of it at least." He looked over at Lillian. "Sorry, Lillian."

She waved a hand. "I've heard worse."

He turned back to Bill. "I believe the DNA analysis will show that the remains belonged to Brian."

"You're willing to halt the search until we get the DNA back?"

"Yes, sir. I know you wanted a second opinion, but I believe the analysis the feds have already provided."

"And if the second analysis shows that it isn't Brian?"

"Then I will take responsibility for the early search termination and will be the first one back in the woods searching for him."

"Okay," Bill told him and took a bite of his burger.

"Okay?"

"Okay." Bill said again. "You are an exceptional deputy capable of making decisions based on the information available to you. You present a valid argument. I agree with your decision to withdraw."

"But you disagree with the feds..."

"I'm questioning them. I haven't been able to disprove them despite my gut telling me there's something I'm missing. That doesn't mean I should ignore the advice of a deputy and put the department at odds with the feds as well."

Simon took another bite of his burger, chewing slowly. "Was the examiner able to get samples before cremation?"

"He had already verified the identity of Wade, but he wasn't allowed near the John Doe after the feds came into the picture. I had hoped he had his samples from the initial autopsy, but the feds seized his lab completely."

"So, your secondary DNA analysis for Brian? What are you analyzing if you don't have samples?"

"We have the cremation remains. The feds are handling the remains for our John Doe, so we may never have verified answers if the victim's family doesn't consent to further testing. But they allowed us to deliver the remains to Brian's family. Rich took a fragment of bone to test and verify, but the feds had already notified the family, so if it's not a match..." He sighed. "If it's not a match, we get to be the ones to break the news to the family that the information they were given was wrong, and we still don't have answers for them."

They ate in silence for a few moments. "I know you feel like something else is going on, that the feds are hiding something, but for Brian's family's sake, I hope we can leave them with closure and to grieve." Simon looked for Lillian, who'd been rolling silverware quietly next to them, listening to their conversation. "Can I get the ticket?" he asked, taking out his wallet.

She held up a hand. "This one's on me, as a thank you for all you did for Brian."

He took a few bills out of his wallet and slid them under the side of his plate. "At least let me tip," he said when she started to object.

"Brownie for the road?" Cole's head appearing in the kitchen window asked again.

Bill looked startled by his sudden appearance; Simon looked intrigued.

"Why don't you box them one each for the road?" Lillian laughed.

"All right!" Cole cheered from out of sight but popped back a moment later with two boxes. "Here you go, boss lady. Enjoy, my mans."

"Thank you for the dinner, Lillian." Simon turned to the sheriff. "I'll see you in the morning." He waved his brownie box in a slight bob then headed out the door.

Lillian cleared away his place and wiped down the counter. She knew the "missing piece" her dad was searching for, or at least the theory she had that could explain all the questions—no matter how far-fetched she still considered it herself—but she knew it was a theory he would never accept. She didn't want to lie to her dad, but maybe a different theory based on truth could help him put aside the feeling in his gut.

"I've been doing a lot of thinking since Ryder was over this morning," she started. "There's something I haven't told you, that might help shed light on Brian."

Her dad raised his eyebrows. "What might that be? And why didn't you share it with Ryder earlier?"

"Like I said, this came to me after he had left. You remember I talked to Rain but couldn't tell you what was said?"

"Of course. Are you going to tell me now?"

She nodded. "Rain told me the feds advised her to change her story, to say she never went into the Mountain."

Bill steepled his fingers above his plate, watching his daughter quizzically. "The feds told us they determined through expert analysis that she never went in. How does this help shed light on Brian?"

"If the feds asked her to say she didn't go into the Mountain, it removes further hype and hysteria where the Mountain is concerned."

"Okay?" Bill wondered aloud when she paused.

"You asked Simon why they wouldn't share the location of the den."

"Right. There's no reason not to tell us where it is so we can investigate ourselves, or at the very least, be able to mark it as unsafe territory."

"But what if the reason they didn't give you the location is because they don't want you to investigate?"

"You mean, if the den is in the Mountain." Bill nodded to himself, considering this new option. "We assumed the feds had convinced Rain to agree by some form or fashion, and *not* that their expert had analyzed her trauma response. I'll admit that all I focused on was that they were covering something up. Why the most obvious thing they could be covering up didn't come immediately to mind, I don't know, but the Mountain didn't feel like what they were hiding. But ... it has always been a very secretive place ... I suppose they could simply have wanted to downplay the involvement of these cases with the Mountain. After all, the more stories associated with it, the more people flock to discover the mystery." He looked up at his daughter. "And Brian is still dead."

She nodded solemnly.

"Rich's results will confirm the feds' because the only thing they lied about is what side of the boundary line the body was found on." He let out a deep breath as the realizations kept coming. "And if Rich's results do come back as Brian, then we have to believe that Paul Slater is the unidentified John Doe like the feds said."

"So, you aren't going to ask his family to verify DNA?"

"If Rich's tests come back with a DNA match to Brian, there doesn't seem to be any reason to bother a grieving family for another DNA test when the feds already ran one." He scooted his nearly empty plate out of the way and tapped the counter. "All this just to keep the Mountain out of the case. Sort of makes you wonder why."

"I think the why is pretty obvious."

He raised his eyebrows in question but didn't ask.

"It's dangerous. Everyone dies that goes in. Rain got lucky somehow. But all the government wants is for people to stay out or they'll get hurt."

Bill patted his daughter's hand. "Even you don't believe the only thing they care about is keeping the public safe from steep cliffs."

"And bears."

The tilt of his head and raised eyebrow showed his skepticism of her response. "I know you wonder what used to go on in there."

"You're right, and despite all the research I've been doing lately, I'm coming up with zilch, so if you come up with anything, feel free to share."

"You've given me some things to consider," he told her as he stood and took out his wallet.

"Dad, don't worry about it," she told him.

"You're running a business. In case you don't remember from your years at college, in order to be successful, you have to sell your product."

"Right, but you're my dad."

"Which is why you'll take extra," he told her, handing her a hundred.

"This is way more than the food."

"Good. Then you'll have plenty left for you." He came around to meet her for a hug. "Don't even think about trying to sneak that back to me. Love you."

"Love you, too. Tell Mom, too."

"I will. Be safe closing up tonight."

"Don't worry, I will."

He stopped at the door. "Did you get things figured out from this morning?"

"I hope so."

He nodded. "Take care of you."

"I am, Dad."

He smiled again, waved, and left the building.

She cleared away his plate and wiped off his counter, moving to start putting chairs away since they weren't likely to get many more stragglers in the short time before they closed. She hoped that the seeds she had planted were enough to satisfy her dad. If she was on the right track, and if the federal agents also knew, their coverup would be airtight. No matter how long her dad's gut told him something wasn't right, it looked like there would be nothing to find. She hated the thought of him being dissatisfied with the case closure, wishing she could share what she thought and help bring him peace. But … she knew her dad. She knew he would immediately dismiss time travel as a possibility. Who wouldn't? He'd tell her the same thing Ryder had, that the articles are coincidental and not enough proof. Honestly, she was surprised Ryder had come around as much as he had in the end, but she just couldn't see her dad doing the same. Knowing there would be nothing to find to feed his gut and that he'd eventually have to let it go and move on to something else would have to be enough.

For him.

She needed to know. She needed to know if what she believed was possible. Could the Mountain be a doorway to another time? Rain had possibly walked through it, but she didn't know anything, and even though she was hysterical about what had happened while she was on the Mountain, Lillian doubted that even Rain would believe that she had traveled backward through time.

But maybe someone did know. Maybe someone had already used it and was here, hiding in plain sight. She needed to figure out who had taken Rain and held her in the dark room. If she could find that person, they could give her answers. She stopped flipping the chair to consider what type of person that would be.

Did she want to meet with someone capable of holding someone captive?

If they had answers, did she really have a choice?

SIXTY-TWO

-Lillian-

Lillian sat at her desk in her Wisteria office and stared at the text messages from Ryder.

I need to see you.

I can't stop thinking… I just need to see you.

She hadn't seen or talked to him in two days… not since he'd kissed her right after telling her to make things right with August.

I don't think that's the best idea…

She and August were back to good, and she didn't want to risk messing things up again. She hadn't intended for things to be taken out of context the last time she was with Ryder, but she was fairly certain she wasn't going to get another chance if things were misunderstood again.

Lilly, please.

A few seconds later a second text followed.

I delivered Wade's remains today.

She hunched in her seat at the finality of their friend's life. It was finished. Someone she'd known for nearly fifteen years, finished on this earth, simplified down to a box of ashes delivered to his family. She thought about Ryder, who'd known him since they were kids, like brothers up until he died. What was he feeling now?

August's words lingered in the back of her mind, calling Ryder opportunistic and taking advantage of a vulnerable situation. It was no secret that Ryder wanted her, but was that what he was doing now? Or was August seeing something that wasn't there because he was jealous of their history and the threat it could pose?

Wasn't this exactly the time to ignore everything else and be there for a friend, no matter what was going on or what other people thought?

I could really use a friend to talk to.

It was as if he could read her mind.

She pictured him the night he stood in her kitchen, looking lost, the night he told her Wade was dead. She closed her eyes and sighed, opening them again to text him back.

Okay. I'm finishing up at work now. Where are you?

My house.

She hesitated to respond, wanting to squash the part of her that was worrying about going to another man's house while she was seeing August.

But I can meet you at yours if you're uncomfortable coming here.

Send me your address.

She was an adult, after all, and could have a meeting with another man without it meaning something more than that she was there for a friend. She'd tell August, out of respect for their relationship, that she was meeting with Ryder, but she wasn't going to be in a relationship where she feared what the other person thought of every decision she made.

She mapped the address that he sent, surprised to find that he lived on the outskirts. She figured him for a middle-of-the-action kind of guy, an urban house, or loft even, within walking distance of anything he wanted, not removed and at the back of what looked like a rural neighborhood.

She shut down her computer and packed her purse, staring at the phone, knowing she needed to let August know that she was going to see Ryder. She found his name and pressed the button to call, knowing a text was her way of chickening out. The phone rang and she twirled her hair around her finger, willing her nerves to stop overreacting. Voicemail connected and she felt a minute sigh of relief.

"Hey August, it's Lillian … which you know, because it showed my name on your caller ID. Um, just wanted to see what you were up to later today. I have some running around to do after work but should be available tonight if you want to do something. I talked to Ryder today and he's pretty down about Wade; he delivered the ashes to the family and needs a friend to talk to. The three of us used to be really close … I'm going to go make sure he's okay. So, if you want to get together later, just let me know. You can call me back or text is fine. I'll have my phone. Otherwise, maybe we can do something this weekend when I'm off work. Okay. I'll talk to you later. Bye."

She listened to the playback of the message, considered deleting the whole thing and starting over, or just deleting it altogether. Instead, she hit the submit button and disconnected, dropping the phone on the desk.

"Stop punishing yourself like you're doing something wrong," she said to the air. "You're just going to be a friend. It's not like you're going over there to have sex with Ryder."

"But that would be much more entertaining."

"Damn it, Lana," Lillian squealed as her door opened. "How long have you been there?"

"Long enough to hear that terrible voicemail and then the pep talk to follow."

She groaned. "I hate leaving messages."

"I can see why." She sat in the chair across from Lillian. "So, why do you feel you have to check in with August?"

"I wasn't checking in…"

"You're an adult."

"I know."

"You can make your own decisions."

"I did."

"And you don't need to answer to anyone else about them."

"I'm not, well, except to you."

Lana raised an eyebrow. "I don't count. You're not dating me."

"Exactly."

"Does August make you feel like you can't do what you normally would?"

"Of course not."

"Then why did you feel like you had to tell him where you were going?"

"It's about respect. August doesn't trust Ryder, and I'm getting ready to go see him, alone."

"But he trusts you."

"Yes, and I want to keep it that way. By letting him know I'll be seeing Ryder, he won't misunderstand later or think I was keeping it a secret from him."

"And would he do the same for you?"

"There's no reason for him…" She paused. "I would hope that he would do the same, but he's given me no reason to doubt his actions."

"But you have?"

"You know Ryder and I have had our moments."

"So, now you have to document every time you two are together?"

"I don't have to, but … I just don't want to give him the wrong idea."

"Sounds to me like you still have feelings for Ryder, feelings that leave you conflicted enough to tell the current boyfriend that it's not a big deal for you to be around him."

"I'm sure there's a point here."

"I'm just saying, if Ryder causes you this much uncertainty, maybe there's a reason for that."

"The reason Ryder causes me uncertainty is because I'm trying to start a relationship and…"

"And you don't want to get rid of Ryder."

Lillian stared at her friend. "That's what August said, too."

"So, what is it that you won't let go?" When Lillian didn't immediately have an answer for her, Lana added, "Maybe you should think about that, and August, too."

"I want to be with August. I know I do."

"But you would be happy with Ryder, too."

She sighed. "Lana, I'm already confused enough as it is. Did you need something?"

"Ouch. Direct shot. No, I just wanted to see how things were going in your world since you've been avoiding me."

"I haven't been avoiding you."

"Yes, as soon as you hooked up with Captain Hotness, it's been crickets for dear old Lana. And I thought we were friends."

"Very funny. But I do have to go."

"Right, Ryder's house. But no sex."

"Correct, there will be no sex."

"Maybe there should be."

"Lana, I'm not having sex with Ryder."

"Right, right. You're with August. I get that. But *maybe* you can't let go of Ryder because you wonder what could be. He surprised you already by having this whole other side to him, and he's apparently an expert in passionate make out sessions. Maybe you need to see which man is better in this specific area."

"No," she laughed. "Ryder is an expert because he has what experts have … a lot of experience. I'm not *sampling* him just so you can have all the details. If you want to know how good he is in bed, you go find out."

"Nah, he's hung up on you. I think that door's closed to all women. At least for a little while."

"You don't even talk to Ryder."

"Just because I don't know him, doesn't mean I don't know people who know him. Word on the street is that he's changed."

"Word on the street, huh?"

"Oh, yeah. It's just bouncing around out there."

"I'm sure," Lillian said dryly. "I do have to go though, so unless you have any other unsolicited advice…"

"Fine, fine, but one of these days you'll realize all of the invaluable guidance I have to offer."

"Mmhmm. Bye, Lana."

SIXTY-THREE

-Lillian-

The drive to Ryder's took her out of town into a peaceful, roomy neighborhood. No peering into the neighbor's yard on either side just by stepping onto the back porch, as it was with her home. People were mowing or tending to their landscaping, offering an absent-minded wave toward her car as she meandered through. The GPS told her to continue when the road changed to a wide, hard-packed gravel lane. She followed the curve of the road, around an orchard, and into a clearing of beautifully maintained grass. The stunning home before her gave strong antebellum vibes.

Certain she was in the wrong place, she parked the car along the circle in front of the house and checked the address. The GPS congratulated her on arriving at her destination. She looked back at the house. There was absolutely no way Ryder lived in this Southern-style gem. As she was about to call him and admit how turned around she'd gotten, he strolled out of the front door and waved to the car. He sat on the top step, his arms dangling comfortably between his legs as he waited for her.

"This is not your house," she called to him.

He looked at the columns and expansive porch surrounding him. "That's what I said, but everyone keeps telling me it is."

She climbed the steps and sat beside him, looking out onto the yard. "Wow," she breathed. "That's an amazing view."

The road that brought her in curved out and around, through one side of the orchard. That much she had noticed. What she hadn't seen from the drive was the extent of the orchard: rows and rows of perfectly lined trees dappled the grass for as far as she could see. There were several acres of cleared, vibrant green grass to stroll through before reaching the orchard. Pavers lined with blooming flowers made a pathway around the house, enticing her to follow and see what beauty lay beyond.

"How does a deputy," she turned to look at him, "with a reputation of being a party boy—don't give me that look—wind up living in a place like this? What do you grow over there?" she asked him, nodding at the precise trees.

"Apples." His gaze trailed from the orchard to his feet on the step below them. "It's been three years since I moved in full-time, and it still feels weird." He glanced at her. "I moved in right around when you came home." He looked toward the orchard, not needing a response. "Wade and I used to play out here when we were little. His dad worked the trees. I had to stay with my grandparents during the summer because my parents were always away. Wade thought I was some spoiled rich kid; I thought he was an ungrateful prick."

"Ungrateful?"

"Wade didn't see the time spent with his dad the same as I did. To me, he got to spend all day with his dad, climbing trees of all things, while mine was states or countries away, and even when he was home, was never really present. All Wade saw was that he *had* to go to work with him every day." He looked at her and smiled. "After the first week of glaring at each other at every opportunity, somehow we wound up fighting over who was allowed to swim in the creek." He motioned behind them where she imagined the creek wound. "I told him it was my grandparents' land, so the creek was mine to swim in. He said I hadn't earned it and that I could go inside to cool off and he couldn't. He had a point, but if I went inside my grandma would find work for me to do, so I was always outside." He smiled at the memory. "I don't remember which of us threw the first punch, but at the end of it we were both bruised, scraped, soaked, and best friends."

"How did I never hear how you met?" she asked, leaning her head against her fist to look at him.

"For one," he said and flashed his signature smile, "I had other things on my mind than talking about Wade. Two, neither Wade nor I wanted to admit who we were. He was the son of an apple picker, which, in his younger years, wasn't something he was proud of."

"And you? What's so embarrassing about all this?"

"I didn't want to be the Apple Prince."

"I don't understand," she said when he didn't explain what the nickname was supposed to mean.

"My mother is a Kingston," he stated as if that explained things further.

She was still at a loss and waited for him to explain further. He sat patiently, expectantly. She'd heard the name before, she knew she had. She wracked her brain as he waited. It was one of the older family names of the town…

"Oh my gosh." She covered her mouth when a giggle slipped through. She turned to all the trees ahead of her and then back to him, another giggle escaping. "Your grandpa is the Apple King! I loved the Apple King when I was a kid!" she gushed. "You would totally be the Apple Prince!" At this point she was laughing completely. "I'm sorry, I know it's not funny," she apologized, blaming her momentary lapse in humor on grief and misplaced emotions, but she remembered back to the silly commercials from when she was young. The commercials and the Apple King were intentionally cheesy, but the right kind of cheesy, that stuck with you years later, but the kind of cheesy that a teenage boy trying to prove he was a man would be embarrassed by.

"Oh, there would be festivals in the fall," she sighed, remembering the hot days but the fun that was had by what felt like the whole town. "I always wanted to be the Cider Sweetie," she laughed again. "I thought all the girls up there on the stage in their dresses were so pretty."

"You never told me that. We went together one year."

"I wasn't about to tell you my childhood wish was to win the apple pageant."

"You would have won."

"Yeah, because apparently I was dating the heir to the apple throne."

He hung his head, but she saw his shoulders rock, and when he turned to look at her, it wasn't just his eyes that were smiling. "You see why I never said anything?"

They both looked back at the rows of trees. She turned back to him. "I was sorry to hear when he passed. If I had realized your connection..."

"It's okay. You and I weren't talking then," he told her. "After he passed away, my grandma tried to keep the business going, but she didn't want to stay here anymore. She'd say it was too much house for her alone, but I think she couldn't be here without him. My dad made comments my whole life about the profitability of converting the orchards into residential or commercial buildings. My grandma knew if it were up to him, everything they'd built would be parceled and sold away." He sighed. "Somehow, she convinced me to move in and watch over the place while she sorted things out. My mom begged her to give it to her, trying to reassure her that she'd keep the dream alive. It was pretty nasty for a while. Grandma offered her a part of the orchard." He turned to look at Lillian. "A test I think, and within a year the land was split, the trees removed, and a new neighborhood was being built."

Lillian pointed toward the lovely neighborhood she'd driven through. Ryder nodded. "Your grandma gave her all that land and she just sold it away?"

"It broke my grandma's heart, but she knew it was better to lose that small parcel than the rest of the orchard and the house, which would have happened if my dad had been allowed to get his hands on this place." He let out a breath. "She rewrote everything into my name, which pissed everyone off, and now..."

"Now you're the Apple King," she giggled.

"We'll keep that to ourselves," he told her seriously, but couldn't keep from smiling.

"Is your grandma still living?"

"Yeah, she gets out here occasionally, tells me the shutters need painting or the porch needs sweeping. She's getting frail, though, and I think it's hard for her to be here without my grandpa."

"It's sweet," she said smiling at him.

He looked at her curiously. "How so?"

"You're keeping their dream alive so she can see it even after her partner in this world has passed on."

"Yeah, well, my dad probably had it right."

"Nah, you won't sell it off. I get the feeling this has always been home to you."

He nodded, watching the trees and all the memories they could tell.

"Wade's death…" He paused. "Wade's death hurts. He was more like a brother to me than just a friend. Sure, we'd go weeks without talking, but any time we got together, it was like no time had passed; we'd pick up right where we left off. It was always easy being Wade's friend … and now—" He looked over at her. "Now we can't ever pick back up. I know he's gone. I helped haul his body out of the water. I delivered his ashes to his family. It's harder than I ever thought it would be to comprehend that he's really, forever, gone. That probably doesn't make any sense, does it?"

"It makes perfect sense," she said softly. "Especially since it was so sudden. Not that any death is easier to cope with than another, but it's not like people knew it was coming, as if he had a terminal illness. At least then you knew how the story was going to end. You'd want to make every moment together count because you knew they were limited. I can't imagine the loss would hurt any less when the time did come, but at least you had some warning. There was none of that with Wade's death, so you have to face it all at once without that opportunity to say goodbye."

He sighed again, looking at the trees that they'd spent so many summers running through. "I thought I'd get Wade involved in the business. He grew up here, too. He knew the way the trees worked, and what they needed. You'd never know it to look at him, but he knew everything about apples. When we were young, he'd pick in the busy season for extra cash, and then when my grandma took over, he'd come help her out whenever he could."

"That would have been really good for you both," she told him, leaning into him and taking his hand in hers. She felt him lean back against her, resting his head on hers. "I'm sorry you didn't get to see it realized."

"Yeah," he said softly, "me, too."

They sat in comfortable silence as they both remembered Wade in their own ways.

"If I bring back the apple festival," Ryder asked after a few moments, "will you compete for Cider Sweetie?"

"Absolutely not."

They were silent a few more moments before he finally spoke again. "Thank you for coming today."

"You're welcome."

"Did you fix things with August?"

"I did," she said. She sat up and scooted slightly, folding her hands back in her lap. "Ryder … I like him, and I don't want to feel guilty for being with him."

He nodded. "And you shouldn't. I want you to be happy."

"Then why did you kiss me?"

"I'm not going to lie that I want you to be happy with me," he laughed. "But I won't kiss you again. I shouldn't have done that, but I acted on impulse."

"And what's to say you won't act on impulse again?"

"I won't. I think you can do better than August, and I'm not going to mess up my chances with you while you figure that out."

"Ryder, don't. You can't just be here waiting for something that may never happen. You could have any woman you want."

"There's only one I want, so your statement is false... for now. I've waited ten years for you, Lillian. I'm prepared to wait for you to figure things out and I'll be here when you do. He's your right now. I'm your forever."

"Ryder," she sighed. "You know we could go back to hating each other tomorrow," she said weakly.

He smiled. "Not a chance. I'm kicking the memory of that stupid teenager out of your brain. You're conflicted about what you knew of him and what you are learning now, so you turn to August instead. You'll come around."

"I see your confidence hasn't changed a bit."

"It gets better with time," he smiled, but then wrinkled his brow. "Which reminds me why I wanted you to come over."

"Wade," she said gently.

"Not exactly," he said standing and reaching down to pull her up. "Come inside. I have something to show you." He looked back over his shoulder. "Don't worry. I'll keep my word and let you come to me."

SIXTY-FOUR

-Lillian-

"Oh!" She breathed out the word when Ryder led her through the double doors of his home and back in time. "Ryder… It's gorgeous." His home was straight out of a magazine, from the chic wallpaper and coordinating paint, the antique spindles along the railings, right down to the fresh flowers in the hallway. "I see your plan is to amaze me with your lovely home," she teased.

"A guy's gotta use all he has," he laughed back. "Really though, I wanted to show you what I found."

He led her through the house, letting her peek into rooms as they passed, each one timeless and unique.

"Your home is wonderful, Ryder," she told him as she followed him into the office.

"Thanks. I have a feeling my grandma has the decorators written into the will."

"Well, she has an amazing vision. I feel like I could look out those windows and see horse-drawn carriages or a sports car. She's blended the old with the new seamlessly."

"She always had a knack for design. I never liked it as a kid, felt too much like a museum. Now though, I guess it's sort of peaceful."

She walked around the office, admiring the shining dark wood of the desk, shelves and tables perfectly accented by the rich tones of the upholstery and pillows. The fireplace wasn't lit, but she could imagine the room was mesmerizing on a dark night with the firelight dancing and the logs crackling.

She joined him at the desk where a stack of papers rested.

He leaned against the desk. "When we talked on Tuesday, I couldn't stop thinking about your time portal theory."

"Oh." Surprise laced the word.

"You thought I would ignore it and move on?"

"Sort of, I guess. It's a pretty outlandish theory to suggest that people can travel through time. It would have been normal to let it go."

"But you haven't…"

"It's my theory. I need to find out if it's real."

"I figured as much." He turned and picked up the stack of papers. "After I was able to talk to Rain and didn't get anywhere by way of her agreeing that she could have known a Paul Slater, I knew there was no way she was going to be able to make that theory stick. I suggested to your dad that Brian must have met him on his own, like you and I discussed, and that we'd have no way of confirming or denying if that really was the case, since, as far as we know, both those people are dead. He didn't like this avenue, but couldn't argue with it, either."

Lillian nodded. "I saw him late on Tuesday night and suggested that the reason the agents were secretive about the den location was because it was beyond the boundary line for the Mountain."

"Yeah, he filled me in yesterday. Good thinking, by the way. I could tell he didn't want to admit that it made sense, but when we got the DNA results back for Brian's secondary analysis, there wasn't much more to debate. I think he's going to officially close the cases."

"How do you feel about that?"

"I think it's for the best. He'd never listen to a theory about a time portal, and this wraps things up neatly in a way he can understand and live with."

"But you're coming around to agreeing with me?"

"Honestly, I wanted to prove you wrong… I'm kidding… sort of. But instead, I found these."

He laid a few of the papers onto the desk so she could see.

"Are these from case files?" she asked him as she read.

"Yeah."

She turned to look at him. "Will you get in trouble for showing me these?"

"Not likely. Look at the dates. These are all beyond cold."

"I'm sure there's something obvious I should be seeing…" she told him uncertainly, "but I'm not sure what that might be."

"Look at cause of death."

She read the page closest to her. "Cardio-Temporal Disruption Syndrome." She looked at Ryder and he nodded to another. "Chrono-Cardiac Hemolysis," she read out loud. "Sounds awful."

He laid more on the desk. "When you start to look, you see a pattern. Just like you told me. These are all years apart, so the likelihood that the same examiner or investigator would notice similarities is slim. Even if they did notice them, there's no telling that they would be able to tie them together because the only similarity is the way they die." He laid the autopsy for John Doe that she believed to be Brian, and then Wade's autopsy report on the desk. "Official cause of death is heart attack. What I know, what the medical examiner told me directly, was that it wasn't just some normal heart attack. Their hearts literally exploded in their chests. What does that?"

"I have no idea. Do these other words mean the same thing?"

"I think they are descriptors used instead because to 'heart attack' just wasn't enough."

She looked at the reports before her and the remaining stack beside him. "And you think all of these could be victims of the Mountain?"

"I do."

"But this just proves that there's something wrong up there…"

"Lillian, if I can't ever convince you to leave August, I'm going to try even harder to convince you to be my partner." He picked up the remaining stack and started separating and assigning a page from his hand to one on the desk.

"You and my dad both," she murmured. "These are found reports," she said, holding two pages in her hand, reading the more thorough descriptions than she had seen in any newspaper article so far.

"I started with the dates and descriptions of the articles you had found, digging out their old case files. The descriptions have several more match points in our case files than were printed in the newspapers."

"I can see that," she said, picking up another pair to compare.

"The dates are too far removed from each other to link them logically, so the individual cases went cold."

"How did you get so many so fast? This amount of research should take days at least."

"You already had several," he said, pointing out some that she had recognized by descriptors. "And a lot of our files have been scanned and keyword coded. All it takes is a few key phrases and you get instant information. Going back further will take more legwork since the really old stuff isn't scanned in yet, but I think this is a decent start to proving your theory."

She sat on the couch nearby, analyzing the reports before her, complete with photos of the deceased, something the newspapers hadn't shared, and if they had, it was never for both the missing and the found in order to compare.

"This is the same person," she said, looking up at Ryder as he came to sit beside her. "This person was found thirteen years before he went missing, and he barely looks any different." She stared at the photo of the young, happy man, smiling from the photo chosen for his missing announcement and compared it to the found photo of the unsmiling photo of very much the same young man. "Thirteen years," she whispered.

"It boggles my brain to think about it," he admitted, "but it's right here. How can we deny this evidence?"

She looked back at the desk and the other examples he'd dug up.

"Thirteen years, Ryder. Wade and Brian were only a week. How…"

"I don't know," he said when she didn't finish her thought.

She stood up to walk, rubbing her arms at the chill she suddenly felt and wishing there was a fire after all. "What's happening in there? How is this possible? Why did Wade and Brian only go back a week, but this one went thirteen years? Why does it change?"

She stared into the fireplace, willing it to offer her insight, but her thoughts stayed just as empty as the perfectly ash-free hearth.

"I know you want those answers. Hell, I do too. But there's one question that is more important than the rest."

She turned to face him, still sitting next to her empty space on the couch. "What's that?"

"Why do they all die?"

SIXTY-FIVE

-August-

"Is everything okay?" August asked after watching Lillian scoot the food he'd prepared around on her plate for a full minute. She'd invited him over and offered to make him dinner, but she'd had a long day at work and seemed drained, so he took over her kitchen and whipped together a simple dinner of baked chicken, homemade mashed potatoes, and roasted corn.

"Of course. Why wouldn't it be?" Lillian asked, glancing up from her plate.

"You've been distracted all afternoon, and you've barely eaten any of your food."

"I've eaten," she said defensively as she looked down at the plate before her.

"Creating a topographically accurate map in your food doesn't count as eating. If you don't like it, I can make you something else. I promise my feelings can handle it," August said.

"What if I'm aspiring to become a cartographer?" she asked, but crinkled her nose. "I'm sorry. I guess I wasn't as hungry as I thought."

August watched as she pushed her plate aside. He reached over and she met his hand, entwining their fingers. "Are you sure everything's alright?"

"Yes. Everything's fine," she told him, placing her elbow on the table so she could rest her chin on her fist.

He watched her across from him, smiling softly, invitingly, but her eyes held a different story, one that was worrisome, a story he didn't feel she'd give up easily.

"How's your outdoor dining project coming along?"

"Very nicely. Fiona thinks we can have everything ready within a month's time."

"That long? Don't you just need to put out some tables and potted plants? That shouldn't take a month to do." He chuckled at her appalled expression. "Sorry … sorry," he said, holding up his napkin as a flag of truce.

"I'm sure this is exactly the reason you gave me Fiona instead of offering yourself as the designer. You must have known, deep down, that you weren't the man for the job."

"I warned you that I defer to the experts. How do you think I found Fiona in the first place? What do you guys have planned?"

"Something a little more permanent than potted plants," she said, crossing her arms in front of her on the table. She leaned forward to discuss plans of large, concrete planters full of overflowing flowers, wrought iron fencing around her patio area and a canopy of twinkling lights that would come on at dusk. She was animated and excitable again, and he couldn't help but smile while she painted her vision in his mind. "Now who's the one distracted?" she asked.

"What do you mean? I was listening to every word you said."

"Then what did I just say?"

"You were telling me that because of the fencing going into the sidewalk in a public area, you'd have to pull permits and get permission first, which will be the longest wait for the project. Once that's all clear, it's smooth sailing from there."

"Well ... all you've proven is that you're as talented as a parrot," she teased. "But how was I supposed to know you were listening when you were smiling and staring away like you weren't paying attention?"

"I was smiling because I was enjoying how happy and expressive you were while talking, and I was staring because you're so beautiful, it's impossible not to stare."

"Oh," she said softly, smiling again and quickly looking away before returning her gaze to his. "I guess I have had some things on my mind."

"Your patio project doesn't feel like what you seemed to be chewing on earlier," he mentioned cautiously.

"Other than dinner?"

He knew she meant it to be lighthearted, but he watched the twinkle fade from her eyes as if a veil had been lowered. The voice in his head told him to let her keep whatever it was that she wanted to herself, but he didn't always do what he knew he should.

"Did something happen yesterday... when you went to Ryder's?"

He watched as she pulled her hands into her lap. "I wondered if you'd need to know," she said neutrally, not looking at him until the words were on the table between them, waiting to be picked apart like her dinner.

He shifted forward in his seat. "I only ask because you've been acting strangely since yesterday."

She straightened her silverware beside her plate as she answered. "Yesterday was rough." Her eyes found his again. "Wade, Ryder and I were friends, you know. Sure, it's been a long time since we were really close..." She trailed off and looked away again. "Time passes so fast it seems. Before you know it, it's been a year since you've talked to someone, and it's not a big deal because you know there's always tomorrow." She tilted forward again, placing her arms on the table, turning her focus back to him. "But then tomorrow doesn't come and one of the three of you is delivering the other one's ashes to the family and needs a friend to remember with."

"I *am* sorry you're going through that, but—" He mentally put his shoe on the table to decide if he should cut it into bite sized pieces before inserting it into his mouth. "You've known he's been dead for two weeks."

"I wasn't aware grief had a timeline."

"That's not what I meant." He dropped his hand to his lap. "This feels different."

"How is it supposed to feel?"

"Lillian," he sighed. "I feel like you're avoiding talking to me about something, and I don't think it's how you feel about Wade being dead. I think Ryder manipulated another situation to his advantage, and you don't want to talk about it because you're afraid of how I'll react."

She pushed her chair away from the table and walked into the living room. August followed immediately. "Or maybe," she said turning to face him, "nothing happened at all other than two friends being there for each other to remember Wade, but because *I* know you don't like Ryder, I feel like I have to explain every second we were together. That's not something I want looming between us every time I'm in the same room as Ryder."

"You don't have to explain what happened while you were together—"

"But I have to reassure you that nothing that shouldn't have happened didn't."

"No." He paused to take a breath that he slowly released. "I don't understand why you're blowing this up. I'm not asking you to explain yourself, or even Ryder. The only reason I don't like him is because he's toying with you. You made your choice, and he needs to respect that."

"He is. He knows how I feel about you."

"But he also knows how you still feel about him."

"Are we going to have this argument every time I talk to Ryder?"

"I'm trying to have a discussion, not an argument."

"I never intended to have feelings for Ryder again in my life. Ever. It was surprising to learn how he felt, that there was something still inside of me that also felt for him. I'm sorry that that hurts you. If I could turn it off as easily as it all came rushing back, I would, but I don't know how."

"You stop letting him in. Eventually he'll fade away."

She crossed her arms in front of her chest.

"Can't you see that it's hurting you to keep him in?"

"Is it hurting me, or is it hurting us?"

"It's hurting you, which leads to hurting us. Can't you see how confused he has you? You've barely carried on a conversation since you were with him yesterday, you stare off into nothing, you pick at your food … what am I supposed to think?"

"I don't know."

"Lillian." He looked at the ceiling and sighed, settling his gaze back on her stubbornly set face. "I like you. I want to be with you. If you insist on keeping him in your life, fine," he conceded. "If you say nothing happened, fine. I trust you, Lillian. What I don't believe is you telling me that there isn't something else going on. It's not Wade, and it feels like you're making a bigger deal out of how you feel about me not liking Ryder to distract me from something more. Something is there. Is it how you feel about me? You've said it's easy to be with me. Is being with me too comfortable?"

"Obviously not right now."

"You know what I mean."

She shook her head and exhaled, her shoulders dropping slightly. "No, I like how comfortable I am with you. I feel connected to you."

"Then why won't you talk about whatever it is you're holding onto?"

"Because I can't, okay?" She sighed, letting her arms fall to her sides. "It's not something I can talk about right now. If that's a problem, then I'm sorry, but I just can't."

"Getting it out might help," he told her gently.

She shook her head again, but she didn't have any words to offer.

"Is there anything I can do or say that'll help you?" he asked, moving closer, taking her hands in his. "I don't like to see you upset like this," he added gently as he pulled her into a hug. "Will you tell me if it's something I've done?"

She nodded against him, holding him as he held her. "There are just some things I need to work out, things I don't understand," she whispered into his chest. She pulled back slightly to look up at him. "I'm not sure if I'll ever understand."

She leaned her head back against him and he stroked her back, using each focused motion to help fight the urge to ask if she'd discussed her confusion with Ryder. "I'm a good listener if you change your mind and want to talk," he told her instead, swaying her gently in her living room to a tune only he could hear. "I won't even stare at you the whole time."

He felt her cheek move against his chest in what he hoped was a smile.

SIXTY-SIX

-Lillian-

The headlights flashed across her living room as August pulled out of her drive. She locked the door and turned off the lights throughout her house on the way to her room, keeping the bedside lamp on for when she returned from her bedtime routine. She stared at her reflection, watching the bubbles form in the toothpaste as she brushed, recounting the conversation with August.

Why had it been so easy to share her theory with Ryder?

Was it because it didn't matter if he didn't believe her?

Did he believe her because he knew she'd never say anything to August, and that gave him another way to stay relevant to her? Or was that her projecting what she thought August would say if he knew?

But he did believe her, and she could talk to him about it now, instead of holding something back.

She rinsed out her mouth. "Even with the proof that you have, August isn't going to believe in time travel," she told her mirrored self, drying the water droplets from the countertop and shutting off the light.

She got into bed and opened the bedside table drawer, taking out the folder that held her copies of Ryder's research. He said he'd get more for her, but did she really need more? What else was she going to learn from more examples of missing and found reports? None of the reports told her why people died when they came out of the Mountain.

She looked through her copies. There were many more "found" reports than "missing" ones, but all that told her was that Ryder could use cause of death as a common search and had yet to find the coordinating "missing" report. She flipped through the pages, looking at the copies from the case files.

She picked up her phone then set it back down again, staring at it as it waited.

"It's just a conversation," she told the phone.

Its blank face gave no objection.

She exhaled, picked up the phone, and hit talk before she could change her mind. It was just a conversation after all.

"Hey." Ryder's voice was sleepy, and she heard him shift on the other end of the phone. "Can't sleep?"

"Hey," she said back, feeling stupid for calling him after all. "I'm sorry if I woke you," she added hurriedly, glancing at the clock, surprised by the late hour.

"You can wake me anytime," he told her lazily, a smile ringing through and she could imagine him in a dark room, eyes closed, lying in bed, holding the phone loosely against his ear. "But it'd be easier to do if you were lying next to me."

"Ryder," she scolded, but there was no bite to her tone as she felt his name on her lips, forcing herself not to wonder at what he wore to sleep, or didn't.

"I was only saying that sometimes I don't hear the phone ring," he added too innocently. "That's all."

"Mmhmm."

"Since I'm assuming you're not calling to invite me over," he said, his voice a little more awake, leaving a little pause before he continued, "I'm going to guess you want to talk about time travel."

"Sort of," she admitted, pausing herself, trying to decide what to share. "I can't get it out of my head. I want it to make sense."

"I know what you mean."

She adjusted the edges of the stack of pages in her lap. "August knows something's not right."

Ryder was silent on the other end for a moment. "Are you going to tell him?"

"I don't think I can."

"You have the proof," Ryder reminded.

"Who would really believe it?"

"I do."

She let his soft words linger over the line. "I'm thankful to be able to talk to you," she finally admitted. "I'm not sure August would look at me the same."

"He shouldn't. He should look at you with awe that you're able to think beyond our small world into possibilities that people only dream about."

"Doctors call that crazy."

"Only because they don't understand."

"And you do?"

"Not at all, but I believe in you."

She sighed, resting her head against the headboard and closing her eyes. "Can you please not be so nice?" she whispered.

"Sure. You're crazy."

"Thank you."

"And I'm crazy about you. But," he continued before she could object again, "we'll save that for another day. What's keeping you up tonight?"

She looked back at the papers in her lap. "I wondered what you could tell me about your conversation with the medical examiner for Wade and Brian."

"Sure, but I don't have much more than what I already told you. They both died from a rupturing heart attack."

"Right, as did the rest of the list that you gathered. Something else that I noticed in all of these reports were excessive levels of cortisol, catecholamines," she said slowly, sounding out the unfamiliar word.

"Way too late for my brain for that big of a word," Ryder joked on the other end.

"I had to look it up," she admitted.

"What did you come up with?"

"It's an amygdala response to a perceived threat."

"More science-y talk."

"Releases adrenaline, among other hormones."

"Yeah." Ryder yawned. "Rich mentioned high adrenaline, said both Wade and Brian, well, John Doe for him, were both probably really scared and that's what caused the heart attacks. Maybe an overload of those things can do that? I can ask him if you want."

"People get scared all the time," she countered. "Why don't their hearts explode?"

"Those scared people aren't also time traveling ... maybe it's the combination of the two?"

"That could be," she wondered. "We'd have no way to know what time travel alone could do to someone."

"Right," he agreed. "Nobody would."

"Okay, but ... what if there are still military people at the base?"

"Don't you think we would have noticed that?"

"It was top secret before. Maybe everything disappeared so suddenly because they went underground, literally. They could have been building tunnels so nobody would ever see them coming and going. The explosion all those years ago could have been them covering up what they're still doing up there to this day."

"Even if the base was still operational, does that matter?"

"I don't know... maybe? Maybe the reason people come out dead is because they stumbled onto the military people. They can't have them talking about them being there, so they inject them with something that causes it to look like a heart attack, something natural, so nobody comes looking." She considered this new line of thinking. "And if someone does come looking, they've already got a coverup that works."

"One problem with your theory. Well, two really," Ryder said. "For one, there were no foreign substances found to support the bodies being injected."

"Unless the excess hormones *were* what was injected. If the amounts were so high it registered as an anomaly during the autopsies, maybe that is what the real cause of death was, and because of such extreme amounts, the heart can't take it and explodes."

"Hmm. I can check with Rich and see if that theory holds."

"If you do that, will it cause uncertainty again for the cases? How would you explain wanting to question the autopsies when the cases are closed?"

Ryder was silent on the other end. "You're right about that. I'll have to think about that one before I take it to Rich."

"What was the second thing?"

"Hmm?"

"You said there were two things wrong with my military theory. What was the second thing?"

"Oh, right, time travel."

"What about it?"

"If the military is operating deep undercover in there, and knows time travel exists, why let bodies out at all? Those missing persons cases are still unsolved and will continue to go unsolved. The only reason I was able to match them with a 'found' report is because this really crazy lady suggested I take time out of the equation. If they really wanted to cover up people being in there and time travel being even a fraction of a possibility, why let anybody out at all? All that does is offer a clue to discovery. If they didn't release the body, there'd never be anything to find and question, just like our cases already show. There'd be no 'found' report somewhere in time that someone with a wild theory could piece together."

She chewed her lip as she stared at the "found" report in her lap.

"If there's no military operation in there still," she said, "then there's still no explanation. There's no reason people go in alive but come out dead."

"You know you don't have to solve this, right?" he asked her after they both silently absorbed that they hadn't figured out anything new.

"What do you mean?"

"You've already figured out a key to more cases than we know yet. If those people were in some other realm of existence waiting for their death to be solved to find peace, you've done that. Hell, I'd have a ceremony with you for each and every one of them if that'll help you with closure for them.

"But what happens if you do figure out why people die when they go through time? Are you going to share the secret to success? You already said that people can't be trusted with that sort of power, that they'd use it for personal gain or to right a historical wrong … whatever. They'd mess up the timeline somehow, and who knows what that does to the present.

"And as far as keeping people safe, if you can't figure out what causes them to die from time traveling, you either have to A, share the secret and its deadly end, which we've already agreed is a terrible idea, or B, convince people to stay away from the area entirely without telling them why, which is already what's been happening for years."

"And people still go in and people still die."

"Right. No matter what you learn, and no matter what you say, people will still think they can win."

"It's not fair."

"What isn't?"

"Knowing what we do, knowing that we could save all those people if we could just get through to them that it wasn't safe. Why know if there's nothing we can do?"

"I don't have an answer for you," he told her gently. "If it makes you feel any better, I'm willing to talk about it any time it gets you down. I'd hold you and tell you everything's going to be okay, that there's nothing to be afraid of."

"I'm sure you would," she laughed.

"It's a sacrifice I'm willing to make. I can help you forget time travel, the Mountain, boyfriends that don't know what they have," he joked back. "Even if I can't claim it for my own," he added seriously, "your heart is not one I'd be willing to lose to the Mountain."

SIXTY-SEVEN

-Lillian-

"Special delivery," Gary sang as he nudged open the door to her office.

"What's this?" she asked as he set a delicate looking vase on her desk.

"It appears to be a token of someone's admiration," Gary said sarcastically, but couldn't help gushing over the gift. "Have you ever seen a vase like this? It's most definitely an antique. There's no way this came from the florist. No, this was handpicked. And oh, look at the colors! You don't even need the flower, which is lovely, but the vase alone is a work of art."

"Gary," she interrupted as he turned the vase around so he could see all angles.

"Yes?" He almost looked offended by her presence.

"Did it come with a card?"

"Oh, yes, but it doesn't say who it's from," he said dismissively. "It only says how beautiful lilies are."

"You read the card," she stated, not surprised in the slightest.

"How else would I know who to deliver this beauty to?"

"The person who handed this to you didn't, I don't know, mention that part?"

He waved a hand in the air. "How am I supposed to know? The little lady comes in, rambling on and on, asking to have someone sign for a delivery. I have my tables to tend to, Josh was trying to help clear a table, I guess I just didn't pay close enough attention."

"Sounds busy out there."

"Oh, you have no idea," he prattled.

"Do you think Josh would appreciate you coming back up front?"

"Hmm? Oh, I suppose…"

"Was there something else you needed?" she asked him since he hadn't moved from his perch on the chair.

"Aren't you going to open the card?"

"I do plan to do that, yes… Didn't you already read it?"

"Of course, but I thought you might be able to figure out who it came from."

"I don't think it's that big of a mystery. I am seeing someone, after all."

"Why wouldn't he sign his name if that was the case?"

"Because he doesn't need to. Bye, Gary."

"Oh, fine," he sighed, getting up to leave the office and leaving the door open as he did.

She shook her head at how dramatic he could be sometimes. The vase *was* quite lovely, as was the singular double lily resting among a frame of greenery. She brought the vase close to smell the barely opened, fragrant bloom. She smiled at the thought behind the gift as she picked up the small envelope that he'd left on the desk. She slid out the card and read the printed message:

Through all of time, nothing is quite as beautiful, Lilly Flower.

She looked back at the neat little display, the lovely vase that Gary swore was an antique. She picked up her phone to text Ryder.

Thank you. But you didn't have to get me a gift.

He responded immediately.

You're welcome.

And it's not a gift, it's a reminder.

A reminder?

Life is fragile and can be cut short, but even in its fleeting time, is still unbelievably beautiful. Don't let things that are out of your control make you forget that and cause you to miss the magic before you.

That's lovely.

I didn't know you were so poetic.

Ryder's response came quickly.

I'm not. I'm sure I read that on a card somewhere… could have been an ad for a magician.

She laughed.

How convenient that your magician had a perfectly fitting phrase to apply to my life.

Exactly what I thought.

A second text followed.

And the card applies, too.

Thank you

The thank you was all she could text back, smiling when he responded with an emoji wearing sunglasses.

"Hey girl–" a loud, abrupt knock and Lana's entrance had her fumbling the phone, causing it to land on the desk and her heart to race.

"Holy Hell," Lillian swore. "You scared the life out of me." Laughing she covered her racing heart with her hand as she reached out with the other to move her launched phone from its resting place.

"I knocked," she stated reasonably.

"Like a jackhammer."

"It was a normal knock," Lana insisted. "You know what I think?" she asked as she took the seat in front of the desk.

"That you always find a way to come in and tell me things I didn't ask?"

Lana laughed. "Of course, and this time I'm betting you were up to no good and got caught in the act."

"I'm literally sitting at my desk working."

Lana looked at the computer. "On what? Screen saver's on." She twirled the vase so the lily faced her. She smelled it, smiled, then turned it back. "That's pretty. Who's it from?"

"I don't understand why me getting flowers is a mystery when I'm seeing someone."

"It's only a mystery because Gary says there was no name on the card."

"Geez, is he still going on about that?"

"Of course he is. It's Gary."

"My name wasn't on the card either, which is the excuse he gave for reading it, so maybe this flower isn't even for me by his logic."

Lana draped herself back onto the chair, studying her friend. "If you don't want to tell me who it's from, I guess I can't make you … but know that I have my thoughts." They both turned their head at the sound of the order ding. "You might want to come up with a story to shut Gary up though."

"It's just a flower, Lana. It doesn't need a story."

"Mmhmm," she mused as she walked out of the office. She was out of sight no more than ten seconds when she popped back around the door. "You'll never guess who just walked in."

"Damn it Lana!" Lillian had jumped at her reentry, her heart racing all over again. "Stop doing that."

"Sorry… Rain's here!" she whispered excitedly. "I never expected to see her face in here again after the way she quit. What do you think she's doing here?"

"I asked her to come in," Lillian told her, getting up to follow her out of the office.

"Why would you do that?"

"Boss stuff," she said elusively. "Don't you have an order to fill?"

"Oh, we'll talk later," Lana promised as she went to her side of the kitchen.

Lillian continued to the front, hoping to intercept Rain before she became too much of a distraction for Gary.

"Rain, thank you for coming in," Lillian said, intentionally interrupting Gary's animated welcome to Rain. "You can come on back."

"Oh, but I haven't even said hi," Gary whined when Rain followed.

"Gotta see what the *boss* wants," Rain pouted to Gary, but followed Lillian through the kitchen to the back. "This better not take long. I have better things to do than spend my time in these walls."

Lillian led the way into the office, hoping their meeting was brief as well. She sat at the desk and pulled out Rain's last paycheck. Rain was standing awkwardly just inside the office.

"You can sit if you want."

Rain closed the door and took the seat. "So, what did you need?"

Lillian set the check on the side of the desk closest to Rain and set a paper next to it with a pen. "This is your final paycheck. The accountant does the last one paper instead of direct deposit, but I couldn't get it to you."

"Right," Rain nodded, picking it up and checking the amount before folding it and putting it in her pocket. "What's this?" she asked, nodding to the form.

"This just says that you've left employment and verifies that you received your last check. I just need a signature for your personnel file."

Rain read the document, which surprised Lillian, thinking she'd just sign and be on her way with a Rain-worthy parting phrase.

"This says I'm eligible for rehire," Rain stated, looking quizzically at Lillian, then back to read the rest of the form. "Guess you'll want to print another."

"It's not misprinted," Lillian stated.

Rain picked up the pen and quickly signed, sliding both across the desk. "Can I get a copy or whatever?"

"Of course," Lillian told her, making the copy and handing it over.

Rain folded the paper and put it in her pocket. She didn't immediately get up to leave, but she didn't say anything either.

"How are you doing, Rain?" Lillian asked gently.

"Fine," she reflexively answered. "Why wouldn't I be?" She rubbed at her chest like someone rubs at a sore muscle, then dropped her hand to her lap, smiling too cheerily. "Doctors gave me a clean bill of health, said I'm not crazy even though they won't look at me too long, and released me back into the world of the normals."

"It'll be good for you to be back with your friends, to get back to a normal routine so you can put all of that behind you."

"Yeah … that's what they said, too. Then again, they believe the official story," she said looking hard at Lillian. "But I'm the one who gets to live the real story, the real life after that."

"I believe your story," Lillian told her gently. She believed in it more than Rain would ever be able to understand.

Rain nodded to the paper. "So, is that the reason you wrote I could be rehired? Pitying the poor girl that nobody believes, that can't even tell her side of the story?"

"You've been through enough, Rain. Everyone deserves a second chance, even you."

"Yeah, well, don't worry too much," Rain sighed. "I won't make you keep that offer. I don't want to come back to work here." She looked toward the front of the building, several walls between her and the dining area. "I'll always know which booth the guys first sat in," she said turning back. "I know I didn't know him long, but I think it'll be a while before I can get his face out of my head, the way he changed and looked…"

"You can talk to me about him, what happened, if you need someone," Lillian told her when she trailed off.

Rain's eyes came back into focus, and she shook her head. "No, I really can't. I can't talk about anything that happened out there." She rubbed her chest again and then clasped her hands together, studying them for a moment before looking up at Lillian. "I think everyone's right. I should put it all away. It doesn't do me any good … and I never want to feel that helpless … that scared ever again."

"The door's always open if you change your mind."

Rain nodded to herself, and stood to leave, pausing with her hand on the doorknob. "Thank you, Lillian," she said softly before turning back to look at her. "For being cool about all this and not thinking I'm crazy."

"You're welcome."

"And…" She looked at the hand still holding the knob before looking back at Lillian. "…sorry for all the…" She waved her hand through the air. "…well, for how I quit. Sorry I acted the way that I did."

"Thank you, Rain." Lillian was genuinely surprised to hear the apology.

Rain turned to leave but turned back again. "Do you think you could help me escape Gary? I don't really want to rehash anything, and he's going to want to know everything. I just can't today."

"Sure," Lillian said getting up to escort her to the front of the diner. They chatted lightly so nobody could interrupt and she opened the door to let her out, thanking her for coming in.

"Thanks," Rain whispered when she was out of the building and walked away down the sidewalk.

"Oh, she's gone?" Gary hurried over from his table as Lillian was entering the kitchen. "I didn't get to talk to her. I have so many questions!"

"Sorry, she must have had somewhere else to be. I guess you'll just have to check in with her after your shift," she said, subtly reminding him that he was on her clock.

He let out a resigned sigh. "I guess … but she is just the worst at checking her text messages," he started.

"Looks like your table needs a refill," she interrupted, nodding, and he followed the direction of her gaze.

"Everyone is so needy today…" he mumbled to himself, but hurried over to tend to his table.

"That seemed painless," Lana called as Lillian walked by.

"Yep, just final paycheck, end of employment stuff."

"Congratulations. Rain is officially no longer your problem."

"Yeah, thanks," Lillian called, offering a light chuckle as she went into her office.

She knew Rain's work ethic, and Heaven knew she didn't want to have to work with her again, but she couldn't help feeling sorry for her after everything she'd been through and what she'd have to live with now. She seemed truly terrified of what she'd experienced, despite being ignorant of what Lillian believed she'd actually lived through.

But what was so special about Rain that allowed her to make it out alive?

Why hadn't the Mountain claimed her, too?

SIXTY-EIGHT

-Lillian-

"You look like you've got quite a day ahead of you," Lillian's dad commented at their Sunday morning breakfast. "Don't typically see you in hiking apparel."

She nodded while she covered her mouth to finish chewing. "August and I are hiking to the falls."

"That's a nice area," he said, nodding and glancing at the map on his wall reflexively. "Can be a little challenging depending on which you're planning to see."

"I'm not sure what he has in mind. He's been trying several of the trails around town and was surprised I'd never been out there. He's assured me it's worth the effort."

"I'm aware of his trekking," he said dryly. "Sounds like he's taking you all the way up."

"Then I guess I'm going on an adventure."

He was quiet as he glanced back at the wall between sips of coffee. "You'll be careful," he told her as he turned back.

"Of course," she assured him, but continued when the crease didn't leave his forehead. "It's not like I've never been hiking before, Dad. I'll have the essentials. August is practically a pro at this and will be with me the whole time." She leaned toward him. "You have nothing to worry about."

The raised eyebrow dad-look was perfected the day she was born, she was sure of it. "I'll always have something to worry about."

"I know, I know, your job is never finished," she repeated what she'd heard her entire life, but smiled warmly at him. "I'll be okay."

He returned the smile, but she knew he'd be anxious until she was back on safer terrain. "When are you going?" he asked.

"After I leave here. August wanted an early start. He's getting the things together for the trip, and I'll meet him at the trailhead."

"Which one?"

"Oh, um … the one closest to the falls?" she said uncertainly.

"You don't even know where you're going?" he sighed.

"I do. I looked at it on the map when he gave me the name. It's written down in my car."

"Lillian—"

"Dad," she laughed. "It's going to be fine. I'll send you the name of the trailhead when I get in the car. I'll text you when we go in and when we get back out. It'll be okay. Oh—" She paused to glance back at the map he'd been looking at, but only out of reference, not out of understanding this far away. "You don't still have deputies in the woods, right? You guys called off the search the other night, didn't you?"

"There's nobody out there," he confirmed. "That doesn't mean I want to start another search party."

She reached over his desk to squeeze his hand. "I promise to be extra careful." She released his hand and started packing up their breakfast trash. "How's work going? Now that all the cases are closed."

"Business as usual. There's always another case." He held out the small trash can for her to toss their mess. "I'm sorry you ended up being as involved as you were."

"Oh, it's alright. I don't mind helping if I can. You know that."

"I'd rather you help on something a little less grim."

"As I recall, you were trying to recruit me," she joked.

"Yeah, but this isn't the life I'd want for you."

She perched on the end of the chair. "Doing this for as long as you have," she started slowly, wondering at the map, "does it get easier?"

"You were close to these cases, connected on multiple fronts. That makes it hard. I wish I could say that it gets easier over time, but that would mean that what I'm doing means less. In a case like this, with so many different pieces separate from each other yet entwined, so many voices unable to speak for themselves anymore ... Someone needs to be that voice. Someone needs to make sure they aren't forgotten and left behind. Someone needs to care. To say that I can do that without a piece lingering when it's all said and done would be to lie to you.

"Hopefully, for your sake, you don't have to worry about this again. You don't have to think about someone's voice not being heard. You'll move on from this. It'll take some time, but eventually you'll realize that it's been weeks since you thought of Wade, months since anyone's talked about Rain going missing, years since a bear attacked that hiker. This will all be a memory that you can set aside."

"But not you," she said, looking at her dad, the lines by his eyes from all that he'd seen, the slight hunch to his shoulders from carrying around the weight of a county. "Not for Ryder or Simon or all the rest of them."

"That's not for you to worry about, kiddo. We knew what we signed up for when we joined the force. We need this." He stood to come around the desk. "Don't dwell on this anymore, okay? The cases are closed, it's time to remember the good things and start to move on."

She smiled because it wouldn't do any good to remind him of all the cases sitting cold with nobody to speak for them, knowing that she'd have their voices calling out through all of time, unable to share it with the world.

"Now, you have places to be and I'm not going to keep you, because the sooner you start, the sooner you can let me know that you're back and safe."

"Please don't worry about me," she told him as she hugged him goodbye.

He patted her on her back. "Please don't make me start to lie to my only child."

"Are we there yet?" she joked after nearly two hours into the hike, completely surrounded by towering trees and boulders as big as she was, but no sight of water.

Ahead on the trail, August chuckled. "I promise it isn't much farther," he called, "but we can stop for a break if you're ready."

She took a drink of her water, watching the path in front of her so she didn't trip. "I'm fine, unless you need a break." She breathed out the words and hoped they didn't sound as winded as she felt.

He turned back to her, a smile on his face, not looking the least bit tired or flushed as she was sure her cheeks were. "I'm in no hurry. If you need a break, we can stop."

"How do you look like you're just taking an afternoon stroll through a park?"

"This is a park," he answered simply, looking at the beauty surrounding them. He reached over to tuck a stray whisp of hair back behind her ear. "Accounting for our hiking rate and where we are on the map, I'd estimate we have about twenty or so more minutes."

"And how are you so sure of where we are on that map?" She eyed the pocket where she knew the folded-up paper was currently hiding.

He laughed at her uncertain expression. "You followed me before, and you didn't even know me then."

"That was a ten-minute walk," she countered.

He smiled, "Yeah, but you didn't know that at the time. Are you worried I've led you out into the middle of nowhere? If you're still concerned that I moonlight as a serial killer, you have nothing to be worried about."

"Oh yeah, and why is that? Because you say so?"

"No," he said seriously. "Because it's not nighttime."

"Oh! Well, then, you're right. I have nothing to be worried about," she laughed.

"Exactly," he said, smiling at his ridiculously corny joke. He moved in close to her, tilting her chin with the slightest brush of his finger along her jaw. "I know exactly where we are. Even without this map, turned around, blindfolded, and in the middle of the night, I could still get you safely out of these woods."

"I'd prefer not to test your theory."

He leaned the rest of the way in, kissing her softly to the song of the birds around them. She poured herself into him, taking his gentle and soft embrace somewhere deeper, the sound of the birds falling away. She felt his arms wrap around her as he met her intensity. When she pulled away, his eyes closed and he rested his forehead against hers. She was pleased to see that his breathing finally matched her own.

"Are you sure you don't need a break?" she whispered smugly, pulling back slightly. "You seem a little out of breath."

He smiled, slowly tightening his hold on her as he leaned down to delicately tease kisses along her neck, his breath warmly tickling her ear. "You may have started it," he whispered, "but I'll be the one to finish it."

She didn't know how long they stood as one among the trees, his hands in her hair, both of their hearts beating at a desperate pace. It could have been seconds as easily as hours.

"Wait," she finally managed on a breath.

"What?" he asked, pulling back slightly to see what was wrong, and they both started to laugh as they came back to reality.

"My hair," she started, trying to turn her head but failing.

"How did you do that?" he asked, lowering her legs from however they wound up around his waist.

"Me? You're the one," she said, trying to step forward from the tree she'd been pressed against, while he tried untangling her hair from the stick that had caught hold. Giving up, he snapped the stick from its branch and pulled her back to their packs on the path, so they'd have more sunlight to see.

"Nature looks good on you," he told her as he finished detangling the stick and picked the extra bark particles out of her hair, dusting her back as well.

She ran her fingers through the strands to get the rest of the tangles under control, then pulled it into a ponytail. He helped her back into her pack and then put on his own.

"For the record," he said as he grabbed her hand and started leading her along the trail again, looking back over his shoulder at her, "that doesn't count as finished."

Her heart gave a little happy dance at the promise of more.

Smiling, she checked her watch. Twenty-two minutes had passed since they had stopped.

"Are we there yet?"

"Can you hear it?" August asked after they'd climbed for what felt like longer than twenty minutes.

She paused to listen, hearing a slight murmur through the trees.

"We're almost there," he called back to her, picking up his pace to scout ahead. After seeing something that satisfied him, he stopped and waited for her to catch up. "Are you ready?"

"After two and a half hours of anticipation, yes, I'm ready."

"Great! You can free-climb right?" he asked, taking her hand and beginning to lead the way again. At her stumbling pull and the nervous glance beyond him toward the unknown, he began to chuckle. "I'm kidding, Lil. Don't worry, the hard part is over."

"You're just full of jokes today," she said humorlessly.

He led her through the remaining trees into the blinding sunshine. She could hear the falls completely, louder now that the trees weren't buffering their call. August strode to the edge of the cliff, holding out a hand for her to join him.

"It's okay," he promised as she hesitantly closed the space from safe to reckless.

When she reached him, she could see there was nothing to fear. While they were on what appeared to be the ledge to a steep cliff, there was actually a natural stairway leading down and toward the waterfall before them.

"From what I can tell," he said as he helped her navigate the rocky path, "this river has several waterfalls along its course, this one being the last big one that you can really get to." He pointed away from the direction they were headed, downriver, and she turned to take in the view. The river surged away from them, wrapping itself around and flowing over rocks, eventually disappearing from view as it curved around an outcropping of trees. "You can't see it from here, but farther down, a little past those trees," he said, pointing as far as they could see, "there's another sort of slide waterfall."

"I've heard about that one. People used to come out and use it like a natural waterpark, but too many kept getting hurt and eventually the conservation people, or rangers—I'm not really sure who—made it off-limits. Now people stay farther down in the pools when the water is lower."

"It was off-limits when I was a teenager, too," he told her, smiling mischievously. "That never stopped me."

"I'm still not sure if I'm mad at you or not for not telling me you were local," she said as they continued their way along the rocky path.

"It wasn't completely untrue," he said as he paused to guide her over a slippery section of the rocks where a stream of water had made its course. "My grandparents were here. We lived here when I was little, moved away, but came back to visit, mostly in the summertime. I've always been the outdoorsy type, so I spent most of my summers on the river or in these woods."

"Again, you could have just told me that when we first met instead of letting me think you were just drifting through."

"Like I said before, it had been years since I'd really been back. My grandpa died about ten years ago, and then my grandma followed a couple years later. It wasn't until all their things were being divided that I made the trip back, found out I had inherited a few pieces of property, decided to build the Overlook and renovate the cabin, and just see where things went."

"Ryder seems to think you own half the town," she mentioned, and instantly regretted bringing him into the conversation, worried it would change their carefree exchange.

"Huh … he's one to talk," August said, but let it go without appearing like the mention of Ryder bothered him. "No, I don't own half the town." He climbed up a ledge and turned to help pull her up. "It's only like a quarter of the town."

"What?" she asked, shocked by this revelation.

"I'm kidding."

"I'm beginning to think I need to know a little more about the guy I'm dating who keeps unraveling more and more mysteries." She gripped his arm when she slipped on a moss covered rock.

He smiled when she set herself right and continued to move closer to the waterfall, holding her hand as he led the way. "That's the point of dating. If I told you everything up front, where would the intrigue be?"

"Right because pretending to be on your way out of town at the drop of a hat, or that you could potentially be a serial killer, or that you may or may not actually have a job, is long-term relationship building material."

"It lured you in, didn't it?"

"Oh, so now I'm a fish?"

"You said it, not me."

"Okay, but in all actuality, I'm not a fish," she said, and he turned to look at her curiously, water droplets spraying onto his hair. "How much closer are we going to get?"

"Pretty close," he grinned. "You're going to get wet on this ride."

"What? August, no!" She squealed as he pulled her quickly to him, scooping her up into his arms like she was weightless, even with her loaded pack.

"You're going to want to stop squirming and hold tight," he warned.

"No, August, plea–"

Her words were drowned along with the rest of her as he jumped into the water.

SIXTY-NINE

-Lillian-

"You could have warned me there was a cave back here," she laughed after he set her back on her feet, her hair and clothes plastered to her. "How'd you know this was here? Another youthful exploration of yours?"

"My grandpa brought me when I was small. I'm not sure how many people know about it since you can't see it at all from the other side. I used to make up stories that bandits would hide out in here, that there was treasure hidden inside."

"Bandits huh?"

"Yeah, you know, like Jesse James?"

"Positive role model," she said sarcastically as she squeezed the water out of her hair.

"Hey, just because he was a bad dude didn't mean the person who found his treasure was, too."

"Is there a story of missing treasure?"

"Not that I know of, but as a kid, I had a wild imagination."

She smiled, trying to picture him as a little boy. She looked around the cavern they were standing in, lit only by the sun twinkling through the streaming doorway of water.

"This is amazing. It's like a dream," she said, watching the water glide down before her, prisms forming in the mist where the sun caught it just right. "It's weird," she told him when he stood beside her to watch. "It feels so familiar, like I've stood in this very spot and done this very thing, even though I know I never have."

"Déjà vu," he smiled.

"Right," she agreed, looking around the cavern again. "How far back does this go?"

"Come on, I'll show you."

"I'm okay," she said, warily looking into the darkness beyond, wondering what they might disturb if they ventured farther than the opening they were in. "Hiking and waterfall hopping were enough excitement for one day. I don't need to add spelunking to the list."

"Come on," he encouraged her, reaching out for her to join him. "I'll hold you if you get scared."

The statement brought Ryder back to the forefront of her mind, remembering the way she felt when he said the same. She wasn't going to allow herself to be confused by him, not while she was having a perfect day with August. She took a step into the dark, firmly pushing Ryder out of her way.

She took August's hand and followed as he headed deeper into the cave, the light quickly fading to where she could barely see their joined hands in front of her. The air was cold on her wet body, and the wall was slick in places. The ground felt firmer under her boots than the mud that had been close to the fall.

"August," she whispered, feeling quiet was needed in this dark space. "How much farther?"

"Just a little way."

"Don't you have a flashlight?"

"Of course," he whispered from ahead.

"Then why aren't we using it?" she whispered back.

He stopped walking, letting go of her hand. "Hang on."

"What are you doing?" she asked when she didn't hear the sounds of him rummaging through his bag for the light. When he didn't respond, she felt her heart begin to speed up. "August," she whispered loudly into the darkness, reaching out for him but finding only air. "August!" she called again.

No answer, no sound of movement.

She began to imagine all the tragedies that could have silently taken him from her. What if there was a crevice that he had fallen into, and she was standing on the edge herself, one step from death?

He would have screamed, she reasoned. *Okay, no cave hole.*

She considered that he could have dropped dead from a heart attack. He was physically fit, but that didn't always matter. They'd been pushing the limits today, maybe that'd been too much.

He does this for fun, she reminded herself. *This was just another day for him. Plus, his body would be nearby, and you would have heard him fall.*

Wouldn't she?

She slid her foot out in front of her and around, reaching out with her hands as well. Nothing but dirt on the ground and a rocky wall beside her.

"August," she hissed into the darkness. "This isn't funny."

Her heart was pounding now, and she was sure it was echoing through the cave system. Where could he have gone?

He couldn't just disappear into thin air.

"Oh, God," she whispered, covering her beating heart with one hand, her mouth with the other. "Oh God, the Mountain."

She didn't know where they were, or how far into the cave they had traveled. Where did the Mountain's boundary start? Had they crossed over and not realized? What if he was gone, lost to time somewhere?

The air suddenly seemed too thin to breathe. She couldn't get it into her lungs fast enough.

Was this how it happened? Was it this simple to just disappear forever? Silently, and without a trace. Wiped off the earth without a warning.

She fell to her knees, leaning over when she felt her head beginning to swim, her already dark vision feeling like it was closing in on her more.

What about her? Was she traveling now and didn't know it? Would she be able to leave this cave like Rain had been spared before? And if so, when would it be?

"August!" she screamed, a desperate attempt to bring him back from beyond.

"Lillian?" she heard him call from nearby and the shuffle of quick but abrupt movements. "Hey! It's okay … Hey, I'm here, you're okay."

"August?" she gasped, gulping at the air that came rushing back with him.

"Yeah, who else would it be?"

"You were gone," she said, feeling her lip quiver. "I called for you and you were gone…"

"I'm sorry," he said pulling her against him in the dark. "God, you're trembling."

"I thought … I thought …" she stammered. "The Mountain…"

"Shh, it's okay. I'm sorry. I wasn't thinking. I just went to check how much farther. I was almost back to get you, and I heard you scream. I shouldn't have left you alone." He was rubbing her arms and her back, talking into her hair as he held her close. "I'm not going anywhere. I'm sorry, Lillian. I'm here. I've got you."

She half-listened to his murmured reassurances, focusing on the feeling of his arms around her, the thudding of his heart against her own chest. She held onto him in the dark, letting his words soothe her back to calm, feeling that he was there and present before her, not barreling through time, lost forever.

"You okay to walk?" he asked after a few moments, when her breathing had returned to a normal speed. She nodded against him. "Hold on to me," he told her as he headed deeper into the cave. "It's just around this turn. Don't let go of me," he reminded her.

She held him tight, feeling along the wall with her other hand. She stopped short when the wall disappeared, and she sucked in a breath at the unknown.

"It's okay. We're here." His hands were on her waist, steadying her. "I left my pack just a few steps away. I'm not leaving you."

"How do you know it's there?" she asked uncertainly, not wanting to let him go again.

"Because I can see it," he told her, and she realized she'd been keeping her eyes closed while she walked since she couldn't see anything anyway.

She opened them, expecting to see an obvious light like he could, but there was only a slight glow coming from nearby.

"You see it?" he asked, and she nodded.

"Yes," she whispered, remembering that if she still couldn't see him, then he couldn't see her nod.

"Wait here. I'm going to get my pack and start a fire."

"A fire?"

"Yes, you're still shivering."

She hugged her arms together when he stepped away, rubbing her hands along her skin to try and warm up. She watched as the glow became brighter as he picked his bag up from the ground and watched it walk farther away then abruptly stop. She could make out the shape of him hunched down and could hear the flick of a lighter. Within a couple of moments, the cavern was flickering with the light of a small fire. She still couldn't see the walls of the room they were in, so she imagined it was fairly large.

"Come on," he said as he returned to where he'd left her and guided her to the fire. He'd laid down a blanket to sit on but stopped her before she could.

Now that they were in the light and she could really see him before her, she began to shake again.

He searched her face, his eyes concerned as he brushed his thumb along her cheek. "Everything's okay," he reassured her. "You're safe. That was stupid and I'm sorry."

She nodded, and tried to respond, but her lips were trembling, and the words didn't come out right. "I… I… d-d…idn't kn-n-n-now–"

"Shhh," he said softly, trying to calm her down again. "We're going to get you warm," he said, and she looked down at the fire that was already heating her legs. "But, you're going to need to take off your clothes."

"V-v-v…very f-f-f-f...f-f-funny."

"Not joking sweetheart," he said gently. "You're soaked and will heat up quicker if you take off the wet things."

She looked back to the fire and around the room that she still couldn't see.

"There's nothing in here," he reassured her. "Just you and me. You've gotta take 'em off."

She nodded reluctantly and fumbled to get her backpack off. He took the pack and set it beside his own, helping her bring her shirt up and over her head. He wrung it out away from the fire and laid it out to dry. He helped her out of the boots first, and then her jeans, squeezing the excess water out of them as well. She scooted onto the blanket and watched as he undressed as well, ringing his own clothes out, and sat behind her, pulling her back against his chest and rubbing her arms while the fire heated them both.

She watched the flames dance in front of them, creating a show in the shadows beyond, drifting in and out, lulled by the crackling and popping of the wood, the occasional escape of a sigh.

"I'm sorry I panicked," she said sometime later when she felt like herself again.

"You have nothing to be sorry about." His voice was soft and dreamy behind her.

He'd been silently stroking her back for the past few minutes when she had shifted forward to rest her head on her knees. The slow slide of skin along skin made her feel like she was in a trance.

"I thought something had happened to you."

"You don't have to explain."

He leaned into her and hugged her from behind. She laid her head back against his chest.

"I feel like an idiot," she finally admitted.

"If anyone was the idiot, it was me. I never should have left you alone."

"I agree." She felt him chuckle behind her.

"With me being an idiot or leaving you alone?"

"Either," she teased, "but there was no reason for me to jump to such outrageous ideas of where you'd gone and work myself into a panic. I've never done that before."

"Have you ever been alone in a pitch-black cave tunnel before?"

"I can't say that I have," she admitted, "but I didn't think I had problems with claustrophobia or irrational fears before."

"That's why they're irrational, you can't rationalize them when they happen. You responded to a situation that scared you, there's nothing to be ashamed of. Besides," he said, squeezing her gently, "I got to make good on my word."

"How so?"

"I told you I'd hold you if you got scared."

"Your plan all along?" she joked.

"Not exactly what I had in mind. Although, I'd be lying if I said the outcome bothered me."

She shifted around to face him, wrapping her legs around him and resting her cheek against his chest, listening to his heart thrum strongly. "Thank you for taking care of me," she murmured.

"Always," he whispered.

She kissed the skin above his heart, where she'd just been listening, and felt his hands halt their caress. She planted slow kisses along his chest, feeling his muscles tighten just beneath the skin.

"Lillian—" he whispered, leaving the rest unsaid as she reached his mouth.

The kiss was soft and sweet, a slow movement in time with the fire flickering behind her. His hands slid along her bare skin, holding her securely, as her hands found their way along his face and into his hair. She sighed when he found her hair, tugging her gently back to taste her neck and along her collarbone.

"Lillian," he whispered again, stopping to rest his head against her chest, listening to the rapid rate of her heart. "We should go."

"Not yet," she begged, bringing his mouth back to her own. "You promised me a finish."

His hands moved along her body, squeezing as she moved against him.

"Not like this," he said, stopping for a breath again, looking at her in the flickering light.

She looked at his eyes, a wrinkle of concern between his eyebrows battling the need for her that she could feel in his touch. She framed his face with her hands, smiling gently before kissing him deeply.

"I'm fine," she murmured against his lips.

"You weren't," he groaned when she shifted against him before kissing him again. "Lillian, please."

"He begs," she smiled as she slowly slid her hand down his chest.

"Lillian." He grabbed her hand firmly before it could travel any further, startling her enough to pause and really look at him.

"What's wrong?" she asked him, feeling his heart race beneath her free hand.

"You just—" He took a steadying breath. "This isn't the time. I'm not using this situation to my advantage."

"Nobody said that *you* were," she said softly, leaning slowly away, the firelight creating a glow over her body, knowing that he'd either have to let go of the wrist he was still holding or follow her down. She smiled slowly and watched his expression go from cautious to ravenous, but he didn't let her go, or follow her down.

He tugged her back to him in a desperate pull. "Tell me you're sure," he demanded, his voice gruff as he held onto her.

"I'm sure," she breathed, her entire being pulsing, waiting.

He let go of her wrist and brought his hands to her face, pulling her to him to kiss her gently, slowly turning her insides to jelly.

She moved in response, and he slid a hand down her side and to her hip, stabilizing her movements. When she tried to pull back and explore his body, he stabilized her again, pulling her back for the slow burn draw of his kiss. She arched against him when he took her breast in his hand and tenderly caressed.

"Please," she breathed.

His chuckle was low, her pleading ignored as he continued to torment her with his slow pursuit, tasting, teasing. His hands glided down her legs, ensuring they were locked behind him before lifting her and laying her gently onto the blanket. She rose up to take him, but he only held her back down, using his free hand to drive her wild as it caressed every part of her with excruciating patience. His mouth was on hers again as his hand inched along her inner thigh. He smiled against her moan as he teased his fingers away once more.

"You're not playing fair," she breathed when he tasted her body.

She could feel his smile against her skin. "You're the one that said you wanted to use me." A quick nip of teeth followed by the smooth warmth of his tongue. "I'm simply following your demands."

"I'm not sure I'd survive any more demands."

"I bet you could," he murmured against her neck as his fingers traced their way down her torso. "I wonder…" he trailed off as she sighed and arched in response to his fingers finally finding their way, but pulled her back from the edge before she gave in and went over, returning to the slow chase as she caught her breath.

"That wasn't fair," she said, trying to free her hands to torment him in the same way.

"I know…" he told her as he pulled her back to the edge, chuckling as he slowed to a snail's pace of exploring her again.

"August," she begged, as she felt the need growing for him again. She moaned as he finally met her demand, the pace he set unnecessary, as she'd fallen instantly.

He laid beside her, his head resting on her shoulder, a leg still entwined with hers, an arm draped carelessly across her.

"This room has great acoustics," he mumbled against her.

"Let's hope it doesn't project them," she told him, running her fingers through his hair.

He shifted and propped himself on his elbow, smiling at her from above. "No need to worry. Even if there were other hikers, the waterfall would have muffled your passionate cries of desire."

"I didn't passionately cry out in desire," she laughed, nudging him away.

"Could've fooled me," he said, rolling onto his back before sitting up. "But what can I say? I'm pretty desirable."

She watched him pull on his pants, admiring how he looked in jeans and no shirt, the fading light providing shadows, outlining each muscle.

"I have a feeling this was all part of a plan."

He paused putting on his shirt. "I don't know what you're insinuating," he said innocently as he pulled the shirt the rest of the way down. "You're the one who took advantage of me. Remember? I was minding my business, trying to keep you warm, and you couldn't keep your hands to yourself."

"Mmhmm. Why did I need to get warm in the first place? Hmm?" she said as she reached out, letting him pull her up. "The waterfall was a sneaky way to get me out of my clothes."

"What can I say?" he asked as his hands smoothed their way along her waist, stopping at her hips to tug her to him. "I do enjoy thinking of ways to get you out of your clothes." He kissed her and the memory of his touch and the excitable torment of what they'd just done spread across her body. She smiled and leaned into him. "Nope," he said, pulling back, laughter in his eyes. "I won't be fooled again so easily."

She pretended to pout. "Not even a little bit?"

"You don't know what a little bit means."

"Maybe you should show me," she said softly, taking a step forward.

"Clothes," he laughed. "The fire is fading and you're going to wish you weren't standing naked in a cold cave."

"Fine," she pouted again, turning and stepping over to her pick up her still-damp clothes. She looked over her shoulder at him to make sure he was watching before she bent over to slowly retrieve an article of clothing.

"It's not going to work," he laughed from behind her.

"What's not?" she asked innocently as she looked over at him again. "I'm only trying to get dressed."

"I can see that ... safely from over here," he chuckled, but watched as she painstakingly replaced each garment of clothing. When she was finally clothed, he moved in behind her as she finished pulling her hair up and kissed her neck. She tilted her head slightly and reached her hand back to his hair. His hand on her hip held her against him while he roamed with the other. "You forgot something," he told her softly before she twisted slightly to kiss him.

"What's that?" she murmured between kisses.

His free hand slid beneath her jeans, a swift jolt as she let out a gasp only to have it smothered as he covered her mouth with his own again.

She leaned into him, exhilarated by his touch, her hips moving in response, her pulse racing to keep up.

"That," he whispered against her lips, stopping his expert manipulation of her body as suddenly as he'd started, stifling a moan with another kiss before it could escape, "was a little bit." He pulled back, leaning down to pick up the string of red lace that was still lying on the blanket, dangling it just out of her reach. "I think someone else had certain intentions for this trip too," he said, bouncing the fabric out of her reach.

"That wasn't very nice," she told him, her body aching for his touch to finish what he'd started. She held her hand out for the panties.

He looked at her outstretched hand and at the stop-you-in-your-tracks red lace. "Neither was your seductive redressing," he told her, balling the panties into his fist and sliding them into his pocket.

"I need my underwear," she laughed.

"You didn't seem to five minutes ago," he said, reaching down to lift up his pack. "You better put some boots on, this fire's going out." He walked over and started nudging the remaining pieces apart, the light they cast barely illuminating their standing room.

"You're really not going to give them back?" she asked.

"We'll see..." he said, chuckling when she gave in on a sigh and sat down on the blanket to put her boots back on. He retrieved the flashlight and handed it to her as she stood.

"I had it the whole time?" she asked incredulously.

"Of course," he said smiling, pulling her pout to him for a kiss. "If you would have checked your bag before we set off, you would have seen that."

"Very funny," she said, grabbing his jeans and tugging him to her. She kissed him quickly as she tried to sneak her hand into his pocket to retrieve what was hers.

"Uh uh," he said, moving faster than she could. He caught her wrists, redirecting them up and around his neck. He pulled her hips to his and took her quick distraction of a kiss into a mind blurring assault. "Time to go," he told her as he stepped back, motioning for her to lead the way with the flashlight.

He spread out the last of the fire and followed her to the tunnel, taking the flashlight in one hand, and holding hers with his other. When they made it out of the tunnel and into the dimly lit waterfall room, they stopped and he repacked the flashlight into her backpack, took out a waterproof poncho and draped it over her and her pack. He turned his bag and retrieved his own, laughing at her expression of surprise as he put it on.

"The whole time," she stated again.

"Of course. Always be prepared."

She smiled, closing her eyes and shaking her head.

He led the way out of the waterfall, her laughter the tune for the shimmering light to dance along the falling droplets.

SEVENTY

-AUGUST-

"Why didn't we take this way to begin with?" Lillian asked him as they neared the trailhead.

The route back, while initially challenging for a novice climber to access from the large waterfall above, took them scenically along the edge of the river, past the slides, and down to a smaller fall. As it was the more accessible and popular destination, the path was well-worn and equipped with distance markers providing a clear way back to the trailhead lot.

"It's all part of the journey. You push yourself to the point you think you'll break, but you know you can't just sit down and quit. You give yourself a pep talk and turn the corner, where all your hard work is rewarded because you've made it! You take it all in, feeling renewed by the wonders this world has to offer, and then you remember that you saved the best for last. You finish out your trip with a leisurely hike with amazing views. You gain a new appreciation for the hike, ending on a high note, thus forgetting you were over it and ready to turn back. It keeps you wanting for more."

"Or you do what normal people do, and go in and out the same way. Both paths are nice and easy, and you never doubt your sanity or choice in extracurricular activities."

"Where's the fun in that?" he laughed. "You got to experience things today that many people may never do."

"You mean recklessly having sex in a cave shrouded from the world only by the veil of a waterfall?"

He chuckled as he looked over at her. "I was referring more to the hike up the unmarked trail to the higher fall. Most people can't make that climb."

"Oh, so sex in the cave … not a first for you. Got it. And here I thought it was impulsive," she teased. "You *were* pretty prepared with the blanket and the firewood."

He laughed up at the sky before turning back to her. "I can honestly say that I've never had sex with another woman in that cave."

"That one."

"Any cave," he laughed again, bringing her hand to his lips and planting a kiss before lowering it, still holding it as they walked. "But I'd be up for doing it again." He dodged, catching her other hand as she swatted, laughing. "I didn't say with *another* woman."

"I should hope not," she cautioned, sighing when her boots crunched against the gravel, marking the lot just ahead. "I can't wait for a shower," she sighed.

"Mine's big enough for two," August reminded her.

"Ryder?"

"No. Ryder is most definitely not invited."

"Stop," she laughed, slightly pushing his arm. "Is that Ryder's truck?"

They crossed from the trees into the gravel lot, where both their vehicles were parked side by side, a couple others parked farther away, indicating other hikers despite not having come across them, and the truck that, now that the view was clear, was unmistakably Ryder's.

"You've got to be kidding me," August swore as the door opened and Ryder stepped out.

Lillian squeezed his hand before letting go, then hurried over to meet Ryder, August strolling up at his own pace. Ryder's expression was serious as Lillian asked if everything was okay.

"Ryder," August stated when he reached them. "What are you doing here?"

"Checking on you," he said to Lillian.

"What? Why?" she asked, confusion ringing through her words.

"Your dad mentioned you were out here."

"Yeah, so? I told him I'd check in. I don't understand. He sent you to check on me?"

"No, he didn't," August guessed, and Ryder turned his glare on him. "But Ryder can't seem to get it through his head that you're with me, and is, yet again, inserting himself into your life."

"August," she sighed in exasperation, but reached over, grabbing Ryder's arm when he shifted to face August. "Ryder. What's going on?" she asked, and he brought his focus back to her.

"What are you doing out here, Lilly? You know how dangerous it is."

"I wouldn't take her somewhere I couldn't keep her safe," August answered instead, receiving a glare from Ryder.

"You have no idea what you're messing with out here," he said, "You could have gotten her hurt."

"I'm fully aware of what's in these woods, and in case you've forgotten, I was the one that led you all through there. Pretty sure I know where she can go and what she can handle."

"Just because you're an expert woodsman doesn't mean you know everything." Ryder turned back to Lillian. "But you. What were you thinking going in there after Wade and Brian and Rain?" He paused. "Lilly, what were you thinking?"

"Ryder, it was fine, really. We just hiked to the falls. Plenty of people go there all the time."

"Do you have any idea how close—" He took a breath and let it out. "Lilly. I've hiked the falls. You should have been back hours ago."

"What she does in her spare time is no concern of yours," August interjected again.

"Why don't you back off, August? She can answer for herself."

"She doesn't need to answer for herself. Last I checked, you don't have any say in what she does, or have you forgotten that? You had your chance ten years ago. You blew it. She's made her choice. Get over it and leave her alone."

"Guys—"

"If you really thought I didn't stand a chance, you wouldn't care that I'm here talking to her. It wouldn't threaten you for anyone else to check in on her, but it does when I do. Why is that, August? Could it be because deep down you know she still feels something for me? Something that can't be pushed out just because some hotshot comes along and gives her a good time for a while?"

"I care that you're talking to her because every time you do, no matter how many times she has to remind you that she's with me, you mix her up and get in her head. If you really cared about her, like you say that you do, you'd leave her alone and stop confusing her to the point that she's distracted for days on end."

"I can't help it that I'm unforgettable, which won't be said for you when she finally realizes what her heart really wants. I can't say that it surprises me that she can't think straight after being with me, but come to think of it, she's never seemed distracted after she's been with you. Why is that I wonder?"

"Because I don't mess with her mind."

"No, you'll just lie about who you really are, make her feel like shit for having emotions, and move on."

"That's your game, buddy, not mine."

"It's *my* game to come into her house, accuse her of sleeping with someone because of your jealous insecurities, and then leave her feeling guilty over something she never did? Sure, that doesn't mess with her at all.

"If you'd stop getting in her head over things she wants to do but won't because she has dignity, she'd realize what she has right in front of her, but you can't let that happen. You use her guilt to your advantage until she proves herself to you, and then you blind her to the possibility of something better because you know if she gave herself to me for one night, you'd lose her forever."

August chuckled ironically. "Ryder, I'm sure if you were worth sleeping with, she would have done it already. Guess you didn't make as lasting of an impression all those years ago, huh? If a one-nighter's all you're after, you can move along. I promise, she's more than satisfied now."

The right hook to his jaw was quick and packed more of a punch than August would have thought. He heard Lillian's sharp breath and possibly a yell as he slid the pack from his back and smiled at Ryder.

He led with a left, catching Ryder off guard, then landed with his right. Ryder threw another, but before August could return, Ryder was coming straight for him in a football style tackle, both of them hitting the ground hard. They rolled along the gravel, some punches landing, others missing, and were completely dust-covered when they finally separated and got back on their feet, both ready to lunge.

"Enough!" Lillian yelled, getting between them before they could pound each other again.

"Lillian, move out of the way," August said, glaring at Ryder.

Ryder grabbed her firmly by the waist, pulling her back and nudging her out of the way. "Lilly Flower, you need to go before you get hurt. We need to see this through."

She turned and swatted at his hands. "Don't you talk sweet to me while you beat each other up." She turned back to August. "I'm right here and you two are fighting about me like I don't have a say in what happens in my own life."

"Ryder's right," August told her, still looking at Ryder. "You should go. We need to work this out now."

"And what happens when you beat each other bloody? The winner gets to come claim his prize?" Neither man had an answer for her as she looked between the two. "Fine. Beat each other up, but don't either one of you come knocking on my door when it's over." She bent down and picked up the swatch of red that had fallen from August's pocket in their quarrel. She turned to Ryder. "Don't ever put words in my mouth again. You don't know what I feel for August. You don't know what happens in my head or have the right to talk about what I deserve." She turned to August. "And you," she said with equal fury. "Not that it's any of your business what happened between Ryder and me when we dated before, but no, we never slept together. We were teenagers. But he was my best friend, and I loved him. That's why it hurt so badly and so deeply when he betrayed my trust. Maybe you're right. Maybe I don't want to let him go because it would feel like losing that friend all over again and selfishly, I don't want to go through that pain.

"I chose you, over and over again I chose you, but if I'm just a prize to be argued over and bragged about, then here's your trophy," she said, and threw the red lace for him to catch. She looked at them both. "But if you are willing to resort to childish squabbles over something neither of you have a say in, maybe I was wrong about both of you."

She turned and stomped away, leaving both men staring after her.

"Lilly!" Ryder called, starting to follow her before August grabbed him by the shoulder.

"No," he growled. "That's not your place."

Ryder shoved off his hand. "As her friend, since that's all I'm allowed to be, it is."

"As her friend that wants in her pants, it's not."

"I won't hit you again, August. I'm not taking the bait and being the one that she casts aside because I couldn't keep my cool."

"Fine, don't hit me." August crossed his arms across his chest and stepped between Ryder and Lillian's car. "But you're not running after her, either."

He listened as she pulled away, watching Ryder's eyes follow her car as it left the lot.

"Let's get one thing straight, here and now," August said when Ryder met his glare. "I know you love her still, and I'm sorry that she doesn't feel the same anymore, but she's with me now, and I'll fight for her until I can't anymore."

"And if she tells you it's over? If she tells you today that this was too much, will you walk away and let her choose?"

"It's always been her choice."

"Would you let her go?"

"Have you?"

Ryder ignored the question, taking a step toward his truck. "You're wrong about one thing," he told him. "She does still love me; she just doesn't want to face it." He took a few more steps and turned back. "The shitty thing though, despite everything I accused you of earlier, is that I'm pretty sure she loves you, too."

Ryder walked on, August heading away as well without a comment, making it to his truck as Ryder pulled up.

"You know what I don't understand? Is how when I met you a few weeks ago, you were still hung up on the loss of your fiancé. You said you'd never stop looking for her." Ryder stared hard at August. "But now you move in on the one that got away from me. You know what it feels like to lose your person, and I wouldn't wish that on anyone, but you… Knowing what that feels like, you're telling me to willingly let go of the one that's still right in front of me." He shook his head before turning to look back at him. "I think you of all people should know that I can't just walk away."

SEVENTY-ONE

-LILLIAN-

"Dad, hey," Lillian said coarsely, when the line connected. She dropped her purse and keys on the table by her door and made her way through the house. "I'm safely out of the woods."

"Well, don't sound so excited about it," he said dryly. "I'm gathering it wasn't as adventurous as you'd hoped?"

"Oh no, the hike was great. August and I had a fantastic time."

"But…"

"But then Ryder was waiting for us in the parking lot, and he and August went at each other like a couple of frat boy idiots."

"Why was Ryder waiting for you?"

"He was worried," she sighed. "He thought we should have been out earlier than we were, and I guess you hadn't heard from me…"

"I didn't send him, Lillian."

"I know. He didn't say that you did," she said, trying to let her anger go. "August took his being there the wrong way, or maybe not, I don't know. Why do guys have to be so stupid?"

"Love can make us that way."

"Dad," she let out a breath as she sat on the chair in her kitchen, trying to untie her boots without dropping the phone. "Just because you're happy I'm dating again doesn't mean that the first contenders are going to fall in love with me. August and I have only known each other a few weeks, and Ryder … well, Ryder and I aren't dating, but whatever this is, is new, too."

"Hmmm," was all he said on the other end.

"Hmmm," she said back, kicking the boot away. "This isn't a fairytale. People don't meet, fall in love, and live happily ever after."

"Not with that attitude they don't. How will your mother and I ever get grandkids?"

She couldn't help but laugh. "Dad," she moaned. "What am I supposed to do with them? They stood there arguing about me like I wasn't there. They hit each other. Rolling around on the ground, punching each other."

"Who won?"

"Dad!"

"I'm just wondering. If August took Ryder, maybe I need to add him to the force. Looks like he'll be sticking around for a while. Maybe he needs a job."

"Oh my gosh, Dad. I'm trying to tell you what astounding idiots they both were, and you want them to work together?"

"Sure. It'll force them to get along."

"I don't think so."

He chuckled on the other end. "If you say so."

"What do I do? I got so angry when they wouldn't listen, and then they were fighting… When I finally got a word in…" She stared at the mess the boots had left on her floor. "I said some things that I probably shouldn't have said and left after telling them that I'd been wrong about them and to leave me alone."

"I'm sure they said things they regret, too. That happens when emotions are high. They'll come around."

"I don't know," she said uncertainly.

"You haven't scared them off for good."

"Well, maybe they need to be for a little bit at least."

Her dad chuckled again.

"What? They acted like little children fighting over a ball. I'm not a ball. I don't think I want to see them right now."

"You will. And you'll figure it all out."

"Gee, thanks. That is so insightful."

"What are dads for, if not to state the obvious? You'll talk with them both. You'll work things out … or you won't. You'll figure out if what was said was reparable or if the words hit too close. Give it time. Let everyone cool off. You'll see."

"You're not going to give me advice on which one?"

"Nope. You know I'd tell you if either wouldn't be good for you, but this is a decision that you have to make."

"I know," she sighed. "I've gotta go, Dad. I need to shower and think."

"Keep your chin up, Lillian. We all do stupid things, but fighting for someone or something you believe in isn't ever stupid. Think about what they believe they were fighting for, and then decide how you feel."

"I will," she agreed, "but for now, I think I want to be mad for a while."

Her dad was still laughing when they disconnected.

Having updated the only person she needed to talk to for a while, she put her phone on silent. She'd think about them later, but she didn't have to talk to either of them until she was ready, and now was not the time.

She glared at the boots and the dirt on the floor around them, wanting to leave them for later along with the boys, but the boots hadn't done anything wrong, and they'd only be another reminder when she washed the day off of her. She picked them up and took them to her backyard, using the hose outside her door to rinse the dirt away. When the water ran clear, she brought them back into the house and placed them on a towel to dry. She swept up the small pile of dirt they'd left earlier, then took the vacuum to the carpet she'd walked across. Unable to leave a singular vacuum row on the carpet, she finished the whole room.

"If only cleaning up all messes were as easy and rewarding," she said, looking at the fresh lines on her living room carpet.

She walked by the phone waiting on her kitchen table, resisting the urge to check it.

She started the shower, letting it warm as she undressed. She grabbed her basket of laundry to start while she showered. The water was heated by the time she returned. Ready to wash away what was left of her day, she tossed in some steamers and stepped under the stream, closing her eyes and letting the water rain over her.

She inhaled slowly and deeply, pushing all thoughts from her head with each outward breath. The scents of the steamers soothed her senses as they dissolved. She let her mind wander as she lathered and rinsed, watching as the bubbles swirled around the drain, as the river had bubbled and frothed over the rocks beneath. She tipped her head back to let the stream flow, feeling the stray droplets splash against her shoulders.

When the steamers had lost their aroma and the water started to remind her of the waterfall, bringing back the memories of the afternoon, she shut it off. Toweling off, she checked her clock. Too early for bed, she noted, wanting to put the day behind her. Deciding to watch a movie, she dressed in comfy clothes and curled up on her couch with a blanket, knowing she was being completely indulgent and ignoring her problems.

She found a mindless movie to watch, something silly and fun that she'd seen a million times that would in no way remind her of her life.

"You're allowed a day," she told herself and pushed play.

SEVENTY-TWO

-LILLIAN-

She woke and the room was dark. Disoriented, she sat up and looked around, wondering why she'd decided to sleep in the living room. The house was quiet, and the TV screen was black. She vaguely recalled her eyes getting heavy during the movie and realized she must have turned it off before she fell asleep.

Listening to the silent room, she heard the sound of water running in the distance. Curious, she followed the sounds to her bathroom door, pushing it open to water streaming steadily, crystals of light twinkling and rainbows dancing. She felt his arms wrap around her from behind, turning into him to kiss him softly. They were in the cavern beyond the fall. Candles created a hazy glow, rose petals were strewn about, a campfire crackled, and champagne chilled in ice next to a blanket on the ground.

"What's all this?" She laughed as she took it all in. "How'd you get this in here?"

"It took more than one trip," August admitted.

"So that's what you've been up to lately."

"Among other things," he said mysteriously, scooping her off her feet.

She squealed, framing his face in her hands and kissing him as he set her on the blanket. They made love as the candlelight made shapes on the wall. He poured her champagne, and she sipped, giggling as the bubbles tickled her nose. She watched as he rummaged through his pack.

"Come back over here," she told him. "You promised to keep me warm."

He smiled and laid down behind her, pulled her closer, and kissed the side of her neck as she dreamily sighed in response. His lips grazed her ear, his breath warm.

"Marry me, Lillian," he said, as soft as the dancing shadows nearby.

She turned to him, searching his eyes for laughter, but all she could see was anticipation as he waited.

"I love you, Lil, and don't want to live without you," he told her.

She smiled, pulled him down to her, and kissed him deeply.

"Does that count as a yes?"

"Yes," she laughed. "People will think it's too soon, but yes. I love you, August."

He picked up the box she hadn't seen him bring over, and he slipped the ring on her finger. They made love before she had a chance to look at it.

They stood at the waterfall again. Light danced off the ring and she hugged him, her laughter a chime as she walked through the water and stood in her kitchen. The sunlight streamed through the windows as August leaned against the counter, his arms crossed over his chest.

"I thought you'd let this go," he said, his voice tired.

"Will you just look at this?"

"No, Lil, because that isn't possible."

"But what if it is?"

He walked over, a firm grasp on her elbows. "Rain is gone. Just because you fought before she went missing doesn't make her disappearance your fault. She's been gone for over a year and she isn't coming back."

"I know," she told him furiously as she slapped the paper onto the counter, a copied picture of a case file with a morgue image displayed. "Because she's dead."

She saw him glance at it and back to her.

"Just because this looks like her doesn't make it her. The dates don't work, Lillian."

"That's what I've been trying to tell you. Something's not right up there."

He dropped his arms and turned away, walked a few steps, then turned back. "Stop it, Lillian. You need to let this go before it drives you crazy. There's no such thing as time travel."

"What if there is?" she pleaded.

He snatched the paper.

"Where did you get this? Lillian," he stated, turning when she hadn't answered. "You went to *him* for this didn't you?"

"He wanted to help," she said defensively.

"Of course he wanted to help. Ryder'll do whatever he can to help if it means getting you back into bed with him."

"That was *one* time," she told him. "It was … I've told you I was sorry. Why do you bring him into this every time you want to change the subject?"

"You brought him into this when you wouldn't leave him out of your life!" he bellowed. He picked up the page, wadded it into a ball, and threw it at the wall.

"I was confused and upset and –"

"And you should have turned to me."

"I tried! You wouldn't listen."

"Because what you were saying was crazy!"

"I'm not crazy!"

"I didn't say *you* were!"

"You just did!"

"I said what you were saying was crazy, not that you were."

"What's the difference?"

"I'm not doing this again, Lil," he said, frustrating her that he wouldn't listen.

"You wouldn't listen then either!"

"Then why don't you run back to him now, like you did then?"

"Fuck you, August!" she turned and stomped down the hall to her room.

"Are you sure you don't want to fuck Ryder again?" she heard as she slammed the door shut.

She turned into the room and rested her head against the door before she moved to the desk. She looked at the pieces of paper, and picked one up at random, reading the frenzied scribble of notes, a spiderweb of words, each individual, but also linked together. *Adrenaline*, underlined. *Why is it always a heart attack?* written in the margins. *Fear?* written and then circled. A page full of questions and disjointed answers.

She set the paper down and looked through more of the pages on the desk. She sat and stared at the mess in front of her and watched as the pen she held moved to the notes page. She circled the word fear again and knew what she was going to write before the words appeared on the page. *Fear is the key.*

The echo of the words lingered as she climbed the path.

"Fear is the key," she told herself like a mantra. "Don't be afraid."

She made it to the crumbling wall. A pull from within urged her to move forward, to cross the barrier, but as she reached out to touch the stone, she felt the hair rise along her arm, individually calling to alert each cell through her body. Her heart raced and her feet stayed firmly planted.

"Fear is the key. Don't be afraid."

She closed her eyes, took a deep breath and let it out slowly as she closed her eyes and lifted her foot.

"Don't be afraid," she whispered and walked into the Mountain.

The fall from the couch jolted her out of the dream. She gasped for breath as she clutched at the burning in her chest. The sounds that were screaming all around her, she could hear in the pounding of her ears. The fear of being lost and alone, unable to find her way back out, shook her now to her core. The pain as her heart raced faster and faster until she knew it couldn't take anymore strain still radiated in waves, aching through her torso.

She leaned against her couch, letting the tears flow, knowing what it felt like to die on the Mountain.

She tried to stand, her legs unsteady beneath her, then sat with a thud as the darkness began closing in on her vision. She reached out for the phone that she hadn't looked at in hours and hit talk.

"Lillian? Hey… I'm sorry for earlier—"

"Please," she breathed out the word, but it was barely more than a croak.

"Lillian, what's wrong?" His tone turned serious.

"Can you—" She cleared her throat. "I don't want to be alone," she whispered.

"What's going on? What happened? Lillian?"

She heard him call for her, but he was too far away for her to answer, and it was too dark after all.

"Lillian… come on, baby, you need to wake up."

She could hear the soft words through her dream, but they didn't make sense in the quiet darkness.

"Lilly," the whisper again.

She felt a hand brushing the hair along her face, and she turned into the gentle touch.

"Lillian," the voice whispered again. "Come on. Time to wake up."

There was an urgency behind the soft noise, pulling her closer to the confusion, pulling her closer to the pain that was in her chest, pulling her out of the soothing darkness that she didn't want to break free from.

"Lillian! Wake up!"

She sat up on a gasp, gulping in air as if she'd been submerged under water for far too long. The dream rushed over her again, and she remembered everything as clearly as if she'd lived it herself down to the moment her life ended. She hugged her arms around her knees, covering her face in her arms, trying to push the dream away, trying to forget what she could still feel inside of her.

"Lillian."

She jumped and turned at the gentle voice and the light touch on her back.

"Holy sh—" She covered her face with one hand, her racing heart with the other. "Ryder?" she asked.

"Sorry. I didn't mean to scare you."

She uncovered her face, studying him as he sat on the edge of the coffee table in front of her couch. She looked around the dark room, lit only by a singular light in the kitchen and the bouncing glow of the TV's idle screen.

"What are you doing here?"

He looked confused but answered softly. "You called me… You don't remember?"

She thought about her dream, the series that had unfolded, the pain after and picking up the phone.

"I'm sorry," she told him, turning on the couch to put her feet on the ground, putting her elbow on her lap and resting her forehead against her hand. "I didn't remember." She looked up at him, still holding her head. "How'd you get in here?"

"Back door was unlocked. Lillian, you want to tell me what happened? Why I've been trying to wake you up for the past thirty minutes?"

"I had a bad dream," she said.

"That was a little more than a bad dream," he told her. "You looked dead on the floor when I walked in. You scared the shit out of me."

"Yeah, me too," she sighed, rubbing her face. She tried to stand, but her vision started to fade again and she quickly sat back down.

"Will you just stay put," Ryder chastised.

"I'm okay," she said, trying to reassure them both. "I just need to get a drink." She leaned forward to try and stand again.

"Lillian, stop. You're as white as a ghost. I'll get you a drink." He stood to walk to her kitchen. "Don't get up," he warned.

Her head was pounding now that she was awake and the throbbing behind her eyes made her thankful for the dim lights. She laid her head back, closing her eyes, listening to him opening and closing cabinets. She was about to call out to tell him where to find a glass when she heard him returning. She raised her head, opening her eyes when she heard him sit on the table.

"Here, drink," he said, handing her the short glass.

"I meant water," she told him, eyeing the brown liquid he was holding out.

"You get water after you drink this."

"That isn't going to help anything, and I already have a headache."

"It'll give you some color again and I have medicine, too," he said shaking the bottle that was sitting next to him on the table. "Drink."

She took the glass, eyeing him darkly, then took a sip, the fire sliding down her throat.

"Another," he said.

She sighed, but took another small sip, feeling it start to warm her from the inside out. She was shivering. She hadn't realized how cold she was.

"Good enough," he said when she handed the glass back to him, and he downed the remaining whiskey in one gulp. He turned his head and swore softly, his eyes glimmering when he looked back at her. "Geez, Lilly, you have the worst taste in liquor. That was straight up fire."

She smiled and let out a sliver of a laugh. "I don't even know where you found that," she told him.

"The trash pile, apparently."

He turned, uncapped the medicine bottle, and shook a few of the tablets into his hand. He handed her the pills and the water, and she gladly drank them down. She handed the cup back to him and he pulled the blanket up and around her.

"Now, tell me what happened tonight."

"I told you. It was just a bad dream," she started.

"And I'm telling you, you're full of shit. I've never moved so fast as I did tonight when I came around that corner and you were dead on the floor."

"I wasn't dead."

"How was I supposed to know? You call, scare the hell out of me, and then go silent. I get here and you're on the floor, unresponsive and white as death."

"I'm sorry," she whispered, remembering the way the dream had seemed so real and how she'd been in so much agony when she woke. She hugged the blanket tighter around her.

"Don't be sorry," he said softly. "Tell me what happened." He paused, studying her face. "Was August here?"

"What?"

"Did something happen after this afternoon? Did he come over here?"

"No," she told him, shaking her head. "I haven't talked to him since the parking lot."

A flicker of emotion crossed his face, but he looked away before she could decipher what it could be.

"Did you take something tonight?" He turned back to her and asked.

"What? Like drugs?" she snorted.

"Something to help you sleep?" he offered.

"No, I didn't do anything out of the usual. No wine, no sleeping pills, nothing."

"When did you eat last?"

"I don't remember," she admitted. "Ryder, I'm fine, really."

"You're not, Lilly. Normal people don't just pass out and then not remember calling people that, if they were fine and thinking clearly, they probably wouldn't have called."

"Why wouldn't I have called you?"

"I don't know, maybe because of the ass I was earlier and the mess I made with your boyfriend... You said you didn't want to be alone... Why didn't you call August?"

"I don't know," she whispered to her lap.

"Lilly—" He paused, waiting for her to look at him. "You chose to call me instead of him. Why?"

"He wouldn't understand."

"Lilly Flower, I gotta be honest with you, I'm not understanding right now either. Help me understand."

She looked away, not wanting to admit what she feared.

He reached over and gently turned her face back to his, his thumb lingering gently before he let her go.

"You can talk to me," he said softly.

She searched his eyes, finding only concern as he waited.

"I think—" Her voice hitched on the words. "I think I know how I'm going to die."

SEVENTY-THREE

-RYDER-

"What are you talking about?" Ryder whispered as he watched the tear slide down her cheek.

Lillian swiped it away, taking a breath as she did. "I felt it," she told him, pressing her hand to her chest. "I felt it happen."

"What did you feel?"

"My heart…" She wiped away another tear.

"You're scaring me, baby," he said, moving to sit next to her on the couch. He pulled her to lean against him and was surprised when she didn't pull away but burrowed against him instead. "Tell me what you mean."

"You'll think I've lost my mind," she said.

"I can handle it." He rubbed along her hair and down her back in long, soothing strokes. "Whenever you're ready," he said, breathing in the smell of her hair, content to stay that way the rest of the night if she needed him to.

The breath she let out was shaky. "I was upset at you and August earlier," she started quietly.

"I remember that clearly," he teased.

"I said I wasn't going to think about either of you idiots."

"I probably deserved that," he admitted when she paused to take another deep breath.

"I turned on a movie and must have fallen asleep…"

"What movie?" he asked when she was silent a moment more.

"What?"

"What movie? Was it scary?"

"Oh… No, it was a rom-com, an old movie I've seen a thousand times."

Ryder nodded but didn't interrupt again.

"I woke up and the movie was over. Everything was dark, but I could hear something, so I followed the noise."

"There was someone in your house?" he asked, tensing, turning to look toward her bedroom and kicking himself for not checking the house when he came in. He saw her on the floor and all of his training disappeared. All he had thought of was getting to her and praying that she wasn't dead.

"No. Nobody was here."

"You're sure?" he asked, wondering if he should make a sweep anyway, although if there had been someone, they were long gone by now.

"Yes, I'm sure," she said pausing again. He settled back, resuming stroking her hair. "There was water, and I went to find it. I guess I thought maybe I had left the shower running. I don't really know. When I opened the door, I was standing on the other side of a waterfall, watching the sunlight peek through."

"Got it, so we're in your dream."

"Yes, and at first it was… nice. Everything was happy and… perfect. Clearly, I should have realized it was a dream, but it felt more like a memory."

"Dreams can feel real when we're in them," he told her, his words calm and quiet. "I've had some weird ones myself, ones I could have sworn happened."

"But you *know* they were dreams."

"Unfortunately," he told her.

"This didn't feel like just a dream. It felt like more." She paused and he waited for her to figure out how to tell her story. "The places in the dream were so real… but the things we were doing were different than what has happened in real life."

"You and August you mean."

"Yes," she said softly. "In the dream, we were in a cave."

"I thought you were at a waterfall."

"The cave is behind the waterfall. We were back in the cave, where we… Everything was different. We said different things, the lighting was different… We were engaged…"

His heart tore a little, understanding the "we" she was talking about didn't include him.

"When we left the cave, we were here in my house. We were arguing. It was angry on both sides. It hurt to hear the words that came out of his mouth, and it hurt to know the words that were going to come out of mine, unable to stop them from flowing, like I was watching a rerun instead of living it out."

She paused again to bring the dream back.

"I got the feeling that some time had passed since the cave and the kitchen," she finally said. "We were fighting about something, and he was mad because he didn't believe me and brought up what happened with you—" She stopped abruptly.

He continued his slow strokes. "What about me?" he asked her quietly.

"He was mad that we … that I had trusted you," she told him.

He felt she was holding back part of the story, but he waited again.

"In the dream, he knew I thought the Mountain's time was askew, but he didn't believe me. He didn't want to hear about it or see my proof. He said it was crazy, and I yelled back and left the room, slamming him out.

"On the other side of the slammed door was my office. There were so many pages of 'missings' and 'founds.' I had notes everywhere, theories…" She pulled her blanket closer and wrapped her arm around him again. "I felt the pen in my hand when I wrote it down and, in the dream, it made sense. It was so clear to me."

"What did you write?" he asked the silence between them.

She shook her head against him. "Then I was in the woods, standing at a broken-down wall of old stone and I knew I was on the border. I knew when I stepped through the opening, I'd be in the Mountain. I knew how it worked. I wasn't afraid. I could prove that it worked."

He felt her body begin to quake softly.

"But it didn't work. I stepped through and everything changed. The air felt electric; I could feel the current and knew the shock would come at any moment. There were no bird songs, no crickets calling. There was no gentle breeze flowing through the leaves. There was no air at all. Everything was stagnant, stale, the air unbreathable. Every breath was like choking on smoke. Immediately, I tried to turn back, but the opening was gone. I clawed at the wall, but the stones were too smooth; my fingers kept slipping. I was all alone.

"I was trapped and hadn't proven anything. Nobody knew where I was. I knew I was going to die by myself. I heard the noises then. They came from all around and nowhere at all… There was a scream… It could have been me… All I could do was run on legs made of burning rubber in the suffocating air. My heart was racing… and the pain… the pain was too much until I couldn't take anymore. I could feel myself giving in, feel the tearing from inside."

"Shhh," he said, squeezing her against him while she cried. "It was only a dream. It's okay now. You're alive and in your house. It was just a dream."

"I can still feel the ache in my chest," she whispered, her body trembling in his arms. "What if it wasn't a dream?"

"But it was, baby, it was. You're right here, right now. You're alive. I've got you. You're here with me. You're not in the Mountain."

"What if the things I saw were memories?"

"They weren't. You said there were things in the dream that were different."

"But what if I was remembering things that *will* happen?"

"Premonitions?"

"Memories."

She tilted her face to his, her cheeks damp from tears.

"It was so real, Ryder. I could feel it all."

"It felt real because in the dream, your brain thought it was. That's all. I promise you, you're safe."

"But what if I go? In the future, what if I go to the Mountain and that's how I die? What if my body just passed me in time and I caught all the memories as it went through?"

He looked at her pleading eyes, the fear in her face, the trembling he could feel as he held her. The memory of her lying cold and white on the ground flashed before his eyes, and a tingle of doubt clawed along the back of his neck. They'd already accepted that time travel was happening. Was it possible her future self had passed by, and in its passing, she picked up the memories? Was that how it happened with the others, but they wrote it off as a bad dream?

"How far into the future do you think your dream went?"

"You believe me?" she asked, and he watched her mouth tug down at the side and another tear escape.

He wiped it away, holding her as she leaned into his hand.

"I'm not sure what to believe anymore," he told her honestly. "But if you believe this, I believe you."

She laid her head against his chest again, wrapping her arms around him.

"Thank you," she murmured.

"What else can you tell me about the dream?"

"That's all I remember," she told him, the trembling slowing.

"You didn't get a feel for *when* in time you were?"

"No," she said quietly. "It was all disjointed, but also not. It was like hopping from one memory to another. I think they were in order, but I don't know. It had been a year since Rain had…" She stopped and lifted her head to look at him again.

"What is it?"

"Rain was dead." She sat up, wiping her face. "August and I were fighting because Rain's disappearance sent me down the path to figure out what was happening with The Mountain. He didn't want to believe that the 'found' report was her body."

"But Rain is alive."

"So… it could have been a dream?" She swiped at another tear. "They weren't memories?"

"Wouldn't you rather it was your brain projecting everything you've been going through lately into some really bizarre dream than the thought that you die sometime in the future and you just somehow downloaded your future self's memories and death?"

"Yeah," she said, smiling sadly and rubbing at her heart again. "But it felt so real."

"Come here," he said soothingly, and she leaned back against him. "I'm sorry."

"You didn't do anything."

"I have. I've added to your stress by not letting you go, and now your dreams are trying to kill you."

She chuckled against his chest.

He was back to stroking her hair, listening to her breathing slowly start to even out.

"I know I should let you go..." she whispered.

"I know," he sighed, bending down to kiss her hair.

He knew the moment she fell asleep when he felt her arms loosen and her head grow heavier against him. He let her lay there a few more moments, telling himself it was for her, that she needed to feel safe and be able to rest.

"Lillian," he whispered when he'd held her for longer than he should.

"Mmmm?" she mumbled.

"Come on," he whispered. "I'll take you to bed."

"Finally," she sighed.

He chuckled, but she didn't seem to notice, her breathing deep again.

"Lillian."

She made a noise that he couldn't make out and snuggled in closer.

"You'll probably be the death of me," he said to her hair, but her breathing didn't falter, and she didn't respond. "What the hell," he sighed. "There's worse ways to go."

He nudged off his shoes and pulled one of her pillows over. He shifted on the couch to lie down against the pillow, and she curled into him as he pulled the blanket over them both. He listened to her steady breathing, trying to stay awake as long as he could. He held on to her, feeling the weight of her as she dreamed, knowing she'd wake up tomorrow and this would all be just another dream. When his eyes were too heavy to keep open, he kissed the top of her head, whispering a murmur into her dreams.

"Love you, Ryde," he heard on a sigh as he gave in to sleep.

He woke before she did, her sounds in sleep a slight purr as she lay cocooned between him and the couch. It was still dark, and she didn't move when he shifted to check the time. 3:00 a.m. He eased into a sitting position, and she reached out, sliding to take over his space, sighing in her sleep. He felt guilty for already stealing so many moments with her and knew he shouldn't push it any further, but every muscle in his body wanted to carry her to her room and wake her up in a manner that would make sure she'd never feel lost, or alone, or scared ever again.

But she wasn't his to have.

He felt for his shoes and slipped them on, reaching for his phone, keys, and gun that he'd set on the table. He brushed away the stray strand of hair that had fallen over her face and leaned down to kiss where he'd brushed it. She didn't stir.

He covered her with the blanket, taking a last look at her resting face and slipped quietly through her house and out the back door, making sure the handle was locked so he couldn't give in and let himself back inside. Each second of the drive home seemed to add a mile onto his normally short drive as he thought about her sleeping form and how it felt to have her body pressed against his.

He trudged up the stairs and headed straight to his gym, knowing that the few hours he had left for sleep would only be torment as he laid awake remembering the smell of her hair, the feeling of her soft skin, the sound of his name slipping through her lips.

The sound of her voice when she called, and the sight of her lying on the floor pushed him through his run. The thought of her dreaming of being engaged to August fueled his fight against the punching bag. The desperation in her face when she thought she knew she was remembering a life she had left to live, begging for him to believe her, almost squashed his push-ups, but thinking of Lillian arguing and putting August in his place kept him going. He dragged himself to the shower and ran the water cold, trying to shock away the image of her face trying not to cry or the sound of relief in her voice when she realized he believed her. He braced his hands against the wall of the shower, wishing the water pelting his back could get colder as he remembered her whispered words as he fell asleep. Words he knew she didn't know she spoke, that she wouldn't remember tomorrow.

He wrapped the towel around his waist and walked to his room, checking the time. 4:30 a.m. He set an alarm for two hours and tossed the phone on the bed. He laid down beside it and prayed that sleep was kind and would come quickly.

SEVENTY-FOUR

-Ryder-

A rapid pounding startled him out of sleep. He woke as he had laid down, the towel still somehow wrapped around his waist, the pillows and blankets undisturbed, as if he'd just sat down. A bird called near his window, an incessant piping without a return.

"Give it up," he called to the bird. "She's not coming." He ran his hand through the front of his hair, then dropped his arm on the bed above his head. "I'd know," he sighed, sitting up on the edge of the bed.

The pounding sounded again.

He looked out the bedroom door in the direction of the stairs leading to the front of the house, then reached over to look at his phone. 8:15 a.m.

"Son of a bitch," he swore, looking at the missed alarm notification, the missed calls, and a list of text messages. "Yeah, yeah, yeah," he told the knocker. "I'm coming."

He pulled open the door before the pounding could rattle the frame.

"Hey, Sheriff," Ryder said, moving aside to let him come in.

"Catch you at a bad time?" Bill asked, eyeing the towel then glancing up the stairs. "You alone?"

Reflexively Ryder grabbed the fold so it wouldn't come loose now.

"Yeah," he said, running his hand through his hair. "Sorry, guess I overslept."

"Hmm." Bill mused. "How does August look?" he asked, nodding to the discoloration along his jaw.

"A little less smug."

Bill nodded to himself. "Get dressed. You're with me today. We've got a case."

"Yeah, be right down," he told him, closing the door behind Bill and taking the stairs two at a time. He tossed the towel on the bed, threw on his clothes and boots, and grabbed his gear, checking his gun before fitting it into the holster he wore on his belt.

"That's a better look for a future sheriff," Bill said when Ryder sat in the passengers' seat.

"I don't know, could win me some votes with the female crowd." He buckled the seatbelt and took the offered coffee. "Who knows, men, too, I suppose."

Bill chuckled as he put the Blazer into drive.

"Thanks for the coffee." He took a sip and winced. "Shit, that's hot."

Bill passed him a sidelong look as he drove. "You'd rather it be cold?"

Ryder sipped again, more cautiously this time. "You didn't have to come out here. I could've met you on scene."

"Sure, if you'd answered your phone." Bill glanced at Ryder. "Rough night?"

"You have no idea … So, what do we have? What's the case?"

"Hiker found a body."

"Anyone we know?" Ryder asked, immediately thinking of the last hiker that brought them to a body, scowling at the second time in less than thirty minutes that August had invaded his thoughts.

"The body," Bill asked, turning to look at him, "or the hiker?"

"Either."

"Don't know. No ID on the victim. Hiker is a nature photographer. Went out early to catch the sunrise, found our victim instead. Female, Caucasian, average height and build from the description Simon provided, maybe early thirties. We'll know more when we can check the scene or have Rich evaluate her."

"Have you seen her yet?" Ryder asked, remembering Lillian lying on the floor, thinking she was gone and her wondering if her future self had died and passed through time. What if she hadn't passed through time? What if she was delivered to this time, last night?

"You okay? You look like you've seen a ghost."

"Have you seen the body yet?"

"No. Simon got the call and went to secure the scene. When you didn't answer your calls, I came to get you on my way there." He looked over at him again. "You know something about this that I don't?"

"No, I—" He paused, not sure what he was planning to tell Bill. That he was worried that this could be Lillian from the future? "It's another body," he said lamely, "so quick after the last ones."

"I don't like it either, but it's part of the job."

Ryder was silent for the rest of the drive, and as they followed Simon on the hike through the woods. Each step was a question.

How far back from the future did she travel? Would she look the same? Would Bill recognize her as his daughter, or discard it as just a resemblance? How would he explain to Lillian that what she was so terrified of last night—what he'd been able to justify away—was actually true? Would he know to look at her how much time she had left? How much time *he* had left with her? Would he have to match her "found" report with the "missing" one in the future and lie to her dad to get him to stop searching for the one thing in this world that he'd never stop looking for?

"It's just over here," Simon called back.

"She," Ryder said gruffly.

Simon looked confused at the sudden remark. "Right … uh … I meant the crime scene, but you're right, sorry. She's a person. She's just up ahead."

In what felt like slow motion, Ryder crossed under the yellow police tape encircling the crime scene, her body discreetly covered with a sheet. She was lying several feet away from the sheer rock face in front of them, as if the cliff had swatted her off like a nuisance fly.

Ryder headed straight for the sheet, dropping to his knees, his hand hovering over the cloth, not wanting to pull it back, already knowing what it felt like to see her lifeless form lying before him. He could feel his hand shaking as he gripped the fabric, his stomach quivering as he slowly pulled it away.

He sat on the ground, dropping his head to his hand between his knees, breathing in deep.

The hand on his shoulder squeezed. "Do you recognize her?" Bill asked gently.

Ryder shook his head, the cloth still in his hand. On an exhale and without further response, he rose and walked out of the taped-off crime scene.

It wasn't her.

He leaned a hand against a tree, feeling the rough bark against his skin, grounding himself in the present, breathing in the air.

It wasn't her.

Lillian was safe.

"You want to tell me what's going on with you?" Bill asked from behind.

"I'm sorry," Ryder said, turning to face his boss. "I thought…" He stopped and ran a hand through his hair, balling his fist at the back of his head.

Bill waited for him to explain.

"This is the third one…" he trailed off, looking in the direction of the crime scene.

"You've seen dead bodies before," Bill stated, crossing his arms. "You've never been disturbed by one. Ever."

"Sure, I have," Ryder disagreed. "You've just never seen it."

Bill shook his head. "This is something else. You were quiet the whole way here. You knew who was in here and were relieved when you were wrong." He paused, watching his deputy. "Who did you think you'd see?"

"Nobody," Ryder sighed, dropping his hands to his sides.

Bill took a step toward him, analyzing, his gaze softening at something he saw.

"Lillian." Bill stated the name gently. "Ryder, you know she's safe. You know she got out of the woods yesterday."

"I…" Ryder paused, wanting to deny that he was right. "I know," he sighed.

"You saw her. You talked to her."

"I guess … I don't know, I guess I was afraid she came back out."

"And you think if my daughter was lying in these woods, there wouldn't have already been a positive ID? Simon wouldn't have said something? You think anyone would surprise me with that? That I wouldn't tell you?"

Ryder rubbed his hand over his face. "I know. I don't know what got into me."

"I do, son," Bill said with a sigh. "You need to pull yourself together now. We need to assess this scene, figure out what happened."

"I know. I'm ready," Ryder told him, pushing thoughts of Lillian out of his head.

Bill studied him a moment longer before turning to lead the way back under the tape, heading to where Simon was standing nearby.

"Everything okay?" Simon asked, looking between the two.

"Yeah," Ryder answered. "Where are we on the map?" he asked, not having paid attention during the hike in.

Simon unfolded a trail map showing different colored routes snaking through the landscape. It reminded Ryder of the one August carried when their digital version wouldn't load. Ryder clenched his fist at the thought of August, releasing it on a breath as he tried to focus.

"We're about here," Simon told them, pointing along one of the green trails, indicating an easier pathway, a significant distance away from the gray boundary line Ryder had been searching for.

"What are your thoughts?" Bill asked him when Ryder hadn't said anything.

"Nothing," Ryder told him. "Just getting the bearings."

"You thought it was another Mountain death."

"It's been the common thread lately," Ryder admitted.

Bill nodded at the observation.

"Sheriff!" Another officer called from the opposite side of the crime scene, coming through the trees and under the tape.

The three of them crossed the distance and met him and another deputy as he held up the yellow ribbon.

"We found her gear."

He led the way along the trail, Ryder noting the numbered cards placed about as Simon stopped to photograph and Bill sent orders back with the second deputy to widen the crime scene. They reached a lesser worn trail with another placard and followed it through the brush to a small clearing.

"Oh man," Simon breathed, photographing the area.

"That's a hell of a way to go," Bill said sorrowfully, looking up at the frayed rope floating freely in the breeze above their heads.

Ryder took in the scene, the broken rope, a pool of blood at the base of the rocks and her body farther down the path.

"An experienced climber would have checked their gear," he said, shaking his head.

"Maybe she thought she did," Bill responded, assessing the scene for himself.

"You think the rope was tampered with?" Ryder asked, looking up at the rocks above.

"Won't know until we can get it down. But no," he said sighing, looking at the ground again. "No, I suspect she thought it would be fine. Too often people think that nothing bad could happen to them." He turned back to the cliff. "She had to have made it pretty far up before it gave way. Maybe she was already making her way back down, realizing her error and trying to get to safety. She could have panicked and ignored whatever training she had."

"If she had any training at all, she'd know better than to be out here without a partner," Ryder countered.

Bill squatted near the landing, pointing out the loose rock nearby. "Looks like the rocks gave way, could have lost her footing or her grip, rope snaps, she lands here, cutting herself significantly…"

"Or is knocked unconscious by the fall, and lays here, bleeding out."

Bill nodded, looking away, back the way they had come. "She comes to, tries to head back down the trail to get help but has lost too much blood already, and collapses where we found her, bleeding out the rest of the way."

Simon photographed the pack left on the boulders nearby. "Why not call for help?" he asked as he unzipped the bag, removing the items one by one, photographing as he did. "Her cell is here. She has signal." He looked over as Ryder and Bill approached.

"If she lost that much blood," Ryder said, looking back to the discolored dirt. "She probably wasn't thinking clearly. Maybe all she could think of was getting out."

"It's a shame," Bill said, opening the wallet and examining her ID. "If she had someone here with her…"

"Let's make sure she didn't," Ryder said.

"Yep," Bill agreed and delegated tasks for each to investigate.

At the end of the day, when it appeared that no foul play had a role in her death, Ryder collapsed on his bed. A life couldn't be closed in one day, but it was looking more and more like bad luck had claimed hers today, not the hand of someone who had meant her harm. And not the Mountain as he'd initially feared.

Was this how he was going to look at every case? Would he always see Lillian waiting to be discovered?

He sat up on the bed, drained from the past twenty-four hours, but he ached to see her face, to hear her voice, to know she was safe.

He could drive to Wisteria… He looked at the clock.

It was still open.

"You don't even know if she's working," he said aloud, trying to talk himself into sense.

He removed his gun, setting his gear on the nightstand. The truth was, he couldn't see her. To see her just made it harder to be without her.

And if he saw her, he'd have to admit how terrified he was that she hadn't only been dreaming, that finding her out in the woods today was too much of a possibility.

Losing her to August was bad enough, but to lose her to the Mountain was unbearable.

If he saw her today, he knew he wouldn't be able to let her walk away.

He stared into nothing, feeling useless. He picked up his phone and scrolled through his contacts, found the one he needed, Stan, the best archivist the station had ever had, and pressed call.

"Hee-yeello?" Stan's chipper voice on the other line answered.

"Hey, it's Ryder."

"Yep. What's up?"

"You working tonight?"

"All night long," he sang.

"You got a backlog?"

"Nada. You got something for me?"

"Yeah," Ryder sighed, running a hand down his face then through his hair, letting out a breath. "I need a favor."

"No problem. Send me the details."

"There's no case number with this one."

"Got it. Your eyes only."

"That'd be appreciated."

The call disconnected and Ryder texted his list.

Very specific. I'll see what I can find.

Ryder knew he'd be thorough and discreet, but he hoped there'd be nothing to find.

The next morning, the sealed manilla envelope was on his desk when he got to work. It was thicker than expected. He wasn't sure if that was a good sign or not.

SEVENTY-FIVE

-Ryder-

Ryder sat on his couch, the packet of papers Stan had put together spread in front of him. He'd been through each picture at least a dozen times.

Did that one have her eyes? Was this one too young … that one too old?

He tried to be specific in his description, but how did you search through time for someone when you had no idea when they left or what they'd look like then?

Would this be his life? Updating his search criteria every year she grew older until one day she went missing in his time or he found her on a page in another?

Was this what it felt like to go crazy?

He turned off the light to the room, leaving the pages as they were, knowing he'd be back again tomorrow … as he had last night … as he had tonight.

He ran his hand through his hair, swatting the lights off as he moved through the house. He paused at the front door to check that he'd remembered to lock it when he came through. He flipped off the lights and started up the stairs, the light rap behind him nearly covered by the creaking of his step. He paused to listen, shaking his head.

"Now you're imagining things? You really are losing it," he said as he started climbing again.

The rapping sounded again, a quick little burst, barely louder than before.

He sighed, heading back down the stairs, wondering if the irritable bird he'd heard before was a woodpecker and had decided to use his pillars as practice. He turned on the lights and opened the door, expecting to see a bird fly away in retreat.

"Lillian?" He looked beyond her at the car he hadn't heard drive up, and back at the woman he'd been searching through time for standing before him. "What are you… Is everything okay?"

"Yes," she told him, standing nervously on his doorstep. "I'm sorry I didn't call," she said hurriedly. "I didn't really know I was going to come over here. I mean, I did, but I sort of thought I would have talked myself out of it before getting here … but obviously I didn't, so here I am." She took a breath and let it out with a sigh. "Can I come in?" she finally asked when he was still staring at her.

"Oh, yeah, sure," he said, moving to let her through. "You look nice," he told her, watching her smile disappear as quickly as it came. "Did you just get off work?"

"No. Yes," she corrected then shook her head. "I mean, yes I worked today, and this is what I wore," she said, smoothing the blouse automatically, "but I've been off work for some time … thinking."

"Must have been some serious thinking," Ryder smiled, trying to lighten her nerves.

"Yes," she replied. "It has been."

"You want to talk about it?"

"Can we sit?" she asked instead, looking down the hall to the only room she'd been to in his house. One that currently had pages and pages of faces of women that matched her description.

"Sure," he told her leading to the stairs. She looked uncertainly beyond him and back toward the hall leading to the office. He held out his hand. "It's more comfortable up here than that old office."

She took his hand, and he led the way, resisting the urge to rub his thumb along her smooth skin.

"Oh," she said when he opened the door and turned on the lights to the more modern living room than the sitting area downstairs offered. She smiled back at him, and he glimpsed the nerves leave for a moment. "This seems much more your style."

"Yeah, I keep the downstairs nostalgic. The upstairs is mine."

He leaned against the fireplace, watching her walk through the room, trailing a hand along the leather couch, stopping to smile at the few pictures he had on the shelves along the wall. He thought seeing her in his space would be medicine for his soul, but he realized, instead, that it was torture. Everywhere she looked wasn't at him. Everything her delicate fingers touched, he wouldn't get to feel.

Still, he hoped she would explore all night.

"Thank you for coming over the other night," she finally said softly, turning to see him watching her from across the room. She picked a statuette from the shelf, a small but heavy piece of silver braids that twisted and wrapped into the shape of a woman's body. She studied it a moment longer before gently replacing it on its shelf.

"I wasn't sure if you'd remember."

She smiled, still making her way through the room. "I wondered how much I dreamed that night," she told him, coming to stand at the other end of the mantle. "How much I imagined… How much I wanted to be real."

Her words were calm, direct. She'd left the nervous Lillian downstairs and the one that stood before him had an intense look he all too often recalled when he dreamed of her.

She was so close, he could have her in his arms in less than a second.

"And that's what you've been thinking about?" he asked lightly, moving to cross the room to where he kept his mini bar, opening the fridge to take out a bottle of water. He held one out in offering to her.

She shook her head.

He replaced the second bottle and opened his own, focusing on the cool liquid instead of the way her eyes followed as he put space between them.

"I've been over and over the dream," she started, waiting for him to nod that he knew the one. How could he forget? "And I think you were right."

"I like the way this conversation is going," he joked. "Please tell me how I was right this time."

She smiled. "I seem to recall you suggesting my brain was projecting and my dream was showing me what I didn't want to face in real life."

He shrugged his shoulders, nodding. "Yeah, that's pretty close," he said, not going to admit to this much calmer Lillian that he'd succumbed to her original line of thought. If she could put it behind her and live a normal life, she never had to know that he'd spend his trying to find her.

"And I realized that the future I thought I had lived was more like what the future could hold if I didn't make a change."

"That's good advice," he said, taking a drink of the water. "I suggest you don't ever go into the Mountain for one," he said lightly, meaning for it to sound like a joke and hoping she could hear how badly he was pleading.

"If you're a part of my life, I will always have to explain why I can't let you go," she told him softly.

"Lillian," he started, not liking the way her tone had turned serious, the finality he heard behind her words.

"It'll always be the first thing that August and I fight about, whether there's truth to anything he fears or not."

He pushed off the bar he'd been leaning against, closing the space between them, realizing now that the confidence he'd seen before was her following through with a decision that she'd made. Coming here to do what she needed was hard until she was standing before him and knew it was almost over. The idea that he only had a few more moments with her in his life went down like acid down his throat.

He thought of the way she'd curled into him when he'd held her as she slept, the way his name had whispered on her sigh. He thought of the comfortable moments beside her, simply being near her when he needed someone to lean on. He remembered the way it felt when he kissed her lips, the way her breath would skip and escape on a gasp, driving him crazy not to have her.

He thought of how if she walked out of his house, she'd walk out forever, and all of those moments would be memories on a shelf that he could never touch.

"Lillian, don't push me out."

"I wish moments weren't as easily discarded like pennies, holding only minimal value while we have them in front of us, thinking we can always find more tomorrow, not realizing their worth. I wish I hadn't spent so long being mad at you, and then so much longer being afraid of how, if I let you back in, you might hurt me again, that you wouldn't need to look for me, the way I needed to look for you every time I knew you were near. I wish Wade didn't have to die for you to finally tell me how you felt."

"I was stupid, back then and now for taking so long to make things right," he said softly.

"I love you, Ryder," she told him just as softly, resting her hand against his face. "I need you to know that I really do, and I wish things had gone differently between us."

"Lilly," he whispered, hearing the sorrow in her voice, the finality. He placed his hand over hers. "Please stay."

She smiled sadly, shaking her head. "I can't, Ryder. I'm sorry. I have to make a change."

She stepped into him, delicately pressing her lips to his. She pulled back marginally and he wanted nothing more than to grab her back, kiss her as if his entire existence depended on it—because surely it must—but she looked into his eyes and her smile was so sad he couldn't bear to bring her more pain.

"Goodbye, Ryder," she whispered. Without waiting for a response, she turned and walked out of the room.

He slid to the floor, his heart tearing itself from his chest, abandoning him to chase after her down the stairs, and out the front door. He heard the car engine start and fade away as she drove out of his life, leaving his heart to flounder, powerless to live but unable to die.

He stared across the room, seeing only her wandering through.

The warmth from her hand was already gone.

The feel of her lips no longer an impression.

Her face before him, fading.

He understood why she'd had to let him go, why he was the change that had to be made. There was too much doubt where they were concerned. She and August had a chance, but only if he wasn't there to mess it up. She'd said herself that she'd chosen August. Repeatedly, she'd made the choice, but he'd never heard it until now.

He'd waited too long.

He put his head in his hands, squeezing his hair with his fists.

He'd had his chance years ago. He could have fought for her then, but he knew she wouldn't have him. He could have apologized as soon as she moved back home, but he'd been afraid she'd laugh in his face, never considering he'd admit his mistake.

The truth was, he thought he'd have more time, and if Wade hadn't died and put things into perspective, would he still be watching, waiting for the right moment to make his move?

If he never made his intentions known…

She'd never know that he had loved her for all these years.

She'd never be confused about how she was feeling now.

She'd never have a doubt about being completely true to August.

If Wade had never died … she'd never have to make a change.

He jerked his head up, realization hitting like a shock though his chest.

"Oh no. Lilly, no!"

He bolted from the floor and flew down the stairs, taking the last three in a single leap.

He jumped in the truck, dialing her number as he raced down his drive.

"Come on, Lillian, pick up."

The call immediately went to voicemail.

He called again. Voicemail.

"Damn it, Lillian. Don't do this!" he yelled to the dash.

He tried her phone again. Nothing.

He stared at the stop sign in front of him and at the phone in his hand, swearing as he scrolled through the contact list and hit talk.

The line connected.

"What do you want, Ryder?" August asked, exasperated.

"I can't get ahold of Lilly."

"Not my problem."

"August…" he paused, deciding to head to her house first, just in case he was wrong. "Is she with you?"

"Why would she be with me?" he asked snidely. "I figured she'd be with you."

"Why would she be with me?" he asked, more confused than August was frustrated.

"Did you just call to gloat? Or can you already not keep tabs on your girl?"

"What are you talking about?"

August was quiet on the other end.

"August. When did you see Lilly last?"

"Yesterday, when she told me she didn't want to see me anymore and won't take my calls. I figured she told you all about it."

"What did she say exactly?"

"What's going on, Ryder?"

"What did she say?"

"Something about you and me and how she was sorry, and that it was time for a change. Then she left."

"Fuck."

"What's going on?" he asked again.

"I can't explain it–"

"Try," August growled.

Ryder considered how much to share, needing August to believe him, needing him to help him.

"I think she's in trouble."

"Trouble how?"

"Her car's not at her house."

"Trouble how?" August persisted. "Ryder."

"The flag's up," Ryder said, his stomach dropping at the sight.

"What? What flag?"

"The mailbox…"

"So? What's wrong with Lillian?"

"The flag was up at Wade's," Ryder mumbled.

"Ryder. Where is Lillian? Tell me where she went."

"I have to check the box," Ryder said, feeling like he was in a trance as he walked to the box.

"Ryder, I'm heading to the woods. Where is she?"

"There's a letter. Oh God, there's a letter."

"Ryder, snap out of it. I'm on my way. Tell me where to go."

"She had to make a change…" Ryder said, staring at his name written on the envelope in her precise script.

"Damn it, Ryder, if you don't tell me where she is, we're both going to lose her forever!"

"The wall," he blurted. "She dreamed of the wall."

"What? Ryder, what are you talking about? What dream?"

"The broken-down wall at the Mountain … She dreamed she … August you have to go. The trail is still marked. She can follow it right in. You're the stronger climber. You have to stop her. She can't go in there. It's not safe."

"I'm on my way. How long has she been gone? How much time do I have?

"I don't know."

"Ryder. Think. How much time?"

Ryder tried to think of how long before she left that he stared at nothing, trying to see her face, trying to bring back the feeling of her touch. How long did he wait before he put it together? How long before he realized that the change she needed to make was not to cut him out of her life, but to stop a death that had changed so much? Bring back one heart to save the hearts of so many from breaking.

"Ryder. Focus."

"Twenty minutes?" Ryder guessed.

"Twenty minutes?"

"I don't know. It may have been longer," he said desperately. "August she can't go in. You have to stop her. I shouldn't have come here first. I can't make it there in time. You have to stop her."

SEVENTY-SIX

-August-

August skidded into the gravel lot, rock spraying into the brush as he threw the truck into park. He moved his pack out of the way and accessed the storage under the seat that only he knew was there, grabbing the emergency pack before heading into the woods.

Her car is here. I can see the tape. I'm going in.

He sent the text and hoped he would be fast enough.

Lillian

"What a great idea this was," she said as she climbed over another rock, sitting as she turned her legs around to the other side. She took a deep breath before she pushed off and kept climbing in.

She found it hard to believe that this could even be considered a trail … or that Rain had made this same trek. She hitched her pack more securely on her shoulders, searching for the next yellow ribbon that had been tied every few feet, marking the way through the woods.

"Come on," she pleaded, her eyes scouring for a sign of movement or a flash of color. She took a few tentative steps in the direction she thought she needed to go, hoping she wasn't getting off course.

The sun was making its descent quicker than she'd liked, the branches casting long shadows. She shouldn't have waited so long after she got off work to go to Ryder's, or spent so much time talking, but she had to say goodbye… just in case… She caught a flicker of movement up ahead as she moved to retrieve the flashlight. She shined the light in the direction she'd seen, hearing a scurrying in the woods beyond.

"It's just a squirrel," she told herself, scanning the distance in front of her and trying not to jump when the shadows bounced in her light.

She caught the movement again, the yellow tape waving her on. She moved the beam to her immediate path, carefully picking her way to the next flag. She had no idea how far she had climbed or how much farther she had to go, but she would make it.

She had to make it. She needed to make a change.

Ryder

Ryder nearly passed the entrance, slamming on his brakes as he slid into the gravel lot, fishtailing the truck and pelting August's with rocks.

He didn't have time to hope one of them scratched that shiny exterior.

He searched through his truck for a flashlight, slamming the glovebox closed on a curse. He couldn't waste any more time going to find one nearby. He glanced at August's truck. How prepared was always prepared?

He ran to the back door, pulling against the locked door.

"Shit!" he swore again, seeing August's pack lying on the seat.

His gun was in his hand, ready to slam against the window. He glanced at the front door, reaching for the handle. The door popped open, and he found the unlock button, pressed it and threw open the back door. He grabbed the pack, rummaging until he found the flashlight, and flicked it on.

He stared at the pack.

If he took it, it would only slow him down.

He slammed the door. August had left it behind for a reason.

He was two steps away before he turned back, ripped the door open again, and threw on the pack. What if they needed it?

August

August knew the trail well. He'd been through here more times than he cared to count when searching for Rain and Brian, and more than that on his own. He took the boulders at a jump, the loose rocks in the path skittering away from his boots to avoid being trampled in his race against time.

She'd be moving slower, having to find her way in the growing darkness and as a less experienced climber.

At a moss-covered log, he waited, slowing his breathing, listening for disturbances. Not hearing anything in the immediate vicinity, he continued.

Lillian

It was fully dark now. The little bits of sky she'd been able to see through the leaves above her faded into a solid dark mass.

She had to be getting close. Surely, she had been climbing long enough.

Her beam flashed against something different. She went around a large boulder, too tall to climb, her light catching as she startled a bird who quickly took flight. Or was it a bat?

"It doesn't care about you," she told herself, immediately imagining it coming back for her, a flutter of wings and tiny claws grabbing ahold and not letting go. She shook off the thought. "It's not the bats you have to worry about."

She turned her light back to the different structure she'd seen before. She could see the shape of the wall in front of her. She moved closer to get a better look.

She reached out her hand, feeling the smooth, cool surface.

It was solid and old.

She shined the light to the left as far as it would go and then to the right. The wall continued in both directions. She looked at the blockade in front of her with disappointment.

There was supposed to be an opening.

All that was in front of her was a wall, turned wild with time. Vines had made their home in the crevices of the stone, climbing along and up the structure. She jumped at the sound of an owl calling nearby, turning to search for the culprit.

A flash of yellow in her beam of light summoned her along.

Ryder

Ryder jumped over the log, his sure-footed landing surprising him as he pushed through the path, his beam flailing wildly in front of him as he crashed through the woods. He hoped he scared off anything that could be considered predatory instead of calling them right to him, but there was no time to be quiet.

He'd lost too much time as it was.

His legs were tired, burning from barreling through the trail, over downed trees, around large boulders. He skirted along sheer drops and tried to avoid the whip of branches, although enough had left their mark against his skin.

Had she made it to the wall?

Had August made it to her?

August

The glow from her light had been in his sight for a few minutes, but he didn't dare call out and alert her that he was close.

If she ran…

The angry burst from the owl above, warning him off of his turf, caused her light to flash in his direction. He took shelter behind the tree, out of her line of sight. Immediately, her glow turned, heading away from him, along the wall.

She didn't have much farther. He didn't have much longer.

Lillian

She followed the wall and the ribbons of yellow tape. Her light illuminated a rock out of place from the rest. She turned her light up to the wall, finding its home.

The snap of a twig and a shuffle of movement sounded nearby. From which direction, she couldn't tell, but it sounded bigger than a squirrel. Her heart beat a little faster.

"It's okay. You're close," she whispered unsteadily to herself.

She took deep breaths, holding them for a couple seconds, and then let them out slowly. If she couldn't control her fear out here, she wouldn't make it in there.

She walked farther along the wall, navigating around more and more downed stones as she went. She reached a pile of stones, glancing up and noting it was the collapsed top half of the structure. Following the length of the wall with her light, the stones became more prominent, the wall more broken. She stepped forward, the stones shifting under her weight. Reaching out, she used the wall for balance.

The hairs on her arm stood straight. A chill ran down her spine.

She stepped up higher on the debris, shining her light over the wall, into the territory of the Mountain. It looked exactly the same.

The stones shifted and she slipped against the wall, dropping her flashlight into a crack between the rocks. She slid to a seated position on the loose stones, reaching for the handle, thankful it hadn't busted against the rocks.

She got back onto solid ground, noting the difficult terrain ahead of her path. She didn't want to risk losing her light or twisting her ankle. She still had to make it out of these woods. If she followed along the outskirts of the wall remnants, she wouldn't get off course and she'd figure out how to get through the stones when she reached the opening.

Startled by a disturbance in the quiet above her, she pointed her flashlight to the sky. More than one flying creature of the night passed over and behind her, skirting along, but never over, the wall. She watched as the last straggler fluttered to keep up.

Could they feel the difference in the air, too? Did the Mountain affect animals the same way as humans, or did they simply have a hunting path, and it was coincidence that they stayed on only one side of the wall?

She swatted at the bugs that had ventured too close to her face, exploring the unusual light source invading their home. She wondered if the bats were scouting the buffet that she was providing by attracting so many curious flyers. She immediately shook the image of bats swarming all around her from her head.

"Focus," she said into the night. "You have a job to do."

She walked around the fallen stones and continued on the route to the opening in the wall. It wouldn't be much farther now.

Her heart beat faster in anticipation.

August

The bobbing of her light heading toward him cast long, dancing shadows, marionettes for a show she didn't know she was conducting. Would the ending be a tragedy or an ever after? Only time would tell.

Ryder

Had August made it to her in time?

What if she'd gone through already?

Was him being here all for nothing?

The questions circled through his head as he cautiously jogged along a clearing in the path, his flashlight searching for any obstacles to slow him down.

She didn't know they were coming. That had to give them an upper hand, right?

What if she went through?

If she went through… He shook his head. He wouldn't think about not having her.

What if August went in after her? He was a jerk, but that didn't mean he should have to die. He had no idea what he was getting into.

Should he have called for backup? What would he have said? How would he explain the urgency?

Ryder pushed harder. He now had two lives to save.

Lillian

She could easily see over the wall at this point, the beam of light bouncing off the face, barely penetrating the darkness beyond. She could climb the structure easily, but she was hoping for a better opening up ahead. She could see a gap in the trees. It didn't appear to be much, but maybe that was the place to go through.

She stepped into the opening. Initially, it resembled a roadway or path leading from the wall. Could this have been one of the guarded entrances?

The clearing was limited to just near the wall, no larger than her pocket of a backyard. The trees that had taken over the rest of the road, if there had ever been one, were tall, mature, with younger saplings fighting for their chance to hide all evidence that anything was ever there.

She turned her light to the wall. The opening was littered with crumbled stones, waiting.

She'd made it.

Her heart raced at the thought of going through. She knew now that her dream was a warning. It was telling her what she had already figured out but couldn't realize on her own.

Fear is the key.

Fear would claim her life, like she'd felt in the dream, unless she could control herself.

Don't be afraid.

The dream wasn't meant to hurt her. It was meant to guide her.

The Mountain whispered to her on the wind, calling her to make a change, to make things right once and for all.

She stepped forward, her breathing slow. She was ready.

SEVENTY-SEVEN

-Lillian-

"Lillian, don't," the voice slid softly through the darkness.

She whirled in the direction of the voice, shining her light on him.

"August? What are you doing here?" she asked, watching him move slowly toward her, his hands raised slightly in front of him in a cautious stance.

"Lillian," he said calmly, taking another step forward, "please don't go in there."

"How did you know—what are you doing here?" she asked again, glancing to the opening in the wall and back to August.

"I'm here to bring you back home."

"Home? No. There's something I need to do. I can't explain it, August, I'm sorry," she said shaking her head and taking a step back from him. "You can't follow me."

"It's not safe up here," he started.

"I'm okay. Really, I am. I've made it this far," she told him, smiling. "I only have a little farther to go, but you can't come with me. It wouldn't be safe for you."

"For me?" he chuckled. "Lillian, come on, let's go home… please."

"How did you know where I'd be?" she asked him warily.

"Ryder called." He took another step toward her.

She wouldn't get to make this climb again. If Ryder had already figured out where she had been going and had called in August, they'd never leave her alone again.

It was now or never. She inched closer to the wall.

"Lillian." His voice was firm. "Please, just stay."

"What did Ryder tell you?" She glanced over her shoulder, unable to see the wall clearly in the darkness, but knew she was edging closer. "How'd he get you to come out here so fast?"

"Nothing," he told her, shaking his head.

"He said nothing," she repeated, disbelieving. "What did he say, August? How'd he get you to rush out here? Did he tell you I'd lost my mind?"

"No," he said calmly. "He was just scared you'd get hurt. He knew I was the stronger climber…"

She panned the flashlight around. "Ryder?" she called into the darkness, turning back to August, who'd come closer when she wasn't looking. She took a step back. "Is he out there? Did he come, too?"

"I don't know where Ryder is. Please Lillian. We just don't want to see you hurt."

"I won't get hurt. Please believe me, August. I'm going to be fine. Please just let me go. Please go home."

"No, Lillian, you won't."

"August–"

"Lillian, I won't lose you again."

"I'm sorry about earlier," she told him. "I know it doesn't make sense right now, but it will. I just have to do this one thing, and then it will all be okay."

"That's what you thought before, too," he said sadly. "Please don't leave me again."

"What do you mean?" she asked uncertainly, her heart starting to flutter the closer she got to the opening.

"I thought by saving Rain, you wouldn't go down the same path. I thought by saving Rain, I would save you, too. But it only sped things up."

"Saving Rain? You mean finding her in the woods?" she asked, trying to sort through the words he was saying. Was he trying to confuse her, to keep her talking while Ryder caught up? Two of them carrying her out would be easier than just one. She took another step, stumbling when her foot came into contact with the remnants of wall splayed along the ground.

August shook his head. "You know, Lillian."

"Know what? I don't know what you're talking about, August. You're trying to confuse me."

"Lillian, please don't go in there. Don't do this to me again. I can't live a life you don't exist in. I won't."

"August, I'll be back. I promise you, I'll be back."

"No, you won't. I didn't believe you before. Please," he pleaded as he stepped forward, "please don't do this again. You won't survive."

"August, I've never—" She stopped, looking toward the wall and back at him. His words finally clicked into place.

Saving Rain.

He knew where she'd be.

He knew her house.

He knew what she liked to eat.

He knew she owned Wisteria.

"The dream," she whispered, covering her mouth with her hand. "The dream wasn't a dream."

"What dream?"

"I dreamed of a life..." She dropped the beam of light to the ground. "Ryder said it was a dream, that it couldn't be a memory," she mumbled to herself. "The cave..." She brought the light back up. "Are we... am I..."

His face was sad, watching as she put the pieces to the puzzle together.

"I asked you to marry me in the cavern behind the falls."

She shook her head. It wasn't possible.

"You said yes, and we were happy for a time."

"No," she shook her head again. "Ryder told you about the dream."

"When Rain disappeared, you couldn't accept that it wasn't your fault. You'd had a fight before..."

She edged closer to the wall, not wanting to listen to the words he was saying.

"You searched and searched for her. You didn't believe she was dead, like everyone else."

"Rain didn't die," she reminded him.

"In our time, she did. You were lost, confused, and I wouldn't listen. I wasn't there for you like I should have been. But then you found her. You showed me the likeness, but I wouldn't see it."

"August, stop. It was only a dream."

"I don't think it was. And you don't either."

She shook her head. "The dream was just... projection. Showing me what I wouldn't see."

"I think you're wrong."

"No. Ryder agrees."

"Ryder doesn't know. He doesn't know that I've lost you once. That if you go through that wall, I'll lose you again."

"No," she shook her head. "No, August. The dream showed me the way. I thought it was bad, but it isn't. It showed me the secret. The dream is a guide."

"Lillian. You will not make it. You will die if you go through. Please stop arguing and just listen. You are going to die."

"Lilly!" They both turned as Ryder walked out of the tree line. "Lilly, he's telling the truth."

She looked uncertainly between the two men.

"He's been telling the truth since he showed up." He turned to August. "You said you'd never stop searching for the fiancé you lost." He looked at Lillian. "Can't you see? He literally went through time for you. Lilly, please don't go in there." He sat on a log, exhaling his defeat for her heart.

"But don't you both see?" she asked, looking at each of them. "If he can do it, then it *is* possible. I can do it, and I can fix things so everything is better."

"You can't bring Wade back."

"Wade?" August asked.

"Wade is what tipped the scales for me to tell her how I felt. If he never died, she thinks I wouldn't be in misery now from losing him first and then losing her to you. She can save me heartache, which also saves her, because even though she loves me now, she didn't know how much she still cared for me before I reminded her. If I never remind her, then there's nothing to stand in her way to be with you. Congratulations, August, she's choosing you again." The words hung in the air between the three. "Lilly," he sighed. "I'd rather live in a world where you're alive and happy with someone you love than to live in one where you're dead."

"It won't change anything," August told her. "Bringing Wade back won't make things right. Ryder will still tell you how he feels. He can't help himself. You're still tormented by your feelings for him no matter what changes."

"The dream." She glanced at Ryder and back to August. "The fight … that's why you thought Ryder and I had slept together. Because in our time we had."

August nodded.

"That's why you don't trust him now."

"Yes. Don't you see? I changed the thing that went wrong in my time, but now it's repeating itself in this time. You can't change anything. It won't work."

She shook her head. "You both are wrong."

"Lilly—"

"No," she said, cutting him off before he could argue. "You're wrong." She took a step backward again. Ryder stood from his log. August reached out a hand. "I'm not going back to save Wade," she said, turning her attention to Ryder, then back to August. "I'm going back to the beginning. I'm going to stop it all."

SEVENTY-EIGHT
-RYDER-

"Lilly, that's crazy. Say you did manage to keep your heart from exploding. You don't know how time works in there, how to use it to get you when you need to be, or even know how far back to go," Ryder reasoned.

"You're wrong," she told him, pulling a paper from her pocket.

Ryder walked over to take the folded newspaper article, shining his light on it to read. It was dated 1965.

"You want to go back to when the Mountain exploded? Don't you think that's the worst time to go back? You're just asking to blow up with it."

"No," she told him, sure of herself. "I'll go back just before. I think this is the key. I think this is when everything started going wrong."

"What makes you think you can go to before then? What if the explosion was the start of the time portal in the first place and all you do is go back to the day it starts and explode with it? Have you thought of that?"

"Yes, I have."

"And?"

"And… I think that whatever caused the explosion messed up something that was already going on. Think about it," she said urgently, looking between both men, who were standing within arm's reach of her. She knew she'd never make it into the Mountain at a run. She had to convince them it was safe. "Nobody knew what was happening when the base was active. What if the reason it was so top secret is because they'd stumbled onto time travel and were trying to learn all they could about it? Only the most trustworthy people could be involved, or the secret would get out and everyone would be after control of time. Harvey told me that—"

"Wait," Ryder interrupted. "You talked to Harvey about this?"

"No. But we *did* talk about the Mountain while I was doing my research. I was looking for information. His wife's family was there. His best friend… He said, the night before the explosion, his friend came to him and told him that they'd meddled with something they didn't understand and to stay away." She looked at both of them. "Don't you see? Harvey's friend is the key. I just need to find out who he is and find out what was about to happen so I can stop him."

"And you think he'll just listen to you, some random person that he doesn't know?" Ryder asked.

"He will when I tell him where I'm from."

"That's your plan?" Ryder asked incredulously. "You're going to risk your life to *hopefully* go back sixty years in the past, find a person whose name you don't even know—not to mention what he might be capable of—just that he's qualified to be part of this super top secret sect, probably with orders to kill anyone on sight and make up a story after, and *tell* him that you're a time traveler from the future, and then ask him to please not do whatever it is that he's about to do because it's going to mess up a bunch of stuff in the future? God, Lilly! Are you kidding me?" Ryder's hand was through his hair, clenching into a fist at the back of his neck. He turned to August. "You've been awful quiet. You want to chime in here? Help me talk her out of this."

August stared at the ground, ignoring Ryder's request.

"Ryder, you know Harvey. He wouldn't have been that close with a terrible person."

"How do you know? How would he know? It's top secret. He can't discuss what he does on the Mountain when he's on duty. Harvey could have been besties with Hitler for all we know!"

"Ryder," she scolded.

"What? That's absurd? So is this, Lilly."

"I think I know who Harvey's friend was," August finally said. Both Lillian and Ryder turned to him. "If you're serious about going," he said to Lillian, "I'm coming with you."

"What? No. We're talking her out of going, not volunteering to escort her through."

"What do you mean, August?"

"Of the three of us here, I'm the only person we know of who has successfully traveled through time."

Lillian nodded.

Ryder threw his hands up and let them fall.

"It's not just like walking through the woods. It's utterly terrifying. The most fear-inducing thing you will ever do, and if you give in, you will die."

"So. Don't. Go." Ryder argued.

Lillian moved closer to August. "You can show me how."

"Yes. But you have to do everything exactly as I tell you. Do you understand?"

She nodded eagerly, ready to move forward.

"Who's the friend, August?" Ryder interrupted.

Lillian turned to look at him and then back to August, the question evident on her face as well.

"I'm not one hundred percent sure," he started, turning his pack around and reaching in to retrieve an ID badge, "but I'm beginning to think my grandpa worked at the Mountain."

Lillian shook her head, studying the image staring back at her. The resemblance to August was uncanny.

"Harvey said his friend died," she told him, handing the ID to Ryder. "You told me you spent summers here with him, that he only died a few years ago."

August nodded. "What if that's what he needed Harvey to believe? What if he left that night and went into hiding, only returning to live here, his hometown, when it was safe again? When it was safe and nobody would recognize him or tie him to the Mountain? My grandpa had secrets. Some of which nobody discovered until after he died."

"The property," she mused, remembering August's story of inheritance.

He nodded. "What if this was the real one, the reason he didn't talk about his past?"

"I can't believe you're considering this," Ryder said to August. "You were supposed to be the one to bring her out, not join her."

"If she's going in, then so am I. Maybe with me beside her, I can keep her safe."

Ryder exhaled, "Fine. Then I'm coming, too."

"What? No!" Lillian exploded.

"Absolutely not," August stated.

"Why? It's okay for the two of you to dive right in, but if I want to join... What, three's a crowd?"

"No," August told him gently. "You have too much to lose."

"And neither of you do?"

"When I came through the first time, I didn't care if I lived or died. I'd already lost my life when my Lillian died. It didn't matter if I went out the same as her. This time, I'm prepared and can help her through. I cannot help you though."

"I won't need your help."

"Yes. You will. Ryder, you have no idea what happens the second you walk through the divider. You'll forget about her standing beside you because all you'll be able to focus on is whatever your fear manifests as. Maybe your skin will be crawling with bugs, ripping at your skin in chunks. You'll watch as your body is devoured alive, and you won't even know that Lilly is burning in her own nightmare beside you. Whatever it is, it will consume you, and you will die."

"What did you see?" Lillian asked gently.

"You. Everywhere I looked, I saw your body, staring back at me with lifeless eyes. You fell off a cliff and broke your neck. I couldn't get to you quick enough to catch you... You laid on the earth, your blood pooling around you, pouring from gashes across your abdomen, staring up at me as the blood gurgled out of your mouth… Your screams chased me through the woods, begging me to save you, begging me to come back and find you. I had to let you go because I had to find you somewhere else.

"I left you alone, again, as I had in real life, and the Mountain used my fear of losing you one last time. Your voice called softly through the wind, just as I was ready to leave. You told me you were still alive, that you needed me to come find you, to help you escape this place. Your screams were a shriek into my soul. I almost turned back, afraid you were lost and still wandering, waiting for me to save you."

"How are you going to keep her safe this time?" Ryder asked, angrily resigned to their minds being made up to go in. "If I stay behind, it's because you *will* bring her back out. How will you keep her alive?"

"I'm going to drug her," August told him simply.

"Excuse me?" Lillian asked.

August turned to her. "I spent years after you died researching the deaths tied to the Mountain. You'd already gathered all the information, and maybe you had figured it out in our time, and I was too dumb to listen, but it was all there in black and white. Massive heart attacks, elevated hormone levels—adrenaline being a primary one. We have to block the body's response to fear, slow the heart rate. It's the only way I was able to make it through. But it will work."

"Okay," she agreed. "I'll take it."

"Wait, Lilly, please think this through," Ryder begged again. "You don't even know what he's going to give you, and you're just okay with that?" When she didn't answer, looking to August and back to Ryder, Ryder turned to August. "Fine, give it to me too."

"I can't."

"Why not?"

"I don't have enough for all of us."

"Lilly, please…"

She turned to Ryder. "I know this doesn't make sense."

"It does," he sighed. "It does make sense why you'd want to fix this." He motioned behind her to the wall. "But I don't want you to. I want to selfishly keep you here with me, and to Hell with anyone else that's stupid enough to go in there and get themselves killed. You're the only one I care about."

"But you already lost Wade," she reminded him gently. She moved to him, and he wrapped his arms tightly around her, breathing in her scent for what he hoped wouldn't be the last time, but that he feared would be.

"Lilly, please. Please don't go," he begged her again, knowing they were just words lying on the ground between them. "You know I've always loved you, right?" he whispered into her hair.

She nodded, squeezing him tightly. "You know I do, too."

"Lillian," August called to her from behind. She turned to him. "You should leave your phone with Ryder. It would cause too many questions."

"Oh, right," she said. She hadn't thought about the minor details. She dug it out of the pack and handed it to Ryder. "I'll be back soon," she told him.

"You better," he sighed, as she turned to August. Resigned, he walked back to his log. He'd see them in, then be on his way. How would he know if their mission was successful? Should he go back to looking for found reports, adding August's description to the list?

August walked over, leaving Lillian standing near the opening to Hell.

"I know how hard this is for you."

"No. You don't."

"I'm going to take care of her," August said, but the words offered no reassurance. "Once she takes this medicine, there will be no turning back. It's fast-acting and will slow everything down for her. If her body isn't stimulated enough, I worry that it could kill her."

"Then don't give it to her. Take her out of here."

"You know she'll come back, and then she'll be on her own, and you know what'll happen then." He looked behind him, where Lillian was waiting patiently. August handed Ryder a package. "Keep this on you any time you come out here. Do you understand?"

"What is it?"

"It's how I was able to save Rain. It's a sedative, a very powerful one. If something happens and the medicine doesn't work when we come back, you need to be prepared to sedate her so her heart will calm."

"Why wouldn't the medicine work when you come back?"

"After this trip, I will only have enough for one more traveler. We will have to split it to come back, and I don't know if it will be enough."

"So just get more while you're back there."

"It's not that easy. I had this made in my time, I don't even know where I'd find it here." He stopped explaining, exhaling a deep breath. "Just tell me you'll keep it ready."

"I will," he sighed. "But how will I know when to be here? Should I just set up a tent and camp out?"

August ignored his comment. "I hope we can come back out as soon as we go in, at least it'll seem that way for you."

"If it all goes according to plan, I shouldn't need to use this," Ryder said, opening the package he was holding. He looked up at August. "There's only one."

"She's all that matters."

Ryder nodded. "I'll be here."

August held out his hand, offering it to Ryder. Ryder shook it, and August turned to talk to Lillian. Ryder watched as she placed the medicine under her tongue. She gave a slight, unsure smile and wave before she turned, ready to cross.

"Lillian, wait!" Ryder ran, dropping the pack.

"She can't," August cautioned.

Ryder grabbed her into a hug. "Come back to me," he ordered.

She was out of his arms, August leading the way. Hand in hand, they stepped to the wall.

He watched them disappear before his eyes as he sank to the ground, knowing that if it all worked according to plan, she'd reset everything, and he'd lose all memory of the moments they'd shared.

EPILOGUE

-RYDER-

She burst through the opening, and all he saw was her. Her screams filled the night and he rushed to her side.

"August!" she shrieked.

He plunged the needle into her arm, and her body immediately softened against him as he lowered her to the ground.

"How long…?" she sighed as her eyes fluttered closed.

She was unconscious before she could hear a response. Her face was calm despite her blood-stained clothes and tear-streaked cheeks. He held her as her breathing slowed and turned to look for August.

THE END

Dear Reader

Thank you very much for taking the time to read my story. I loved writing it and I truly hope you enjoyed reading it.

As an indie author, word of mouth is everything! If I could ask one thing of you, it would be to leave a review for the book or to recommend it to another reader.

If you LOVED it – REVIEW it! (It'll make my day, and it'll help someone choose their next read!)

If you HATED it – RECOMMEND it to your enemy! (But be sure to hold the evil laugh until after they start reading.)

I appreciate whichever you choose!

Again, thank you so much for reading.
-Angela Franklin-

You can connect with me on social media:
@author.angela.franklin or www.akfranklin.com

Made in the USA
Monee, IL
08 May 2025

aab9ecac-3bf4-4ff3-8630-dfbf8af826d7R01